HARD
MONEY

Also by Michael M. Thomas

GREEN MONDAY
SOMEONE ELSE'S MONEY

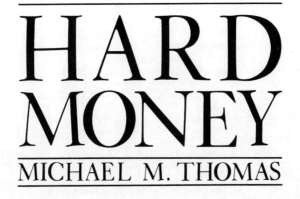

HARD MONEY

MICHAEL M. THOMAS

ELISABETH SIFTON BOOKS

VIKING

ELISABETH SIFTON BOOKS · VIKING
Viking Penguin Inc., 40 West 23rd Street,
New York, New York 10010, U.S.A.
Penguin Books Ltd, Harmondsworth,
Middlesex, England
Penguin Books Australia Ltd, Ringwood,
Victoria, Australia
Penguin Books Canada Limited, 2801 John Street,
Markham, Ontario, Canada L3R 1B4
Penguin Books (N.Z.) Ltd, 182–190 Wairau Road,
Auckland 10, New Zealand

First published in 1985 by Viking Penguin Inc.
Published simultaneously in Canada

Grateful acknowledgment is made to Chappell/Intersong Music Group–U.S.A., for permission to reprint lyrics from "Thousands of Miles" from the musical production "Lost in the Stars," words by Maxwell Anderson, music by Kurt Weill. Copyright © 1949 by Kurt Weill and Maxwell Anderson. Copyright renewed, assigned to Chappell & Co., Inc., and TRO Hampshire House Publishing Co. International copyright secured. All rights reserved.

LIBRARY OF CONGRESS CATALOGING IN PUBLICATION DATA
Thomas, Michael M.
Hard money.
"Elisabeth Sifton books."
I. Title.
PS3570.H574H37 1985   813'.54   84-21916
ISBN 0-670-53110-3

Printed in the United States of America by
R. R. Donnelley & Sons Company, Harrisonburg, Virginia
Set in Janson

For Barbie

Spiders eat one another, and, for their continual design of eating, are paid by a continual dread of being eaten . . . the young ones, after the example of their fathers, use the same trade. The danger, as well as fear, is common to all. There is little regard to relation or families; and for that reason, like pikes in a pond, none ever takes a prey, but he turns suddenly round, lest another should take him.

—Roger North, *The Life of the Honorable and Reverend Dr. John North*, 1744

HARD
MONEY

CHAPTER 1

The butler said the Ambassador would be with me in a moment.

"Ambassador"? Now that surprised me. Maybe X really had become foolish and pompous in his old age, unlikely as I would ever have thought it. There was, after all, the evidence of his behavior in New York right after his retirement, those two foolish years as "Gotham's Número Uno Socialite," as the gossip columns had put it. He wouldn't have been the first old lion I'd seen whose brains had turned to oatmeal and teeth to clay, and whose libido and ego went bananas. But I would never have thought it of X. Ambassador, my foot! Not X, I thought, even though it had been almost twenty-five years since I'd seen him in the flesh.

The title was his to use if he chose. His three-day stint as U.S. representative at an international telecommunications conference in Dublin had technically carried ambassadorial status, but that was a thin sop for the real ambassadorship he'd come so close to getting. The English always liked titles; they'd sleazified their own Honors List pretty thoroughly, and X had been a big hit when he'd moved to London seven years ago; his womanizing and party-giving had been as fascinating to *The Tatler* and *The Daily Mail* as they had been to *The Daily News* and *W*. But then he'd vanished, gone underground, dropped from sight—more completely than might ever have been expected of such a looming public figure.

Sitting there in his London house, I supposed that it was possible that all those years of work building and sustaining GBG, and the terrible grief he felt at losing his second wife, Selena, had finally taken their cumulative toll. It was conceivable he could have become a foolish, trivial old man, like most of his peers and contemporaries, seeking some kind of affirmation in dusty medals and faded ribbons. His son, Abner, who ran the company now, had asserted that X was out of touch with what was going on, something else I found hard to believe of the sharpest, most pulse-sensitive man I'd ever known. Well, if he had, I wanted to see it for myself. I didn't believe it. "Ambassador," indeed! That was strictly "Palm Beach," as X used to say, and whatever else I might have figured him for, it wasn't Palm Beach.

X's full name was Xenophon Horace Hubert Monstrance, although he'd dropped the "Xenophon" decades earlier, long before we met. Apparently the name reminded him of his father, a stuffy, classics-spouting Boston lawyer of small distinction. X was not fond of his father; he wasn't fond of any of life's failures, large or small.

Although most people—indeed, the world at large—called him "H.H.," he had always been "X" to me, from the moment I first met him, looming over Abner and me at the kindergarten where we were classmates, an imperial figure, splendid and imposing in his uniform with its badges and ribbons. Abner had introduced me as his new best friend.

"Well, we'll be best friends too, Sam," he'd said. "You just call me X. That's what my best friends call me. That's what I call myself, when nobody can hear me." He'd laughed in that growly way of his, with his clever little eyes sparkling in his big, tanned, tough face. I remember him reaching down and shaking my hand firmly, making me feel very much a man, but a man in the presence of something larger and greater. In those days I thought there was only one God, and He could only be found at Sunday school. Later, when I learned what fathers could mean and do to their sons, I knew there were other gods up and about in our lives, and I understood better what it was that I felt when X first took my hand.

That had been 1945. X had just returned to New York from Washington, where he'd ended the war as Deputy Director of Air Force Intelligence. Abner Monstrance and I had just finished our first year of school together, the first year of our friendship. Circumstances had thrown us together, and we'd hit it off immediately. At that time, Abner and his sister, Eugenie, lived with their mother in a cavernous, gloomy Park Avenue apartment not too far from where I lived with my mother and grandfather. Abner's mother was "sick"; whenever I was taken there to play, the only grown-ups I saw were Mam'selle and various maids and cooks and the white, rustling presences of nurses moving in spooky silence to the back of the apartment where the sick lady lived.

Soon after X came back from the war, Abner and Eugenie, who was two years older, went to live with him in his opulent duplex on Fifth Avenue, which was where, for the next dozen years, I came to play and hang out. They ceased to speak of their mother, and since I had only one parent myself, I thought the world worked that way, so everything seemed normal. X had a lot of lady friends then; he had been born in love with womankind. They seemed to change with the seasons, and some of them were famous, actresses mostly, whose pictures I recognized from *Life* and *Look*. We three children knew, however, that in the long run none of them had a chance. No woman did, until years later, when Selena came into his life.

I looked around the high, square English drawing room. X had bought the distinguished house on Chelsea Embankment, a landmark of Victorian architecture built by Sir John Soane, fifteen years earlier, when he anticipated being named Ambassador to the Court of St. James's. The Ambassadorship was going to be the most glittering of X's myriad glittering presents to Selena, and this house was to serve as the stage for their conquest of Great Britain. Selena had rejected the official residence in Regent's Park. As far as she was concerned, Winfield House had been sullied beyond redemption by the taste and occupancy of a lower caste of multimillionaire.

This was a very impressive room: a monument, I was sure, to the incomparable taste of the late Selena Harding Cromwell Maffett Monstrance, who had been, in her own way, no less a legend than her husband. She was rumored to have been the paramour at one time or another of most of the world's richest and most powerful men, and the insistent perfection of her judgment in fashion and decoration, as well as her faultless powers of organization and persuasion, still lingered in the memory of that part of society which venerated such things.

The room was openly, intentionally ambassadorial. The furniture and objects gave off a fine lemony whiff of great houses and ducal pedigrees. It was famous furniture, much-reproduced in magazines and guides, museum-quality stuff. Solid, noble English furniture: handsome tapestried wing chairs and settees, glorious fat sofas, richly polished secretaries and sideboards and tables. Stately pieces suitable for the public moments and private satisfactions of great persons. Pieces which seemed to speak to each other like gentlemen in clubs: in deep, secure voices expressing a considerable pleasure in finding themselves in each other's considerable company.

I got up and examined the paintings. To my mother's despair, I had never developed much of an eye or memory for furniture, habitually turning a dull, unknowing gaze on people who rushed up and flapped their arms and shrieked in high, precise little voices about "that wonderful set of Adam chairs at Fibblesden." I did have a feel for pictures, thanks in no small part to X, for whom paintings were as important a part of the properly comported life as food and wine, suits from Huntsman, and Charvet shirts, as essential to his well-being as the adulation of other men and the love of beautiful women.

I recognized a few old friends on the walls: a Braque still life and one by Chardin, a Bonnard screen hung as four separated panels, the big Brittany landscape by Gauguin, the famous Van Gogh and the nearly-as-famous Cézanne portrait of the dealer Vollard. Interspersed with them were a clutch of English pictures: a couple of conversation pieces by Devis and Zoffany, a dashing Gainsborough of a young couple perched on a stile, a Canaletto of Somerset House, a good-sized Constable river scene. It was bigger and more finished and better than *my* Constable, my rarest treasure, a tiny oil sketch that had been a legacy from my grandfather. Like X's much grander painting, my little picture was the distillate of everything an Anglophiliac sensibility required.

It was hot for May. The doors to the rear garden were open and I walked across to them, attracted like a bug to the buzzing blaze of the bright day outside. I wondered if much in the room had been changed in the dozen years since Selena's death. Probably no more than the absolutely necessary darnings and touchings-up, I guessed. And had X been darned and patched up too? There would have to have been some touches of restoration and repainting. After all, he would be close to seventy-five and he had always been meticulous about appearances, in himself and others. Cracks on the surface, he had been fond of telling Abner and me, often signaled chinks in the inner man.

At a table placed near the French windows, a photograph in a vermeil frame caught my eye. I picked it up. It showed X and Selena, in all her pale, studied elegance, flanked by Eugenie and Abner. I guessed the photograph to have been taken just after X and Selena were married. Abner would have been about twenty, in his sophomore or junior year at Yale; he stared at the camera intently, trying almost painfully to look adult. He had narrow, dark good looks, vaguely Mediterranean, which were obviously derived from his mother. There was none of X's ruddy, broad confidence in his features. The only resemblance was in the eyes; he too had those small, bright, black eyes glinting with intelligence and acquisitiveness. In X's otherwise genial features they seemed surprising, out of keeping; in Abner's, they harmonized with a general dark tenseness of brow and jaw.

Next to Selena, Eugenie stood awkwardly, taller by a good six inches than her stepmother. As a girl, she had been on the plain side, with agreeable, pale features made dreary by a general lack of liveliness. She was not a clod, and in those days, of course, her frame was not grossly padded out with bloat as it was now. She looked at the camera restlessiy, uncertainly; the photograph captured her characteristic expression: a sheepish apprehension, as if she were about to be placed on probation for life for being less than beautiful. Even now, in her mid-forties, that insecurity lingered, at least in the newspaper photographs I had seen.

X was naturally the center of the picture, fit, tanned, and beaming; he seemed to gleam, every inch the radiantly self-confident legend. The legendary tycoon, entrepreneur, impresario, financier, charmer, warrior, seducer.

I put the picture down. I'd seen so many photographs like these, although perhaps none of so perfect, so ideal a family. The Monstrances had it all: blindingly successful father, lustrously brilliant stepmother, agreeable and intelligent children.

The garden was pretty and formal, neat rows of bright flowers. A trellis of roses. Box hedges. A pair of slender shade trees. A table and chairs and a settee of white-painted iron. An admirable place for reading and reflection or for quiet, exquisitely cultivated talk before lunch; for a glass of sherry or hock and a biscuit; for coffee and more talk afterward. I let myself be washed by the warmth of the day. I felt suddenly drowsy and sat down.

My mind went back to the family photograph. Once upon a time my life had been so closely entwined with the Monstrances that it had been as if we were strands of a single cable. There had even been a point at which X had asked my mother to marry him. For thirteen years, from the age of five, Abner and I had been very close, virtually inseparable friends, from kindergarten right through Starbuck Academy, where Abner's name had been added to the carved list of "First Boys," the roll of the school's immortals, his name in marble not far from his father's on the plinth of the Memorial Chapel. The summer we graduated, our last as inseparable chums, our two families had celebrated with a trip to Europe together: Mother and I, X and Abner and Eugenie. We moved across five countries like capitalist Panzers, in a big chauffeured Daimler followed by a Buick station wagon with the luggage. The continent spread its cloak to ease X's passage; the rest of us pattered along behind, happy to be in his wake.

At the end of July, however, when we disembarked from the *Constitution* and shook hands and kissed cheeks on Pier 84, the cable unraveled. Perhaps, as later seemed likely, my mother's rejection of X was the catalyst. It was perhaps inevitable that Abner's path and mine would diverge. I went to Harvard and he followed X to Yale, and then adulthood uncovered fundamental differences of ambition and inclination. So that was the last time I saw X. Nor did I see much of Abner afterward, except in a glancing way, until coincidence, not then perceived as fate, brought us back within each other's orbit many years later.

I wasn't surprised that X, even in retirement, had been able to track me down in what I thought was a bolt-hole. In the old days, of course, it would have been a routine job for one of the three secretaries and two assistants sequestered with him on the thirty-fifth floor of Granite Tower, the skyscraper he'd built in 1958 a few blocks north of Rockefeller Center. In those days, when X still had all his claws and tentacles, there were literally thousands of people around the world poised to please or perform at a crook of the Monstrance forefinger. That was before Selena was killed and he seemed to lose the will to keep at it. By then, he had built GBG from a few New England radio stations into the most commanding presence in American entertainment and communications, bigger and more influential than CBS, more "commercial" and profitable than ABC.

He'd started the company in 1932 with three radio stations, which he'd bought with a bank loan guaranteed by a college classmate and what little was left to him as his portion of a diminished family fortune. When he retired from GBG the company owned five television and eleven radio stations, it numbered its network affiliates at over two hundred, and it had established its leadership in book and music publishing and in recorded music and across the entire technology of entertainment and communications; GBG Laboratories ranked with Bell Labs and Polaroid as a center of applied research. For over forty years, X had beaten off shock wave upon shock wave of high-minded critics and sociologists decrying the influence of broadcasting; challenged by new technologies and fashions, he swallowed them whole or made them his own; the trustbusters loosed on him by six Presidents had been sent whimpering by the courts to restudy their briefs. When he quit, GBG had consolidated revenues of $4 billion, and the value of its shares on the New York Stock Exchange aggregated nearly $2 billion. In the drift of time, X had won himself a place in the nation's commercial pantheon, one with Edison and Ford, Sloan and Watson.

That had been his legacy to Abner, the realm he'd handed over to his son nearly a decade ago. Under Abner's rule, the kingdom had become an empire. The throne X had abdicated now commanded a realm, renamed AbCom Inc., which was nearly twice the size of X's Granite Broadcasting Group. GBG had been reshaped and reoriented by Abner through massive investments and acquisitions in the areas of financial services, telecommunications, computer software, and real estate. The GBG broadcasting network remained the core of AbCom, its single largest generator of revenues and profits, but its importance was diminishing, much as X's own legend seemed to be engulfed in the faultless rush of his son's accomplishments.

I had seen X's televised farewell press conference; I had watched his final appearance at the Television Hall of Fame Awards; I had read all the valedictories in the press. The theme was consistent. He was too old, tired, and grief-stricken to continue. He felt obsolete; the world was spinning too fast for old heads and old hands.

And so he left Granite Tower and moved across town to the East Fifties townhouse in which was lodged the Monstrance Foundation, owner of eight million shares of AbCom common stock. There he was said to busy himself like any other high-powered retired executive, whiling away his daylight hours with the activities appropriate to a senior plutocrat: he served on boards and did good works, presided over commissions and committees, and lunched in clubs with old friends and acquaintances. After business hours, however, things were different. According to the society pages and gossip columns, he led a social and sexual whirl that would have killed an entire younger generation. He gave and attended dinner parties five nights a week; he appeared at charity functions with starlets on his arm; in tune with the season, he was seen at all the fashionable resorts, from St. Moritz to Sardinia. He was swarmed over and nibbled at by parasites—social climbers, fading beauties with one throw left, young people on the make—all seeming to want to borrow a cup or two of reflected glory by being seen with him. He kept to his word, however, and stayed away from his company. In April, a messenger went across town bearing a signed proxy for Abner on the Foundation's eight million shares. He was presumably available to render advice upon request, but it appeared he meant it when he said he was quitting.

Then, suddenly, he decamped for London. The plug was pulled on his old life. The Fifth Avenue apartment was mothballed, its famous paintings sent on extended loan to the Metropolitan Museum, of which X had been a trustee and treasurer. The Georgetown house, scarcely lived in, was sold. On Little Gourd Key, the spacious compound with its private seaplane dock and diesel sportfishing cruiser was rented out. So was Dunecrag, the great, slouching "cottage" on the East Hampton oceanfront. X gave up his shooting and stalking leases in the Highlands and his fishing rights on the Test and the Restigouche. Sold, too, to Germans and Arabs and honorary Monegasques were the jewel-like pied-à-terre on the Île-Saint-Louis, with its effulgence of Louis XV furniture and Nattier portraits and naughty Boucher screens; the villa near Siena, with its vineyards and olive groves and frescos by Ghirlandaio; and the ski lodge at Sun Valley.

After a quick whirlaround, X dropped from view. He ceased to be news, even to the trivialists, and was soon forgotten. The modern world moves swiftly, and memory is unequal to the constant push for change and novelty, so the missing tend to be as quickly turfed over as the dead.

I hadn't thought about him at all until his call came. I'd been in Scotland, in the Highlands north of Inverness, where I'd fled for some rest and whisky-assisted recuperation from professional exhaustion and misfortunes of the heart. I was, among other things, an enthusiastic—some said avid, others said fanatical—golfer, for whom there were no more healing distractions than to resume, on a great links, my lifetime's study of the baffling dynamics of hitting a three-iron into a high wind and, afterward, to ponder the day's findings with useful applications of single malt whisky. To be, as I was, a magazine writer believing himself to be falling out of love with the wrong woman for the wrong reasons required the strong medicine that only Scotland could provide.

The electronic paw with which X had once seized the time and attention of popes and presidents had reached out and tapped me on the shoulder at the old links at Brora, a half hour north of Dornoch, where I was staying. Brora was a traditional course, so much a part of the working landscape that the greens were electrically fenced to keep off grazing sheep. It was a raw morning, with a damp wind blowing in off the North Sea at about ten thousand miles an hour. I left the links not at all displeased with having shot an only mildly dishonest eighty-seven. Stuffed in my street shoes I found a note saying it was urgent that I call a London number I didn't recognize.

When I got back to my hotel in Dornoch, I checked my address book to see if the callback number might be one of my magazine's U.K. string-ers, sent to track me down by the editor, whom I had thoughtfully not provided with an address, since I had brought my "account" with him into balance. Only Mother knew where I was, and she was sworn to secrecy, but my editor was a willful fellow and he might well have broken her down, strong as she was. The number didn't match any I'd been given, but my native curiosity insisted I call, and when I did, an en-gagingly snippy Sloane Ranger accent bade me to do H. H. Monstrance the honor of taking lunch with him at my convenience the following week. He wished to speak with me on a matter of greatest urgency.

I was booked to fly back to New York directly from Prestwick on Mon-day, in time to interview a suspicious, secretive tycoon who was rumored to be fronting for the Mafia in a Manhattan building project. The inter-view had been a bitch to arrange, but I found myself accepting, without a moment's hesitation, lunch with X in London for the following Tuesday. The editor would have a fit, but after all, this was H. H. Monstrance calling; more than that, this was X.

On the flight from Inverness to London, I continued to wonder what X wanted. He probably had some kind of ghostwriting job in mind. Not autobiographical; he'd already published a bland and disappointing ghostwritten recapitulation of his career at GBG. More likely, I thought, he'd been holed up all this time hatching some great scheme for the so-cioeconomic salvation of the Western world, and now he needed someone to put it into writing. There was a lot of that sort of mush around these days. Even our magazine, not exactly a puff organ for the plutocracy, received probably a dozen tycoonish submissions a week, from men who'd made a pile and seemed to think that wealth licensed them to prescribe for the problems of the rest of us. The trouble was, as my editor said, it was difficult to justify printing nostrums written by the very chaps whose piggishness had gotten us into this mess in the first place. He sent them back with a pleasant note advising that the Op-Ed page of *The New York Times* would probably prove a more hospitable and effective sounding-board for the interesting, yea, provocative views of Mr. ———, which it invariably did.

Well, if that was what X wanted, I would have to disappoint him. I'd been writing for over twenty years now, since I'd joined *Newsweek* right out of Harvard, and at last I felt I was on level ground as a writer. I'd worked through my grudges; I'd reached the point where I flattered my-self that I got more of the words right than I got wrong; and I felt, or at least had, until the problems with my lady arose, that I knew myself and life well enough to start making sense out of things. So I wasn't currently available to put my words under other people's names.

I especially liked working for *Manhattan Spectator*. I was born curious—Mother, less kind, called me downright nosy—and irreverent and suspicious—others said cynical—of the motives of men in high places, and the *Spec* gave me plenty of room to feed and indulge these vices of personality. The magazine had been founded to penetrate and puncture the cant and persiflage that everywhere abounded. We thought of ourselves as a brave little band; our editor, hardly ever a profane man, once described us as "right out of *Beau Geste*, brave Legionnaires manning a Fort Zinderneuf of realism in a Sahara of bullshit."

After sixteen years at *Newsweek*, I'd come to the *Spec* five years ago, attracted by the fact that its twenty or so contract writers were not required to specialize. I had written book reviews and theater notes and squibs on Wall Street and the advertising world, and features on everything from a crisis in the management of Lincoln Center to the heartbreaking degeneration of the "idea" of the New York Yankees. Recently, I'd been taking a close look, thanks to chance, at "the new Manhattan establishment," as *New York*, with whom we loosely competed on occasion, glowingly categorized the congeries of social climbers, stock market papermongers, real estate shills, and assorted other virtuosos of hype and blather who seemed to dominate public awareness in the city. It was promising territory, comprising a miserable collection of shameless opportunists and gratification seekers: the men were principally paper merchants gorged on inside info and big lines of credit; the women were marked by a social ambition so obvious as to be unconscionable; the whole lot were vulgar, loud, unlettered, parasitic, and marked, above all, by an insecure, humorless self-esteem based on and derived from possessions. The fact was I found myself among them more than I liked, thanks to Cass, which I tried to excuse away by telling myself it was all in a good cause, that I was suffering fools in order to harvest material against the day when I would blow them all to journalistic kingdom come, when I would tip over their golden rock and show the world the slimy slugs and crawly beetles underneath. That's what I told myself in the mirror. The truth was that I was going out among the socialites and troglodytes as a labor of dying love, because I was once again connected up with Abner Monstrance, through his wife of two years, who happened to be the sister of my girlfriend of three.

The day hummed drowsily in X's garden. The traffic along the Embankment was barely audible. I was sticky and thirsty. I wondered where the butler was; an iced tea or a beer would do very nicely. I wished X would come down. How would he find me? I asked myself nervously. The last time I saw him I was a kid of eighteen; now I'm a kid of forty-three. I started to think of the way things had been.

"Sam! By George, this is grand!"

He'd come out suddenly while I was woolgathering. I scrambled up.

"Hello, X." For an instant we hesitated, both uncertain what the form should be after so long, until he reached out his arms and we embraced, just as in the old days. We stood back to examine each other, to appraise the damage.

He looked just fine. He'd put on some weight, and the bulk of his torso appeared to have shifted a few latitudes to the south, but the man after all was coming up on seventy-five. His once sandy hair was now dead white; when I'd last seen him, it had been merely flecked with gray. He was as tanned as ever; the tan looked legit. No sunlamps and Estée Lauder bronzing glop for X. His eyes were the lively, bright, dancing black marbles I remembered; the wrinkles and crinkling in the surrounding flesh seemed to have acquired a richer, more fascinating complexity. X wasn't tall, but he was a big man, large dimensioned; his monumental head, Roman in scale if not in particulars, was delineated by broad robust features, but there was nothing crude or peasantlike about him. He looked older but not aged; the only clear evidence of his years was a slight stoop to his shoulders, as if seven decades of bearing that massive head had taken its toll.

He saw me look him over; a flash of doubt fled across his features, a quick shadow against the sun.

"I've gotten fat, haven't I, Sam?" He laughed. "It's these damn lotuses I've been eating. They've too damn many calories!"

His hoarse, surprisingly high voice and laugh hadn't changed. Sounds bumped out of X like pinballs, tumbled like gravel in fast water. His voice was free of any conscious affectation, but yet there was something there instantly recognizable as Old Boston, Old New York, Old Philadelphia: something implacably, impregnably patrician.

"You look just great, X," I said. "It's pencil pushers like me who turn into slobs."

He looked remonstratively up at the sun. "It's hot out here. Too hot for May in England; hell, it's always too hot for May in England. How about a drink?"

He led me back inside.

"I hated to put air conditioning in this house," he said. "Selena wouldn't let me when she was alive, but the boys from the National Gallery said I ought to think of the pictures."

That was the X I knew talking. Whenever something needed doing, there had always been "boys" on call to do it: boys from the Met to rehang the paintings; boys flown in from Miami if the twin Chryslers on the fishing boat started missing; boys from the GBG Labs to fix the television set.

His uniform hadn't changed either. Still a soft dark-gray suit, one of probably fifty; a shirt patterned in minute blue checks, the collar latched under the small knot of a navy blue knitted silk necktie by a gold safety pin; dark brown slip-on shoes polished to a mirrorlike gleam that matched the depths of the patina of the spectacular Chippendale bookcase which dominated the drawing room. Keep it simple, boys, he used to tell Abner and me. Simple and good. Don't dress like a salesman: no Windsor knots, no patterns in the suiting. Being classy's nine tenths a matter of discretion.

"Scotch, Sam, seeing as you've just come from Scotland?" He brandished a decanter at me. "McAllan here, and if that's too pale, there's some Laphroig out back they keep for polishing the furniture—or, if a malt's not to your taste, we pour Famous Grouse in this house."

"No whisky," I said, "at least not till the sun goes down. Besides, you better hoard what you've got. Supplies are going to be short, inasmuch as I just finished drinking up all the whisky north of the border."

He poured me a Cinzano, finishing it off with a splash from a siphon as expertly as a bartender at "21." That surprised me. In the years I'd been close to the Monstrances, I'd never seen X do anything for himself. Not once. There had always been valets and pilots and fishing guides and butlers and chauffeurs and housemaids and barmen to do everything from gaffing a marlin to skewering an olive.

He poured himself a glass of champagne from a bottle reposing in a large silver bucket.

"Well," he said, raising his glass, "cheers. It's been too long." He sipped his drink. "You look fine, Sam. The writer's métier clearly becomes you. How's Marjorie?"

"She's fine; she's retired, you know. She lives in Bridgehampton year round now."

"She still smoke too much?"

"Absolutely. Sometimes it worries me."

"Ah, Sam, one must forgive a small vice in a woman otherwise so extraordinary. So she's finally sent in her papers. Good. I could never understand how an intelligent and beautiful woman could want to become a lawyer. I detest lawyers."

I raised my glass. "Here's to that—with no offense to Mother."

"Well, I envy her Bridgehampton. I miss that part of the world." He sipped his wine and looked me over again. "And I hear you've been seeing something of Ab?"

"A fair amount." I wondered how he knew. According to Clio Monstrance, her husband hardly ever spoke to the father-in-law she'd never met. "I take out his wife's sister."

"Quite a coincidence. You and Ab didn't see much of each other after Starbuck. It's a sad thing when friends lose touch. Ah, well, that's what life's mostly about: coincidences. And how do you find Ab?"

"Very well. Clio seems to have brought him out."

I wanted to keep the family aspect strictly on a personal and social level. If X wished to talk about Granite/AbCom, let him bring it up.

"Has she now? She must be quite a girl."

That Clio was, although my feelings about her effect on my life and pursuit of happiness were definitely, if not mixed, confused. When Cassandra Hargrove and I first started seeing each other, Clio had been no more than an occasional voice on the telephone from San Francisco, where she was married to a banker. Then it was Cass who was the star turn of the Hargrove sisters, who had recently been promoted head of the Department of Nineteenth-Century American Paintings at a major auction house and had co-authored the definitive study of the landscapist Jasper Cropsey. It was Cass who bent supportively from her pinnacle when Clio lost her only child to leukemia and her only husband to someone in his office and came back to New York, Cass who got her sister the job behind the reception desk at the Sandler Gallery, which was where she first met Abner Monstrance. To me, Clio was little more than a dim presence, to be taken dutifully along to cocktail parties and openings: quiet, with attractive, blond good looks that I found too blandly, pattern-book perfect, besotted as I was with Cass's dash and bite and her sharp dark beauty.

Abner Monstrance could have married a stone and, because of who he was and what he commanded, that stone would have automatically become a force in Manhattan social life, if it so chose. Clio was surely no stone, but few, least of all her sister, would have figured her for the social comet she became. Suddenly she was in all the papers and magazines, which reported on her clothes, her entertainments, and her comings and goings in extravagant, worshipful detail.

As if reading my thoughts, X said sharply, "She certainly gets her name in the papers a great deal."

"She does indeed," I said. I was surprised at his critical tone. If one wanted to talk about seeming to court and bask in social publicity, it would have been hard to top X's performance during his courtship of Selena Maffett and the years of their marriage. Back then, I was discovering that "publicity" was almost as much fun to observe as baseball, and I had followed the Monstrances' busy social life with an avidity I'd once reserved for Roy Campanella's batting average.

X being X, and Selena being Selena, all their publicity didn't seem surprising. But neither Abner nor Clio was the sort of person I would have ever picked out as being in the least hungry for social celebrity. Cass disagreed, and although it would have made our life together more bearable and possibly more durable, I couldn't consider her attribution of social ambition to her sister and brother-in-law as anything more than sour grapes. I might not flip out for her, but I admired Clio. She struck me as basically calm and steady. She had gone through a lot, and I could hardly imagine that she was seduced, fooled, or fazed by the silly people in whose company she was regularly reported. Abner, moreover, was reserved to the point of stiffness, uneasy in any company unless discussing business; he had never been notable for his small talk.

"I don't think all this publicity's doing Ab any good," X said. "If he keeps it up, people will cease to take him seriously. They'll write him off as a lightweight. I've seen it happen before." He spoke with a sudden sourness.

"To tell you the truth," I said, "I don't think they chase after it. Abner's complained about it to me once or twice. You know how it is, X. There's always some jerk ready to fink to the gossip columns in exchange for a mention." I did not add my growing suspicion that among said finks was my own lady fair. "Besides," I added, "it's harmless."

"Don't be too sure of that," said X.

Is it possible he's jealous? I thought. For him to criticize Abner in this matter reeked of what my late grandfather used to call "the ancient pot-kettle relationship." X had flaunted his affair with Selena, his pursuit and capture of her, and the circumstances of their married life together right up to the day the GBG jet had crashed into the Potomac. Their life was recorded in a veritable Bayeux tapestry of columns, snippets, articles, and interviews. I had no doubt X had truly loved Selena, but she had also been one of the prize trophies of our age. When she and X commenced their affair on the Onassis yacht, she was reputed to be the mistress both of the incumbent President and the richest man in Texas, reason enough to rile up X's legendary, unstanchable, competitive juices, especially in matters erotic. Which could account for his perceiving Clio as a challenger to Selena's memory.

Poor Clio, I thought; her motives and accomplishments were being mightily impugned on all fronts. People who shamelessly hustled invitations to her parties invariably knocked her the next morning for pushiness or extravagance. I was willing to take Clio and Abner at face value: they were in love, he was rich, they wanted to have a good time, and this seemed to be the way rich people had a good time. After all, Abner had been working fourteen hours a day for a decade, and her life hadn't exactly been a barrel of laughs. Clio had a talent for entertaining that had been germinated and nourished by Abner's money and position. The dozen or so parties to which Cass had taken me had been very nicely executed, almost permitting me to overlook the sort of people who made up her guest lists.

I didn't really enjoy their parties, or any of the others given by the connections Cass had developed through Abner and Clio. There was no variety, to begin with. The same faces talked at me and at each other, night after night, like a tired repertory company dragging itself from town to town. These evenings were too assembled, too constructed; it was hospitality as taxidermy, a display of human trophies. The atmosphere was seldom comfortable. The men seemed uneasy with their importance; the (typically) new wives seemed uneasy with their men. It was oddly asexual, curiously dull. No one flirted or drank too much, and in place of conversation there was rendered, one by one, what amounted to a series of position papers. Not at all my scene, but I was trying to hold things with Cass together, and this took up little enough of my life and none of my modest fortune, so I went where I was told and sat where I found my name, and made agreeable noises, and solaced myself with Abner's or whoever's Beluga and Dom Pérignon.

The abiding problem was Cass. She took vituperative offense at her sister's success and good fortune. Clio's wealth and celebrity grated on her, which in turn grated on me. If it had been a simple matter of envy, I might have handled it better, but Cass had become intoxicated with Clio's world. She wanted to belong to it in a big way, which meant ingratiating herself and, by extension, me, with a group of people I knew I would detest—and detest myself for seeing—if we became regulars. My dear late grandfather had described the upper crust as "a bunch of crumbs held together by dough," which certainly covered this crowd. Yet here was Cass, bitching about Clio's nouvelle richesse and complaining that Clio was rubbing her social success and celebrity in her face—and nevertheless cultivating these rich new acquaintances. This had been going on for a year and a half now, and I was faced with the embarrassing conclusion that I had once again fallen in love with the wrong person.

I looked up to find that X, too, had lapsed into private thoughts. Our conversation needed redirecting, so I asked him about his life in London.

It was fine, he said. Like everything else in life, not what it had been.

"I remember first coming here back before the war. I stayed with Rosa Lewis at the old Cavendish Hotel in Jermyn Street. Champagne for breakfast, white tie every night. What times those were, Sam! It's still civilized, but the bread is salt and the stairs are steep, as they are for all us exiles." He grinned at me.

"Dante?"

"Right! The seventeenth canto of the *Paradiso*." He grinned more broadly. X liked to toot his little flourishes of erudition. He thought they kept him from being taken for a mere businessman, especially one whose immense fortune had been built on the taste of the masses.

"And how's New York?" he asked. "I try to keep up through the papers. It sounds pretty ghastly. Who's this Trump chap I keep seeing puffed up in the *Times*? Does he have something on the Sulzbergers? I gather even Nixon's welcome in polite society."

"He seems to be. Trump's a builder who's made about a trillion dollars using tax abatements to build million-dollar apartments for Arabs. All perfectly legal. Hell, these days, everybody's a builder. Or a paper merchant. That's all New York's about, now: real estate and moving pieces of paper around. Deals, deals, deals. Anything goes, everything's for sale, including three quarters of the people you meet. People are making sums of money that are frightening—they make more overnight than you made in forty years at GBG—and yet the city gets noisier, dirtier, angrier."

"You sound bitter."

"I'm not happy. I walk around a lot and I look at things. I try to calculate which is growing faster: the number of limousines or the number of people living in the street. This winter a guy lived on a steam grate down the block from my apartment. If I go over to Columbus Avenue, I can buy a pair of Italian shoes or a dress made by some Japanese fag, but I can't find a newspaper or a quart of milk. They're knocking off the neighborhoods one by one. All in the name of laissez-faire. Eldonomics."

"Eldonomics, eh?" X smiled, more to himself than at me. "My goodness gracious; who'd have ever thought it possible." He sipped his coffee thoughtfully. "I know all about Eldonomics, Sam. That's one of the things I want to talk with you about." For a moment he stared past me at his Bonnards. "Do you remember Jake Polhemus?"

"Sure." Jacob Polhemus was X's oldest friend and a legend in his own right.

"Jake came through London a few months ago. We try to get together once or twice a year, especially since at our age we can't count on being around forever. He sounded like you. He says that nowadays in America the mere fact that a man has a lot of money is grounds for respect; that it doesn't matter how he came by it or what he does with it, only that he has it."

"He's right. People seem to think that spending money is an accomplishment."

"Well, there've always been those, but in a properly ordered society they're kept out of sight. Eldonomics, eh?" He snorted.

"I'm not that old, X," I said, "but for the first time I can remember, money isn't merely talking, it's screaming!"

"It has a way of doing that," he said patiently. "The trouble with money is that it does its job too well. Jake said that it reminded him of these fungicides that are promoted as a boon to mankind and end up poisoning everything on God's earth. Anyway, it must be grist for your mill as a writer. Nothing about people is as revealing as how they relate to money."

Their own and other people's, I thought. I asked, "What about socks? You always told Abner and me to look at a man's ankles if we wanted to know the truth about him."

"The world was lighter-hearted then, Sam. Speaking of which, I like that magazine you write for. Someone around there has a sense of humor. You seem to be making things hot for the people who deserve it. Someone's got to. I don't know what's happening to *The New Yorker*, and that other magazine seems to be mainly about zucchini. By the way, I thought your book was quite amusing. I intended to write you about it, but I never got around to it. There was quite a long time when it seemed I didn't get around to anything. But that's enough of me, at least for the moment. Tell me what you've been up to."

I had the feeling he knew all he needed to know, but I told him anyway, about my years at *Newsweek* and about the *Spec*. I was surprised he'd read the book. It had been a trendy, smart-ass, postadolescent novel about the thinly disguised goings-on among a bunch of thinly disguised celebrities in a thinly disguised East Side hangout. The critics' enthusiasm was restrained, but I made some money from it, and since in those days I was in the last flush of the writer-as-stud phase, the book also earned me a decent return in the moist, fleshly coin of the writer groupies who hung out at Elaine's and P. J. Clarke's. It made me shudder to recall that period of my life. I'd been almost disgustingly writerly, all pose and little production, scouring New York for a vintage Royal typewriter to pose with me in the jacket photograph.

The novel had been my last intentional flirtation with the smart and easy way out—as a writer, and as a lover, a son, a citizen. My friend Buck "the Arb" would say, "Go with the flow to make the dough," and perhaps he was right, along with all my friends who finally settled back and let life take them on its terms.

Now I was on the lookout for a really heavy subject. In Scotland I'd had the idea of doing a big series on the effect of money—TV money, new-owner money—on sports. When I told X about it, he smiled.

"Still a fan, eh?"

I still was. Sports meant a lot to me. I was a holdover from an era when sports meant something to the people who played the games, even the professionals, and so they meant something to us in the peanut gallery. The old days, when the sports pages were about line scores and world records and locker-room gossip instead of drug busts and contract disputes. Once, in the course of a spat, Cass had told me that for a grown man to love sports the way I did was silly. I nailed her in my best Rhett Butler manner. "My dear," I said, "my love of sports is the urn in which I keep the ashes of my youth." Even she had to admit it wasn't a bad line.

"Remember the seventh game of the 'fifty-five World Series, Sam?" X asked. "Wasn't that something?"

Something I'd never forget.

In his imperial fashion, X had commanded a day off from Starbuck for Abner and me. We'd been picked up by a GBG Convair at a nearby naval air station and flown through a brilliant October morning to LaGuardia, where a limousine waited. We had lunch at the Stadium Club and then went to the GBG box right back of first base, so close to the field that I felt I could reach out and touch Moose Skowron and Gil Hodges. The scene was as vivid as yesterday: the big ball park sparkling emerald and blue; the red, white, and blue bunting draped from the field boxes and the facade; the league pennants bristling in the fresh wind; in centerfield, the monuments to Gehrig, Miller Huggins, and the Babe glistening in the sun. I remembered Podres, pitching for the Dodgers, as intent in his work as a surgeon, making a two-run lead stand up; I remembered Amoros going halfway to Riverdale to catch Berra's fly and then doubling McDougald at second—X and I chomping hot dogs and hooting and hollering and squeezing our knuckles white.

Abner hadn't shared our excitement. He wasn't a fan at heart. He preferred being watched to watching; he wanted the crowd's eyes to be on him. Moreover, there was a debate with Exeter scheduled for Saturday; being made to come to New York had deprived Abner of an afternoon's debating practice. Not that the issue was ever in doubt. X was X; the school would have seen that Abner obeyed his father's summons.

Perhaps if I had been wiser or more experienced then, if I hadn't been feverishly obsessed with the game that afternoon, I could have looked at Abner more closely and seen in him the man he would become. His natural shyness was already consciously being reworked into aloofness, as if he knew that only by drawing apart could he protect himself against being drowned in his father's vitality and genius and celebrity.

The butler came to announce lunch.

After we were seated, I asked, "That's not the same butler you had in New York?"

"Good heavens, no. You're thinking of Hobson. He left me a year or two after Selena died. He didn't approve of my new group of friends. I heard he ended up in Beverly Hills, so he got what he deserved." X chuckled. Then he blew out his breath sharply. "This fellow's all right, although he insists on calling me 'Ambassador.' I'll bet you did a double-take when you heard that."

He couldn't hide his rue. Ambassador to the Court of St. James's. The only promise X had made to Selena that he hadn't been able to keep. The appointment was set, all fixed up in Washington, the leave from GBG arranged, the house on Chelsea Embankment complete down to the last goblet and finial.

But then GBG News had uncovered the business about the President's brother and some military contract payoffs. It wasn't the biggest scandal in history, and X could have killed the story, but he was who he was, and he let GBG News go for the jugular, and out the window went London. According to Mother, Selena's chagrin had been so great she'd threatened to leave X. "Poor Horace," Mother told me later. "He tried to buy forgiveness with that house in Georgetown, to create a grand Washington presence; let her try to outdo Pamela Harriman."

The big house on M Street. Selena Monstrance had been close to finishing it when the GBG JetStar carrying her and her decorators to Washington had fishtailed into the ice-crusted Potomac with, it was reported, several hundred yards of Colefax and Fowler fabric.

The butler brought a decanter of wine the color of old straw. X brightened.

"Now this should be something," he said. "Montrachet 'sixty-two. The only white wine that seems to get better with age. Why can't men be like Montrachet, Sam?"

"They can." Now it was my turn to grin. "Provided they're explorers."

"'East Coker'!" His delight was obvious. "My goodness, you still remember it. Good for you!"

Of course I remembered "East Coker." It was X's favorite modern poem. I'd first heard it when he read it to Abner and me one night on the porch of his salmon-fishing camp. I was fifteen and it didn't make a great deal of sense to me then, but there was no mistaking the enthusiasm with which he croaked the dry lines. In the background, through the darkness, we could hear the steady murmur of the Restigouche moving toward the sea. He'd promised us each a new Bogdan reel from Abercrombie & Fitch if we learned the last section by heart. The brass reel, never to be used, had my name engraved on it. I supposed it was in a carton in Mother's attic. I still had the poem, too. I wondered if Abner had kept either.

The nutty vapor of the wine was powerful enough to walk on. The butler appeared with potted shrimp and toast points.

"Tell me, Sam," X asked. "I was interested in what you said about money and sports. Do you ever see Eugenie?"

"Once in a while. If you read the sports pages, she's hard to miss."

Which was certainly true. Eugenie Monstrance had bought or created franchises in football, baseball, basketball, and ice hockey, each one of which was a consistent loser. Dogged as they had been by bad luck and worse management, two of her clubs, the football Vandals, based at Shea Stadium, and the baseball Boroughs, which played out of the new ball park at the Nassau County Sportsplex, could have been contenders. The other two were hopeless.

Eugenie's defeat-riddled teams, collectively known to the bar crowd at Runyon's as "the Empress Eugenie's meat rack," were a mystery. By comparison with most of her fellow owners, Eugenie was generous, concerned, considerate, and retiring. I couldn't remember her ever holding a press conference or otherwise thrusting herself into the limelight.

But, for all her virtues as an owner, her teams lost—and lost—and lost. There was no doubt she was her own biggest problem, a victim of her own noble intentions. She badly wanted to win, but she wanted to win honorably and wanted her teams to reflect the highest traditions of sportsmanship and gentlemanly behavior. She paid her people very well, she exhorted them in every known way, and she fiddled ceaselessly with her rosters. She seemed to have an uncanny gift for making the wrong move at the wrong time: trading this outfielder, cutting that defensive lineman, bringing up this defenseman and sending down that wing, trying this natural small forward at guard. And she seemed to have a penchant for drafting troublemakers: kids with personality or dope problems, great athletes with lousy behavior patterns that sat crossways to Eugenie's ideals of sportsmanship. One after the other, she let them go and lost in talent what she gained in moral uplift.

In any case, she could afford it. A recent AbCom proxy statement showed Eugenie Monstrance as the beneficial owner of 4.9 million shares of AbCom. The stock was selling in the low fifties, so she was worth some $250 million in AbCom alone.

"It's funny, isn't it?" X said. "Eugenie was such a determined, competitive, able girl. And by no means stupid. Twice as bright as Ab, if you ask me. I can't understand why these teams of hers keep losing, and why she still keeps trying. Women have no business owning teams anyway. Poor thing, I gather she's made a mess of herself?" He didn't sound truly sympathetic or concerned.

What he gathered was true. Physically, Eugenie was a mess. Nerves, presumably, had created a sugar dependency that took the form of an addiction to soda pop. She was reputed to drink a case a day. Apparently it didn't matter what; she was carbonationally omnivorous for Coke, Pepsi, Nehi Grape, Dr. Brown's Celery Tonic, Mountain Dew, Dr. Pepper, any brand of orange pop, root beer, cream soda. She looked as if a three-inch layer of kapok had been glued to her frame. Her teeth had rotted; her breath would have scared off an iguana.

"It must kill Ab to see our name associated with all those losing teams," X said. "It certainly bothers me. I can't understand how she could let herself go so completely. I don't imagine she has any beaus?"

"None that I've heard of." There was no point in repeating scruffy, snickering barroom speculations as to whether the Empress got it on with her players, or the inevitable rumors that she was a lesbian. Talk like that went with the territory.

The butler returned with a cheese soufflé and a platter of thin French beans dressed in butter. It was a perfect meal for the day. X hadn't lost his old flair. He overwhelmed you with the rightness of his touch.

"I must say," X said as he helped himself, "that it's a bit of a relief to me to see these teams of Eugenie's do so badly. There was a time I used to lie awake nights worrying whether I'd made a mistake about Ab and Eugenie, whether I'd made the wrong decision about Granite."

"What do you mean?"

"Well, of course you wouldn't know this, but right after you and Ab graduated from Starbuck, I decided I had to make a decision about Granite's future, about who would run it if something happened to me. It was the only fair thing to do. Both Ab and Eugenie were in college; they had a right to plan their lives. We controlled enough stock to keep Granite a family company, which is the way I wanted it when I started out.

"Eugenie was doing extremely well at Wellesley: business manager of the paper, president of the student union, head of the laundry, all those sorts of things, and getting fine grades in the bargain. I was quite impressed. She was a demon for work, with a good practical head on her shoulders, and a quick study. She had worked a couple of summers at Granite and had done me really quite proud. Everyone liked her. She had a nice way with people.

"Ab was quite different. He did brilliantly at Starbuck, of course, although he seemed a trifle grim and mechanical, and a business like Granite depends inordinately on instinct and flair. He had real drive and ambition, though, even if he wasn't easy with people. In short, his temperament wasn't exactly what I would have designed for a future head of Granite, but he was my only son, and in the old-fashioned world I was brought up in, sons had the right of succession. So I decided it would be Ab who would eventually take over, and starting then, in his first year at New Haven, I groomed him to succeed me. I had to tell Eugenie, of course, and she took it very badly. I must say I was surprised. I can't imagine how she ever let her expectations rise so high. She carried on so that she made me feel quite guilty, so I made over a large stock interest to her, thanks to which she's become one of the richest women in America. It's all worked out for the best, thank heavens, but there were moments. On the whole, Ab's done very well. I'm quite pleased with many of the things he's done, although I'm not sure I grasp them all. Ah!"

The butler had appeared with a decanter of red wine. X swirled and sipped it ruminatively, looking into his glass as if the wine's depths held secrets and answers.

"Mmmm. Very good. I thought, Sam, this being such a special occasion—our twenty-fifth reunion, you might say—that we should have a go at the last of the 'forty-seven Mouton. Here, just taste this, and let's talk of shoes and ships and sealing wax. This is far too lovely a wine to insult with talk of money or children."

I sank my nose in the glass. It was, indeed, magically complex and powerful.

For the rest of lunch we exchanged chatter. We were like insects encountering each other on a vine leaf, flicking and probing with our antennae to establish identity and territory. It wasn't surprising that we were somewhat tentative; it had been a long time.

I was uneasy without being nervous. X was obviously up to something. In his complex, manipulative dramaturgy of life, things had to be arranged just so and all in good time, his good time. He hadn't just suddenly thought of me after all these years and felt an irresistible need to see me again. I wasn't family. There were no accounts still open between us. What the hell, I thought; no point in letting puzzlement spoil this excellent meal.

CHAPTER 2

After lunch, X led me upstairs to the library study, a tall room over-looking the river, lined to the ceiling with bookshelves; the windows were open to the sultry afternoon and the narcotic *whoosh* of traffic along the Embankment.

"This is where I spend most of my time," he said. "You'll have to excuse me for a minute. At my age even the best wine goes through with hardly a fare-thee-well. Take a look around. You're a bookman at heart."

The shelves were filled with books for reading. No bookseller's "fur-niture": no resplendently bound, unopened sets of Scott and Conrad and the Victorian poets, no histories of Northumberland, runs of *The Edin-burgh Review*, illustrated memoirs of long journeys to desert lands. There was a Nonesuch Dickens, about half of Trollope in a motley of editions, a few Russians, some Waugh, all of Anthony Powell and Faulkner, most of Hemingway and Fitzgerald, Proust; a lot of history, Tocqueville, *The Fed-eralist*, a clutch of volumes on the Civil War, Macaulay, biographies that ranged from Lincoln to Gordon Liddy; there were shelves of books on current events, mostly of the "what has gone wrong" variety; two shelves of adventure stories, "boys' books," with a shelf of Henty: *With Gordon at Khartoum*, *Win by the Sword*, *By Pike and Dyke*, and a score more; beneath them Conan Doyle, Buchan, Dornford Yates, *Beau Geste*, the Sussex Kip-ling, *Penrod*, and a complete run of Owen Johnson: *Stover at Yale*, *The Tennessee Shad*, and the rest. There were thrillers and atlases; art and refer-ence books; a little bit of everything. It was a good library for voyaging in—rich in memories and resounding with possibilities.

A number of the books sprouted slips of paper. I took one down idly: *The Hart-Davis–Lyttleton Letters*, Volume 1, a book I didn't know. At the first marker, a fine line had been drawn under a comment quoted from Justice Holmes, apparently about Virginia Woolf: "It was like watching someone organize her own immortality." On the facing page was underscored: "It is not what old men forget that shadows their senescence, but what they remember."

I replaced the book. X came back into the room.

"As you can see, after fifty years of radio and television, I've managed to learn to read all over again. How about some coffee?"

He gestured me to a place next to him on a maroon leather chesterfield and offered me brandy and a cigar. I declined. The big wines had done enough damage, and we were coming, I knew, to the serious business of the afternoon.

X took a sip of his coffee and put the cup down.

"Before we talk business, Sam, let me give you a little quick autobiographical sketch, just bring you up to date on these last few years. A brief spiritual autobiography, you might say.

"When I retired from Granite, I was pretty down personally; losing Selena that way was a terrible blow. You never knew her, but she was a goddess. When the plane crashed, I thought it was the end of the world. I could barely make myself get out of bed. So I handed the company over to Ab and tried to keep busy to forget, which meant that like most old men I did a lot of damn foolish things and spent a lot of time with a bunch of ninnies who kissed my feet. I should never have left Granite; that was the dumbest thing I did. Here I'd lost half my life, and I just walked out on the other half.

"Eventually I wised up and came here. London's a good place to think. Not like New York. Nobody thinks in New York, they only react. When I wasn't thinking about Selena, I thought a lot about Granite. I was out of it, so I pillowed my head on my memories. At first, I was pretty darn pleased with myself. Looking back, I could say I'd done something damn few men had done: I'd changed the world!"

He sipped his coffee and smiled to himself.

"You're too young to remember a world in which television wasn't right there at the center of life, Sam. I used to think of that time as a kind of Dark Ages out of which I'd led the world. I always had a vocation for broadcasting. We made money at Granite our first year, and we never stopped after that. I had a real aptitude for radio, but I think it's fair to say—and, mind you, I don't want to sound immodest—I had a genius for television. The first time I saw it, right here in London in 1938, when I was relatively still a kid, it was as if I'd been given Aladdin's lamp."

His voice registered the excitement of that long-ago revelation. But there was a trace of sadness, too; recognition that the first bright, pure moment was now only a memory, its fresh excitement irretrievable.

"I don't need to go over Granite's history for you," he continued. "I think it's fair to say we changed the way people lived, the way they understood themselves and the world, what they saw of life and wanted from it. People had the world opened up to them; they were entertained at their convenience; they got to see things they'd never seen before and couldn't have ever hoped to see: The coronation of queens and the inauguration of presidents. Joe DiMaggio and Ted Williams hitting home runs. Jack Kennedy's funeral. A man on the moon. They learned what war really looked like. Frank Sinatra and Bob Hope and John Wayne and Billy Graham and every president and king and dictator came into their living rooms to make them laugh, or rejoice, or think."

He smiled to himself and shook his head slowly.

"It wasn't ever just a business, don't you see? It was like the motorcar or the airplane or, in a way, the atom bomb. It touched so many lives."

"For better or worse," I said.

X grinned. "We'll come to that in good time, young man. Let an old man tell his story. You can imagine how exciting it was. It worked out wonderfully for me personally. It gave me everything I ever thought I wanted. I became rich; I became famous; I suppose you can say I became powerful. I was Number One: unbeaten, untied, and unchallenged. I'd licked Bill Paley and the Sarnoffs hollow. There wasn't a place in the world I couldn't wangle an invitation to, and that included Buckingham Palace and the Kremlin. I ate shark fins with Mao Zedong and fettucine with four popes. I drank gin with Hemingway in Havana and anise with Picasso in Saint-Tropez and vodka with Stalin at the Black Sea. I got whatever I wanted when I wanted it, including one of the most extraordinary women who ever lived, and I got, I thought, the one thing I wanted most out of my life."

He looked at me expectantly, wangling a cue. I obliged.

"What was that?"

"Immortality, Sam. A place in history. Most businessmen—let's face it, that's what I was—live and make a lot of money and die and that's that. What names live on? Not so many: Edison, Ford, Rockefeller, Watson. And me. Granite was my stamp on posterity. As a Starbuck man you'll appreciate that."

I knew what he was talking about. For nearly two hundred years, Starbuck Academy had instructed its matriculants that a main part of the great business of life was to bid for a place in posterity.

"Well," said X emphatically, "I'd done it! I'd opened all those magic casements for all those hundreds of millions of people, and history was going to know about it, and thank me for it, and love me for it!"

"There's no question you'll be in the history books, X," I said.

He shook his head sadly. "That's probably true enough, but not in the way I planned."

"What do you mean?"

"For a few years there, after I left Granite, I was sort of a boat without a jib, a top without a gyro. I was sort of spinning along on the surface, listening to all those people tell me how great I was. When I got here, and started to calm down and think things through and spend time with people from Oxford and Cambridge and the London School of Economics instead of from Park Avenue and '21,' I began to see things differently. As I told you, I started to read again; my mind began to turn over, like an engine firing up after a long cold winter on blocks. It took quite a few tries to get it going, but then it just zoomed ahead. The more I read, the more I realized how blind I'd been about myself and what I'd done."

He poured himself another cup of coffee. I had the feeling he was going carefully, working from a much-rehearsed script. The gist of his mea culpa was almost too obvious. I couldn't see the point. Perhaps it was no more than it seemed: an old man pouring out his mind-ache.

"Do you remember what John Stuart Mill said about Jeremy Bentham? He said that Bentham committed the mistake of supposing that the business part of human affairs was the whole of them. Well, that was me! I'd been mentally anesthetized by being so busy, so competitive! I'd been so preoccupied with beating Paley and Goldenson and the Sarnoffs in the Nielsens, so busy wanting to be admired by Wall Street and the *Times*, so pleased with being 'Man of the Year' this and 'Businessman of the Year' that, that everything else had been knocked out of my head. I had been hailed for thirty years as the man who created commercial television. Now, all of a sudden, I was confronted by my creation!"

"You and Dr. Frankenstein," I said boldly, hoping I didn't sound impudent. I liked X's drift. I hated television.

"Anyway, the more I read and pondered, the more I saw things with new eyes. The English still keep a pretty tight rein on television hours, and I asked myself why. Mind you, I'd spent thirty years at home listening to how our programming was vapid, opportunistic, violent, salacious, and downright evil, but people seemed to lap it up and so I shrugged the criticism off as just so much mush from the do-gooders and bleeding hearts. Just jealousy, I thought. Jake used to say that envy breeds 'constructive criticism' and 'moral outrage' the way a swamp breeds mosquitoes."

He got up again and took a scrapbook from a shelf. He carried it back and set it down beside him on the sofa, unopened.

"I started to look at television with new eyes, and I was appalled."

"You must have been if you were watching the BBC. Six hours of snooker isn't high in entertainment value."

"That's not what I watched. Television over here is about where we were in 1950. It has an innocent quality I rather like. No, I watched the hot new shows, the hot new Granite shows. I got a service in New York to tape them for me."

"A service? Why not just get them from Abner?"

"People at Granite might have taken it in the wrong light. People are always suspicious of retired chieftains, and I'd made it pretty plain that I'd gone for good. Look at what's been happening at CBS. Anyway, have you seen something called 'The Dumpsters'?"

I had. Once. It was GBG's highest-rated sitcom, about a racially mixed family obliged by poverty to live in a trash module. It was a mean, stupid, mildly racist show which made a tasteless joke of poverty and misfortune. Its popularity stemmed from the fact that it was known to be the favorite show of the President of the United States, who frequently alluded to it.

"Well, I watched that show, and I was mortified to think that Granite was reduced to putting on this sort of thing."

"'Reduced'? They're making millions off that show."

"There is a point at which profit has to defer to decency, I fear. Besides, this isn't a solitary instance. I've watched all the Granite shows—and the others! At first I was simply appalled as a matter of taste: the writing was awful, the stories nonexistent. But none of that mattered beside the terrible dumbness of it all, the total lack of any underlying concern except self-gratification."

"We are a country dedicated to self-gratification, X. It's become the American way." I didn't add: Thanks to you.

"Precisely," he said, suddenly thumping his thigh as if to punish himself. "Precisely! I watched this garbage, Sam, and as I did, I swear the screen turned into a glaring, accusing eye, looking right at me. And then I knew."

I said nothing. He was on a tear.

"I knew that I had gotten it all wrong, Sam. I had built this company, this industry, into what I flattered myself into thinking was a monument for the ages, and what had I really built? A golden barge named GBG floating atop a great, poisonous, stinking tidal wave of garbage. I had seduced the nation into relying on television for its understanding of the world and for its values, and I had given it lies and delusion."

"Aren't you being a little melodramatic? Christ, X, you weren't the only one. If you hadn't come along, someone else would have. There were other people in the business, smart people. And you gave the audience what it wanted, right?"

He shook his head.

"Not right, Sam. The audiences came to demand what we acclimated them to wanting. Before television, don't you see, there wasn't any such thing as a television audience. There was no law of nature that decreed that we were obliged to give our viewers garbage. Taste comes from above; taste and inspiration and values. That's the point of an elite. That's why there's a Starbuck. We started out giving them good solid stuff: 'Playhouse 90,' and 'Texaco Star Theater,' and 'Person to Person,' and 'The Granite Players.' A trifle naive, but so was the country. But then we saw it was easier, and just as profitable, to sell personality instead of story and character; to copy the next fellow's success; to take the easy way; to cut corners."

So what? I thought, It's the way of the world. How about my own line of country? "It seems to me it's the same in every form of popular entertainment, X," I said. "Just look at what makes the best-seller lists."

"Don't get me started on publishing. It sickens me to see what they're doing at B and B. When I bought them, they were the finest publishers in America. Now I'm embarrassed. Sam, the fact is, an audience is like any other animal: If you continually feed it garbage, it develops a taste for garbage, just like a raccoon. All it wants to do is eat, and it doesn't much care what, after a while."

"So change the menu."

He grinned at me. "We always did understand each other, Sam. I can see you get my drift. I'm tired of living with my conscience. Damn it, it clanks around my head like Marley's ghost, howling for retribution. I may be an old man, but my batteries are charged up, and I can give it one more good shot. I'll be honest: I want posterity to clap me on the shoulder and say, 'H.H., well done!'"

It was clear to me now what he had in mind. It was a ghostwriting job, after all. Some sort of manifesto, a call for right thinking from one of the titans. I'd seen them in banking, in automobile and steel manufacturing, in advertising, so why not an admonitory voice from television's past, a hand from beyond the grave proffering a torch to show the true way? Why not, indeed? Yet in terms of probable effect, why? The world was up to its ass in manifestos and prescriptions; it hardly needed another. I felt vaguely disappointed and began to formulate a means of extricating myself.

"A lot of people want to reform television, X. Admittedly, it's a vast wasteland—about the size of China. Where do you start?" I tried to sound interested. In the back of my mind, I began to wonder if I could get a seat on the late Pan Am flight. I snuck a look at my watch; it was only two thirty. If I played my cards right, I could be out of here in twenty minutes.

"Jake always said that the best way to deal with a cause was to concentrate on its effects. Watch!"

He rose quickly and crossed the room to a cabinet against the far wall. It contained a video monitor and an array of electronic equipment. From a shelf he took a video cassette and inserted it into the player. The screen filled with electronic confetti, then displayed the Presidential Seal, succeeded by an image I knew all too well: the familiar smiling face of Eldon Erwitt, President of the United States of America, the Great Smoothie, the Great Disclaimer, "Eldon the Blameless," and above all the patron saint of "Eldonomics," the Administration's euphemism for economic bigotry disguised as stimulus.

I didn't like Erwitt. Not for any particular political reasons; I had no deep convictions about his advocacy of the gold standard, or his tax bill, or his policy in Honduras, or his defense budget. I disliked him because I thought him duplicitous. He had a way of making a complex, dangerous world seem safe and simple. The metaphorical igloos of his constituents were packed with iceboxes he had sold them. As I watched Erwitt slide into his pitch, in this case a soothing address to the UAW elders, I found my gorge rising. The truth was, I didn't just dislike Eldon Erwitt; I despised him.

What I thought didn't matter. Erwitt, now in his second year as President, was riding high. His rise to the White House had been a genuine American political myth, the stuff of fable. He incarnated the values and epistemologies of the television era; he was, in fact, the creature, creation, and personification of the medium in which he had risen to prominence, and which had been the principal instrument in electing him. Born and raised in Iowa farm country, graduated from a land-grant college, exempted from World War II, he had started out on a small Des Moines radio station doing local news and events; shortly after the war, he'd been hired by a Chicago radio station to read the regional farm news.

Then someone discovered that Erwitt had a natural aptitude for television, a knack of speaking with ingratiating, easy friendliness directly to the camera, as if to a friend met on the street; the camera, in turn, figuratively slung its electronic arm around his shoulders and embraced him like a buddy. He was truly telegenic: sincere, soothing, reassuring, comfy, pleasant-looking. Oddly, however, he projected more effectively when speaking against something rather than for something, perhaps because he was so agreeable about it, and to exploit this special twist, his writers developed a monologue for him, first merely as a lead-in to his reading of the news, but later as the substance of the show. To please the antediluvian politics of his middlewestern audience, the monologues centered on a genial disparagement of colored people and foreigners and amiable diatribes against the Internal Revenue Service. He handled potentially explosive or inflammatory material in a jolly, almost offhand way which lulled even his most violent adversaries into apathetic grumbling. "It was," wrote one early critic, "as if Will Rogers's material had been written by Josef Goebbels."

In time, as his audience grew, the scope of his material widened to pander to any conceivable right-wing grudge against Washington and the East. His sponsors brought him to New York and he was taken national, on GBG first, as it happened, and then, for his glory years, the decade between Kennedy's assassination and Nixon's resignation, on CBS. From time to time, he offended segments of his audience. In lieu of apology or justification, he developed a trademark style of brushing off and defusing complaints, invariably starting with a winning smile and the disclaimer, "Did I say that?"—itself to become a trademark—followed by folksy digressions, mainly anecdotal, calculated to reduce any issue, no matter how passionately held in the hearts of its adherents, to evanescent irrelevance. It was a technique which continued to serve Eldon Erwitt well as President.

His audience became in time a legitimate political constituency. His kind of plausibility was a rare asset; its political possibilities were first grasped by a secretive group of Lake Forest and Skokie millionaires shrewd enough to sense they had a potential standard-bearer; they introduced Erwitt to like-minded friends in Los Angeles and Long Beach, who in turn passed him along to sympathetic circles in Dallas and

Amarillo. He became a popular speaker at high-level business get-togethers, at the Greenbriar and the Bohemian Grove and Boca Raton, reiterating what those audiences wanted to hear: that all the world's troubles, all its evil, could be attributed to those tripartite forces of darkness: poor people, foreigners, and government. Cadres of money drew up, ready to be mobilized when the time came.

His political roots grew deeper in the conservative ideological loam of his home state. When opportunity knocked, his followers were in a position to pressure the Governor of Iowa to appoint him to fill the unexpired term of a suddenly deceased United States Senator. Two years later, he was reelected on his own, having become a national political figure with an irresistible recognition factor. Toward the end of his term, he seized control of a party that was ideologically in shreds, dominated its television-captivated convention the following year, and won the presidential nomination. The issues and momentum were on the incumbent President's side, and he should have beaten Erwitt easily. But pride got the best of him: damned if he was going to be seriously challenged by "a TV pitchman." The President made the mistake of taking Erwitt on in a televised public debate, and when the following January arrived, there was Eldon Erwitt being sworn in on the steps of the Capitol, with his wife Darlene, a former Chicago weather girl, beaming behind him.

I returned my attention to X's tape, which recorded Erwitt's recent Good Friday speech to the National Association of Christian Manufacturers. God had begun to loom larger in Erwitt's rhetoric, brought in as a sort of divine chorus underscoring a cascade of conventional laissez-faire pieties. A thematic breakdown of the President's remarks would have been something like: the free market is God's invention, and America is the bastion of the free market, so God is on America's side; the aim of the free market is individual wealth, which means that some will win and some will lose, but if life is harder on some than others, that is God's way, that is the American way; let no man deplore Christian charity, but God wasn't speaking of handouts either. God is good; America is good and great, and nothing can go wrong; so don't listen to the naysayers, who are mouthing the words of the Evil One, the composite Democrat with horns and cloven feet, whose handiwork was big government. Amen.

The tape ended with a question-and-answer period. Erwitt was asked about something he'd said in his campaign about social justice. The questioner was obviously antagonistic, a plant, and the audience's mutterings and hisses were audible. Like Casey at the bat, the President raised his hand and grinned affably. There was no denying his easy charm.

"Did I say that?" he said with a smile, and launched into a story about an alligator and a pickaninny. The tension of the moment dissolved in chuckles; the question lost its point.

X got up and turned off the VCR.

"Well," he said, "how do you feel about that?"

"Dyspeptic. He may have sold a hell of a lot of automobile batteries and cancer insurance in his time, but that's not the same thing as running the country. Frankly, he scares me."

"How?" I knew X had led me into the channel he wanted, but there could be no harm in going along.

"I have this feeling that Erwitt's been on the other side of the cameras too long. Maybe the klieg lights have blinded him; maybe he's read too many scripts. I don't know, it's just a feeling that he doesn't know where make-believe ends and the real world begins, which is ketchup and which is real blood. Nine times out of ten, that would be harmless. Not in a President, though; his finger's on the button, and Erwitt's likely to press it someday thinking it's all just part of some big videogame, that he's back doing a cameo on 'Lost Worlds.'"

"Precisely!" said X triumphantly. "I knew you would understand if anyone did. I feel the same way, only ten times worse. You know what I was telling you just now about my guilty feelings about television? Well, they're all crystallized in Eldon. I invented him, you know."

I'd forgotten. Of course: Erwitt had started in television on Granite's Chicago station.

It was shortly after the war, X said. He'd gone to Des Moines to visit the family of a Yale classmate who'd been lost at Leyte.

"I woke up early, and turned on the radio in my hotel room. Purely a professional reflex. The first voice I heard turned out to be Eldon, reading crop reports and giving the local social news: Four-H meetings, Grange suppers, that sort of thing. I listened for a minute or two, till my ears started to wiggle and I sat straight up in bed and said to myself, Hey, this fellow's got what it takes! After a few more minutes, when I sorted out my reactions, I knew exactly what Eldon had: pure, absolute, totally projectible confidence. Listening to him recite the price of corn made me feel that the world was in good hands. I thought, If a fellow can make radishes and rutabagas sound reassuring, heaven knows what he can do with something that's really important!

"I asked around about Eldon. He was just in his early twenties then, a local boy. I didn't like it that he'd managed to sit out the war, but it was

1946, and the war was over, and it was back to business now, so if this fellow had what it took, well . . ."

X shook his head. He would have undone the past if he could.

"I arranged to meet him and disliked him at once. He was like a lot of 'naturals' I've known; all God-given technique and ability and nothing underneath. His microphone manner was like Bob Feller's fastball; there wasn't any explaining it, it was just there. He absorbed material like a sponge. He could read anything and make it work over the air, but he didn't know anything; I doubt that he does now. No history, no languages, no literature; all Eldon had in his head were received opinions and prejudices that he'd picked up from the local gentry whose company he coveted. He parroted them because he thought it pleased. He was just another small-town boy casting envious looks at the country club and the big houses on the hill. Right out of an O'Hara novel. Off the air, he was simple and vulgar. I recall that he kept taking out a pocket comb and fixing his hair."

"He still does. The voters lap it up."

"It was disgusting: like a woman putting on lipstick in a restaurant. Anyway, I'd discovered this broadcasting *idiot savant*, and whether I disliked him or not was beside the point. I could see he could make a lot of money for Granite. Listening to him, I could barely tell where the farm news ended and the commercials began; I knew the sponsors would love him. He wouldn't be a big star, of course, not in a league with Benny and Fulton Lewis, but I could see putting him head to head with Kaltenborn and people like that. All I had in mind then was radio; I signed him for a song and brought him to KCHI."

"Where it was discovered that he was dynamite on television?"

"Right. It was the grin that did it. People trusted him; he'd smile at them through the camera, and speak right to them, and they'd listen and believe. Sponsors liked that—although, as you say, it's one thing when the sponsor's selling toasters and another when he's selling ideology, but we'll come to that. Back then, we were toe to toe with CBS and NBC, and the DuMont network was still alive and kicking and hungry for stars. The Sarnoffs had taken a broken-down top banana and turned him into Milton Berle, and I thought we could make something pretty important out of Eldon if only we could hit on the right formula. That's when I came up with the monologues.

"You're too young to remember this, Sam, but during the Depression, Eddie Cantor had a financial misadventure with Goldman, Sachs, and he wouldn't let them off the hook for a long time afterward. Well, we did the same thing with Eldon, except we used 'the man from the IRS,' and 'the fellow from Washington,' and so on. It worked; nine tenths of our audiences consisted—consist—of frustrated people looking for a scapegoat, and they loved Eldon. Then we had the idea of building in a straight man—a straight woman, actually, a grandmotherly type who'd say things like 'Eldon Erwitt—are you actually saying that Margaret Truman sings like a neutered cat?' and Eldon would answer 'Did I say that?' with this ingenuously wicked grin he had, and repeat the slander all over again, only humorously, and then he'd segue right into a pitch for dishwashers."

"As he did just now on the tape. Who wrote his stuff? I can't imagine he did."

"At first, I did. I'm a hell of a scriptwriter. Then I put a team together, and after that we just kept bringing in people. Between his time with Granite and then at CBS, I imagine that a hundred different writers were at one time or another paid to put words in Eldon Erwitt's mouth."

"Why did he move over to CBS? Money?"

"Not really. I'd have paid Eldon what it would have taken to keep him. He was a good, dependable moneymaker for Granite, and he was a star, although strictly of the second magnitude. He was happy at Granite, but he wasn't happy with me."

"I don't think I follow you."

"Eldon never got over his boyhood dream of belonging to the country club, and that dreary little wife of his was a terrible social climber. I suspect that's why there's so much pomp and circumstance in the White House. So when Eldon became something of a national celebrity, he thought that he and his wife would automatically be included in Selena's and my private life. They expected to be our friends, to stay at Dune-crag, to dine at our table. Can you imagine? Even if I hadn't found them so uninteresting, I kept a very strict line between Granite and my private life, and in any case Selena wouldn't have people like that around her; she wasn't what you'd call 'a good business wife.' Eldon came to see that, and when his contract was up, he signed with Bill Paley. I guess he thought the Paley doors would be thrown open to him, but Bill's wife, Babe, couldn't stand him either, so there he was under a lifetime contract to CBS with his nose still pressed against the window. But by then he'd gotten to know some people who had a great deal of money, and a great many political antipathies, who needed a spokesman. The rest, regrettably, is history. Which brings me to my main point."

"I gather you feel some responsibility for Erwitt's becoming the leader of us all?"

"I do. Without television, the notion of someone like Eldon becoming President of the United States is preposterous. As you said yourself, in a world as difficult as today's, the fact of Eldon becoming President is more than preposterous, it's unacceptable! We're living in a hair-trigger world, Sam. I'm not just talking about missiles and the Russians and Eldon's Wild West notions of foreign affairs. It's the social fabric I'm worried about, and not just this idiotic business of paupering half the world to save the face of a few New York bankers who ought to be horsewhipped for their recklessness. I'm an old-fashioned capitalist, Sam, and a patriot. I like being rich, and I love our country for making it possible. I don't think the opportunity should die with this generation. I doubt that's what Jefferson had in mind, or Lincoln, or FDR. I don't really think that's what Eldon's got in mind either, but he's too ignorant to know better. The dumbest people I know are rich, successful men; they spend so much time making money, which really isn't very difficult if you make the right connections, that they can't see past their bank accounts. People have far more tolerance than they should for being treated unfairly, but when they finally wake up, they tend to react violently, and then you end up with either Hitler or Lenin. I've been reading my history, Sam: the process always seems to start with a well-meaning, manipulated boob like Eldon who's anxious to please his rich friends. Friends who have absolutely no idea of 'enough,' even if it's for their own eventual good."

"Perhaps they have no idea of 'eventual.'"

"That's well taken. They don't seem to. In any event, it seems to me that the whole world's coming closer to the knife edge. Someone's going to have to lead it back from the abyss, and let's hope it's America. But if it is, then America needs to know the truth about the way things are, and to understand what's being done to it, and what it's doing to itself. We must face some hard truths; we must know how scared and worried we ought to be. What we mustn't believe is the sort of emotional disinformation Eldon and his people are peddling."

"Emotional disinformation?"

"All this smooth, reassuring talk about how we're the best. This refusing to face reality. This refusal to recognize that the only way to get well is to swallow the tough medicine for the ills we've brought on ourselves."

"That's not something America has ever been very good at."

"I'm afraid that's no longer an acceptable excuse, Sam. You have it right about Eldon. He can't tell the difference between script and reality;

he never could. That was his strength, when it came to selling soap powder, but it's a dreadful, fearsome weakness in a President. I've been watching him for over a year now with mounting horror. He hasn't changed. He doesn't realize that in real life the red light stays on, the cameras keep rolling. If Lebanon gets out of hand, or Brazil erupts, or the schools can't teach hungry black children to read, as far as Eldon's concerned it's simply a matter of dousing the lights and striking the set and keeping the writers up all night to rewrite the lines so it can be reshot tomorrow to come out right. That's why Eldon's got to go."

"And, if I follow you, you're the one who's going to do it?"

"Put it this way, Sam. I think I've got a lot to answer for. It's no fun being this old and feeling about your life's work what I've come to feel. I joked with you about lotus eating. Well, for the last year or so, gall and wormwood have been on the menu pretty regularly too. I'd like to redress the account, pay my alms to posterity, make sure Asclepius gets his cock. I don't want to die with Eldon on my conscience."

"What do you plan to do, shoot him? I've thought once or twice that if the doctor gave me only a year to live, I might trot down to Washington and do a little housecleaning with a submachine gun."

X chuckled. "Interesting idea. No, nothing so violent. What I have in mind is peaceful and perfectly constitutional. As I said, I built television, and I invented Eldon, directly and indirectly. They're two open books I know well, because I wrote them. I intend to fix Eldon!"

"Fix him?" I asked.

"See to it that he's not reelected. And while I'm about it, I intend to see if I can do something about fixing up television. Call it a crusade." He sounded very optimistic.

I tried not to be impatient or skeptical; I wanted to sound positive, helpful. I didn't succeed; my realism got the better of my politeness. "Crusades are tough these days, X. How are you going to go about it, write a piece for the Op-Ed page, write a book? It's been done a hundred times, and it doesn't work. Books don't get it done any longer, not unless they're about becoming rich or thin. You're going to need a better white horse to ride than that."

He smiled patiently at me. "I'm not a fool, Sam, you know that. I've got all the horses I need; I've got Granite!"

I suppose I looked as startled as I felt. I know I didn't say anything for a moment. X seemed to study my amazement with high good humor, waiting for me to say something. Finally, I did.

"What about Abner?" I asked mildly.

What about Abner indeed? I thought. It was Abner's company now. It wasn't Granite Broadcasting Group any longer; it was AbCom, Abner's glory, pride, obsession, life. X wasn't even a memory around the company any longer, not according to the people I talked to. Abner had waited for his chance, and when it finally came, when X gave it to him, he seized it. Forget that he'd effaced X, that he'd put his own stamp on the company, elected his own board, purged the management. The important thing was that Abner had transformed the company, given it new, wider horizons, brought it to new heights of wealth and profitability. Abner Monstrance was the darling of Wall Street and the idol of his stockholders, a cover boy on *Forbes* and *Fortune* and *Business Week*, an admired, adored leader of the business community, an exemplar of all that was right and good about American capitalism.

Beyond that, Abner was a pillar among Erwitt's supporters; as a senior co-chairman of the Bilateral Liaison for Economic Equity and Progress, or BLEEP, he was a highly visible and vocal spokesman for the private sector's remunerative support of Eldonomics. Abner and Clio dined frequently at the White House. It was rumored that in the next Erwitt Administration, assumed as fact although the election was still two years off, a seat at the Cabinet table already had Abner's name on it, as Secretary of the Treasury, perhaps, or Commerce at the very least. And after that? Well, there were presidential noises, one or two small balloons being selectively inflated.

X knew all this as well as I did. He watched me gnaw on these considerations. But none knew better than I how Abner had hungered to be out of his father's shadow. Finally, his father had gone and taken his shadow with him. I could hardly imagine Abner would consider stepping aside for his father now. I doubted he would even let X in the building.

"You know," X said finally, "it was always a dream of Ab's and mine to work together. Not as father and son but as partners, in harness together."

"X, let's be realistic. Abner's a big deal now. He's his own man. He's made—" I couldn't bring myself to say AbCom—"the company his own. He's Number One now."

"Sam," X said wheedlingly, as if he were talking to his son instead of me, "it's not a question of being Number One, don't you see? I don't question that it's Ab's company, but his heart's really in his stock brokerages and computer businesses. I don't know anything about that. I do know about broadcasting, and Granite could use some help there. The ratings haven't been all they might be. I'd stay downstairs, out of Ab's way. I'd help rebuild the schedule, and take care of Eldon, and then I'd come back here and read Gibbon until the time came for me to turn my toes up."

Don't be disingenuous with me, I thought. I said, "X, Eldon Erwitt is Abner's political patron. Abner's not going to let you turn GBG upside down to do a number on Erwitt. As for letting the camel get his nose under the tent at GBG, yours is larger than Jimmy Durante's!"

He laughed at this, then turned serious.

"Well, all I can do is talk with Ab. I'm sure I can persuade him. I've heard all this talk about how he's Eldon's favorite boy, but in the end class always tells. There's only one thing Ab and Eldon Erwitt have in common, you know."

"What's that?"

"I invented them both." He chuckled and stood up. Our audience was over.

My hand was on the front doorknob when I thought to ask him where I fitted into all this.

"You're a writer. This could be a hell of a story, Sam. To bring you in on it was the least I could do. Besides," X said, rather grandly, "all great enterprises should have their chronicler. A Froissart, a Xenophon, a Cabeza de Vaca."

"You have a point. I'll take it under advisement."

"Do. Mind you, I don't want a propagandist, only the true story, the way it happens."

I started to say, If it happens. Instead, I said, "That's all I can guarantee, if I do it."

The late-afternoon outside was bright. I felt fuzzy from the wine and the intensity of X's conversation. He saw me down the steps.

"You said you might be back for Wimbledon," he remarked as we shook hands. "We can talk further then, otherwise in New York." It was obvious he was settled and bound upon his endeavor. He winked conspiratorially. "In the meantime, let's you and I just regard what's been said here as our secret: deep graveyard."

He winked again and squeezed my hand. "Deep graveyard" was X's old way of saying "top secret," especially top secrets having to do with surprises for Abner. We'd shared other such secrets in the past. It had been "deep graveyard" between us when he'd bought Abner the Boston Whaler and the Patek Phillipe; "deep graveyard" when he'd arranged for Abbott and Costello to entertain at Abner's eighth birthday party and for Jackie Robinson to umpire the eighth-grade interclass baseball game.

I walked along the Embankment toward the Tate Gallery. The air seemed drier; the morning's threat of rain had passed. As I walked I wondered about X's motives and became confused. The tangle of possible threads seemed too complicated to sort out. I could understand the business about Erwitt, mainly because I was sympathetic to X's point of view. I couldn't escape the feeling that it went further than that, past politics and money, past fame and posterity, past all calculable matters to the place where we live and eat our hearts out. To be sure, as the poet suggested, old men could be explorers, but they could also be monsters, consuming and consumed with a burning envy of their sons' lives and loves.

CHAPTER 3

"Welcome back to the United States, Mr. Mountcastle."
The customs inspector handed back my passport, scrawled
something on my declaration, and waved me on. I looked idly at the
passport as I stuck it in my pocket. It reminded me how even so apparently random a matter as the way a name is spelled could make a big
difference in life.

The name on my passport, birth certificate, and driver's license was
Stephen Armitage Mountcastle VI. My father had been Stephen V; my
grandfather, the late lord of the sprawling, faintly dilapidated apartment
on Eighty-third Street off Lexington Avenue, where Mother and I also
lived, was Stephen Armitage Mountcastle IV, and so on back into the
mists. When I was born in 1939, my parents sensibly surmised that three
concurrent Stephen Armitage Mountcastles, even with numerals, would
be too many and too confusing for an already troubled world, so my
initials were contracted and I became Sam. It was a happy decision, if
only because it spared me from the curse of "Young Steve," or "Steve
Junior," or "Little Steve." My readers knew my byline, "S.A. Mountcastle." Strangers sometimes called me "Samuel."

By the time I was seventeen, however, I was the sole proprietor of
"Stephen Armitage Mountcastle." Four years after I was born, my father,
a correspondent for a small news syndicate owned by my mother's family, was killed by a German sniper in a Sicilian orange grove. He was just
thirty. My grandfather made it to the allotted threescore-and-ten with
quite a bit to spare. He was still bouncy and active the night he was run

down by a taxi on Park Avenue on his way home from a dinner at the
Union Club celebrating Eisenhower's reelection. To lose Grandfather
nearly broke my heart. He had lavished on me all the love and hope he
had reserved for his own son, and he was, even though X was by then
very much a part of my life, the most estimable man I knew.

I remained Sam. Mother wasn't one to try to cut her losses with a futile
rhetorical gesture like renaming me Stephen. She took little time out for
mourning her father-in-law, whom she loved as devotedly as I did. She
drowned her grief in work and made her law practice her emotional balance wheel.

Mother and her sisters had some money from the sale of the family
business to Dow Jones right after the war, and there were three smallish
Mountcastle trusts, so we were quite well off. She made a good living
from the theatrical and literary law practice she had shared with Grandfather, and we lived in the right neighborhood and I went to the right
schools, which was how I came to know Abner and his family.

It started in kindergarten. M-O-U followed right after M-O-N, and thus
it was ordained that for thirteen years Abner and I would line up next to
each other, in gym lines and bus lines and cafeteria lines, in classrooms
and assembly halls, on playing fields, at dining hall tables, in camp dor-
mitories, and respond to "Monstrance, A., Mountcastle, S," over and
over. "Monstrance, Mountcastle, Monstrance, Mountcastle." For over a
dozen years, we heard that litany, right up to the June afternoon when I
followed Abner onto the stage of the assembly hall at Starbuck to receive
my diploma. I often pondered whether our recurring physical conjunction, produced by sheer alphabetical accident, wasn't the principal reason
Abner chose me for his best friend. He liked things well-ordered and
convenient. We did have certain things in common. We were both dili-
gent students, although our motives were different. I liked to study for
what was learned and taught. To Abner, the grades were the challenge.
We were both private people, vaguely uncomfortable in large groups.
Neither of us was boisterous or boastful or pushy, and those were the
qualities we most disliked in others.

Yet our differences seemed more considerable. Abner found little in
life to laugh at, while most things struck me as at least possibly humor-
ous. Later in life, when I got to the point where one starts asking oneself
the great existential questions, I concluded that any enduring relationship
must have as its basis a shared sense of humor. Either one laughs at life
and oneself or one doesn't, and the twain are difficult enough to bring

together, let alone keep together. I was having that problem now with Cass, who seemed to be losing her sense of humor.

In any case, as far as Abner was concerned, I was dependable, loyal, and convenient. He didn't want confidentiality in his friendships, he wanted company, and I supplied that. Even as a small boy, Abner looked for a decent return on and a high degree of control of his human investments, neither of which he got from his relationship with his father.

I had, of course, no problems with X. We understood each other right off the bat. His celebrity didn't daunt or seduce me. Thanks to Mother, I was used to seeing the living room of our apartment filled with great lights of the Broadway stage and Nobel and Pulitzer prizewinners. Grandfather and Mother had drummed into me that the only celebrity worth admiring came from individual creative achievement, from published books and produced plays and films, and scrapbooks full of good reviews from critics one valued. Accomplishment: the same thing I admired in my earliest personal gods: Peewee Reese, Jackie Robinson, Campy, the Duke. Only later would I learn that nine times out of ten the power and the glory ends up in the hands of agents and impresarios, that the world belongs to the middlemen.

X was something special, of course. When he came to a school game or parents' tea or Christmas festival, the waves parted. People made way as if his aura had sharp edges. I was then far too young to have any comprehension of the unbelievable power of money and institutional connections. About money, I knew only that it took fifteen bucks—or more than one birthday, at a dollar a year—to buy a Marty Marion fielder's glove at Davega's. That was the outer limit of my financial sophistication. Of institutions as such, all I knew was that it was great to be a hated Yankee and better to be a Dodger. It was beyond my grasp that people might hope that, by making up to X, something would come their way: money, perhaps, or some type of commercial advantage, or, at the minimum, a quantum of reflected glory, esteem by association. I would have given my right leg to have my picture taken with "Oisk" and "Newk"—and X saw to it that I did, and kept my limbs—but it never occurred to me that grown men and women would give almost as much to be seen talking with Abner's dad.

Mother understood. She knew all about X; she had dealt with GBG on behalf of a number of her clients. She didn't make it a big deal, as a lot of parents would have, when I asked if I could have Abner Monstrance over to play or when I was asked to Fifth Avenue or Dunecrag for an afternoon or an overnight or a weekend, or even when a GBG limousine picked me up to take me to LaGuardia for a junket to Canada or Little Gourd Key. She didn't grill me about who else was invited, and how many were there in staff, and what did the curtains look like, and the silver and china, and did Mr. Monstrance appear to be "seeing" anyone? She didn't come to fetch me, flusteredly hopeful that the great man would ask her in for tea. She simply said she hoped I'd had a good time and had I remembered to say "thank you."

Mother and I were close, but we weren't truly intimate. Our relationship never included the sentimental hooks which—I would later be informed by a series of lovers undergoing therapy—were the necessary core of a suitable, fruitful relationship between parent and child. Mother didn't go in for a lot of kissing and hugging. I was sure she loved me the best and only way she could, and since she was the only parent I had, I had no choice but to take her as she was. We had a very good time together; she took me places, and showed me things and sights, and shared her pleasure and knowledge with me; and I felt neither loss nor deprivation for all those unexperienced embraces.

Through my boyhood, a number of men attempted to succeed my father in Mother's arms and estimation. I suppose X came the closest. My mother was a striking woman, which attracted him to her as over the years they found themselves side by side at school pageants and awards ceremonies. Their romance flared only briefly before dying out. With Mother, what was over was over, so I never really had a chance to decide whether I liked the idea of X as a stepfather.

I suppose in general I would have approved. X, after all, was the dominant adult male in my life. On the other hand, it might have turned out to be another case of a good friendship spoilt by passion. Relationships, like most things, have a way of needing to be just so. I never went into the matter with Mother. All she was willing to tell me, long, long after the event, was that it had been a beautiful night at sea and that X was always highly susceptible to dramatic settings. Beyond that, the curtain came down. Occasionally I wondered whether she had slept with X, but only occasionally; I was no puritan, but it seemed to me that one's mother's sex life was well beyond the pale of curiosity, even in an age as shameless in its values as this, even to a nosiness as rapacious as mine.

Mother lived alone now. Some years earlier, she'd merged her practice into a larger firm, and her surviving clients had gradually been farmed out to younger associates. She still looked after a dwindling list of "ewe lambs," dosing them as needed with tea and sympathy. She had now reached the age when each day seemed to bring fresh disaster reports: another friend dead, sick, broke. She wrote letters of condolence and small, helpful checks in her house in Bridgehampton, talked on the phone with her remaining friends, read late into the night, smoked too much and ate too little, and, in the winter, took solitary, reflective walks along the deserted beaches.

I was looking forward to seeing her. We made a point of seeing each other once or twice a month, and this would be our last time together before she left for her annual summer vacation at the Oregon writers' colony where she kept a tiny cottage. Mother hated what the South Fork of Long Island became in the summer; each year her sojourns on the Oregon coast seemed to last a few days longer. We would be alone for the weekend. Normally I brought Cass, but she was in Italy, scouting new artists for the fashionable West Broadway gallery she'd joined six months earlier as Director of Exhibitions—going from Cropsey to crap, as I put it. It was just as well she was not coming; she and Mother had never hit it off.

I pulled the rental car into the building Friday traffic on the Belt Park-way. I'd thought about my meeting with X most of the way across the Atlantic. Even if he got only a fraction of the distance he intended, it was potentially a hell of a story, rich in large reverberative issues, everything from the condition of modern man to a father-son conflict that Aeschylus would have coveted. I was no different from any other writer; I burned to search out and describe the big verities, to use my art and intelligence to diagram the unified field, the double helix, the figure in the carpet. And X had sensed a responsive chord in me; he'd judged me aright, but then he always had. I too thought something had gone terribly wrong with the country. Something had soured and tainted so many of the aspects of American life that I remembered from boyhood as having been fresh, innocent, and wonderful. Maybe X was right: maybe it was television. There were other candidates: the computer, OPEC, inflation, Eldonomics, Vietnam. Temporal and spiritual leadership and management had col-lapsed. American life was pervaded with meanness, avarice, and in-civility. I'd read a piece in which an eminent historian had mourned the disappearance from the national discourse of certain resonant words, old, valuable American words: "community," "posterity," "happiness," "vir-tue." Starbuck words.

It was hard to pin down. Perhaps a fundamental brutishness, too long appeased by bountiful nature and kindly geography, had at last broken through now that the chips seemed to be down. Perhaps we were just reverting to type after a thirty-year postwar free ride. No longer the spoiled fat kid with the big allowance and the bodyguard, we were uncomprehendingly angry that something had gone wrong for us, and sought now to lodge the blame elsewhere. What sort of people were we, to look for leadership to a television emcee? Maybe we didn't want leadership at all; a certain logic suggested that a nation of two hundred million people sincere in its desire for real leaders would have produced at least one or two. Perhaps we had declined to the point where we gave ourselves what we truly craved: the cottony delusions of an Eldon Erwitt.

X's game was definitely worth the candle, although in my heart I doubted he would be able to change things much. Look at the prospective foe: the White House; the television industry, which was doing quite well, thank you, just the way things were; and Abner. Who would be X's allies? The press? The press frolicked around Erwitt's legs like puppies. The great unwashed public? Only if X could reach them, and that brought me squarely back to the problem of Abner.

Abner wasn't a boy any more; he wouldn't roll over and play dead. X was right about Abner not being much concerned with the network, which meant he would have less than no interest in X's ideas about reforming television; and as for making electronic war on Eldon Erwitt— well, X wouldn't even be able to mention it. The Monstrances had never really been on the same wavelength. By now, I was certain, the gap between them would have widened unbridgeably. X would want to talk about values, about issues. Abner managed by the numbers; his bottom line was ethically and morally neuter; he was a "price" rather than a "value" man, who prized only those things that could be promptly and accurately measured: ratings points, return on investment, body count.

It didn't seem to me that X sufficiently appreciated the work Abner had put into making the company his own. Apart from renaming it, he had joined with a major developer to build One AbCom Plaza on Central Park South; the company would soon be quitting the Saarinen-designed skyscraper on Sixth Avenue that had brought X a slew of architectural awards thirty-five years earlier. Even the old building was now renamed AbCom Tower. Perhaps, as I had surmised before, even Abner and Clio's high-visibility social life was meant to efface the memory of X and Selena's exquisite, sculpted existence. I hoped not. Abner had his own considerable, admirable capabilities, but this wasn't one of them. The style with which X and Selena had lived didn't have much to do with buying power, and therefore it was beyond the conceptual reach of Abner and Clio and their shiny new friends, aspire though they might, spend though they did. Of course, I reminded myself, I was one of those people who still referred to "Sixth Avenue," who still said it was spinach and to hell with it, who had too much to drink and grieved for the way it used to be.

Which brought me to the matter of Cass. Mother would want to know. The exit sign told me I was abeam Center Moriches, which gave me a little over an hour to figure out my answer. I'd have to tell her about X, just to get her viewpoint, but sooner or later we'd get to my love life, and I was damned if I was going to let her gloat again.

Cassandra Hargrove and I had been with each other going on three years. Technically, we didn't live together, but we were definitely a couple. From the moment I'd been introduced to her, all systems had seemed go. We were a perfect match. Her looks were the looks I wanted in a woman: dark eyes and hair; a firm mouth, the lips a touch on the thin side; slender but with good, heavy breasts. She wore a perpetual expression of barely concealed amusement, as if she was in the grip of a wise inward chuckle. She could make noises and behave like a grown-up, but she could also fool around like a six-year-old. She knew about the right things. When we met, I was full of Mark Twain and going through a phase of intense nostalgia for the bucolic peace of nineteenth-century America. Since the selection of an object of desire is to some extent a function of one's current emotional affectation, there was no way I wasn't going to fall in love with a charming, darkly lovely, knowing woman who knew about Cropsey and William Merritt Chase and John Frederick Kensett and Eastman Johnson and all the other imagers of that idealized, spacious, good-hearted, late-afternoon harvest world. Her ideological feet seemed planted squarely in the past, giving her solid ground from which to sniff curiously at the oddities and pretenses of the present.

On top of that, in the first hour we were together, Cass and I discovered that our tastes and humor were the same; we liked and laughed at the same things. It seemed we used the same lens to see through life. So congruent were we with each other, not to have immediately fallen in love would have been a sin against nature and God's divine plan; so powerful was our mutual compulsion, it was out of the question that we might be filling each other's transitory emotional requirements—that we might be role players, cast by coincidence to fill up phased empty spaces. Not us: we were destiny incarnate.

So naturally we missed, or chose to overlook, the warning signs. The reliance on bed as the ultimate panacea, for example. Even now, when things were rocky between us, we could still have at each other as groaningly and juicily as ever and convince ourselves for a half hour or so that things were as they had been. We worked too hard to sustain our initial rapture; it got to be tough, exhausting work; we were "too hot not to come down" and it was difficult to devise a steady output of new intimate excitements and private jokes. That we came up with so many logical reasons not to move in together should have told us something, as should the restraint shown by friends who knew us both well when we told them of our infinite good fortune at having found each other. No one actually came out and said anything, and if they had—well, what the hell did they know, and who the hell were they to talk? Our tastes meshed and matched so perfectly, and in a world in which style counted for so much, were we completely foolish to take for granted that a common taste for Sargent watercolors must be a reliable earnest of a deeper, perhaps a final, once-and-forever entwining?

Probably.

At first, I took the easy explanation. It was Clio's fault; it had to be. Sibling rivalry. Being an only child, I hardly qualified as an expert on the subject, but I knew Cass to be very competitive. She'd told me that she and Clio had been forced by their parents to compete with each other in every conceivable way: for grades, prizes at dancing school, boyfriends. Cass had apparently come out on top about ninety percent of the time, which made perfect sense; she was the more driven of the two.

Up to a point, I could understand her taking Clio's capture of Abner, and all that Abner entailed, as a defeat in abstract terms, even though the notion was somewhat foreign to me, since I wasn't fixated on winning. Minor irritation changed to major aggravation, however, when it began to dawn on me that Cass was specifically jealous of her sister; it drove her crazy that Clio dined at Mrs. Astor's, that Clio sat in the front row at Bill Blass's show, that Clio employed squadrons of young men to roll grapes in Roquefort to be gobbled by Henry Kissinger and cadres of Rothschilds, that Clio sat on the right hand of every Ancient of Days celebrated in *Women's Wear Daily*. I thought these people, and the way they lived and comported themselves, were jokes, often in questionable taste, and I thought Cass would too. I couldn't have been more wrong.

I could take any kind of bullshit in small doses, but increasingly I was being served king-sized portions. We seemed to be spending a lot of time with people whom Cass had met through Clio, people who'd made a pile in real estate and columbium futures. Cass claimed that it was all in the interest of her gallery, that these people represented potentially important clients and collectors, although it was my considered judgment that not one of them would have known a real work of art if it bit him on the ass. As ever, an entire army of people existed whose sole function was to help the newly rich spend their money in the right way. There were people who knew about toile de jouy and velvet, who knew about which orchids and soufflés were currently "in" and which little country wines and legumes were "out," and which were the "right" periods of Jasper Johns and Billy Baldwin, and what "this year's" flower beds should look like, and what columnists to cultivate, and who could help get people into what clubs, and what it would take, and which charities to support and committees to strive for. It was now possible, in no longer than it took to write the check, to acquire for oneself what it had taken other people years to learn about and assemble and cultivate, from wine cellars to friends to gardens. There was no such thing as right by precedence, no point to connoisseurship. No man's island of taste and sensibility was his own, to savor and take pride and pleasure in; someone was now always on the fringes, ready to trump your ace with his checkbook if he liked the look of what you'd put together.

Arrayed behind the purveyors of instant glorious living, and plugged into them, stood a vast machinery of gush, positively humming with a thirst for material. Glossy life-style journals, gossip columns, special Sunday supplements in the *Times*, now the life-style journal of record. The ink on the check would barely be dry; the last clever gewgaw from the Pimlico Road would have barely been uncrated and arranged ever so artfully; the last painting of Jack Russell terriers would have been straightened to plumb over the Adam mantel ripped from some great country house; the white-gloved Ganymedes from Glorious Food would have been stationed, Pouilly Fumé in hand, behind each chair, when *Architectural Digest* or *House & Garden* or some breathless androgyne from some Living section somewhere would appear, trailing florists and photographers, to declare the assemblage one for the ages, of a piece with Sissinghurst and Ferrières and Dunecrag. I thought it a game played by whores and tipsters. Cass wanted to play it, however, and so far I'd gone along, concealing first my slow rage and now my second thoughts.

It will pass, I kept telling myself, with more hope than common sense, even in the face of her new job, even in the face of a desperate anxiousness to please people whom I would have consigned to the fiery furnace. It's worth keeping together, I told myself, trying to suppress awareness that my principal motive was a horror of the dismal, draining process of having to start over again with someone else. I knew for myself that I couldn't face the prospect of ever again waking to see a new pair of buttocks twinkling across the bedroom in the morning light on their way to the john. Well, I thought, if Mother asks, I'll just try to stonewall. Why not? I didn't know what the answer was.

I turned off Route 27 at Southampton College, to dodge the traffic, now already slowing up this far out, which meant a jam around Water Mill. As I usually did, I would cut around by Flying Point and take a look at how far the destruction of the landscape had come. This was my part of the world; I'd been brought here as a child, to a house Grandfather rented in Wickapogue, where I was watched over in my busy round of sand and sea's edge by a succession of nannies. For ten summers, Mother had tried on houses all over this part of the world, until she found one she liked in Bridgehampton. I was very proprietary about this place; I loved it desperately, which was why, despite many misgivings, I'd let Cass talk me into renting a house in Water Mill for the summer. I thought, too, that the fact we'd forked over close to fifteen thousand dollars might act as a force to steer us through our current difficulties.

It was only Memorial Day weekend, but the streets of Southampton were already filled with a sorry preview of summer, upwardly mobile human detritus, cheeks distended with cuds of Juicy Fruit, stuffed like sausages into tennis clothes. No wonder Mother fled to Oregon, even allowing that she rented her house for $75,000 to a Hollywood sitcom writer who liked to hang around Bobby Van's and try to cadge invitations to the Sag Harbor literary softball games.

It was late afternoon when I turned off onto the road that ran through the rye fields to where Mother's house overlooked a finger of Swan Creek. I wondered how many more crops these fields would see. Farming was never an easy dollar—all the less so, I thought sourly, now that some stockbroker was always right there to fork over a hundred grand an acre so that his wife could make an architectural statement.

The five o'clock light was fiercely clear. The fields on either side ran flat and brown toward the glittering silver punctuation of the inlet. To my left was the line of the dunes and the rooftops of the houses hunching beneath them like sheep; at this distance the architectural atrocities were at least unobtrusive, but each year the drive through the fields became more of an exercise in visual masochism. The line of the land was broken here and there by the shapes of new houses abuilding, pustular wooden eruptions defiling the spacious, shallow planes of sky and fields that gave the place its rare and special loveliness. I doted on the shape and line of the land, on each trickling finger of bay and creek, on the swans which lorded it over the creeks and marshes, on the impudence of the gulls, on the stands of chestnut and maple, on the fences and farms standing amid horse-dotted fields. All now under siege.

I crossed the last little bridge over the neck of the creek, took the final turning of the road, and there were the familiar high trimmed hedges fronting the tall maples and, beyond those, barely showing, the roofline of Mother's house. The hard, pure light sharpened the edges of leaves and shingles. As the car crunched to a stop on the gravel drive, I heard a rackety clamor overhead, as a flight of Canada geese made its descent into the adjoining field.

Mother was on the porch; I was sure she had been there for some time, although she would make it appear she had only just come out, having heard the car on the gravel. She looked better than the last time I'd seen her, more rested, less fragile. The only evidence of her age was a hint of transparency when she became tired. Otherwise, she was still slim and unstooped in her light pullover and tan trousers. The perpetual cigarette burned in her left hand.

"Hello, darling." We embraced each other. I drew back and looked her over closely, scrutinizing for new rips and tears. I couldn't see any, not on the outer woman. Her hair remained light chestnut, although she by now admitted to helping nature every now and then; her bony, sharply de-fined features looked the same as ever, perhaps drawn a hint more tightly. People had forever told me how much we looked alike, but she always seemed to be in good form, whereas when I got tired a general disorder set in.

She inspected me as if I had just come down from boarding school.

"You look tired, darling. Goodness, what a dreadful necktie. A present from Cassandra? How was Scotland? I gather you never got to Munich?"

"It just didn't work out." All I'd told her in my cable was that our trip to Munich had been scrubbed. In fact, I'd quarreled with Cass in Lon-don, where she'd insisted that we have breakfast, lunch, and dinner with her new friends Bud and Marie, the latest flaming stars in her ever-en-larging social constellation. The exchange had left me in no mood to spend a week in Munich looking at modish pictures, especially in the shrill company of her associates from the gallery.

"That's too bad. Munich should be lovely about now. You and I should go there by ourselves. We could go on to Vienna." She smiled wickedly.

"Very funny," I said, smiling myself. I had a thing about Vienna, which Mother well knew. I'd never been there; I was saving it as the last shelter for the ultimate rainy day of the soul, the place to take the one, true, perfect, final, and only love. Cass had been a strong candidate; I'd almost broken my vow of chastity and taken her to Vienna. Thank God I hadn't; Bud and Marie would have tagged along; they were probably there now, buying up the Kunsthistorisches Museum and the Staatsoper and Demel's and Sacher's. Papering the city of my dreams with Bud's checks.

Grandfather had created the magic image in my head; his grandmother had been Viennese, and he made the city sound more enchanted than Oz. A trip to Vienna should be a great occasion, he said; it should be entered at the height of your life, with your true love or deepest friend by your side. He meant to take me there himself, until fate, in the form of Orestes Branquillo, hack license number D-4869, had rudely intervened. Vienna wasn't like Paris or London. To appreciate Vienna took character, depth, true growth of the soul, he said. To illustrate, he'd played Viennese music to me by the hour, everything from Schubert *Ländler* to waltzes by Lanner and Strauss, the singing of Richard Tauber and Julius Patzak and Grete Keller, operettas by Kalman and Lehar. He'd created a pleasing addiction in me; whenever life got to be too much, I simply plugged in and checked out, flying away in my head to the drizzly, wondrous city on the Danube. But I still wasn't ready to risk the real thing. For the time being, Vienna was off limits, except to my imagination. Mother knew this.

"The place looks great," I said as I carried my bags inside. "When do the Beverly Hillbillies arrive?"

"Next Thursday afternoon. I'm taking a noon flight to Portland; one of the policemen will drive me to the airport. Is there a chance you might come out later this summer?"

"Hard to say. It depends how things go."

"With Cassandra? Don't tell me there's trouble in paradise?"

"I wouldn't give you the satisfaction. Let's just say some adjustments are in order. I've got a lot of work, too. I owe them about five long pieces." That was a lie. "How about a drink? I've had a long and dangerous crossing."

"Why not? You can make me a little vodka over ice." She lit another cigarette; drawing the smoke in made her cough. The cough sounded like it had sunk hooks in her lungs.

"You sound really great," I said. "Are you training for a road company of *Camille?*"

Nothing I could say would matter anyway. Mother's cigarettes were as much a part of her as her fingernails.

"We're dining here tonight," she said. "I hope you don't mind. It's that time of year already. Looking at those people just takes my appetite away."

"Speaking of which, have you looked at Southampton recently? There's something going up on Wickapogue Road that looks like the TWA terminal at JFK. And what the hell's going on in those fields off Mecox? I'd say Lipshitz has had a hell of a busy winter." I'd appropriated the name from a singularly awful house I'd seen in Wainscott the year before; Lipshitz was my generic term for all the despoilers of shore and skyline, Huns in BMWs.

"You know how I hate it when you say that. It demeans you. Actually, that particular monstrosity is being built for some people from Texas."

"OK, Tex Lipshitz, then. It's just a name, for God's sake; it suits. I see Popinski's fields are staked out. What's that about?"

"He sold ten acres to a developer. They're putting up seven houses on three of them. They call it 'cluster zoning.' I doubt the water table will stand it. It's called progress and the redistribution of wealth. It's been happening to people like us for hundreds of years. Now, about dinner. I think we'll manage. You know how I am about cooking, so I had the fish shop steam the lobsters. Between us, we should be able to handle salad and the rest. It's still too early for corn, and most of the decent vegetables seem to come from California, which I reject. I did get some new potatoes and a dozen Little Necks for you. I had the Seafood Shop open them. So make us both a drink, and then you can have a bath; you must be exhausted."

I fixed her vodka and made myself a stiff Scotch.

"Be quick," she said. "I'll be on the deck. I feel like talking. It's been rather a lonely winter. Most of the people I used to be able to talk to have been inconsiderate enough to die."

I obeyed orders. The bath and the Scotch did wonders after the demeaning rigors of air travel and the Long Island Expressway and the terrible sights I had glimpsed in Southampton and along the road. I shaved and put on a sweater and a pair of khakis and joined Mother on the deck she had built to look out on Mecox Bay. She'd brought up a tray with bottles and ice; I made us another drink. She leaned on the rail and stared out at the bay and the flatlands between, drawing deeply on her cigarette. She looked very intent, as if she was trying to suck in the scene before her, to make it permanent within her.

I could never get over the difference a mere nine feet of altitude could make in flat country. The view from the deck swept west to east. From beyond the dunes, the ocean's rumbling drone carried to us; over by the inlet, where the great houses of the captains and kings crouched among hedges and copses, lights twinkled. Out over the ocean the moon's three-quarter disk was halfway up the sky.

For a while, we talked of nothing in particular. Our wheels needed greasing; old imprinted triangulations needed replotting. She talked of the books she was reading, of friends quick and dead, of the way of the world.

Finally, when it grew dark and the bugs had become a nuisance, we went downstairs to supper; we ate quickly, in relative silence. I dumped out shells, put the dishes in the washer, and poured us another glass of white wine. Mother lit a cigarette and drew on it as deeply as if to force the smoke through the soles of her feet.

"Well," she said, sounding reluctant to bring up the inevitable subject, "I suppose you'd better tell me about Cassandra. I always like to get unpleasant subjects out of the way."

"Let's say, for the moment, that it's not one of our better patches. Cass is having a tough time sorting out what she wants. There are a lot of things tugging at her. I'm in the middle."

"Is she jealous of her sister, the one I read about in the papers?"

"I don't know. You could tell me. Jealousy's more of a female thing."

"That's a dumb remark. Actually, jealousy's not altogether a bad thing; in its way it can be quite a creative emotion. It all depends on its object. but don't say things like 'a female thing.' It makes you sound like an ass, and you know how I hate you to sound that way. You're not going in for this business of the 'Return to Chauvinism' that the *Times* says will be the rage this fall?"

"I might as well. Chauvinism would suit me, don't you think? According to which of the women in my life I happen to be talking to I'm already by turns anti-Semitic and homophobic, and now I'm a jackass."

"Now, don't be testy. The poor thing is probably jealous. She can't help it; it's in her genes: her parents were the most awful climbers. And I suspect all those gay men she hangs around with don't help. They're the biggest bitches and troublemakers in the world. I could see their influence on Cassandra last fall: all that waving about of her hands and talking so loudly. My God, the world's gotten noisy!"

"Which is precisely why I went to Scotland."

"Well, I wish you luck with her, although I'm not so sure that luck isn't a rather precious commodity to be using up there. What's her sister like, anyway? I think somebody told me she was quiet and actually very nice, although you wouldn't guess it from the papers."

"Clio's not bad. My problem is that I can't help thinking there's got to be something wrong with her for her to see the people she sees."

"Maybe that's all the choice she's got. People who are rich above a certain level tend to be more comfortable only with other rich people or with servants."

"Paid and unpaid?"

"Naturally. Either way, they can talk about money without being embarrassed. Do you ever see Abner? How's he turned out? I read about him all the time: boy wonder, captain of industry, and so on. It must be—what?—twenty-five years since I've laid eyes on him. He was a bit of a stick as a boy. So unlike Horace. I was always surprised Horace anointed him his heir. The girl always struck me as having more on the ball. Now she has all those ridiculous teams. Anyway, let's get back to your love life. I do feel sorry for you, because I think you care. Poor Sam, love is even harder to manage than childhood."

"You said something nasty about Cass's parents. Enlightenment, please. How come you never said anything before?"

"I did. You didn't want to hear me, so you didn't. I never knew the Hargroves myself, but I heard about them at the Colony, and your grandfather knew him at the Brook. He was with the old Fulton Trust, but bankers aren't usually very good about money, so they were always a bit hard up, barely able to pay for the girls at Chapin, and only if they cut the odd corner and got a little help from an aunt of hers. Clara Hargrove eked out the family income as an amateur social secretary. I don't think there are many of those left, since there isn't much left of society, but in my day there were quite a few. They took care of invitation lists, arranged parties, oversaw the debutante business and the holiday dances. I think she was in charge of the Junior Cosmopolitans when you were in school. Frankly, one reason Mrs. Hargrove did it was to get her girls to parties to which they might not be invited or which otherwise they couldn't have afforded. A clever, ambitious child like Cassandra would have been acutely aware of how things were. It probably embarrassed her."

Cass had never mentioned that her mother moonlighted as a party planner.

"Then there was a whiff of scandal. There was talk at the Colony about Frank and Clara Hargrove helping certain people get into certain clubs."

"For money?" I asked.

"Who knows. Generosity takes many forms. You help me and I'll help you. There's always someone inside and someone outside, and as long as that's the case there are favors to be done. At least in those days it took a certain amount of guile; nowadays all it seems to take is the prospect of commissions. I was in town three weeks ago and was taken to a ladies' evening at the Brook. I think your grandfather would resign from beyond the grave if he could see what's become of that place. It used to be quite elegant. Now it's full of people selling mutual funds to each other."

"Get back to the Hargroves. This is interesting."

"Don't you find it most interesting that you don't know any of this? I grant that the present age doesn't seem to put much weight on where people come from, but you're supposed to be a journalist. Try as they may, people can't live lives unconnected to their past. That was Freud's point. Character isn't wholly an individual thing, darling. It runs in families. It can be institutionalized."

"Fair enough."

"The first time you brought Cassandra here, I suspected from the way she sized everything up that she was on the make, probably without knowing it herself. She'd grown up having to watch her mother plan parties for Rockefellers and Stillmans and, quite possibly, Monstrances. It wasn't exactly the same thing as having to take in washing, but to a certain kind of child with a certain kind of mind, it wouldn't be very different in terms of shame. When she got away from home, Cassandra probably buried those emotions. When her sister married Abner—"

"They all came back."

"Just so. There she was: on the outside again, peering through the glass at the other girls in their party frocks. Jealousy must have risen from the depths of her like one of those horror movie things. She can't help it, and though I hate to say it, I'm bound to think there's nothing that you can do about it except go along or get out. The decision you make should tell you quite a bit about what sort of person you are. Give me another drink."

That was a signal to change the subject. I was happy to. The question of what sort of person I was hadn't been yielding answers I liked.

"I saw X in London," I said. "After all these years. He ran me to ground in Scotland."

"Now, that's news," Mother said. "You know, I was thinking about Horace the other day, wondering if he'd died and I'd somehow missed it."

For a moment, she said nothing. The smoke from her cigarette curled and hung about the overhead light. The night outside was full of small sounds.

"Well," she said, "I suppose I can't stand the suspense. How was he?"

I told her all about my meeting with X. The only secrets Mother and I kept from each other were about ourselves. X's "deep graveyard" stopped at Mother's property line.

She chuckled after I finished. "Lamenting mightily and rending his garments, is he?" She shook her head. "How like Horace. Well, he can always get some new ones from Huntsman if he tears these up too badly. Does he still affect those dreary gray suits? He used to think they diluted his flamboyant personality and gave him the air of a banker. It always embarrassed him to be thought of as show biz. Poor dear Horace. Alone with his *mea culpas* in that big house. It must be touching. I almost wish I could see it."

"He sounded pretty sincere to me."

"Horace Monstrance could fool Parson Weems. No wonder he sees through the President. They're two of a kind."

"I don't think X'd like that. Aren't you being a little tough?"

She looked at me indulgently. "Of course I am. Horace has too much flair for his own good. It's like very good-looking men; they have a terrible time being taken seriously. There's absolutely no similarity between Horace and the President. Except, of course, that they both got where they are because of television."

"X said that only someone who understands television as well as Erwitt does can knock him off."

"Well, he has a point, and I'm certainly all for getting rid of Erwitt. I started out thinking those people in Washington were merely déclassé. Now I'm not sure they're not, in a strange way, absolutely bonkers. Your grandfather turned Erwitt down as a client, you know."

For the second time in two days I was dumbfounded.

"Stop gaping," Mother said. "It doesn't become you. It's true. It was just before your grandfather died. Horace sent him to us. They'd brought Erwitt to New York from Chicago, and he felt he needed a lawyer here. Your grandfather took him to lunch at the Praetorium. After lunch, he came back to the office and called Horace and begged off."

"Why?"

"He said Erwitt was a combination of cupidity and stupidity and he wanted nothing to do with him. Life was too short, he said, to take on people like Eldon Erwitt. Poor dear, if he'd only known."

"Cupidity and stupidity. I like that. I'll have to tell X."

That could be the motto of the Erwitt Administration, I thought. Like *Lux et Veritas*, or the Starbuck motto, *Fidem Praestare*, from Cicero: "Outstanding in Loyalty." I wondered what it would be in Latin. *Cupiditas et Ignorantia?* I asked Mother if she still had my old Loeb Latin dictionary.

"It's probably in the attic with your other things. Are you going to see Horace again? You must say hello for me."

"I may see him in early July. If I go back for Wimbledon. He wants me to be the official chronicler of his great crusade. I don't know if the magazine will spring for it."

"Well, they should, provided Horace gets it off the ground. I somehow doubt that Abner will cooperate, but then Horace always did have the Indian sign on Abner. Be careful around the Monstrances, Sam. They're tricky people."

"You should know. You came close to marrying X. I'm not proposing to do that."

"Came close is all," said Mother quietly. "I'll admit I was extremely fond of him for a time. Don't ask me if I let him sleep with me, because I'm not going to tell you. Suffice it to say I didn't want to be another scalp on an already terribly crowded belt, and I wasn't about to exchange what he wanted from me for a wedding ring."

"Are you suggesting it went beyond a mere craving for your pale white flesh?"

"It did. What he really wanted was you."

Life was getting too full of sudden revelations. I said, "I have no idea what you're talking about."

"I suppose I never told you this. Everything was over and done with, and there didn't seem any point. The thing about Horace, you see, is that if he wants something, he won't take no for an answer, not even from fate. The way he saw it, he'd been dealt a cruel but not necessarily irreparable blow with his children. They were not to his specifications. The qualities he wanted in a son were vested in his daughter. She, poor child, lacked the only things he wanted in a woman: charm, taste, wit, and beauty, beauty, beauty."

"You think Abner was a disappointment?"

"I know he was. He tried so hard. Too hard, in fact. Horace thinks that a good sixty percent of doing anything is making it look easy and instinctive. Does he still go around quoting Castiglione? Anyway, Abner toiled away—he certainly wasn't stupid—and won all those cups and things, many of which Horace himself had won thirty years earlier. It wasn't enough. Horace used to complain that Abner just didn't have it, whatever 'it' was. I always thought it extremely unfair of him, not to say unkind. But Horace thought you had it. I guess he meant style. It's too bad he never saw your room."

"So he proposed to you to get me? Why didn't you accept? I could have used the money. I could be living in Southampton and buying friends instead of having to make them. That was very inconsiderate of you."

"Don't be a jackass. You were all I had. Horace would have spent the next twenty years weaning you away from me, and he might have succeeded. You'd probably be running his company now, and peeing on redwoods at the Bohemian Grove, with these Eldonomics people, instead of writing and reading and mooning about girls."

I must have had a very strange expression on my face. She laughed.

"Don't look so deprived, darling. I wouldn't have married Horace anyway. He had such a terrible attitude about women."

"Those scalps on the belt?"

"That's right. In one of those Anthony Powell novels you sent me, *Temporary Kings*, I think, there's a man who has a necktie, or perhaps it's a pillow, woven from the pubic hair of all the women he's slept with. When I read that, I wondered if Powell ever knew Horace. I should have looked more closely at his neckties."

"You needn't have bothered. They're all the same: navy blue silk. He probably has a hundred of them."

"That's Horace. He probably had a hundred women, too. Women give him the only reassurance he finds convincing. Much more than money, fame, or influence, not that he doesn't like those too. Every man I've ever known had at least a corner of his self-confidence that was a little rickety, that could only be propped up with a certain particular support. In Horace's case it was the conquest of women. The psychoadrenal rush does the trick; slam, bam, a quick vaginal fix to make him feel good about himself!"

"Mother, please!" I said sarcastically. "What about Selena?"

"As far as Horace was concerned, she was the ultimate woman as object. It made no matter she'd been in half the beds along the Eastern Seaboard, so had he. She suited his requirements perfectly: a beauty, a good horsy family, that famous taste, and she belonged to another man. Two, if you counted the President. That alone would have acted like an aphrodisiac on Horace."

"Obviously it did. I always heard she was a class act."

"She was indeed. The elastic in her knickers was selectively loose, but, really, the sleeping-around part had nothing to do with the price of eggs.

All that counts in that department is whom you sleep with, and there Selena was very selective. Only intelligent, powerful, cultivated men. No stable boys or polo players. She was truly upper class, and she had perfect taste, the way some people have perfect pitch. For Horace, so determinedly genteel, even though he's tough as a boot, she was transcendent, a goddess. He was always a bit embarrassed that he'd ridden to fame and fortune pandering to the taste of the public; it drove him crazy to be lumped with Sarnoff, who looked as though he'd come to fix the stove."

She lit another cigarette. The first puff set off a paroxysm of coughing. "You're going to kill yourself," I said.

"At least I'll do it on my own time. How about a brandy to settle the catarrh?"

I went over and poured us a couple of snifters of cognac.

"Anyway," she said, raising her glass, "here's to Horace. May he succeed, because for all his small faults, he has some great virtues. Poor man. He lived all those years in a sort of Ptolemaic daze, thinking the sun went around him, and now he's discovered it doesn't. A hayseed he found on a farm somewhere has become the most powerful man in the world, and the son he never much liked has not only made a great success but has even scrubbed the poor man's name off the door. I think Horace has all the incentive a man needs. Whether he can put together the wherewithal is something else."

We'd covered a lot of ground, and I was suddenly tired. It was about four A.M. for me. I said good night. She offered her cheek and told me to enjoy my golf game in the morning, and I climbed upstairs to bed. I just had time, before I fell asleep, to regret that Mother and I talked like this so seldom. There was so much information, if not advice, she could have given me, that she owed me. I wondered how much time remained to make up for all the things that should have been said between us.

Downstairs, I heard the sound of the stereo. She would sit up most of the night, I knew, smoking her endless cigarettes and listening to Schnabel playing Beethoven and Schubert. Night was the enemy of old people, something to be outlasted; a time for hearing their lives creak ominously, like the planking of old houses.

The next morning, Buck Buchanan and I were out on the National with the dew sweepers. We got around in a little over two hours and were finished well before ten o'clock.

We had a good match, a dollar Nassau played the way golf used to be played, before it became an interminable, mechanized, executive recreation. Buck was unconscious for the first seven holes; on the eighth tee he was two over par and three up on me, but then he awoke, Justice and Decency descended from Olympus and declared for me, and incredibly skillful play on my part brought me back to even after sixteen holes. Now the gods turned wroth and loosed a storm of evil luck on my head, while equally undeserved good fortune attended Buck's spastic slashings and pokings, so that his half-topped eight-iron bounced off the flagpole and dribbled onto the edge of the final green from where, thanks to the deflections of various spike marks and worm casts, he ran in a putt of at least five hundred feet for a winning bogey.

Actually, I didn't mind losing to Buck. He was a big jock, after all, and real athletes were supposed to beat us amateurs, even ones possessed of my naturally graceful, lissome swing. Buck had also made me quite a lot of money. As he put it, "most ever'thing he did, he did good," starting with high school days back in Covington, Georgia, when William Jenkins Buchanan had been recruited by fifty colleges and had chosen Dartmouth, the only Ivy League school where he wouldn't have to take the straw out of his ears. He'd been a two-time consensus All-American defensive back with the Big Green, followed by five years and three Pro Bowls as free safety for the Jets, until a knee went for good against the Oilers. Buck was eight years younger than I was and a trillion times richer, which I suspected was evidence he was a trillion times shrewder. I'd known him for a long time, ever since *Newsweek* had sent me up to Hanover to do a sidebar on this second-round draft pick with a *magna cum laude* degree and a Phi Beta Kappa key. We'd liked each other from the go-off and became close friends, especially when the fortunes of the draft brought him to New York to play for the Jets.

He'd hit the town running. Football wasn't going to be his life, he said, if only because there wasn't enough money in it. Buck wanted to be real rich. He knew how to exploit the ass-kissing jock groupies from Wall Street who packed the bar at Clarke's and Weston's, and he parlayed his down-home, kick-the-dog and where's-the-grits, red-clay Georgia accent into an off-season job at a well-regarded brokerage house, where he married the boss's daughter, a Briarcliff girl with a master's degree in whining and a Ph.D. in shopping. After ten years, he'd quit both the job and the marriage and started an arbitrage pool with ten million dollars happily put up by former customers for whom he'd done "right well" and "real good" as a broker. That had been three years ago. He hit the takeover boom right on the nose, and now he was said to be personally worth $15 or $20 million. Still, he took my four dollars as if it meant something, which explained why some people make money and others don't. To get rich, Buck said, you just had to want "ever' dollar in the world, ever' last one. You got to think ain't nobody out there got a right to a nickel." His Dartmouth degree was in English literature, but it suited him to speak like an extra on "Hee-Haw," despite the fact that the snootiest maître d's in town bowed and scraped as they showed him to the best tables at Le Cirque and the Four Seasons. Perhaps the fact that he had a direct wire to the Sultan of Oman had something to do with it.

"I need ever' penny I can get," he said when I paid over my bet. "She's at it again." He raised his eyes heavenward. "She just flat will not trust my accountants' word that I'm broker'n a country preacher on Saturday night."

Buck's ex-wife sued him for more child support about once every two weeks, with the enthusiastic backing of Manhattan retailers. The only times I ever saw her, she was towing a Corgi into Bloomingdale's or Bendel's, thin and sour-faced, burning with a rage to spend. She and Buck had a couple of kids, and she used them to club her ex-husband on his wallet via his heart.

I asked Buck if he intended to pay the latest matrimonial Danegeld.

"'Course. Summer pussy is at hand; I can smell it in the air, and I'm gonna need all my right considerable powers of concentration to do it justice, so who can fret 'bout money at a time like this? They used to say when they was recruitin' me to play at Tennessee: 'Billybuck, you ain't hardly lived until you've seen the spring humpin' in the Clinch Mountains.' Those ol' boys oughta seen what goes on down here. When them stews hit them Westhampton discos, it fair beats a grunion run!"

We went into the clubhouse, showered and changed, and ordered a couple of beers. I wanted to pick Buck's brain on the subject of AbCom. Buck understood corporations and the men who ran them. He attributed this to his "ol' possum hunter's nose for fun"; Buck's game was arbitrage and its ugly stepsister, "greenmail." He made his money on takeovers, the reality or the threat. Most of the time it was a question of betting correctly that A would get B, no matter what evasive action B took, unless C stepped in and paid a higher price for B, in which case Buck's several hundred thousand shares of B would be worth that much more. But he got a bigger kick out of greenmail. He had great news for weakness of character in a given management. He claimed his years playing the likes of Lance Alworth and Paul Warfield had given him a sense of who he could come up on and who lay back off. "Nothing I like better than the smell of chickenshit," he'd say, as he took a hefty position in the shares of a company whose management, he felt, would fork over whatever it took in the way of the other stockholders' property to get him to go away.

I had mixed feelings about the greenmail part, even though, as a tiny fractional investor in one of Buck's arbitrage pools, I'd made a nice turn on the little bit of money I'd given him. There wasn't any question that Buck and his colleagues in the racket saw it as a game and played it in that spirit, but it seemed to me that the human stakes were higher than they were prepared to recognize. On the other hand, it was pretty satisfying to watch a brace of corporate fatcats turning slowly on the spit, to see the fear in their jowly faces at the prospect of those million-dollar salaries flying out the window, not to mention the arrogated perks of office: jets and limousines, executive dining rooms, and girlfriends stashed in company apartments.

I asked him what he knew about AbCom.

"Not too much. 'Course I don't follow stories."

I knew that. Buck didn't sit around reading the dissertations of security analysts about earnings prospects. The action he was interested in came in bigger pieces. When he set up on his own, he had told me, "I don't care doodiddle whether General Motors' earnings are going from nine fifty to ten fifty this year. What I want to know is if there's sumpin' going on that'll make that sumbitch pop fifteen percent one way or t'other. If there ain't, don't call me."

He thought for a moment.

"Now, when you're talkin' AbCom," he said, "you're basically talkin' Abner Monstrance. It's all his. Folks say he's one smart sumbitch, although he ain't exactly a barrel o' laughs. About as much fun as an Eskimo's dick on Valentine's Day. He used to work about a hunnerd hours a day. Now you hear different. Since he married your gal's sister, the Street says he's kinda slowed up around the store, jes' like every other guy I know who suddenly found out you could do something with it other than use it to piss. Seems I heard there's a big institutional report coming out on the company. I'll send you a copy."

"The Street loves him, doesn't it?"

"About as far as the Street loves anybody. The Street loves you up to about ten seconds past the point you stop doin' better'n good. Just ask the boys at Warner Communications. That's why I don't buy anything that ain't swimmin' around in a barrel with me standin' over it with a twelve-gauge shotgun. Shit, old buddy, they ain't but about five hundred institutions that run the market. Which means maybe fifteen hundred people making the decisions on half a trillion dollars' worth of investment portfolios, most of which don't pay no taxes, so it don't matter diddley squat to 'em if they own a stock five years or five minutes. If they get nervous about a stock, like as not they blow it out their ass and then ask questions. Look what happened to IBM last year. One day you're the prettiest girl in town; the next you're yesterday's douche bag. Right now, old Abner's in fat city. Fartin' through silk, as my dear old daddy used to say."

He paused to think. As I'd hoped, I'd gotten him started on a train of thought. Asking Buck a question about a stock, despite all his disclaimers, was like tapping into a computer.

"AbCom's real hot right now," he continued. "More for what they ain't done than for what they done did. They stayed out of videogames and they stayed out of the dirty end of cable, and that was a big plus. They shut down the movie studio jes' when the dentists started to get in the business. They got into real estate—a little big and a little late for my money—but if a boy's patient, real estate 'most always works out. They're into financial services, discount brokerage, and so on, and every stockbroker's got a rooting interest in that. Folks jes' love Direct Mail— all them catalogs. The TV network's doin' OK, although it ain't like it was when the ol' boy was callin' the shots. Computer software's hotter'n a coed's pussy on Alumni Weekend, and it looks like they got themselves a big winner in that business communications hookup, BizNet. The whole thing looks good from here. Of course they borrowed a whole bunch of money to expand."

"How much?"

"I seem to remember order of magnitude six to seven hundred million."

"That's a lot of money."

"Uh-uh. 'A whole bunch' ain't the same thing as 'a shitload,' which is order of magnitude ten digits minimum. Folks don't even turn around these days for less'n a bil. These banks have gone plumb crazy. Some kid from Continental Illinois called me up jes' the other day beggin' to lend me two–three hundred million just to leverage my plays. And this guy don't even know me."

"Would you be a buyer of AbCom here?"

"Nope. No play."

"Meaning no takeover?"

"Correct. The family owns thirty percent of the stock, so there can't be no unfriendly takeover. This ain't Disney. You couldn't root Abner Monstrance outta there with a backhoe. He's got his own board; he votes the family stock; and people who know him tell me he was born convinced that God has only one thing He wants to do with His life, and that's to help old Abner Monstrance out!"

We said goodbye in the parking lot. He promised to send me a bunch of stuff on AbCom.

Later, I accompanied Mother to lunch over in Wainscott with a playwright who was an old friend and client. He was almost translucent with the cancer that was killing him, but he managed a gaiety that made us all grateful. Every gesture, every hard-won breath, every dwelt-over recollection was a tiny celebration: of a life he'd loved, of the times and memories he'd shared with some of those around the table, and of what he'd accomplished. No one is ever happy to die, I suspected, not even amid the most tear-wrenching pain, but at least this man had completed enough of his life to go out whole. The books were on the shelf, there to outlast the worst that death could do. He had what X was after, a lock on posterity.

Mother must have seen what I was thinking. We were almost home, crossing over through Sagaponack by the back road, when she turned and said, "I don't want you to think I'm down on Horace, darling. He's an extraordinary man with a singular talent who took something that ordinarily should have been a very small part of our lives and managed to blow it up until it literally changed the sort of people we are, for better or worse. It was quite an achievement, any way you look at it."

"He now thinks it's a mixed blessing."

"I can understand that. He's old enough now to know what really counts. Horace knows the group he wants to be included with: people like George Kennan, Jake Polhemus, and Averell Harriman; Jack McCloy and Bill Fulbright. A pretty sad lot it is that's behind them."

"Ah, well, take heart. There may yet be giants in the earth."

"Let us pray. You say Horace wants you to act as his scribe in this project?"

"Something like that."

"But not to write his revised standard memoirs? Did you read that book of his? Horace hallucinating his own version of history. Who wrote it for him?"

"Some guy from the *Times*. He admits it was pretty bad."

"Good for him. I must say, I'm pleased to hear that someone, even

Horace, can still feel even a modicum of shame and contrition. I thought those were emotions the modern world had declared obsolete."

Lunch had been sumptuous, so we made ourselves a pickup supper later in the evening and sat on the deck with coffee and a nightcap. I slept well that night.

The next day I lazed around, planning to leave after lunch, when there would be a hole in the city-bound traffic. When the time came, Mother walked with me to the car and watched me stow my bags.

"I meant what I said about going to Vienna," she said.

"I know you did."

Geese in close formation circled the farther reach of Mecox Bay. She hugged me and pecked a darting kiss at my cheek and then stepped back to look at me.

"I can see he's got you, Sam. Well, you're old enough to take care of yourself. Just remember: at this stage in his life, Horace hasn't got much to lose."

I leaned out of the car window. "Look," I said, "about Vienna—a lot of things can change. Take care of yourself out West. I'll call you every Friday morning."

"Say hello to him when you see him again."

Driving out, I looked up briefly and caught a last glimpse of her in the mirror. She raised a hand to signal goodbye; it was a gesture more tentative and forlorn than I could ever recall seeing her make. Then I went round a corner and she was gone: house, maples, all. I thought to myself that there is a point in life, like a dare line drawn in the dust by a bully, and when we cross it, everything is at risk. She was telling me I was at that point. I didn't think so.

CHAPTER 4

Home is where you know what to do with yourself on Sunday. In foreign parts, Sunday can be a tiresome, desolate proposition, either parry-and-thrust with wearied weekend hosts who've run out of amusing ideas, or pointless, lonesome walks in the Bois de Boulogne or Leicester Square, or too many solitary Camparis and coffees at the table in the *piazza* or the *platz*. At home, Sunday is a time for established routines, with predictable options and familiar local rules.

On most Sundays, I rose early, between six thirty and seven thirty, depending on the ravages of the previous evening, put Bach or Palestrina on the stereo as a gesture to the notional holiness of the day, and padded to the door to gather up the *Times* and the *News*, which I read in sequence. The New York papers no longer took up a full mind and morning these days, so after I finished, it still being early and Cass or whoever, if anyone, still asleep, I would ablute and dress and wander over to Seventy-second and Broadway for a supplementary ink injection: *Newsday*, whichever out-of-town papers seized my fancy, the bluebird edition of *People*, *Barron's*. I would skim these at my coffee shop of preference and let myself go in the eggs, bacon, sausage, and English muffin department. I was fairly skinny, but the spirit of the age was to think thin, so Sunday would be my one major-league breakfast meal of the week. The other days it was just a glass of juice and a slice of protein toast, unless I took a "working" breakfast: coffee and a croissant at someplace like the Regency Hotel, to watch the real estate barons bartering away the common weal and listen to some guy try to persuade me to wield his hatchet for him.

Breakfast is life's great meal, and I considered myself a connoisseur; nothing could beat a really great coffee-shop breakfast, aswim in grease, unless possibly breakfast at the Dorchester in London, and the problem there was that in England there weren't any English muffins.

Until recently, Cass slept over every Saturday night. When I got back, she would be sitting up in bed, dressed in one of my shirts, coffee steaming beside her, intently studying the gossip pages. In the old days, those columns were an incitement to laughter. "You won't believe this," she'd say. No more. Now her face would knit darkly as she discovered in Liz Smith or Suzy mention of some function at which Clio had starred. She didn't take it well when I cheerfully noted that she read the columns with the same vocational avidity as out-of-work actors poring over the casting calls in *Variety.*

By eleven thirty on this particular Sunday, two weeks after Mother had left for Oregon, I completed my routine more quickly than usual. The state of the world continued dismal: bombings, famine, missiles, riots. The obituaries included a former Mississippi Senator, a Hall of Fame third baseman, and an early abstract expressionist. The sports pages were as usual principally concerned with contract disputes and litigation, with franchise financing and TV ratings and declining audience shares. For blood-and-guts action, the thrill of victory, the agony of defeat, one now turned to the business section to read about the latest takeover war.

I went back through the *Times* to make sure I hadn't missed anything in my first sortie. I hadn't. I now knew how things used to be in Finland, what BLEEP thought the President should do about depreciation, why the Yankees were in last place, seven amusing things I could do with roast peppers, what inspired six black lesbian writers, whether George Bernard Shaw was gay and Mozart a depressive, and what was doing in Ljubljana.

I flicked on the television set, which was now pretty much left tuned to WGBG as a sort of halfhearted homework. "Newsmakers in Focus," GBG's equivalent to "Meet the Press," was on. A plausible-looking man in a blue shirt with a white collar was doing a lot of earnest talking, mostly with his hands. I recognized him as the head of one of the country's biggest banks and paid attention as he piously explained why his bank's billion-dollar loan losses were somehow the fault not of his management's misjudgments but of the American political system, and that it was therefore meet and equitable that Uncle Sam and the electorate pick up the tab.

Amazing, I thought: the country demanded less of its bank presidents and senators than it did of its quarterbacks and centerfielders, which explained why the athletes now all sounded like bank presidents and senators, and played about as well, too. In a properly ordered world, a jerk like this, whose ego had damn near busted his bank, would have his ass kicked up and down Park Avenue or be pilloried outside the University Club. Instead, here he was, on national television in a $1,500 suit and a $100 haircut, earning a cool million a year, scratching his chin and pontificating about "adjusted market forces" and "interventionist free markets." Well, I thought, what could you expect? Nowadays outfielders got paid a million a year for batting .250, so why not bank presidents? When I was growing up, guys who hit .250 stayed in the Three-Eye League and banks didn't go broke. In exasperation, I ran the dial; finding only Jimmy Swaggart and Jerry Falwell, I turned off the set and put on the Poulenc *Gloria*.

The music helped my irritation pass. I was perfectly content: alone, dressed like a bum in the tropics, the air conditioner whooshing away, scrunched up on my overstuffed sofa amid neat, carefully organized stacks of books and magazines and the half-dozen yellow pads on which I made running notes for the pieces I was currently working on. A few days earlier, I'd established a new one, marked simply *X*. Living alone demanded orderliness, and so the discarded newspapers were already out the back door, laid out like plague corpses. The main, the only, purpose of Sunday was reading. The printed word was as succulent to me as roast pig to a Chinaman. I read just about a hundred periodicals with some regularity, so Sunday was necessary. I was glad Cass was still in Europe; she'd developed a nasty habit of accepting invitations to Sunday lunch parties at which all I seemed to do was drink too much and blow away the rest of Sunday in a haze.

I looked around and admired my studied order. I lived in three big, sunny rooms facing the park. The apartment was high enough to give me a vista, yet low enough to keep the details in focus. My living room looked out over the Sheep Meadow; I was almost directly across Central Park from Cass's apartment. The next largest room I used as a workroom/guest room/food-serving room; Buck had put in a lot of time on the studio bed there during the last turbulent months of his marriage. Then there was my bedroom, a perfectly good bathroom with all the basics, and a kitchen of sorts. When it came to entertaining for more than one, I was the king of takeout, for which the West Side was paradise enow. If there was sun, the rooms were especially pleasant; on cloudy or rainy days, the spacious overview of the park was something of a solace. At sunset, when the bastions of plutocracy lit up over on Fifth Avenue, the view was as beautiful, and just as romantic, as Rome from the Quirinal.

Everything was in its place. I rather resented my mother's remarks about my boyhood room. My books were put away in some semblance of order in the bookcases that lined all but two available walls. Notes, bills, and papers were stacked tidily in folders next to the typewriter on my worktable. At home, all I wrote were letters and checks, and occasional beginnings and endings. I did my meatier work on the computer screen in my office at the magazine.

Most of my furniture had come by descent from Grandfather, from the old apartment. I wasn't sentimental about wood and upholstery, not one to moan and weep over the final passing of a favorite stuffed chair. I had a high-class sofa Cass had made me get from some decorator, and a worktable I'd had built by a place in Sag Harbor. The rest was purely functional: ordinary tables and armchairs and bureaus supporting the photographic potpourri of my life: family, friends, Cass in various metamorphoses and poses, me. In the living room was a really good stereo system and a television-videotape setup which was more technology than I needed; the stuff in the kitchen seemed to work; the queen-sized bed handled two people very nicely, in any configuration they were likely to choose.

I had my special small treasures. There was the tiny Constable oil sketch I'd inherited from my grandfather. It was as if someone had jig-sawed a few square inches out of a perfect English morning and somehow gotten it into a frame. There was a first edition of *A Shropshire Lad*, in which Housman had written his name and the date, 1896; it had been a Starbuck graduation present from the Monstrances: the card, signed by X, Abner, and Eugenie, was still in it. To celebrate that occasion, Mother had given me a small watercolor by Fairfield Porter, which perfectly caught the special light of the South Fork. There were some things I'd bought for myself: a lithograph, very handsome, of Prestwick Links in Scotland; a first edition of *Scoop*, signed by Waugh, purchased on impulse for too much money at an antiquarian book fair in an Amsterdam Avenue synagogue; signed photographs of Richard Tauber and T. S. Eliot and Red Barber and Bobby Layne and Jackie Robinson; an autographed copy of *You Know Me, Al*; and a framed letter from S. J. Perelman to Ogden Nash. It was a particular comfort to have such wise, witty, and crafts-manlike genius in the room with me, even by proxy. Each of my few treasures, in fact, was alive with memory and aspiration.

Memory was also represented by a red leather Mark Cross scrapbook, stamped with my initials, containing photographs of my father and his journalism. It wasn't a lot, but it reassured me that I came by my small gift for writing honestly. Judging by the photographs, I was bigger than he had been, taller and therefore probably twenty pounds heavier, but at first blush no less slender; I had my mother's thin features, but there was something of him in the slope of my shoulders, a kind of perpetual hunch as if I were getting ready to punch someone, and in my outsized hands.

I fiddled away the forenoon. I couldn't make myself get to my books and papers, even though, unlike Bellow's Sammler, I was pretty sure these were the right books, the right papers. I was twitchy with apprehension and unresolved business. Betwixt and between in my emotional life; knowing what I probably ought to do, yet afraid, for convenience's sake as much as anything, I supposed, to take the big step. Edgy about X, which made no sense at all. This was just a story, a big one, handed to me on a platter, if it ever came to pass, which was conjectural. Perhaps it was just that suddenly all the forces and figures that had played large in my life had charged me like Zulus, howling, pointing their fingers, pressing their claims. For Christ's sake, I thought, you're forty-three years old. I ordered myself sternly to sort it out like a rational grown-up. I made myself sit down and started with Cass.

A look around the apartment sufficed to remind me how reduced a presence she had become. A book of hers lay on an end table. Her picture, laughing with me in front of a Berkeley Square restaurant, was on my desk. I knew that a change of underwear was pushed into a corner of a drawer in the bedroom bureau, that there were a few women's things in the bathroom cabinet, and an old raincoat and a pair of jeans in the front hall closet. The cooling remnants of our radioactive romance, cinders of feelings.

It had probably begun so hotly out of mutual desperation. When we met, I had been lonely, and fretful, and looking for an impossible combination of passion and regularity, eager to push down roots, to get my emotions bedded down and cuddled. She was no better off. When well-meaning friends, priding themselves on their ability to mine meaningful relationships from unpromising terrain, introduced us, we went through all the usual motions. We told each other identical tales; we exchanged similar sorrows and attendant commiserations. She was coming off a long, intense relationship into which she'd put everything and had been emotionally savaged for her troubles; I was coming off a series of six-month stands which, in talking to her, I elevated to an emotional hegira

that would have embarrassed Schiller. We thought of ourselves as mutu-
ally drained and tender. We saw in each other what we liked to think
about ourselves. It was destiny.

I think, in fact, we would have fallen in love simply as a courtesy to the
friends who brought us together, so vulnerable, needful, ignorant of self
were we. We went through the whole attenuated minuet. First, a lunch
date, a stroll through the American Wing of the Met, Cass telling me
about Cropsey and I telling her about Emerson, each feeling the way
through the other's delicate condition, appreciating the other's gorgeous
sensitivity; a final soulful, silent, inwardly sighing pause, aquiver with
imagined mutuality, before Durand's "Kindred Spirits." Then a second
date, dinner this time, at Elio's, both of us highly sexed but knowing that
the rules required prolonging the torture at least one more time, so nothing more than a kiss in the taxi; she went away for ten days to look at a
bunch of collections on the West Coast, and I found her absence curiously
tearing and woke up in the night erect, sweaty, amorously entangled with
the pillow, muttering passion. Lots of phone calls, to fan the flame,
which was under no circumstances to be allowed even to flicker. She
returned; a third date, a long and boozy dinner, again at Elio's, now as
sacred and refulgent of deep, right feelings as Combray or the Ritz, and
this time I got out of the taxi and we had each other's clothes off before
the rickety elevator reached her floor. No aphrodisiac is as potent as that
sense of Kismet.

The ringing of the phone interrupted my recapitulation. As if my
thoughts had flown the Atlantic, it was Cass, calling from Düsseldorf.
Now we went through different motions, but we had our lines pat.

Miss you.

Miss you.

(Did I catch a pause there?)

How was Munich?

Nothing, nothing, nothing! But Bologna! *Favoloso!* We found two of
the most extraordinarily wonderful talented fantastic painters, and we'll
show them this fall; how's New York?

Busy; it's turned very warm.

I'll be back Thursday. The TWA flight from Rome.

I'll meet you.

No, don't bother to come to the airport.

(So why'd you bother to tell me the flight?)

OK.

Can it just be the two of us that night? So much to tell you. Have you seen Clee?

No. Of course we can just us two. Hurry back.

I can't wait, darling.

Me either.

Love you, love you.

Love you.

The whole charade. We hung up. I turned the tube back on without the sound. The last round of the Open wouldn't be on for another forty-five minutes. I clicked until I found a USFL game on a cable channel. I didn't recognize the teams. Who cared anyway? The league was just a front so its richest owners could bully their way into the NFL and go to the NFL commissioner's Super Bowl party. It was still football, though. I watched a wide receiver go flat out down the far sideline, reach out as far as he could, and snare a fifty-yard pass. Magic. The sports pages might be about nothing but money, but there was still something inescapably wondrous to me about a man running full tilt half the length of the field and then looking up into the sky to find a ball descending to his finger-tips, a ball thrown there by another man trying to find him over the arms and howls of half a ton of charging, thumping linemen. A splendid con-junction now bisected by the crassness and crudeness of money. The new geometry that casts all in doubt. Yet the game would survive, just as we survive our misguided affections, I thought. I put Cass to the back of my mind. There was work to do.

The day's study materials were arranged on the coffee table. As prom-ised, Buck had sent along a bunch of stuff on AbCom: boilerplate statis-tical sheets from Standard & Poor's and Value Line; a copy of the company's last annual report and proxy statement, along with the first quarter report, and—to be saved for last—a lengthy institutional re-search study.

I was officially assigned to the X story now. My editor, the terrier in gold-rimmed spectacles who banked and doled out the *Spec*'s writerly capital, had given me the go-ahead to stick with X right to the end.

He'd thought it over for a couple of days and then taken me to lunch at the Praetorium, a great fluted limestone block on lower Madison Avenue which had been founded in the mid-nineteenth century as a bastion for writers and artists. Once the club had functioned as a clearinghouse for the higher culture. It still did, in theory, although now the great McKim, Mead and White dining room had largely been taken over by lawyers talking air rights and tender offers, as if, by transacting their low business here, it would acquire a metaphorical varnish of decency.

The editor was recognized as a pillor of probity, and he worked at keeping up appearances. In addition to his bankerish spectacles, he wore high laced shoes and clerically dark, vested suits, which looked as natural on him as his subtly dotted bow ties. As we were seated, he looked around the room, sniffed that the cafeteria at Davis, Polk must have overflowed, and ordered for both of us.

Over indifferent curry he laid down the rules. Under his severely cut hopsacking beat the heart of a secret swashbuckler, a man who moved knowingly in the shadows. The fact was, the editor liked to model himself on Le Carré's George Smiley.

"House rules, now," he said to me, as if he were Alec Guinness briefing a mole in a Lambeth safe house.

"Of course. I think he's straight."

"This could be gold, but a man can get too involved, lose his perspective."

"Got to talk to both sides, too. Trust no one."

"I know."

He pushed at his curry and filed Smiley away for a moment. He smiled. "I must say that the prospect of bashing that miserable, bigoted, ignorant SOB in the White House warms me all over."

"Now, George," I said kiddingly, "in our work we can't have feelings."

"Seriously," he said, "it's rare that we get to look at a big business story from the inside. See it whole: people, institutions, the works. Don't miss a thing, Sam. This could be about the biggest thing we've ever done, and business is on the front burner right now."

"I don't think the deal includes writing the inside stuff as it happens. He's not talking current events. He wants a record, something after the fact."

"I understand that. I see a three-, maybe a four-part series."

"I see a book."

"Everyone wins on this one. Just keep our name out of it, will you, until we're ready to publish? I don't want a lot of phone calls from lawyers."

"I know my tradecraft, George," I said, grinning. "Don't worry."

What he said about business being on the front burner was right. Money was on everyone's mind, in sums that could only be abstractions to the average reader. Corporations were front-page news, not for their commercial or technological successes or failures but as prizes in the greatest paper chase in history. Wheeling and dealing had long since replaced making and selling as the perceived nexus of the economy. It was strictly an insider's game, though. It was all duly and dutifully reported and analyzed in the business press, but without much point; the journalists weren't adequately trained to penetrate the alphanumerical smokescreens thrown up by dealmakers, so the public was left to clutch at figures as hard to grasp as moonbeams. That was the point. The meaningful action, the hard bargaining over confidential numbers, took place on the other side of locked doors impenetrable even to the most informed and conscientious reporter. We reporters, and the public in our care, were left to interpret leaks sifting under the doors of executive suites and boardrooms, like wisps of smoke, or to ponder runic press releases handed to us after the fact. This wasn't true of other news, although the Administration had tried. We could still report real war as it unfolded, but then what was war but a matter of blood and honor? X's story had it all: politics, money, corporate warfare.

I looked over my pile of homework. I'd photocopied the entries from *Who's Who* on Abner and his father. I picked up Abner's:

MONSTRANCE, Abner Jacob, corp. exec.; b. New York City, March 12, 1939, s. of X. Horace H. Monstrance and Irene (Calixter) M.; Starbuck Academy, 1957; B.A., Yale College, 1961; M.B.A., Harvard School of Business Administration, 1963; A.M. (Hon), Pace College, 1983; m. (1st), Sophia Mary Lewis (June 22, 1963); children: Horace Jacob, b. 1964; Frances Sophia, b. 1967; m. (2nd) Clio Hargrove Gresham, 1980; inv. mgr., J. R. Polhemus & Co., Boston, 1963; mktg. mgr., KAJM-TV, Chicago, 1964; gen'l mgr., KHHM-TV, Los Angeles, 1965–66; gen'l mgr, WGBG-TV, New York, 1967–68; v.p., network sales, Granite Broadcasting Group, 1968–69; sen. v.p., finance, dir., mem. exec. comm., 1970–73; chmn., pres., ch. exec. off., ch. exec. comm., AbCom Inc. (formerly Granite Broadcasting Group), 1974–; tstee., New York Public Library; tstee. Council for Broadcasting; tstee and treas., Metropolitan Museum of Art; tstee., Starbuck Academy; dir., Monstrance Foundation; dir., Advertising Alliance; dir.; vice-chmn., mem. exec. comm., Bilateral Liaison for Economic Equity and Progress (BLEEP); mem. Presidential Commission on National Literacy; mem. Mayor's Council; clubs: Uptown Quoit and Squash, Gorse, Brook, Maidstone, Blind Brook, National Golf, Bath and Tennis (Palm Beach), Everglades, Seminole Golf, F Street (Washington), Bohemian (San Francisco), Yale, Harvard, Augusta National Golf, Augusta, Ga.; home: 774 Park Avenue, NY 10021; "Westover Cottage," Cooper's Neck Lane, Southampton, NY 11968; "Briarfence," Upperville, VA 22176; "Seahorse,"

216 North Country Road, Palm Beach, FL 33480; office: 1237 Avenue of the Americas, New York, NY 10020.

Rereading the entry made me realize how much I'd forgotten about Abner's life as a man. I'd forgotten that there had been two children from his first marriage. I now recalled Cass having mentioned that they lived with their mother in New Orleans and almost never saw their father. Small wonder: children, even if on the verge of being grown up, didn't seem to fit with Abner and Clio's way of life. Did Abner, I wondered, have any plans to bring his son into AbCom and steer him right to the top, the way X had done with him? I doubted it.

And still a joiner! Abner would have made a great Eagle Scout; he would have liked all those merit badges. At school, he'd always signed up or hustled for every campus organization worth belonging to, from *The Weekly Starbonian* to the Good Citizens Club, the Student Council, and the Library Committee. His membership in BLEEP and on charitable boards thus didn't surprise me. What did was his list of "social" clubs.

Of course, many of the clubs he listed were hardly "social" any longer. Like the Praetorium, they were mainly milestones of executive progress. I was surprised to see so many golf clubs listed. Abner must have known, from his wife via Cass, that I was fanatical about golf, but he'd never mentioned the game to me, let alone invited me to play a round. Anyway, there was golf, and then there was executive golf. I wondered in passing what his entertainment industry associates would think of the notorious anti-Semitism of his Palm Beach connections.

I'd also forgotten that he owned a place in Virginia. The name "Briarfence" tinkled in my memory. Then I remembered; "Briarfence" had been where Selena had lived with the husband from whom X had amputated her. Interesting, I thought.

I tried to summon up an image of Abner's first wife, but all I had in my head was a dim vaguely remembered snapshot that one of Mother's sisters had saved for Mother's and my return from Europe one summer. A pleasant-looking, obviously suburban girl, I recalled.

I read the entry through again. Abner had worked for Jacob Polhemus when he got out of business school. He was partly named after Polhemus, X's best and oldest friend. In fact, Polhemus was Abner's godfather and had been something of a buffer between the two Monstrances. He had come up quite frequently to Starbuck, and he and Abner dined alone together.

Polhemus, of course, was a legend on a par with X, and the only man I ever heard X speak of with real admiration. X had few idols, if any, but he could discourse at length on his friend Jake's loyalty, generosity, straightforwardness, tolerance, unselfishness, and, above all, his cultivated taste and manners.

Polhemus had put the seed money into X's fledgling Granite, and he had had numerous other successes as an inventive investor and entrepreneur, having built a handsome inheritance into several hundred million dollars. He had backed Polaroid and Digital Equipment and was known to prefer New England businesses. GBG had been his greatest success; various Polhemus entities still held about 9 percent of AbCom's common stock, slightly under six million shares, worth over $300 million. Much of the original stake had been given away, I knew. I wondered how Polhemus would fit into the developing puzzle.

Unlike X, Polhemus had been a notable public servant. A dollar-a-year adviser to Roosevelt, vice-chairman of the War Production Board, and Undersecretary of War for Air. Later, he had been a special envoy to NATO, Deputy Ambassador to the United Nations, a governor of the Federal Reserve Board. There had been a profile of Jacob Polhemus about ten years ago in *The New Yorker*; I made a note to dig it out.

I picked up the photocopy of X's *Who's Who* entry and read through it. Most of the facts were by now familiar to me: the two marriages; the boards, trusteeships, honors, decorations, degrees; the clubs; the homes; much space was given to X's military phase. X had always liked to show off his medals, the Bronze Star, the Order of Merit, the Légion d'Honneur, to talk of the good times at AFORAD or SHAEF. He'd had a "good war," Mother said once.

By his own lights he certainly had. It was the only even remotely lively part of his ghostwritten autobiography, which I'd struggled through during the week. The book was written in a flat, lifeless tone that lay over the potentially glamorous material like a coat of sludge. I'd hoped to get a clue as to his reactions to Erwitt's defection from Granite but had been disappointed. There were many possible facets to X's feelings about the President, and I didn't want to miss one. The war certainly came into it; X thought of himself as a warrior, and, though he hadn't gone so far as to say it in so many words, I was sure he considered Erwitt a shirker, possibly an outright coward and draft dodger. The Granite issue was another, but the two paragraphs devoted to Eldon Erwitt merely expressed a mild, unretributive disappointment with an ungrateful employee, a person of another class who had lived down to his background. Of course, X's book had been written when Erwitt's public career was no more than a glint.

I put the Monstrances aside and looked over the stuff Buck had sent me. The S&P and Value Line tearsheets were standard statistical compendiums, interesting only because they went back over ten years and showed in concise form the dramatic arithmetic of AbCom's growth. Interestingly enough, although the company's most recent annual revenues of some $6 billion were nearly triple what GBG had taken in during X's last year at the helm, operating profits of slightly over $800 million were less than twice what the company had earned under its founder. It was obvious a lot of wheels had been spun in the name of "market share."

I picked up the most recent annual report, a glossy, heavily illustrated booklet of thirty-odd pages, read quickly through the summary financial statements, and turned to Abner's letter to the stockholders. It was predictably self-congratulatory, for AbCom's stockholders had every reason to be pleased with what their management had wrought. Revenues were up sharply; profits, earnings per share, and dividends had all increased nicely. AbCom's traditional lines of business were perking along, and the company's more recent diversifications were delivering exceptional growth in tandem with the promise of a splendid future. The letter concluded with a rousing statement in support of Eldonomics and harsh words for regulators and consumerists. A Martian reading it would have inferred that we were still living under wartime rationing and controls, instead of the free-for-all, *sauve qui peut* economics the Administration had unleashed two years earlier. The political aside didn't surprise me. Abner was recognized as a leading private sector spokesman for Eldonomics, and it was to be expected that he would use any reasonable forum to get in his ideological licks. What was somewhat surprising was the skill with which the stockholders' letter was written. The language and phrasing were smooth and happily free of the usual bizspeak fumblings, pretensions, and solecisms. There has been a professional at work here, I said to myself, someone who has respect for the language.

Accompanying the stockholders' letter was an Avedon photo of Abner looking intent, reflective and solidly visionary, and a shade humorless: a good, responsible face, reassuring to investors; a carefully composed face, which he'd started to develop as a schoolboy and now had down pat. He'd lost his intellectual and moral baby fat earlier than most, and he'd started working on his image while still a boy.

I moved on to the main part of the report, a copiously illustrated recitation of AbCom's operations. The company was organized into four principal operating groups, each reporting to a senior executive vice-president: Broadcasting and Entertainment, Communications and Information Technology, Consumer Interface, and Financial Assets Management. Broadcasting and Entertainment was the largest of the company's operational components, accounting for 30-odd percent of revenues and slightly over 50 percent of operating profits. It comprised the company's five owned-and-operated radio and television stations, network operations feeding 239 GBG affiliates, the film library which had survived the disposition of GBG Films, the recording and publishing subsidiaries, the production and distribution of video cassettes, and three cable-TV systems. The jewels in the crown were the owned-and-operated television stations: WGBG, New York; KHHM, Los Angeles; KAJM, Chicago; WGRA, Washington; and KABI, Houston.

Communications and Information Technology was described in an upbeat, almost breathless manner saying clearly that here was the apple of the corporate eye. Almost $500 million had been invested in this segment in the last two years. It was contributing less than 15 percent to sales and profits but was growing at 100 percent annually. The group consisted of BizNet, which interconnected and interfaced business machines and offices through a series of regional microwave and satellite-fed networks, and AbCom Software, which developed and marketed computer programs to do everything from tertiary calculus and ballet notation to space games and checkbook balancing. As far as I could grasp, the hottest item in the group's electronic smorgasbord was what sounded like the most laid-back way yet discovered for Apples and IBMs to talk to each other.

Consumer Interface consisted of direct selling operations, ranging from fifteen different catalog merchandising operations, which offered everything from bodybuilding equipment to Victorian lingerie, to some thirty "shopper" newspapers in demographically "hot" areas and a telephone survey network using "matrix-linked 800 numbers," whatever those were, and a party-plan cosmetics and weight-loss operation. This sector was still relatively small potatoes, accounting for less than 10 percent of sales and profits, but it was growing very rapidly. Reading between the lines, it seemed to me that the objective was to trap the upscale consumer at home. In an increasingly noisy and dangerous world, this seemed to make good sense.

Financial Assets Management included AbCom's real estate holdings and its financial services subsidiaries. The former consisted of shopping malls, office buildings, and undeveloped commercial acreage, mainly in cities like Dallas and Tampa, as well as One AbCom Plaza, and a syndicated real estate fund marketed through AbCom Discount Brokerage,

Inc. The financial services businesses, which provided the group with most of its handsome profits, were a hodgepodge of what had come to be known as "paper entrepreneuralism": a Florida savings-and-loan, a nationwide discount brokerage house, a commercial and industrial finance subsidiary that lent "mezzanine money" to leveraged buy-outs, a mutual fund, a Cayman Islands trade bank, a dealer in commodity and financial futures. The figures confirmed how healthily one could suckle at the swollen teat of high-velocity credit and mass market speculation; together, they accounted for a little over 25 percent of AbCom's pretax earnings and were closing fast on broadcasting and entertainment. In terms of current financial fashion, they seemed to touch all the bases.

Each group breakout was accompanied by a sidebar which highlighted a particular aspect or segment. Idly, I turned back to the Communications and Entertainment report, remembering something X had said in London about creating entertainment by computer. Sure enough, the sidebar carried a glowing account of something called AbCom Creative Technologies, full of phrases like "interactive response positings," "protagonistic typologies," and "situational projectables." Technology's answer to the monkeys who would write all of Shakespeare if they just had the time.

I went to the numbers. It always surprised people that a writer could read financial statements. When I first started to work in New York, however, Mother had insisted that I learn something about accounting. She said that might make me unique among practicing journalists, and she'd turned out to be pretty nearly right. But then, I wrote by and large for people who weren't vocationally concerned with writing, publishing, or criticizing. What I was trying to do was show how the world seemed to work, at least in the shape I found it, and this world worked on money, which chose—most of the time—to speak in numbers, if not always straightforwardly.

Buck had put it more succinctly, with his usual feel of the relationship of ideas to cash in the bank: "Good buddy, they's about ten million liberal arts B.A.s ain't got the slightest idea of what is a debit and a credit. The real weird thing is, they's proud of it, which is why most of 'em are broke, which they ain't so proud of, as far as I can see."

AbCom was in stout financial shape. Working capital was almost right at a billion dollars, although short-term debt had climbed sharply. The company was into its banks for $976 million, up nearly $400 million from the previous year. Nevertheless, the company's total debt of $1.6 billion was cozily perched on a cushion of $3 billion plus of book net worth, and that last figure didn't come close to what I guessed its assets were really worth. The accounting was no more or less debased than had come to be standard for large corporations. A cursory check of the footnotes to the financial statements showed another half billion in debt off the balance sheet, trying to pretend it was something else. The company's unfunded pension liabilities seemed manageable, which meant well short of impossible. Over the next five years, AbCom was going to have to pay off nearly $1.3 billion of debt, but its cash flow was already at flood levels and seemed to be rising, and the banks were in there for so much anyway that they'd have to go wherever the horse took them.

The inside back cover of the report listed the company's officers and directors. None of the names on the executive masthead meant anything much to me except Fergus Duncan, senior vice-president for corporate communications, who was known to me as the author of the "From the Tower" columns, the feudalist AbCom "advertorials" that shared a regular place on the Op-Ed page of the *Times* with Mobil, United Technologies, and the National Rifle Association. Even if their viewpoint wasn't mine, the columns were well written. I guessed Duncan's was the graceful, invisible hand behind Abner's letter to the stockholders.

Duncan was a guy who got around, a regular Mr. First Nighter, always at a good table in all the right hangouts: "21," Elaine's, Giulio's, Clarke's, the Four Seasons, the Tea Room. He was a balding, stocky guy in his middle fifties, with a little brush mustache, who affected a pince-nez, regimental ties, and Mr. Chips tweeds, as if trying to pass for an Oxford don. Duncan had been pointed out to me any number of times as an example of talent gone rotten, mostly by other writers very much aware of the quarter of a million a year that AbCom was said to pay him. I'd heard that AbCom lent Duncan to BLEEP from time to time, to help polish up the apologias for Eldonomics, which had led *The New Republic* to describe BLEEP as "Erwitt's brownshirts in pinstripes."

There were fifteen members of the AbCom board. Five were officers of the company, including Abner; two were "family" members, Eugenie Monstrance and Jacob Polhemus; seven were outsiders: a woman from the Harvard Business School; two chief executives of large industrial companies; a black rabbi (two tokens for the price of one); two attorneys, one a highly regarded Washington fixer, the other Arnold Plume, best-known merger lawyer in New York; and a partner of First Stuyvesant Company, AbCom's investment bankers. Nothing exciting or unusual about that. The fifteenth name, however, was someone special: Henry

"Hank" McNeery, perhaps Eldon Erwitt's least distinguished predecessor as President of the United States.

Like Erwitt, McNeery was also the stuff of presidential myth. His term had lasted seven days, the so-called "Two Hundred Hours of Henry McNeery." An obscure farm-belt Senator, serving as president pro tem of the upper chamber, he had been out of Washington when a sudden mild but incapacitating botulism laid low his predecessors in the presidential succession. McNeery's brief term had been notable for avoiding armed conflict and for the flood of favors and dispensations which had emanated from the White House. When the rightful President recovered and reclaimed his office, McNeery resigned from the Senate and entered the private sector. His two hundred hours had been all he needed to pave his way with purest gold.

If Jacob Polhemus exemplified the best traditions of selfless public service, McNeery incarnated its vast potential for sleaze and opportunism, the notion that the point of public service was not to steward or improve the general interest but to prepare a man for a prosperous afterlife in corporate America. He wasn't the first to see that a sojourn, however brief, at or near the heart of the greatest power in the land could be cashed in for real money. Next to the venality of Hank McNeery, however, men like Ford and Kissinger looked like pikers. He rejected nothing that had a buck or two in it, and seemingly infinite were the opportunities that came his way. First came a lucrative string of consultancies, directorships, and adviserships. Then he went brand name: south of Sarasota, the President Henry "Hank" McNeery Pro-Celebrity Golf Tournament was inaugurated, to publicize a condominium development in which the ex-President had been given a substantial carried interest. His beaming, prognathous face could be seen from Colorado's I-70 touting a resort community near Glenwood Springs. There was little McNeery wasn't offered to endorse; nothing that he refused.

Many found him ludicrous, even contemptible. Herblock cartooned him as "Boob McNeery." He bid fair to replace Scrooge McDuck in the popular mythology of avarice. And yet he grew in power. His much-mocked obviousness about money was likened by many in the press to a sailor on leave. Some of us saw his success as symptomatic of something more ominous, however. In his greed, in his evident contempt for financial decorum, in his shamelessness, McNeery might tell us something about himself; that he not only got away with it but was cheered and admired and welcomed by the people in power told us worse: that we were a culture and an era to whom effrontery and vulgarity were no longer bad.

McNeery had linked up with Erwitt early on. This connection served him well and brought him even greater wealth. It was said that only Darlene Erwitt and Hank McNeery could walk into the Oval Office without an appointment. When BLEEP was organized, to counteract a growing public and media uneasiness with the deep social disruptions inherent in Eldonomics, it was inevitable that McNeery appear as Chairman, in which capacity he functioned as a go-between at the highest level, a sort of corporeal diplomatic pouch, carrying messages from big business to the White House. Messages, said some. Others, watching Eldonomics unfold, thought "orders" was the right word.

McNeery's presence on the AbCom board prompted me to look quite carefully at the AbCom proxy statement. I wanted to see how AbCom's outside "independent" directors made out. American capitalism had come a long way from the days when my grandfather had been paid $100 cash for attending board meetings of Intercontinental Brands, a chicken-feed fee to assure his independence of mind.

Times had certainly changed. Each unaffiliated AbCom director received a base compensation of $20,000 a year, plus $1,500 for each bi-monthly board meeting, plus an additional $1,500 for each meeting of the various board committees: Audit, Compensation, Ethics, etc.—a total of six such committees. Each outside director was on a minimum of three committees, which met three times a year each. If a director answered the bell every time it rang, that added up to $41,000 a year for openers. Figuring time spent in preparation and actually in the boardroom, including lunches catered by Le Cirque, the base pay worked out to just under a thousand dollars an hour. Not bad, especially considering that, according to *American Lawyer*, Arnold Plume, who was the most expensive attorney in the country, billed his time at about a third of that amount.

Directors and committee fees were just the beginning. In the preceding fiscal year, the lady B School professor had received an additional $42,000 in consulting fees; the two law firms had been paid fees of $1,687,000 and $2,063,000 respectively; the investment banking firm had received $867,000 for "advice and services rendered," although a recheck of the annual report showed no transactions which would normally have required an investment banker's services or expertise; even the African rabbi had been financially serviced, through a $75,000 contribution to the

Yeshiva Amiri Baraka in Crown Heights. McNeery had taken down $80,000 for advising AbCom executive forums.

Nor did my heart bleed for AbCom's management. Exclusive of stock option profits, Abner's compensation package came to a shade over two million dollars. The next three top-paid executives each earned over three quarters of a million. "It's real crazy," Buck had observed a while back. "These boys nowadays pay themselves ever' year in salary what folks thought was a rich man's capital when I got started in this business."

I put down the proxy statement. On the TV screen, footballers were running up and down the field in normal USFL fashion; it looked like a game of campus touch, a Chinese fire drill. I debated turning up the sound to find out who was who, and what the score might be, but decided instead to put on a record of English operetta arias. The sprightly songs seemed appropriate to the busy rotations of the little men on the tube.

I picked up the investment report. It was printed on rich, creamy stock, embossed with a logo of a sunburst and, in large, clean letters, INSTITUTIONAL EQUITIES ASSOCIATES, INC., RESEARCH SPECIALISTS. According to Buck, IEA was among the hottest of the score of investment boutiques which, along with the research heavyweights like Merrill Lynch, Morgan Stanley, and Goldman, Sachs, dominated institutional perceptions of individual stocks and stock groups. Veronica Pfannglanz, the IEA partner who followed AbCom, was on a real roll right now, Buck told me: she had called the earnings breaks in Warner Communications, Coleco, and MCI and had urged her clients to load up on Metromedia before the buy-out. Her bullish report on AbCom, by his reckoning, had already added 15 percent to the value of AbCom shares; in aggregate market value, with AbCom at $53, that added up to nearly $500 million. That struck me as power.

I read the report twice. The opening page summarized the company's investment basics, listing its stock market symbol, ABI; its recent trading range; dividend and price–earnings statistics and ratios; and a recapitulation of its stockholder profile. There were 64.8 million common shares of AbCom outstanding. Of these, 21.3 million, roughly a third, were owned by insiders: the Monstrance Foundation held 8 million; Eugenie had 4.9 million; various Polhemus accounts had 5.7 million; X still owned 1.7 million personally; and Abner and the other officers owned 1 million in round figures, exclusive of options and stock purchase units. An indeterminate number of institutions owned 27 million shares, or approximately 42 percent; the 25 percent balance, 16.5 million shares, was in the hands of some fifteen thousand individuals, ranging presumably from odd-lot-ters and people like me with a few hundred shares to individuals who had traded businesses or properties to X and Abner for GBG or AbCom shares and held the stock in multiples of a hundred thousand shares.

Ms. Pfannglanz wrote in a sonorous, ponderous style, heavily freighted with profound-sounding jargon. Wall Street technobabble didn't faze me. It was just a way of making something essentially simple seem complex. In defense of its self-esteem, Wall Street, like education, like the social sciences, had developed a *Haussprach* that resonated with expertise, complexity, reconditeness, significance; a semantics that filled both initiate and outsider with awe at the monumental mystery of what was, at bottom, the process of buying and selling pieces of paper.

The first section of the report reviewed AbCom's first-quarter results, breaking the company down into considerably smaller segments than had the annual report and emphasizing percentage changes rather than dollar absolutes, a method that usefully equalized mountains and molehills and made the company's glamour spots look even better. Overall, first-quarter earnings in the current year had risen from $1.78 to $2.30. After reviewing this in detail, Ms. Pfannglanz wrote:

> ABI's dramatic increase in first-quarter earnings suggests that the re-positioning of the company, initiated when the new management team took over thirty-three quarters ago, is now taking hold. A combination of business lines restructuring and the implementation of a well-concep-tualized long-range operations/investment strategy has convinced us that ABI is now set firmly on a course of reliable and dramatic long-term growth. This appears borne out by first-quarter results.

So management longevity was now measured in quarters instead of years. I read on:

> Broadcasting: Management attributes the relatively undramatic per-formance of this area to a combination of general economic conditions, heightened competition for a diminishing network audience, and un-usual expenses occurred in repositioning network programming, in both TV and radio, to a more constructive market posture. Beginning with the fall season, the GBG Network will place exploitative scientific em-phasis on increasing market share through demographically proven sub-jects targeting such audience-proven taste spectra as socioeconomic polarization. Under previous management, GBG programming deci-sions were largely made on the basis of imponderables such as taste

and intuition. GBG's fall lineup will reflect state-of-the-art psycho-modularization testing techniques developed in conjunction with Stanford Research Institute. Two "Dumpsters" spinoffs, "Watermelon People" and "Ron's Limo," look very promising. In addition, GBG's old reliables, "Shield 262," "Resort," and "River Oaks," continue to move from strength to strength, with the addition of well-known entertainment personalities in continuing roles. Great things are also expected from a six-hour miniseries adapted from Khalil Gibran's *The Prophet*. In daytime TV, tertiary syndication, and major league sports, GBG reigns supreme, having in the last case recently extended the ingenious profit-sharing arrangement originally negotiated by previous management.

This needed to be taken with a grain of salt. Buck had once said that forecasting how movies and TV series would do had killed more security analysts than Henry Kaufman's forecasts of interest rates. I liked the ring of "psychomodularization testing techniques." Grade AAA cant. I wondered what "previous management," ensconced in his grand London house amid his volumes of *The Federalist* and Gibbon, would make of that.

The report continued with an analysis of the rest of the Broadcasting and Entertainment Group. The record business looked good; apparently GBG Records had come up with its own dusky hermaphrodite to cash in on the Michael Jackson phenomenon and was selling over a half million albums a week. The film library had proved to be a cash cow, being again and again recycled to cable television and now to the videocassette rental market. As a writer, I was especially interested in Ms. Pfannglanz's view of AbCom's publishing business:

Trade Publishing: After efforts to sell the company's Bailey & Brothers trade publishing subsidiary collapsed, management determined to reshape the 150-year-old firm, a legacy from previous management, into a viable component of ABI's overall communications symbiosis. New management headed by the former marketing director of B & B's elhi textbook group has sought to cut back and eliminate obsolescent or marginal lines of publishing product, principally of the literary genre. In the future, new publishing investment will be directed to product with demonstrated financial reliability. Two lines of videogame storybooks, distinguished from past such product by a variance in the ratio of linear to imaged semiotic material, will be introduced at the forthcoming Consumer Electronics Show. In a more traditional vein, the company has cut back on that part of its sales force dealing with the fractionated, largely uneconomical independent bookstore market and will concentrate on working with the chains. In terms of the individual market, a promising departure from traditional, low-efficiency outlet selection would appear to be the establishment of Realization House, which will publish a new line of paperbound self-improvement books to be rack-jobbed at the rate of three new titles monthly in nontraditional outlets such as jogging shoe and health food stores and gourmet food shops.

I wasn't sure what "linear semiotic material" was, although I expected it might be Pfannglanz for "book." In London, "previous management" had indicated his considerable displeasure with what was going on at B & B. X loved B & B; it had been part of Granite/AbCom for a quarter century. I could remember X boasting about the B & B tradition: how Isaac Bailey had published anonymous first books by Thoreau and Emily Dickinson and the Abolitionists, how Frost had worked there as a copyeditor, and how so many other great names had come to public notice and critical recognition under the B & B imprint. As a writer, I had identified B & B as synonymous with good writing, good bookmaking, and the highest standards of editing and publishing. No longer. Friends at B & B spoke of themselves as galley slaves.

"Realization House" rang a bell; I thumbed ahead to Pfannglanz's comments on Consumer Interface. Sure enough, AbCom had developed three "Realization House" direct mail catalog lines devoted to the burgeoning technology of solipsism: jogging and physical training gear, personal stereo products, and ten-speed bicycles and accessories.

The report reviewed every slice and sliver of ABI's operations, with much in the way of supporting statistical material: bar charts, pie charts, moving averages, market-share breakdowns, valuation models. As I read, I developed a better feel for the company's strategy under Abner, its governing ambitions. AbCom intended to stake out a profitable, significant position in every conceivable sphere or market, established or emergent, of communications: from satellites to cellular radio to data processing, from comic books to old movies to limited-edition recordings of Toscanini. It was constructing a weblike, diversified outreach, virtually impossible to escape in one form or another, to bring upscale institutional or individual customers within its orbit. In the world according to AbCom, the company would service those customers' higher-margin investment and spending requirements, from purchasing an espresso machine to making a straddle in columbium futures. It evoked images of capitalist Big Brother, relentlessly pursuing us through all our communications orifices: mailbox, phone, television, radio, and, of course, computer.

Ms. Pfannglanz's conclusion was positively rhapsodic:

Conclusion: As our clients are aware, we have for some time now been impressed by the pace and agility with which ABI management has worked to consolidate its objectives. This constructive feeling has been enhanced by the superimposition on ABI's corporate culture of a new goals-oriented, quantity-based management matrix. What until eight years ago was essentially a proprietorship, whimsically (if admittedly successfully) managed by a cadre of creative experimentalists, has been converted to a thoroughly modern, diversified, personnel-deep, markets-aggressive organization in the true sense of the word. Now the numbers are coming through. ABI appears poised on the verge of an earnings breakout not yet fully reflected in the price of the shares. For the current fiscal year, we are projecting $7.50 to $8.50 per share, an estimate which could prove as much as 15% on the low side, depending on year-end accounting adjustments and the deployment of reserves. Currently selling at less than 8 × our lowest-case projection, in a lackluster market environment, we believe the shares will achieve a material upside price and multiple adjustment.

ABI is a stock for this era, just as U.S. Steel and General Motors were investments for their time, now passed. In time it may become a holding for the ages, like IBM and General Electric, a permanent citizen of virtually every portfolio. For the present, it should be owned by any investor with a vestige of faith in the future, as that future can now be discerned.

WE RATE ABI (NYSE) AGGRESSIVE BUY/NO LIMIT

> V. Pfannglanz
> Executive Analyst
> Media/Communications

Impressive and positive this report certainly was, yet it left me with a bad aftertaste. There was something of Big Brother in this vision of Ab-Com creeping into every cranny of my existence. It was all so heartless and mechanistic, so programmed; and I was as much a part of the program as any widget, and without so much as a by-my-leave. I didn't like its political and economic implications. Abner's objective seemed to be a wholesale exponential intensification of the nation's present mindless, pell-mell consumerism. Eldonomics preached the same thing: spend yourselves happy, you who have it. A nation is only as strong as the unleashed buying power of its wealthy.

I also didn't like it that qualities such as "taste and intuition" were disparaged as nonmanagerial, beyond the pale. What about imagination, X's imagination, the public's ability to imagine, the seeds from which the billion-dollar beanstalk grew? I thought of my own boyhood; it might not have coincided with mankind's greatest golden age, but from here the communications "technologies" of those days, books and records and the radio, and the primitive allurements of early television, looked awfully good. They enhanced our imagination; they made no effort to replace it.

Mother was probably right. X's visionary skills had indeed taken something that should have been a small part of our lives and made something monstrous of it. Abner proposed to make it even more monstrous, more pervasive. X was the last best chance there was to slow the process down. Both believed in their cause. The prize was glittering, and the motives and connections a web of conflict and contradiction. There had to be a collision, people pulled this way and that, relationships turned inside out. It might come to no more than a skirmish, so entrenched did Abner seem. It might also come to more than that, and then, given the passions involved, and the past, it could be bloody.

It was all too troublesome to contemplate on the one day of the week that was invented for peace of mind, notwithstanding that I had quandaries of my own to sort out. I looked at my watch. Time for the Open. I changed channels, and Pebble Beach swam into view just as Nicklaus sank a great long putt on the first and the leaderboard graphic showed he was now trailing Watson by two, and five or six others were still in the hunt.

The Open was step one. I needed a still higher level of escape, to retreat to the most impregnable fortress of imagination. I crossed to the stereo and put on a tape; music filled the room, Schwarzkopf singing "Artist's Life." Who needed the real thing? To see Vienna plain might burst the bubble. The streets might be filthy, the people surly, the pastry stale, and the cream thin.

On the television, Watson sank a thirty-footer and the hunt was on. Beside me on the sofa were books and magazines that could take me all the way to sleep at the end of the day. Life could be worse, I thought. I had Strauss and Schwarzkopf, and Nicklaus and Watson, for company, and in this fretful world, with its complexity of Monstrances and loved ones, who could ask for more than that?

CHAPTER 5

"It therefore appears reasonable to expect continued growth for AbCom, given our diversified markets and our strong position within them, on the order of twenty-five to thirty percent a year. Thank you."

Applause rippled around the paneled dining room. Abner bobbed his dark, intense features in acknowledgment of the vigorous clapping that greeted his upbeat closing words. It was plain he had given the crowd exactly what they wanted to hear. The mood in the room was bully and conspiratorial.

"Played 'em like a banjo, he did," muttered Buck.

I agreed. It had been a very impressive show.

We were sitting with a hundred men and women in the largest private room at the Gorse Club, where Institutional Equities Associates had sponsored an invitational presentation by the top management of AbCom. Abner had been the final speaker, following his chief financial officer and the four group senior executive vice-presidents. There had been a heavy helping of *son et lumière*: a fifteen-minute filmed overview of the company that someone behind me whispered, approvingly, had cost a million dollars; clips from GBG TV shows; another film, about One AbCom Plaza, with many grabbing sunset angles; promos for AbCom's distribution and financial services units, including a dozen mail-order catalogs and brochures describing a score of investment programs; self-help books published by B & B; record albums; and a signed photograph of the stars of "River Oaks."

We had been shown a lot of charts, and every line, bar, and squiggle on them went up, up, up. The self-satisfaction on both sides of the rostrum was thick enough to spread on bread, glutinous, almost tangible. In the last fortnight, the market had suddenly burst out of its lassitude and tacked a hundred and fifty points on the Dow on huge volume. People were talking "major bull market." Everyone was suddenly richer and, I knew, just as suddenly feeling smart and confident. One could smell it. I recognized the scent; I'd caught it before, in the mid-sixties, when I was starting out on *Newsweek* and checking facts for the financial desk.

The people who had been assembled to hear Abner were surprisingly young, mostly in their middle thirties, neatly dressed in the uniform of the day: three-piece suits for the men, "dress-for-success" matching blazers and skirts for the women. Everyone wore a cravat of some sort, the women favoring floppy bow ties of Rembrandtesque proportions, the men subdued four-in-hand neckties. Here and there among the youthful, confident faces a grizzled head could be seen, nose and cheeks finely webbed with the evidence of too much drink and pressure and disappointment, eyes that had seen too many ups and downs, flashes and fizzles: veterans from the sixties, who'd somehow hung on in the brave new age. They were few and exceptional, however; the game once again belonged to the new breed, the young tigers from the hot money-management firms, the cool-eyed boys and girls who now ran the mutual funds and bank trust departments, the specialty analysts like Ms. Pfann-glanz, our host for the evening, who called the tune on the big stocks.

These were the people who technically controlled AbCom. Over 40 percent of the company's stock was held by institutions; over 65 percent of the shares not controlled by insiders. At dinner, Buck had hazarded that 20 million shares were represented in the room. There had been a lot of accumulation in the last year, he said, as Abner's transformation of the company had begun to take hold of the Street's perceptual machinery and catch its fancy. Abner was "these people's kind of folks," Buck said. He had a point; the empathy was obvious. Abner was coolly objective, "all business"; he had reshaped Granite Broadcasting Group into the kind of conceptually compelling company their concept-compulsive souls could vibrate to.

I assumed that, among the older men in the room tonight, there were one or two who'd originally bought the stock because of X. I wondered what they thought of the transformation, not that it mattered.

The meeting broke up into smaller knots. Abner and his cohorts began to work the room. In this crowd, he appeared completely at ease, even happy; usually somewhat stiff in groups, he seemed to disport himself in this audience's approval like a seal, sleek and almost frolicsome. He didn't look like a man who'd jump at the snap of his father's fingers.

Of course, how could you tell? Abner's youth had been dominated by X's shadow, by his father's great black noisy wings flapping overhead, blotting out the sun. He'd taken refuge in restraint; who could say what knots of personality were hidden behind that circumspection, or whether time and success had at least partly undone the tangle?

Partly at best, I thought; I found Abner a bit stuffy, a bit too pleased with himself. Once or twice I argued the point with Cass, commenting that I thought Abner's success was silting up his personality. She invariably accused me of being jealous, pointing out that AbCom was one of America's great companies, which obliged me to respond that it had been one of America's great companies as GBG, thirty years earlier, forty years earlier, when X was running it. It had occurred to me just this morning that I seemed to get pretty proprietary, almost defensive, about X/Granite vs. Abner/AbCom. Perhaps Mother had a point; there might well be a special bond between X and me.

"Quite a story," I commented to Buck. The rest of our table had gotten up.

"Real good. Not that stories are worth diddley squat these days. This ain't that kind of market, hasn't been for right nigh ten years now. Old Graham and old Dodd, they dead, D-E-D, dead! You either hot or you not. It's almost mystical; they love you or they hate you, starve you with neglect. Kinda like gettin' a divorce. Right now these folks jes' love ol' Abner. But it can stop jes' like that!" He snapped his fingers. "And when it do, bang! They pull the trigger fastest they can and afterward wander on up to see what it was they shot."

For the moment, however, it was obviously a love fest. The group around Abner formed and re-formed with the insistence of groupies besieging a rock star.

"Come on," said Buck, rising. "Le's jes' wander round an' see can we pick up sumpin' to make us some real money."

Abner saw me get up.

"Sam!" He came across the room, a practiced grin on his face. Some of his group followed, adhering to him like remoras. "What are you doing here? This isn't your line of country." He explained me to his coterie: "Sam Mountcastle's one of my oldest friends and a very distinguished journalist." He chuckled his stamp of approval. The four or five people around him nodded. I felt relieved; I had made it past the border patrol.

"S. A. Mountcastle?" said one of them. I recognized Fergus Duncan. "I'm a big admirer of yours." He introduced himself and stuck out his hand. I shook and then, figuratively, put my heart in it; writers eat praise for breakfast just like anyone else.

I introduced Buck to everyone and saw my stock climb another two points. This was getting to be fun.

"I'm doing a piece on institutional ownership, Abner. I was going to call you when I got far enough into it. Terrific job tonight. You know, it's the first time I've caught you in uniform. I thought it was a great presentation."

"Well, thank you," he said generously. "Coming from a distinguished writer, that's quite something."

He meant it well, I was sure, but there was something in his tone that I found offensive; I kicked myself mentally for being so touchy.

"You remember what Dad used to say," he continued, sounding just a touch too jocular. "'French cooking is ninety percent presentation.'" I detected a little catch there, as if he hadn't wanted to mention X, but the words had forced themselves to his lips regardless. "Anyway, Sam, you ought to let Fergus here put you in the institutional picture. They just bring me in every now and then to keep them sullen but not mutinous, as Herman Hickman used to say at Yale." Abner chuckled again.

Another of X's favorite quotations, I thought. Herman Hickman was just a memory in New Haven when Abner matriculated.

Other people now attached themselves to our little group, including Ms. Pfannglanz, a stern, late-thirtyish woman with gray, scolding eyes and ironed dirty-blond hair. When she'd introduced Abner after dinner, I'd made her for one of those people who practice toughness as a virtue. In her case, I suspected, intestinal fortitude was equated with statistical accuracy.

Abner made ready now to transfer his attention, in a way that was almost mechanical, like a great crane being repositioned. His height, well over six feet—he was much taller than X—reinforced the impression. Before he turned away, he said, in a tone that unmistakably denoted gravity of subject, "I gather Clee and I will have the pleasure of seeing you and Cassandra in three weeks' time? At the Shrecks' for the Cornaras?"

I nodded. Even though I could see that Abner's tacit admission of social intimacy had sent Mountcastle shares soaring through the top of the charts, my pleasure was mitigated by the prospect of an evening to be spent with or around Bud and Marie Shreck, as well as by my realization that, quite contrary to my expectations and, frankly, my hopes, Abner appeared to take this social stuff seriously.

"Give me a call," said Fergus Duncan as Abner now turned away to reply to a question. He scribbled a number on the back of an elegant, somewhat outsized vellum card which said simply: "Mr. Fergus Mac-Pherson Duncan." No company name, no logo, no commercial information; a British gentleman's visiting card. "Say," he said, "that was a pretty good line about presentation. Who said that, Brillat-Savarin?" He pronounced the name as "Brillit," joined by a hyphen to a brand of coffee.

"Actually, I think it was Escoffier," I said, trying very hard not to sound downputtingly upper-class. There was something I instinctively liked about Duncan.

"Yeah? Well, I gotta put it in the quote base. Say, I really liked that piece you did last week about the mayor. What a weirdo!"

I agreed that the current occupant of Gracie Mansion was indeed eccentric.

"You're telling me?" said Duncan. "I grew up listening to La Guardia *read* the funny papers. This guy's right *out* of the funny papers! Or the funny farm!"

Duncan's voice and accent were incongruous. Taken together with his elegant tailoring and studied, Anglicized appurtenances, from pipe to jaunty paisley pocket foulard, the effect was like David Niven speaking with Buddy Hackett's voice. In a way, Duncan reminded me of Buck. The way he spoke had little relation to the way he wrote; he talked street but expressed himself on the page with an Augustan grace and rigor, just as Buck talked like a redneck but—I doubted—surely didn't think in those terms, not that he was ever about to let me know.

"Anyway," Duncan said, noting that Abner had moved away, "I'll give you a call. Take a lunch, maybe. The Tea Room or the Numbers, whichever you like. You can pick my brain all you want, and then maybe we can talk about something worthwhile, like how come nobody writes English any longer?" He hustled over to stay close to Abner.

Buck and I parted on the steps of the Gorse. So far this June we had gone through six or seven microclimates. The night was pleasantly cool, early Octoberish, although July Fourth was exactly eighteen days off.

"Ol' Abner's not exactly Mr. Casual, is he?" Buck observed.

I thought I'd give Abner the doubt. "He's spent most of his life holding himself in," I said. "His old man was a pretty strong cup of tea." I was careful to say "was." Deep graveyard.

"Is the old sumbitch still alive?"

"I think so. I think he lives in England."

"Damn," said Buck. "Jes' shows how short-memoried we all are. I used to admire the damn out of old Monstrance. When it came to TV, that old boy could pick 'em up and put 'em down. Reminded me of the Juice. Two of a kind, them two was. I tried to go one-on-one with the Juice once, up in Buffalo—man, it was colder'n an old nun's pussy—and he like to left me for dead on the forty. Jes' like Abner's old man left CBS for dead. NBC, too. DuMont he jes' left dead, period!"

"I didn't know you were such a keen student of the history of American broadcasting."

"I ain't." Buck's voice turned softer, earnest. "But I'll tell you sumpin', good buddy. If it weren't for the TV, I'd prob'ly be sittin' on the porch in my overalls, pickin' pecans for a living, or maybe, if I was real lucky, workin' at Pop Deitz's Sun station. If wasn't for old Monstrance, and Paley and them others, I wouldn't of known there was a world out there."

We shook hands and parted. As I walked uptown, I thought how pleased X would be, to know that in at least one heart and mind and memory he'd gained the kind of appreciative posterity he wanted.

The editor liked the idea of a piece using professional tennis as a symbol for the decline of civility in Western life, so he approved my going to London for the second week in July to catch the last three rounds of Wimbledon. All the highest-priced juvenile delinquents would be on display, and the metaphoric pickings looked promising. I sent a cable to X to tell him I'd be there, in case he wanted to see me.

The day before I left, I had lunch with Duncan at the Russian Tea Room: "21" was too heavy for me at lunch; too many tycoons and painted ladies, too many Buds and Maries.

He was already seated when I arrived, at a table near the front of the large room, with a half-finished vodka in front of him.

"The shmucks and the day-trippers think it's a big deal to sit in the bar," he said when I sat down. "For my money, where Sam Cohn sits is where I want to sit." He nodded discreetly at the next table, occupied by a woman I recognized as a successful new playwright and a bespectacled man in a sweater. "I'm telling you, Tolstoy and Dostoevski and Turgenev and Chekhov could reserve for four here, and you know who'd still get the best table? Sam Cohn." He drained his vodka and signaled for another. It was brought with a promptness that was testimony to Duncan's own high rank among the samovars.

Over lunch, we barely touched on the subject of institutional ownership, which suited me fine; I'd only broached the subject as a cover story, to explain away my presence at the IEA dinner, and while I was interested in the subject in principle, as I was interested in everything under the sun except how a radio worked and what mc² equaled, I had visions of getting mired down in one of those unwanted predicaments that big lies and small fibs invariably seem to lead to.

Nor, mercifully, did Duncan shill the party line for AbCom or BLEEP. He was obviously a good loyal soldier, an experienced corporate courtier. He'd taken Abner's shilling, and so he was Abner's man, and that was that. When he spoke of Abner, "the boss man," it was with the appropriate degree of reverence, but by no means worshipful. About himself and his life, to which he devoted a good part of our two hours together, he was frank, reasonably irreverent, and not overly impressed. I found myself liking him more and more.

He had graduated from CCNY with a degree in English. Two years in the mailroom at Ted Bates followed, writing the great unpublished, unfinished New York novel—just one of fifty, he said, being written at that agency alone. Moved over to BBDO as a junior copywriter. Ten years there climbing the ladder, until he was switched into account work, which he hated, so he went into financial advertising at Hill and Knowlton, where he developed a taste and uncovered a hidden talent for corporate public relations.

"Sometimes I think I shoulda stuck at that," he said, "the money those assholes in Wall Street PR are making these days off these takeovers."

Someone at Citibank had spotted him as a comer, and he'd had a stint there, which led to five years in the big-time, working at Mobil for the legendary Herb Schmertz. The trouble was, there wasn't room at Mobil for two Schmertzes, so Duncan had gone freelance, but the solitude got to him, and when Ben Sonnenberg had recommended him to Abner, he'd jumped. He was now fifty-four years old.

"That freelance bit did one good thing for me," he said. "I knew I'd never be able to stick it out and write my novel. Man, that was lonely! I had this office on Madison and I used to just sit there, shitting in my pants about where the next job was gonna come from. Of course, you wrote your novel when you were a kid, so you got on the track early."

I reassured him that there was always time. Sooner or later, if you had something to say and the inclination to say it was real, the time would come when you could get it out. It was like a slow, meandering train.

Our talk drifted onto the subject of the city. We came from opposite poles, but being born and bred in New York was like a tropical fever in the blood, impossible to purge.

"I was your basic Upper East Side kid, only too far up and too far East for P. S. Six. My old man worked in a shoe store on Third over under the El. He was nuts about the Philharmonic—listened every Saturday—so I went to Music and Art, and then to CCNY, where those bastards broke my heart. I goddamn near quit!"

I asked for clarification.

"Maybe you're just too young. Naw, you'da been ten–eleven then. You know, the fixers, the 'fifty-one team, CCNY, the guys that shaved the points: Warner, Lane, Roman. There was four or five of 'em. You gotta remember, Sam! They won the NCAA and the NIT both. Beat Bradley both times. Bradley had a guy named Unruh, Paul Unruh, same last name as that guy went batshit in Camden and blew half the town away. Anyway, we put 'em away two times in the Garden, none of this shit about playing the big ones in some dump like Salt Lake City, but the next year the wise guys got to the coloreds—and a couple of the white kids too, let's be fair—and they got caught shaving points and that was all she wrote for that dynasty. The only starter they didn't get was the captain, Dambrot, Irwin Dambrot, best jumpshooter in the clutch I ever saw, till I saw this kid King, plays for the Knicks—and Bird, of course."

It was hard to believe this was the voice behind the icily precise phrases and pretensions of the AbCom "advertorials." I asked Duncan what it was like working for Abner.

"The boss man's OK. Fair, plays by the rules; works his own ass off before he asks for yours. Likes a little backscratching now and then, but who doesn't?" He grinned at me, raised a finger, and a fourth vodka was brought.

"A little bird says you write those two-page BLEEP ads," I remarked.

He didn't try to be cryptic. "I help now and then with the English. Most of these moguls don't write so good."

"What about the Op-Ed pieces?"

"The boss man sets up the subject, makes a rough draft, and I english them for him, get rid of all that shit he learned to write at the business school."

"And you have nothing to do with the content?"

"Nothing. Politics bores me. All I do is get the boss man's words right. Plus I supply the quotations. You ever notice something?"

"What's that?"

"Well, a lot of what the boss man's got to say comes from BLEEP. They kind of set the notes, and the boss man fits 'em into a melody, and then I sort of do the harmony. It's the same for the White House. I've helped out in D.C. a couple of times, but that's off the record. You know something weird? Erwitt gives maybe fifty speeches a year, and he never quotes anyone. He doesn't even quote Lincoln, for Christ's sake! Can you imagine that? I got curious and started going back, looking at Presidents' speeches all the way to Wilson. Christ, even Harding quoted from Lincoln! You got two hundred years of great quotations out there, and Erwitt doesn't even use one!"

"Our President is not an intellectual," I commented. "History does not concern him. Where's McNeery fit into all this?"

"He's in it for the dough. He's no dummy, though. He's no different from the rest of them, just quicker on his feet. The barn door's open, but nobody knows for how long, 'cause sooner or later someone's gonna find out just how open—"

"I believe that economic theory is popularly known as Eldonomics. Are we going to eat?"

We ordered and, when the food came, threw ourselves upon it. When coffee came, along with a schnapps for Duncan, he said, "You've known the boss man a long time, he tells me."

"Most of our lives."

"Which means you must've known his old man?"

"Up until we got out of boarding school. Say twenty-five years ago."

"What was he like? People around the shop talk about him like he was Babe Ruth."

"He was pretty impressive," I said mildly, making it try to seem that I was dredging up withered memories.

"He was a goddamn genius!" declared Duncan. "I used to hear about him when I was with the agencies, and Sonnenberg used to talk about him all the time, like they were the best of friends. I read that biography the old man wrote. What a piece of shit! I wish I could've worked on it for him. I'm not kidding: you go around the shop, especially down where the TV and radio guys are, and you say 'H. H. Monstrance,' and everybody crosses himself."

"In front of Abner?"

He grinned and called for the check. "No comment," he said.

"When they're not crossing themselves, what do they say about him?"

"Oh, just about what you'd expect the average citizen of Assisi to say about Saint Francis. How he was a genius; how great he was to work for;

how people weren't scared of him, the way everybody at CBS was scared shitless of Paley; what a class guy he was; how he lived bigger and better than the Queen of England; how he made it with the ladies."

Duncan had risen halfway out of his seat; now he sat down and leaned forward, lowering his voice.

"You think that part's true?" he asked.

"What part?"

"About the broads. Guys say he was about the biggest swordsman ever lived. They say he put the meat to half the women in the company. Like he'd bang half a floor of secretaries at lunchtime. Anchorwomen, weather girls, actresses looking for a shot at the soaps, the old kielbasa never cooled off, the way they tell it. You know ———" Duncan named a famous actress who had recently collected her third Oscar. "A guy told me the janitor came in one night and found the old man putting it to her dog-style on the goddamn boardroom table!" His voice was filled with admiration.

I refrained from comment. X's erotic adventures had been well and fully chronicled, factually and *à clef*, by better-briefed journalists than I, ink-stained Leporellos who made a living counting the grunts and thrusts of the great and famous. Instead, as we walked out on to Fifty-seventh Street, I asked Duncan if Abner fooled around.

"The boss man? You got to be kidding. Even if he didn't just discover what it's for, which means he's still reserving it for the one who showed him how, he doesn't get his rocks off with women."

"Men?" I asked facetiously.

"Cut it out. Numbers are what turns the boss man on. Business. He gets off on the company, Sam. AbCom's where he lives. Sometimes he pushes too hard, although I think the new wife's calming him down, or at least wearing him out with this society shit."

"What do you mean, 'pushes too hard'?"

"Like he's fighting something. His old man, maybe. You remember Eugene Field?"

"Sure: 'the little toy soldier is red with rust—'"

"That's the one. Well, he used to work for *The Denver Post* as a drama critic, and some limey came through town doing Shakespeare, and after watching Lear, Field wrote, 'Mr. So-and-so played the king as if someone else was about to play the ace.' The boss man gets that way sometimes."

"Does he ever talk to his father?"

"Never. The old man stays away. If he's playing any head games on the boss man, I don't know it. It isn't like it was over on Fifty-second Street, where they finally had to lock the goddamn doors to keep the old man out! When H. H. Monstrance went, he *went!*"

We left each other then, promising to reconvene at some point after I got back from Wimbledon. It was Duncan's thought we could burn down a few Third Avenue bars together.

Wimbledon was no better or worse than I expected, but I was deeply glad to be there. Over the long July Fourth weekend, Cass and I had moved into our rented Water Mill house. Hardly had we struggled in the kitchen door with the last bag from the A&P, and stowed the last mixed case of Italian rosé and Spanish champagne, than the clouds moved in and the skies opened in a steady slow rain that lasted three days. Barely had the rain begun when the phone started ringing: the guys from the gallery; Marie Shreck; Clio, installed up the highway in the big Southampton house she and Abner had bought and fixed up the year before. By the second morning, the notorious seaside damp had penetrated everything. I was trying to finish up a couple of book reviews that I was late on, but the paper drooped languidly in the typewriter roll and the ink blurred like watercolor. The phone kept ringing. By the time I left on Monday afternoon, it looked as if we were fixed up right through August of the year 2000.

It was obviously going to be a long summer, I prayed for good weather. If the sunny outdoors was denied me, the vast escape of beach and ocean, Cass would wear me down unto death with socializing, unless I took a walk, which seemed a dumb thing for me to do, what with nearly eight grand tied up as my half of this project. I suppose I still hoped that Cass would wake up one morning and be as I thought she was when I met her, but I was realistic enough to realize that, for that to happen, Saint Jude was going to have to work nights and Sundays.

So London was, surprisingly, a respite. I checked into the hotel I'd been tipped to a few years earlier by a pal on *The Tatler*, a Victorian pile in Knightsbridge known only by its address, 15 Walton Crescent Gardens, and murmured to be owned on the quiet by British Intelligence. The editor would have loved it. There were about fifty rooms, tended by a staff described irreverently by the hotel's owner as "the Spanish touring company of 'Upstairs, Downstairs.'" It was convenient, unfussy, and fairly priced, just the place for people whose sense of self didn't need to be affirmed by Connaught-scale prices. You just came and went; there was no "hotel life"; the place didn't even have a bar.

As expected, all the truants, tarts, delinquents, and pop-offs made it through to the round of eight. The English press was loaded for bear, and the players didn't let them down. It was a pity, because some really great tennis got overlooked in the commotion. McEnroe went out in the quarterfinals after putting on an exhibition of truculence and profanity that would have made a Hell's Angel look like Lady Windermere. In a semifinal match, play was halted for ten minutes while the world's third-ranked player lay prostrate on the court and kicked his heels and beat his fist on the ground over a line call that cost him a point in a 40–love game in the third set of what turned out to be a 6–1, 6–1, 6–0 win.

Between saying "screw you" to the linemen, these kids showed some shots I doubted Tilden could have imagined, let alone executed. That was the sad irony. Fifty years from now, when fans would discuss the all-time greats, it would still be Tilden and Budge and Kramer, Gonzales, Hoad, Rosewall, and Laver who would be extolled, none of whom could probably have touched McEnroe on one of his good days, but who were sportsmen, who said things like "good shot" and bit their lip when the out calls went wrong. These kids probably didn't care, but if they didn't watch out, they'd wake up forgotten, their tickets to Valhalla canceled by their ill manners.

Not that I really cared. Tennis wasn't for me, even though I'd had about ten thousand lessons as a kid. I liked golf better, as a game, and for watching; I just couldn't turn on to tennis, as I couldn't for hockey. The players didn't really interest me. I liked the "idea" of tennis: long, late, green afternoons punctuated by the decorous plonking of balls back and forth between ladies in long skirts and gentlemen in boaters, but those days were one with the dodo bird.

At least I wasn't in rainy Water Mill. I endured the women's final, won by a testosterone-fortified veal sausage from Copenhagen who survived a medical protest by the loser, the Wimbledon doctors attesting that the victor had the proper convexities and orifices, all more or less correctly situated. On Saturday afternoon, a glowering runty cretin from Mamaroneck outlasted the latest pride of Texas: a twitchy postadolescent with a knob-shaped head that evidenced a heavy hand on the forceps. At the press conferences following their victories, the winners confirmed my general impression that most sports could now be played at world-class levels with less than a dime's worth of mental furniture.

Tempting as it might have been to watch the swart Westchester monkey waltz with a hundred and sixty pounds of Scandinavian calf, I decided to pass up the victory ball in favor of a quiet dinner and a good book. A friend with a car offered me a ride back to Knightsbridge.

I hadn't heard from X during my five days in London, nor had I called him. I was operating on the theory that if he wanted me, he'd find me. Nor had I dropped everything I was doing. X's enthusiasms had been known to pass with the suddenness of a summer squall, so I had done my homework and was now seriously involved in touching up what I thought was a pretty good article on the new economics of Broadway.

I had barely gotten into my room when the phone rang. The voice was the same clippy Mayfair chirp that I'd spoken to from Scotland.

"Oh, Mr. Mountcastle," it said. "Mr. Monstrance regrets telephoning you this late, but he wonders if you might be free to dine tomorrow evening. He's having just a few people in that he thought might amuse you. Eight thirty, at Chelsea Embankment, very informal. He very much hopes you'll be able to make it."

I said I'd be pleased. As Willie Nelson should have put it, one night of anything will make up for two nights alone.

I was the first to arrive at X's, which gave us a few minutes together. It was all set, he said. The Polish couple who looked after Dunecrag had been instructed to get everything spic and span by the first of August. As far as anyone knew, X said, he was simply coming back for six weeks. The party line was that homesickness had got the best of him. This would give him plenty of time to huddle with Abner. He'd had a checkup, and Harley Street had pronounced his blood pressure and prostate to be those of a teenager, more than up to the prospective stresses of his great enterprise.

I told him that I was at his beck and call. He cautioned me to say nothing to anyone; as far as the world was concerned, he and I still hadn't seen each other for twenty-five years. He'd fix things so we'd encounter each other on Long Island and play the part of reunited long-lost friends.

"I know you're a good actor, Sam," he said. "I saw you in *Pinafore*." My brilliant theatrical career had consisted of playing the patter roles for the Starbuck Savoyards.

The doorbell rang. As he rose, he said, "There's someone coming to-night I want you to meet: Margarita Clerc. Unfortunately she's bringing her husband, who's one of those Frenchmen who makes you want to firebomb Paris. She's in on this with us. I'm bringing her to New York in September, got Jake to fix up a lectureship at Columbia for her. She's become a tutor to me on the decrepitude of the land of my birth. I knew her mother, a wonderful, dotty old girl, must be ninety, who lives in Venice and paints the most awful watercolors. Ah, Prime Minister—"

The guests turned out to be a former Labour prime minister and his wife; a writer for *The Economist* and her husband; a well-known theatrical director; a celebrated pair of duo-pianists, horsy-looking, austerely dressed sisters in their fifties; and the Clercs, Pierre and Margarita.

I noticed when X took the Clercs around that he introduced her with a faint but discernible pride of possession, as if she was to be admired as a trophy. Whether he had bagged her mind or her body, I couldn't say. I thought back to Fergus Duncan's encomiums on X's prowess as a lover; anything was possible.

Margarita Clerc looked to be about my age, possibly a few years older. Her features were strong, intelligent, "foreign"—the sort of looks the fashion magazines called "striking" when describing some Milanese contessa. She was neither buxom nor particularly tall, yet she had a largeness of presence that made her seem bigger. Her complexion, eyes, and hair were dark, darker than Cass's, yet there was a definite similarity. Give Cass another fifteen years and ten pounds, and a return to seriousness, and this was how she might turn out.

Her husband was a thin, faultlessly turned out Frenchman, about the same age as she, who gazed languidly around the room, pricing X's furniture and paintings, evaluating the potential for his own use of the faces in the silver-framed photographs and the people to whom he was introduced. He looked as if he smelled excrement somewhere but couldn't quite locate it. They made an odd couple, bringing to mind a writer's observation that Englishwomen, while quite discriminating about whom they sleep with, will marry almost anyone.

When we went in to dinner, I wasn't surprised to find myself placed next to her. X was back to his old game, laying down the chalk marks in other people's lives.

We started by swapping summary biographies. Her father had been American, an Oxford-educated expatriate lawyer; her mother was Anglo-Italian. The family had lived in Zurich, where her father represented a well-known New York law firm, until 1940, when she was ten, when they'd moved to London. During the war, her father had been involved with British counterintelligence. He'd died of a heart attack the day Kennedy was shot. She had been educated in a succession of English elementary schools, at boarding school in Lausanne, and at Oxford and the Sorbonne, where she'd met her husband. She taught American history at London University. The odd thing was, she'd never been to the United States.

"It's strange, isn't it," she said, when I commented on the fact, "but I really never had much desire to go. In a way, I was educated against it. Father loathed his native land. He never stopped saying what a terrible place it was. Part of that was just Europhilia, of course. But much of it was very deeply felt. He said America would be the death of the West. He wouldn't let Mama and me have American passports. I've never even claimed my right to citizenship!"

"I gather you're about to break the string," I said. "Your father must be turning in his grave."

"Horace told you, did he? Well, the time has come; I'm past fifty, and there's probably no harm that can come to me now. Besides, you know how Horace is about getting his way."

She had a lovely, sexy voice, English and precise, somewhat at odds with her smoky, volatile looks. Women could turn me on with their voices as much as their beauty. Margarita Clerc was turning me on.

She asked me what I did and I told her. The question and reply were mere courtesies. I was sure X had briefed her about S. A. Mountcastle and his expected role in things. I asked her how she'd met her husband.

"In Paris. Father was rabid about languages. He said if I could speak one or two besides English, no one would possibly take me for American. Pierre was teaching economics at the Sorbonne. He was older, frightfully overeducated, very demanding; I was still young, impressionable, frightfully ignorant about certain things. Pierre hated America too, in that silly way the French have, although then I thought it terribly clever. I suppose he reminded me of Father; most girls would prefer to marry their fathers, don't you think?"

I nodded. I thought of Eugenie Monstrance. Mme. Clerc had a point. Then I thought of Cass. Maybe she didn't.

"Horace tells me you're very good at puncturing balloons," she said.

"I try. I think of myself as in the parasite control business."

"I like that. Father used to say that unless one planned to be an academic, the main point of education was to be able to tell when someone else was talking rubbish."

"He had a point."

"I thought so too. Later I found out he'd cribbed the idea from a man who'd taught him at Oxford."

"That doesn't make it any less true."

"I suppose not. How do you think I'm going to like America? Father always said what he disliked most was that Americans had no use for the past."

"I wouldn't disagree with that. How are you going to like it? It's hard to predict. Most visitors get terribly excited about what they call 'vitality' but which seems to me to be mostly commotion. I think you'll find there's not much sense of place: people do what they want, where they want, when they want; it doesn't matter if someone else got there first. We seem to regard right of trespass as a Fifth Freedom."

"Well, I hope I can count on you to show me around. Are you taken, as they say?"

I didn't know the answer to that, so I said I wasn't sure. I inferred from the question that things weren't all that great in the Clerc household. Later I would learn that she and Clerc lived apart most of the time: he in Paris, she in a small house in Hammersmith. I found the inference exciting; she was exciting; the possibility of being with an older woman was exciting. She smiled at my reply, unsurely, as if looking into herself and her own life with some misgiving. I noticed small wrinkles at the corners of her mouth and eyes, tiny stratifications brought on by trouble which gave a tiny, enticing hint of vulnerability.

"X knows where to find me, and so does the magazine," I said. Suddenly I wondered whether I could be grown up enough for a woman like this; the essence of my affair with Cass, at its best, had been its childishness, a shared feeling that life and the great big adult world were just something to poke mischievous holes in. I wasn't sure I was up to playing the man, or that I wanted to.

For the rest of dinner we made small talk, ignoring our other dinner partners, who didn't seem to mind. This wasn't the time and the place to huddle conspiratorially about X's war on the evil empire of Eldon Erwitt, as I had come to think of it. From time to time I caught X watching us, mostly as if checking that the machine he'd set in motion was ticking smoothly but another time, when Margarita laughed at something I said, with an expression that was distinctly proprietary. Again I speculated as to their connection: was she his mistress? Could a man that old still do it?

When dinner ended, X led us from the dining room. The Clercs left shortly afterward, and soon after their departure I said my own good nights. Outside, I saw that the sky had clouded over, but it didn't feel like rain. I decided to walk back to Number 15. As I set out on the route that would take me back to Walton Crescent Gardens, it occurred to me that I might take Margarita Clerc to lunch or dinner. My Monday was my own. I had a bit of shopping to do, and I planned to visit the British Museum and look at the Dickens and Yeats manuscripts, just to douse any literary hubris that might be building up in me, and to see an exhibition at the V&A, and to lunch at the Garrick with a friend. No, I thought, life was too complicated right now as it was. The best thing was just to let events take their own momentum and direction, not look for new entanglements, and be wary of them if they came. Leave things as they stand: a pleasant London night, the streets feeling safe, and me going home to my own bed, alone—and glad of it.

CHAPTER 6

I returned to find that New York had become a cauldron. Air conditioners shuddered helplessly against heat that shouldered its way through the walls. It was weather made for tension. The streets literally percolated hostility; the asphalt bubbled and squished underfoot; tempers boiled over nothing; the newspapers reported angry exchanges between pedestrians and drivers that resulted in fatal shootings. Water Mill, despite the likelihood of a stressful seven weeks, looked like the promised land. But first there was the Shrecks' dinner party.

There was no way of getting out of it, since one of the purposes of the party was to honor Clio and Abner. Why, I wasn't sure, but in this set it never seemed enough to invite a few friends in to eat, drink, tell a few stories, and maybe flirt a little. Every party was always "for" someone, probably to justify an entertainment deduction; I got the feeling that accountants were now as integral to top-level Manhattan hospitality as cooks and bartenders.

Bud and Marie's dinner had two other purposes. It was to be a housewarming, the social inauguration of the couple's newly refurbished Sutton Place triplex. And there was another pair of honorees: the Cornaras, whom Abner had mentioned that night at the Gorse, who appeared to be standard-issue Eurotrash but very, very rich. When I asked Cass whether I should anticipate a toast to Bud's discount-store fortune, which had paid for the apartment and its furnishings, she was not amused. I expanded my thinking to include Marie's remarkable bosom and behind.

"Bud's a big real estate man," I observed. "He knows better than any of us what a fellow's got to pay for right of access. Too bad about inflation, though. I understand it only cost Marie's first husband a plate of ribs and a Diet Pepsi to get her in the rack."

"That's not very funny," Cass said. Bud and Marie were serious business to her. The rich always hang together, and though the cast may change, it does so as the money changes hands. I had been brought up among and around well-to-do people, what was said in those days to be gentry and were, compared to what was currently on offer, but I remembered people complaining that the wrong people had all the money; observing Bud and his tycoonish ilk, I began to understand why. These new great fortunes were based on a rabid determination to accumulate all the money in existence, a determination which simply left no room for art, philosophy, or the like, except as accessories of the high life. As a result, the Buds of the world did not make for stimulating company.

I had taken to needling Cass, to whom the high life seemed to be the thing, more and more about her new friends, of whom Bud and Marie were simply *primi inter inferiores*. I suppose I hoped that I could push her far enough to do the right thing by both of us, to cut the cord outright, which I was too chicken or indecisive to do myself. She seemed content to keep me on. A reasonably well-known writer was a useful enough bangle to flash in public; I also thought that she was as uninterested as I in the prospect of starting over with someone else. And I persisted in the illusion that some divine wind might blow all these croaking frogs out of our life and restore us to that golden time of spaghetti dinners, going Dutch, arguments about politics and painting, real books about real life. So I continued to perch on spindly gilt chairs; to drink the latest wine poured by a white-gloved cup-bearer in a bolero jacket; to discuss, as if seriously, the latest delicate howl by Renata Didion or Nora Steinem, invariably with some jumped-up stewardess who had been told by the chintz merchants that this, sweetie, is gracious living, and don't let anyone tell you different, darling.

"How come they have to do this now, in the middle of the heat wave?" I asked Cass. We were at her place; I'd come across the park to change there, since it had been one of those days where a hundred-yard stroll sweated through two shirts. I was just out of the shower and was standing damply in the middle of her bedroom wrapped in a towel.

"It's just a small private party for their good friends," she answered patiently. She was sitting on the edge of the bed in her underpants, combing her hair. "It's not as if Bud and Marie asked us to drive back into town. Anyway, I think it's very gracious of them to include us."

"'Gracious'?" I said. She'd done it again. "What kind of word is 'gracious'? Gracious Bud and gracious Marie, graciously welcoming their guests, half of whom are there hoping graciously to make a sale of some kind, including you, to their newly—what?—'gratiated' home. What's the verb for 'to make gracious'?"

She tossed the brush aside. "Sam, don't always be such a prick. Grow up. New York isn't *Stuart Little* anymore. Life changes. People change. Grow up, for God's sake! Bud Shreck is a very interesting man. I think you're missing a bet; you ought to do a profile on him."

This had become a small issue between us. It had even gone far enough that I'd had a call from the Shrecks' publicist asking if I wanted to set up an interview. This had led to a real screamer with Cass. I drew the line at bartering my professional resources for the dubious gratitude of a *shvitzer* like Bud, I said—loudly. When it finally blew over, I thought weakly that, yes, I might actually do a real number on Bud and Marie, leave them tattered and eviscerated on the page. That mood soon passed. The editor probably wouldn't print it; hatchets weren't my weapon of choice; to pick on the Shrecks for their vulgarity would be like what my bird-shooting friends called "beating up on the cripple"; and I had a rule that I didn't disparage those whose hand fed me, even if I only ate their gilded crumbs out of emotional *force majeure*. Besides, I knew deep down that in the end whatever I wrote about the Buds and Maries of this world would make no difference, and what was the point of writing if it didn't? The world in which they dwelt was impervious to value criticism; bucks was how you kept score, not old-fashioned knee-jerk stuff like good, true, and beautiful.

"I'm sorry," I said. "It's the heat. I want to get to the country."

I saw as I said it that the issue was already dead with her; her mind had moved in its dragonfly way to other matters of personal concern. Cass's self-absorption could be maddeningly skittish.

"I wonder what he's like," she said, putting the question not to me but to life in general. "I can't wait to meet him." She didn't even try to keep the calculation out of her voice.

I didn't need to ask who. The news of X's impending return for August had burst on the New York–Long Island social scene like a thunderstorm on a sleepy bay. I, of course, played mum and dumb.

"Me either," I said. "It's been twenty-five years since I've seen him. We used to be pretty close." I was quite happy with my performance.

"Did you see this?" she asked, gesturing to *The Daily News*, lying opened on the bed. My old relation to X was of no interest to her; in her current frame of mind, it was past imagining that someone in my anti-social frame of mind could possibly share close acquaintance with an H. H. Monstrance.

I had already seen the gossip column:

> The planned August sojourn of H. H. Monstrance, founder of the great communications empire now ruled by his dynamic son, Abner, at his showplace East Hampton cottage, Dunecrag, has smart Hamptons so-ciety agog and a-twitter, which is agogging and a-twittering aplenty. Abner's wife, Clio, surely New York's most inventive hostess, is laying plans for a glorious Southampton party over the Labor Day weekend to cap the return of the patriarch. The affair will be a real wingding, boys and girls, and those unlucky enough not to be invited had better make plans to be in Beijing or Addis Ababa. For those on the list, however, it's strictly all systems go. Ladies, man your ball gowns!

"How thrilling," I remarked. "What courage to face the future it must give the good people of Astoria and Bedford-Stuyvesant who make up the principal readership of this paper." I also knew all about Clio's party. Cass had told me after Clio had told her. I wondered if Cass had tipped the news to the columnist. Christ, I said to myself, don't become another one of those women who spills other people's beans.

"I wonder what Dunecrag is like," she said, shrugging into her dress. She made it sound like Mecca. "Clee said she'd try to get me invited."

"I thought Clio hadn't met her father-in-law," I said. I was getting pretty good at disingenuousness.

"She talked to him on the phone. He wants to give some lunch parties. Meet the new people. Clee's helping him with the list."

I looked at my watch. "We better get going." This is quite an artful Trojan horse X is building, I thought. The new people, eh? Well, X was supposed to have a good eye for a bosom; Marie would probably pass very nicely.

Twenty minutes later we were on our way up to the Shrecks' terraced penthouse overlooking a broad lawn which ran down to the East River. The cost of the paneling in the private elevator alone would have ex-hausted my capital. I could tell the evening was going to be heavy on the *luxe* and *volupté*, if not on the *calme*.

Cass and I were ushered into a long mirrored hall. Marie stood before a massive marble table receiving her guests. She was a flashy woman in her mid-thirties, with a lot of mouse-colored hair, slightly dull, overexperienced eyes, and a brightly painted mouth rumored to be capable of sucking the chrome off a fender. The creamy cantilevering of her famous breasts supported a necklace that probably cost the yearly gross national product of someplace like Ghana. Next to her stood Bud, about thirty years older, burnsided and bejowled and beefy, definitively of the butter-and-egg persuasion, from his pointy Italian slip-ons to his altogether too extravagantly ruffled evening shirt. Next to them was Clio; beside her was a woman with piles of shiny raven hair, made up like a Lebanese houri. While Cass kissed her way through the small receiving line, I took a quick look around, peering past Bud into the drawing room.

I got a shock. The "gracious living" engineers had indeed been at work with a vengeance. This had been one of the city's notable apartments, in the same family since the building had been put up by Starrett and Van Vleck in 1917. It had been famous for the scope and sophistication of its woodwork and moldings, especially for its double-storied drawing room paneled in painted boiserie reputed to have been made for Madame de Pompadour.

Now, I saw, that was all gone. Surfaces once graced by pale garlands now glowed with the porcelain sheen of coat after coat of industrial lacquer. The second-story windows had been replaced with a thick paning that looked to me like glass brick. The overall effect was sanitary, disturbingly like a giant men's room; I found myself looking around the walls for gargantuan faucets and flush levers.

"Sam," said Marie, "I want you to meet one of my dearest friends, Mme. Cornara. Mr. Mountcastle is one of our most distinguished journalists, Lucienne." Marie's voice was thin, fluty, wispy. Vocal gentrification had exiled Little Rock to the distant reservations of the past.

"Just another head on the wall," I mumbled, releasing Mme. Cornara's extended hand and risking a sharp look from Cass. I embraced Clio, acknowledged Bud's "How's it going, fella," with a torpid handshake, and passed through into the living room. Cass had already swept in ahead of me and was deep in animated conversation with a pair of men whom I recognized as Marie's decorators. Their North Atlantic Line decor, heavy on etched glass and slick surfaces and lots of art deco furniture, which they had bought on the cheap when the last Cunarders were scrapped, was currently all the rage.

I looked around. It was the usual group. These people worked like a repertory company: they played each other's dinner parties the way Edwin Booth used to play the mining camps of the Old West. The thought recalled Fergus Duncan's quotation from Eugene Field and caused me to chuckle. I looked around; the faces were familiar. The usual dowagers, representing the old money, the way things used to be, had been planted together on a sofa, where a stream of anxious young men buzzed about them, bending knees and kissing hands. They turned up because they liked the attention and because they could tell themselves that it was a good cause, that they could milk Bud for a little six-figure something for the Public Library or the Arboretum. They might be right: Bud was very clearly one of those men to whom it was more important that the IRS get none of his money than that his children, say, get any.

I saw a couple of newspaper colossi across the room. That was common these days; journalists like caviar and champagne as much as the next fellow—look at me—and if it made them sleepy on patrol, what the hell: the war was over; Eldonomics had seen to that. In a group admiring Bud's new Monet I thought I caught sight of the rice-terrace coif of a former Treasury Secretary. I acknowledged a faint, unenthusiastic wave from a guy I'd known pretty well in the old days, before he'd gone big-time. He was hanging on to his new wife, a woman with a lot of hair and a reputation for glottal virtuosity second only to our hostess's. She was talking to another woman I recognized as the hopped-up ectomorph whom the trendy fashion papers had anointed "the Duchess of Delight." Cass swept up to them, and the three women launched into a conversation conducted with an aggressive exaggeration of expression and gesture designed to let the rest of us know what a keen time they were having talking to each other.

Behind them stood four guys making stock exchange noises about eighths and quarters. Fascinating. I helped myself to a glass of Dom Pérignon and a couple of pieces of toast loaded with good gray Beluga and began a tour of the walls. All the right names were represented, none of them particularly well. It was what these days passed for a "collection." Like Marie's guest list, Bud's art was a sprinkling of the names of the moment, sold to him by a socialite dealer who guarded the Shrecks' custom with the ferocious solicitude of a she-wolf. I could see him smiling and stroking his way through the crowd. All the right species were represented: one de Kooning, one Rauschenberg, one Stella, one Johns, and so on. The de Kooning had sold at Sotheby's for close to two million; close up, it didn't look so hot. History is going to be tough on Mr. de Kooning, I thought. I looked for traces of Cass's handiwork on the walls—I knew she'd made a couple of sales to the Shrecks—and recognized two of the oversized ripoffs of Dubuffet in which her gallery specialized. The crowd had moved on, and I inspected the Monet. It was all right; what you get from a very great master when his muse has taken the day off. Accessible: lots of poppies. Who couldn't like poppies?

I heard someone call my name and turned. It was a guy named Jerry Caster. We'd been at Starbuck and Harvard together and had seen quite a lot of each other in the early years, when everybody was just starting out in New York, young and striving and decently broke whether on Wall Street or Grub Street, and our principal wherewithal was a lot of laughs and a few shards of principle and self-esteem. Some years back, Jerry'd hit a big strike in financial futures, and after that I hadn't seen much of him. He was said now to have also struck it rich in venture capital, but it had been quite a while since any of the old gang had heard from him, and we no longer asked each other, "Anybody know what's happened to Jerry Caster?" Like a swimmer sucked under by a riptide, Jerry had literally disappeared into his new money. I had heard that he was a sort of social point man for people like Bud, acting as an intermediary between new money and old clubs. Shades of the Hargroves! I wondered what a guy like Jerry expected from someone like Bud for putting him up for the Meadow Club or the Brook.

"Hey, Sam, how's it going?" he said jovially. I'd already heard that line once tonight. "Where you been keeping yourself? I assume you know Jules Cornara? He and Lucienne are thinking of buying the old Grover place, right down Gin Lane from Bud and Marie and Clio and Abner."

We shook hands. Cornara was an unappetizing, sallow runt in an over-tailored tuxedo with a lot of embroidery on the lapel facings. He and Bud obviously took from the same tailor. He gave me a gloomy, uninterested smile; he was clearly a man who could separate the sheep from the goats in the pastures of self-interest and net worth.

"Well, Sam," Jerry said, "let me give you a bell next week, buy you lunch. I'd like to catch up on you, find out what you're up to."

"I'm going out of town," I lied. "I'll call you." Spare me, kind gods, I said. When guys like Jerry said they wanted to catch up with people like me, what they meant was: I'll buy you lunch at "21" and tell you how much money I've made.

"Do that," said Jerry. He and Cornara resumed their discussion of the outlook for titanium, and I resumed my inspection tour.

Upstairs I discovered the master suite. I peeked around. A large bedroom with a four-poster the size of a hockey rink, all done up in frilly swags, just the place for Marie to practice her matchless oral ministrations. Off the bedroom were dressing rooms, two baths, hers with swan faucets, a bidet, and a small icebox. I opened it; it contained one bottle of Dom Pérignon and one of cheap domestic champagne. I hazarded that the purposes of the latter were strictly cunnilingual—or worse, from what I'd heard about Marie.

I nosed about for another ten minutes, checking the bric-a-brac. There was a nice Meissen suite of *commedia* figures. A couple of Fabergé pieces; a few decent enough export plates in a lighted cabinet. Downstairs, Bud and Marie pretended to have outgrown their early period, with its *Town and Country* aesthetics, its Boehm birds and Ispanky figurines of ballerinas, but up here, away from prying eyes, was the stuff I suspected they really liked and understood. I checked the family photographs. Ghastly children, probably either his or hers, souvenirs of less glamorous marriage no longer acknowledged. Faded old small color prints of mommas and poppas. The haunting past. Not like the big, lavishly framed photographs I'd glimpsed in the living room: Bud with Kissinger, Bud with Henry Ford II, Bud with Golda Meir, Bud with President Erwitt.

There were more people in the living room when I went back down, now including Abner, who stood talking to a man I thought I recognized. Abner introduced him as Eric Shaughnessy.

I knew about Shaughnessy. GBG hadn't been notable for breeding entrepreneurs, but he was one exception. Number three in the company behind X and Abner, he'd quit the year after X left and started Communications Network, Inc., CNI, which began by tying corporate information centers together by microwave and was now a billion-dollar operation that linked the computers of the world's largest enterprises by satellite. AbCom still had a similar business, BizNet, which Shaughnessy had started, and which did slightly different things with blips and beeps, on a much smaller scale. A profile of Shaughnessy in *Fortune* had reported that he'd left Granite/AbCom because Abner tied his hands on BizNet. The fact was, AbCom had put up a significant part of CNI's seed capital.

"Sam's just back from Wimbledon," Abner said. "How was it?" He didn't sound at ease.

"As you might expect, the shits. Those kids need a touch of the old belt buckle."

"Along with most everyone else." Shaughnessy laughed.

"Eric and I were just talking about institutional investors, Sam. It seems we have rather divergent views on the subject. As it happens, Eric, Sam's very interested in the whole question. You were saying . . . ?"

"Just that anybody who thinks he'd doing himself some good by sucking up to the institutions is pissing into the wind. All you're doing is spilling your guts to a bunch of emotional postadolescents who are nothing but hot-sheet artists. They'll sell you out tomorrow, if there's a buck in it. The little guy, he tends to be a believer."

"I don't agree with you," Abner said. He sounded as though he were reading a prepared statement. "We find it so much more efficient to deal with investment professionals. They speak our language."

"The only language I want my stockholders to speak," said Shaughnessy, "is the language of love. I treat 'em like every day is Mother's Day. We even still have preemptive rights. They get first crack at all our goodies."

I was curious. "I don't mean to interrupt, but are you saying you discourage institutional stockholders?"

"Theoretically, yes. Obviously there's not much you can do; it's a free country. The best we can do is try to keep it within limits. Mainly by treating them no different from any other investor. No special peeks at our numbers; no executive sessions; no trips to Disney World; no dinners at the Gorse, on our tab or theirs. They don't like that, and it helps maintain a general lack of enthusiasm on their part."

"The stock's been great, though."

"Well, there're six or seven people in the wire houses who follow CNI closely, and if they talk us up to the insurance companies and pension funds, there's not a hell of a lot I can do about it. Plus we don't hoard. Our cash flow is great, and what we don't need I pay out one way or the other."

"Doesn't not kissing the institutions' asses sort of cheat your other stockholders out of a lot of upside buying power?"

"I think it balances out. I've heard all the arguments pro and con. I can't run this company exclusively, one hundred ten percent, for the stockholders, which is what institutions seem to expect. We've got customers we need to sell and service, projects to carry through. My people can't do that if they're worried the institutions'll sell us out like they've sold out some other pretty good managements."

"Well, Eric," said Abner, "I must say I disagree. We've no better stockholders, none certainly more loyal and sympathetic, than our friends in the banks and pension funds." He sounded quite pompous. Just then Clio came up, smiled at Shaughnessy and me, and led Abner off to meet someone.

"Nice girl, that," said Shaughnessy.

"Very."

"In a funny way, she reminds me of the old man's wife, Selena. You ever know her?"

"No."

"She was really something. She could make a boy feel as pert as a yellow tie on a spring morning. She and the old man used to put on 'at homes' that make this look like a church supper. Clio's got the same kind of class. Of course, she doesn't have the old man. Now that old bastard had juice enough for ten men. He could run flat out fifty hours a day, and anyone who wanted to run with him had to keep up. Selena could."

"That's what I've heard. I was interested in what you were saying to Abner about institutions. Do you think it's really that ominous?"

"I don't think it's a good thing. 'Course, Abner's in a different position. The family controls the company, so he doesn't have to sweat it. But that's not really the point."

"What is?"

"The point is, the little guy always counts in the end. Sooner or later, and it's getting later, he insists on it. There're too many of him. The point is to handle things so that he's in the picture and doesn't wake up one morning and feel inclined to chop off a few heads. There's millions of them out there, from guys on the line at the River Rouge plant to old women trying to live off annuities. Those are their savings we're talking about. The guys in the institutions act like it's their money. They don't give a merry screw as long as the portfolio's up on the day they calculate their management fees."

"I thought that was the point of the exercise."

"Only part of it. One day a lot of people are going to figure out what overinstitutionalizing the market has really cost this country: in jobs, in wasted resources, in management habits. Then it'll be Katy bar the door! Guys like Abner, though, all they see are the numbers. His old man wasn't like that, and the numbers he put up on the board weren't exactly shabby!"

"Nor are Abner's."

"Agreed. But they're nothing like they're going to be the day Abner decides to stop spending twenty-three point nine hours a day trying to outdo his old man. They're two entirely different people. Abner's smart and talented, but he doesn't run on the same voltage. When the old man used to walk into a room, every guy there, and every woman under the age of ninety, felt like someone had run an electric wire up their ass. He had a tiger in his tank!"

Shaughnessy looked around.

"Who are these people?" he said. "This isn't Abner's scene. Why's he here?"

"Why are you here?" I asked, knowing Shaughnessy wouldn't take it wrong.

"No choice. Like it or not, I'm in bed with Cornara."

He explained. He was trying to get a ground station network established in North Africa. The American ambassador, one Arthur Mismer, had tried to help, but he was a nincompoop who only screwed things up, and so Cornara, who had connections, had been recommended to CNI.

"Isn't Cornara in the oil business?" I asked.

"Cornara?" Shaughnessy snorted. "He couldn't find oil in his crankcase. He makes his money on the telex. He's a fixer, a middleman. Come on, Sam, this is the golden age of the middleman. Look who's making the real money. Guys like me who invent things and build companies? Nah! Investment bankers make it, and guys who know people, like Cornara, and lawyers with pull. I pay Cornara, and he sees it gets to where it counts. We start to lay down our first installations next month. I don't mind paying the money. I do mind having to turn up and act like Cornara's a friend of mine."

"I thought payoffs were illegal."

"In this Administration? Are you kidding?" He shook his head.

"Where'd you find Cornara?" I asked.

"Through Abner. Actually through McNeery, the former President, who's one of Abner's directors. He's expensive too. Plus I had to ante up for BLEEP, which I didn't want to do, but you play the game according to what the guy who owns the football tells you."

We were called to dinner.

"Nice seeing you," said Shaughnessy. "Come by the office sometime." I said I would. "Say," he added as we separated, "I hear the old man's coming back. I wonder how he is." I said I didn't know; it had been twenty-five years. Secret agent Mountcastle at work and play.

At table, I found myself next to a young man from the decorative arts department of the Met. He was a typical art careerist, up from the sticks with a doctorate from the Fogg or NYU, trawling for invitations and the sponsorship of rich old women or, even better, younger women on the make. Apparently, he advised Bud and Marie. It seemed they were trying to buy the *trompe l'oeil* wall paintings from the Villa Malcontenta to put in their new Southampton house.

"Won't the sea air wreck the murals?" I asked.

"Not at all. The house is completely sealed and climatized," he answered. "They'll be safer there than they would be in the Louvre."

"What's the point of having a house on the beach, then?" I asked. He turned impatiently to his other side. Across the room, Cass was jabbering busily into the ear of a fragrant-looking man whom she would later identify as Bud's trichologist, the man who tended the thinning up-parted locks of many of Bud's ilk.

The woman on my left, my former friend Jerry's wife, went through the usual platitudes of how it was really too bad we didn't see more of each other, but then wasn't that the way it always seemed to be now, what with the pace of New York and all. I thought she looked a little beat up. It takes a lot of energy to ride shotgun in the speed lane.

Cass had told me I could look forward to Bud and Marie's food and drink as being strictly major league, and she hadn't been kidding. Although it wasn't exactly what I might have chosen for a scorching July night, it was three-star all the way. I suppose I'd been expecting the usual double-gaited menu: kiwi fruit and veal birds stuffed with Gorgonzola and scallops vinaigrette tastefully arrayed on plates the size of Yankee Stadium. Instead we were given oyster soufflé, followed by a huge, crusty game pie made from one of those nineteenth-century recipes that begin "take forty partridges and two brace of stags," and on to a cheese board which had arrived that morning on the Concorde. The wine was up to the food. Chablis was followed by Clos Vougeot '64, followed by '59 Château Latour, followed by a great Yquem with the dessert extravaganza: a spun-sugar oil derrick, bedded in geological strata made of sherbet, from which dribbled a flow of Godiva chocolate sauce, pumped by a tiny motor. It didn't even daunt me. With food like this, how vulgar could you get, really!

Someone tapped firmly on crystal. I drained the last of my Château Yquem and prepared for the worst with a fresh glass of '73 Dom Pérignon. Over at the A table, Marie rose. The moment I had learned to dread had arrived, the time for toasts; I signaled an ephebe to refill my glass.

"It's always wonderful to have good friends and family," said Marie.

Her wonderful breasts jiggled in the candlelight. I realized the wines had made me tipsy; I felt altogether too benign.

"It's wonderful to be able to bring them together and to try to make them happy. Of course, Bud and I are especially delighted that our first dinner in our new home could be in honor of our dear friends Lucienne and Jules, who entertained us so generously this spring on their beautiful yacht in Bodrum . . ."

She paused to let the rest of us beam upon the Cornaras.

"And in honor of those lovebirds, Clio and Abner Monstrance. . . ."

Marie put down her Lalique goblet and clapped prettily.

"Of course, none of this could be possible without my dear, darling Bud, who has made me so happy and blessed among women, and who works so hard to make all this possible."

She cast a glance at her husband, a look of such collusive lewdness he actually blushed. I wondered what Marie looked like without any clothes on. I was definitely a touch blitzed. I wondered what Mme. Cornara looked like naked.

Marie was followed on her feet by Bud, and then by the Cornaras in turn, and finally by Clio and, last, Abner. Clio spoke well and calmly. Abner seemed oddly nervous before this audience, not at all the man I'd recently seen transfix a roomful of gimlet-eyed investment professionals. Clio looked very beautiful, I thought. I wondered if she looked like Cass without any clothes. Blonder down there, probably.

After dinner, I worked at keeping my mouth shut until it was time to leave. Cass insisted I go home with her. She was a little tipsy too, and I knew she wanted to talk. She was probably feeling sexy.

Undecided whether I would stay the night or not, I accepted a brandy and sat down next to her on the sofa.

"That was quite a production," I commented.

"It was wonderful. What a wonderful apartment."

I needed to keep the mood level and tranquil, so I agreed and hymned the cooking and the wine.

"Wasn't it, though?" she said. "So imaginative." It was the kind of *House & Garden* observation that had been creeping into Cass's conversation lately. "Bud and Marie do everything so beautifully." She shrugged off her jacket and tossed it over a chair.

We talked for another half hour. Even planed smooth by drink as I was, I found it difficult not to react. Cass was being so stupid, so trivial. The worst part was, she was beating herself over the head. I could hear it in her voice. Beneath the honey, her tone said that Marie's admired walls were paneled in wormwood and the cut-crystal decanters had held vintage gall. I wanted to say, Why not just let it go, and come back to me? You're never going to have fifty million bucks or whatever it takes, so just stay with me and let's live the life we can. It wasn't half bad before, was it?

I didn't, however, and we finally arrived at a familiar emotional crossroads: either I could leave or we could quarrel or we could make love. Separation would have been best, possibly even healing, so naturally that was out of the question. A quarrel would be too distasteful, too exhausting, and so we threw ourselves into moist oblivion. It started off well enough; both of us were raw-nerved enough and had drunk enough to get the ball rolling. In getting each other's clothes off, in tonguing and stroking and getting to a quick level of excitement, we performed wonderfully, almost thrillingly enough, at least for me, to overcome my awareness of what it was that had brought us to this point. We were out of sync, however; buoyed by my own excitement, willing to mistake my engorgement for passion, I insisted on entering her before she was quite ready. What I had drunk now hindered us in overcoming this brief mechanical problem. Finally, we got ourselves properly fitted together, and ground and thrust away on the sofa, separated, I was sure, in our fantasies, until I couldn't bear the friction and attenuation any longer, and came, but managed to sustain myself firmly and artfully enough inside Cass until she gave a long sigh and found her own release, or so she sounded, and so I hoped.

Afterward, we leaned on each other and made our way down the hall to the bedroom. I buried my nose in her hair and we held each other like real lovers, the way we had before, B.C. When she dozed off, I lay awake thinking. Now there was something in the room with us; it lurked in the shadows like a child's bad dream and cast its own long shadow between Cass and me. I did not think it unconquerable, however. If our life had been changed for the worse, it surely could be changed back to its earlier pure, happy state. She would see the light, and our past paradise would be put back together, and all would be as before. Sure it would, José.

I stayed there most of the night, hoping osmosis would implant some of my own wavering certitude in the sleeping mind beside me. When the first streaks of dawn appeared over the water towers and battlements of Queens, on the far side of the East River, I took the promising appearance of the new day as a good omen, dressed quietly, and made my optimistic way home through streets already reeking with heat.

CHAPTER 7

Water Mill offered small respite. Daytime was all right on the whole, except on weekends, when the lunch cycle cranked up, but the evenings were hell. Our life seemed stuffed with people, wiggling, wailing, howling for attention. Either it was Gus and Ken from down the road, popping in for monkfish on the grill and a good "dish" about all the goings-on, or else it was off to Southampton, where the florid palette of entertainments seemed infinite. I spent my evenings in the dressed-up company of tycoons, simulacrums of Bud, who liked these occasions as little as I did but who were equally too daunted by their women to mutiny. Heftily gaudy in their peach silk jackets and lemon trousers, they seemed somehow forlorn, hunched and huddled amid the noise and chatter, gross insects drawn into the alien glare by wives and mistresses, lured from the shadowy recesses where they hatched their vast and complex schemes.

My lot was worsened by the fact that the mysterious, implacable biogenetics of wealth had replicated Bud and Marie in the appropriately named Getsmores, Martha and Sherman, Marty and Shermie to their "inties," among whom Cass had achieved full membership during the short week I'd been in England. I shouldn't have been surprised; this crowd was notable, if for anything, for the speed with which new friendships were cemented fast. The insecurity of the wealthy acted as a powerful emotional adhesive.

Marty Getsmore had the money in the family, inherited from a father of whom suspicious things were muttered when her back was turned.

She was an anxious woman in her late thirties, one of those who seemed to feel that a lot of hair, baroquely arrayed, might compensate for terrible failings of personality. Shermie, much older, was obviously delighted to find himself with a visa to paradise. He functioned in relation to his wife's money more or less the way Marie Shreck did to her husband's pile, adding the light, frivolous touch: she spending enough on clothes to keep her favored couturiers in catamites; he making sure the Alouette was at the helipad and that there was always plenty of Cristal. He knew his onions, though; as maître d' of the Getsmore helicopters, he was in a position to spare one an inconvenient drive to the city or the horrors of the Long Island Rail Road. In no time at all, he was taken into most of the better Southampton clubs, where he could indulge his most deeply felt longings, golf and backgammon.

July wore on toward August. I was uneasy about the prospect of X's presence in all of this; I feared he could prove to be a catalyst for tensions as yet undreamed. Cass spent a good part of her time scheming access to him, but as the only invitation he was known to have accepted was to Clio's Labor Day party, she was fencing in the dark, as were all her subdermal sisters up and down the Montauk Highway. The very prospect of X had produced a condition of near social hysteria, working as it did on the rich basis of anxiousness which was anyway integral to high Hamptons summers. If the local neurasthenia could have been described in the phrases of a ski bulletin, one would have said that a fresh six inches of anxiety had fallen on a hundred-inch base of insecurity.

Our household wasn't the only one to feel the tension. Abner showed it too.

"Well, Sam," he said to me one steaming Sunday night, "it'll be quite something to have Dad back." We were standing together on the Shrecks' lawn, sweltering in makeshift cowboy outfits, watching an ox being charred in honor of a visiting Munich shoe designer. It had been a long, yea endless, day. Lunch at Marty and Shermie's: Bellini cocktails mixed by a bartender flown in from Venice; cuttlefish risotto and vitello tonnato under Pratesi umbrellas; sour, warmish Pinot Grigiot and a sun so close overhead that the brain fried. It did not remind me of Harry's Bar, which Bud Shreck was reported to be buying, as indeed he was reported to be buying everything.

"It certainly will," I replied to Abner.

"How long has it been since you've seen Dad?"

"Twenty-five years," I lied. I felt like a traitor.

"Well, we'll have to have a regular reunion, won't we?" His voice said he hoped the Concorde bringing X triumphantly home would slide into the Atlantic, like a needle into Lake Agawam, a silver sliver vanishing into depths beyond the reach of God. In the light of the gas torches, his face bore an expression I knew well, a mixture of uncertainty, impatience, and apprehension. I'd often seen it at Starbuck, when the proctor came to tell Abner that X was on the phone in the house master's study. X always had a way of interjecting himself into Abner's life at unguarded moments; it was as if he picked up signals from the ether. Perhaps those signals lingered still, like the radioactive blinkings of otherwise invisible stars.

I had little time for the troubles of others, though, and that was perhaps why I could fib to Abner with such ease and lack of regret. The world was too much with Cass and me; even the greenery conspired against us. The soft-drink magnate who lived next door appeared to be competing in a *concours d'élégance* of hedges; each morning, early, his gardener set to work on the privets with a hedge trimmer that would have powered a 747, enveloping the day with a teeth-grinding whine. When he finished, and silence came, other signals went out and the contract service would show up to mow our lawn. I began to miss the silence and shut-awayness of the city. I wanted Mostly Mozart and Indian food and cool movies that were not about plastic dolls.

Overnight, I became sexually apathetic toward Cass, although she barely noticed, sequestered as she was in her cocoon of plans and ambitions. I took to the beach early, where I peered lewdly at the slim young girls from behind my sunglasses and—plugged into my Walkman—spent hours suspended contentedly between the odd polarities of sea and sky and Richard Tauber singing of Old Vienna: *"Liebliche Weise, Walzertraum. . . ."* It was like going under an anesthetic. The world drifted away, replaced by mirages. Above the waves would appear an image of St. Stephen's Cathedral, comfortably gray and chilly. *"Frühlingsverlangen, Gluck ohne Ruh'/Hoffen und Bangen, Liebe bist duh. . . ."* Pillowed by the thought of nonstop happiness, I would drift off. *"Einmal noch beben, eh' es vorbei/Einmal noch leben, lieben in Mai!"*

The last weekend in July I played with Buck in a local golf tournament. We qualified in a good flight, won a couple of matches, and then got jumped on by two kids who hit two-hundred-yard five-irons and said "Too bad, sir" every time we missed a putt, and that was all she wrote for the great team of Buchanan and Mountcastle. I didn't mind losing. The match had gotten me out of a beach picnic Cass was throwing in honor of her gallery's resident conceptual minimalist sculptor. The Getsmores had already forked over $40,000 for six bricks laid in a row in their brand-new imitation Gertrude Jekyll rose garden. I was happy to be spared the beach, the shrieks of gulls and gays, the plop of paddle balls, the sight of Bud noshing a plateful of lobster salad.

Buck and I bought our conquerors a couple of Cokes and sent them on their way. We ordered club sandwiches and rum Southsides and sat on the clubhouse porch and shot the breeze. Spread out below us, the tournament's remaining matches struggled over the course. The golfers' bright clothes formed cheery blots of color against the grass and dunes. In the far distance, clouds fluffed up over Peconic Bay. For the first time in weeks, I felt at one with the world.

"You still interested in AbCom?" Buck asked out of nowhere.

"Sure."

"I heard sumpin' th'other day. Not what you'd call a story. More like a titty-tickler."

"Oh?"

"Guy I met says ol' Abner's maybe thinkin' of closin' down the GBG Network."

"I don't believe it!"

"That's what my guy says, and he seems to know. Abner kinda thinks the network's more trouble'n it's worth. He don't like it when the guy owns the affiliate in East Pissant calls up and bitches about the Nielsens. He's thinkin', Why not go independent? Keep the O and Os; maybe even buy a coupla more stations, now that Uncle Sam says go to it, boys! Shit, he's got the NFL. He can auction it off game by game, market by market. The new contract lets him do that, you know. He can get into syndication. Make some of his own shows. Hell, good buddy, why not?"

I thought of how X would greet this news. "Where'd you get this," I asked, "one of your moles?"

Actually, Buck called them his "monitors," listening posts, supported by cash or kind, in corporate and regulatory America, in Washington, Houston, Atlanta, wherever decisions were made that might significantly alter the value of a company or the Street's perception of that value, or which might hinder or expedite a deal in progress. Buck's monitors, he freely admitted, were where he ate.

"Uh-uh," he said. "Got this from a fellow I never saw before. Ran into him at McMullen's. He'd taken that fatal extra glass of beer, and you know how them boys get when it hits 'em they're talking to ol' Number Forty-four. Nice guy. All duded up, but talked like a runner."

Duncan, I thought. Out looking for hormonal relief in the bars. I said nothing.

"Jes' thought you'd like to know," Buck said as we walked to the parking lot. I watched his Maserati vanish down the hill. Should I pass this on to X? I wondered. No: I was neutral, just an observer, there only to receive impressions and information.

X made his reentry into New York/Long Island society right on schedule, on August first. One of the local New York stations thought it newsworthy enough, just because of who he was, to film him coming out of the Concorde jetway and through the British Airways terminal to a waiting WGBG helicopter, which flew him directly to Dunecrag; a special dispensation permitting it to land right on the lawn had been negotiated with the East Hampton town council by AbCom's legal department. The process reminded me of the "Court Circular" notices in the London papers, reporting that So-and-so was conveyed to Such-and-such "in an aircraft of the Queen's flight." Indeed, X *was* royalty.

The atmosphere in our small corner of the world now became electric. Cass was so wound up I felt I would set off sparks if I touched her. She ached to get to X's, to penetrate the ceremonies of the elect, but so far no soap, even though inescapably overheard fragments of sisterly chitchat indicated that Clio was doing her best. Obviously, I couldn't help.

I was disappointed at the bits and pieces I heard about the doings at Dunecrag: the big Sunday lunches on the porch above the dunes, the black-tie dinners on Friday and Saturday nights. X seemed to be trying to take the place by storm, and his listmakers had dredged up the usual lot: the acid-pink-and-green-swathed Maidstone gentry, the Shreck-Getsmore sodality, the always available remnants of the Austro-Hungarian Empire and the Troisième République Française, the occasional Arab. Trojan Horse stuff, I guessed; mingle with them, gorge them to the point of euphoric loyalty, disarm them. I hoped so; at the back of my mind lingered a suspicion that the waltzing old fool of the post-Granite years had been in some great measure the true X, the now and actual X, the man he had become.

As a half-shares tenant, though, I had to be tolerated in my house, even though I pushed it; each passing week rubbed the thin coating of civility thinner, and a strain of native meanness was brought nearer my surface. My favorite subjects were the Shrecks and the Getsmores. The argument always followed the same pattern.

"What's Latin for 'I buy things, therefore I am'?" I'd ask innocently. "'*Teneo ergo sum*'? Something like that?"

Cass would half hear me. She'd be busy slicing zucchini or riffling through *Architectural Digest*.

"How about 'I have helicopter, therefore I am'? Nope; Descartes didn't know from helicopters. Anyway, it's too long."

Down would go the knife or the magazine. "What in heaven's name are you talking about?"

"Well, Bud and Marie" (or Marty and Shermie, the order of naming being determined by which partner had the money) "have been so generous, I thought I might have a little gift made up for them. A coat-of-arms. One of those painted and gilded things. I don't think the Shreck family crest is on file at Somerset House, so I'm using a little Yankee ingenuity. A fancy Latin motto. '*Teneo ergo sum*.' Then you could have a golden ladder, standing for social mobility, and dollar signs rampant and—"

I usually didn't get much farther than that. This was serious business, and Cass would spring to the defense, attack—whichever.

"You're just bitter. All you intellectuals are! Bud's a success. Just because he didn't go to Harvard—"

That would be my cue.

"No," I would say evenly, with each passing day less surprised how easy it was to be even with this woman for whom I'd once have killed (or the contemporary chivalric equivalent). "No, I'm not jealous of Bud. There is nothing about Bud that tempts me. If being rich means I have to be like Bud Shreck, I will arise and go now, and go to Chad and live in a mud hut."

"What have you ever done? Bud's a success! And look how generous he is! He offered you his helicopter last week when you had to go into New York!"

"Which I declined. Unlike some people around here, I don't equate my convenience with my principles. I wish to have no obligations, real or felt, to Bud Shreck. I have nothing to sell him. I don't crave his company."

"You don't hesitate to drink his wine."

"And very good wine it is." This was my moment to sound lofty, like Paul Henreid, or sneeringly superior, like Stewart Granger, depending on the inflection of the moment. "But I remind you I drink it only because you insist on bringing me along."

That would generally do it. Bang would go the screen door; her car would growl into action, tires would spray gravel.

I suppose if we'd continued in this vein right through August, we'd have killed each other. Mercifully, autumn began to be a presence, like the Manhattan skyline glimpsed through a late summer haze, and Cass spent the middle of each week in town, getting the gallery ready for the fall whirl. Her absence left me fuddled, strangely enough. I had taken the summer off from work, except for a few book reviews; now, with the focus of my feelings and wordplay absent for considerable stretches, I had trouble thinking up things to do with myself. There were always the novels, three or four notebooks of random thoughts, ideas for plot and character, pithy observations and apothegms. Finally, as much out of desperation as anything else, I contacted an old client of Mother's, a once-famous film director now being maintained in hard times by a young film buff with a lot of inherited money and a big house in Amagansett. I thought there might be a profile there. People still seemed interested in the old days of Hollywood.

Like many old men, he liked to subject others to his eccentricities. His vestigial power trip took the form of being willing to talk only right after sunrise. He and I would sit on the roof deck of the house where he was kept "like a goddamn stuffed animal," beginning at around six in the morning, the tape recorder between us, watching the sea and sky change color, and talk. By eight thirty or nine, age and three or four vodka-laced grapefruit juices would seal up memory and reflection for the day, and I would drive back to Water Mill.

One morning I found myself meandering along the back roads of East Hampton for no good reason other than a generic hatred of the Montauk Highway. As I drove along Further Lane, I saw the mass of Dunecrag. I passed by Maidstone and kept moving west. Finally, at Georgica Beach, I ran out of road and stopped. I left the car and climbed through the dunes to the beach.

The morning mist was just burning off; to my left I could make out the rooftops of the mansions fronting Lily Pond Lane. The ocean was like glass: soupiness of air and water promising a real scorcher. I walked across the sand to the water and let the dull, warm ripples play at my feet. On the blurred, distant line where sky and ocean met in a lusterless conjunction, a fishing boat slogged its way eastward. Faced with still and vasty Nature, I tried without success to summon up appropriately deep thoughts. There had been a time, before I learned how unlike poetry most of life is, when Wordsworthian or Byronic conjecture came to me with Pavlovian dependability. No longer.

I didn't hear the figure approaching up the beach until a voice said, from a few yards away, "My goodness, is that you, Sam?"

I turned to find Margarita Clerc smiling at me. She was wearing a dark blue one-piece bathing suit; in her left hand she held a book and a glasses case. A scarf was thrown over one shoulder. She looked polished and tan. I wondered if she was staying at Dunecrag; I asked her how she liked our beaches.

"They're ravishing. We don't get this sort of ocean in Europe. The North Atlantic's freezing, and full of Germans, and the Mediterranean's a cesspool. How are you, Sam?"

"Fine. The better for finding you here. Have you been in the country long? Where are you staying?"

I knew a good bit more about her now, having looked her up in the British *Who's Who*. She would be fifty-two in November. She held degrees from Oxford and the Sorbonne. She had taught at Bologna before the London School of Economics. Her bibliography included scholarly papers and articles, in the most recondite learned journals, and two books: *Cain's Absolution: Ontogenies of Envy in Contemporary Society* and *The Institutional Dilemma*. I couldn't recall having seen either on X's London shelves. I hadn't read either myself.

She had been married over twenty-five years. That bothered me; Abner and I would have been mere kids, being tucked in, figuratively, at the Georges V at perhaps the very moment when she'd first taken Pierre Clerc into herself.

Without thinking, we fell into step and started up the beach. She was staying with friends: a chemist from Chicago who'd sold something he'd invented to Procter and Gamble for enough to buy a house on Lily Pond Lane. X was probably keeping her out of sight, too, I speculated. I asked her how she liked America.

"So far everyone's been terribly kind. I do find New York a bit of a push."

She was staying in an apartment off Park Avenue in the Thirties. I inferred X had gotten it for her. She asked me where I was staying.

"We rent a house in Water Mill." The Freudian "we" was intentional.

We had come several hundred yards. It was suddenly as hot as noon. She laid down her book and stepped quickly to the water, flurrying her hands in, cooling her face. Her bathing suit rode up, revealing a band of pale flesh. At the suit's elastic edge, a few dark strands could be seen, threads against thighs that were firm and unmarked. I wondered if they were an earnest of the rest of her; the body under the sleek suit took form in my mind; I visualized its sharply defined hollows and puckerings, its dark, hidden patches. Suddenly I experienced one of those fierce erotic epiphanies brought on usually by heat or hangover; my libido got busy; I needed to step quickly across the brief space between us, push the fabric of her suit aside, and penetrate her from behind like an animal. The urge was incredibly powerful, breathlessly pure. Then it fled, leaving only a faint quickness of the breath as evidence that for an instant something not human had occupied my skin.

"Is it always this steamy?" she asked, drawing a wet hand across her forehead. I wondered if she'd felt the same urgings.

"Not really. The wind's from the southwest now. It'll change. How are your lectures coming?"

"Well enough. I'm going to be speaking about what inflation does to altruism."

"Sounds interesting. I'm planning to come."

"Oh, I hope so. Horace said he'd be there. At least he did in London. Today, who knows? He's very mercurial, isn't he?"

"He defines the word. Have you spoken to him since you got here?"

"My goodness, no. He swore me to secrecy. I'm on Mr. Polhemus's payroll. And you?"

"Not a word." That we were co-conspirators was now acknowledged. "X likes his games," I said. "I suppose when you've done as much as he has, that's all that's let to give it a thrill."

"Possibly." Her tone took me to task. "Actually, I think he's very serious about this, and I applaud him for it."

"Don't get me wrong," I said. "So do I. No one dislikes Erwitt more than I do. And I hate television."

"Personally," she said, "I don't much care for your President. He's let the rich behave so badly. They should know better. It's their own children's lives they're gambling with."

"Don't get me started on the rich. I've had a summerful!"

"So have we all. I had a rich lover one summer. Before Pierre. An Italian count. A beautiful boy. He could afford to be a Communist; his family was very rich. They owned vineyards."

"Which meant you could toast Khrushchev with the best vintages of Barolo?"

"Exactly. Tell me, Sam: do you think Horace has said a word to his son?"

"I doubt it. As far as I know, all X has done is give lunch and dinner parties for a lot of jerks. Cover, I suppose. I think he is going to have a very big problem with Abner."

"He seems not to think so."

"He's absolutely wrong. Abner's spent a lifetime getting out of X's shadow."

My mind went back to our Starbuck graduation. The principal handed us our diplomas under the two-hundred-year-old horse chestnut that stood on Academy Lawn. Afterward, Abner stood next to his father, receiving congratulations for all the honors he'd carried off. I noticed, however, that while people shook Abner's hand, they bent to X, and I could see then that there was another shadow stretching across the dappled June afternoon, longer and darker and chillier than that cast by the great flowering tree.

"What will X do if Abner doesn't give in?" I asked.

"I don't know."

"Do you think X does?"

"I don't know." She looked at her watch. "Gracious, it's a quarter to ten! I'm supposed to play tennis in three quarters of an hour." She began to walk quickly back up the beach. I fell in beside her. When we got to where my car was parked, I offered her a ride, which she refused. I said I'd see her in New York.

"Oh, I hope so," she said. "If not before." I liked the sound of that.

When I got back to the house, Cass had just arrived. She waved hello, but she looked unenthusiastic. Once again I felt like a jigsaw piece that had gotten mixed into the wrong puzzle.

By the last week in August, I had to get away. The air pressed so closely, it seemed it might shatter and break. I needed a break from cocktail parties and striped tents, from being asked to check my brain at the door. Cass and I were skating on a tenuous veneer of pretense and blather. When the boys from down the street burst into our house yelping about begonias and galantines, I felt lesions grow in my mind. Even X, still a presence rather than a person, added a quantum of uneasiness. And nature had turned on me. The sun, so delicious and revivifying in July, was now a relentless, baking punishment. I was worried about Mother, too. She'd sounded rotten on the phone, coughing and rasping; it had been a filthy wet summer in Oregon.

I needed surcease from dancing on my nerve ends, and I had an inspiration. Eugenie Monstrance's pro football team, the Vandals, was in training camp in the Berkshires. I knew the guy who was the club's assistant general manager pretty well, so I called him up and got cleared for VIP treatment, to eat with the team and so on. The Vandals ranked with Tanglewood in the local economy, and a room was located at a motel in Great Barrington.

So far, so good; then my friend called me back. He had good news and bad news and worse news, he said.

"The good news is everything's all set, which you knew. The bad news is that the boss lady overheard me talking to you, and asked was that you. Apparently you two know each other. I'm gonna put you through in a minute. The worse news is she wants you to stay at her place."

I was connected with Eugenie, and we exchanged pleasantries. Nothing would do but that I stay at her house. She would try to make it up while I was there, but she couldn't be sure. Her baseball team was in the doldrums and she might have to fly to St. Louis to fire the manager. It was too gracious a favor to refuse graciously, and I accepted.

Her house was in South Egremont, about a half hour from the prep school where the Vandals bunked and worked out. The place was right out of Edith Wharton, redolent with memories of languid afternoons: tea and croquet and parasols. The domestic requirements of the place were seen to by a trio of elderly Irishwomen, faintly menacing descendants, in dress and general gloominess, of the pale presences who had tended Eugenie's mother long ago.

I spent most of five gray and gummy days hanging around the team. Football interested me, both in the particular and the abstract, even when exemplified by a team as listless as the Vandals. They had already lost two preseason games. The number-one draft choice, a burner out of Texas A&M, was cooling his heels in Beaumont while his agent argued contract. The team should have been better: there were ten years of high draft picks on the field, the coaching staff had won conference championships at Buffalo and New Orleans, the quarterback was experienced enough to know where his receivers were supposed to be, and there were a lot of big, quick people running around out there on the field.

After a while, however, I could see that this was a team that had been snakebit often enough by its front office to believe that its bad luck had been institutionalized; certainly the Vandals' recent history had been one of bad trades, bad cuts, mistakes in player evaluation, bad firings. Eugenie obviously tried too hard, and her own effortfulness had turned on her and atrophied the psychological ligaments of her players and staff. Every sportswriter I'd ever known had told me that there had been damn few owners who could build consistent winners, damn few Al Davises, but that ninety-nine out of a hundred who bought into pro sports could come up with consistent losers.

One night I ate out at a local place with the offensive line coach and the girl who covered the team for *Newsday*, Moira Riley. I always read *Newsday* in the summer, mainly because they closed up the sports section later than the city edition of the *Times* did, and I knew her stuff. Riley was good—direct, knowledgeable, unawed, and unfazed—and pumped no bullshit. She knew her way around, too. The day before, at the end of practice, she'd gone into the locker room and been confronted by the starting tight end, six feet four of ebony gristle from Ohio State, his biggest muscle hanging between his legs like a cruiser's hawser. He'd stared at her with this challenging, shit-eating grin for about thirty seconds, while she stared at his crotch, shaking her head in obvious disgust, until the towel came down and he told her what she wanted to know.

I asked the coach how come, with three first- and second-round draft choices tackle to tackle, it looked like I could get through to the Vandals' quarterback.

"We just missing a couple of quality people at the skill positions," he said. He was a typical career journeyman; a baked-out, thin-haired beaky man in his fifties, with a Vandals cap tilted at the back of his head; it was the sixth such team cap he'd worn in the NFL. By now he had the answers pat.

Oh, bullshit, I thought; you've got two Outland Trophy winners on the same line.

"Oh, bullshit!" said Moira Riley. She was a pleasant-looking young woman, in her early thirties, I guessed, with a sprightly face hidden behind enormous red-framed glasses. "Bullshit," she repeated. "What this team needs is a quality player at the owner position!"

The coach looked nonplused. This kind of talk wasn't covered in the Media Manual. I stepped into the breach.

"So could three quarters of the teams in the league."

"I'll buy that," said Riley. "They ought to make 'em pass a licensing exam."

And the same goes for presidents and poets, I thought.

"The thing is," she continued, "that your average owner's a meathead, or on an ego trip, or too dumb or too broke to do the right thing. This is one smart lady; she's got more money than God; she knows the game."

"Miz Monstrance is indeed a fine woman," said the coach. "I'm proud to be associated with her. She's given us ever'thing we ever asked for. She's just done got real bad luck."

"Luck, good or bad, is the residue of design," said Moira Riley. "Branch Rickey said that. Amen. You want to know my theory? The lady hates men; men hate to lose; the lady sees to it that her men lose. Period, end of analysis. Think about it!"

I was still thinking about it the next day when about fifty feet of vintage Bentley nosed up next to the playing field and Eugenie got out, a can of Pepsi in her hand. Practice came to a halt. Minions scuttled across the field and practically rolled paws-up in the grass. When they had finished and the scrimmage had resumed, I went over to her and said hello.

Her appearance was shocking. It had been some time since I'd seen her. Her face was mottled and puffy, although her eyes were sharp and clear. When she embraced me, it felt as if I had been submerged in foam rubber. She was wearing a bright blue caftan-shaped garment with the collar and trim of a child's sailor suit. The intended girlish effect was lost on this scale; the effect was ludicrous, sad.

She was so evidently pleased to see me that I was glad I had come for that reason alone. She asked after my comfort at the house, and I said I'd been very comfortable. We watched practice together for about an hour, during which she followed up her Pepsi with a Dr. Pepper and a Mountain Dew from an enormous monogrammed cooler which her chauffeur produced from the trunk of her car. Great crescents of damp formed under her arms; the furrows of her neck became tiny creeks of perspiration.

Her comments on her team were knowing and enthusiastic. She sounded to me like she wanted to win; I tucked Moira Riley's theory away as one of those female things. There was something agreeably un-grown-up about Eugenie's involvement with her team. She was a couple of years older than Abner and I, but next to her I felt quite the man. I wondered if her soda pop addiction might represent a subconscious wish to perpetuate her baby fat, her presumably happy suckling infancy. Possibly so, but several thousand calories a day of sugar now only added the suet of middle age, grainy, veined, and coarse.

After a while, she excused herself to go back to the house. It had been a hot, long drive, she said.

When I returned after practice, I found her on the screened-in porch, working at a hoop of embroidery. Amazingly, the work was very fine; her swollen fingers appeared not to hinder her.

She looked up and said, almost apologetically, "It's something Mama taught me."

"It's very beautiful."

We ate at seven, a surprisingly sophisticated meal cooked and served by her starched Gaelic Furies. Earlier, I'd wondered if this was perhaps some kind of lesbian den she'd built for herself amid these pleasant hills. I dismissed the thought; the idea of Eugenie entwined in strange arabesques with her three servants was too preposterous.

"I spent last night at Father's," she said after the soup.

Really, I thought. Hmmm.

"He gave rather a grand lunch. All sorts of Pooh-Bahs. Abner's wife was there. She's such a nice woman."

"I like her too."

"She brought her sister. A very striking girl, much darker and more vivid. Father was very taken with her."

Now I was really hmmming to myself. "Cassandra? Was she there?" S. A. Mountcastle, the Old Dissembler.

"Is that her name? I barely met her. She talked quite a lot. As I say, Father seemed most taken with her. He even moved the wife of the Italian ambassador so she could sit next to him. Father really shouldn't do those things. Signora Grazielli was very upset!" It was also clear that Eugenie was very upset that her father should make such a fuss over another pretty woman.

"How is X, anyway?" I asked, figuring I might as well play this hand for broke. "You know, I haven't seen him since that summer we all went to Europe."

"He's fine. Full of himself as always, and it doesn't help that everyone makes such a fuss about him. There was the most awful woman there with a lot of evil-looking hair who talked like a fishwife. He practically had to get the caterer's men to pull her off."

Marty Getsmore. X was coming down in the world. It was maddeningly obvious, infuriatingly clear, that Eugenie had been given no idea of the notional connection between Cass and me. By no one—which included Cass.

After dinner, courtesy of Eugenie's satellite dish, we watched her Boroughs, under a new manager, drop a 13–2 squeaker to the Cards. I couldn't keep my mind on the game. Irritated as I was with Cass, I was madder at myself for being so irritated with her. I'd resolved not to care. A hundred hours earlier, all I thought I wanted was to be quit of her.

Now the news that she was flirting with X set me aquiver with feelings I didn't care to identify. A woman's emotion, I'd said to Mother. Hah!

It took me awhile to go to sleep, and then I awakened again about two, aware that someone was in the room. I had been dreaming, deep down in the lightless caverns where the best dreams happen, and I wasn't immediately certain where I was. I turned on the light and found Eugenie sitting on the edge of the bed. Her robe had fallen open; her small breasts had sagged with age into pendulous tubes; beneath the pushed-up foldings of fat of her stomach I could see the dark hair of her pubis.

"Oh, Sam," she said. "I just thought . . . I'm so sorry." She began to cry, small sounds for such a large woman. I wanted to be sympathetic, to comfort, to say the right thing.

"Has it been a long time, Eugenie?"

The sobbing stopped.

"Not really . . . just with someone nice . . ."

I tried to be soothing and held out my arms. She closed her robe around her and came within my embrace for only a minute, laying her cheek against my shoulder. Her hair was surprisingly fine and cleansmelling. I felt her lips press against my skin; then she disengaged herself, pulling back to look at me intently with sad, intelligent eyes, big gray eyes, not the black Monstrance marbles of her father and brother. I heard her heavy tread move down the hall, heard the light switch and her tread on the stairs: going to the kitchen, I thought. I felt immensely sad for her.

The editor had liked the piece on the old director and decided to move it up, which meant a last fast rewrite, so I had to detour into Manhattan on my way back from the Berkshires. The air conditioning in the car quit halfway down Route 22, so when I finally reached the city, my epidermal temperature had risen to match my soul.

I had what Buck would have called "a major-league case of the red ass." I was mad at Cass, mad at X, mad at the prospect of this last summer weekend, and each of these rages, which lapped against each other like a confluence of tidal pools, was intensified by confusion. In each case, try though I might—and I spent most of the drive down talking out loud to myself—I couldn't accurately describe my own feelings to myself. Just who was I mad at and why? What did I feel? In the end, I chickened out and decided to let the course of events tell, since I seemed so inadequate to the task myself.

It was probably impatience that led me to reject Bud Shreck's Cass-arranged offer of an aerial ride to the Hamptons. I was in a mood for self-flagellation, and four hours in a hot car on the Long Island Expressway was just what Torquemada Mountcastle had in mind. Admittedly, I was a little short with Bud—with his secretary, to be exact—but at least I remained consistent with my principles. Principle over convenience, I repeated, as I crawled past the Center Moriches exit three and a quarter hours after I left the garage.

When I finally crawled into Water Mill about eight, the steam was coming out of my Cassie's ears.

"Are you crazy! Bud's very upset!" She didn't bother to greet me.

"I don't give a merry f—— if Bud's suicidal!" I shrieked back. "What'd he do, call you to complain? Just tell him writers aren't reliable."

She looked a trifle shamefaced. "Actually, Marie called. Bud's still at LaGuardia. Something went wrong with the plane, and then they lost their slot."

"So he takes a car."

The whole thing was explained. The Shreck limos were here. The Shreck choppers were there. I suggested a taxi. Surface transportation was unthinkable for Bud. As I listened, I got angrier. When my turn came to speak, I wanted to put a proper steely edge to my words.

"Let me tell you something, sweetheart." A nice touch of Bogie. "I can't stand Bud and Marie. I hope their f—— plane crashes on f—— Riker's Island! You know what's wrong with you, honey? You've got a rare disease. It's called TSA, Terminal Social Anxiety! It strikes insecure women between the ages of thirty and fifty, especially on the South Shore of Long Island, but it's been known in major cities and in places like Newport. It may be incurable. It manifests itself in a desire to associate with certain people simply because those people have a lot of money!"

My anger was getting hard to sustain. My tendency to wisecrack always got in my way, and this subject was too dead to be gone over again. A line from Wodehouse swam into my head. "I spit me of the Shrecks!" I declared vehemently, smiling. This was going to be, after all, a very long and full weekend, and ours was a small house, and there were guests due to arrive. "I spit me of the Getsmores too!"

She wasn't listening; I doubted she'd heard a word. In that way of hers, she'd flown off on yet another tangent of self-involvement.

"I went to H.H.'s for lunch," she said.

"How was it?" I asked. I did think for an instant about saying I knew, but I couldn't find a point to it. I didn't want her on her guard. On the other hand, she must have known that Eugenie might say something, although when Cass was thinking about Cass, there was precious little room in her awareness for others to claim.

She told me about the lunch; about the guests; about the house; about X, about X, about X. It was clear within a minute or two of her recital that she was in the grip of a massive crush on H. H. Monstrance, a man twice her age.

"I used to know him, you know," I said.

"That's what H.H. said. He asked how you were. He said he always liked you, but that it had been years since he'd seen you."

"And he's still got the old charm?"

She wasn't listening. "I think I'm going to write a book," she answered. "Foster Greenglass was on my other side. He was very interested."

There is no uniformly correct response to the web of problems posed by a declaration by the woman in one's life that she proposes to take pen to paper. I took the easy route.

"What about?"

"Life. Working in the city. Something satirical. The art world. Love. Disappointment."

"Sort of *Haywire* meets *Heartburn*, huh?" It figured. Foster Greenglass was the publisher of the moment. He specialized in the outpourings of women with a gripe: the quarrelsomely indiscreet, questionably accurate recollections of the bitter offspring of celebrities; the autobiographical ravings of neurasthenic heiresses; nervous little epigrammatic novels. The smart guy who wrote the *Spec*'s monthly book column had once parodied Greenglass's entire spring list under the title "Vintage Whine."

"Well," I added in a placatory way, "you've written one book and you're a smart person. Give it a go."

Again she didn't hear me. Her heart, or maybe it was something else, clearly belonged to Abner's daddy. She was on the scent, I could tell, and she would have neither nose nor ears nor eyes for anything or anyone else. For however long this fancy lasted, I was as good as dead.

As we got ready to go to Clio's summer-capping party, I suddenly became nervous at the prospect of seeing X. For most of the last month, he had been no more than a name in other people's conversations, so distant from me that he had, I realized, become unreal. Now I would have to confront him, greet him, take my cue from him, and carry off whatever pretense he had in mind for us. Would he be the slightest bit nervous as he looked in his mirror? I guessed not. X was completely at home in his games, even though the pieces on the board were the lives and feelings of other human beings.

Clio gave it her all, I must say that. In the face of the accumulated ennui of three months, she managed to entertain people who had looked and babbled at each other since Memorial Day; who were tired, sun-struck, impatient; who were mentally into a new hustle, a new season with new attributes and demands; who were congealed, as in an old George Price cartoon of subway riders, into a single enervated glob of flesh and neuroses.

A huge tent had been erected between the house and the dunes. Its ceiling panels bore the AbCom logo: a stylized **A** superimposed on the lightning bolt which had been the symbol of the old Granite. I had seen the tent before, on television, at the U.S. Open, when the camera had panned over the small city of corporate hospitality tents. Around the perimeter of the dance floor were richly flowered tables; squadrons of waiters circulated among the arriving guests with cocktails and canapés.

Clio and Abner received with X in the high, spacious living room. In the front hall, giant blowups memorialized high points in X's life and career: a young slick X behind a bank of GBG microphones; X in uni-form, a major, with Bus Beal, his wartime CO; X, a colonel now, with Hap Arnold and Eisenhower; X with Burns and Allen; a blowup of the family picture, X, Selena, young Eugenie, young Abner; X with Paley and the Sarnoffs and Nixon, on the White House lawn, at a ceremony commemorating twenty-five years of commercial television; X being sworn in as Special Ambassador by President Ford; X on a dais, looking on as Abner spoke from the rostrum; X and Walt Disney; X and Franco, King George VI, Pius XII, Jackie Robinson. Ironically: X and Eldon Erwitt, then a young man, grinningly on the make, in a flashy double-breasted suit.

At each place was a large rosette, like an English political badge, from which X's face beamed with its customary huge confidence. The matchbooks bore his initials and the date. This was a major celebration—in honor, I guessed, as much of summer's end, of X's presumed depar-ture, of Abner's relief, as of X's presence among us.

Cass threw her arms around him and kissed him, trying, a bit too obviously, I thought, to show off her intimacy with the great man. Then he looked at me.

"By God, Sam Mountcastle! Now this is a surprise! I was just asking Ab what had become of you!"

"X!"

Mike Nichols couldn't have directed it better. We carried it off perfectly, I thought: two people who'd lost track of each other to whom the
simple fact of reunion demanded a public display of feelings out of proportion to the true emotional consequences of the event. He grasped my
elbow; we talked about getting together the next time I came to London;
with visible relief, he turned to the next arrivals and Cass and I passed
into the throng.

It was evident that the guests were all charged up for the occasion, that
all remaining resources of gaiety and gregariousness had been husbanded
for one final roll. The tent was alive with chatter. I looked around; all the
expected crowd was there, down to the whores working the room to try
to coax a last small profit from summer's cinders. Bud was up to his
withers in an ebb and flow of commission agents and art and antiques
dealers. Cass was in there pitching, too. Her practiced crystalline laugh
pierced the noise of the crowd, carrying over the music and the tinkle of
plates and glasses.

Dinner was good; I worked my way with happy determination
through the five wineglasses at my place. At the head table, Clio, between X and—to my surprise—none other than former President Henry
"Hank" McNeery, smiled and made polite conversation, glancing now
and then around the tent to make sure everything proceeded as planned
and paid for. I now noticed a number of young square-bodied men with
emblems in their buttonholes, McNeery's Secret Service escort. I returned my scrutiny to the head table. X had apparently taken over the
conversation; McNeery nodded carefully in time to X's expansive
gesticulations.

After dessert, microphones were set up under the bandstand and Clio
got up. She smiled warmly over the crystal tintinnabulation that prayed
our silence. She really was a very handsome woman.

"I want to ask you to toast two very special men," she said. "It's wonderful for me, as I'm sure it is for you, to see Abner and his father together again." She turned toward Abner. "Darling, I love you," she said,
glass high. And to X: "And I love you too. Don't stay away for so long
next time." There was a great burst of applause; chairs squeaked as we all
got to our feet. X got up.

"I just want to thank Clee and Ab for this beautiful party. It's been a
wonderful thing for an old man to see so many old friends and to make so
many new ones. I've been threatening Ab to make this an annual affair. I
want to ask you to drink to them now: to Ab, whom I've always been
proud of, but never more for anything than for bringing me this beautiful

daughter-in-law. And to Clee too." He raised his glass amid general applause and sat down.

Now it was Abner's turn. He thanked his wife and said a few agreeable words about his father. Then his expression turned almost pious. I knew what was coming.

"We're very fortunate to have a great American with us tonight, a man who, like most of us here tonight, understands the American way and is in there fighting for it, a wise counselor who's become a good friend. Ladies and gentlemen, President Henry McNeery!"

McNeery got to his feet and went to the microphone. As he thanked our hosts, I looked at X. He gazed at the former President with a polite indifference that I was sure masked contempt. Have we come to this? his expression seemed to say.

The tables now dispersed. The music began in earnest; people danced. I went to the bar. Cass had disappeared in the melee.

I felt a touch at my elbow and heard a familiar voice. Margarita Clerc smiled up at me. She was darker than when I'd seen her on the beach; it was obvious she'd put in a good many hours in the sun. She looked tan and sexy.

"I told you we'd see each other again," she said.

"I didn't see you. How'd I miss you?"

"We just got here. Pierre's plane was late."

"You're staying at Dunecrag?"

They were. We went onto the floor as the music changed to something manageable. She was a good dancer, but she responded uncertainly as I drew her closer.

"How is it at X's?" I asked her hair.

"Very grand. I met your lady. She's very striking."

"Isn't she." We circled the floor, making small talk, not advancing our intimacy. She felt very right in my clutch. At one point, over her shoulder, I discovered X looking at us. He saw me and winked conspiratorially. Deep graveyard. After a bit longer, Margarita asked to be taken back to her table. Reluctantly, I did; Clerc was there, sipping champagne, looking foxy and superior.

It was nearly four when Cass and I and our houseguests got back to Water Mill. As we undressed for bed, she asked, "Who was that woman you were dancing with? You never dance."

"In the black dress?"

"Yes. With the bosoms." She cupped her own, as if offering them for comparison.

"She's called Margarita Clerc. She teaches at Columbia. She's a cur-
mudgeon—like me!"

"She was at H.H.'s today for lunch. He was very attentive to her. How
old is she? She has a husband."

"I didn't know you'd gone to X's today. I thought you just went to East
Hampton to Dean and DeLuca."

"Well, you were playing golf and H.H. called just as I was going out,
so I stopped by."

Her business was her own, but I found myself thinking about X's
relation to Margarita. Cass turned the lights out.

"I'm glad you like the idea of my book, darling. I've been thinking
about it a lot." She reached for me. I pleaded the weariness of age and
evening, but she, tipsy, was insistent. It was the least I could do. I
thought of Margarita and other girls I'd loved, and she thought of X, or
whoever, and so we made love for what I expected would be the last time.

And that was how I spent my summer.

CHAPTER 8

It was good to be back in New York, but not as good as I'd hoped. Cool air would bring clarification, I thought, but summer lingered on for several weeks, and so did my confusion. I liked certainties in my life, but now I was aswim in ambiguities, mostly about what X was doing to nearly every meaningful aspect of my existence. My collusion in his surreptitiousness had put me on his side in something with which I had no more than an abstract ideological quarrel. Feelings were going to be hurt, possibly people, himself included. I had expected to be parted from Cass cleanly, but with her on board the good ship X in a role not yet clearly defined, that seemed unlikely too. We'd said our goodbyes, with the same efficient finality with which we'd cleaned and closed up the house. All very adult: just good friends now, who'd keep in touch, with dinner every now and then, and possibly, if the mood was just right, bed afterward (no point in throwing the baby out with the bathwater). I'd be around for the odd escort job; no, I wasn't going to rush off and fall in love again; I promised. Chums forever, a firm handshake, not so much as the tiniest glint of tear in the eye, and such good memories. Right?

Wrong. Not that she knew it; not that she was aware we were both marionettes on X's strings. She'd gone blissfully off to Paris to watch Marie shop. It was left to me to stew. I had always hated the responsibility of carrying other people's secrets, but this was the worst yet.

I tried all the usual remedies, vocational and seasonal, beginning with what friends advised me would be endless fruitless negotiations for the recovery of the security deposit on the Water Mill house. I asked the editor for assignments and fielded everything he threw at me, from snippets about publishing parties to a prospectively long and significant piece, which could take a month or so, about a huge new development planned for Kennedy Airport. He too was waiting for X to drop the other shoe, and I sensed he was holding me back, keeping me in reserve. It had never occurred to me to wonder what exactly X intended, in the unlikely event that Abner went along with his ideas. Would I move to AbCom on some pretext, to observe and take notes? Would I stay where I was and receive regular briefings? Neither the editor nor I had focused on the mechanics of the arrangement, although I was certain that he had concocted a whole apparatus of Smileyan tradecraft for when the call came, if it did.

I tried to divert myself with autumn in New York. There was the struggle to recover the security deposit on the summer house. About me the city chimed with the sound of crystal slippers being cobbled for the feet of the Cinderellas it was the new season's duty to provide for Manhattan's amusement. I could pick and choose from a multitude of busynesses: gallery and boutique openings, book parties, restaurant promotions, little dinners and big, pub crawls, boys' nights out. But my heart wasn't in it, so I simply treaded water in the dull apathetic sea of Indian summer and waited. I knew X was around, presumably on the pretext of wanting to savor a few last delights before going back to England. The papers reported him at the Mayfair Regent; he didn't want to tip his hand, I assumed, by opening up his Fifth Avenue apartment. To do that could lead people to believe X intended to stay around longer than he said, and then they might ask why. Of course, judging by the gossip columns, he was playing Mr. Frivolous to the hilt, perfectly in phase with people's expectations of him, in perfect consonance with the perception of himself he had created to hide behind.

Sooner or later, the next step, in some direction, would have to be taken, but my patience was being tested. I liked to know that the path led from A to B to C; irresolution wasn't my strong suit. Finally, however, in late September, the wheel spinning stopped. X called on a Saturday morning and asked me to meet him at his hotel for lunch. By coincidence, the night before, the weather had turned cool in a way that seemed to have a quality of finality to it.

I walked through the park and down Madison Avenue. The fresh day had set the city's retail juices to bubbling. The avenue was crowded: the upscale rabble was out in force, VISA cards at the ready; tennis whites had overnight given way to Ralph Lauren corduroys and tweed jackets.

The cruel Darwinism of fashion was powerfully evident: Italian shoes no longer dominated the windows of the smart shops; they had been replaced by raggedy Japanese sweat clothes at nine hundred dollars the copy. The only constant was exorbitance.

X was waiting for me in the hotel lobby, which I found odd. He obviously wanted to talk.

"I need some air before lunch," he said. "How about a short stroll?"

A short stroll it was. Disappointing, too; when he'd said lunch at the hotel, I'd naturally assumed that meant Le Cirque. In fact, I'd already digested, mentally, a perfectly grilled filet of flounder and an ambrosial field salad. Instead, we crossed Madison, walked over to Fifth then uptown a couple of blocks, and entered the grand old apartment building to which I'd first come to play many years before as a small boy. The doorman greeted X as if he'd never been away.

A Chinese houseman admitted us to the apartment. I saw at once that it had been brought back up to concert pitch, aired and cleaned and polished. We went into the living room; the light from Fifth Avenue sparkled on crystal sconces. On the walls the paintings that had been on loan at the Met had been rehung: four little Klees that whistled with spiky originality; a Degas double portrait; the large Matisse "Atelier Rouge"; a Cézanne landscape of Lake Annecy; the Géricault "Fusilier"; prime still lifes by Gris and Braque; a suite of great Picassos, three of which I knew—the early "Clowns and Acrobats," a breathtaking analytical cubist painting, "Saxophone et Tambour," and a monumental symphony of nudes from the early 1930s—and a late head of a woman, dated 1965, which I'd never seen before. It was a strong, exciting work; like most people, I'd assumed Picasso's last years to be a waste of time, but a picture like this threw that viewpoint out the window. It also said something about the confidence and quality of X's eye.

To my surprise, they had been joined by some of the paintings I'd last seen at Chelsea Embankment. The four Bonnards were back in their old place on the wall behind the piano. The Cézanne portrait was on the end wall; I knew without checking that the Gauguin would have returned to X's little study down the hall and that the Van Gogh was once again in the bedroom. There had been some changes, too. In the dining room, where I seemed to remember a Monet "Lilacs," a vacant Bud-and-Marie-type picture that I'd never fancied, the imposing Constable now held sway. It was obvious that X was back for good.

"Well," I said, "it looks as if your talk with Abner went the way you thought. I wouldn't have guessed it. Congratulations."

He grinned. "Champagne?"

"Absolutely."

I raised my glass and drank to his health and the success of his mission.

"Actually, Sam," he said, "it's your judgment we should be toasting. My little chat with Ab went the way you predicted it would. Why, he practically threw me out of the office!"

He gave me a moment to recover and then described his meeting with his son. To hear X tell it, he'd been the very breath of reason. He'd merely offered his services to help fix up AbCom's slipping ratings, where, after all, he did have something of a track record, and, while he was about it, do a little something in the area of public service programming. He had not mentioned President Erwitt. He'd made it very clear that he wanted no executive responsibility, just something on the order of a consultancy. The last thing on earth he intended was to interfere in management. Just give him a small office down on the eighteenth floor at GBG News. The way he saw it, it shouldn't take too long to get things straightened out: a year at most, surely no longer. Then he could go back to London to die. It would be a partnership for the good of Granite/AbCom. The partnership he and Abner had always wanted, that they'd always talked about.

And Abner would hear none of it.

"He actually got quite nasty and personal," X said. "I begin to grasp how Lear felt about his daughters. Serpent's tooth and all that. Poor Ab has developed such a conventional mind! He went on and on about obligation to the stockholders, responsibility of management to maximize values, not to engage in charity, the company not a force for social or moral good or bad, and so and such, blah blah blah. He used a great many of those words he learned at the business school. I was a fool to let him go there. After he came back, I never again really understood what Ab was thinking, let alone what he was talking about."

"So where do you go now?"

"I asked him to think it over. To sleep on it. I said he owed me at least that small courtesy."

"And will he?"

"Sleep on it? Oh, yes. Soundly, I dare say. Reconsider? Absolutely not!"

X's voice was amazingly cheerful. He beamed at me. I could see that he relished Abner's obdurate defection.

"Ab's absolutely stuck on his position," he declared. "And he's getting a good healthy dose of stiff backbone from his wife, if you ask me. She's a fighter, that girl!" He spoke with real admiration. "Quite handsome, too," he added.

"So, assuming Abner won't change his mind, what's next? From the looks of things around here, I wouldn't say you're preparing to beat a hasty retreat."

He looked at me gravely and slyly, impregnating the moment with inescapable significance.

"I've given Ab until Tuesday to reconsider. If he continues to be recalcitrant, then he and I will simply have to settle our differences the way gentlemen do in a free and democratic society. At the ballot box."

"A proxy fight?"

"There ought to be a more dignified phrase, don't you think?"

"X, you haven't got a chance!"

He looked at me patiently.

"Sam, I know you're quite impressed with the way Ab seems to have consolidated his position. But there are many ways to skin the proverbial cat. I've done a little arithmetic. Between Jake and myself, there's over ten percent of the company right there. I've talked with Jake. He has some serious reservations about some of the things that have been done at Granite, and if push comes to shove, we are the oldest and best of friends and Jake's the sort of fellow to whom loyalty still means something. And then there's Eugenie. And the Foundation."

He was counting his daughter on his side, but as far as I was concerned, Eugenie should be considered a complete unknown in something like this. How she went would depend on which of her contending resentments had the upper hand when she signed the proxy. As for the Foundation, which I could only assume would have complicated legal and fiduciary interweavings, it seemed likely, on the basis of what I'd been seeing in the papers of other cases, that Abner could keep its voting rights tied up in court until the second coming. Which I supposed this was, in a way. I told X of my doubts.

"There's no question you have a good point with respect to the Foundation. I have a few ideas there, however. Are you familiar with the concept of hubris?"

"Indeed. The sin of overweening pride."

"And often a very useful petard with which to hoist an overconfident young fellow like Ab. Ah, lunch. Let's change the subject. There's nothing that can be done until we hear from Ab."

From the way he said "we," I knew that he counted me as one of his soldiers.

At lunch, he talked about New York and the way it had changed. Too many men in vests, he complained. And so much money around! It made him feel positively poor. Then he switched to the subject of President Erwitt. It was plain he'd studied the President in considerable depth. He pointed out something to which I hadn't given much thought: Erwitt practically never allowed himself to be engaged, in public, on a one-to-one basis with other human beings. Give-and-take had been virtually eliminated from presidential communications. Everything was staged and scripted. "To take care of Eldon," X remarked over dessert, "I'll have to lure him out of his electronic lair, get him out from behind that damned TelePrompTer."

We went back into the living room for coffee.

"You know," he said, "I guess I never did understand Ab."

He went over to the piano and lifted the cover. I recalled that he considered himself a gifted salon pianist.

"There was a wonderful show years ago," he said. *"Lost in the Stars.* Kurt Weill and Maxwell Anderson, from a damn good book by a South African. I tried to get a piece of it for Granite." He played a few chords, sketching out the beginning of a tune. "It had a fine song in it."

He began to sing—in his fashion. Actually he talked the words, hoarsely, in rough time with the notes.

"How many miles to the heart of a child, thousands of miles, thousands of miles. . . ." He really didn't play badly. His emotional commitment outweighed his technical deficiencies. Then he launched into the Starbuck hymn. It was oddly suitable music for the moment.

"Once to ev'ry man and nation
  Comes the moment to decide;
  In the fight 'twixt truth and falsehood . . ."

Hearing those words, I saw in my mind Memorial Chapel, the boys in dutiful rows along the nave and, at the entrance to the choir, the kneeling figure of a marble knight, blind and brave, a fitting image to take to heart at the outset of a great crusade.

That was the way X thought of it, and so did I. Abner saw it differently. The next day he telephoned X to inform him that if that was the way he wanted it, a state of war now existed between them.

CHAPTER 9

Even in a day when corporate strife had become universally big news, the family angle to the proxy contest for control of AbCom was something special. X's announcement at a press conference that he intended to seek proxies to elect a new board burst over the world of business and entertainment like a star shell.

The media went to town. "Family Feud Goes Prime Time" reported *Variety. Time* dwelled on "the dark Sophoclean overtones of the coming battle for AbCom." *People* reached into its photo morgue and pasted together a hasty article on the family, including one singularly unflattering shot of Eugenie in a Vandals T-shirt and a picture of Abner and Clio in evening dress, looking rich and glamorous, disembarking from a limousine. The visual inference was clear: this was "Dallas" come to life.

X's opening salvo had been intentionally general and ambiguous. At the press conference, he indicated an objective of reemphasizing the company's traditional broadcasting businesses and took a sideswipe at the low estate of GBG's programming quality, emphasizing children's television. The financial community's first reaction to the former was favorable. Everyone knew what a mess RCA had made of diversification; overnight, the alchemy of fickleness turned Abner's golden triumphs into lead. X's criticism of programming standards was designed to enlist the sympathies of the moralists out there.

As I expected, the press was all over the lot. X was variously characterized as "a retrograde financial anachronism" (*Wall Street Journal*); "the last good hope for quality and morality in television" (*The New Republic*);

"an old-style rootin'-tootin' founder-entrepreneur" (*Forbes*, which also praised him highly for his knowledge of Burgundies). Abner, "the cool-eyed scion fighting off what strikes many as a bid to return a great company to the Dark Ages" (*Fortune*), was criticized for having "pushed a people biz too far in the direction of high tech" (*Ad Week*), although it was agreed that "from the point of view of most stockholders, the younger Monstrance's stewardship has been a rousing success" (*Business Week*), despite the fact that "there has been some grumbling among institutional investors about too far, too fast" (*Barron's*).

Abner had responded to X's press conference by coming across as all business; speaking as "your management," he condemned his father's act as "disruptive and contrary to the stockholders' interests." The implication was that he would swat this patriarchal gnat and get on with the great business of getting and spending. I thought Abner was making a tactical mistake; he had opened the door for X to portray himself as a heroic crusader, a lone hero pitted against the massive, malign forces of a huge impersonal institution.

The fact was, apart from Jacob Polhemus's resignation from the Ab-Com board, no surprise in view of his closeness to X, there was no immediate hard news. No cash was at stake, even though AbCom stock rose for a day or so and then dived, sharply, on the rumor and subsequent denial that Abner had offered to buy his father and the Foundation out at a fat premium. Following the initial uproar, and after about a week of excited speculation and publicity in the press, public attention subsided as the two sides began to assemble their order of battle for what promised to be a protracted paper war. Unlike most proxy contests, in which the challenger spends weeks, even months, lining up his legal and financial ducks, this one had been precipitated virtually overnight, born of pride and overconfidence, and the other ruinous feelings which set parents and children at each other, and not from calculated commercial ambition. That much I knew from the inside, at least. It struck me that if Abner tried too hard to persuade the public that this was about money, and followed the rhetorical line of cheese X had laid down in his press releases, he might end up piping his own way into the trap.

I had moved quickly to open a line of communication to the enemy, as I couldn't help thinking of Abner's side. Fergus Duncan liked to have a kindred soul to talk to, and he responded to my "what the hell's going on" with chapter and verse on the company's defense strategy. What he told me was a surprise. I had expected to be informed of complex, toxically expensive legal stratagems. From what Duncan said, Abner was going to run on the merits, period. According to Duncan, Abner had come to an understanding with X, using Jacob Polhemus as intermediary, concerning the ground rules. Only those three knew what the rules were to be. All Duncan knew so far was that the incumbents would be using white proxy cards: "White for the good guys, get it?" Maybe so, I thought, but Abner was throwing away a tremendous built-in advantage in resources and field position. It brought to mind what X had said about hubris.

The world didn't wait long, however, to find out how the Monstrances planned to do battle. I learned about it at a meeting at the offices of the Monstrance Foundation, the bunker from which X would conduct his campaign.

About a dozen people were at the conference table. There was Frank Hillhouse, a chubby, fortyish partner in Bouverie, Marcus and Company, the old-line firm that had been AbCom's investment bankers until three or four years earlier, when Abner had replaced them with the trading-room whiz kids of First Stuyvesant Company. Hillhouse was something of a whiz kid himself, who had recently come over to Bouverie, Marcus from Lazard to bring the firm's merger activities into the twentieth century. He radiated a smug antiseptic toughness. On either side of him sat a matched pair of aides, male and female, calculators, yellow pads, and Cross pencils arrayed in front of them like dueling pistols.

Across from Hillhouse was a rumpled, owlish man in his early sixties, smoking one cigarette after another and putting them out angrily with stubby, tarred fingers. He turned out to be X's answer to Arnold Plume, the takeover lawyer who would be handling Abner's defense. He too was flanked by acolytes.

Across and down the table from him was a natty, dark-haired man who was introduced as Meyer Bishman. He was X's hired gun in the area of public relations and proxy solicitation; he passed around a fistful of business cards, which described him as a "specialist in shareholder response." Bishman had something of Duncan's superimposed Old World elegance, but his effort was too much and too obvious. He glistened with polish and pomade, blazer buttons gleaming like bullion; it was plain his eyes had been nipped and his skin sanded. I surmised that he kept his tan on a shelf in the bathroom, along with the patently artificial auburn of the thinning hair parted north from below his ear. I had an idea that Bishman was probably no more than five years older than I was, but he looked a good sixty. Next to him was a blowsy woman with gray-streaked, messy dark hair, a cigarillo dangling from her mouth, bejeweled framed glasses perched above her forehead, and about $200,000 in gemstones on her fingers. I assumed from the obviousness of the jewels that they had to be real. This was Bishman's ex-wife, Audrey, but "still his partner on the biggies," as she put it when we shook hands.

X introduced me as just what I was, technically: a well-known journalist doing an article on the proxy fight. The implication was clear that through pure but fortuitous coincidence, my interest in the general subject and the specific instance of his bid for AbCom had been simultaneous. No one seemed surprised or particularly interested. Corporate warfare had long since moved out of the business pages as a subject of general media-worthy interest.

He thanked us for coming. "I'm going to have to rely almost totally on you ladies and gentlemen. This sort of operation isn't my line of country, really, but you've all been very highly recommended to me, and I hope— I know—we'll make a strong team together."

He looked around the table and got what he wanted, a ripple of ingratiating, supportive nods.

"First, however," X said, "I should brief you on what I have agreed with my son, Ab, with respect to ground rules."

What he told us provoked several low whistles of surprise and assorted murmurs of approval and dismay. A special meeting of AbCom stockholders would be held on December fifteenth in New York. That was a surprise; incumbent managements facing a proxy challenge would be expected to force a call for a special meeting into the courts and then, if compelled to hold one, to do so in some place like Billings, Montana.

X would be furnished a stockholder list. A second surprise: Abner had somehow been persuaded to surrender a prime tactical advantage, the proxy fighter's equivalent of high ground. There were roughly seventy days between now and December fifteenth; what little I knew about these matters suggested that X's side, if left to its own devices or, again, reduced to the courts, would normally be expected to use up a good part of that time just in finding out who exactly AbCom's stockholders were, in order to plead the insurgent case directly.

When X outlined these two conditions, the mood around the table perked up considerably; the general feeling, I could tell, was that the old man had sure as hell put one over on his imperious kid. Next, however, he outlined the two main concessions he had made, and a certain restiveness returned to the room. First, he said, he had agreed to neutralize the Foundation's eight million shares. These would be voted in accordance with the way the majority of the remaining fifty-seven million went. It was clear from his tone of voice that X wanted this to be seen as a noble gesture, an emblem of moral amplitude, superiority. Hillhouse's face, however, registered disgust; he plainly thought the old man had chucked a 13 percent voting advantage, almost a quarter of what would be needed for a clear majority, out the window.

The other concession was the zinger and brought expressions of shock to the features of lawyers and investment bankers alike. There was to be no bidding for or buying up of AbCom stock, by either side, and there was to be no litigation, period. This contest, X said, was to be fought out on the merits, not with money or lawsuits.

"That's the way Ab and I want it," he said.

I was sure Abner would be catching some of the same flak from his advisers that X now got. From where I sat, the deal the Monstrances had cut looked about even Stephen. X had given up a hell of a salient by sequestering the Foundation's shares; on the other hand, if he could make his case effectively, he was assured the access and time to make direct contact with every AbCom stockholder of significance. The agreement was rooted in and redolent of each of the two men's high opinion of himself; X was betting on his ability to persuade and manipulate, Abner on his record and the strength of his institutional connections.

"Could we get copies of the agreement?" asked the attorney.

"I'm afraid there isn't any written agreement. Ab and I shook hands on it."

The attorney's expression spoke volumes about his opinion of his client's sanity. Handshake deals, even between father and son, had gone out with the dinosaurs, obsoleted by the *sauve qui peut* ethics which the seventies had brought.

"Don't worry," X said soothingly. "It'll stand up. I know Ab, and he knows me."

No, you don't, I thought, but I also knew X was right that the agreement would stand up, because it had been made between two men of Starbuck, to whom that connection counted deeply, as it did to me. It was a way of behavior and belief that was probably old-fashioned to the point of incomprehensibility to these expedient men.

X returned his attention to the room at large. "Before I turn the meeting over to Mr. Bishman, who seems a logical choice to act as team captain, given the nature of our undertaking and the rules which have been established, has anyone else anything to add?" X looked around the table.

"It wouldn't hurt, would it," asked Hillhouse, "even though I know you've agreed not to buy any stock, to line up a credit facility, say two or three billion?" He spoke the sums in the voice I would use to describe buying a newspaper.

"Why?" asked X.

"Well, these things change. Suppose the bad guys play dirty and we have to bear-hug 'em?"

I caught Hillhouse's drift, which was pretty self-serving. Investment bankers of the new breed got rich on having two or more contenders exchanging volleys from their checkbooks in a price-driving bidding war, not through negotiation of the sort X proposed. Hillhouse preferred to negotiate with his own client, to persuade him to open up his wallet as wide as it could go.

"Well," said X, "that's not likely, but if it should come to pass, it's certainly something we can explore at the appropriate time. Incidentally, sir, as you have the floor, would you bring us up to date with respect to the Wall Street aspects of our situation."

Hillhouse reported that although the initial heavy trading volume generated by the public announcement of the proxy contest had to some extent subsided, ABI was still up almost five points. The arbitrage faction seemed to believe that some form of bidding war would develop and had bought almost seven million shares, on and off the Exchange floor, in the ten days since the declaration of war. The betting on the Street was that both X and Abner were lining up financing preparatory to a stock feeding frenzy and that First Stuyvesant had been authorized to find a "white knight" for AbCom if things got desperate.

"As that is patently not the case," X said, "it would seem appropriate for Ab and me to make a joint public announcement."

"I wouldn't do that, sir," said Hillhouse. "The stock'll come off maybe six or seven points, which'll cost the arbitrageurs maybe fifty million. They'll hate you for it."

"It seems to me," X said, "that they'll hate us both for it."

"Actually," interjected Bishman enthusiastically, speaking for the first time, "when a stock takes a tumble, nine times out of ten it's blamed on the management. I think Mr. Monstrance has a point."

"Besides," X said, "I've had an opportunity to meet some of these arbitrage people this summer. They strike me as a seedy lot. Sharks, sir, feeding on offal. Anything else, Mr. Hillhouse?"

Hillhouse recapitulated the research picture. The analysts who followed ABI were mostly watching and waiting. Merrill Lynch and Prudential Bache had taken ABI off the "Buy" list pending clarification;

Shearson continued it as a "Hold." He'd spoken with Ms. Pfannglanz at Institutional Equities Associates. She'd definitely go with the management. There was talk she'd been offered a high-level job in corporate planning at AbCom just before this broke out.

Bishman took over. He asked his wife to review the stockholder picture as we knew it at the moment. Around the table, pencils—including mine—were poised over scratch pads.

"OK, Bish. Start with sixty-five million shares in round figures." Audrey Bishman had a crisp, unpleasing accent. Midwestern I guessed, probably Chicago; it was as if she tucked a "y" in front of her vowels.

"Knocking off eight million for the Foundation leaves us fifty-seven million less change. That breaks down as follows: Mr. Monstrance here, a million seven; Polhemus: five million seven, which makes seven million four off the bat for us good guys. AbCom management and board shares round out at just over a million, which leaves us, say, forty-eight million plus to compete for. We need twenty-nine million for a majority, so we have to get, say, twenty-two million of the float. Everybody got that?"

Around the table there was a faint patter of calculator keys being punched.

"So: forty-eight million up for grabs. The biggest single block of that is Eugenie Monstrance: four million nine. That's family, and that's up to Mr. Monstrance to bring into camp. Which means ball park we're talking forty-three million for the rest of us to get." She paused to check her figures. "That stock, I forgot to say, includes two million in various ABI pension funds, which we can write off as solid for management, so let's say we're talking forty-one million walking around theoretically uncommitted. Got that?"

Everyone nodded.

"Now we won't know until we see the stockholder lists, which will be sometime early next week, but Bish and I had a talk with a little bird we know at the transfer agent's, and it looks like that forty-one million breaks down roughly sixteen, sixteen five, with individuals, which leaves the rest, say, twenty-five million shares, with the institutions. That's strictly ball park, though. Until we get a look at the stockholder list we don't know shit from Shinola. Bish?"

Her ex-husband took over. Briskly, he described how his outfit functioned. On delivery of the stockholder list, the Bishman Organization's computer would break it down every which way: geographically, demographically, institutionally. This would make possible a targeted canvass of AbCom's stockholder population through a continuous solicitation effort. It sounded to me like a charity phonathon: Bishman described a complex communications fabric utilizing automatic dialing, mail drops, 800 numbers, stand-by arrangements with Federal Express and Purolator, and so on.

From his pocket he produced a pale pink proxy card, marked in alphanumerics, slotted in computer Braille.

"It all comes down to this." He waved the card at us. "Ten weeks from now, there've gotta be pink cards representing twenty-nine million shares in the hands of Certified Guaranty. More pink cards than white. Pink's our lucky color. We've never lost one using pink, right, Aud?"

Mrs. Bishman nodded. "Right, Bish." She looked around the table. "Our behavioral people tell us pink is a good, friendly color. We used to use buff, but after we lost on Premier Oil, we sent the behavioral types back to the drawing board. Mr. Monstrance here wanted to go with dark blue, but people don't like to write on dark colors."

Of course X would go for dark blue: Starbuck and Yale.

Bishman recapitulated what others would do by way of direct solicitation. Bouverie, Marcus would tackle the big hitters: Wall Street, the bank trust departments, professional money managers, pension fund trustees and advisers, anyone who held real or discretionary power with respect to any holding of fifty thousand shares or more.

"I hope you're feeling strong, Mr. Monstrance," he said. "We may have to send you out on the road before this is over. You're the ace in the deck. We're gonna have to bring home the bacon with the little guys."

"I agree," said X. "If you ask me, we're going to win or lose this thing with the small stockholder, with the man on the street. I can tell you Ab feels exactly the opposite. He's counting on the funds to carry him through. He may have a point. A lot of these institutions are johnny-come-latelies to Granite, and I don't know them. I do think it's vital that the fellow with ten shares think he's worth just as much trouble, expense, and attention to us as an insurance company with half a million."

I saw Hillhouse start to demur, then think better of it, and settle back in his chair.

"Well," asked Bishman, "anybody got any further questions? Nope? OK, let's get the show on the road." He sat down with a faint jingle of gold jewelry. X again thanked everyone, and the meeting broke up.

I stayed behind. There were a few questions I wanted to ask.

"What did you think?" X asked me before I could say anything.

"Interesting. I trust you noticed that all these experts talked about was methodology. No one seemed to want to know exactly what you proposed to tell the stockholders to induce them to throw Abner out on his can. Just throw anything into the hopper and it'll work. The salesman, not the product."

"You can't blame them. They've seen it work for Eldon. If it'll work in a presidential election, why not here? Actually, you've touched a nerve. One thing I'm not going to ask our stockholders to do is to chuck Ab out. I intend to make it perfectly clear that I want him to stay, that even if I come back in, there'll be no substantive change in the company, that he'll be operationally in charge. I think that's a pretty good selling point. More bang for the same buck, as they all seem to say!"

"Speaking of which, this is going to cost a lot of money, X. Who's picking up the tab for your side? You personally?" I knew that Abner could draw on the depths of the company's pocket.

"Ab and I agreed that the Foundation may bear a portion of our expenses. It was not a decision about which Eugenie seemed enthusiastic. Bishman tells me, however, that it shouldn't run more than three or four million, now that we've cut the lawyers out except for the drafting and filing."

I knew from my homework that X's "persuasion" of Abner and Eugenie had been academic. The Monstrance Foundation's bylaws empowered X with two and a half votes to their one apiece. There was one more thing I had to ask him.

"X, how'd you get Abner to agree on the no-litigation no-bidding stuff? Christ, he's thrown away a lot of firepower. He could lock the Foundation up in litigation for a decade and see that it couldn't spend a dime. He could make you go to court to get a stockholders' meeting, let alone a list, which the court might not give you. Instead he volunteers them. He can write out all the checks he wants on the company's account. What'd you do, put a spell on him?"

X chuckled. "A spell? Gracious, no!" He chuckled again.

There was no hiding a fact that both of us knew. A spell was exactly what it was; a bewitchment that had held its power for over forty years, then over a boy, now over a grown, powerful man.

"I didn't cast anything on him, Sam," X continued. He was just talking. "I let him do it himself. Ab has a tendency to see his life as a moral imperative, as if the rest of us were put on earth to fulfill his wishes. So I just let him do the talking. It didn't take him long to convince himself that he could thrash me for the first and final time. And I don't doubt that he could, if all that was bound up in this was simply corporate policy and the price of the shares. But there's more at issue, which Ab just doesn't see."

"Because you just haven't told him," I said. X simply smiled druidically, savoring his little mysteries and mystifications.

As Hillhouse had predicted, the public disclosure of the Monstrances' unique ground rules pissed off quite a few professionally and financially concerned folks. The American Bar Association issued a statement declaring that the compact between X and Abner, by outlawing litigation, very likely deprived AbCom stockholders of possible financial benefits of due process. The next day, a derivative action was begun on these grounds in Philadelphia. A day later, the chairman of the Securities Industry Association opined in the *Journal* that the agreement precluding a bidding war was "a possible first step in the dismantling of free-market capitalism as we know it." But the loudest wails came from the arbitrageurs, because this was costing them cash.

"What the goddamn booger-lovin' shit is goin' on here?" shouted Buck over the phone. "You know these folks. Is they crazy? I never heard such bullshit! Abner's gotta be out of his mind."

"How's the stock?" I asked, with deliberately irritating calmness.

"Off two and a quarter so far, which makes nearly six since last night on the Coast. Took 'em half the morning to get it open. The specialist saw it coming and decided to take an early lunch. He ain't been seen since. Shit, boy, I'm out fifty thousand big ones and it ain't even noon. I did get a little off in Zurich about four this morning."

"Fifty thousand dollars? And you're worth fifty million? My heart bleeds for you. And for me, since about two dollars of that loss is mine. Serves you right for speculating."

"Man, this is serious!" His voice went away from the receiver. I imagined he was punching away at his quote machine. He came back on. "That sumbitch is down to fifty-five and a half! I'm eating dogshit!"

"According to Arnold Plume, the well-known takeover lawyer, 'Arbitrage is a perversion of capitalism.' He said so in an article."

"He ain't sayin' so today, and if you don't think so, jes' ask old Arnold about a certain account in Geneva and see what *that* lying, pompous, two-faced, hypocritical sumbitch has to say about arbitrage! Anyway, what's the old sumbitch up to?"

"Which sumbitch?" I was having a good time. Buck was a great fellow, but like all driven moneymakers, there was no such concept as "enough" in his canon.

"Cut it out! I heard one rumor says if he got in he was gonna break the sumbitch and sell off the pieces. I heard another Abner was gonna buy out the Foundation at five points over market. Now they talkin' like it's some doohickey election for dogcatcher! Goddammit, Sam, nobody just has a proxy fight any more! I figured this one for a lock six ways from Sunday. Now all I got is a pair of squeezed nuts plus I still got eight thousand shares! Goddammit!"

To some extent, Buck and Abner shared a similar sense of moral imperative, a conviction that life consisted of their rights and other people's obligations. Buck counted his in money.

I told Buck to stop whimpering, it didn't become so manly a figure, and went back to work.

My own sense of superior apartness lasted exactly four more days, and then all hell broke loose about my head. Mother was the first to call.

"Well," she said over the telephone, making no effort to hide the sarcastic fun she was having with something she knew would really bother me, "so you're going to be a war correspondent. Just like your father. And a leading light of the gossip columns. How pleased Cassandra must be! All along you've been just her sort of man!" Her relish at my discomfiture disappeared in a harsh cough. She'd just returned from Oregon on Columbus Day and still complained of feeling generally lousy.

The item had appeared in Liz Smith's column in the *Daily News*.

David McClintick, step aside! It's been learned that S. A. Mountcastle, the respected magazine writer, has been given a privileged track on the inside dope on Wall Street's version of *Hamlet*, the proxy fight being waged for control of AbCom, the multi-billion-dollar entertainment and computer conglomerate, by Abner Monstrance, the White House's favorite high-tech businessman and power that is in the company, and his father, the legendary H. H. Monstrance, who started AbCom fifty years ago as Granite Broadcasting Group. Publishers are running up each other's backs trying to nail down rights to the book which Mountcastle, a longtime friend of both Monstrances, has got in the works, and which should make *Indecent Exposure* look like *Nancy Drew*.

I told Mother, somewhat pointedly, that the item had been a plant about which I knew nothing and that, incidentally, Cass and I were no longer an item, and hung up. Now I knew exactly what Buck meant when he talked about "a major-league case of the red ass."

There were about six different veins of aggravation and anger I could draw from. I despised people who courted publicity, and indeed the whole machinery of hype, and this made me out to be part of it. If there was anything in life that particularly enraged me, it was someone arrogating to himself the right to speak for or about me in public, and whoever had tipped Liz Smith had done that. My money, obviously, was on X.

Then there was a whole lot of unwanted attention. Publishers were on the horn; I referred them politely to my agent when they wouldn't take my denials for an answer. Cass checked in; I had reserved a dollop of suspicion for her too. No one was saying much to my face, but I'd picked up enough rumors to know that she was acting as the official hostess at 841 Fifth Avenue, and one couldn't rule out the possibility that a fragment of pillow talk had been passed on to the columnist.

And I was especially embarrassed for Clio and Abner. I read the item as implying, in neon, that I had been on the case for some time. I didn't want to leave them with the feeling they'd been nursing an asp in their bosom, even though I had to admit that it was difficult to deny. The fact was, however, that I hadn't written anything yet, had no notes, and was in the ambivalent yet perhaps defensible position of being an insider without declared allegiance. Defensible? Perhaps: but it wouldn't be easy to explain what I was doing in the basement of the House of Lords with this fellow Fawkes; the best I could hope for was that the fact I didn't actually have any matches on me might be taken as proof of innocence.

I had to counterattack, I thought. After all, it had taken me twenty years to come to terms with the risks and possibilities of living as a writer in the real world, of spending most of my time not with other announced writers, making writerly noises and assuming writerly attitudes, but with people who played golf and worried about the Dow Jones. I didn't want publicity and celebrity, or to be known as one of the company of New York writers, a guildsman, although there had been a time, in my twenties, when I thought a good table at Elaine's more important than a good notice from Gore Vidal. I didn't want money, even though I was pretty certain I knew what buttons to push to bring the so-called reading public baying. I realized that writing about the current sad sea-change of a world I grew up in could be seen as a form of betrayal, but only by those who held no fixed values, to whom truth and beauty were unquantifiable and thus empty abstractions. What I wanted now was to write well and for what I wrote to make some kind of a difference, to change a world I found grasping, smarmy, sleazy, illiterate, shallow, choked. Just what X said he wanted to accomplish: to make television better, and to have it make our lives better by revealing things the way they were. No matter what people said, I wrote out of rage, not pique; out of reflection, not envy. It was as I had tried to explain to Cass often enough: in an age which makes a state religion out of euphemism, a realist will be damned and demeaned as a cynic. There are always naked emperors about, and they always have their tailors with them.

All this was now called into question, I thought, perhaps overreacting, by the gossip column. My life's work, my vocation, my standards, my karma had been compromised, possibly irredeemably. A vigorous defense, indeed a tantrum, was in order, if only for cathartic purposes. So I called Abner and made a date to see him, intending to put a better face on things. I stormed into my editor's office and futilely accused him of colluding with X in planting the item. I was just blowing off steam, but there was something in the tone of his disavowal that caught my ear, a troubling hint that my straw man might not be so porous. X seemed to have everyone's number, so why not the editor's? The Monstrance road to greatness was lined with fallen pillars of probity, broken and shattered.

Then I called X. It was impossible to stay angry, enraged as I was at him. He seized control of the conversation and dismissed me in a voice he would use for a troublesome child, talking over my protests and accusations, denying any part in the matter, and implying that anyway it was just a tempest in a teacup, minuscule potatoes compared to his great concerns. And his momentous news.

"You remember how it's been suggested that I add a woman to my slate of directors?" he asked.

I sputtered my recollection. I was the one who'd brought it up. The dissident slate was the usual grab bag: an Ivy League college president, the head of a medical foundation, a law school professor, a retired Cabinet secretary piling up private-sector cash, an ex-NASA bigwig, a London insurance broker, the president of an airline, his attorney. Jacob Polhemus had turned him down, unwilling to visit another hurt on Abner.

"Well," he said triumphantly, "I've got one!"

My curiosity got the better of my vexation. "Who?"

"Eugenie!" I could visualize his triumphant grin.

"Jesus Christ, X! Eugenie's on Abner's board!"

"Not any more." There was a new vindictiveness to his gloating, a mean edge which I found unpleasant. "She sent her resignation over to Ab an hour ago."

I asked him how he'd done it. I had an idea, which he confirmed.

"I've got her slotted for a larger role in the company's future. The idea appealed to her."

"I'll bet it did." I hope she got it in writing, I thought.

"I told you I always knew she had ability. Well, here's the chance she never had. Ab never really gave her a chance either, bless her. If we get in, I'm going to make her Senior Vice-Chairman with, and I'm quoting, 'oversight responsibility for the company's noncommunications businesses.' Rolls right off the tongue, doesn't it? Bishman thought it up."

"What does 'oversight' mean? Is that a fancy word for 'executive,' or is it just words? Is she actually going to be in charge of something?" I tried to get my angry contentiousness into this new subject. My other rage had been hopelessly deflected.

"Indeed she will! At the very top level!" He spoke with real conviction. I could see one gift he'd passed on to his star pupil, Eldon Erwitt. They each believed what they said at the time they said it, absolutely. "Of course," X added jovially, "Eugenie has no real interest in day-to-day operations; she's more of a strategist, and she has too many interests of her own, although I'll try to get her to extricate herself from those teams of hers."

"Does she understand that?"

"You bet she does! And I've sent word to Ab that the other five places on the board are his, provided he'll come to terms."

"You mean surrender. Christ, X, the first shot's barely been fired. Abner's not going to go for that."

"Of course he isn't," said X. He sounded very pleased.

He wanted total obliterating victory over his son. He was willing to play on his sad daughter's frustrations and longings to get it. I hated the whole business, yet it was suddenly borne in on me that not once in the course of my fierce reactions to my imagined predicament had I considered telling the editor to stuff the story and telling X to get lost, to go back out of my life. This old man was beating up on his children; he had made a virtual concubine out of Cass, which caused me all kinds of retrospective embarrassment, as I chose to term the ambiguous reaction I felt to their suddenly burgeoned relationship; yet here I was, still signed on for the duration. Perhaps the nobility of the cause excused the duplicity, the manipulation, the arrogance. I preferred to see it that way, certainly, but then, too, I knew deep down that perhaps that wasn't the way things were at all. About all I could do was to hang on, as to a bucking horse, and find out.

CHAPTER 10

Two days later I had lunch with Abner in his office at AbCom Tower. The dark granite building had retained its distinctiveness across a quarter century; it looked spare and elegant in comparison with the modish, kitschy ostentation of its postmodernist younger neighbors. Abner occupied the forty-fifth-floor corner office that had once been his father's. One of the three secretaries announced me, and I was promptly shown in.

It had been a long time since I had seen the Monstrance throne room, the seat of kings, but I was struck at once by the change in style and mood. X's office had been a jumbled magic toyshop, loaded with the latest gadgets: stacked television screens, recording equipment, record and tape players, wire recorders, radio transmitters and receivers, phonograph records, and reels of tape the size of dinner plates stacked all about. Abner's office was severe, not a hair out of place. I had expected banks of video monitors, but the only screen in the room was attached to a computer terminal next to his otherwise bare steel and crystal desk. X hadn't gone in for a proper desk, preferring to work at a round rent table and a stand-up desk he'd been given by Hemingway. Where there had been a calculatedly relaxed array of stout, stuffed sofas and chairs were three or four skeletal modern pieces, limbed in chrome and covered in tan linen and black leather. There were no paintings; in X's time a witty Miró and a large wild Picasso drawing had been on the walls.

Under Abner, the place had been stripped of the personal touch. The only gestures to informality were three uniformly framed photographs: of

Clio in an evening gown; of Abner's two children, stiffly posed; and the photograph I had first seen in London of X and Selena, Abner and Eugenie.

Before I could launch into my carefully thought-through apologia, Abner led me over to the window and pointed north, where a spiky ossuary of cranes and structural steel marked the progress of One AbCom Plaza.

"We should be moving early in the year, March perhaps. It'll be a lot easier to work there. We've really outgrown this place."

"What are you going to do with it?"

"I have an offer from IBM. I'm also thinking of essentially gutting it and doubling the floor space. We think we can cut the plaza downstairs in half and still keep the city happy. Some idiot's talking about making this a Landmark building, but I think we've got that blocked in the City Council."

I started to speak again, but again he cut me off. He took me over to his desk and punched several keys on the computer keyboard. Rows of green figures rippled into being.

"I've got the whole thing right here, Sam. Plugged into what we called our 'war room.' Pretty apt name, don't you think, what with this ridiculous business with Dad?" He sounded confident and expansive. "Funny," he said, "I guess it happens to everyone."

"What's that?"

"Senility. Aging."

"Actually," I said, "that's what I wanted to talk with you about. This thing with X. There was that item in the *News*—"

"Look at this, Sam." He punched the computer keyboard. "There's not a hair of this company I can't part." Glowing alphanumerics appeared on the screen.

"Our time sales for the next three seasons." More keystrokes. "Assets Management's real estate bank."

He was obviously very pleased.

"The system's programmed to flag any aberrants from norm or plan. If a problem comes up, it flashes here and we get right on it."

I wondered if the computer flashed sick hearts and disappointed hopes, laughter and tears and frustration. Did it track the emotional inventory of a company that rode on the spirit and morale and talent of its people? I started in again.

"Look, Abner, I don't want you to get the idea—"

He looked at me without exasperation but with an obvious effort at patience, like a teacher obliged to take a pupil through an equation over and over, unsure whether the student is obtuse or stubborn. I found his expression maddening; I would have liked to punch him right in the middle of his smugness.

"That business in the paper? Don't give it a thought. That's just another one of Dad's tricks. It's an old game of his, trying to make me think I don't know who my friends are. Like this business with Cassie. What's she doing with Dad, with a man his age? Clee's pretty hurt, I can tell you. It's very disloyal of Cassie. Anyway, if you end up doing a piece on this, just call over here for anything you need. AbCom's an open book. How about lunch?"

He led me down the hall to an elegant, spare dining room where we were served an elegant, spare meal. Well, screw you, I found myself thinking. This business between the Monstrances was like two bull elks bumping in a forest clearing; the thing to do was to stay to one side.

Over a salad of radicchio and sliced oranges, Abner remarked, "I guess Dad just can't stand to see the changes we've had to make around here."

"All I know," I said, no longer feeling treacherous in the face of Abner's complacency, "is that he seems concerned about your television operations."

"Dad and his Nielsens." He shook his head sympathetically. "I feel sorry for him. That was yesterday's game. There's nothing wrong with the network, Sam. We just have to face facts: people are sick of old-style television. They want something different, a new form of gratification. We're going to give it to them. We know more about the American people than they know about themselves. Give us another five years of demographic engineering, mate it with what we've already got in the database, and you'll see a whole new era of television. Up at AbCom Interface, we're marrying software with psychological testing and programming to produce a whole new technology of viewer satisfaction. Last year we spent ninety million!"

"Sounds like Big Brother to me." He didn't seem to hear me.

"Dad's day is past," Abner said, "and he can't stand the fact. He doesn't understand what we're doing around here; he's old, he's scared of dying, he wants attention; and he's jealous of what I've accomplished. Lord knows, when he turned up this summer, which I knew would be a bad idea, I tried to make him feel good. We gave him all the perks: a helicopter at his disposal, cars, one of the jets any time he wanted. Clee made a terrific effort. I wanted to do anything but pick a fight with him, and now look what's happened! Well, our work here is a lot more important than Dad's hurt feelings. It's not just pride on my part. I've got employees to think about. I've got stockholders to take care of. There's an entrepreneurial and technological revolution going on in the country now—thank God, we've got some people in Washington who understand how things have to work if we're going to get anything done—and I've positioned AbCom at the cutting edge. Another ten years and we'll be bigger than IBM! Dad thinks we're still selling breakfast food and Uncle Miltie."

A waiter brought a mixed seafood grill. I decided to change the subject and get back to matters of fact and tactics. Besides, Abner's evangelism was spoiling an excellent lunch.

"I was surprised that Eugenie bolted," I said.

"Were you? In a way I was glad, and I certainly wasn't surprised. Eugenie's been a real pain in the keister. Not that losing her shares won't sting."

"By my count, that puts X up to around twelve million."

Abner looked untroubled. "Counting Dad's stock and Uncle Jake's, which I guess you have to, they've got twelve million, yes, but that's about all they'll get, and they need another sixteen to seventeen. I had the Harris people run a flash poll the night Dad announced the proxy fight, and we have an approval factor of eight–nine percent overall, and ninety-six percent with our institutional holders. There's always some shrink-age, but that's a base of close to forty million shares right there."

"Some people think the institutions can be pretty fickle."

Abner chuckled, a bit too jovially. "You're thinking of Eric Shaughnessy," he said. "Eric's a bit too much of a maverick. He likes to stir the pot, to annoy people."

"What about the people these institutions represent?" I asked.

"What about them? They've been very well served by their fiduciaries. They want to see the value of their accounts increase. We know what our friends in the institutions want: good results and no surprises. That's what we give them. Our five-year plan is set. Around here we don't plan for surprises, and we don't permit them. What's Dad got to put up against that? I don't think he even knows."

"Intangibles have been known to make a difference." I didn't want to sound contentious, let alone hostile, but Abner was getting to me.

"They used to," he said. "No longer. That was in Dad's day. People on the Street tried to get the measure of the men who ran companies, be-cause they didn't have the concreteness, the measurability we've got now. So we'll get through this, and then we'll get on with our real business."

"What about the individual stockholders?"

"They tend to be reflexive and vote with management. Otherwise, they're a nuisance: expensive, whining, uninformed, acting as if they owned the company."

Before I could respond, he did a ninety-degree turn in midair.

"Tell me, Sam, do you think Cassie's jealous of Clee?"

"It's hard not to be," I hedged. "That they're sisters probably aggravates the situation." The answer seemed to please him.

"I think you're right. Clee's really wonderful, isn't she? The trouble is, though, if you do things well, people get on your case. Eugenie's so jealous of Clee it kills her. I think that's the reason she went over to Dad. He's jealous too, I think."

"Do you really? Why?"

"In his heart he knows that Clee's the real McCoy, a real person, unlike Selena. You never knew Selena, did you?"

"No."

"She was totally superficial. All she ever thought about was clothes and what to serve for dinner. She was the shallowest person I ever saw. I wish you could have seen the people she surrounded him with. I think that's why he started to go soft. That's what kills Dad: he sees Clee doing all the things Selena did, and doing them better, and being a fine, sensitive person in the bargain."

There wasn't anything I could say to that. To comment on the people they saw, Bud and Marie and the Cornaras and the Getsmores, would have been offensive. A ginger sorbet was brought, followed by coffee. We finished up with pointless small talk.

The lunch left me with a bad taste in my mouth, however, which could easily translate into a rooting interest for X. Abner's new breed was beyond my appreciation, almost beyond my understanding, with its cocksure assumption that people like me, little people, subconsciously defined in his mind as all of us who didn't lodge in forty-fifth-floor suites with three secretaries and helicopters on ready alert, were just so many manipulable bits of data, minute fractions of information to be summoned at will from the innards of his computer and reshaped and reorganized to suit the requirements of himself and the other power people.

This feeling was reinforced a few days later when I paid a visit to the offices of the Bishman Organization, X's proxy solicitors.

Bishman had called almost daily with progress reports. They had received the AbCom stockholder list, and he was anxious to show me how he could "massage" it. So on a pewter-colored afternoon, I took a walk down to the nondescript old office building off lower Park Avenue where the Bishman Organization was located. Bishman met me at the elevator and led me past banks of computers and telephone consoles operated by busy, intent men and women. Bishman was in a genial mood; he was confident of ultimate victory, mainly because he had time to do some real digging.

"The kid's a schmuck," he said. "He shoulda told us: OK, we'll give you a meeting in three weeks. He'd of killed us. Now we got a shot."

The stockholder list was a computer printout about the thickness of four Manhattan phone directories, listing the stockholders of record. I went to Bishman's office to see how he "massaged" it. AbCom's records showed several million shares as being held in "Street names," amorphous nominee designations under which banks and brokerages held their customers' stocks. Bishman's object was to break down these aliases to identify the real owners.

He sat me down at a terminal in his office.

"We're hooked into the big mainframe out there. Lemme show you the process." He punched the keyboard. Like Abner, he was totally delighted by and involved with his gadgetry. "OK, here's Horn and Co., which shows six hundred and seven thousand four hundred thirty-two shares. Now that's a nominee, what we call a 'Street name,' in this case for Certified Guaranty Trust, which is holding the stock for God knows who. That's where we come up against a wall we got to break down. I wanna know whether the Certified's acting for, say, the Steamfitters Pension Fund or some widow in Palm Beach. Got it?"

"So far. Isn't that a bitch to do?"

"Used to be. Things have been easier the last couple of years. This guy Erwitt's the greatest thing that ever happened to the proxy business—to the securities industry, period."

"What's the President got to do with it?"

"The word out of Washington is anything goes, just don't get too greedy or crooked, or don't get caught."

"I don't follow you."

"It used to be guys were scared to talk. Passing out inside dope was something you went to jail for. Now a guy gets caught, he gets made Chief Justice or put on the SEC. So there's no damper, see?"

"Not really."

"Look, say there's a hypothetical guy working for AbCom's transfer agent or registrar, for Certified Guaranty, and this guy owns maybe five shares of AbCom, or maybe he doesn't even own any, but he's got this burning interest in stockholder democracy, kind of an ideological thing, like he learned in school. Now you got something like this proxy fight comes up, and how you gonna have due process for the stockholders unless you know exactly who they are? Get it?"

I thought I did. I asked, "What does it take to create a burning interest in stockholder democracy?"

Bishman shrugged, then winked lewdly. "The old man said to cut you in on everything, so here goes. It takes maybe two weeks at Dorado Beach, or a line of credit with a bookie, or whatever. But it's for the greater good. Sometimes you just kind of swap information. Like you find someone in a need-to-know spot who's cheating on the expense account or knocking off a little nookie on the side. One way or the other, we get the goods. Look!"

He tapped the console. On the screen, the nominee's holding was broken down by specific names, with addresses and telephone numbers, arranged by zip code.

"Once we got that," Bishman said, "we can go right to work six ways from Sunday, which is what we're doing now. Name a city."

Kansas City, Missouri, I said. He punched out one line, then another.

"Six-four-one-oh-one zip," he said. Orderly green rows emerged on the terminal screen.

"OK, you got the Missouri Trust Company holding stock for these accounts. You got small companies, like this one here: Ludwell and Gaines, eighty-five shares; usually not worth a personal call."

"What's your break point on making personal contact?"

"Usually a couple thousand shares. On this one the old man's all fired up about the small stockholder, and he's buying, so everybody's gonna hear from us. Plus we're probably gonna pay brokers to solicit their accounts. Put enough in it for a broker, and he'll sell his accounts outta IBM at a buck!"

"Is that within the ground rules?"

"Ground rules, shmound rules. Mr. Monstrance wants to win this thing. When we get down to the short strokes, around Thanksgiving, we'll see who knows from ground rules!"

"How do you plan to use Mr. Monstrance?"

"Not sure yet. We may have to dog-and-pony the old boy around the country. No whistle-stops at first, just the big ball parks: Boston, Chicago, Houston, Frisco. Nail the guys with more than a hundred thousand shares head to head. We can do a lot of personal-touch stuff from here. Like anyone with a thousand shares or more gets a personal letter signed by Mr. Monstrance; anybody with five thousand or more gets a personal phone call from him. If it gets hot and heavy, we'll put him on the road: set up a bunch of lunches and dinners around the country and invite everyone with ten thousand plus. Plus Europe too, probably. Right now, it's too early to tell. We still got nearly six weeks, and we don't want to leave our fight in the locker room."

The period through the first week of November was what X described as "the Phony War." Silence descended on the battlefield, punctuated only by desultory cannonades in the form of full-page advertisements and mass mailings of proxy materials. These were, on the whole, gray and uninspiring, standard financial public relations pap. On Tuesday, the *Journal* would run an ad extolling "your management's record." On Thursday would appear counterclaims by X's side, promising to put GBG back on top. The public and press grew bored with so little action. There were times when I asked myself whether in fact this was real.

Not that there wasn't plenty to keep me occupied. I did a piece on the private life of a pillar of the banking world that finished me off with most of my few remaining friends in business. I didn't know the man, but his actions in this instance had been foolish and endangering, and it was my job as a writer to cast some light on them. It was a good article, but even Buck said that if I kept this up it was going to be tough to be seen with me in certain places.

I kept in touch with AbCom through Duncan. Things looked good from over there. Every day brought new assurances from one massive institution or another that a white card would be marked for management.

"The trouble is," Duncan said, "the sonsabitches won't vote until eleven fifty-nine and thirty seconds. They figure something'll come up and leave 'em with egg on their faces. Hell, even if they sign a white card now, they can always sign a pink one later on, and only the last one counts."

I didn't see much of X during this period. Cass was with him constantly, I knew, and I guessed it made her uncomfortable to have me around. That wasn't what I wanted, anyway; I went to movies, plays, did a little light sleeping around, just testing the waters, and sat in on Margarita Clerc's lectures at Columbia.

Duncan commandeered a company limo and went up with me to hear the first one. He had struggled loyally and manfully with my copy of her book on envy. It was not, he reported, "a page turner." He was in good fettle. He liked what he was doing.

"Beats the shit out of just being the guy who lights the matches in the bathroom," he remarked, as we emerged from the park at 110th Street. It was, I thought, a fairly accurate description of the function of his Op-Ed pieces.

He was evidently interested in Margarita.

"I hear she's some kind of guru to the old man. Got him all hopped up against advertising and product safety and the rest of that crap. Think he's pronging her?"

"Such language," I replied, trying to sound coolly disinterested. "Who knows?"

"I hear he's back banging away for all it's worth. That old sonofabitch is gonna need a computerized zipper if he keeps it up."

X's sex life was a subject of consuming interest and wonderment to Duncan. Where did Cass fit into such a busy and complex erotic life, I speculated?

Duncan turned to the subject of the proxy fight.

"I tell you, Sam, this f—— thing's going along too easy. If the meeting were tomorrow, I think we'd pull forty million shares."

"Taken some more bloody ground, have you?"

"Yeah, the Mellon looks like they're in. That's three quarters of a million. Forstmann-Leff's gonna let us know Monday, but I talked to Tony and they're a lock. Same thing with Sarofim in Houston."

"So why is there no smile on your lips?"

"Because the f—— meeting's not tomorrow! Because every new day is a day something lousy can happen."

"Or something good."

"No. The good we know. In Wall Street, there's no such thing as a good surprise, unless some guy makes a bid for you. Look at RCA yesterday. Earnings up twenty percent; the first time in ten years those clowns have done one f—— thing right, and the stock sells off a point! I don't get the old man, either. Where's the heavy artillery? What's he waiting for?"

Margarita looked well and spoke effectively. She was dressed severely in a dark suit over a pale gunmetal blouse, which somehow made her look a good ten years younger than her age. Her lecture, the first of a series to be concerned with the moral basis of American executive culture, dealt with the evolution and degeneration of basic emotions like shame in the face of aggrandizement by values based on expediency and competitiveness for its own sake. Emerson came in for a hard time, as did, expectedly, Veblen and fundamentalist religion. It was a good, meaty talk. I looked forward to the rest of the series.

Duncan was also impressed, although less with the content than the lecturer.

"That is a real woman," he muttered. "No wonder they say the old man's got a hard-on for her that a cat couldn't scratch."

Afterward I went up to speak with her and saw, to my dismay, irritation, and surprise, that Pierre Clerc was standing there. I complimented her on the lecture, introduced Duncan, and, being unable to propose dinner, and seeing that she was distracted by the usual postlectural crowd of exegists and second-guessers, said I would call her next week and slunk off.

Duncan dropped me off outside my apartment. I declined his invitation to "beat up on a little Third Avenue quiff" and went upstairs. I was feeling oddly paranoid, as if all New York was against me. I made myself a drink and put a record of Schwarzkopf singing operetta arias on the stereo. "*Wie Mann sich Rosen . . .*"; the strong, lovely voice filled the room. I settled in my chair with my drink, thinking about the Monstrances, and about Margarita and Cass and Clio and Fergie Duncan and Bishman and all the other worrisome presences in my life, until the music finally pushed the phantoms from the room. That was one thing Vienna was great for: chasing ghosts.

The "phony war" ended on the fifteenth of November, exactly one month before the special stockholders' meeting.

X opened up on two fronts, but it was soon apparent that the first was essentially high-minded persiflage intended to distract from the gutter action that I was sure he was really counting on. A series of advertisements, headed AN ABUSE OF PUBLIC TRUST in blaring block letters, appeared in the general press, giving a bill of particulars indicting AbCom for ethnically pejorative programming, for a deficiency of public-interest and quality children's broadcasting, for a concealed commitment to divert "premium quality" matter such as sports and movies to an elitist cable audience, for neglecting its responsibility as an investigative watchdog of the public interest, and for exerting a corrupting influence on family values and preferences and favoring the haves against the have-nots.

From *Time* and *The New Yorker* to *TV Guide* and the principal newspapers in each of the two hundred top television markets, X seemed out to tickle the cozy, cosseted guilt of readers who were on the whole immune to the slings and arrows of ordinary life. His call for a higher level of moral and intellectual content in daily programming was cleverly addressed to the sort of person who assumed that the average American family, or at least a family entitled to the vote, subscribed to *The Atlantic* and enjoyed Vivaldi.

The gutter campaign was aimed squarely at the rank and file. Bishman had done his work well. He had the names. Now his computers spat out letters to active and retired members of hundreds of labor organizations, from the Carpenters' District Council of New York City to the UAW; to the members of associations of federal, state, and city workers; to participants in a wide spectrum of corporate benefit plans. The mailing went out to over a million names. It went to any individual the Bishman organization had been able to identify as having a direct or indirect holding in AbCom, even the most fractional contingent portion of a huge institutional position.

"This is what the computer was invented for," Bishman said proudly. We were standing in the mailroom of the Bishman Organization, watching machines fold, sort, stamp, and bundle thousands of pieces per minute. "Most people who got a lot of data stored up, it goes through 'em like shit through a goose and does about as much good!"

"Will people read it?"

"Sure they will! It's very personal-looking. Good stock. High-grade print job. Letter quality. People are going to be surprised to find out what they own. See here."

He picked one up at random. It was addressed to a man in California. The first paragraph informed him that, as a participant in the Los Angeles County Employees Retirement Association, he had an interest in how the Association's officers and fiduciaries voted the Association's 53,812 shares of AbCom common stock. Those shares were managed by four firms, which the letter listed, together with the names, addresses, and telephone numbers of the concerned money and portfolio managers, as well as the retirement association's officers. The recipient was urged to contact those individuals directly.

"Greatest job we ever did around here," crowed Bishman. "Half those phone numbers are unlisted."

It was the content of the letter that was inflammatory. X was out to rouse the rabble by attacking Abner's compensation and the way he lived. The letter was designed to enrage small stockholders and to encourage them to vent their wrath by leaning on their investment fiduciaries. It pointed out, in capital letters, that Abner's salary and bonus, which had exceeded two million dollars in AbCom's most recent fiscal year, had risen to that level at almost twice the inflation rate for the preceding five years. The implication was clear: Abner was personally an engine of inflation. It was because of people like him that black children went hungry and steelworkers lost their jobs. And someone had suborned Abner's accountants; the last sentence asserted that for the last five years, Abner had paid a total of just over $18,000 in income taxes.

The next paragraphs were even uglier. They were devoted to Abner's use of his expense account and company perquisites, and to the grand style in which Clio and he lived. There was a chronological list of some of Clio and Abner's fancier dinner parties, emphasizing the luxury of the occasion and the triviality of the guests. It didn't take much imagination to reckon the effect on a Sun City retiree of learning that a recent menu had included "five pounds caviar, $3,000; two cases 1962 Haut-Brion, $4,600" served to the likes of "Simon Bastion, floral designer; Electra Pourdemain, glove editor, *Vogue*." The conclusion was unmistakable. AbCom's stockholders were picking up the tab for a decadent, homosexual-ridden life-style while around the country, millions of people were lining up for handout process cheese.

"Good, huh?" said Bishman.

"Lenin would be proud of it."

He didn't take notice. "What you gotta do, you see, is relate the numbers to the guy in the street. People like you and me, we spill a few grand here and there, so what? Some schmuck embezzles five grand from a bank and we read about it in the *News*, what's the big deal? To you and me, five grand's movie money. But for a lot of these people, living on pension funds and social security, five bucks is a big deal, especially when the high point of your day is to go down to the store and pick up a can of Alpo for dinner."

"This is a pretty selective guest list you're quoting," I objected. "I've been to a few of those dinners. There've been some pretty high-powered types on hand."

"This isn't journalism, kid. This is a proxy fight. We wanna hit the guy out there in front of the TV in his undershirt with a Bud, the kind of guy still says 'homo.' There's a lot of places still that queers don't go down so good. We aren't putting out this shit to win the White House vote, get it?"

The menu-guest section was followed by excerpts from the trip logs of AbCom's fleet of jets and helicopters. The former included landings at

Palm Springs, Nassau, Palm Beach, Nice, and St. Moritz, all annotated "Mrs. M and guests," each apparently paid for by AbCom. The helicopter entries left little doubt that Abner had commuted to Southampton courtesy of his stockholders and that Clio wasn't above using the three Alouettes as delivery boys. Pains were taken to point up the fact that the AbCom helicopter fleet was of French manufacture, with the suggestion that this had cost hundreds of jobs in Stratford, Connecticut, and Amarillo, Texas.

The mailing piece ended with X's avowal to put the company back on the path of balance and frugality. If given a mandate by the stockholders, he would reduce executive salaries and put a lid on travel and entertainment expenses.

"That's bullshit," I said to Bishman. "He's told Abner he and his people can stay on even if the dissidents win. And you don't cut back T and E in a business like television. Deals fall apart on limousine privileges."

Bishman shrugged. "So what? Right now, executive compensation is what plays. By the time this is over, it'll be something else."

I couldn't argue with that. The editorial pages were full of grousing about the seven-figure salaries the top men in corporations, endorsed by rubber-stamp boards, were paying themselves. Especially since the results, overall, didn't seem to justify the outlay.

I had one last question for Bishman.

"I assume you can back this up? It seems to me to verge on libel."

"Whaddya want? You want flight logs? I got Xeroxes up the ass. You want florists' bills? You name it, we got it!" He quivered with excitement, setting off tiny clangs from his jewelry.

Duncan thought X's strategy would backfire.

"All this is gonna do is piss off the money managers. This business that the rank and file makes a difference is dipshit! The fund managers are in bed with the guys who pass out the gravy. Two or three times a year they take the honchos from this or that to Vegas or Freeport, give 'em walking-around money, get 'em laid, whatever. That's the way it is."

Buck to some extent agreed when I called to get his reaction.

"I think it's a riot. You're asking is it going to make a difference? I don't reckon so. The stock's actin' a little nervous, though. It opened late, up a point and a quarter, which just means some asshole's bettin' that this proxy fight's goin' to turn into a bid war."

"I don't see that happening."

"Me either, Sam. So all this means is that Abner's a mite more delicate than he was yesterday morning. I heard a bunch of ol' boys at the Recess sayin' they'd heard ol' Abner'd gotten kind of fagified by the new wife."

"Fagified?"

"You know—queers everywhere."

"Since when did you become so antihomosexual?"

"I ain't talkin' about homosexuals, ol' buddy. I'm talkin' 'bout fags! There's a difference."

I didn't debate the point. If investors were edgy about this sort of thing, I asked, how could this affect the way things turned out?

"As long as things go along smooth, old Abner'll be OK. I've been tracking this just like it was being arbitraged, like you asked me to, talking to my buddies and all. Right now, the way it looks, the management's strong with about three quarters of the institutional stock, say close to twenty million shares right there. With his own stock, that's twenty-one million, which leaves seven to play for out of sixteen million kicking around in Street names. A mite over forty percent of the float, and I ain't never heard of a management doin' worse than seventy percent, so right now, old Abner's walkin' in the tall cotton, provided there ain't no bad news."

"Any chance the dissidents could manufacture some?"

"Wouldn't put it past them. But they got laws about that, and this'd be one case where the old SEC might just do something. Abner's tighter'n stink with the White House. I don't see it. And I'll tell you one thing, old buddy, that old sumbitch has given a couple of institutional guys I know a major-league case of the red ass. The last thing anybody wants is some greaseball from South Succotash calling up the Madison Fund and telling 'em to vote for Monstrance 'cause his son has queers to dinner. It's like when them Yale kids tried to tell the Morgan not to vote for anything in South Africa. The Morgan like to shit."

But, as I remembered, Yale had gotten its way.

"South Africa?" said X, when I discussed Buck's observation with him. "That's just the point. You realize, of course, that this is exactly what the people behind Eldon want?"

"What? To get Yale out of South Africa?"

"No. To turn this country into South Africa. Anyway, we're certainly on the offensive now, and in the limelight."

There was no doubt of that. The press had had a field day with X's mailing piece. "Why watch 'Dallas' or 'Dynasty,'" wrote *The Washington Post*, "when you can watch the Monstrances without commercial interruptions?" Others were not so jocular. Speaking for BLEEP, as well as in his capacity as an incumbent director of AbCom, former President McNeery appeared on "Today" to excoriate X for blemishing the high traditions of corporate discourse and urged viewers not to lend themselves to "this shabby business." Duncan succeeded in getting Joe Granville bumped off "Wall Street Week" to make room for Abner, who gave a good account of himself to a highly partial panel. *Forbes* editorialized that X's revelations concerning Abner's life-style represented a threat to management morale and might impair the determination of managements everywhere to act in their stockholders' best interests.

X relished the excitement. There was a lot going on in his life. As I got up to leave the apartment, he asked me to come and look at something in the dining room.

The Constable had been taken down. In its place hung a large modern picture, about five feet square: the background was a flat and angry scarlet, on which, crudely delineated in coarse black strokes, were the outlines of two dancing figures. Diagonally across the surface a line of what appeared from this distance to be small seashells had evidently been glued and then smashed. In the upper right quadrant the canvas had been slashed, so that an unpainted flap, on which some sort of magazine cutout had been cemented, hung down loosely against the scarlet ground.

"It's a Stronzo," X said proudly. "The new young Italian. One of his latest series. Cassandra found it for me. It's got real pictorial cleanliness, don't you think?"

"It's very interesting," I said politely.

At the door, he said, "By the way, I assume you saw McNeery's statement. I think Eldon's weighing in on Ab's behalf. I gather McNeery's been talking to the banks, telling them the President will cast a favorable eye on anyone who helps Ab out."

I could see he liked the challenge. He still thought only of Erwitt the man, not the institution, as, perversely, he thought of his son as the institution, not the man.

On the weekend before Thanksgiving, Abner and I went back to Starbuck for Alumni Weekend, when he would be presented with the Starbuck Medal, the school's highest alumni award. I flew up with Clio and him in an AbCom jet. We landed, ironically, at the same airfield to which X had dispatched his Convair more than twenty-five years earlier.

I had expected a gloomy flight, but neither Abner nor Clio said anything about the proxy fight or X and his slanderous attacks. Abner was full of the upcoming weekend, eager to see old classmates, anxious, I thought, to lose himself for even these brief hours in fond protective memories. The weather was fine and nippy; the campus, in the last vestiges of autumn, seemed splendid and poignant. On Saturday night, we gathered with others from our class before dancing fires in the public rooms of the Starbuck Inn, talked of the changed but undiminished strength of the Starbuck tradition, and commiserated among ourselves, over whisky and brandy, on the passing of the golden years.

The next morning, Abner received the Starbuck Medal. With the innocence of most academics with respect to real life, the principal spoke of his "great pride to be able to present this medal, which this Academy conferred just twenty years ago on your illustrious father, X. Horace H. Monstrance, like you a great Starbuck hero and benefactor," and so on. Seated next to Clio, I felt her clench briefly.

We then all congregated in Memorial Chapel for a service in memory of Starbuck's honored dead. The headmaster read from Psalms and the familiar verses of Housman: "Life, to be sure, is nothing much to lose/But young men think it is, and we were young." I let my eye travel around the chapel. At the foot of the choir, the sightless marble knight still knelt in his vigil, shield at his side, both hands before him, grasping his broad, righteous sword. Above the stained-glass windows of the Beatitudes was a row of well-varnished wooden shields on which had been painted the names of those sons of Starbuck who had fallen for their country, from Hoskins, Wm., Jr., Class of 1802, killed at sea in 1813, to Murphy, R. P., Class of 1962, killed near Da Nang. In my four years at Starbuck, I had passed away the droning Sunday mornings memorizing those names: boys and men killed at Antietam, at San Juan Hill, along the Marne, and, in an olive grove near Palermo, Mountcastle, S.A.M., V, Class of 1928. The strongest of all links to a valued past.

We rose to sing the school hymn. "Once to ev'ry man and nation"—the headmaster's strong voice led us into the music—"comes the moment to decide." We sang too loudly, as if our lives depended on it, as if somehow we could stave off the mortality written high on the walls. Abner's deep, clear voice, squarely offkey and a beat behind the tune, rang out stronger and more confident than any other.

CHAPTER 11

As Thanksgiving approached, the skirmishing became more intense, as the two sides increased the velocity and aggressiveness of their rhetoric. Abner stayed wedded to his original course. He was making sure of the loyalties of his big stockholders and letting inertia carry the day with the small ones. There wasn't an expert on Wall Street who disagreed with his tactics. Every day now, he and the other members of top management addressed emphatically select gatherings of money managers in the private rooms of the best restaurants and clubs, stressing and restressing the company's unarguably admirable record of growing profits and assets. At Duncan's behest, I attended a couple of these sessions. The mood was much what it had been five months earlier at the IEA dinner: clubby, collegial, elitist. Among these people, X's charges of corporate high living seemed thin and strident. They too were living high off the entrustment of the savings and equities of anonymous masses huddled somewhere beyond the horizon.

Abner refused to get down in the gutter with X. Not once did he attack his father on anything approaching a personal basis. Once or twice, from one or another of Abner's associates, I picked up passing condescending reference to X's age, to his being out of touch with contemporary reality, but nothing more.

X, being less well known to this generation of investors, endured a schedule that would have felled a Percheron. He devoted the first three weeks of November to a fifteen-city tour, appearing at a series of "AbCom Town Meetings" organized by Bishman's people. The latter had done their work well. They had stuck their electronic pick into crevices and fissures, and unearthed AbCom's real owners, one by one. Bus drops and car pools were organized, and X addressed full houses. The night before Thanksgiving he left for Europe, for a week of being put on display by Bouverie, Marcus. He showed me a page from his schedule. It was frightening: "Geneva, Nov. 22, 9 AM: Pictet et Cie; 10:30 AM: Lombard Odier et Cie; 11:30; Ferrier Lullin et Cie; 12:45: lunch with Leonard Hentsch of Hentsch et Cie; 2:30: Banque Privé . . ." and so on right through dinner. He took Cass with him. Her role was evident: who could doubt the vitality of a man accompanied by a vivacious, sexy, obviously smitten young woman? I began to understand that she, like me, like Bishman, like all of us, had her uses. Somehow I found the realization comforting.

Not that X neglected the institutions. He called on them before and after the "Town Meetings" and, oddly, he seemed equally able to carry his message right to the dark-paneled hearts of the trust departments of the great money-center banks. Not that it made any lasting difference, I thought, once he'd left the room, but he had this rare gift, unique in my admittedly limited experience, of converting every human encounter into "you and me against them." He made listening to him, and by implication following him, seem a matter of deepest self-interest. In a way, it was like hypnosis. It worked while he was onstage, but only that long. I doubted that it would make a lasting impression on these tough young men and women, to whom the bottom line was the supreme, the only reality.

It made a strange picture, as Mother observed, this New England aristocrat campaigning on the stump like a backwoods politician, pleading for the votes of little people, relatively poor people. We both admitted that X was a man of infinite contradictions.

Mother found it difficult to accept X as a populist. "A bigger snob than Horace never drew breath," she said over a martini at the Veau d'Or. "I suppose that's not the point, though. Is it working? It very well could, you know. Horace really does have the common touch."

We were having what passed for Thanksgiving dinner. During the fall and winter, she tried to come up to the city twice a month for two or three days, to have her hair done, see whatever worthwhile plays might be on, visit her diminishing circle of friends, look in on the law firm into which she'd merged the family practice, and have a meal with me.

"It's too early to tell. The consensus seems to be that X needs a couple of breaks." I looked at her. She looked worn down, and her cough still racked her. "Have you been to Dr. Postley? You look lousy."

"How *galant* of you, Sam." She shook her head. "Don't worry, darling. It's nothing but a cold I caught in Oregon and haven't been able to shake off."

She took an approving sip of her cocktail.

"Quite as good as your grandfather used to make," she pronounced. We called the waiter over and ordered. "It really is such a waste, this business between Horace and Abner," she said.

"That's what Jake Polhemus says."

"Jacob? My word, I suppose he's still alive, too. Have you seen him?"

I had. I'd taken him up on his invitation to call and had flown to Boston to have lunch with him.

We met at the Somerset Club. Over a sherry, we talked casually about the shape of the world. Polhemus was not pleased with the state of things.

"I'm rather worried about how important money's become to everyone," he said. "It seems almost a sort of *eminence verte*, if you will, the power behind every screen. I think Xen feels the same way—now. He didn't once. Oh, there was a time when Xen was no different from the rest of them; he wanted to make every penny there was to be made in the world!"

He sounded pleased that his old friend had at last seen the light.

"I'm very much for Xen in what he's doing," said Polhemus. "Not that I entirely approve of the way he's treating Ab. Ab's a better man than his father thinks. He always was. I don't like this fellow Erwitt at all, though, and there I come down squarely with Xen. I can tell you I've had some pretty sharp talks with Ab about it. Not that Erwitt hasn't been good for my pocketbook, but I had more than enough to start with. I do think a nation that reserves its welfare for its rich is heading in a very bad direction."

"I gather you tried to make peace between them."

Polhemus chuckled. "Indeed I did, and have—for forty years now. But there'll be no peace between those two. Xen likes a fight, you know. The biggest thing in his life was the war. He had what the English call 'a good war.' He loved every minute of it. I rather envied him; I hated it."

"How do you think it's going to come out?"

"Badly, no matter what happens, mainly because I think they both want this quarrel, which practically guarantees that it'll go too far, one way or another. Xen's always been extreme, I'm afraid. He was violent on the subject of his own father, you know."

"Who was also a tyrant, I gather."

Polhemus laughed out loud. "Good heavens, no, he was just a poor, fatuous little man who wasn't very good at much of anything. It was his mediocrity Xen couldn't bear. I love Xen dearly, like the brother I never had, but he does want everything so many ways."

"I remember you were like an uncle to Abner."

"More like a father, actually. Ab could talk to me; at least I let him finish his sentences."

That rang a bell. How many restaurants had I been in with the two Monstrances, where the waiter would ask Abner what he wanted, and Abner would start to order, and X would say "Steak." We were back on that old subject, I saw, endemic to these kinds of families; fathers who wanted different children; children who wanted different fathers. I recalled Mother once having said that we marry the wrong people in order to get the right children, or vice versa.

"Anyway," said Polhemus, "you asked how I think things will come out, and you deserve a better answer than I've given you. My people think that Ab will win the proxy, as do I, although I somehow doubt that matters will end there. It doesn't look good for Xen. There just aren't enough of our generation left in the saddle any more; they're all off playing golf or bridge at Hobe Sound and Santa Barbara; I call at a bank and get some young man who stares right through me with his voice, although at least very respectfully, thanks to the size of my account. Anyway, there are bound to be scars from all this, and they won't be good for anyone. We never learn, do we?"

"I think it depends on the teacher."

"I suppose so. Every father has once been a son, and every son may someday be a father, and still no one seems to learn. The baby boy looks up from his crib, sees his father bending over him, and believes he has looked into the face of God, and that impression stays with him the rest of his life, for better or worse, usually the latter. It's one reason I'm glad I don't have children of my own. A wise man once told me that hell is the condition of knowing through eternity exactly what your children think of you, or forever hearing their words and reading their thoughts, of at last knowing them, but from beyond the grave, from the other side of some transparent, impenetrable curtain."

"So you've taken the world as your child." It was a fatuous statement, but I was in the presence of an acknowledged great man. I felt something of his greatness myself. What, specifically? I couldn't say. There was just something holy about him; I felt as if all the rest of us, his friend Xen included, were just scrabblers in the muck.

Polhemus smiled. "You've been reading the Sunday supplements. They persist in making me out to be like that little green plastic creature in the films. If I've become an old philosopher, it's only because I've really had little else to do. I'm like a eunuch in a harem, listening to the girls' troubles and giving them my wise old uncle's advice while pinching their bottoms. Sometimes they don't take it. Ab didn't."

"How do you mean?"

"I told him that there was no question of my not voting with Xen. Simple loyalty demanded that, even if there weren't some question on the merits of the case. But I advised Ab to be tough, to play hard. And he didn't. He wants to show his father up, so he made that agreement, and that was silly of him. A man must always take whatever rules are in force and play within them. The other side will, if it gets the chance. I'm afraid the old sporting tradition was moribund even when Xen and I were schoolmates. The playing fields of Eton have long since been turned into parking lots. Ab should have stayed here, working for me. The pace was right. He would have flourished. You know, he had about six months here before Xen made him return to Granite, and I do believe he was happy!"

Over lunch, we talked about X. I commented on his strange ability to find the right denominator, highest or lowest, with all stops in between.

Polhemus replied, "Ah, but that's his native gift. Xen knows exactly how another man should be talked to. It's not just flair, mind you, much as he tries to make it seem so. He's observant; he's calculating; he reads other people uncannily well. It's a very specific genius he's got."

"Which Einstein said was an infinite capacity for taking pains."

"Actually, it wasn't Einstein, Sam; it was some Victorian woman." He corrected me apologetically, as if he had lured me into error. Polhemus's genius was for politeness. "That's neither here nor there. In the world in which Xen and I were brought up, it was considered as vulgar to be seen counting as to talk about money, not that it wasn't just as important then as now to get your sums right, or that money didn't matter as much. Life is just as much a matter of seeming as being, and Xen's terribly good at that part. Just as the President is. He was Xen's aptest pupil, I suppose."

"I somehow don't think X would like that."

"Of course he wouldn't. I stand corrected: doesn't. That's why he's trying to do what he intends to do. The President's a perpetual admission of error to Xen, you see. I've never known a man less able to live with error than my old friend."

"It seems to me that X is doing more than correcting an error."

Polhemus sipped his coffee. "By my lights and yours, yes. By Xen's: no. He doesn't live badly with his own mistakes only; not Xen. If God makes a mistake, that's just as unacceptable to him."

On the last day of November, a windy, dull morning, ABI opened with a nuclear bang: the tape printed a cross by Goldman, Sachs of two million shares at $67, up a point.

Twenty minutes later, the Dow Jones ticker announced that Communications Network Inc., Eric Shaughnessy's company, had purchased just over 2 million shares of AbCom and might increase its position. The market reacted by promptly bidding ABI up to nearly $70. I called Buck for comment.

"Hot damn," he said. "Away we go! I didn't get the word till after the close yesterday, so the best I could do was buy a few thousand after the opening. Got to have somethin' in the game! I hear some boys got rich buying options on the Coast last night. The word is that Shaughnessy's going after bear, that the standstill agreement's off, and that ol' Abner's all over town lining hisself up a three-billion bank line! Hot damn!"

The word, however, was wrong.

Two hours later, Shaughnessy issued a clarifying statement. CNI had purchased the shares purely for investment, he said, "in the belief that the market for AbCom undervalued the company's assets and earnings prospects under either of the two likely management scenarios." The statement emphasized CNI's close business and personal ties to the Monstrances and declared—a bit too piously, I thought—that CNI had no interest in disproportionately affecting the forthcoming proxy vote. Accordingly, the statement said, CNI's holding would remain neutral, on exactly the same basis and terms as the Monstrance Foundation.

The market promptly marked ABI down a point and a half as the arbitrageurs bailed out. I called Duncan.

"I told the boss man we oughta sue. Somethin' stinks here."

"How come? Shaughnessy's going to sit on his hands, the same as the Foundation."

"My ass! The two million shares he just bought came from six institutions, two of 'em f—— whores who'd promised us their proxies. That's maybe a million eight shares out of our count. Jack Young at Merrill tells me there's more stock where this came from!"

"So where does this put you?"

"The numbers are still good, but every time the institutions clean out, that's more weight to Mom 'n' Pop, and that ain't good. This f—— William Jennings Bryan act of the old man's is tough to fight. We got a call from a bank in Chicago. Some f—— woman's investment club in Winnetka went to some prayer breakfast or something and called in to tell the bank to proxy their shares, maybe fifteen hundred, for the old man."

"That's peanuts."

"Peanuts, acorns, what's the difference? The old man's done a number on us, and the boss here is just gonna sit and take it like a gentleman: lying down!"

I worked out the numbers. I couldn't see that Shaughnessy's insulation of two million shares made all that much difference. The needed majority was now reduced to just over twenty-seven million shares, but, according to Buck, Street talk still projected the incumbents to pull around eighty percent of the unaffiliated stock, which would give a total for Abner of thirty-two million, a huge margin as these things went.

Perhaps more significant, although entirely imponderable, might be the effect on wavering minds of Shaughnessy's statement that he liked ABI's outlook under either of the two contending "management scenarios." Shaughnessy was a high-visibility figure, characterized in the business press as the Robert Redford of commerce. His tacit support might do X a lot of good. I decided to go and see him.

CNI World Headquarters proved to be a smallish suite of offices in a recently renovated building a block north of the Yale Club, just across from Grand Central. When I entered, a pleasant-looking young man looked up from a copy of *The Paris Review* and asked if he could help.

He led me down a short corridor onto which two small offices opened; one was occupied by a copying machine, a telex, and a computer station, the other by a pretty girl at a typewriter. Shaughnessy's own office, at the end of the hall, was a decent-sized room. Against one wall ran a long teak-colored table, about waist high, which was stacked with books of all sizes. Above it hung a poster for a Manet show at the Metropolitan. On the adjacent wall was a Matisse gouache that I thought I'd seen before.

"Recognize it?" Shaughnessy asked. "It used to be the old man's. He sent it to me for good luck when I started this business, with a note that said it was important to have a pleasant office, especially at the beginning, when it tends to get lonely."

I took a seat across from him. He reached over and pushed a button, shutting off the telephone console.

"You answered your own phone when I called," I said. "I didn't think tycoons were supposed to do that." *Forbes'* annual rating of the four hundred biggest rich had pegged Shaughnessy at number 207, fifty slots ahead of Cass's friend Bud.

"Why not? Nothing ever happens around here." He gestured toward a paperback lying on his desk. "Matter of fact, I've been reading Gibbon. Getting ready for the deluge."

"You think it's that bad?"

"I think it's out of control. Guys five years out business school running around buying companies for themselves for five hundred million bucks, with bank loans! Everybody wants a deal; nobody wants to work. Pretty soon we better start using the country's money to build things again."

"Like CNI?"

"Well, at least there's a thousand new jobs in Silver Springs and Tulsa and a half-billion bucks' worth of new computers and microwave towers across the country."

"Not to mention a whole new information technology."

"I'm not sure that's the best thing in the world. We blip all this data back and forth, inundating these companies with information they say they've got to have, and I frankly can't see that it's done a whole lot of good as far as making things better. It comes too fast. No one has a chance to think it over." Bishman had said the same thing.

I asked him why he'd sided with X. After all, Abner was a friend too. I recalled Shaughnessy telling me how useful the Abner-McNeery pipeline to the White House had been in North Africa.

"I owe him one. He was my mentor; I was one of his bright young men. When he quit, he told me that if I saw something I wanted to do on my own, he'd arrange it with Abner so I could get some seed money from AbCom. I had this idea, and Abner kept his father's word. More or less."

"What do you mean?"

"I needed fifteen million bucks to get going. Abner said they'd cough up ten million, but I had to get another five myself, which was OK by me. Abner'd been running the company for about a year then. It was still called Granite. So I went running around Wall Street, but the Arabs had a lock on things, and the Dow was around six hundred, and everybody told you there was never ever going to be any business ever again, because it was the end of the world, and the last thing there was any of was venture capital. Today, I could raise five billion in thirty seconds and they'd be fighting to give it to me.

"Anyway, I ended up going to the old man, and even though that wasn't his best time—all he could talk about was vintage wine and pussy—he got his pal Polhemus to go fifty-fifty with him on five million for five percent of the stock. The whole deal was done in an afternoon. I've got the piece of paper here somewhere."

"What's that five percent worth as we sit here?"

"Forty million. Polhemus gave his piece to Yale a few years ago. I think the old man's still got his."

"Anyway, tell me about AbCom."

"So I go back to Abner waving his old man's check for five million dollars and he congratulates me in a kind of a bloodless way and we shake hands on a a ten-year loan at fifteen percent, with a bunch of warrants, and terms that are about as flexible as a body cast, and then I almost go broke getting it on paper."

"How come?"

"He sends over a task force. Kids: lawyers, accountants, MBAs, none of them over twenty-five. Boys and girls together, nitpicking me damn near into Chapter Eleven. First they want to review my business plan. Then they tell me what's wrong with it. And so on, and so on, and so on. Meetings? They didn't have this many meetings at the Council of Trent! I've got stuff on order, customers signed up, people signed up who've quit good jobs to come on board, a deal with ComSat on a couple of transponders for which I kissed half of Washington's ass, and I can't take delivery or deliver until I get my AbCom deal signed on. I go to the banks for some interim money and they call AbCom and some kid with the ink not even dry on his MBA tells them 'There are technical problems with the stock purchase agreement' and nothing turns the banks off like that. Here I'm trying to start a company and every time I open my mouth some kid pulls out a pocket calculator and second-guesses me.

"Finally I go to Abner. Abner, I say, these kids of yours are trying to make a gold star for their potty chart and they're making it out of my skin. I've got to get off dead center. Eric, he says in that way he's got, you must understand, we can't run a corporation of this size like a candy store; we have procedures. Well, I choke back what I want to say and somehow I get through it, ending up with a loan agreement that ties me up tighter than a galley slave all because some Tom Swift with an MBA wants to be a hero. And you know what?"

"What?"

"The reason this place works is because I've run it just exactly like a candy store. I watch the cash. I smile at my customers and pat them on the head and worry how they're feeling and is there anything they need, and every now and then I give them a little free goody, just for their being so nice. You know where I get a lot of my trainees? Disney World. I hire away kids that are used to smiling and being polite and run them through a six months' technical and sales training program we set up in Salt Lake City, a good healthy place where they don't think Donald Duck is a sadomasochistic symbol, and they come out winners."

"So dealing with Abner left you with a bad taste, and this is your revenge?"

"Revenge is for the movies. I just owe the old man for saving my ass. He's a mensch. Abner's not a bad guy, but he likes to think of himself as Mr. Cool Customer, all business, like one of those isotope machines; he measures everything right down to the last microcurie. Besides, either way it comes out, it's a good investment."

"And giving up the vote?"

"It makes my life easier. I still do business with Washington. Abner's leaning on me to put McNeery on my board. Abner's very big with Erwitt's people. I have to think about that. I hear the President's going to take a position on this pretty soon."

During the first week in December, I had an erotically noncommittal dinner with Margarita Clerc. Somehow we'd let November slip by without seeing each other. I'd been in and out of town chasing X, and busy between, and so I'd missed her lectures. She was equally preoccupied, it seemed. Carelessness and negligence of this sort are New York commonplaces. Then we just happened to run into each other at a show at Wildenstein, and we made a date. We had an agreeable three hours together, which left what I hoped was a residue of warm, good feeling to be capitalized on later, and parted cordially. December looked to be full of possibilities.

When I got home, there was a message to call Buck at his apartment, whenever.

His voice told me that my call had caused a most unpropitious disentanglement. He was breathing hard.

"Thought you'd want to know, good buddy," he panted. "The shit could hit the fan for ol' Abner tomorrow. It's all over town that American Micronumerics's going in the tank."

He filled me in. American Micronumerics had been the fastest-growing computer software company in the world, riding the coattails of Apple and Big Blue to sales of nearly half a billion dollars. The stock had risen from five to sixty, but in the last three weeks had backed off into the mid-forties. The company denied any difficulties, but the tape, it was known, never lied, and something had to be going on. Now, according to Buck, the morrow would hammer investors in American Micronumerics with a multiple rabbit punch. The company was going to announce that its accountants were forcing it to take huge write-downs relating to receivables and inventory, as well as to reverse certain reported transactions. The effect would be to turn the most recent quarter's results from a $15 million profit to a $70 million loss. There were rumors that AMNU insiders had recently sold 600,000 shares; there was talk of New York Stock Exchange and SEC proceedings and that the company's creditors had shut down its lines and were making Chapter Ten noises.

"I don't see what this has to do with AbCom," I said.

"Old buddy, tomorrow the Street's going to want to never have heard of software. They goin' to throw these companies out with both hands. And who's got 'bout half a big, big one tied up in that area? You know who. . . . Now, honey, you stop 'at!" He suddenly groaned with delight and hung up.

He was right. By the time AMNU began to trade, down almost 80 percent, the carnage had spread throughout the software sector, including any company even remotely connected with the business. Up in flames together went good and bad, solid and speculative. The usual rumors fed the conflagration. IBM was announcing a totally new operating system. No, Apple was. Floppy disks caused cancer. Software dealers were overinventoried by a factor of ten. AbCom's new database product was full of glitches. At the close, AbCom was off six points, to a fraction over $60. The day had cost its stockholders nearly four hundred million dollars.

I was summoned to a meeting at the Foundation. When I arrived, the mood was jubilant.

"This could do it!" Meyer Bishman declared elatedly. His ex-wife grinned like a mastiff.

X came in. I hadn't seen him since his trip to Europe; he looked as fit as ever. He moved around the table, shaking hands, gripping elbows, patting shoulders and arms, every inch the inspiring captain about to send his team out for the last game of its college career. When he came to me, he grinned.

"Sam! By God, what a day! I always said I'd rather be lucky than smart. How've you been? I've just been so darn busy! Meyer's been keeping you up to speed, hasn't he?"

He promptly turned the meeting over to Bishman, who asked his former wife for a recap.

"Well, after today, a lot of bets are off. As of Friday, it didn't look all that great. We've made two passes through the list in the last week, and obviously we haven't had a chance to factor in today's good news, but on our last count we were getting clobbered. Actually, we were probably doing better than it looked, but we wouldn't know that until right up to the gun, which is too late. I have a feeling we were making some headway with the big hitters."

"As a matter of fact," said X, interrupting, "I just got off the phone with a friend who's on the board of the Second Cattleman's National in Fort Worth. He says that on the basis of this news, he thinks he can have another word with the head of the bank's investment committee. I believe they have over eighty thousand shares."

"Way to go," said Audrey Bishman. "Now: as of Friday, all we could count on was twenty million shares, of which twelve is our own. Of the other eight, there was three five pledged by institutions, a million in early pink cards, and we extrapolated the rest. Between us and Bouverie, we figure the other guys for like eighteen million institutionally, with maybe another two known to be leaning. So there's fourteen million we don't know about, nearly all of which is individual. We can figure sixty percent, minimum, of that to the bad guys, say seven million shares, so what's still up for grabs is like five million. Until today's news. Friday, it looked tough. Today? Can do!" She sat down.

Bishman looked at his ex-wife lovingly. He asked Hillhouse for a report from the Street.

"They printed over eight hundred thousand today," said the investment banker, "and my trading people guess they did maybe twice that off the board. Say two million. Merrill pulled the stock off the Buy List, and we hear Goldman's going to make it a Sell."

"What about Institutional Equities Associates?" someone asked.

"No word. We're trying to set up a meeting with Pfannglanz. Get her together with Mr. Monstrance."

Now that, I thought, could have interesting possibilities.

For the first time, I felt that the positive note on which the meeting broke up was less than nine tenths bravado. At Bishman's invitation, I rode downtown with him to his offices. He had a stretched bottle-green

Lincoln elaborately fitted out electronically: telephones, computer console, television.

"Thought you'd like to get a close-up look at the thunder of battle. Man, this is a lot better now. Now we get to shovel the shit on Abner. Make him look like he's not only a crook, he's a meathead! Negative is always easier to push in this business than positive, especially from the outside."

Upstairs, he led me into a large, brightly lit room. It had once apparently been a cafeteria or storage room: the greenish paint on the walls was dilapidated; the linoleum on the floor cracked under our tread. Two large tables ran the length of the room; each was divided by a row of telephone consoles, at which perhaps forty people were sitting, twenty to a table, ten to a side. Some were talking on the phone; others were reviewing what I took to be tear-offs from computer printouts. At each telephone station was a computer terminal.

"Took this space temporarily," he said. "This is my repertory company. Check 'em out."

I looked at the people. They were young, old, black, brown, yellow, and white. There were granny types in spectacles and sinewy young men who seemed to have just returned from a run around the reservoir. There were stringy young men and chubby young men, shrewd faces and open ones. Dark Italian looks and jolly Scandinavian blonds.

"My A Team," said Bishman. "Actors Equity, every one of them. I got the idea from Lehman Brothers. Now I rent it back to them, and to half the firms on the Street. Greatest bunch of door openers in captivity!"

He explained. The trouble with telephone solicitation was that it was too depersonalized. What it needed was to match solicitor with solicitee. He'd hit on the idea of developing a corps of solicitors vocally, ethnically, and morphologically versatile enough to match any individual solicitation. He cross-referenced his acting company with the millions of stockholder profiles in his computers. Thus a little old lady in Ossawatomee, Kansas, with fifty shares of AbCom would be wheedled to vote for X by a twangy, grandmotherly voice. According to Bishman, the system was damn near foolproof, as long as he had something to sell.

"Shit," he said, "I know more about these people out there than they do about themselves."

"Do you think they mind?" I asked, trying to sound kidding.

"Who knows?" Bishman said. "Besides, what business is it of theirs?"

CHAPTER 12

Just ten days before the stockholders' meeting. I was conscripted by Cass to be her escort at the gallery's final show of the season. All the chips were on this one, and she was nervous and irritable. One of the reasons, I was sure, was that X was otherwise occupied. He had promised to look in, she told me at least fifty times, but he was having drinks with some Italian bankers and dinner with some Wall Street people. I could understand her chagrin; in her mind, she'd been pointing for just such a night, her gallery's triumph, its breakthrough, with X at her side; instead, he was off with Bishman courting AbCom stockholders.

I hadn't really seen Cass in a couple of months. When X got cracking on their social life, Abner and Clio had understandably—but regretfully, according to Duncan—put a lid on it, and I was no longer on their list anyway; I guess by then Abner had put my name in the "business" column of his personal ledger. So I was glad to see her again, to catch up, and in a way flattered to be even her escort of second choice.

She made angry, irritated little noises at her living room mirror. I knew she had plenty of reason to be nervous. She and her partners had bet house, car, and boat, as Buck would have said, on the exhibition opening that evening: "Ettore Stronzo/Raffaele Sporca: A Retrospective." It was a late opening, even though New York now remained active through January, and I had heard that the gallery had been obliged to come up with close to a million dollars in advances and guarantees against future output to keep Stronzo and Sporca out of the dreaded hands of a major Fifty-seventh Street competitor. The art world had become just like everywhere else. Artists' careers had become phenomena in and of themselves, almost separate from the body of work, as "relationships" between lovers often seemed to be aloof from passion, and were publicly evaluated in terms of money and celebrity, brought to fruition by hype as much as by accomplishment. I was discreet enough not to ask if X had put up the money, or guaranteed a loan or a bond, as something Duncan had said implied. This evening I was determined to be diplomatic, helpful, and soothing, a regular old comfort.

"What do you think?"

"You look absolutely wonderful," I said. "Don't worry. This is going to be a knockout."

I'd kept my opinions of the artistic merits of the Signori Stronzo and Sporca to myself: that I thought they were meretricious, posturing, and crude, that I thought as painters they stank, would not have been useful to the occasion. I was quite proud of myself. I was learning tact; perhaps this was what was meant by being grown up.

"I think your hair's terrific too." I meant that.

She had had most of her thick, shiny, rough-curled mane cut off. The new shape, short and severe, worked well with the narrow angles of her face; she looked knowing, ominous, intense: the incarnation of her Euripidean namesake.

There was little I could say about her costume. She was wearing a stained, puke-colored sweater caught up in a series of loose baggy folds that ended just above her knee. The garment was torn, frayed, and patched, so that one elbow stuck out, and a rip along one side bared a dark-stockinged leg almost to the hip. It was as if the Michelin Man had rolled in a grease pit, blown his lunch over himself, and then lost about half the air out of an old suit. On her feet she was wearing rubber winkle-pickers which seemed to have been fused from the shreds of old tires. The ensemble had probably cost her close to a thousand dollars at some Mercer Street boutique. If we owed the Japs one for Pearl Harbor, I thought, we owed them another for the new couture.

"Thank you, sweet." She came over and kissed me lightly. "Tactful but reassuring. I needed that." She looked at her watch. "We'd best be off. God, I wish this proxy thing was over!"

So did we all. The American Micronumerics thing had wounded Abner, but no one could begin to guess exactly how much. The confidence voiced by both sides had a hollow ring; we were all suspended in a solution of uncertainty, which had gone on too long; everyone was tired of it. The Street at least had other diversions; a bidding war had broken out in the oil industry, with many more billions on the table and in hard cash, so the action and attention had moved away from AbCom, leaving everyone involved feeling faintly foolish and superfluous. I was keeping busy on the side; an article on the books-cooking of a well-known Broadway producer had caused the sort of finger-pointing stir I relished, and I was just finishing up a piece on social public relations, based on the accumulated disgust of a leading PR man now retiring, that ought to have them wetting their pants on Sutton Place. For all that, however, I was too much a part of the AbCom affair; I had been overexposed to it and burnt by it.

On the way down to West Broadway, Cass jabbered about the show. According to her, its financial success was assured; every painting in the show had already been sold or reserved. That could well be true. The amount of money chasing art, any art, was boggling. The two Italians' prices started at $45,000; two years earlier, I knew, a few hundred dollars would have taken the lot.

"Aren't these guys a little young to be given a retrospective?" I asked. Sporca, the elder, was twenty-six.

"Their last retrospective was over a year ago. Things move faster now, darling. This isn't the Quattrocento, much as I know you'd like it to be."

"I saw the picture you sold X."

"Isn't it terrific? H.H. was lucky to get it. It's one of the last two left of Ettore's 'Blu del Blu' series. Bud and Marie got the other one. Isn't the energy fantastic? He's really got the most incredible visual rubato. I love the rage!"

I nodded, forswearing the opportunity to note that X had commented on the picture's clarity and collectedness or why, if the series was "Blu," X's painting was red. As always in the art world, the bullshit was piled higher than an elephant's eye, but for tonight I had vowed to leave my shovel leaning against the barn wall. I said, as mildly as possible, "There was certainly a lot going on visually. I have to say it looked as though it had been painted very quickly—it was sort of crude—but I gather that doesn't count anymore."

She gave a patient laugh. "Still got a chip on your shoulder, darling? Still hate everything that's new and successful?"

"Most, I guess." I was tired of this line of argument. Better to buy peace with an unmeant admission.

There were few people at the gallery when we arrived, but by eight, it was packed clam-tight, with people eddying in irregular whorls about a number of vortices. There was a crowd around the artists, young men with pitted, pale complexions dressed in the uniform of the day: punk-chopped hair, black-framed glory-hole Ray Bans, Armani fatigue jackets, baggy twill pants gathered at the ankle, every currently stylish formula of dress or chatter. The entire party, in fact, seemed as much a convention of personifications as a gathering of people. I drifted about in a slurry of acidic white wine and clever finger food.

Out of the babble, a voice at once known and unfamiliar suddenly exclaimed, "Sam Mountcastle, is that you?"

The woman who had spoken was smiling at me with a look that intimated long and fond acquaintanceship, but I couldn't place her. She was pleasant-looking, brown-haired, a bit on the chunky side, wearing a dark skirt and blazer; her eyes twinkled behind clear-lensed horn-rimmed glasses.

She saw that I was having trouble.

"Oh, Sam, I am disappointed. Have I really gotten that old and fat? You don't remember me, do you? It's Florrie, Florrie Grosvenor. Actually Florrie Grosvenor Nuywaerts da Sola Basto, although that all got so complicated I've gone back to being just plain Florence Mary Ashley Grosvenor. It's really enough as it is!"

"I'll be a son of a bitch!" We fell upon each other. "Where the hell have you been? And what the hell are you doing in this zoo?"

I hadn't seen Florrie since college. For most of our childhood, we had been bonny and boon companions. We were almost exactly the same age; the Grosvenors had lived in the apartment building across the street and had summered in East Hampton. She'd entered Radcliffe a year after I'd gone to Harvard, but then she'd vanished; *Gone to Paris to paint* was what she'd scrawled on a postcard, which had been the last I'd heard of her. Florrie and I had paddled together in kiddie pools, gone to Sunday school together, danced together, played tennis together. When we were sixteen, we'd suffered through romance and passion; one night, behind the cabanas at the Maidstone pool, Florrie had done me the initiative honor of taking my engorged and aching member in hand. The next afternoon, she took it in her mouth, which proved (fortunately for her, I always thought) the affair of an instant's confused delight before I rendered sticky evidence of my potency. That same afternoon, I had been permitted to insert a tentative wiggly finger in her faintly fleeced vagina.

Episodes like this bond people forever in memory. Seeing her again flooded me with recollection and affection; she returned to memory as easily and naturally as if I'd last seen her only that morning.

We hugged each other again, making the small exclamations appropriate to such a reunion. She smelled expensive and was very smartly put together. The Grosvenors had been rich.

"Where the hell have you been?" I repeated.

"You name it: Paris, Delhi, Brussels, Zurich, São Paulo, London. I'm living in Washington now. I've gone to work for the IMF. Making sure Brazilian peasants starve so that Walter Wriston looks good in his annual report. I'm a banker now, can't you see?" She spread her arms to let me appreciate what posed as a standard-issue "executive girl" dress-for-success outfit, but which I was pretty certain had been confected to measure on the Faubourg Saint-Honoré.

"Look," I said, "can we sneak away?" I was free; Cass had only wanted someone to come in the door with; my utility had ended the instant she'd thrown herself on the first arrivals.

"I can't, I'm afraid. I'm here with someone. How about lunch? Saturday?" We made a date.

She left and I pushed my way through the crowd toward the bar, coming suddenly upon X, flanked by Margarita and a severe-looking woman whom I recognized as Ms. Pfannglanz, the stock market's oracle on AbCom. Ah hah, went my nasty mind.

I said hello. Cass arrived and began chattering busily and possessively to X. He seemed delighted by the attention.

"Can I get you a refill?" I asked Margarita.

"I'll come with you," she said. No one seemed to notice our departure. Cass nattered on, checking the room out of the corner of her eye to make sure she was observed talking so familiarly to X, who seemed absorbed by what she was saying, but not so absorbed he didn't place a hand on Ms. Pfannglanz's elbow and draw her into the conversation.

We squeezed our way through the crowd to a bar where perspiring ephebes in bun-tight white ducks poured drinks.

"I owe you an apology," I said. "I missed your lecture again."

"I know. I looked around for you. I enjoyed our dinner."

"We must do it again. How about tonight?"

"Alas, I'm on duty. Horace wants an ally in dealing with that formidable lady he's got with him. She's apparently very important in this proxy thing."

"She is. How about tomorrow?"

"Worse: I'm going back to London tomorrow night for Christmas, and there's just too much to do. Perhaps when I return." I noticed she sounded tired and discouraged. There was a hint there that she might not be back.

"You are coming back, aren't you?" I asked.

"Of course I am." She smiled. "I'm just tired, and New York at this time of year is too much. I've got four more lectures, after all. Horace is very tiring too. The more complicated things get, the faster he spins."

I walked her back to where X was standing and talking with some people I didn't know. He gathered up Margarita and Ms. Pfannglanz and made ready to leave. Just before he did, he muttered to me.

"The Bishman people picked up a lot of good news today. It looks like we've got 'em on the run, Sam. Got a darn good break with that software company going bust. Of course, a boy's got to make his own luck. Give me a call. I haven't seen you away from the battlefield in too long." He punched me lightly on the arm.

About eleven, the last hopeful hanger-on had been dispatched into a rainy, chill evening and Cass closed up shop. I went along with her and the boys from the gallery to a fashionable bistro on Bleecker Street, where we screamed above the din over Beaujolais and indifferent sauerkraut, and much triumphant waving and flamboyant kiss-throwing took place. It wasn't my right to be impatient: Cass and her gang had just played the equivalent of a concert; this was their form of walking off the residual nervous energy, so I sat and sipped my St. Amour until it was time to go home.

At her place, Cass led me right into the bedroom. Her nervous energy was still running high, and it was clear I had one more function to perform. It was all right with me; there had been a long spell between beddings with anyone. I suspected she intended to wield my body against X as a vengeful weapon for his desertion of her in her moment of triumph. Well, that was all right too. As we undressed, she chatted about the evening, obviously on a high. The only sour note came when she mentioned Margarita.

"I saw you talking to her. She's always around H.H. these days. Does she have anything to say? I suppose I ought to read her books."

"They're very heavy going."

"I'm not surprised. She always looks so serious. I hate people who always look serious! So does H.H. I'm surprised he likes her."

This was not the time for a disquisition on the difference between being serious and looking serious. "I wouldn't be jealous, if I were you," I said. "It looks to me as if you were firmly in the saddle."

She liked that, and repaid the thought in bed. Not that it was as good as it had ever been, that would have been impossible; but given the technical and psychological limitations, it was plenty good enough.

On Saturday, I met Florrie Grosvenor at an Italian restaurant around the corner from the Morgan Library. We ordered a couple of Camparis and caught up with each other. It was really good to have her back in my life. She hadn't lost her quirky, elegant way of putting things, and she was still appealingly pretty. She'd had quite a life. After dropping out of college, she'd lived in Paris for a while, trying to paint and living off the nice stipend from home that arrived each month at the Morgan bank in the Place Vendôme. Boredom and her command of three languages had caused her to drift into Eurobond trading with Lehman Brothers on the Avenue Montaigne; the job was convenient for lunch at the Relais Plaza. After that, in the way such financial careers develop, she moved from one job and firm to another: with Citibank in Delhi, where she'd met and married a Belgian who worked for Solvay; then back with him to Brussels, which she couldn't stand, and where she'd fallen madly in love with this dashing Brazilian who worked for Goldman, Sachs; she'd run off with him to Zurich, and followed him when he went back to São Paulo, where she got another job with Citibank; then he'd left her and she'd gone to London, to a job at Salomon, too ashamed to return to New York but wanting the comfort of her native language.

"Being married to a dashing Brazilian is like having sex with an elephant." She laughed. "Everyone should do it, but not more than once!"

Now she was in Washington at the International Monetary Fund. "You might say I've spent twenty years working for the chickens, and now I'm working for the roost."

"Is it interesting work?"

"If you like the Perils of Pauline, yes. It's challenging. You have no idea of what these banks have gotten us and themselves into. I've learned to say 'deep shit' in six languages. One of these days, there's going to be a collapse, especially now that they've discovered the oil business. But that's boring; tell me about you. I've done a little research since the other night. Is it true you're living with Cassie Hargrove?"

"Was. Sort of was. We actually never lived together, but I admit we went steady. It's over now."

"Well, you don't seem brokenhearted."

"That probably says something."

"Probably. I couldn't believe it when I heard it. Easygoing, soft old you and hard-driving Cassie Hargrove! Humph!"

"I don't like the tone of that humph, and I don't like that 'soft old' business. How'd you know her, anyway? She's a lot younger than us."

"Eight years, to be precise. The Hargroves were friends of Mummy and Daddy. Actually, until he died, Daddy was one of Cassie and Clee's trustees. Not that there was much to trustee. Well, tell me about Cassie. She ran on envy the way a car runs on gas. And now Clio's married to Abner Monstrance? That must kill her!"

"Let's just say it didn't help our relationship."

"I'm not surprised. Cassie's so competitive she makes Ty Cobb look like a pussycat!"

"How do you know about Ty Cobb?"

"From you, sweetie. I learned a lot from you, and not just behind the bathhouses at Maidstone." She reached her glass across the table and clinked it to mine. "Does Cassie still dislike her sister?"

I paused. That was an interesting question. "I'm not sure," I said. "I don't think so. All I ever saw was sweetness and light. What makes you say that?"

"It's just the way they were as girls. Cassie was a year younger than Clio, and she was always trying to outdo her sister and couldn't. Clio was the favorite. Her parents doted on her. She had these perfect blond looks, kind of blah, if you ask me, but that's what the Hargroves wanted. Clio looked as if she came out of the womb in a twin set and pearls. Anyway, the parents lavished what little they had on Clio, and that was bad enough, but what really drove Cassie crazy was that Clee didn't seem to care; she kept trying to give all the stuff to Cassie, but of course it was always the wrong color or cut or something. Cassie acted as if she was the one who was spoiled. Mummy told me that after the Hargroves lost most of their money in 1958, and Clio was perfectly happy to leave Bennett and go to work at Saks, Cassie wouldn't even take a scholarship to Wellesley! They had to scrape and practically take in boarders to send her to Vassar, because they were such snobs too! I'm glad for Clio, though, if she's happy and has a nice rich husband."

"Did you see Cass last night? That was her gallery, you know."

"It was? You know I thought I did. Was she hanging all over an older man, a stocky type with a great big head right out of a Karsh photograph?"

"That was her. The man, ironically, is Clio's father-in-law, H. H. Monstrance."

"The H. H. Monstrance? The television man? My God, and Clio's married to Abner!"

"None other."

"That must make life thrilling. You know, I've read all about this busi-

ness with the tender offer and all, but I just never made the connection."
She shook her head. "So that's the famous H. H. Monstrance. He practically took my clothes off with his eyes. Hmmm! Is Cassie his mistress
now? That's the perfect role for her."

"I don't know whether she is or not. He likes to keep his personal
relations ambiguous."

"And—don't tell me—she dumped you because you weren't fancy
enough."

"Patient enough is more like it. Forbearing; tolerant. This is a new
world we're living in, filled with wonderful new people."

"Now don't sound so sarcastic. I must say, I'd been told SoHo was
bohemian, but all I saw last night were men in suits talking about depreciation." Her face softened. "I'm really glad for Clio, you know. She's
very nice, and it hasn't been easy for her.

"She and I were sisters in misfortune, you know; we both got knocked
up. I didn't dare tell Mummy and Daddy so I hightailed it for Paris. You
didn't believe all that garbage about art school, did you? I can hardly put
on lipstick straight, let alone draw a line. All for naught, though. It
turned out to be ectopic, and I ended up leaving half my insides and
any delusions of motherhood on the floor of the American Hospital at
Neuilly."

"Clio lost her only child too. Leukemia. I think I agree with you. She is
a nice woman."

"I gather they live very lavishly."

"They did, until this thing started. Frankly, I didn't like that. I thought
it was causing a lot of trouble for me and Cass, and I blamed it on her.
Now I'm inclined to think it was more him."

"It usually is," said Florrie. "Half the men I know in Washington pretend to be homebodies, but they'd die if they weren't out every night—
with a wife to blame. Abner's in Washington quite a bit, I understand."

"So I gather," I said. My journalistic reflex took over. "He's close to the
White House. What's the scuttlebutt down there about this proxy fight,
anyway? Do you hear anything?"

"Nothing much. Obviously the Administration's rooting for one of
their own. Come to think of it, I did hear something to the effect that
there's no love lost between the President and Abner's father. Didn't Erwitt work for him once upon a time?"

"A long time ago. Have you met the President?"

"Nobody meets the President, Sam, except his old cronies, heads of
state, and about a dozen New York fairies who are friends of his wife. I

don't think he knows half the Senate to say hello to. He stays in the White House and makes speeches on television. God knows, it seems to work."

We promised to stay in touch. I thought I might as well meander uptown. It seemed a good day for surveying the traffic at the busy intersections of my life. The December afternoon was cool and clear, although the weather was turning; a wall of gray clouds advanced from the west, and the morning's sunlight was being drained from the sky. The rest of my weekend was clear; compared to the activity of the last month, the prospect of forty-eight hours clear stretched before me like an open, verdant meadow.

Five days before the stockholders' meeting, Duncan invited me to an "all-hands" meeting at the AbCom offices. I could tell from his voice that the home team was edgy. In the weeks or so since the American Micronumerics collapse, the market's first regurgitative hysteria had abated in favor of a watchful pessimism, but AbCom shares continued to drift lower. The stock was now selling in the high 50s.

As they had feared, Duncan said, Ms. Pfannglanz had turned tentative on the stock, and the institutions were scaling back their positions. I'd seen the report; X had messengered it to me at the magazine with an exuberant note.

The report, headed FLASH!!!! reiterated her continuing belief in AbCom's many sterling investment characteristics; it was the concluding paragraph that did the damage:

A number of clients [she wrote] have requested our views on the proxy contest being waged between incumbent management and a group organized by the company's founder. Our normal inclination would be to vote automatically with present management, which has done an outstanding job in taking ABI into new areas having attractive long-range growth characteristics. Stockholders should be aware, however, that the dissident slate has reiterated its intention to retain incumbent management and to channel its own efforts into improving the results of ABI's (traditional) broadcasting operations. This is an area in which the dissident group has previously demonstrated inspirational expertise. While we make no recommendation in this area, we do believe that ABI stockholders should carefully weigh the possibility that a victory for the dissident slate may well leave them with the best of all possible worlds.

I told Duncan I'd seen the report. He was obviously discouraged. The more I knew him, the fonder of him I became. For all his brisk, street-smart patter, he was a sheep in wolf's clothing, loyal, sentimental, ideal-istic. He tried to hide the fact he was scared.

"Think the old man ate her pussy to get her to write that?" he said. "That sonofabitch is clever. You know he f—— us over on American Mi-cronumerics."

I didn't.

"Well, he did. I clapped on the old deerstalker and went investigating. The old bastard called in a due bill on some chickenshit bank in Massa-chusetts that was in the AMNU credit. Chase was the lead bank, and apparently they had a new loan agreement all worked out, everybody nervous but going along, and then this bank up in Worcester backed out. You know how it goes in these things: lose one and they all head for the exits. Next thing you know, Peat Marwick craps in its pants on the ac-counts and all hell breaks loose. Anyway, we're gonna roll up the big guns now. The biggest!"

He looked at his watch.

"Time to go. Needless to say, you're here off the record."

It was the first time I had been in the AbCom boardroom. A forty-foot teak slab ran down the middle. Full-length portraits of X and Abner faced each other from the end walls, the stylish *beau sabreur* of the old days confronting the determined technocrat across and over our heads, above the slick paneling and the banks of TV screens and chart racks and ex-ecutive gadgetry, above the fat leather and brass chairs and the cups and pads and onyx pencil jars marked with the AbCom logo, above the mur-mured chatter of the men and women taking their places at the table. I felt that the rest of us were involved in another, lesser reality: that even our most desperate concerns were nothing next to what was happening between the Monstrances.

I looked around at the others in the room, recognizing the fleshy, osten-tatiously elegant figure of AbCom's counsel, Arnold Plume, eyes masked by tinted glasses. Across from me huddled a team from First Stuyvesant, Abner's investment bankers. The others I took to be from Abner's equiv-alent of the Bishman Organization.

Abner came in and sat down at the head of the table. He was accom-panied by former President McNeery.

"Well," he said, "why don't you start by bringing us up to date, Fer-gus." Abner looked paler than usual. Of all the people engaged in this business, I thought, only X looks healthier by the day.

Duncan got to his feet and took a sheet of paper from his inside pocket. "We've taken some casualties." He read a short list of turncoats, including the Fort Worth bank which X had identified as a possible switch. "We still look good, though. About nineteen million in the bag, according to yesterday's phone poll. There's no way we'll do worse than sixty–seventy percent with the individuals, but say nine million there, just to be safe, which brings us up to twenty-eight million minimum, plus another million around this table, which adds up to home free but nowhere near the margin we wanted."

I studied McNeery. At closer range than I'd seen him at Abner's party for X, the shrewdness beneath his oafish exterior was apparent. There was something frightening about McNeery; he exuded greed and calculation the way other men exude cheerfulness or confidence. "One of them boys that's in life strictly for the bucks," was the way Buck had put it about someone else.

Someone at the table asked Duncan about the effect of the dissidents' mass mailing.

"It's hurt in spots. We heard from one of the banks in Detroit, with maybe three hundred thousand shares. They're catching some crap from the UAW Council, which is catching crap from the rank and file. We got a roomful of mail downstairs, which is jake with us, since if they write us it probably means they haven't leaned on the guys they oughta lean on. Most of it's been sound and fury, though."

He sat down. Abner looked around.

"This has been a difficult time for us all. We've endured some pretty rotten allegations from the other side. There are certain compensations. I think when we come out of this next Wednesday, we'll know who our friends are. One of the best is sitting here next to me. I think you'll be pleased to hear that President McNeery has agreed to work with us these last few days."

This announcement produced an outburst of throaty approbation; one could almost see upper lips stiffening. Arnold Plume's meaty features took on the sort of sanctimonious expression I had seen in Counter-Reformation paintings of saints and martyrs being angelically conveyed Upstairs. Even the hotshots from First Stuyvesant looked impressed.

It surprised me that Abner had waited so long to play this card. Of course, he would have preferred to go it alone, but he was practical enough to realize that if things got close he'd better let fly all the arrows in his quiver. McNeery would bring to bear the considerable inferential weight of his White House connections, not to mention BLEEP's network of corporate affiliation and obligation. Clearly, Abner's team had sensed that the tide might be turning; McNeery had been brought in to play Canute.

"I think you'll all be pleased to know that, thanks to President Mc-Neery, we understand that President Erwitt himself has taken an interest in the situation and will be making a statement."

Which he did, the very next day. At a televised White House ceremony at which Erwitt presented five fatcats with the second annual Presidential Medals for Corporate Excellence, the President remarked, "These awards represent a confirmation of the direction and policies we're following that's made America great again. I don't know why—"

The President paused, with a big genial grin, looking for and getting a round of jolly applause from spectators, laureates, and press for this obvious allusion to his old signature monologues.

"I don't know why, though, some people just can't stand progress. You know, it's sort of like this business up in New York with AbCom, the old TV company, where I worked for a while when I was just a poor boy getting started. Now there's progress even in TV and communications, which is why the average person is getting better programs today than ever before. Anyway, here's a management, which like these gentlemen here could very well have a Corporate Excellence medal pinned on them, doing a good job for their stockholders and all, something this country can stand straight about and look anyone else in the eye, and there's a bunch of old-fashioned people—well, I won't say that maybe jealousy comes into it, but the kind of thinking that got this country into forty years of trouble—and they're trying to get in there and turn the clock back, just when it's all coming together and America is putting some mighty proud numbers up on the great scoreboard.

"I don't think we have to have that. I've told the trustees of my blind trust to mark my proxy card for the management at AbCom!" And with that, on national television, the President of the United States took a white proxy card from his pocket and waved it with the grin and vigor of a kid waving a toy flag on the Fourth of July.

Ordinarily, this would have been a thunderbolt. The President of the United States declaring himself for one side of an internecine corporate fight? It was unheard of. Watching, I expected the press to jump all over him, but as *The Washington Post* reported the next day, Erwitt had rendered the reporters docile with an anecdote about a boyhood lemonade stand. The only adverse reaction was a spate of editorial small-arms fire here and there around the country. It made me ashamed to be an Amer-

ican; it also ended whatever doubts I may have had about which side I
wanted to win.

The bills for the final days of the battle for AbCom must have run into
the millions. As in most of life's great matters, events acquired a momentum of their own, irresistibly sucking up time, money, and energy in a
way that obliterated all sense of proportion and relative value. Perhaps
fifty thousand telephone calls were made; couriers were dispatched as far
away as Bahrain to pick up proxy statements; it was estimated that the
AbCom proxy fight alone would substantially increase the quarterly
earnings of Federal Express and Western Union. Every AbCom stockholder was contacted at least twice by phone or mailgram. The contending forces worked around the clock right through the weekend; there was
always some time zone somewhere in the world where a few hundred
shares of AbCom could be located—and argued for as passionately as a
few feet of ground at Antietam.

On the eve of the meeting, it was too close to call. Institutions were
changing their minds every five minutes. There would be disputes over
proxies, Duncan promised me. The stock had been selling ex-proxy, to
assure the best possibility of a quick and orderly decision, but a New
York court had granted a stockholders' petition to keep the proxy polls
open until twelve midnight. Trading volume in ABI swelled by a few
hundred thousand shares a day. Both sides and the SEC were scrutinizing
the tape for straw men. There were a hundred rumors.

The night before the meeting, I dined with X at 841 Fifth Avenue. I'd
been in at the beginning, he said when he called; I might as well be in at
the kill.

I wasn't surprised to find Cass there when I arrived. The two of them
were in the drawing room, admiring a mess of electrical cable which
looked like something a hasty electrician had left, but which, I would
learn, had cost X $40,000 at a gallery in Rotterdam. Cass was really
getting her hooks in. Several times, X put his arm around her waist or
patted her fanny possessively. He was in strong, keen fettle, his quick
little eyes dancing with expectation, his voice clear. We dined by candlelight on a series of miniature courses, little more than fragments of
French and Chinese cooking: thumb-size dumplings and parings of
crayfish and tiny roundels of veal with baby ravioli and infant vegetables.
X did most of the talking.

"I want to say this, with you two as my witnesses," he announced suddenly. "Win or lose, I will not forget what Eldon Erwitt said last week. He is going to regret that as long as he lives. I am going to hound him from office if I do it with my dying breath! You may take that as an oath." He spoke in a cold, blusterless voice.

I felt oddly uncomfortable, despite my own anger at Erwitt's intervention. It was now beyond doubt that X wanted me around not simply to chronicle and compile but to bear intimate witness to something that might well get out of hand.

At precisely ten o'clock the next morning, Abner called the stockholders' meeting to order, speaking from a dais on which sat AbCom's other directors. The Cotillion Room of the Pierre was packed with stockholders and thrill seekers and members of the press. To groans of disappointment, the meeting was recessed at five past ten. The tabulation of proxies was proving to be a longer, more difficult business than had been expected.

Duncan had warned me, so I hadn't even bothered to show up.

"It'll take a week," he said. "We got guys gonna go over every ballot with a fine-tooth comb, and so does the other side. The bank tells me on the QT that their rough cut shows sixty-five million shares voted out of a total of around fifty-five eligible. Some guys voted five or six times, changing every time the wind blew. So that's gotta be sorted out. If I was you, I'd go out and get laid or something. I'll call you when the time comes."

He sounded confident. The word on the Street was that the Erwitt statement had put the doubters to rout. I went back to work not sharing his confidence. Erwitt was the Street's man. I thought, and hoped, that X had tapped into other constituencies.

Six days later, Duncan woke me up at midnight. He sounded a little drunk. The meeting had just been reconvened; it was over, he said.

"And?" I was struggling from sleep, trying to organize my feelings into a semblance of caring one way or the other.

"The other side won. By six hundred thousand shares." No, there was no possibility of a recount. The proxies had been counted six times. Duncan said he was too tired to go into it now, but call him next morning or next week or next month or next year and he'd fill me in. I said I was sorry, and, strangely, I was. I'd wanted X to win for all sorts of larger reasons, big brave reasons of conviction and ideology, but there were people on the other side I cared more about personally. I liked Duncan;

he played fair; he mourned the same world I mourned. And Abner hadn't really asked for this. After forty years, wasn't he entitled to his dreams, his turn at bat? Clio came to mind, and Jacob Polhemus, and finally X. Did any of this touch him personally, or did the great mirror of his ego blind him entirely?

Should I call him now to congratulate him? Should I call Abner to commiserate? Was this like a death? I supposed for Abner it must be.

Above all, I felt depleted by anticlimax. X had painted word pictures of a war and I had gone along, persuading myself with rich bloody images of the grandeur of what, in the end, came down to bickering over pieces of paper. So much had been expended. Yet there had been no occasion for gallantry; there would be no elegant surrender, no handing over of swords. After all that had happened, there had been no grand final gesture: no tattered banner tacked to a mast. The issue had not been settled in one last fierce, mad, suicidal charge. There were no howling crowds in victorious headquarters, or jigs outside a railroad carriage, or confetti storms on Broadway, or mushroom clouds spreading against the sunrise, or even tearful, brave speeches of concession. None of that: just a bunch of accountants and lawyers and clerks haggling and tallying in the basement of a bank, and agreeing on a figure, and that was that.

I saw now that this wasn't a war at all, not a huge human enterprise which bound up the survival of millions. The great emotions inherent in this kind of contest were reserved to the few people who had something measurable at stake: money, prestige, standing, influence. I wasn't one of them, and this made X's victory less to me than I had expected. Only X himself could now make it something more.

CHAPTER 13

"You have to say this for McNeery. He was a real trouper. He kept the heat on right up to the end. Really busted his hump. But the f—— widows and orphans killed us, and the rank and file, and who'd have figured the f—— affiliates." Duncan took another long pull on his Old Granddad and paused in the middle of his monologue. He'd invited me over for an evening of booze, postmortems, and send-out Chinese food. The food was still in the kitchen in cartons; it was close to ten o'clock and he was pretty drunk.

He finally got to his feet and wandered to the kitchen to bring out dinner, which gave me a chance to look around. His apartment was something of a surprise. He lived in one of those faceless East Side monoliths. I expected to find four or five low-ceilinged rooms done up in middle-period Bloomingdale's Olde Englande: antique globes and plenty of brass and recently distressed wood, hunting prints on the walls; the furniture covered "in menswear," as Mother might have said.

Duncan's place was as minimal as Abner's office, after which it might have been copied. Its original four rooms had been merged into two. The walls were white; darkly monotonous stained wooden floors were spasmodically interrupted by pale area rugs around which a few stark pieces of furniture were organized.

The bedroom contained only a low platform bed, a sort of enhanced futon; the table next to it supported a small quartz alarm clock, a functional reading light, and, on the bedside table, copies of *The Ages of Man*, the old George Rylands Shakespeare anthology, and Schell's *Fate of the*

Earth. The closet door was ajar, revealing a row of brambly racetrack tweeds and plaids. Ever nosy, I checked the bathroom cabinet but didn't find the economy-size Valium bottle I halfway anticipated.

In the living room a low rank of pine bookcases had been built along one wall. As usual, I examined them. Duncan's books were interesting for their limitations; they seemed to fall into only three categories. There were two shelves of "social" works: books by Cleveland Amory, Jerome Zerbe, Stephen Birmingham, Lucius Beebe, Cecil Beaton; novels of society by Edith Wharton, John P. Marquand, John O'Hara, Louis Auchincloss; and "prep school" books: *A Separate Peace, The Second Happiest Day, Love Is a Bridge, P. S. Wilkinson,* a run of Owen Johnson, just as I'd seen at X's. I could imagine Duncan immersing himself in these cicerones to the trappings and inwardnesses of an upper-class life, a world he'd never made. Then there were shelves of Shakespeare, in a variety of editions: the Arden, the Pelican, the New Cambridge, the familiar blue soldiers of the Yale, an India-paper Oxford like the one my grandfather had given me on my sixteenth birthday, but just the works, no commentaries, as if the Bard was a totem to be collected in many images, the way others might accumulate bronze owls. And, surprisingly, there was a group of books devoted to thermonuclear holocaust, everything from *On the Beach* through Herman Kahn, evidence, I thought, of a puzzling obsession.

The only picture in the room was a large calligraphic Twombly print nicely framed. Beneath it, a card table held a computer terminal hooked into a modem. On top of the bookcases, a decent stereo was tuned to a classical music station. The apartment's impersonal spareness was completely contrary to Duncan's customary flamboyant presentation of himself.

While we ate, I asked him about his interest in Shakespeare. There was everything in the Bard, he said, everything you needed to know: it came in handy in preparing his Op-Ed apologias. He told me about "Quotebase," into which his computer was plugged: a data file and program put together at Princeton, a massive assemblage of quotations and information that could be summoned at a keystroke to put a good light on laissez-faire and the free market.

"It makes me feel like f—— Glendower," he said, "I summon Adam Smith and Milton Friedman from the vasty deep. Know what I got in there? I got the whole f—— *Harvard Concordance* to Shakespeare!" He laughed, got up, and poured himself another stout dark bourbon. We got back onto the subject of the proxy fight.

"The f—— affiliates were what really put the old sonofabitch over the top," he said.

I knew what he meant; *Barron's* had run a fairly comprehensive analysis of the voting. The several hundred affiliated stations that constituted the GBG radio and television networks ranged from individually owned outlets serving one or two markets to clusters of major market stations owned by substantial public companies like Taft and Capital Cities. In the course of tallying the proxies, it had turned out that—whether independently or in collusion—some fifty GBG broadcasting affiliates had purchased nearly two million shares of AbCom and voted them for X. There had been other unusual aspects of the AbCom vote. No less than 94 percent of AbCom's eligible shares had been voted; over 90 percent of the registered holdings of five hundred shares or less had voted, and X had gotten almost half of these. These were unheard-of percentages.

"The affiliates want the old sonofabitch back!" Duncan said. "They bought the stock off the board, a lot of it through Jeffries out West; nothing we coulda done about it anyway, except get the wind up. I can see their point. The affiliates don't give a shit about diversification, they don't wanna know from f—— computer software; they want ratings! And ratings is what the old sonofabitch is supposed to be the best there ever was at. They figure he gets back in, they can start marking up the rate card. ABC ate our f—— lunch in the last sweeps. They don't wanna hear Abner talking about real estate; those f—— want points in the Nielsens!"

"Two million shares is a lot of stock. Where'd it come from?"

"F—— institutions, naturally. Bunch of whores; a guy told me the money managers figured that, whoever won, the stock'd come off and they'd buy it back cheaper, which is what they're doing right now."

"What about the rank and file?"

"Oh, they ate our f—— lunch! Abner just looked right over them. I told him not to be such a f—— big shot, but he doesn't want to know from guys that don't have corner offices and three secretaries and a chopper on the roof. His wife told him to cool it too. She could see it coming, that number the old f—— did on her. Made her look like a hooker on the make. It was a smart move. Ever since all that shit went down at Bendix, the nookie angle's dynamite with stockholders. You want another one?"

He got up and made us another drink, wobbling.

"And who could figure these guys writing their pension funds? I mean what's the f—— point of a f—— money manager, if some shithead out in East Jesus's gonna wanna vote his own f—— stock in the f—— pension plan!" He was really drunk by now; the profanities dribbled from him like spittle, uncontrollable. "You know what happened?" Standing, he swayed, and put a hand to the chair arm to steady himself. "You know what happened? You're never gonna f—— believe this! Some f—— jigaboo in a three-piece suit flew into New York from Detroit and f—— ordered f—— Alliance Capital to vote four hundred thousand f—— shares in the f—— Chrysler pension plan for the old man! Can you believe that! A f—— burrhead in one of those bright green three-piece suits! Erwitt killed us with the f—— unions!"

He sat down heavily.

"Still," I said, "it was a little over one percent that decided it; that's not much."

"So f—— what?"

"So what now?"

"Who f—— knows? Maybe we all go down to f—— Fraunces Tavern and have a f—— farewell dinner with the boss man. Maybe he stays. I hear the old sonofabitch asked him to. I hear his old lady thinks he should. Shit, the old f——'s seventy-f——-five years old!"

"And you?"

"What do I think? I think he oughta take a walk. Who needs this shit!"

"What I meant was, what do you do? Open your golden parachute and float gently to earth?"

He grimaced and belched. "Hah! What f—— golden parachute? The boss man didn't believe in 'em. You know Plume, the lawyer? F—— guy's like Shakespeare when it comes to lining his own nest! He had this plan all worked out that would've put everyone over vice-president in fat city for life, plus the f—— directors, and the boss man turned it down. Wouldn't even listen to f—— McNeery! Said it wasn't in the stockholders' interest. Plume damn near shit his drawers. Me too. I was in for close to two f—— million!"

"So what are you going to do?"

Duncan leaned forward, with a loose, sly look on his face that I'd seen on every other intoxicated man I'd ever known. I'd seen it in my mirror a few times. The whole wide world's a secret, it said, and only you and I know it.

"You wanna know something?" Duncan said. "I weep for the boss man, but I'd give my f—— left nut to work for the old sonofabitch! I'm a little loaded now, maybe, but I'll tell you one thing: I'm f—— good at what I do, and I'm a loyal f—— soldier! You know him, Sam. How about putting in a good word for me?"

His thoughts drifted elsewhere, onto higher planes. It was that time of night and drunkenness; one's mind seemed to grasp everything.

"Hey," he said, "maybe this's the wave of the future. The little guy's comin' back. F—— Erwitt's a f—— Nazi! He's f—— sold us the idea the f—— country belongs to about five thousand rich people. Somehow, we just f—— forgot about the little guy. We could do f—— anything to him, and he wouldn't say shit. Look at the f—— spades. Kick their f—— black asses out in the street. Starve their f—— kids. Ninth grade, they can't even speak the f—— language! And they never said shit. Never voted. Never kicked ass the only way they could. Now maybe that's gonna change!"

That was CCNY in the fifties talking, the old street liberalism, The Way We Were; the alcohol was carrying him back.

He got up suddenly and lurched across the room, obviously off on another tangent. He pulled a book from the shelf.

"Not that it f—— matters," he said, shoving the book at me as he sat back down heavily. "You know this book?"

It was *On the Beach* by Nevil Shute.

"Greatest f—— book ever written!" he said. "Greatest f—— movie, too! Ava Gardner, that was a f—— piece of ass! A guy told me the old man and she . . ." I watched him struggle to regain the line of thought. "Gregory Peck, too. Australia. F—— Australia; you ever been there? Anyway, the f—— world's coming to an end. F—— Erwitt's gonna blow us up, every f—— one of us! Not me, though. I'm f—— prepared. I got my pill! I'm . . ."

"You're what?" But he'd drifted off, eyes closed. I reached over and took the glass from his hand and put it on the table, turned off the light beside him, and left.

Over thirty years, man and boy, I had learned one thing for certain about Manhattan women: the nigher Christmas draws, the crazier they get. Even when Cass and I were a couple, I played it solo between Hanukah and Christmas Eve. This year, I was truly alone, so I had dressed up warmly to ward off the wintry gusts of consumerist hysteria ravaging the streets and got my shopping done early. A London dealer I knew was in town with a trunk show of Victorian drawings and watercolors, and he took care of most of my problems. I bought Mother four pretty aquarelles of gentians which would go well in Bridgehampton. I decided it would be gentlemanly to say thanks for the memories, so I spent a couple of hundred dollars on a Pickwickian Christmas scene for Cass. For the most important person on my list I got a good-sized study of sunset on the Dornoch Firth. I wasn't worried about the recipient's reaction; I knew I'd love it. It brought back fine memories of looking down from the eighteenth fairway at Royal Dornoch and seeing early twilight make purple shadows on the great sickle of beach.

Two nights before Christmas, X had a big party, a combination victory bash and holiday celebration, very grand and ornamental, the apartment done to the teeth in fir and holly and mistletoe, in gilt and silver, and in notionally or genuinely important people, a good many of whom I'd seen at Abner and Clio's parties. It peeved me to see X surrounded by the likes of these; he reminded me of a good old oak crusted gray with lichen. Cass, obviously the hostess of record, buzzed about noisily, blowing kisses at all and sundry. I found it all depressing, and knew no one would miss me, so I replenished my champagne and followed my memory down the hall to X's little sitting room where I guessed I would find a television set. The Knicks were playing at the Garden, and the game was on cable. When I went into the room, there was Eugenie, staring morosely at the screen. I wasn't surprised to find her there; her Westchester Buckets were the evening's opposition.

"Well, hello," I said, "and Merry Christmas. What's the score?"

She got to her feet awkwardly. She was wearing a black gown that barely shrouded her swollen frame. The ill-suited dress emphasized her size, reminding me of Cass's observation that one reason Eugenie looked as badly as she did was that she insisted on wearing clothes scaled up from Paris originals designed for ninety-pound mannequins. The lines couldn't handle the extra hundred pounds.

She kissed me on the cheek.

"Merry Christmas, Sam. We're losing again, I'm afraid. By eleven points."

"Not enjoying the party out there?"

"You know how I am about parties. Who are all those people?"

"That's what your father said when he came back from London. Now they all seem to be his friends." There was something companionable about holiday bitterness.

"Cassandra seems to find them for him," she said; once again her place in his house had been usurped.

"It's just as well," I said. "X has better things to do with his time." I pulled up a hassock next to the set. The legend at the bottom of the screen told me the Knicks were now up by eighteen. I felt emboldened. "I wish you hadn't traded Beeney," I said. "He looked like a good one."

Orpheus Beeney had been the Metros' first draft choice two years back. He had hands like lacrosse sticks but very little personality; he wasn't a crowd-pleaser. The Buckets had let him go to Detroit for a flashy veteran guard who was known to be something of a troublemaker and frequently to play out of control, exactly the sort of player one would never expect a Eugenie Monstrance team to want. Now Beeney was racking up nightly triple doubles for the Pistons, and the swagger man was still playing out of control—in a drug rehabilitation clinic.

"You may be right," she said. "I just didn't think Orpheus was going to develop into the kind of catalyst we needed, fine young man that he was. The coach argued vehemently with me against trading him."

That had been two coaches ago. On the Buckets, turmoil was institutionalized.

Our conversation was interrupted. X came into the room.

"Ah, Sam, Eugenie," he said jovially. "I thought I'd find you sports buffs in here." He settled on the arm of the settee on which Eugenie was sitting. "My word, it's noisy out there." He sipped his champagne and looked without interest at the game. The Buckets had been on a short roll and brought it back within six. As we watched, Bernard King buried three straight stroboscopic jump shots to kill the fire.

"Listen, dear," he said to Eugenie. He patted her on the shoulder, as if consoling a six-year-old. "I've got to have a little chat with Sam, do you mind? Game's almost over anyway. Why not rejoin the party; they're just putting supper out."

She did as she was told. X pushed the door shut. He left the television running.

"Dammit, Sam, I can't think why she has to keep on with this sports foolishness. It doesn't do any good."

"Maybe she's trying to make a statement, X. You're a pretty tough act to follow."

For the next five minutes, he talked about nothing in particular, just gabbed. He had nothing to talk to me about. I got the feeling that his only purpose had been to interrupt Eugenie, to force her back into orbits in which she was plainly uncomfortable and off-balance, and to pay her the small insult of showing himself to be more confidential with me than with her. I was embarrassed for myself and shocked that he would repay her loyalty to him so shabbily. That she took it without protest didn't say much for her, I knew, but still I wished that X wouldn't keep showing me his smaller side. "Well," he finally said, "I should be getting back to the party. Coming?"

He wasn't asking, he was giving me an order. I was damned if I was going to jump. I wasn't one of his children or one of his vassals. I told him I wanted to see how the game came out, and kept watching. He stayed. Down the hall came the yammering din of the party. I suddenly wanted to get away from here, from him, from what he was, from this world, these people: I wanted to be home alone, with a good book, or a good game, or Strauss or Schubert or Lehar on the stereo. If I were really in Vienna now, I thought, I could be at the opera, and later at Demel's, and the next morning walk in the snow and watch the pigeons and, after coffee and the papers at a café, stroll to the Kunsthistorisches Museum and look at the Titians and Correggios.

There was thirty seconds left in the game, and the Buckets had somehow come back yet again and tied it up. Ten seconds left; King missed from the high post. A Bucket grabbed the high rebound and headed downcourt, where Ray Williams fouled him. Both free throws went in. Williams threw up an airball from midcourt and that was the game: the Buckets by two, a major upset.

X crossed to the set and snapped it off impatiently.

"Too bad Eugenie didn't see that," I said. I followed him back up the hallway toward the racket.

"Don't worry about it," he replied. "She wouldn't get much of a kick out of it. She only likes it when she loses."

He stopped suddenly.

"Well, Sam, what a year it's been." He lifted his glass. "Cheers and your good health, sir, and happy holidays. May the New Year profit us and our friends and discomfit our foes." I raised my glass. I had my doubts.

As always, I spent the three days around Christmas with Mother in Bridgehampton. This year, she had a surprise for me. She was going south for the winter, to stay until late March with a friend on Boca Grande, an old-money hideaway off the west coast of Florida. She wasn't feeling well, and the East End landscape, in whose winter bleakness she usually rejoiced, now looked forbiddingly cold and lonely. I agreed with her decision. Three months in the sun with little to do except widows' bridge and genteel shelling and being tended by servants paid for by a usefully ample Du Pont stock inheritance could do her a world of good. I promised to try to pay a call.

Like most people, I hated going out on New Year's Eve; like most people, I felt the only thing worse was staying home, so I had accepted a surprising invitation from Abner and Clio, surprising only because I couldn't imagine having a party at all under the circumstances. I wasn't sure what to expect: something on the order of a wake, perhaps, the guests consisting mainly of the few true friends and last hangers-on who hadn't been nimble enough to switch allegiances, or, worse, a "brave front" awash in sympathetic noises and upraised chins.

Actually, it was a perfectly agreeable evening, with excellent food and plenty to drink and company no worse or better than usual. At midnight, Clio drank a gracious toast to her husband, and we all pecked each other in a fine, friendly fashion.

Around twelve thirty, I felt a hand on my shoulder: Abner. I judged him to be in the same condition as me; he looked a little loosened around the edges.

"How about a quiet glass together, Sam, for old times' sake? Come on, I know where there's some champagne."

He led me up the twisting staircase and down a hall to the master bathroom. He flicked on the light switch: the room was lined from floor to ceiling in green marble and mirrors. A large marble tub, of a size usually found only in good English hotels, was set in the middle of the floor.

"Over there." Abner gestured to what I saw was a small icebox standing against the wall, just like I'd seen at Bud and Marie's, presumably the current fad. Abner opened it. Inside, several bottles of Pol Roger were chilling. No bottle of cheap champagne as at Bud's.

I took two glasses from the cabinet and poured. Abner sat on the john and I established field position on the edge of the bidet. A lank lock of hair drooped against Abner's forehead.

"Cheers," he said.

"Happy New Year. I know it's been a tough one."

"It's been pretty brutal, Sam." He scrunched his lips and shook his head. "Do you know, he actually thinks I'm going to stay on?"

"I think he hopes you'll stay on."

"Is that what he told you?" There was no suspicion in his voice, no mistrust. He smiled, as if upon a benighted heathen. "Well, with Dad, hope and conviction are about the same thing. You know, Clee thinks I ought to stay too. I don't know, though. What do you think?"

"What are your alternatives?"

"I've had a lot of calls. I've been offered the CEO's job at two Fortune Five Hundred companies. There's always BLEEP, especially with the election coming up in two years. I could go to Washington now, if I wanted. President McNeery's fixed up something pretty big at Defense, but frankly I'd rather wait for a seat at the Cabinet table to open up. I just don't know. Clee and I are going to Virginia next week for about ten days. I'll make a decision then."

He looked up at me suddenly. An expression of helplessness appeared on his face, like a little lost boy's. It lasted for two or three seconds at most, as if a concealed door had suddenly flown open, disclosing the guttering black landscape of his private hell.

"The thing is, Sam"—his face recomposed—"I'm probably marked as a loser now, a second-rater. Once a loser, always a loser, Dad always said."

"Come on," I said. "They pulled every dirty trick in the book, and on top of that, you had a couple of terrible breaks, and the thing still turned on a few hundred thousand votes out of fifty-odd million."

He looked at me curiously. "I thought you were a hundred percent on Dad's team," he said.

"I tried to explain to you about that. He got me involved, it's true, but only as a kind of observer."

His hand brushed away any thoughts I might have had of going into it.

"You know," he said with sadness, "I really liked working for Uncle Jake. Running the portfolio. There weren't all these people to have to quarrel with. We analyzed situations, and we bought and we sold, and once in a while we talked to a management, but it wasn't the same thing as having to deal with them. I loved doing it; I loved Boston; I loved Uncle Jake. I should never have listened to Dad."

I guessed there were a lot of people who could make that statement. I said, "X can be pretty convincing."

He grunted in agreement. "I'll say! He told me all this stuff about how it was my family duty; I was his only son, et cetera, et cetera. What could I do?" He spoke calmly, but what I heard was a cry from the heart.

"He talked to Uncle Jake, too, and you know how they are. So there wasn't any choice. So here I am. Was." He held out his glass. "Funny thing: I never could have believed Uncle Jake would have sold me down the river by going with Dad." He shook his head at his own naiveté.

"Somebody once told me that generations stick together closer than families," I said.

"I suppose so. The thing is, once I got used to it at AbCom, I got to like it. I saw what could be done, that you could run it much more efficiently just by treating it like a giant portfolio. Buying and selling; moving the pieces around. I couldn't sell that to Dad, of course, but then when he retired I could do what I wanted, and I did, and it worked. Dad promised he'd stay away, that it was now my company. Then Dad decided he was bored in England—he always gets bored—and here we are!"

"I thought X only wanted to work with your television people. You couldn't have handled that?"

"You didn't actually fall for that garbage, did you? As long as you've known Dad! Sam, you know with him there's no such thing as half a loaf. I suppose he fed you that foolishness about the President, too, about how what's going on now is a threat to the American way of life? As if Dad knew the first thing about the American way of life!"

For the next five minutes I had to listen to Abner extol Erwitt for having brought the nation back from economic collapse. He sounded like an ideologically barnacled old fart in the smoking room of the Gorse Club. I heard him out. He suffered that duality I'd seen before in other young men at the top, that vacillation between exploration and preservation that could make an Abner Monstrance by turns seem a brilliant, adventurous, foresighted manager or a mingy, retrograde, feudal relic.

"Well, what do you think you'll do?" I asked when he'd finished. I was not going to get into a debate on Erwitt. "If I were you, I'd take my chances on X's good faith." I was tipsy enough to have absolute faith in my wisdom.

"I don't know. You may be right. I told Dad I'd let him know by the end of January. He's gone to Little Gourd, and we've got to close up the fiscal year. I don't see how I can work with him, but I hate to leave AbCom. My blood's in the place. We're hoping to move to One AbCom Plaza in April. I'd like to be around for that."

His face brightened.

"At least there's this: I didn't let Dad haul me into the gutter with him. I was tempted. It got very confusing. In the end, you know, I wasn't quite sure what winning was worth. I think I do now. Ah, Sam, losing feels terrible!"

Sentiments I hadn't felt since Starbuck welled in me. I was actually proud of him. This whole thing had gotten itself backward. X had fought for the high good, and won, by getting down in the slime where the Arnold Plumes and the whiz kids from First Stuyvesant had wanted Abner to draw his line of battle. Abner's principles had been nobler than his cause, and he had lost. In each case, principle had been hammered, and so I suppose the right side had won, if anyone had.

It was getting late. Clio's voice came from down the hall, calling to tell Abner that their guests were leaving. Abner reached over and clicked his glass against mine.

"Well," he said, "Happy New Year."

"And a Happy New Year to you," I said, and I clicked my glass to Abner's just as Clio entered the bathroom and saw us sitting there and began laughing.

Just as soon as I thought I had January organized just right, X called to invite me to Little Gourd Key for a few days in the middle of the month. I accepted; I was curious to go and see what had really become of a place that was full of good memories, and I liked the idea of the sun, and the dates proposed by X dovetailed nicely with the Super Bowl, which I would be attending as Buck's guest. I further justified the trip on the grounds of business: alone with X, I could begin to get chapter and verse on his specific plans for AbCom and GBG, now that the company was his once again to rule. I had begun to write the story of the proxy fight and to interview a number of people who had figured in it.

Bishman had furnished me a cross-section of AbCom stockholders, a list of about fifty, and I intended to talk to them all. So far, the half dozen I had interviewed over the phone had mirrored Duncan's liquid analysis of the outcome: they had voted for X as the champion of the little guy, the disenfranchised; most of them thought that all Abner did at the company was spend their money on parties and jet airplanes. Talking to them, I began to sense a larger story, something I now saw that X had seen; these were people embittered by a decade of hopes and realities destroyed by inflation. A number of them had voted for Erwitt, because he looked and sounded like one of them and because he promised that things would be better. But things didn't seem to be, even though all the numbers about GNP and suchlike were good; no one they knew was doing much better except the stockbrokers.

I planned next to start a canvass of the institutions. I was particularly interested in the interplay between the professional fiduciaries and the pensioners and policyholders whose interests they stewarded and spoke for. I was excited, because I sensed a big book here, about America and the transformation of its capitalism; I felt that I was starting to see it come clear. At the same time, it was important that I stay on top of the new story that would be breaking, and I told myself it was important to go to Little Gourd. That it would be sunny and warm, and the sea blue, made it just that much better.

First things first, however, so I continued my interviews and, when I was sure she had returned, made a date for lunch with Margarita.

She insisted on Le Cirque and announced that it was her check.

"Absolutely," she said. "Horace has put me on the payroll as of the first of next month, as a consultant."

Rude thoughts as to possible types of consulting services crossed my mind. Across the room I caught sight of Bud Schreck dealing ferociously with a plate of pasta. I could expect to find him on Little Gourd. The Shrecks' new tropical house had been in *Architectural Digest*, together with a suite of photographs of Marie impersonating various Balanchine ballets under the palms.

"He's led me to believe that you'll be coming over too, although more as an observer," she said.

"At AbCom? I fear he's led you incorrectly. I love X, but I keep my distance. You can find me at the magazine, although I'll be around sniffing." I told her a bit about my interviews and the excitement I was beginning to feel. I could see that she, too, was on an upbeat, so I asked, "Tell me, are you liking it any better here?"

"I think so, now that it seems to have quieted down. I had a lovely time in London, though. And then I went to Venice to stay with Mamma for New Year's. We had the *acqua alta*: the Piazza San Marco was flooded. It was wonderful! I wish you could have seen it."

I didn't want to sound too flirtatious. "I wish I could have," I said. Naughty thoughts crossed my mind. Outside it was howling; a nice afternoon with a fire . . . my apartment had a good fireplace—in the bedroom. I added, "I'm glad you're liking it better here. You're a considerable ornament."

She sipped her wine and studied the tablecloth as if truth was somehow woven into the linen. She reminded me of X in London, staring into the ruby depths of his glass of claret, peering for auguries.

"Well, that's very complimentary," she said at last. "I'm not sure I understand it."

"What in particular don't you understand?"

"For one thing, I don't understand New York dinner parties. No one flirts and no one argues. They simply talk about the price of things and their itineraries. Lions sit next to lambs, and no one except me thinks it's peculiar. I went to a dinner just before Christmas with Horace. A very elegant party given by a very admired lady. Apart from the usual tycoons and favor seekers, the guests included that man who was let go by the *Times* for giving stock market tips and two people I was later told had bankrupted really quite large companies. Isn't there such a thing as disgrace any more?"

"Not really. Not here. No shame, either."

"How do you distinguish the two?"

"The concept of disgrace means you don't invite people like that. The concept of shame holds that people like that don't show their face in public." I was quite pleased with the remark.

"And I have to tell you," she said, "that I am completely baffled by the behavior of the press. They all seem to be best friends with the sort of people they should be on the lookout for. I suppose there's nothing wrong with them mixing; in London, after all, it's not uncommon for the editor of the *Times* or the *Observer* to find himself at dinner with some pirate from the City, but the next day he'll like as not savage him. Here, it seems, he simply writes something agreeable about the host's wife's table linen."

"That's what the lion's claws have become; to borrow your metaphor: instruments for scratching the lamb's back."

"Well, I think it's very limited and really very unhealthy. No one in England talks about money. Not at a dinner party, at least."

"Now you're sounding superior. You need only remember what they say on Wall Street: happiness can't buy money. Did you see anything in London that you liked? How's the Neapolitan show?"

We finished lunch talking about books and the state of capitalism and movies and fashion. I liked her conversation; she infused the lower subjects with a nice sense of larger meaning, finding in them serviceable metaphors for more significant considerations, yet when she veered onto the high-minded, she tempered her phrases with the sharp bite of gossip, personalization, and balloon-puncturing. As Bill Klem, the great umpire, said of himself, she called 'em as she saw 'em, which is how I thought of myself, and so I felt an additional good bond, a ligature as strong in its way as the erotic pull, grow up between us.

Outside the restaurant, I asked, "Can I walk you home? This is a large and dangerous city. I'd even come up for tea. I could even stay for dinner."

She looked at me levelly. "That might be fun. But not today, sadly. I've some meetings, and I've committed myself to colleagues for dinner." There was not a breath of teasing I could detect.

"When I get back then? I've got to go south for a few days."

When we parted, she stood for a moment watching me go. I knew also that if she was to come seriously into my life, on any basis, there could unequivocally, absolutely, be no one else. I was unsure whether I could handle that, was ready for it, or wanted it.

Almost forty-eight hours later to the minute, the AbCom Gulfstream passed over the southern edge of the cloud cover that covered the stretch from Boston to Nassau like a solid blanket of suds, and started on its final approach to Little Gourd Key. As we swept in over the island's eastern edge, I had only a moment to seize the impression that the place looked much more civilized and settled than I remembered.

I wasn't surprised. I had read articles in *Harper's Bazaar* and *W.* I knew that the ramshackle control tower toward which we now taxied contained equipment that NASA would envy. I knew that it had been acknowledged for over a decade now, by those to whom such intelligence was crucial, that the place to be from January to Easter was Little Gourd Key. I knew, from hearing Cass talk, that it was now pronounced "Cay."

Little Gourd was the smaller of a pair of bulbous islands about two flying hours south of Miami, twenty or so square miles of what had once been white beaches ringing scrubby savannas. When I had first gone there, thirty years earlier, the trip had involved a forty-minute flight from San Juan in a Grumman Mallard belonging to the Little Gourd Key Club. If the weather was down and the seas were running, the trip over by boat could take six hours. Now it was four hours from New York to an all-weather jetstrip.

Great and Little Gourd Keys were separated by a channel about half a mile across, punctuated with shifting sandbars; sometimes a line squall would flash in across it, obscuring the view of Great Gourd from the spit of beach above which X had built a rambling fishing lodge. A spindly dock had been built fifty yards or so out into deeper water, with a thirty-foot outrigger Chris-Craft tied up alongside. In those days, Little Gourd was still essentially what it had originally been settled as: a sanctuary for perhaps a dozen reclusive Philadelphia millionaires, who had invited X, whom they knew from salmon-fishing on the Restigouche, to join their loose contributory confederation, the original Little Gourd Key Club. They had put in a basic infrastructure of roads, docks, and power lines. It was strictly a man's place, then: black tie and backgammon in the evenings, a life essentially on and in the water. Then the first wives and mistresses had come, and so it went.

In the comfortable little terminal, I was treated to a display of native-style forelock tugging, had my luggage cleared without inspection or question, and was led to an air-conditioned Lincoln.

Our trip took us the length of the island, through what now resembled an opulent Miami suburb. The palms had been replanted into an alignment as precise and formal as Versailles. By the side of the white crushed-shell road, black men poked aimlessly at hedges and fronds. I lowered the tinted window, to the chauffeur's evident consternation, and the warm, richly scented air, with its remembered hint of dampness, flooded in around me. Some things don't change, I thought thankfully. There's not a man on earth rich enough to reorganize the feel and smell of this air, the beat and color of this sea.

After about twenty minutes, we drove up to a whitewashed ironwork gate with a huge painted escutcheon, and, in gilt letters of Trumpian dimension and ostentation, a sign reading LITTLE GOURD CAY CLUB, and past a guard box manned by a native tall enough to play power forward for the Celtics. He was uneasily decked out in a bearskin busby and a tropicalized Guards uniform. He smiled and saluted. Inside the gate, my apprehensions mounted in the realization that I was in for an ordeal by money.

We passed a boring-looking golf course and a cluster of tennis courts. Low-roofed villas hunkered down among artificial-appearing clumps and clusters of spiky tropical trees and plants and beds of flowers too bright to be real. We passed at least three armed security patrols in what looked like armored golf carts. The club itself, once a rickety, inconsistent collection of conical thatched-roof pavilions, was now a large stucco edifice fronted by a sweeping white gravel driveway; at one side, a tower, some sort of condominium annex, I guessed, was in the last stages of construction.

We turned down a road I thought I recognized, paralleling a wide white beach that curved out to a point marked by a stand of trees.

"We be heah, sah," said the driver.

There was nothing I found familiar about this house. The place I remembered had consisted of three simple blocks around a lush, devil-may-care wild garden with a spring. We had eaten and lounged around in the largest, a room open on three sides to the sea and the sunset; the others contained bedrooms and rudimentary bathrooms. The house I now entered was a whitewashed stone and plaster mansion swooshing with the blast of air conditioning. I followed a uniformed major-domo past a formal little library that would have been more suitable for a freezing weekend in Dorset and past a long high living room, double the dimensions of the original, done up to the nines in bougainvillea chintz and shell-framed mirrors and lamps. He led me down a wing to a sunny, cheery room overlooking the beach.

"Mistah Monstrance to lunch ovah Mis' Getsmore, sah," advised my guide. "Miss Hargrove too, sah. He say you join theah or he see you heah after, sah."

I said I'd be happy to unpack and stick around; it was not great news to hear that Marty and Shermie were on the island, but whither Bud and Marie goest, I thought, so went they. I put on a bathing suit and went out to the pool. It was nice to undo the trauma of moving so quickly from the dull, pewtery skies of New York to the soft brilliant light of the tropics.

The butler offered me caviar and champagne, but I settled for a sandwich and a glass of beer. While it came, I took a plunge. The pool had been built where the wild garden had once been. On my other visits, all the swimming was in the lagoon or the channel, or on the south side of the island, in the ocean. Little Gourd was surrounded by reefs which kept out the sharks. We'd swum naked off the dock, and fooled around on the beach, and stayed on the water until we were burned the color of wood. Now I might as well have been poolside in Locust Valley or Santa Monica.

The day was so pleasant and calm I figured I could stand the worst the place could throw at me in the way of Shrecks and Getsmores and all they entailed. I was only due to be there for four days, and X had promised to find me a free ride over to Miami.

I ate my sandwich and then took my towel and went down to the beach and lay on the baking sand. I found myself thinking of Margarita, shifting languidly in response to small twitches of excitement as my drowsy thoughts turned erotic, obscene. Around a quarter after three, noises from the driveway signaled the return of the houseparty. I got up and went to say hello.

There was X, Cass, a couple I'd met in East Hampton, and Loomis Hartley and his wife. Hartley was the great shining star of television newscasting, the reason ABC had taken the lead in the evening ratings. Like Erwitt, he had been a protégé, a creation, of X's, but his twenty years with GBG had ended in a contract dispute with Abner. Now, I had read, he was in a fight with ABC about money.

We shook hands and kissed cheeks and chatted briefly. They were all a little bleary from what I gathered had been a long lunch accompanied by torrents of white wine. It was agreed that we would foregather on the living-room veranda around eight, after a nap and a bath. We were due, it seemed, at the Getsmores for cocktails, after which there was another "little cocktail" at the club and then back here, augmented by the Getsmores' household, the Shrecks, and some others, for dinner.

I returned to the beach until I knew I was risking incineration and went back to my room. A few minutes later, there came a quick tapping at the door and Cass came in. She was obviously horny.

It was all very businesslike, but no less exciting for that. She shrugged off her shirt and the bathing-suit top underneath and crossed the room and put one arm around my neck, looking up at me with an odd purposeful glint in her eyes. She slid her other hand into my trunks.

"Don't think I didn't see you all hard when we came back," she said. "Were you thinking of me?"

There was no point in saying I hadn't been. Besides, she'd had two years to learn how to turn me on, and I liked the idea that she obviously wasn't getting adequately serviced by the man of the house, and we were sober, and so we had a pretty good time together. Afterward, I watched as she got back into her shorts.

"I've always heard that's the trouble with power fucking," I remarked conversationally. "All power and no fucking." She looked at me curiously, as if she'd just emerged from a dream or been caught sleepwalking. This must be tough on you, I thought. It can't be easy. I got up and gave her a hug. "I loved that," I said. "Don't worry, I won't say a thing. Provided you don't make me sit next to Marty Getsmore."

She giggled and left.

The evening dragged by in snatches of overheard dialogue. I felt I was hearing lines from every comedy of manners ever written: ". . . Said we could take the chopper over to Lyford for lunch . . . awful husband of hers couldn't keep his hands off me . . . not keeping the money supply tight enough . . . Arnold plays golf all day long, so what am I supposed to do? . . . look, I said, honey, you keep getting me off three times a night, you do whatever the hell you please . . . Ben's got the G-Three here so I might go to Palm Beach for some clothes . . . the last time I saw emeralds that big was at Persepolis, and you know what happened to them! . . . drinks too much and he's spent every penny she had . . . what do you suppose Getsmore was before it was Getsmore? . . . well, if you like that sort of thing, Jamaica's all right, but I think that Tryall crowd's a pretty dull lot . . . heard he made a hundred million on the Marathon deal alone

. . . she knew the rate for doing a cocktail party was forty, and yet she offered them a hundred, and you know how poor these people are . . . I gave each of the kids a mil and after that they can goddamn well take care of themselves . . . when's Bunker getting here? . . ."

The Getsmores had built themselves an imitation Hyatt House; I couldn't believe my eyes when I saw that the sign at the end of their driveway read "Hog Heaven." But I restrained myself from making any remarks about death wishes of the rich and steered myself through the events of the evening with tact and agility. Looking around, however, I took small confidence from the fact that the collective bank accounts of this collection of second-raters added up to a respectable fraction of America's liquid capital.

I had been looking forward to Caribbean food at X's—rum punch, grilled fish, key lime pie—but we were served crêpes de volaille and wines that walked with a heavy tread. I tried to make conversation about the weather in Fez in May and what one paid a gardener in Southampton. I endured a plenitude of toasts. When I went to bed, Cass came to my room, as she did each night that I was there.

I felt no ambivalence about sleeping with her, no feeling that I was cuckolding a friend or patron. I asked for no pillow talk, and she didn't volunteer it. Several times, in her embrace, I imagined I was making love to Margarita, once even to her sister, Clio, and I felt no shame about these fantasies either. Somehow our roles vis-à-vis each other were now defined. This was what we had to give each other; this is what it always had been. Now we could enjoy it, our bodies said, for this brief time, without emotional trills, ornamentation, or complication.

By day it was different. Then I felt, again, like a piece in the wrong box. There was no time to be alone with X. He spent his mornings alone in his room or closeted with Loomis Hartley, and when at noon he appeared on the beach or at poolside, it was in his role as resort baron: all pasteled, mindless affability. He laughed over rum punches at Shermie Getsmore's complex jokes and made solicitous rumbles of sympathy at Marty and Marie's hairdressing difficulties. After one or two tentative stabs, I saw that he really had no intention of serious conversation with me; he just wanted to be sure I was around, the way an old lady checks her china cabinet.

Ordinarily, this would have irritated me terribly and I would have huffed about work I ought to be doing, but the weather was good and I was here with no way to get back, even if that had made sense. I could see Cass was unsure of how to fit me into the whirl, so I saved her the trouble. I took myself to the island's beaches with my Walkman and listened to *Csardasfürstin* and plowed through a couple of good thrillers I'd brought and made notes for my pieces on AbCom. In the evenings I put on my best bright trousers and my best bright face, now considerably ochred by the sun, and nibbled at whatever it was whichever jet had brought in that morning from E.A.T. or Dean & DeLuca or Fauchon or Dallmayr's. It wasn't great, but it was certainly bearable.

Eugenie arrived on my third day there, on short notice, with a great many attaché cases and, apparently, a lengthy agenda of AbCom matters to discuss with her father. He had invited her down reluctantly, at her insistence, but having her on the island, in his house, was evidently as far as he was prepared to take it. In front of all of us, he rejected her request that he give her an hour or two later that afternoon. He wasn't going to miss the Getsmores' croquet tournament, he said. They'd flown in two pros, specially, from Palm Beach.

So she ended up spending only one night on Little Gourd, which was a blessing for me, since I could hook a ride over to Miami with her the next morning. She hadn't planned to go over until Sunday, the day of the game, but X's message was clear, and so a flurry of phone calls produced an invitation to spend two nights with friends in Del Ray.

That night, Cass said to me, "I think it's very exciting that you're going to be working with H.H."

"You're the second person who's under that misapprehension," I said. "Where's this coming from?" The question was obvious, so I corrected it myself. "What's X saying about me?"

"Maybe I got it wrong," she said. "I thought I understood that you were going to work at AbCom."

"Well, I'm not! As a matter of fact, I'm about the only person on this island who does not seem to revolve around X like the solar system. You people are like Saint Francis of Assisi in reverse; you've taken the vow of wealth!"

She didn't say anything for a minute. I must have sounded pretty testy.

Then all of a sudden, for no good reason, I got really angry. I was abruptly, uncontrollably furious with X's presumption, and at him and Cass, and at what had happened to this island, and at the Shrecks and the Getsmores and everything else, beginning with life in general and going on from there. And Cass was the object nearest to hand.

"What happens when I leave tomorrow, anyway?" I whispered. "Do you have one of the tennis pros lined up? Or that big buck who rakes the yard? Or is it back to business as usual? What do you do, play with yourself while he watches? Or do you play with him? I can't imagine he can get it hard enough to get in! Or is it the old 'Roman Charity' bit; do you let him suck on those big tits of yours? Like this. . . ." I reached over.

She sat up straight. "You are hateful," she said. "Think of all he's done for you! What a bastard you are!"

"Done for me?" I started to recite my list of grievances, but she was out of the bed, halting at its end for a moment, a wraith in the darkness; I thought I heard her make a sound, a sob, a whimper, and then she was gone, and I was left talking to the vague hum of the air conditioning.

CHAPTER 14

After the mealymouthing of Little Gourd, it was oddly comforting to plunge into Super Bowl Weekend. This was the other side of the coin of the New Prosperity: white-minked, open-collared, gold-chained, blow-dried, down-and-dirty, peel-off-the-C-notes America. Buck had rented a large apartment at the Palm Bay Club for the weekend and had promised a wingding. I was ready.

Eugenie's limousine dropped me at the club. I asked if she'd be at the league party the following night.

"I don't think so. I will be at the Dolphins' party Sunday night after the game. Will I see you there?"

"If there is any decency in life, I expect to be dead by then. After Little Gourd, I need a transfusion of real life, and I have a way of doing these things to excess, so the reaction may be severe. If we miss each other, I'll call you in New York." I thanked her for the airplane ride over from Little Gourd and watched the beige Rolls pull away.

I had found our few hours together interesting. She had a very classy plane, a spic-and-span new Gulfstream III. My friendship with the Monstrances was turning me into a regular connoisseur of private aircraft. I complimented her on the plane's interior.

"I'm glad you like it," she said. "Do you know this chintz?"

I didn't.

"It's what Selena was going to use in the drawing room at Upperville. Do you know, she had a hundred yards with her when she crashed. McMillen had Colefax and Fowler make up a new lot for me." The vindictive satisfaction in her voice was unmistakable. It sounded sick to me. These people didn't even leave the dead alone.

"Whatever happened to that house?" I asked neutrally. I thought I knew the answer, but I couldn't come up with it.

"Don't you know?" she said. "Father sold it to Abner." Now her tone was bitter. "Or Abner asked to buy it. It doesn't really matter which, does it?"

There was no suitable answer to that, so I simply nodded as sympathetically as I could and looked out the window. The ocean below gleamed bright, clear green; it seemed to me that I could look right down through its depths to the heart of the earth. Little Gourd was a dull, sand-colored stripe disappearing behind us.

"I understand they've taken up riding to hounds," Eugenie continued acerbically.

"Really?"

"Yes. I gather Clio cuts quite a figure on a horse." Her voice softened abruptly and she shook her head, as if remonstrating with herself. "I shouldn't go on like this. I'm really very fond of Clio. Tell me, how did you find Father?"

"To tell the truth, faintly ridiculous. I don't think much of his equatorial court. I like to think of him as different; the idle rich don't suit him, not that they're exactly idle on Little Gourd."

"I despise that place," she said strongly. "I always have. I remember the three of you used to go there. He certainly didn't have much time for me, after I flew down specially to meet with him. There's a lot we have to talk about."

I felt myself being put into an uncomfortable position. I didn't want to be the Monstrances' all-purpose confidant, most certainly not when it came to their personal feelings about each other. To some extent, it was inescapable and—frankly—even useful, but I didn't want to seem to encourage it. I knew that curiosity could all too easily be taken for, mistaken for, sympathy or partisanship, and I wanted to skirt that trap, so I treated her question like a sucker punch and tried to slip under it by simply saying "Really?" as noncommittally as I could.

"Yes." Her voice was proud now. "Father and I came to an understanding when I agreed to give him my proxy. I'm to be in charge of all of AbCom's nonbroadcasting activities. I've been reviewing them since the final tally was determined, and I've really got quite a few ideas." She gestured across the aisle at a small stack of obviously expensive leather attaché cases. "But he said he didn't have time just now to discuss them. Can you believe it?"

I could. X had merely talked of agreeing with Eugenie about "oversight" of certain operations. I asked myself whether neutrality precluded a little mild family diplomacy, decided that it didn't, and said, "I expect he's waiting to hear what Abner's going to do."

There was patient certainty in her voice. "Oh, Sam, everyone knows Abner's going to go to Washington."

I nodded as if to agree and returned to my scrutiny of the horizon, on which I could now see more trouble brewing. She, too, seemed to feel that we had taken this subject as far as we could; with a sound approaching a resigned sigh, she reached for one of the briefcases, pulled it to her, and began to study a folder of closely typed pages filled with figures. I got out my thriller, and we continued in this mode all the way into Miami.

Her limousine vanished around a corner of the driveway, and a boy came out of the club and took my bags. I was swept into a welcoming cacophony of tinkling glasses and noisy, anxious, boisterous voices, a kaleidoscoping display of loud-voiced women with too much hair and deep tans, replicas of Marty Getsmore minus twenty years and a few hundred million; the expected knockout airheads, stewardesses, New York and Miami and Dallas models, Rodeo Boulevard beach babies, surrounded by puffy guys, young and old, bulging in linen and poplin, medals ajangle; up against them were cohorts of good-looking thin guys, mostly younger and surely less flush, in brightly colored golf shirts with club insignias: Augusta, Cypress Point, Seminole. This was the kickoff of a seventy-two-hour Happy Hour, the longest and most exuberant in the universe.

Over the loudspeakers came a counterpoint I'd heard before, the last time I'd already been to Miami for one of these, Colts vs. Cowboys, 16–13, in 1971: "Paging Joe Namath . . ."; "Paging Roone Arledge . . ."; "Tucker Frederickson, please call the operator. . . ." At a table in the corner, looking as though he hadn't ever left, was a nice-looking man in string glasses surrounded by a dozen empty glasses and a pleasingly diversified selection of what I took to be Pan Am flight staff. "What a way to go!" he shouted to no one in particular. "What a way to go!"

A glow of contentment settled on me. It might not exactly be the most uptown setting I could choose, and certainly about the least intellectual, but after the attenuations and edginess of the proxy fight and the dopey pretensions of Little Gourd, it would be good to be an animal for three days. Across the room I saw Buck, up to the gunwales in tasty-looking women, and so, shouting the modern equivalent of *Joyeux garde!*, the chivalric battle cry, I plunged in with both feet, hands, and anything else that reported for muster.

To the extent I remembered it, the Super Bowl itself wasn't much of a game, but then it seldom was, and the game wasn't the point of the weekend. One team or the other always seems to lose its edge or wits or both in the two weeks leading up to the contest. The papers later told me that the Saints won 31–14, which was OK by me. On the eve of the game, I had been reintroduced to the delights of cannabis, and so I sat there like a tailor's dummy in the Orange Bowl, adrift on a crest of good feeling and a sense that the world was turning at the rate of about one foot a year, so thus it was only faintly that I recalled George Rogers taking about six hours to complete a sixty-six-yard breakaway for a touchdown, and the kid playing quarterback for Denver throwing a couple of big interceptions, the ball staying up like the Goodyear blimp, while somewhere in the enormous distances in my head a band played the "Blue Danube Waltz."

Buck always took a group of clients and sources to the Super Bowl, with the express purpose of "strengthenin' ties with them good ol' boys in the investment community through screwin' and drinkin' and doin' a lot of real good dope." It was a good scene for him; he sounded like a character in Dan Jenkins's *Semi-Tough*, which was bigger than the Bible with most of his guests. "The only way to get them big blocks of stock," he told me in a rare moment of mutual lucidity, "is to beat the institutional traders into submission with sex and liquor and other fun things. 'Cept the Canadians, of course; they just take cash and stay back home in Montreal and ice skate, or whatever it is they do." He had everything arranged to suit his guests; lest their charms prove less than overwhelming, our group was soon joined—indeed, overrun—by a group of New York and Miami "models" whose ready susceptibility to the attractions of the traders was remarkable.

We were headquartered in a condominium overlooking the club pool with a fine sideways view of Biscayne Bay. It had five bedrooms, plus a pair of kitchens in which relays of caterers' men kept the food coming. My age and intellectual standing put me in the small single by myself; the others were shared by a varying cast of three to five institutional investment types and whoever they were pairing off with, in couplings successful or unconsummated, at any given moment. The best bedroom was occupied by Buck and his consort of the weekend, a sharp-faced ex-model who did PR for a Manhattan specialty store. She was stuffed with cocaine when I got there, and stuffed she remained, wafting febrile and ghostlike in and out of the smoke-fogged rooms.

"Strictly role-playing," Buck said, showing me to my room. "I wouldn't diddle that old dawg with someone else's dick, but those guys think them skinbag model types are the best, and they put me down as a real class act."

On and on and on it went. I thought wistfully that Duncan should be here and made a mental note to introduce him to Buck in proper fashion. As a party it was great; as a logistical feat it was awesome. Cases of wine, beer, and liquor arrived almost by the minute; the food, which ranged from stone crabs to tacos, was replenished just as frequently. I didn't do cocaine myself, but one expert from the equities desk at Security Pacific estimated that $50,000 worth of the sweet white powder went up the group's collective tubes on Saturday night alone. Occasionally we shifted venue; there was an afternoon at poolside in which memory drowned in a vat of mimosas, a bus trip to Sea World that was underwater the whole way. Basically, however, it was one single-spaced, seamless revel: a continuum of intoxicated waking and carousing broken only by tiny intervals of restless sleep.

It was, as expected, hardly stimulating to the mind. Conversation tended to be limited. One guest, a senior investment VP from an old-line Worcester casualty company, sat drooling in a corner muttering "f——bumper," whatever that meant, over and over for nearly thirty-six hours straight. The "What a way to go!" man joined us for a while. In the background were the usual marginal types: a few veteran studs, retired players from Buck's years in the NFL, who came, saw, licked their lips at the free meat on offer, and set about them, sword and buckler. It was not in fact a halcyon time for adherents of the Equal Rights Amendment. Then there were the nervous nellies who kept whining "what's next" and thought they'd try just a small toot, looking anxiously over their shoulders as if the narcs were about to kick the door down, and the football addicts who never left the television and spent their hours soaking up every marginal or trivial particle about the game.

I wandered around semi-dazed. It never got dull. Especially when I ran into Moira Riley, the reporter from *Newsday* I'd met up at the Vandals camp. She was having a terrible time. The paper had sent her down with some jerk from the psychology department at Hofstra who was writing a serious study of the ethical dynamics of professional sports. We were going through one of those awful periods when sports were picked up on by sociologists in search of metaphors.

"This guy is really an asshole," she said. "Can you believe he's got a contract with Oxford University Press to publish that shit?"

I persuaded her to come up to Buck's to share a demijohn of Mt. Gay rum I had discovered and secreted under my bed. Then it seemed like an awfully good idea to go over to the NFL party at the Doral, so we took a twenty-dollar taxi ride out to the Beach and found a tentful of jerks in terrible neckties and funny haircuts all standing around trying to look as if they knew something, so we took another twenty-buck ride back to Palm Bay, where we were sure we'd be safe from assholes, as she put it, and after we smoked a joint and had at a little more Mt. Gay, it was "why not?" time.

It was the only instance in my life I could remember, thin though my memory of the occasion would prove, when making love to a woman could be fairly described as "neat." Moira had a cute little face, after the glasses came off, and after we'd gotten as undressed as seemed absolutely necessary, or as pure impatient lust permitted, she proved to have a neat little body, with neat little pale and pink breasts, and a neat, snug little whatever tufted with a neat little reddish bush, and she seemed to think everything was neat, too, and so it was. She left me while I slept, with a note saying *Thanks—gone to work.* I figured I'd catch up with her in New York.

After the game, I flopped. The next thing I knew, about what seemed like a century later but turned out to be just after midnight, the phone was ringing, beating like Big Ben against the rusty recesses of my head. My mouth tasted as if the Syrian army was on field maneuvers between my teeth.

It was Cass calling from Little Gourd.

"Where in the world have you been? Didn't you get the message?"

I mumbled something.

She went on angrily, spilling words, confusing me. I tried to pull my awareness together. Abner had had an accident. In Virginia. A bad accident. A terrible accident. He was unconscious. He was worse than that; he was critical. They were flying there now. X was. She and X were.

I shook my head as she talked on, practically screaming at me. It was like a voice in a nightmare, and it wouldn't stop. Did I have a pencil? she screamed. Yes. Yes. I wrote down the address of a military field north of Miami. Yes, yes, I would be there in an hour.

Like a Pavlovian dog aroused by a bell, I got up, dressed, packed, and telephoned for a taxi. I did so automatically, which should have told me then what I didn't figure out until well on the way to the airfield, in the musky, still, Florida night full of sounds and the sickly intimations of decay. They had called, X had called, and I had jumped. Jumped to attention like a servant, an obedient child. I knew then that it was worse than I thought, that after twenty-five years the old knots still held, that I was still part of them, and, very likely now, for good.

CHAPTER 15

Throughout our mercy flight north, X alternated between extreme vexation and moderate concern, often as if he, not Abner, had suffered the accident. His expectations and assumptions had been disarranged; to X, this was the same as if his own life had been turned upside down. Several times he repeated to me, to Cass, to the cabin at large, "I don't see why this has to happen now. I was counting on Ab. This throws everything out of kilter." Only once did he show even mild contrition, when he remarked that none of this might have happened if he'd stayed in London. For most of the trip, he remained closeted with himself, staring at the cabin roof, drumming his fingers on the folding table; from time to time he fiddled with a paperback of Emerson's *Essays*, pretending—I thought—to study it with intentness of a country priest at his breviary. Finally, as we started our descent into Dulles, he said, "Well, now that Ab's out of the picture, I'll just have to manage some other way," and looked at me significantly, which sent the hairs on the back of my neck tingling with warning.

All we knew was that Abner had been thrown from his horse, struck his head, and was unconscious in a northern Virginia hospital. It took us the better part of an hour to drive through the freezing dawn on roads slick with ice; when we got there, Abner was still unconscious, his pulse and vital signs steady but his electroencephalogram filled with confusing signals. Clio looked wrecked with mingled grief and fatigue and confusion. When Cass rushed up to her and started the full Lillian Gish routine, she pulled back, hunching up within herself, too full of strain and tiredness to play the game. The arrival of the great H. H. Monstrance was obviously an event; the hospital administrator appeared, followed by the attending doctors, and all but genuflected to X, drawing him aside, leaving Clio, Cass, and me to fend for ourselves as they briefed their illustrious visitor on his son's condition.

X exuded grave and great concern, nodding soberly, knowingly, as the physicians talked and gesticulated, making it clear by his close attention that the doctors were speaking to a professional kinsman, a man who had been a trustee of greater hospitals than this, who was on a first-name basis with the noblest names in medicine. Predictably, when the doctors had finished, he asked to use a phone. I knew the form; he would be calling chiefs of service at Columbia-Presbyterian and NYU Medical, summoning them to Abner's bedside to render their verdict; an H. H. Monstrance needed the opinion and artifice of better than country doctors, even for a nosebleed. His world of medicine was peopled not by doctors but by "top men." I recalled when Abner had broken his arm our first year at Starbuck, a simple break, little more than a greenstick fracture; the GBG Convair had hurtled into Portsmouth NAS and disgorged half the senior orthopedic service of the Hospital for Special Surgery.

As X went down the corridor to the administrator's office, I saw Clio watching him with an expression that, if translated into heat or energy, would have melted him to jelly on the spot. I returned my gaze to my shoetops. I didn't want to draw her attention to me, to be included by inference among her enemies: the father-in-law who had disgraced her husband and the sister who was his—what, concubine?

X returned shortly. Dr. Bloom, Professor of Neurology at Physicians and Surgeons and head of service at Columbia-Presbyterian, the "top man" in New York for this sort of thing, was just now leaving for LaGuardia, accompanied by two senior people from NYU. An AbCom Learjet would be able to land at the local airport only fifteen minutes away. As an afterthought, he added that the plane could take me back. Once again, I found myself feeling that I had become a sort of mandatory ornament in the Monstrances' lives, of no special value except for the mere fact of my presence.

We waited for two hours. There was no change in Abner's condition; the oscilloscopic information transmitted from his brain remained perplexing.

At one point, X took me aside.

"It doesn't look good," he said. His solemn assurance was worthy of Dr. Zorba. Why don't we wait for the real doctors? I thought.

"If Ab can't cut it," he said, "I'm going to need some help. Someone I can trust." He sounded like Caesar looking about himself for men who slept o' nights. He put his arm across my shoulders paternally, collusively. "I meant to discuss this with you in Little Gourd, but there didn't seem to be any urgency. Now . . ."

I could see he was leading up to what both Margarita and Cass had hinted at. I decided to try to cut him off before he got started.

"X," I said, "a couple of little birds have whispered in my ear that you've got an idea I should come over to AbCom with you on some pretext. Is that right?"

He didn't say anything. I continued.

"This is obviously the worst possible time and place to discuss this, but we might as well get it out of the way. First of all, that wasn't our deal. Second, I like what I'm doing; I like the magazine; it's important to me to at least appear disinterested. If I don't, what I write won't be worth a shit, and neither of us wants that, least of all me. I admire what you're doing; I applaud it, although I have to say I wish it could have been done without spilling so much blood. This is potentially the biggest story I've ever had, but so far it's just the beginning, and I've got a half dozen other pieces I'm working on that I want to finish." I debated momentarily whether to list them, and decided, time and place notwithstanding, that there was no point in demeaning him by lumping his great crusade with reporting on a shopping-center scandal, rumored kickbacks in the art trade, and the change of command at Macy's. "You and I understand each other, X. You've always said that. I want to watch, and get it right, and write it down so that it will mean something. But I have to do it from a distance. I can't do it on your payroll; it doesn't matter where my heart is, or my allegiances, or my affections; I'm a journalist, and you know what that means, and what it can cost."

He nodded slowly. "You're right," he said. I watched him think it over. He knew what I meant; he'd once given GBG News the green light and it had cost him an embassy. "Well, it was just a thought." He went over to a bench and sat down by the two sisters. Instinctively, Clio edged away. X took out his Emerson and scrutinized it fiercely; I watched him build a mask of quiet concentration behind which, I was certain, his mind was working feverishly. I was sure he was furious with me, but that was one of the risks of life. We put people in imagined positions without asking their permission, without really even seeing them, and lose our tempers at them when they choose to walk away.

A while later, the New York doctors arrived and went into consultation with X and Clio. There was no further use for me here, if there had ever been.

"I guess I'll be off," I said. The taxi that had met Bloom's jet was outside. I could see that it was light now. Icicles had formed on the bare limbs of the trees on the hospital lawn. "I assume you and X will want to stay here with Clio," I said to Cass.

She looked at me as if I'd spat on the pope.

"Are you insane? That's Selena's house. H.H. could never stay there. There are two or three good inns around." She had acquired that Monstrance assurance; the best rooms would always be available, as a matter of right; it would have been so if X had shown up in Bethlehem.

I shrugged and started for the door. Clio came down the hall alone. There would have to be more tests, she said, but Abner was showing signs of emerging from his coma.

"I'll drive you to the airport, Sam," she said. "I've become sort of a supernumerary around here. A little air'll do me good. You'll be all right, won't you, Cassie?"

As we drove through the still-sleeping countryside, Clio told me about Abner's accident. They had gone for an early ride, as they always did on Sundays. She had a gift for description I'd never noticed, or hadn't listened for, or hadn't chosen to hear. Her words made the scene vivid. The morning had been cold and fine; the frosted ground crackled under the horses' hooves. They had paused at the high end of the gentle valley in which the farm sat. It had been quiet, the horses' snorts the loudest sounds for miles. Suddenly a rabbit had broken from a nearby coppice, scooting under Abner's horse and startling it. Abner had been talking to Clio, with an easy hold on the reins. His horse shied and bolted, ran perhaps fifty yards, and then stumbled, precipitating Abner over its head. He had crashed head first into a stump. She hadn't known what to do. She'd covered him with her quilted vest and galloped to the stables and called an ambulance. Everything else we knew.

I said the usual things.

"Was it nice on the island?" she asked, her voice now flat and tired. "We were supposed to go next week. Abner was going to tell his father. . . . Oh, hell, it doesn't matter, does it?" Her voice broke.

We drove the rest of the way without saying much of anything. It did matter, and I did want to ask what decision Abner had reached, but for one of the few times in my life, a sense of propriety overwhelmed my curiosity and I kept silent.

I thought about it further on the flight to LaGuardia. Outside, the pink-streaked morning became cold, blue, desolate, as if the sun had been filtered out. As we crossed over Manhattan, I looked down and saw the floodlit skeleton of One AbCom Plaza; in the dreary light it looked like a giant monument to forlorn hopes and abandoned dreams. She's right, I thought; it really doesn't matter now, does it?

Although Abner was unconscious less than forty-eight hours and out of the hospital in ten days, up and walking about, it was soon apparent that the stump against which his runaway horse had pitched him had dented more than his skull; it was as if a piece of delicate machinery, a typewriter, say, had been dropped onto a hard floor from a small height: the visible damage didn't look all that bad, but the critical machinery was surely not working as it should. According to Cass, Abner was afflicted by periods of forgetfulness, by intervals of impenetrable distractedness; on the other hand, she reported, his overall mood had changed for the better: he smiled a lot, and laughed, and seemed, if possible for Abner, even carefree much of the time.

The doctors called it "a neurological transient," she said. Clio was going to take Abner south, to Palm Beach, to recuperate. As it stood, there was no way he could return to AbCom, but after a month or so of rest and sun, who could tell?

I didn't see X for quite a while. In paranoid moments, I assumed he was put out with me for turning him down. The fact was, he had moved into AbCom and it was taking up his entire life and concentration. This I got from Duncan, who called, exultant, to thank me for putting in a good word with "the Chief," as he seemed to call X. I hadn't liked the way I'd left things in Virginia, and I could understand X's predicament and need; he would want an ally, a confidant, a point man, a dogsbody, the kind of man for all functions and seasons that people like X seemed to rely on. I thought the least I could do for X was to propose a substitute for myself, and so I wrote him a note telling as much as I knew about Duncan, and what I thought of him, emphasizing my sense of his loyalty to king and country, CEO and corporation, and left it with X's doorman.

My life turned quieter and, frankly, unspeakably duller without the Monstrance circus. One way or another, first with Abner and Clio through Cass and then with X, I'd been involved with them, in an escalating way, for almost two years. Now: zero. I can't say I missed the strident buzz of the high life, but I was aware of its absence. From time to time, I had a drink with Duncan, and the relish and excitement in his voice as he described the authority and panache with which X was recapturing AbCom from his son's memory sometimes left me wondering whether I'd made the right decision. I knew I had; it was just that I felt the odd twinge, the ounce of doubt that made one say: if I had gone to that party, after all, maybe the girl of my dreams would have been there.

The weather didn't help. Winter wore on in a skein of unrelieved gray dampness. I was suddenly bored with my work. My subjects were all so negative: malfeasance, corruption, cheapness, tawdriness, pretension, vulgarity were the lines on which this washing was hung. X at least was—would be, presumably—on to something positive, enhancing, classy.

I did manage to live in control, obeying the precepts of Mountcastle's First Law of Urban Existence, formulated shortly after I turned forty. It held, simply, that only about 70 percent of life, no more, was essentially controllable. The balance—leukemia, airplane crashes, defraudation, no laundry pickup—wasn't, and therefore one should not go bananas trying to make it obey. I'd watched too many friends go down one set of tubes or another, or wear themselves to an enervated frazzle, trying to put a handle on every particle of their lives, so I put 100 percent of my effort into the 70 percent and took my chances with the balance.

I spent a lot of time with other men: Buck, Duncan, other writers, guys from the Street, art dealers. This was in obedience to another of Mountcastle's Great Life Truths, not so much a law for living as an insight for eternity. It held that every notionally, chronologically adult male is actually part boy, part man. I wasn't talking about Peter Pan syndromes and not growing up, just that the boy part needs the companionship of the boy parts of other adult male personalities, while the man part constantly needs to be confirmed through the affection and erotic submission or seduction of women or, in some cases, other men. Which was a roundabout way of justifying a string of pub crawls and midnight hamburgers at Clarke's or scampi at Elaine's, and a whole bunch of time at Madison Square Garden where, one night, at a Rangers game, I encountered Moira. She had in tow an earnest young man in a three-piece suit and one of those cubical legal briefcases.

Circumstances did not lend themselves to a detailed, public recapitulation of our hour of passion at the Palm Bay Club, so we talked sports.

"How about those Buckets?" she asked. Eugenie's basketball team had been on a tear, winning eight out of twelve since mid-January, with a recent four-four split on a road trip. "What'd I tell you? All they needed was to get their owner put in quarantine."

She explained. The word was that Eugenie had become so completely wrapped up in AbCom that she was practically never seen at the Twenty-third Street headquarters of her sports complex.

"It seems the son and heir's come out of his deep sleep with only about forty of the required fifty-two cards upstairs. The Empress has jumped into the breach. Best thing that ever happened to the basketball team. I can't wait to see what it does for her others."

The next day I called Duncan and found him in his usual sunny mood. "The Chief" had canceled the AbCom "advertorials" in the *Times*. The space was being taken over by the National Rifle Association. I asked him about Eugenie.

"Oh, lord, she's all over the place. Ordering reports, holding meetings, busier than ten beehives. Five or six times a day she asks to see the Chief about some big report or study she's made, and once in a while he sees her and listens to her, but nothing's changed yet, and it's my guess nothing's gonna change until he and the lady professor are finished thinking through whatever it is they're thinking through." I wondered whether it was sobriety or the influence of "the Chief" that had banished profanity from his discourse. He now spoke with the circumspection of a Scottish presbyter.

As he'd brought the subject up, I asked him about Margarita.

"She's around. They have a lot of meetings and spend a lot of time in the screening room watching tapes of our shows. It's obvious they're hatching something." There was no hint of prurient connection in his words.

I'd meant to call Margarita, but my mood hadn't been right. I wanted to serve myself up to her perfectly prepared, and an evening watching Bird and King go one-on-one, which is all I seemed to want to do these nights, probably wasn't the right setting.

From Cass, I heard little about X but much about the life of which I was no longer a part. She seemed to call like clockwork, and once or twice dropped the hint that a night together might be a resounding success, but my mood for that had passed on Little Gourd—forever, I hoped—and I valued our chats mainly for the reports she brought of life on the front lines.

Certainly the city's social inanities continued unabated, which was both diversion and distraction. In the mysterious fashion of such fads, the movers and shakers had discovered *fin de siècle* decadence and fallen to it with a vengeance. Sets of Proust and Wilde walked out of the better bookstores to keep company on the choicest night tables with the Seconal

and the K-Y. Cass described to me a "Come As a Proust Character" dinner given by the Schrecks following a new Joffrey ballet of *Within a Bud-
ding Grove*. All the women had been in velvet and the men in ruffled shirts
and pipestem evening clothes. I imagined Bud had looked particularly
appetizing. She described giant torchères blazing in the perfumed night.
"The path of Swann leads only *du coté de chez* Schreck," I remarked, but
she didn't get it. Nor, I saw somewhat sadly, did she perceive the true
paradox of the evening: that how truly corrupt and degenerate was the
spectacle of these people playing at what they thought was "make-
believe" decadence.

But in this way I got through February, the dreary worst of winter, and
that, in New York, was at least something. The end of the month also
marked the finish of what might have been called X's period of gestation
within AbCom. Things started to pop. Early in March, Duncan called
with the first bulletin.

"The Chief's canned every outside consultant on our payroll. You
know how many that is? Seventy-three! We were taking from twenty-two
outside firms telling us how to run our business. McKinsey; Booz, Allen;
SRI—he said, Throw every one of 'em out of the office. Bust their
meters, he said. 'No more chin scratchers,' that's what he said, his words
exactly, 'No more chin scratchers.' Guess what we were spending on con-
sultants?"

"A million a year?"

"Five mil. Can you believe it? The staff payroll here last year was over
fifteen million, and still we paid a bunch of jerks in pinstripes five million
dollars to tell us what to do! You know what the Chief did with their
reports?"

"No."

"He told the Senior VP–Administration to get rid of 'em, so the guy,
one of those real think-for-himself MBA types, asks should he have them
shredded? The Chief says no, just send 'em over to CBS; the way things
are over there now, they go in for this sort of . . . foolishness!" It was
tough for Duncan to completely manicure his speech; like a lot of people,
profanity was for him less a matter of expression than of native rhythm;
the epithets corresponded to the ticks of a metronome.

The next blockbuster, this time public, fell at the end of February, and
brought me back in contact with X. It was announced, with much fan-
fare, that Loomis Hartley would be rejoining the network, coming back
from ABC at an estimated $3 million a year to anchor "The GBG Eve-
ning News." An interview in the *Times* quoted X as saying that the hiring

of Hartley was an effort, pure and simple, to beef up the ratings by injecting a heavy dose of star quality.

That ran exactly counter to what X had originally complained about in London, the vaudeville character of television news, and certainly didn't square with his repeated assertions to me that he intended to change the style and practice. Of course, the heady air of network competition might have caused X to welsh on his commitment to me, and to himself, but I wanted to know. This was the sort of thing that could be central to the story, so I called and made an appointment to see him.

Getting to the AbCom Tower left me in a vexed state. It was a grimy sort of day, a Wednesday crowded as always with theatergoers; plus the carte blanche which the real-estate developers had been given had injected several hundred thousand additional people into an eighteen-block area, threatening to rupture the desperately strained membrane of service and civility that was supposed to hold city life together.

X had taken over his old office, the one in which I had met with Abner barely five months earlier. It had been transformed. Abner's stark ambiance had been succeeded by an agreeable, opulent disorder. The walls had been paneled; two sides of the room were faced with bookshelves. A piano stood in the corner opposite a paper-cluttered antique partners' desk. The electronic jumble I remembered from years before had returned updated: four television monitors, recording and tuning devices, stereo equipment, laser players. There were a couple of large couches set at right angles around a coffee table. The room was careless, casual, welcoming, and comfortable, part sanctum sanctorum, part a Renaissance studiolo, part a college master's study. It was a little too pat, however: about 40 percent X and 60 percent carefully pieced-together setting for a constructed persona.

He watched me look around.

"Quite a change from the way Ab had things, eh? I felt as if I was in a jail cell!"

"I'll say. How's it going?"

"I'd rather expected you to ask that question before now. Cassandra tells me you've been in a pout. Have you been put out with me?"

"I thought it might be the other way round. Frankly, I've been pretty busy, and from what Duncan tells me so have you."

"Good man, Duncan. You were right about his loyalty. He breathes Granite, eats and drinks it. I like that. I still wish you'd reconsider about joining me. It's not as if I was asking you to lay down your life."

He really didn't see that in a way he was.

"I'm sure that we could come to some arrangement that would suit us both."

"I doubt that, X, I truly do. Let's stay friends. Tell me about Loomis Hartley. I thought the one thing you really hated was what news broadcasting's become. I think the word you used was 'vaudeville.' I saw the story in *People*. Duncan must have planted it. All about Hartley's yellow neckties and his Samoyeds." I stopped just short of saying "for shame!"

"I could answer that for you, Sam," he said, trying not to talk down and not really succeeding. "I will admit that Loomis should give us an immediate three-point jump in total share, and for what I have in mind, it's critical that he start with the largest possible audience. I don't want to say more than that just now. It's better that Loomis explains himself."

I guess my expression said I expected him to clap his hands and make Hartley materialize in a puff of pink smoke from a nearby bud vase.

"No, not to you in person"—he chuckled—"but from the screen. Much as you hate to watch television, as you've often enough made clear, I want you to do me a favor. I'm putting Loomis on the air Monday night next, and I want you to watch our evening news for a week. I'm going to send you tapes of the other networks. You'll be wanting to make some comparisons. Just give me about six hours of your time, and then tell me whether you think I've broken faith."

I agreed to watch.

As he showed me out, he remarked, "You know, Ab actually brought some fairly capable people on board, even though at first I was never quite sure what they were talking about. They kept going on about 'corporate culture,' whatever that is. But I've got them started speaking and thinking in English again, and I'm pretty happy with them. Granite's a good place to be, Sam. We're bedrock."

On the way out, I asked a secretary for directions to Duncan's office and followed a maze of hallways until I heard him speaking loudly over the telephone. His office was obviously in the middle of redecoration. Duncan was standing at a desk or table covered with a dropcloth. When he saw me, he hung up.

"What's this deal with Hartley?" I asked.

Duncan opened his palms. "How do I know? The Chief's not saying. Isn't he in great shape? What a guy!"

We agreed that he was indeed that and promised to get together to swap our reactions to the all-new "GBG Evening News with Loomis Hartley."

Afraid that I might miss some point or subtlety, I taped Hartley's first five newscasts myself and watched them through twice. Then I watched the tapes of ABC, CBS, and NBC which X had sent over after Hartley's first week. Then I repeated the process. And again, before I got it. Hartley wasn't the point. Nor were the events and images that made up the news he reported. Hartley was there strictly for the reason X had said he was, purely as bait, to draw viewers away from Reynolds and Jennings, Brokaw and Mudd, and Dan Rather, to ensure the largest possible audience.

The big story of the week was President Erwitt's trip to the prairie states. As hard news, it was strictly a non-event, just another fuss cooked up by the White House to keep the President on camera. As usual, the networks threw almost a quarter of their allotted twenty-two noncommercial minutes into covering his trip through Kansas and Nebraska.

But not GBG, which took me three passes through the tapes to realize, and which left me shaken at the atrophied condition of my perceptiveness.

Over the five Hartley newscasts, a hundred and ten minutes, roughly, of total air time, "The GBG Evening News with Loomis Hartley" devoted exactly two segments of one minute each to the Erwitt procession across the wheated plains. None showed Erwitt. Each was put on just after the first commercial break. Each was devoted to shopworn sentimental images: threshing machines and the skyline of downtown Omaha. For each, Hartley's voiceover was approximately the same: "While the President's ceremonial tour moved to Wyoming today, the attention of the nation turned to the more important business of . . ."

It was quite simple. X intended to reeducate the audience as to what, in fact, was news. I doubted that the audience would realize it was being done to them, which I told X when I called to congratulate him.

"They may not, Sam," he said, obviously exuberant, "but I can assure you Eldon does. I've already heard from the Communications Office of the White House. They're hopping! This is just step one!"

"What's next? I saw you put on more economic news."

"Right on! Money's on everyone's mind. Then we added a minute or two on Central America, where it seemed justified, and on Congress. It's like a martini, Sam; it's all in the proportions. In television, thirty seconds here, fifteen seconds there can change the way people see the world."

That was the sweet irony, I thought. By telling the audience that their attention was turning, Hartley was turning their attention. The truth was in the supposition.

"Am I wrong, or did the other networks start to scale down their Erwitt coverage toward the end of the week?"

X laughed robustly. "Got that, did you? Good for you! The preferred
form of competition in America is imitation. I had Arbitron run confidential overnights beginning Monday. We picked up share every night
after the first. I made sure the news about the ratings leaked over across
the avenue."

"So where do you go from here?"

"A number of places. Miles to go before we sleep, Sam. Robert Frost
came to Starbuck and read to us, you know."

He'd come to us too, I thought.

"Our policy now is that simply being President isn't a news event of
itself. If Eldon does something that's honestly newsworthy, we'll carry it.
If Iacocca does something earthshaking, or that boy that plays for the
Mets—Raspberry?—we'll cover it. The world's making news twenty-
four hours a day in every latitude and longitude, and we've got twenty-
two minutes three times a day to digest it."

I asked him if he expected trouble. Not right off the bat, he said. The
other networks would either follow him all the way, in which case they'd
hang together, or they'd revert to the old pattern, in which case there
could be no complaint, what with three out of the four networks following the usual pattern of showing the President doing everything but going
to the john.

"I think Eldon's popularity as a television star is now going to be put to
the test. Let's see if the people demand him. We'll know soon enough. I
remember the letters NBC got when they took Berle off the air. We'll just
have to see what the public says."

"And Erwitt, and BLEEP?"

"Oh, those two absolutely!"

He spoke with relish.

Just two days later, now restored to the good graces of the lord and
master, I went to a dinner party at X's for a French banker who, according to Buck, "had 'bandoned the land of his birth for the money he
loved." My real reason for going was that X had promised that Clio and
Abner would be there, as Abner had come north for a few days to be
examined by a new team of top men, this time from Mount Sinai. I was
anxious to get a firsthand look at Abner, and, to be honest, I wasn't put
off by the prospect of seeing Clio again.

Cass was not there. She and her partners were in Sarajevo, trying to sign up a collective of conceptualist pottery makers on whom they'd been tipped by someone from the Met. To my doubled pleasure, it turned out that my late consort's place as X's designated hostess was being filled for the evening by Margarita, very dark, tan, and sexy in long black crepe.

She came up to me at once, carrying a glass of champagne. I guessed that she was nervous in this unaccustomed role; she drank her wine quickly, in staccato little birdlike sips.

"I've missed you," she said. "I thought we'd made a date."

"These have been times that try men's souls," I said. "I've been in hiding, playing schoolboy. I do it every so often. I think it keeps me young."

"Really," she said. A waiter brought us more champagne. She looked at me appraisingly. I had a feeling a decision had been taken; I hoped it was what I thought.

She tipped her glass toward me; a few drops speckled X's Aubusson. She looked almost wicked. "I'd like to catch up. Horace says I'm only on duty until after dinner. Why don't we go somewhere, then, and have a drink."

I thought that was a good idea, a wonderful idea.

Abner and Clio arrived shortly thereafter. The change in him was immediately apparent. He looked about the same, still good-looking, still tall, a commanding sort of man, but the lines of his face seemed to have softened; he looked boyish. He came shyly into the room, smiling as if just glad to be in the same place as the grown-ups but not quite sure exactly what to say or how to act. I watched him embrace X, watched X step back and look at his son, beaming as if to tell the rest of us, Look here; see how, at last, thanks to God, I have exactly the kind of son I have wanted and deserved. His affection, strange to say, was almost cruel.

Clio had also altered. Her troubles had attenuated her solid good looks, giving the stretch of skin over bone a newly taut, almost saintly refinement. Her eyes seemed larger in her face, more luminous, more knowing. She had become, I thought, very beautiful, a testament to the transforming power of martyrdom, a Castagno saint in an Oscar de la Renta evening dress.

She saw me and came over.

"Hello, Sam. How are you? We've missed you."

"How are *you*? Abner looks well. Is he?"

"He's all right. No worse than can be expected." Her voice sounded strong. "We've been in Florida; it seems to have been good for him, at least for his body."

Abner came over. "Hello, Sam," he said. "Gosh, it's really great to see you." He made it sound as if we were meeting back at school after separate vacations. The stentorian bonhomie was gone, the sense of the big man orating down. Much as I knew what it cost these two people, I somewhat liked the change. This was an Abner I'd never seen. It was as if a pumice stone had been taken to his mind and personality, polishing down the edges, smoothing the individuating crags and irregularities. Listening to him, I wondered whether, as he lay unconscious and his mind was left free to find its own way, it hadn't erased that nexus of pride and tension that had driven him from childhood. He seemed perfectly aware of what was going on and made reasonably good sense. I suppose I'd expected him to drool or to lapse into unexpected vacant silences, staring at unseen horizons within himself, but there was none of that.

Dinner was announced, and we went in to X's gleaming dining room. I had been placed next to Clio, which pleased me. I took it for granted we were good enough friends not to have to fence around.

"I guess he won't be going back to AbCom," I said.

"No." Her voice was bare of regret, and of other feelings.

"It's probably just as well."

"Is it? It was his life."

"That was the problem. For both of them. One company, and two lives depending on it."

She looked down the table at X. The set of her lips told me that nothing more need be said on this subject. Watching her, I thought how like Cass she was, and how unlike, and that the similarities and the differences were the right ones.

"So what will you do next?" I asked.

"I'm not sure. It depends on how he does. We'll stay in Palm Beach through the end of the month. He likes it there. He's got his golf and the ocean and his clubs, and everyone's been quite understanding. The doctors say it may change. We'll just have to see. Tell me, do you miss Cassie?"

"Sometimes."

"What a good answer. I think you were good for her, Sam."

"For a while. She's found other pastures now: larger and greener." I cast a meaningful look around the dining room, taking in the Stronzo on the end wall, the glistening silver candelabra, the Adam mirror above the sideboard, the celebrated guests.

"I wish her well," Clio said. "Cassie's very ambitious. Perhaps they go well together; they both treat people like Kleenex. Cassie wasn't that way originally, though."

"I'm afraid it's an easy trick to learn."

There were a lot of questions I wanted to ask her. Personal questions, about her life and her feelings. I watched her look diagonally up the table at Abner; she gazed at him with the sad pride I'd often seen in mothers, full of awareness that the child now carelessly at play must grow up into a world and into a self likely to be full of trouble and ingratitude. In Abner's case, I saw, the direction was reversed; Clio was staring at a memory.

There was a sudden tinkling of crystal, and Abner got to his feet. I looked at Clio. She smiled patiently, as if to say: it's all right.

"I just want to thank Dad for Clee and me," Abner said. "This has been a nice evening. I want you all to know that I'm coming along fine." He spoke genially, his words edged with a modest but obvious effort at getting his inwardly rehearsed lines out the way he'd memorized them. "Dad's been just great through all this, especially about taking over . . ."

He paused. He'd lost the thread. Possibly with the word "AbCom" on the brink of utterance, something inside had pulled the switch, shut down the synapses. At the head of the table, X beamed expectantly. I looked sideways at Clio; she smiled at Abner reassuringly.

". . . taking over," he repeated, searching the files, "taking over at . . ." his face screwed up momentarily, its strong features becoming confused, until he finally smiled and gave up and sat down. Not ashamed; he'd just forgotten something, but he'd remember it next time.

"You see," said Clio quietly.

After dinner, the thirsty fever of anticipation I felt at Margarita's invitation subsided. Talking with Clio was part of the problem. So was the apparent fact that numerous doors of emotional possibility had all simultaneously drifted ajar. Come on, I said to myself. Here is Margarita, this older woman who's been in your fantasies since you met her, and who's a real, unencumbered grown-up, sounding interested in you. Don't always go mooning after the long shots, trying to change people and their circumstances.

X had put his car at her disposal. She was still living downtown, in the Murray Hill district, in a hotel apartment owned by the Monstrance

Foundation. It was a bitter night even for March; the sludge-pitted streets were empty; we slid easily along through a city that might have been lifeless.

"It's sad about Horace's son, isn't it?" she said. Intermittently the light from streetlamps outlined her profile. The extra bit she'd had to drink had loosened her features and voice, adding a hint of sluttishness that was tantalizing. We were both charged up. Frustration makes its own electricity.

"I agree. Once he had a lot on the ball. How is it at AbCom now, pretty exciting?"

"It is if you have a taste for what they all call 'action.' Horace certainly does."

"What are you doing for him?" I asked the question in a certain way. She turned and looked at me.

"Not that, Sam," she said patiently.

"I didn't mean *that*," I said weakly.

The limousine slid through the Park Avenue tunnel and turned off into Thirty-fifth Street. It stopped in front of a small hotel that was supposed to be one of the treasures of the city. I followed Margarita into the lobby. She got her key and a couple of message slips and led me to the elevator.

Her lodgings consisted of a nicely furnished sitting room, a compact kitchen, and a bedroom.

"I brought you a belated Christmas present," she said. She handed me a glass. There was no mistaking the smell and the strong, idiosyncratic taste.

"Bowmore," I said. "From Islay."

"Horace said you had a keen taste for malt whisky. This is my favorite."

"Mine too."

"I know. I brought you two bottles from Millroy's in Greek Street. Merry Christmas!"

I smiled and raised my glass.

She sipped her drink. "Horace is so very confusing," she said.

"In what way?"

"It's almost as if he were schizophrenic. I spend a great deal of time with him, you know. He's close to being a genius, Sam. The ideas he has, my goodness! And yet when he leaves the office, he closes the door on that genius and becomes someone else entirely! It was never that way in London, at least not when I knew him. He surrounded himself with people from the Cavendish Laboratory and the LSE, men like Lord

Rothschild, the one or two good minds in the City, top journalists from Fleet Street. Those people tonight weren't good enough for him."

"They're what's available," I said. "They're easy to come by. He's an older man, working at an exhausting clip, and still he likes company. In New York, this is company."

"It really is, isn't it," she said. "London is so different. In London, people talk!"

"In London people talk," I said, "because in London people read. Here, not even the writers read. No one does. They're all busy making deals and chasing publicity, moguls and writers alike."

"*You* read," she said.

"When I'm not making a horse's ass of myself running around worrying that I'm missing something."

"Unreal," she said, sipping her whisky. "Unreal. Unreal people in an unreal city." Her voice, her whole personality, seemed as smoky as the liquor. She looked across at me, nodded something to herself, and said, as conversationally as if calling on a student to recite, "Sam, would you come over here and kiss me? It's been such a very long time."

Kissing her was like being drawn into the interior of some wild, rich flower and enclosed in its blossom. The world was shut out. There were noiseless soft hints of damp secrets.

"Please . . . ah, yes, please." She shifted to give me access. There was to be no practiced sequence, no commonplace ritual of sexual procedure. Movement slid liquescently into movement; under her skirt my hand drew her tights down, rose to stroke her sex, bedded in hair like silk, a moist sweet purse. Somehow my own clothes were off now. I entered her as surely and smoothly as if all my life had been practice and prelude for this moment. As I rose and sank above her, her breath came louder, faster, became a moaning and then something rougher, although hers or mine by then I could no longer distinguish, because every infinite capacity for sensation was gathering in me at a single microscopic point of tickling pain. I heard her muttering, voice rising to perhaps an octave shy of a shriek, a rattle in her throat of pain, delight, pure sensation, but now I was wound down to a point a shadow short of being turned inside out, and I told her so, and she said "Please" once more. Then there was no more possible restraint, and I felt the spasms opening into a long, sweet spreading flow, and I heard her snort and roar and say something and felt her twitch and then it was my turn to tumble, untethered and breathless, through half the black length of the universe.

Later, both of us blinking in the light back in the bedroom, she stepped out of her dress. All she had on was a black brassiere. Her hair had shaken loose and flowed to her shoulders, darkly sweeping years away; now she did look thirty, even younger. She let me look at her for a minute, admire the legs and the startling patch of nightshade at her crotch; let me watch her slide off her brassiere: her breasts showed few giveaway puckerings and blemishes. I reached up and she came down to me and I commenced, without thinking, a routine practiced over many years in many beds on many bodies.

But she said, "No, no, please, no games, please." She brought my head back up and made me kiss her mouth while her hand slid low and got busy, until she shifted me over her again, taking me in. This time was more for her: better for her, longer, the deep noises came earlier to her throat and continued, until I was once again strung out, reduced like mercury balanced on a needle, and couldn't hold it a second longer, feeling in the last fractional instant as if I held within myself the entire moment of all creation.

We fell asleep. When I awakened, the clock by the bed dully showed 4:07. Her breathing was soft in the room. I lay there nursing my thoughts. Margarita was certifiably the first "older" woman I had ever slept with—excepting those weary South Boston hookers who stood honor guard to the lubricious rites of passage of Starbuck seniors. I had expected, I guess, wiriness and blotches, dryness, everything a bit rough, a bit strained and stringy, and yet she had turned out to be as juicy as new fruit, as fresh and passionate as a milkmaid.

I lay there, hearing her breathe, and thought things over. This was close to an ideal woman: ripe and smart and handsome. And yet something was wrong, missing; the wrong people were in this bed. Just as I had come, my mind had fixed on a scintillant flashing vision—now just a memory of a memory—of drawn paleness, dark, calm eyes, a frank, clear voice. It was treasonous to think of someone else, I knew, but how could it be helped? Pondering that, I fell asleep.

When I clambered back into life the next morning, Margarita was sitting up, reading the paper, dressed only in a pair of shell-framed half-glasses. She caught me staring at her body; even in the illusionless light of the morning after, it was as good and tempting as I remembered.

"There's coffee in the thermos on your side," she said. "And some grapefruit juice; it's all I had."

"Thanks. I—"

"You needn't say anything, Sam. It was marvelous for me too." She giggled. "Goodness, that sounds presumptuous, doesn't it."

"Why? Those are the facts."

"Let me just say this. Let's neither of us take any of this for more than it can possibly be. Certainly not just yet."

"I agree. Let's concentrate on the tangibles. Such as replenishing on our vital bodily fluids and letting old dogs show their best tricks."

Perfect teeth in a perfect smile. "Now that sounds spot on!"

I put my coffee cup down on the night table and looked her over carefully. She returned my dirty-minded stare, then carefully took off her glasses and put them on her night table; with her other hand she tossed the newspapers on the floor. She pushed the sheet off her hips and slid down the bed, bringing her knees up and opening her legs.

"As you put it here in the States," she said, her smile already beginning to decompose with excitement, "be my guest."

In the middle of March, I went south on assignment, to spend a long weekend in Palm Beach watching polo. The editor had a hunch that here was a new craze rich in all kinds of phoniness; since I was our notional sports expert, he put me on the case. I asked him for a couple of extra days and took the long way round, flying to Tampa, where I rented a car to drive down to Gasparilla Island and pay a call on my mother at Boca Grande. Outside of Sarasota, a roadside sign announced that Eugenie's ball club was playing the Tigers that afternoon; I had plenty of time, so I detoured to the ball park and watched for six innings. The Boroughs played with spirit. I took that as an indication that Eugenie's attentions were still fixed on AbCom. The team might be fun to watch this year, especially with this good-looking kid they'd found to play shortstop.

The first night on Boca, I dined alone with Mother at the Gasparilla Inn. It was the beginning of spring vacation, and the dining room was full of blond kids, the flower of what was left of Old New York, Old Wilmington, Old Whatever. Mother looked better; her color was good; it didn't seem she would splinter when she coughed. The terrible bone-deep exhaustion which had weighed on her seemed to have slipped away.

"Emily Bowcrest's son John was down here last weekend from Washington. He's got a pretty high-up job in the Commerce Department. He says there's a lot of talk in Washington about this new gimmick of Horace's."

"What, cutting the President's exposure on the news?"

"Exactly. Apparently Mr. Erwitt's quite upset. The White House is trying to figure out what to do."

"There's not much they can do. I saw the letter X wrote the White House press office. He compared himself to an editor making up the front page. You don't see the *Times* putting Erwitt's picture on there every time he tries on a war bonnet."

"Young Bowcrest spoke of Horace as a traitor to his class. It took me back forty years. The dumbest people in New York used to say the same thing about Roosevelt."

"I don't know young Bowcrest, but I can imagine what sort he is. You know, X fired all the MBAs AbCom hired over the last eight years. Forty-three of them. That'll really make him a traitor to his class, whatever's left of it."

"Not much, although we daren't say that too loudly around here. How's Abner?"

"Not good."

I told her about X's dinner. If I had time, I thought I might give him and Clio a call in Palm Beach. I didn't tell her about Margarita.

The next morning, I took an easy amble across Florida on Route 80. I got to Palm Beach at dinnertime and checked into the Brazilian Court Hotel. I was tired, so I ate in the hotel, put off making any phone calls, and went to bed early.

The next morning was bright but gusty. I breakfasted late, grazing ruminatively through the New York, Miami, and Palm Beach papers. The "Shiny Sheet" reminded me of the total hermetic triviality of Palm Beach life, further confirmed by a stroll along Worth Avenue. Polo might come and polo might go, but shopping would always be the sport of choice in this part of the world. It was such a weird place, Palm Beach. I had just done a long piece about it when I met Cass. She loved it, and me for it, then; now I wondered how she'd feel. The place had its ugly side too. That morning's papers were full of letters about anti-Semitism. Apparently, a couple of nasty incidents had brought to light what everyone knew flourished here like some rank vegetation in the deepest shadows of the brushed and combed palm trees; by night people dined and danced at the homes of Jewish friends whom by day they wouldn't let into their clubs, and everyone accepted it. Weird.

Around lunchtime, I got in the car and headed back across the bay toward the polo complex that had sprung up to the west. I didn't know much, if anything, about the sport. I vaguely remembered being taken to an indoor match in the Park Avenue Armory as a kid. I had seen photographs of Tommy Hitchcock and Pete Bostwick and Louis Stoddard and Stew Iglehart riding against England at Meadow Brook, of wooden-bodied station wagons drawn up to the edge of the pitch, champagne in buckets, and polite applause. I knew that the Prince of Wales and the Duke of Edinburgh and a lot of Argentines played the game, presumably in a setting of a piece with the golden days before the war. I was put off, therefore, to find myself entering a sort of Condo City, where, like some golf resorts, the game was little more than cheese to trap buyers of vacation homes.

I was armed with an arsenal of passes and badges which let me roam throughout the complex. The general atmosphere was dauntingly up-market. The buffet would have graced a cruise ship. It was all effortfully tony and self-satisfied.

The afternoon's featured match pitted a team of Argentines sponsored by a fat widow with a lot of Pensacola real estate against a team of Argentines sponsored by a fat widow with an inherited chain of convenience stores in Kansas and Oklahoma. The winner would play a team of Argentines sponsored by a fat widow who owned an important Brussels brewery. At risk was a trophy given by some watch company. Fat widows appeared to be the social and economic linchpins of the sport, as they were of the area. Buck claimed to have once attended a dance in Palm Beach given by a woman so stout that she was moved from table to table by a fork lift.

Midway through the final chukker, I heard my name being called. I looked around and couldn't see anyone; then I saw waving, and there were Clio and Abner a few aisles over. She hand-signaled to meet them downstairs at the conclusion of the match.

By the time we parted, I had agreed to go with them to a dinner dance that evening and play golf with Abner the next morning at Seminole. I'd come fully prepared for Palm Beach: I had a dinner jacket with me, and my golf clubs were snug in the trunk of my rented car. Only my attitude was wrong.

I showed up at their house a little after eight. It was a big French-looking place off North County Road, set close to the ocean. A properly deferential houseman opened the door for me and showed me out to a terrace. The days were lengthening now, and traces of sunset lingered in the sky, pink on the low horizon deepening into purple and then black at the sky's highest pitch. The air was refulgent with tropical odors from the flower beds lining the walk to the pool. The wind had died down.

Clio was sitting on the balustrade, looking out at the ocean. It was very effective, almost too perfectly posed, and yet I somehow knew she hadn't arranged herself for effect.

"Abner'll be down in a little while," she said, pouring me a glass of champagne. "He insisted on going over to Everglades to hit practice shots, so his nap was later. He won't be fifteen minutes."

She looked wonderful in a deep green dress. It would be all too easy to fall in love with her.

"Hit shots! That sounds as if the old competitive juices are flowing. Is that a good sign? It sounds like it."

She shook her head. "I'm afraid not, Sam. He said he didn't want to let you down by playing badly. No, what you see is what you get. Abner now is the best Abner's going to be."

I fumbled to say the right thing and made a mess of it.

"No, Sam, don't get me wrong. It's not all that bad, and it could be much worse. He might have been crippled. It does mean our brilliant career's over, I'm afraid, but there are compensations." She looked out at the ocean. "It's a nice house, isn't it?" she said. "It used to be Selena Monstrance's—when she was first married. Abner bought it from an estate."

"Has Eugenie been here?" I asked.

"You just missed her. She had to rush back to New York. Something about something Abner's father's done at the company. She's been a real rock through all of this."

"Well, Sam, are you keeping Clee happy?" Abner came out onto the terrace. "Bringing her up to date on all the New York gossip?" He looked very handsome in a white dinner jacket, the way he'd looked as marshal of the Starbuck Spring Ball.

There was a large maroon Rolls in the driveway, but Clio insisted that we take my car. "I hate to drive and so does Abner," she said, "and besides, it'll be an early evening: the food and wine should be all right, but it'll be deadly dull. You can drop us back here afterward. If it's not too late, we'll even give you one for the road."

She was right about the party. We left shortly before midnight, thanking our host, an expansive Bolivian with piranha-perfect teeth. "That's the new 'in' group down here," said Clio. "Old narcotics money."

Back at their house, they invited me in for a nightcap. I gathered Clio wanted to talk to someone; anyone over the age of twenty would do. Abner's continual jolliness must be tiring. Champagne was produced. After one glass, Abner rose and excused himself.

"It's really grand having you here, Sam," he said, shaking my hand warmly. Then he made a fist and playfully nougied me on the bicep. "Just like old times. I'll pick you up at your hotel at eight. That way we can be off at nine and back for a lateish lunch. That's all right, isn't it, Clee?" He kissed his wife on the cheek and left us.

"Thank you for staying, Sam. It's so good for him. I just need someone to talk to, someone who isn't part of all this."

On the table next to her stood a large photograph of X in a vermeil bamboo frame. It showed him perhaps twenty years earlier, in his prime, grinning toothily, a real bear. Clio picked it up and studied it.

"I hate this man for what he's done to us. I wish I could get even. I hope he gets cancer." Her voice was calmer than her words.

"Isn't it better just to move on?" I asked. "Nothing can be undone."

"I suppose you're right. I didn't know what I was getting into, Sam. I was so desperate then. There's such poison between these people, such a thirst to bury each other! Was it that way when you first knew them?"

"Certainly nothing like this, although I suppose the potential was there."

I let her talk. She told me how Abner had insisted on the high life they'd led. My supposition had been correct. Abner had set out to efface the memory of X and Selena's glamorous life.

"I'll be frank, Sam," she said. "I enjoyed it at first. I was down in the dumps, and I hadn't had much fun in my life, or much money, and for a while it was thrilling. I loved meeting all those famous people. But then it got boring. The same crowd, night after night, but Abner insisted we keep at it, keep having them around and feeding and feting them and getting our names in the papers. It was as if every notice in Aileen or Liz was like another nail in this coffin he was building for his father. He never said anything—you know Abner—and of course H.H. was just an idea to me; that's all he was to me, an idea! What I didn't see was that Abner wasn't in control of his own life, our life together. H.H. was—through Abner's feelings about him, his resentment, his jealousy. When I finally saw it, it was too late. It was like a snowball!"

"X always had the Indian sign on Abner, but I must say I thought that was over."

"So did we all. And he's such a damn charmer, H.H.! You don't see the monster underneath until it's too late! I was very taken with him when he first got here. He's come on to me, you know. His own son's wife!"

"Don't let that upset you. It's automatic with him. He's always loved the ladies, and now he's an old man."

"That's the only good part," she said. "That's what I told Abner. We might not devour H.H., but time would. It had to!"

We both looked out at the ocean. The night was full of small noises.

When she returned her gaze to me, she said, "Will you keep a secret for me, Sam? Abner always said you were the best keeper of secrets he knew. He said his father thought so too."

Well, I figured, what could one more square foot of deep graveyard mean, especially if it was Clio's? I nodded.

"I'm the one responsible for Abner's injury," she said. "We had a quarrel while we were out riding. Abner was determined to leave AbCom. He was going to Washington. Or he was going to start another fight for the company from outside. He said he had people willing to commit money to him, hundreds of millions, billions! That awful McNeery had something to do with it. It made me so angry! I was so tired of it all. I told Abner if he felt that way he should stay there, try to work with H.H., stop trying to destroy each other. H.H. is an old man. He'll die soon. I couldn't stand the idea of another war."

She shook her head.

"I don't know what got into me. We were stopped on the rise, quarreling about it—it was all we did then, quarrel about H.H. and the company—and I just got so angry, Sam! I never lose my temper, never even at Cassie all those years. But I couldn't help it. I hit at him with my crop. I hit him again and again, and I guess I hit his horse, and the horse got scared and bolted."

We both sat silent for a moment.

"And Abner doesn't remember any of this?"

"If he does," she said, "he's said nothing. I don't think he does. Poor dear, he's such an open book."

"And such a closed one for so long."

She walked with me to my car. Leaning in the window, she said, "He's my destiny now. Forever, I suppose; not that I would have wanted anything else; that's why I married him. But not this way, Sam, not this way!" It seemed for an instant that she might cry, but she got hold of herself. "Have a good game tomorrow. Take care of my husband. He really is a sweetheart, but he needs tending."

I did. I played with Abner the next day and saw him safely home, and then I went to the airport and flew north with the spring, Clio's secret safely within me.

CHAPTER 16

April came, the leavings of winter melted away, the days turned fine; it was bluebird weather, good enough to make the most cast-down heart sing, and mine did. For many reasons: I loved the city in the fullness of springtime, liked the way the whole world seemed to have crawled out of a dank cave with me on its back, relished the return of the baseball season and the gradual greening of Central Park outside my window. My emotional life was at least orderly; Margarita and I were not in love, but our high companionability had its exquisite moments, and these occurred often enough to keep us happy. At least I was happy, but each hour in her company convinced me that this was the wrong place for her; the hurly-burly grated on her, and I guessed that sooner or later she would simply up and leave, unable any longer to stand the noise and pushiness. I knew this also with a certain sense of relief, admittedly shameful, because when that time came it would neatly sever a relationship that was always trying to deceive us into making more of it than it was or should be.

On the whole, life seemed pretty manageable. My visit to Clio and Abner receded in my mind; her secret became just another agreeable responsibility to a friend. I occupied myself with a fifteen-thousand-word rough draft on the AbCom proxy fight and liked what came out. Another cut at it, and it would be in shape to show to the editor. I had written it so that the aspects having to do with X's motives, which would be reserved for the book at the end of the road, could be cut without unbalancing what I thought was a very clear and analytical recitation of the proxy fight: good enough to be run on its own.

Life and work seemed to be humming along very nicely, thank you. I should have known, of course, that it doesn't work that way, not in God's revised, post-1970 plan for the Western World. On the day before I was to leave for Georgia to cover the Masters golf tournament, I was summoned by the editor and peremptorily informed that all my other work was to be shelved; I was being sent on special undercover assignment to AbCom.

I blew up, with a force that surprised me. It was naive to expect that I could cover X's retransformation of the company and its best-known business without spending a lot of time around him. Yet the editor's announcement got to me in a number of ways, making me feel powerless, futile, foolish, a dupe. I had turned X down on the matter of going over to AbCom; I had rejected both Cass and Margarita when, obviously prompted by hints from X, they had queried whether I was going to work for him.

"Technically, I don't have to do this, you know!" I said, trying to muster a steely, tightly wound tone of voice.

"Technically, probably not," he said. "But then, technically, man is a kindly, loving, generous animal, and technically, *Hamlet* is a mess as a play. Technically, there are alternatives available to me. I have a feeling there's more going on at the Department of Agriculture than meets the eye. Certainly enough to justify a five-part series with a lot of field work; I've actually laid some of the groundwork for you. Could you be ready to leave for Wichita by Sunday? I should think you could finish up by—oh, Labor Day at the latest."

He knew he had me. "I hope you notice I'm putting on my surliest face," I said.

"I do, and a very fine surly face it is. Your cover will be an indefinite temporary leave of absence from here. You have been hired by AbCom as a private contractor, to write a history of the company, and will be given an office there in order to collate background material. You will also be available to them for intermittent special consultation on press relations. Mr. Monstrance and I thought that a rather nice touch; it'll explain away your admittance to the company's inner circles, should anyone within AbCom ask. Your principal contact will be a man named Duncan, whom I believe you've become quite friendly with. Actually, you can read all about it in 'Page Six' of the *Post* this evening. I fed them the story an hour ago."

I could see he was enjoying the spymaster angle. He had on his Smiley face.

"And if I refuse?"

"Then it will be Wichita, Sam. I'm not kidding. You and I and this magazine are married to each other. I can't lose you and you won't quit. Do you think you'd be happy working for Shawn, or back on *Newsweek*, or writing about croissants for *New York*? You'd hate it. And I don't want to lose you, and you know it. But this is a terribly important story, important to this magazine and to me personally, and if you refuse, I'd have to take a position and that means Wichita!"

"Why is this story so important to you personally, may I ask?"

"Sam, it may be that Mr. Monstrance and I are just two old men flailing away fruitlessly, trying to change a world we feel some responsibility for having allowed to drift to its present miserable state. I hope not. It seems to be important to him that you be there, right on the scene, so as not to miss a beat or a note. This is a small thing for us to do, you and I."

"Easy for you," I said. "What about my journalistic integrity? People are going to take me for a flack like Duncan!"

"People will take you for what you write. As for your integrity, Mr. Monstrance wouldn't have asked for you, nor would I consider lending you, if we both weren't sure on that score. You won't be working for AbCom; you'll remain on our payroll, although you will receive a monthly fee from them, strictly for the sake of appearances, which you'll be expected to contribute to our bonus pool. And you will have a right of appeal at any time. I have no intention of committing you to servitude; I'm merely asking you to give it a try. I might also remind you that it was none other than S. A. Mountcastle himself who came to me some months ago anxious to pursue this story right down to the last figment."

I was in a box. X had outflanked me on a salient I hadn't thought to guard, and the editor was right about my own interest in the story. What the hell could I do? If I set aside the fact that my ass was burning at the fact that X had won the initiative, my objections seemed merely rhetorical and academic. It was agreed that I would present myself at AbCom when I got back from Augusta.

The Masters wasn't a tournament I particularly liked. The beauty of the venue was unarguable; few places could be as lovely as Augusta National in April—the air soft, the tall pines awesome, the banks of flowers aflame with color. The course itself was basically a string of seven wonderful holes beginning at the tenth, and the rest pretty boring, redeemed only by their putting difficulty. It wasn't a layout that compared with Muirfield or Seminole or Royal Dornoch for variety or character.

I hadn't gone to Augusta to write about golf, however, but about corporate America at an annual apogee of self-approval. Masters Week was strictly Stuffed Shirt à la carte. "You know," Buck had once said, after returning from an outing there, "I took one look around that ol' dining room, with all them darkies grinnin' and all them old boys dressed up in them club blazers lookin' jes' like a bunch of fat green penguins, and I said to myself, Billybuck, if you want to bring America back, jes' plant a bomb in here the night before the fourth round of the Masters, 'cause them's the boys that got us in the shit in the first place."

I was staying about twenty miles northeast of Augusta, in Aiken, just over the South Carolina border, in a house that had been lent to me by friends. Aiken was one of those places that brought joy to my retrograde heart. It seemed to exist out of time: like Prouts Neck and Northeast Harbor in Maine, parts of Nantucket and the Vineyard, Boca Grande, the Adirondacks, places I'd heard about in North Carolina and the Michigan Peninsula and north of San Francisco. Places too distant and homely for the fast-trackers who crowded the Hamptons.

On the last practice day I was wandering around the club looking for Buck, who was hosting a group from the Morgan Stanley trading desk. I crossed by the pro shop and went into the main clubhouse in search of a beer. Just out of curiosity, I went through the small lounge and peeked into the dining room. At a corner table, Nicklaus was eating with his wife. Another table attracted my attention. At its head sat former President McNeery; around it were ranged a baker's dozen worth of *Forbes* and *Fortune* covers. It looked like a rump session of the executive committee of BLEEP. There was probably a half-billion dollars in GBG advertising revenues sitting around that table. I thought what perfect cover the Masters provided, an ideal exclusory setting for the big boys to get together under the umbrella of sport and put the economic and political blocks to the rest of us.

I took my beer outside and wandered through the ropes down toward the ninth green. A now familiar voice called my name.

"Hello, Moira," I said. "Have you taken up the ancient Scots game?"

"Are you crazy? I'm here strictly on the cuff. A guest." She made a sweeping gesture. "Did you ever see such bullshit in your life? How about these characters in the green coats? This isn't a sports event, this is some kind of religion."

"You're too young to have a proper appreciation of cultural values," I said. "I doubt those shorts you've got on would carry the day in the members' dining room."

She looked at me reproachfully. "More respect, please. Have you forgotten that there was a time not too long ago when you and I meant a whole lot to each other? Somebody told me you were a born-again chauvinist. Anyhow, I'm here with someone."

"Not another sociologist of sport?"

"Nope. I'm running a test pattern on a guy I met at McMullen's. He does interest rate swaps at Salomon Brothers. He told me he made over a mil last year. He's twenty-five, two years younger than I am. At first, he pissed me off, then I said, hell, Moira, you know second-string shortstops who make a mil a year. We came down in a little jet. How's your love life?"

"Mixed."

I told her to bring her beau up to Aiken for dinner. A little later I found Buck at the practice tee watching Weiskopf hit one sovereign two-iron after another and invited him. By the time I got through, I'd assembled about a dozen people for the evening. I used a pay phone to alert the cook and headed off in search of a liquor store.

My "at home" turned out to be a success. Most everyone got drunk fast and thoroughly. Unfortunately, Moira's kid from Salomon Brothers didn't pan out. Confused by finding himself in a crowd which essentially didn't give a merry screw about money, he tried to bigtime us with exciting tales of recent interest rate switches, but since a couple of us had seen Ted Williams hit homers, compared to which saving Mitsui "a hundred basis points" was pretty pallid stuff, he was soon left to talk to himself about the fractions he found so consoling.

"I know, I know," said Moira, arms raised in mock surrender. "He looked better in McMullen's. I don't think you've got so much to talk about, anyway. Didn't I see in the *Post* you're checking out? Going over to some company? Funny, Sam, you're the last guy I ever thought would take a dive for money."

This was exactly what I didn't want to hear, but I figured I might as well practice, at least until I could come up with a decent possible face for it.

"It's just temporary," I said. "Something for an old family friend. I've known the Monstrances for years, and the son's had an accident, and the father asked me to do a history of the business now that there aren't likely to be any Monstrances to run it. The father's seventy-five. It's a six-month assignment, tops. I had to beg my editor to let me go." I hoped I'd made the closing line convincing.

"No Monstrances, huh? What about Eugenie? Or doesn't she count?"

I'd had about twenty drinks, and my need to get involved in an equal rights argument was minimal. Fortunately, just at that moment, Buck came up.

"Monstrances? Damn, Sam, you gonna have yourself a ball over there! The Street's just goin' batshit over the old man! They figger he can pick them TV shows like no man ever could, and that come next December them ratings'll glow like Uncle Fester's nose at Christmas. IEA's talkin' one hundred fifty on the stock down the road."

"Pfannglanz?"

"None other. She's done and gone wet her drawers over Abner's daddy.

"Say," he said, looking at Moira, "who are you? You're as cute as a button."

"Of stainless steel," I said, and introduced them.

Buck recognized her name. "Well, come here, you cute thang," he said, "and les' jes' go talk about whether the three-four's better'n the four-three, or mebbe some other number." They went off, leaving me feeling better. Buck's enthusiasm was catching, and as a liar I wasn't half bad.

The following Wednesday I went to AbCom Tower and was informed by Duncan's secretary, to whom the protocols of subterfuge concocted by X and the editor directed me to present myself, that Mr. Monstrance awaited me. She led me down a hall lined with empty offices; the last time I'd been here, I recalled, a number of them had been occupied.

X was expansive, almost bursting with enjoyment of our little game.

After we exchanged pleasantries, he told me to follow him and led me to the other side of the floor to a pleasant large office with a downtown exposure.

"I'd like to have given you a corner office, Sam, but we can't be too careful. One step at a time."

This was all really strange. He watched as I looked around. Already I missed the overgrown cubicle at the magazine. Everything here was simple and in good, expensive, neutered taste. I resolved at once not to introduce one iota of my own personality into it. I was going to fight it to the death—or whenever.

"I think you'll be happy here," X said. "You can change anything you don't like. One of my girls will take care of it pronto." He drew open the curtains; the office had a fine view south; I could see past the World Trade Center almost to the Jersey docks. "Nice, eh? Now, let me show you a couple of things."

He went over to the bookcase. Its bottom shelves contained the paraphernalia expected to be found in the office of a communications-entertainment oligarch: two TV monitors each hooked up to a VCR, one Beta, one VHS; audio equipment—tape decks, compact disk player, laser disk player, turntables, amplifiers, and the rest of the works—all operated by a button-studded control box on top of my desk. Someone would be around to teach me the tricks.

"Now this, Sam, is really deep graveyard."

He opened a drawer at the bottom of the bookcase and beckoned me over.

"I got the idea from Nixon. Purely in the interest of history, you understand, because I certainly don't approve of wiretapping or any of that other surreptitious stuff, although I hear Eldon's people aren't quite so fastidious. Watch!"

The drawer contained a small cassette recorder.

"Instant history," X said, obviously pleased. "It's connected to voice-activated microphones I've had installed in my office and in the conference room and the boardroom. Just like the White House, you see, although obviously an improved model, thanks to my boys up at the Labs."

He closed the drawer and locked it, tossing me the key.

"Now only you have access to it. Come here." He went to the desk and picked up the electronic remote control. From a desk drawer he produced a pair of what looked like Walkman earphones. "All you do is plug these into this." He showed me.

"I don't follow you," I said.

"Just put them on when you hear the beep." He grinned and went out the door, obviously satisfied with himself. I waited.

A minute later, I heard three sharp beeps. I put on the earphones. My ears filled with the sound of a piano and X's exultant roar: "Once to ev'ry ma-a-a-n and nation . . ."

I noticed a tiny red light blinking on the light switch next to the door. X continued singing for another stanza; then the earphones were silent and the red light went out. In a moment, he was back in my office.

"Pretty super, eh? For your ears only, though, Sam. We don't want anyone thinking they're on to some kind of Granitegate, do we?"

"Very ingenious, X."

"I thought you'd appreciate it. Come on down to my office, and we'll get you started on some other stuff."

As we walked up the hall, I asked him who else was on the floor.

The company president, he said, and the chief financial officer, and Duncan, Margarita, the kitchen and dining room staff, and now me.

"Eugenie?" I asked.

"I put her down on thirty-eight. I thought it would make her feel more a part of things, but she doesn't seem to like it."

We reached his office. In just the few minutes he'd been out showing me the ropes, sheaves of message slips had blossomed on his secretaries' desks. He acknowledged their existence with a nod and an impatient flick of the hand.

"I'll do those in a minute, Mrs. Dunbar. Nothing important, is there, Miss Sproulle? Good."

He put me in a seat across from him and took two papers from a manila folder on the desktop. He gave one to me.

"I want you to get into the stream of things. Read this and tell me what I ought to do about it. It's Duncan's draft of the letter to the stockholders for the annual report. He drafted it for Ab, and actually I intended to let Ab sign it."

"Now wait a minute," I said. "I'm not here to work, just to observe."

"The thing is, Sam," he said, intent on his copy of the letter, "the tone's not quite right. I want something with a little more snap, a shade of irony. Nobody understands irony around here, not even Duncan. You know that piece you wrote about the United merger; well, I thought you got the tone just right."

I took my copy of the letter and got up. He was busily scratching out sentences and inserting changes in his unexpectedly crabbed, small handwriting. As I got to the door, he looked up.

"Don't forget to listen to the beep, now."

As the days passed, the beeps became too frequent to ignore, as I had childishly resolved to do on leaving X's office that first day. Within hours, my curiosity had gotten the best of me and I took to reviewing the tapes at the end of each day, especially since, after the flurry about the stockholders' letter, I didn't have much to do. X was now concentrating almost all his effort on programming. Early May was traditionally the time for setting the fall lineup. The town was crammed with producers, studio shills, and agents.

The annual meeting of GBG's affiliates was scheduled for the end of May in Los Angeles, and X was obviously preparing a few surprises for them, but on these the tapes were silent. I was surprised, because I knew he planned to make a major speech and I had halfway expected to be asked to help with it. Instead, he closeted himself with Margarita and Duncan, sometimes separately, sometimes together. It irritated me to be excluded; part of it was that I was sitting around with little to do; another part, which I grudged to admit to myself, was that X favored the others more.

It was fascinating, however, and in a way elevating, to overhear him at work. Now I could observe the admirable X, brilliant, purposeful, dedicated, a man to be taken seriously, not a foolish old king with a kennel of parasites and courtiers.

The programming "reformation" of GBG began with its four hottest shows, each of which served as a cornerstone for an entire evening's schedule. They were: on Monday night, "The Dumpsters," the only sitcom still in the national top ten; on Wednesday, "Shield 262," a kaleidoscopic precinct-house series whose disorganized plot and extravagantly rapid crosscutting were regarded as the acme of prime-time artiness, which ranked number five in upscale markets; on Friday night, "River Oaks," a glitzy knockoff of "Dallas" and "Dynasty" which now outranked both of its ancestor competitors; and on Saturday, "Resort," a multiplot hour showcase for a changing cast of slightly shopworn stars who could be got cheap.

I listened in "live" on a couple of X's meetings with the independent producers of these series. I had cased the "guys from the Coast" in X's reception area; they seemed cut from the same bolt: suave, overbarbered Jewish men in their late fifties named Bernie, Isaac, Fred, and Leo, artfully and precisely casual in dress. Over the microphone they sounded wound up: they spoke rapidly and roughly in gentrified Bronx accents, pushing out the vowels; they were very sharp and quick with figures; and their wordplay alternated the hip and jargonistic in a kind of fingersnapping fugue.

X always began by saying how appreciative he was that a busy man would come in especially to see him; Bernie's (or Fred's, Isaac's, or Leo's) response would confirm huge respect, an awareness that he understood himself to be in the presence of a giant, not some mere network putz. Invariably, some small attempt at ingratiation was made. "Nice to see you

again, Mr. Monstrance. We met before, you may remember; Santa Barbara, I think, in '56 or '57. I was working for Selznick then. *Farewell to
Arms*, you remember?"

"Of course I do, Bernie. God, weren't those the days! Wasn't David
something! His type is sorely missed; if it wasn't for you fellows, I don't
know what we'd do for product. Which is what I wanted to talk about
with you, share some of my thoughts with you, a few ideas I've been
thinking about since I've been away from the business."

"Mr. Monstrance, if I can say so, the business hasn't been the same
without you. I mean, without you, and now Mr. Paley's out across the
street, it's just a lot of kids with calculators, if you know what I mean." I
could envision shoulders shrugging under $1,500 of pale Huddersfield
flannel jumpsuit.

"Bernie, I appreciate that. I think I know what you mean. You've made
exactly the point I was going to make." X used his most patrician inflection in these meetings, clearly intending to let his listener know that as far
as X was concerned, he the Brahmin and Bernie the tummler shared a
real kinship. He established at the outset that no matter how cheap and
meretricious might be the shows Bernie produced for GBG, those were
the last adjectives one could apply to Bernie himself.

"Bernie," he'd say, and I could just imagine that big, cheery face
screwed into an expression of grave, confiding sincerity, "we've got a
problem. We're losing that audience out there. I think you and I understand that unless we do something about upgrading the quality of what
we're putting on the air these days, this audience erosion is going to
continue. We all laughed at cable, and admittedly it hasn't changed things
the way people predicted, but it's cutting into you and me. We're driving
our audience away. We're not showing them the world as it is. Fantasies
don't draw the way they used to, Bernie, because as far as the average
man's concerned, his fantasies no longer work out in real life."

About here, X would pause, to let Bernie give himself a teeny push
toward the side of the angels.

"Well, how do you see it, Mr. Monstrance?" Bernie would ask, thinking the question largely rhetorical. X would be ready for him.

"Bernie, it's not very complicated. We've got to take these wonderful
characters and situations you've created in 'River Oaks' and change them,
so subtly that the viewer doesn't sense it, and give them a new reality, a
new moral dimension."

"People don't go in for preaching, Mr. Monstrance. If satire's what closes on Saturday night, morality generally doesn't make it past the matinee."

This would produce a hearty, companionable guffaw from X. Then: "Bernie, just hear me out. . . ."

X would start to speak about the program, displaying an astonishing and flattering grasp of its details, even quoting dialogue from episodes aired several seasons earlier. He made himself sound like the greatest fan of "River Oaks" ever, the kind of fan who clipped pictures and started newsletters, who knew what Bobby and Judy ate for breakfast, and how Harold and Carolyn really hated each other off the set, and the real name of Miss Winnie's real-life husband, and that Carter Hubbard, so handsome and dashing on the show, was really a homebody who collected stamps and kept gerbils. As X talked about his ideas for the characters, they came alive in his words. He talked about how he might change this, reemphasize this, reweight that, so that the show's cartoon emotions would be scaled up, enriched, given weight and dimension.

I could almost hear Bernie squirm. Here he had something that played to a 22 rating. You don't tinker with success. And yet he was thinking: it's H. H. Monstrance that's asking me to change it! This is a fifty-million-dollar property I've put together, Bernie would be thinking, but this guy was bigger than Sarnoff or Paley or Goldenson!

Which is when X would launch into what I came to call his "Dickens shtick."

"Bernie, people like you are to this age what Charles Dickens was to his. The great entertainers and the great lesson-bringers. Dickens entertained—millions of people waited for the next installment of *Oliver Twist*, and when Little Nell died, all England mourned—and yet he preached too. I've watched every episode of 'River Oaks,' and, Bernie, that show is the *Bleak House* of our time, the *David Copperfield*, the *Tale of Two Cities*! Entertainment, yes, but with a point!"

Bernie liked being lumped with Dickens. I could almost hear him purr. And then X, as swiftly as a good lightweight, would shift his feet and pop him with the money punch.

"Bernie, I believe I'm correct, and I'm prepared to pay to prove it. Let me propose something for you to think about. I'll guarantee to pick up 'River Oaks' for four more seasons. We'll work out a bonus tied to the ratings. At the end of that time—that's two years from now—if we don't renew, and you have trouble syndicating those shows, you can put them to us on some kind of formula we'll work out. How does that sound?"

Bernie hadn't come to own two acres on North Canyon Drive in Beverly Hills, plus matched Rolls-Royce Corniches for himself and the wife and a Brentwood condo for the girlfriend, plus numbered accounts in Geneva and Zug which not even his lawyer knew about, by jumping at the first offer.

"I hear you about the money, Mr. Monstrance. What I don't hear is how what you're talking about gets implemented." He'd pronounce "implemented" carefully and with relish; it was a very authentic tycoon-type word.

"I want to be in on the script process. I want to assign one, perhaps more, of my own writers to your team. I want the right to sit down and discuss the show with you. Bernie, you and I are both experienced professionals of good intent. I think we can shake hands on something that will suit us both."

It was my guess that it had been some years since Bernie had regarded a handshake as anything more than a nominal convention of politeness. But this was H. H. Monstrance, a class act, inviting him to step up in class, with an insurance policy yet. I could hear the wheels turn. What the hell, Bernie would be thinking, there's five mil socked away at Lombard Odier so if it all went down the tubes it wouldn't be exactly like starting all over again in the William Morris mailroom. I listened as X batted four-for-four, as Bernie ("River Oaks") and Isaac ("The Dumpsters") and Fred ("Shield 262") and Leo ("Resort") went for his deal, handshake and all.

"So far, so good," X said at lunch one day. He ate in the office every day, sometimes alone, sometimes with some combination of me, Margarita, and Duncan, sometimes with executives from other parts of Ab-Com, as he absorbed the details of Abner's diversification, and with people outside the company he was looking over. Gradually, the empty offices on the floor began to fill up, mainly with broadcasting people: a few old cronies lured back from retirement or consulting work or academe, as well as a sprinkling of comers wooed away from CBS and ABC and HBO. In the three months following Abner's accident, he had recentered AbCom around broadcasting. Now he began to ponder AbCom's other components, riffling through them like a croupier checking a deck.

"The question before us is whether Financial Assets Management has a place in our particular little universe," he said one morning. He looked around the table, at Duncan, at Margarita, and at me. He had started talking about the three of us as "my brain trust," and we breakfasted with him every Friday.

"If the answer is no," he continued, "then what is the best way to use it? It's certainly profitable, but given our forthcoming policy position, we simply can't continue to be in those businesses. And given that time is now somewhat of the essence, I think we must declare our intention to divest ourselves of financial services."

I was still in the dark about the "forthcoming policy position." I had tried to wheedle something out of Margarita, even in the throes of passion and excitation, but she wasn't talking. I'd gotten Duncan drunk one night and gotten him to spill a few, discreet beans. There would be a blockbuster policy statement at the affiliates' meeting, which would have something to do with both advertising and finance.

I was frankly irritated that Duncan and Margarita knew something I didn't. It was a small punishment but an effective one, more effective and stinging each day. The message was clear: OK, hotshot, you sniffed at corporate power, now see how you like being left out. I'd now been at AbCom for just over a month, and the fact was that I loved it. I was surrounded by energy and influence of a reach, magnitude, and variety that I could never have imagined from a distance. An outsider by trade, I had never even guessed at the power of an institution like AbCom, nor had I wanted for an instant to entertain the thought that such power might exist. I began to sense the repercussive possibilities of these entities, the way they amplified stupidity and ambition, and inherent defects of individual character and ego, and resonated them, and sent them crashing into millions of lives. Looking out from inside the monolith, I could understand, in a way both real and graspable, what might flow from the presence in the White House of an ignorant man, or a venal one, or one too clever by half, or too susceptible. I saw what X had seen, looking at Erwitt, and knew what he would know, if to a lesser degree, because all I had done was stand on the bridge while X actually knew the feel of the rudder.

For the first time, I was close to the exercise of real power, a humming, glowing, radiant core of institutional cause and effect that sent its reverberations across continents and through lives. For the first time, I perceived, in ways that weren't conceptual or theoretical, how people could become intoxicated by the experience and the association; how they could become arrogant, self-involved, hubristic, dangerous. I could see how power had its own momentum in and of itself. This was the real thing, and it was thrilling. It made me wonder exactly what the rudder felt like.

"I think I know what I want to do with that group," X continued, "but Fergus thinks we should get a second opinion, so I told our Finance people to put some figures together and talk to a couple of investment banking firms. They'll be coming in next week, and we'll listen to what they have to say. I'd like you to sit in on those meetings, Sam."

He changed the subject.

"Morale around the place seems pretty good, doesn't it?"

His personal magic had worked its way back into the fiber of the company. Initially, according to Duncan, the atmosphere had been chilly with apprehension. But as X began reaching out and bringing others into his aura, the general uneasiness began to melt away. It was natural that there would be pockets of resistance, and these X moved swiftly to root out and eradicate. Sometimes he leaned toward overkill but pulled back: he reconsidered his decision to fire every MBA employed by AbCom when he realized that such a move would decimate his financial departments beyond functionability. He established his credo for the company in the Annual Report:

> AbCom will be reoriented to its original roots, as a profit-making enterprise dedicated to and committed to the creation and communication of information and entertainment. This is our last; as good cobblers, we shall stick to it. The resources of the corporation will be dedicated in the future to the development, expansion, and renewal of AbCom's original and traditional business.

Thus, into the plush suites formerly occupied by AbCom Interface's demographic design laboratory, and its sociologists, pollsters, and trend dowsers, went his newly assembled Writing Group: forty men and women, novelists, mystery writers, biographers, of all ages and persuasions, all of whom had published well-received books but who were barely getting by in this bad age for books. He had recruited them through talent and literary agencies and college faculties. Each was paid $3,000 a month, with a one-year guarantee, for which AbCom got ten days a month of their time and imagination. I sat in on the meeting when X outlined their mission to them.

"All I want from you," he said, "are ideas and treatments that you and I can transform into quality popular entertainment. I want programs that are amusing or exciting or uplifting or instructive to watch, with literate scripts and plots that knit, that have real connections with real life, that indicate that there is something more to life than sex, money, violence, and buffoonery. There's not one of you in this room that doesn't think the world has treated your great talent with unkind indifference while schlock artists have prospered. Well, here's your chance: you're prospectively addressing an audience perhaps fifty times larger than even James Michener's."

The mention of the sacred name caused a murmur. People shifted in their seats. "That's a pretty tall order, Mr. Monstrance," said someone.

X smiled, warmly patient. "Dickens didn't find it so," he said.

Afterward, he told me it reminded him of the great days in Hollywood in the thirties and forties, when writers like Faulkner and Fitzgerald and Raymond Chandler worked in the bungalows of studio lots. He had a hunch, he said, that if the excitement in the entertainment business got back to coming from stories and scripts and not from deals and packages, we'd start to see better shows and movies and we'd get bigger audiences. He bet me five dollars on it.

He got a kick out of the fact I was getting hooked. It showed, I knew. The odd thing was, I didn't seem to mind.

CHAPTER 17

May was X's month for making things hot; he began by changing the management of B & B Publishers and ended with his address to the GBG affiliates' convention in Los Angeles, and along the way he jolted the cosy preconceptions and assumptions of a lot of people around the company. It was as if, to make sure that his mastery of AbCom was complete, he had taken it by the scruff and shaken it one last time, like a terrier with a rat, to rid it of any lingering thoughts of resistance. In doing this, he gave me my first real taste of executive power.

It began with the proposal to rename B & B Publishers AbCom Verbal Technologies. X called me into his office.

"AbCom Verbal Technologies! Can you beat it?" He leaned forward on his worktable and said, collusively, "Sam, next to Duncan, you're the house word expert, and you might as well see the sort of decisions a fellow running a company has to make. I want you to take a good hard look at B and B for me and tell me what you think. This fellow Cutter strikes me as a smarmy little piece of goods; I can't imagine why Ab hired him."

I liked the sound of the assignment. Most writers I knew considered what had happened to B & B a disgrace. Harold Cutter, who ran it, was a marketing hotshot whom Abner had brought in from Time-Life Books; in the trade, despite a grudging respect for B & B's glowing bottom line, there was considerable conjecture as to whether Cutter knew how to read. His right-hand man, editor-in-chief Friedel Glemp, had been hired away from Doubleday, where popular rumor held that as a child he had been given piss to drink instead of mother's milk. He certainly looked as if he had; I often saw him lording it over a favored corner in the Four Seasons, a shriveled runt in Darryl Zanuck dark glasses.

Among the faddish, best-selling categories of trade publishing, Foster Greenglass had a lock on the celebrity heartache market, but B & B led in the others: diet and self-help, shlock fiction, get-rich-quick, books which could be evaluated and sold 90 percent on the basis of talk-show promotability; at B & B these days, literary or intellectual merit or interest was strictly a throw-in. As someone said, B & B under Cutter and Glemp made Simon & Schuster look like Oxford University Press.

"They're having some kind of a planning *Schützenfest* in Montego Bay next week," X said. "They invited me, but I turned 'em down. Then I called this morning and told this fellow Cutter that you were doing a company history and I wanted you to sit in. He doesn't like it, but he doesn't have much choice."

I had a question. According to the organization table, to which X still paid selective lip service, B & B fell under Eugenie's notional supervision. Did he want me to report back through her? I certainly didn't want to get between Monstrances.

"Eugenie?" he said. "Why?" He brightened. "Oh, I see. Well, don't you worry; I'll cover your back, Sam."

I can't say that I went to Jamaica with my ax sharpened, but it wouldn't be truthful to say that I attended the B & B Sales and Planning Conference in an exactly objective frame of mind. I did my homework; I skimmed the books from B & B's last list and found the quality of editing and proofreading, where existent, deplorable; I read a year of back issues of *Publishers Weekly* and made notes on the many public pronouncements of Harold Cutter, who fancied himself a spokesman for the industry. When I got off the plane in Montego Bay, my pockets were bulging with ammunition.

Cutter was out of sorts on the flight down. Mainly, I thought, to irritate the B & B president, X had denied Cutter his accustomed use of an AbCom jet, which obliged him to fly commercial with the help. He was a small man who affected a loud basso, as if forcing his voice an octave or two lower might add a desperately wanted inch or two to his height—or to somewhere else. He tried, in a halfhearted way, to soften me up, using a lot of phrases like "word projects" and "publishing product"—never once "book"—and then tired of the job and went off to flirt with the stewardesses. Glemp took over; he was an oily little piece of birdshit, equally given to technobabble, who spoke of "B. Dalton exit polls" and boasted of the prospects for several TV-show spin-offs, like a "Resort" beauty plan for computers, on which he would be billed as "executive producer."

I sat through the three-day sales conference, sharpened my ax, and wrote up my recommendations for X. It turned out he'd done some homework of his own, as I learned when the beeper sounded and I tuned in to eavesdrop on his meeting with Cutter and Glemp.

He started by discussing a new, radical diet book for which Glemp had paid $500,000.

"I'm told by Jack Abraham, who's the top man in nutrition up at Columbia, that this diet will probably kill a dozen or so people. Obviously we can't publish it." I heard Glemp start to say something, but X had moved on to address Cutter.

"I'm not happy with B & B, Mr. Cutter," he said.

Cutter took the bait. Reaching for new depths of orotundity, he challenged X. He pointed to B & B's profits and spoke glowingly of the innovative techniques that had made them possible, "internal target ROIs per line item," and "time-weighted author costing."

"I'm afraid that's completely beside the point," said X. "What is apposite is this. Last year, Mr. Cutter, B & B spent a mere eighty-two thousand dollars buying poetry and first novels. Last year, Mr. Cutter, you paid your executive chef over a hundred thousand dollars. Mr. Glemp's expense account at the Four Seasons, which I have closed this morning, was in excess of fifty thousand dollars. I understand that you have given Mr. Glemp an advance of over two hundred thousand dollars for a novel he is writing; quite apart from the fact that this is arrant self-dealing unheard of in the history of publishing, I can find nothing in the books Mr. Glemp has edited which suggests he is capable of writing a literate English sentence."

I heard both Cutter and Glemp start to say something.

"Please, gentlemen," X said. "All this is also beside the point. What matters most to me, Mr. Cutter, is that you appear to take great pride in your profits and none whatsoever in the books you publish. They are mostly garbage, and—in the bargain—they are filled with misprints, errors of fact and typography, and solecisms. They are a disgrace to publishing and to literacy and an affront to the reputation and history of a very distinguished house."

As I had recommended, he fired them both. I felt exultant, as if I had struck a brave blow for all writers everywhere. Exultant and powerful. It didn't occur to me then that it wasn't really very brave, this business of writing memoranda and then hiding. For a time, I was plain intoxicated with myself and the great, throbbing, unstoppable engine of which I now fancied myself an integral part.

Mother started calling me "Mr. Valiant-for-Truth's little helper," which I didn't like.

"Why don't you cut it out?" I said. I wasn't going to admit the possibility that I might have been showing off.

"Why don't you?" she answered back. She was tired, I thought. The sun-kissed bloom I'd seen on her in Florida had faded away after her return to Long Island. "You've taken to punctuating your sentences with Horace's name instead of commas. It's very tiresome. Is it necessary?"

Margarita was upstairs napping. Mother made a small, dismissive gesture and looked meaningfully at the ceiling. "That's a very nice woman you're with. Are you smitten again? You must be, the way you're behaving. Where's her husband?"

"France. They have a sort of . . . arrangement."

"How agreeable for you. She seems to like you a lot, Sam. She certainly makes it known."

I know I reddened. Margarita's lovemaking was noisy and demonstrative. The night before, we had been pretty rambunctious. Our physical attraction remained intense. Often we made love in the office. That morning, alone on the beach, we had simultaneously felt the urge and sprinted up to the shelter of the dunes, where I had taken her as I had first fantasized, from behind, her skirt pushed up her back, her underpants shoved roughly aside, a matter of no more than seconds.

That evening, after a good dinner cooked by Margarita, Mother asked about AbCom.

"It certainly must be very busy around there these days. I just got something in the mail informing me that Horace is going to give us stockholders the right to buy shares in his brokerage businesses. That's very unusual these days, you know. Stockholders' rights have all but gone the way of the woolly mammoth. Why's he spinning it off, anyway? I thought it was one of Abner's crown jewels. Or is that itself the reason?"

"No, he doesn't think it fits."

"Which is another way of saying it bores him."

"No, he's got some plans for the company, and this kind of business just isn't compatible." I couldn't say more than that, although by now X had taken me into the confidences he'd been sharing with Duncan and Margarita. "You're right about his giving his stockholders first crack. The investment bankers hated the idea."

"Not enough money in it for them, I expect." She sniffed.

"That's about right," I said. "Actually, X tried to trade Financial Assets Management to Eugenie for her AbCom stock, but she turned him down."

"Like to get her out of the company, would he?" said Mother. "I shouldn't wonder. I'll wager she's a terrible nuisance. But he'll never root her out, if you ask me."

Who could tell? There wasn't any question that Eugenie had over-played her hand, although her misinterpretation of the situation was, I supposed, perfectly understandable. When X fired Cutter and Glemp from B & B, Eugenie tore up to his office and there was a real blowout. On my tapes I heard her rant, wail, weep, and stomp; B & B was sup-posed to be under her supervision, she howled; in fact she had endorsed Cutter's idea of changing the subsidiary's name, and yet X had gone right around and over her. I felt sorry for her; she didn't get the picture. She believed she had bartered her vote to him for a real, live executive role at AbCom, the first step in the short staircase that must someday lead to the top of the company, especially with Abner out of the way. X believed his part of the bargain could be met by simply indulging her, allowing her, on sufferance, to play a part, to dress up like an executive and command the writing of hundreds of memos to which neither he nor anyone else would pay attention.

Her tantrum determined him to get rid of her. Financial Assets Man-agement looked like the perfect chip for a trade, and he had offered it to her in exchange for her five million shares of the parent, now worth nearly $400 million. He probably ought to have given her a chance to cool off, because she turned him down on the spot, not taking ten seconds to consider his offer.

"She's a damn fool, that girl," said my mother. "She's pushing fifty and still can't see that Horace will never love her the way she wants. And he's certainly never going to let her run the company."

"I guess he sees her as a threat," I said.

"Certainly not. He sees her as too unbecoming, too plain. When it comes to women, Horace is strictly one for externals. What else is he up to?"

If Margarita hadn't been there, I might have told her what I knew about two new shows that were in preparation. Right now, scripts were being polished under X's personal supervision, and filming was sched-uled to begin in a matter of weeks at GBG Studios in Ventura. The graveyard on these was deeper than the Marianas Trench. All that was known, even by us in the brain trust, was that one was a series about life, love, and work in a big bank, and the other was a statehouse comedy-drama.

Instead I told Mother about the meetings with investment bankers I'd attended in connection with the spin-off of Assets Management.

X had instructed the chief financial officer to solicit presentations from two firms: Bouverie, Marcus and First Stuyvesant, the whiz-bang, high-visibility house that had handled AbCom under Abner. He said he wanted a second opinion in the interests of objectivity; the way things turned out, I concluded that he really wanted to give First Stuyvesant a good, painful tweak, to pay them back for having worked against him in the proxy fight. In the event, I learned a hell of a lot about the mental and ethical principles of investment banking.

First Stuyvesant sent their merger experts to the meeting. One was tall and thin and wore cowboy boots and jeans, an open shirt, and a big silver buckle which, he was at pains to point out, had been given to him for winning a big old-industry imbroglio. His sidekick was a fat little messy bundle of nervous energy who did most of the talking, while his colleague sprawled in his chair looking laconic, Gary Cooper with an MBA. X wasn't impressed; he'd known the real Gary Cooper.

From his Hermès briefcase, the little one produced a thick sheaf of computer printouts which he proceeded to thumb portentously. "We've done our homework, Mr. Monstrance, and we think we've got a pretty clear view of the direction we're prepared to recommend."

"Yup," said the tall one in confirmation, nodding slowly, and slouching farther down into his chair.

"We've done a DCF, using various IRRs, plus a couple of database matrix runs for line-of-business congruence, and where we come out, Mr. Monstrance, is that at four hundred forty-two million, which is the gross valuation our corporate appraisal department has placed on your financial businesses, we'd recommend looking for a third-party buyer. We're prepared to approach Bank of America, Travelers Insurance, and Paine Webber. We think those institutions offer optimal complementarity within what we see as likely fit-price parameters."

X looked appropriately pensive. The little one puffed up. I expected the thin one to pull out a jackknife and start whittling. Duncan leaned over to me. "As boys play with flies . . ." he muttered.

"And on what basis would your firm propose to handle this, assuming we decided to take you up on your recommendation?" asked X innocently. He looked expectantly at the two men. There was a pause. I thought of an observation Buck had made: that in the eyes of investment bankers, the sole point of a big corporate transaction was not its business, economic, or social good sense but the fees it would generate for them. I knew those fees had now risen to heights so ridiculous that even the brassiest banker could hardly bring himself to quote them without reddening.

The little one steeled himself.

"Well, sir, we've looked over some comparisons"—he proffered a computer sheet—"and feel that a fee of ten million dollars is indicated."

"Ummm," mumbled his partner.

"Ummm," said X. He scratched his broad chin. "Tell me, does 'indicated' mean the same thing as 'justified'?"

"Yessir," said one.

"Yup," his partner mumbled.

"I see." X steepled his fingers, looked at his buffed and polished nails, smacked his lips conclusively, and said, "And tell me, if I sell the business to Paine Webber, say, what will happen to the people?"

"People?" The two bankers looked at each other askance. This was an alien concept.

"Indeed," said X. "My son attracted some very good people here. They're used to running their own show, and from what I hear, that chap who runs Paine Webber would make even me look self-effacing. Ab got a lot of these people to become part of this company on the understanding that they'd continue to run their own show. To sell them out would be keeping bad faith with my son's word, don't you see?"

Expecting to be dealing purely with price, and confronted with a question of value, the First Stuyvesant team fell momentarily silent.

X continued amiably. "So while there's no doubt that a very favorable sale could be made, it wouldn't be in the spirit in which this company bought these businesses and induced their owners and managers to throw their hands in with us. For that reason, I'm going to offer our stockholders an opportunity to buy the financial businesses on an attractive basis. Are either of you gentlemen old enough to remember something called a rights offering?"

They looked perplexed. They had come to peddle slick new technology and this old man was talking war clubs.

"Well," X continued, "I've decided to let the stockholders of this company have the opportunity to buy shares of the Financial Assets Management Group on a basis which will value the group at three hundred million."

"But that would be leaving nearly a hundred and fifty million on the table!" the short one objected.

"Would it?" X asked blandly. "I don't really think so. Offering it to our stockholders at a favorable price doesn't really strike me as 'leaving it on the table.' I believe it belongs to them as it is. Our stockholders have, on the whole, been loyal and supportive, and this strikes me as deserving of some recognition."

Neither of the First Stuyvesant men said anything. X continued.

"Now, as our family foundation will be entitled to subscribe to a great many shares of Financial Assets Management, ownership of which doesn't quite jibe with my sense of the Foundation's longer-term interests, I propose to arrange for those shares to be made available to management of the financial services group, with the Foundation possibly providing some sort of assistance in helping them finance the purchase."

That was that. Fifteen days later, Financial Assets Management was spun off in a rights offering underwritten on a standby basis by Bouverie, Marcus. It resulted in an immediate market profit, for those stockholders who exercised or sold their rights, of close to $100 million. A week after that, X set off another financial starburst by selling a 51 percent interest in BizNet to Eric Shaughnessy's CNI for $200 million cash. He negotiated the deal himself, with no finder's fee, which didn't add to his popularity in the investment-banking community.

But the research and investment side of the Street loved him. They wallowed in and echoed Duncan's flowery chatter of "long-range strategic divestments," "optimal asset redeployments," and so on. X put it somewhat differently.

"I'm going to need a war chest," he told me.

As we came up on the affiliates' meeting, AbCom was really humming. The pace and excitement were intoxicating. Each success, each new direction taken, seemed to fire X up more. Ideas spilled from his office; lights burned late up and down the building. Rumor fanned the flames. The pilot for the new bank series, now known to be titled "First National," was said to be fantastic, but no one could be found who'd actually seen it. Along the corridors flew excited talk of a top-secret casting directive X was said to have given with respect to "City Hall," which someone had heard was what the other new series, now in preproduction on a closed set, was to be called. It was rumored that Network Sales was having to beat back anxious advertisers clamoring for a look at the pilots. The word was out from Madison Avenue to Burbank: the old man was still at the top of his game. The magic was back. On the New York Stock Exchange, the price of ABI soared above $85.

Duncan was doing yeoman service with the institutions. No longer required to editorialize, he principally concerned himself with the investment community, where he had allies and where he could speak the language. It didn't hurt, of course, that Ms. Pfannglanz of Institutional Equities Associates, so coolly positive on AbCom under Abner, was now practically soft and giggly on the stock.

"That's the thing about lady security analysts," Duncan said, "once in a while they fall in love with a stock, usually because they get a wide-on for the management, and when they do, they never let it go."

X was less enthusiastic about our rising institutional constituency, now well over thirty-three million shares, up by 25 percent since he'd taken over. He sounded like Shaughnessy.

"We've got two or three years of hard work ahead of us here," he said, "and that's too long a time for what's gone up not to come down. The reasons don't have to be of our own making. The Street's fickle. It gets bored easily, too easily. We mustn't forget that these people who've been avidly buying our shares were in some conspicuous cases the same people who voted against us."

Duncan didn't share his skepticism. He read the Street's enthusiasm as a testimonial "to the Chief's drawing power." He had a point, as I learned when I sat in on a couple of institutional briefings Duncan conducted in the back room at the Four Seasons. Sooner or later, after the grave talk of ratings, and the increase in advertising rates, and the company's strong balance sheet, with a cash position now exceeding half a billion dollars, and after all the spread sheets had been unfolded and examined, with much deep, purse-mouthed, talmudic talk of "beta" and "best case/worst case," and after the calculators had been duly punched, Duncan would get going on the subject of "the Chief," and his eyes would shine and his voice would sing, and around the room could be heard the heavy breathing of the faithful.

Duncan had surrendered completely to hero worship. Time after time, he regaled me with hymns to X's genius, his diligence, his capacity for work, and, naturally, his prowess.

"Can you believe the Chief," he'd say. "He gets to his office at six thirty. Watches videotape and the morning shows for an hour and a half. Eight thirty, Bernie Rusker's in from LA to discuss 'River Oaks'—which Chevrolet just signed up on at a quarter mil for thirty seconds, four spots an episode. Their agency went apeshit over the fall previews. Bernie leaves and Isaac Tellman comes in, just to kiss the old man's ass, and it goes that way until twelve thirty. Then he has, say, lunch with you and me, or with someone else, or alone in the office. Either way he fits in an hour's worth of poontang; then more meetings, until about six, when Hideki comes to give him his massage and he watches the local news. He's gonna kick some ass around WGBG, I can tell you! Then home, where he's merely giving a seated dinner for forty for some asshole from Milan!"

"C'mon, Fergie," I needled, "how do you know about the poontang? I think that's all bullshit."

"Oh, yeah? I heard it from Miss Sproulle. She said they put a layer of soundproofing on his door. You ever notice that his girls always go out for lunch when he comes back? The switchboard takes his calls? You know why? 'Cause their delicate ears get embarrassed. He bellows like a f—— bull when he gets off. Last week he had that girl from 'Shield 262' in there, you know the one, little blonde with the big hogans, and you coulda heard him all the way up to the f—— Tea Room!" Duncan's efforts to rinse his vocabulary had lapsed.

"My doctor says it's physically unlikely at his age."

"Your doctor's full of shit. Why do you think he's going to the Coast alone on the Gulfstream? Alone, my ass! I happen to know who he's taking."

Our talk turned to the upcoming affiliates' meeting in Los Angeles. Every one of GBG's two-hundred-odd affiliated television stations would be represented, and all but a handful of the radio outlets; it promised to be a wingding.

"I'm surprised he's taking Abner," I said.

"Why?" asked Duncan. "You know the kind of guy the Chief is. The kid deserves a whole lot of credit, even if some of these guys never quite got the picture about software and the rest of that stuff."

I didn't say anything. I wasn't the only one who was concerned about X making Abner accompany him to Los Angeles. Clio was furious. I'd spent the previous weekend with them in Southampton. On Saturday, Abner and I had met Buck at Shinnecock, and Clio had come along for the walk.

I was assembling a delicate filigree of half-topped five-woods down the right side of the twelfth hole, trying to observe the indifferent golfer's first commandment, to keep the ball in front of me. Abner and Buck were hacking their way down the left side, about forty yards away. Clio came up to me.

"How is it, working for him?" she asked in a cold voice. "I was very disappointed that he got you too, Sam."

"I didn't have much choice," I said. "He fixed it up with my editor. It was either go over to AbCom or look for a job on *House and Garden*. I'm sort of an undercover agent."

"Oh," she said, "it's none of my business. I'm not mad at you. I'm sure it's very interesting. It's just so frustrating, watching him always get his way! Is it ever going to end?"

"I take it you're referring to the Los Angeles junket?"

"Exactly. You've seen Abner, Sam. What does his father want? To parade him like a slave, like something out of *Aïda*? To make him come into the room like a child and shake hands with the grown-ups? Can't he leave us alone?"

I had no good answer. I bought a little time by studying my next shot. Setting my feet, I addressed the ball, took the club back smoothly, snatched it from the top, and sent the Titleist scuttering a foot above the ground about seventy yards in the general direction of Greenport.

"I don't always know what X has in mind," I said weakly. I felt, powerfully, that I didn't want Clio to think of me as one of the other guys, of "them."

"Abner's not up to it," she said.

I agreed. Just in the few weeks since I'd seen him in Florida, he seemed to have regressed. It wasn't exactly what you'd call deterioration. I'd always thought that Abner had locked up his childhood within himself, imprisoned its carefree innocence behind bars of gravity and purpose. That knock on the head seemed to have jolted loose the hasp.

"It won't be too bad," I said. "I'll watch out for him."

"Thank you." Her voice was dull and resigned. Then she shook her head; the sunlight on her hair added an incongruous bright note. "I'm sorry, Sam. Do keep an eye on him. You're his last true friend, which makes you mine. I'm counting on you."

I liked that.

The affiliates' meeting was a combination of Christ's entry into Jerusalem on Palm Sunday, the reunion of Napoleon with his marshals, the Apollo astronauts' confetti-drenched progress up lower Broadway, and a revival meeting. There were times during the four days in Beverly Hills that it seemed to me that well-dressed, obviously prosperous and self-assured men and women pressed in on X to touch the hem of his garment, imploring him to lay on the hands they'd just kissed. It was as much a convocation of the faithful as a business convention.

It had been skillfully scheduled and organized, orchestrated to produce a euphoria nicely balanced between mindless fun-in-the-sun and satisfaction brought on by the tangibilities of sales and profits. There were previews of the fall lineup; the affiliates were shown new episodes of "River Oaks" and "Shield 262" and "Resort." The word of mouth was terrific. The shows were credited with new depth of characterization and better stories, without sacrificing an ounce of commercial appeal. Large general sessions were held in the ballroom of the Century City Hotel to hear a lot of blather from GBG's senior staff management; smaller working parties convened to formulate high-sounding resolutions to cosmetize various aspects of turning a fast dollar; above all, there was food and drink.

The entire four days pointed toward the final evening, when X would address the assembled throng at a black-tie dinner. In the meantime, his hours and minutes were disbursed with infinitesimal precision, calculated to build up camaraderie, community, and anticipation. He turned up everywhere: huddling in the Polo Lounge with major market operators whom AbCom had made as rich as he; hugging the blue-haired wife of a station owner from Palatka, Florida; swapping smutty stories with a bunch of Oklahoma broadcasters. Along the way, he revealed bits and pieces of his new plans, turned up edges and corners here and there, fueling leaks and gossip and surmise, setting the stage for his exhortation to the troops.

GBG put on a show. A hundred limousines bore the motley around Los Angeles, to ooh and aah at the Rodeo Drive boutiques and to dig away at mountainous buffets, at acres of ham and lakes of Zinfandel, conducted on GBG's Ventura soundstages, where they rubbed up against the stars of GBG's hit series; they were convoyed to Malibu for a clambake catered by Spago and to the Chandler Music Center for a grand reception. Through it all, X moved, aflame with presence, radiating excitement. The occasion was emotionally meaningful for him too. Some of these people were true comrades: veterans from the old days and old wars. He sat up long and late with them, exchanging lengthy, fond reminiscences of the glory days of the fifties and sixties, when the world was their oyster. They might be old men now, but by God, they had done it once and they would do it again!

As Clio had feared, Abner was on exhibit, a trophy. These people were not Abner's people, never had been. As first they were tentative with him, but when they saw he was harmless, they bore in on him with a familiarity that seemed almost vengeful, slapping his back, winking and punching him lightly on the biceps, and he winked and slapped and punched them back. Had Abner really been aware of the undertones, I would have felt sorry for him, but he seemed delighted by the attention. I was glad Clio was back in Long Island.

I asked Duncan how these affairs had gone under Abner.

"Christ, you can't believe the difference. The last couple of years, Abner'd just fly in, do a duty dance with the biggest independents, give a speech about ratings, and hurry back home to get back with his financial people. The numbers were never too bad, although we never quite caught up to CBS and ABC. But shit, this is f—— Easter Sunday in Saint Peter's Square!"

He and Margarita and I were billeted three floors below X in the Beverly Wilshire. The rooming arrangements for the convention were made according to precise socioeconomic gradations that comprehended the entire spectrum of Southern California lodging. The GBG top brass was mostly two miles north at the Beverly Hills Hotel, comfortably ensconced in an atmosphere of fast talk and phones at the table. The representatives of the big independents, the owners of GBG's larger nonowned affiliated stations, were at the Bel Air and the Westwood Marquis, hotels chosen to encourage them to think of themselves as "old money."

Margarita and I found time to tour Los Angeles on our own. She was in a terrible mood, cranky and distracted, untouched by the carnival gaiety of the occasion. I wondered if she were homesick. Only at night, when I came to her room, did she seem to reconnect with happiness. We were approaching a moment of crisis, I felt, when the fever would either break or not. I felt no lover's anxieties, however; what was troubling her wasn't caused by me, or us, or our situation. We were playing roles in each other's lives, and we understood that and were happy enough with it.

X's performance at the final dinner was described by the *Los Angeles Times* media critic as "stirring, a clarion call to a new dignity for television." It was a good, strong speech; the four of us had worked over it for long hours, shaving, pruning, turning phrases just so. By the time he came to deliver it, the expectant mood of his audience had been nudged and drummed to a quivering pitch.

He came through the crowd toward the dais like Muhammad Ali entering the ring. As he passed, people rose applauding from their seats and cheered this old man for whom the honors of venerability, wealth, and reputation were evidently not enough. Along the way, he paused, letting this or that table savor his vigor or bask in the radiance of his grin or exult in a comforting, declarative pat of nape or shoulder. I felt the excitement.

When he rose to speak, he wasted no time on introductory platitudes. His tone was just right. He knew his audience. He spoke briefly of television's alleged deficiencies, his language and voice neither accusatory nor abashed. We have been careless, he was saying, but our role is too crucial to the mental and spiritual life of the nation to dwell on that. Let us move forward.

He talked about programming. This was a dollar-and-cents bottom-line audience to whom each Nielsen point gained or lost was a matter of millions. He discussed programming, emphasizing that Granite—the old name sent a thrill around the room—was working very effectively with its principal suppliers to upgrade its existing successes. He alluded to new shows, entertainment that would knock the socks off the competition in the ratings; on those, still in preproduction, the affiliates would have to trust him, to take his word. His audience would, and they wanted him to know it; they clapped and stamped and whistled.

He touched on GBG's unparalleled position in sports programming and news, dwelling on the network's ratings strength, on its showing in the recent May "sweeps." Not all this could be credited to him, he said. He called Abner to his feet, and a great wave of applause swept the ballroom. He had them purring.

Now he moved smoothly into the ideological meat of his speech. The time had come for GBG to exercise the potential for community leadership that should accompany prosperity if the system that had enriched the GBG family was to survive. The time had come for GBG, for the entire medium, to show its critics and the nation—indeed, the world—that it was capable of responsible self-government; that acceptable, even enviable profits could be earned in a manner compatible with the public interest. That deregulation—promised by Erwitt to his cronies in the industry—would be of lasting value only if those who were deregulated took it as a responsibility and not simply an opportunity for quick profit.

He began by talking about children's television. Margarita and I had argued that this was the safest place to begin to soften them up. Children's TV was old hat, a burying ground for bromides. I felt the audience relax.

"In a world of latchkey children," he said, "children whose only constant companion is the television set, it is up to us to act *in loco parentis*. We didn't ask for the baby-sitting job, but we created the need for it, the impulse for parents to work, both of them, in order to realize the possibilities of the rich life we show them. These are often poor homes, poor people, and we are wealthy, so we must do something for them."

The audience stirred. X moved on. Now came the fun part.

First he quoted Robert Heilbroner, words to the effect that the most pernicious, self-destructive force within capitalism was advertising. I'd found the quote in *The New York Review of Books*. It was pretty provocative, and Duncan and I had argued about including it, but X left it in. He paused and let it sink in; his listeners shifted uneasily in their seats.

He wasn't suggesting, he said, that GBG bite the hand that fed it. But he believed his audience must also recognize that it dealt from a position of strength; that as long as GBG entertainment ranked at the top, the network could be selective. Commercial television was neither the designated (or self-appointed) guardian of public virtue and morality nor its principal enemy, X said, but it was obliged to be on guard against proselytizing for substances unmistakably harmful to the body corporeal or the body public. He pointed out that twice, in its recent history, commercial television had been legislatively obliged to withdraw from lucrative sources of advertising.

"In the case both of cigarettes and hard liquor," he said, his voice rumbling roughly from the loudspeakers, "this industry had its mind made up for it. We are now faced with another narcotic, which to our minds at Granite threatens the public health in ways no less insidious. Not all narcotics can be identified and proved harmless by physical measurement, my friends. Others are more subtle. I refer to the wholesale, heedless expansion of consumer credit and speculation and the highly stimulative and effective advertising that has accompanied it!"

He paused. The room murmured. Merrill Lynch and American Express and the banks bought a lot of time.

"Such advertising," he continued, "which represents the effective commodification of money and credit, encourages borrowing and consumption and discourages saving to a degree which is by any conceivable standards irresponsible, and which demonstrably and adversely affects the economic health of this free society. Some form of control, of the stimulus as well as the disease, is necessary; some form of control is inevitable. It is better that we take the lead now before it is taken for us."

He had their whole attention now. This was potentially strong medi-

cine. There were people in this room who'd ridden the coattails of inflation and the money explosion to mega-fortunes. X was talking about
where they lived. I felt that he had moved them to the knife edge of
unhappiness, but now he deftly switched subjects.

"In the same vein, I fear that there can be little doubt that we have
failed in our responsibility as citizens of the larger community when it
comes to politics. I can assure you as of this moment that we have under
way a serious review in depth of the way we cover and report politics,
and there will be significant changes in the manner in which we report
the great and serious business of the American political progress."

The audience stirred. They could guess at some of these measures: no
exit polls, no predictions, no before-the-fact reporting. All the tired old
stuff like those articles in *The New Republic* complained about. So what.

"I can't say whether what we do will influence our competition, and
thereby change our industry's approach to the system and process of
American politics. Perhaps so; perhaps not. No aspect of television's history as a medium is as bright as its role in reporting electoral news and
comment, nor is any aspect as fragile."

Then he got down to specifics, and now he shook them.

Effective immediately, he announced, GBG would limit clearances of
time for paid political advertising on its owned-and-operated stations to
one minute per commercial hour, and this at rates any serious candidate
could afford. Nor would GBG make more than that amount of network
time available. A disapproving murmur rippled around the room. X held
up his hand. In order that GBG affiliates not be exposed to financial loss,
a subsidy arrangement would be worked out. That explained his war
chest. Besides, he said, grinning, the economic consequences would not
be great: advertisers were lined up the length of Madison Avenue to buy
the GBG fall schedule.

In the same sense, he concluded, similar limitations would be imposed
on advertising that encouraged the speculative use and availability of
credit and investment vehicles. The continuity department at GBG
would take responsibility for this. He emphasized that this area was a
matter of degree and selection. The audience relaxed. Obviously, American Express's fatuous galleon could continue to cruise the seas; Merrill
Lynch's bull could continue to stalk its maze. I could hear minds click like
abacuses, counting the cost. Credit cards? Thank you, Paine Webber? All
the come-ons to borrow? But the mood of the evening was too upbeat to
trouble them for more than a moment. Give the old boy a hand; it won't
really cost. Even the credit card people will work something out.

He gave them five more mesmerizing minutes, speaking in his dauntingly patrician way of generalities like change and challenge and opportunity. I was proud of him, proud to be of his party. I looked at Abner, gazing raptly up at his father, a blank happy grin bespeaking his adoration and dependence. The audience was pillowed in self-satisfaction. Tomorrow couldn't come soon enough, and that was the way I felt too.

CHAPTER 18

A premonition that something wasn't right stirred me from sleep; the bed beside me was empty. I sat up, collecting myself. My watch told me it was just after seven. I parted the cobwebs which shrouded my awareness and remembered that it was Sunday; a phrase from Wallace Stevens's "Sunday Morning" came into my head: "complacency of the peignoir."

Margarita was standing naked at the window, looking out at Central Park. The cool hiss of the air conditioner pebbled her skin. Beyond her, I could see by the light that the day was making up for a real scorcher. Summer had jumped us like a panther; one day the weather had been mild, with clear, bright skies, the air soft and faintly breezy; the next, the sky had turned thick and rheumy, the atmosphere dense and clotted with damp heat.

"Is something wrong?" I asked. I knew there was; I suspected I knew what.

She turned and looked at me, leaning back, her hands on the sill. I let my eyes run the length of her body, tracing the fond descent of breast to belly to the thick, black patch at her crotch. Raising my gaze to hers, I saw that she looked thoughtful and unhappy, and that she looked her age.

"Couldn't sleep?" I said. "Thinking about the play?"

The night before, we'd gone down to the Village to see a new play. It was much touted but had turned out to be just another wry, gaggish little exploration of love and sorrow, going no further than contemporary audiences were willing to go in the way of introspection, with a heavy reliance on a sound track of pop and hard rock, dramaturgy as disc jockeying. Afterward we'd had a rather morose supper, and bed had been no better than fair to medium good, say C plus, B minus.

"Come over here," I said, patting the warm space next to me.

She shook her head, obviously gathering herself. She took a deep breath and said what for the last month I had been expecting to hear.

"I'm going home, love. For good, I hope."

"'Hope'? Christ, that makes me feel great!"

"It's not you, dear heart. I think you know that. It's just that this country has worn me out."

"Do you want to talk about it?"

The words spilled from her. "I thought I could find something here I couldn't get at home. But there's no moral center here either, and there isn't anything to make up for it. Oh, Sam, I've come to hate it here. Why do you all have such contempt for each other, as if there were no one else in the world but each one of you? You trespass in each other's lives as you please, in search of whatever it is you want or think you're entitled to, no matter that someone else may be there before you, and all that matters is that you get what you want now! You despise the past and begrudge the future. You can't assimilate anything or anyone unless you make a fad of it, and then you discard it and rush onto the next new thing. You dump your refuse, your noise, your appetites into other people's lives and think that's your God-given right, your Fifth Freedom. People can't live that way, Sam! I try to look the other way, try not to hear, but I can't any longer, don't you see?"

"That's quite a bill of particulars," I said. "I had a feeling you were unhappy, but I hadn't guessed how much. Come over here."

She crossed the room and sat on the edge of the bed. I reached over and laid my hand on her forearm. She felt hot.

"I'm going to miss you," I said. I knew there was no point in arguing, in trying to catch her up in some kind of logical debate.

"And I you, terribly." Her eyes were genuinely sad when she turned to look at me. "You do understand, don't you, love? It's probably not as bad as I paint it; I'm probably just homesick. But I'm tired of talking about money, and I'm tired of vulgar people, and I'm worn to the bone with everyone's indifference. Doesn't anyone care?"

I knew what she missed. Conversation that wasn't about getting and spending. The small, sometimes inconvenient courtesies which make it possible for numbers of people, large numbers, to exist side by side more or less peacefully.

"I care," I said. "X does. He's going to miss you too." I wasn't going to fight her.

"I've done all I can for Horace," she said. "That's part of the problem, don't you see?"

"Have you told him you're leaving?"

"Friday afternoon. He wanted me to come down for the weekend, but I simply couldn't bear to see those loathsome people one more time, and I really didn't want to have Horace badgering me. I wanted to be with you."

Getting it out relaxed her. She swung her feet up on the bed and sighed.

"What finally decided you?" I asked.

She smiled and shook her head.

"A funny, small thing. Do you remember when we had dinner last weekend, there was a young couple at the next table? Handsome young people; very much on the way up, I should have said."

"Vaguely."

"I couldn't help overhearing them. The young man was obviously trying to seduce her, and I think he was succeeding. From what I overheard, he was with some investment bank. She was very taken with him; they're probably just waking up now, and wondering what it all means. Anyway, when they finished dinner, he paid the bill with a credit card, and, do you know, he very carefully kept the receipted check! Folded it and put it in his billfold! He was going to seduce her—and then deduct her! You might say something cracked in me then. I knew at that moment I couldn't stay here, even if I thought Horace wasn't doomed to failure."

"Come again?" I asked.

She laid her hand on my arm. "I want to give you some advice, my love. Disconnect yourself from this crusade of Horace's; it's futile."

"What do you mean?"

"He's misjudged his enemy, Sam. He thinks he can mobilize this country against Erwitt and what he secretly and openly stands for, and he's wrong. He's wrong because he believes in something called the American spirit; he believes in all those schoolboy words about fair play and equality and concern. He thinks there's a wave of resentment out there that he can ride, and he's wrong! There's no resentment out there, love. No one cares, really! The wealthy think they're insulated; they've bought off the politicians. And the poor have given up. There's smugness out there, and despair, and nothing in between."

"X would say that makes the battle all the more worth fighting."

"No battle is worth fighting if it has no chance of being won. I mean no chance, none at all; zero; null; nil! If there were a thousand other Horaces to line up shoulder to shoulder with him, it might be different, but there aren't. Horace thinks Erwitt's a joke, and in a way he is, but people thought Hitler was a joke too, with that silly mustache, and Mussolini, with that chin. The people behind Erwitt want the country a certain way, and Erwitt's job is to induce the lassitude, the selfish well-being that will open up the vacuum. Horace doesn't see what's at stake. He thinks it's ideas. It isn't, love, it's money—and I find that so discouraging it's driving me back to England. We may be a sad, sick old country, poisoned with our own kind of sleaze, but we have our graces too."

"What can I say?" I said. It was grown-up time.

She smiled again and placed her hand on my thigh.

"I'm very proud of you and me, I really am. We've had a wonderful, delicious, exciting time together, and yet we've managed to avoid confusing preoccupation with love the way a great many people I've known do, the way I have myself once or twice. You've been a dear, Sam: amorous, attentive, ardent. I wish it might have been big enough to have changed the way I feel about staying here, but it isn't, and you know that as well as I do."

"And X? There are other aspects to him."

"That always bothered you, didn't it? You needn't have worried. Oh, there was one time, before you and I became lovers, but it really didn't come to anything. He's very sweet and avid, but he's too old now, I fear. He's a great man when he puts his mind to it, but no longer in that way. Make love to me, will you? I'm feeling awfully lonely."

Three weeks later, I rode with her in X's car out to JFK to see her onto the London Concorde. We chatted amiably, one old chum seeing another off. X had taken the news of her departure agreeably. I had raised her objections with him, and he had brushed them off.

"Resentment, Sam?" He'd laughed at the thought. "Of course there's no resentment. Not now, there isn't; Eldon's done his job too well, by George! He's put an entire nation to sleep. But just what do you think television's for? First, we have to create resentment, which we shall! And then and only then can we put it to work. We have to show the man sitting hopelessly in front of his television set just exactly the contempt Eldon's people have for him, and for the rest of us, and how Eldon hides that contempt. We'll turn things upside down and show Eldon for the malevolent stooge he is! It's not hard to transmute his contempt into the viewer's hatred, if you know what you're doing, and I think I do. I'll miss Margarita. She's been a great help. But there's man's work to do now, Sam, man's work!"

I kissed her goodbye in the car. The babel and confusion of the airport precluded doing the Paul Henreid–Bogart–Bergman bit, mist on the runway, etc. I was barely able to watch her long, lovely stride carry her into the British Airways terminal before a cop came along to shoo us off, and I was left alone in New York for the summer.

There had been worse prospects facing me in my life. If I chose to flee the city, I had plenty of options: there was Dunecrag, if I chose, although I too had no patience for the troublemakers and favor seekers who pussyfooted around the rim of X. I was sure I could cadge a weekend or two with Abner and Clio, Buck was in a fancy new rental in Southampton, and I had an open invitation from Gus and the guys in Water Mill. In other quadrants were other chances: Fire Island, Maine, the Berkshires, the Cape.

Summer was a good season for the city. I liked Saturdays and Sundays in the park, just wandering, watching ball games on the Great Lawn and the Heckscher Playground, kite-flying on the Sheep Meadow, croquet, breakdancing, rollerskating, the vagrants whose mumbling, overcoated delirium knew no season. Summer in the city was manageable, however, only if you were alone or absolutely, desperately, foamingly in love, which was sort of the same thing. Aggravation must be denied; there was no room for a case of Buck's red ass, for the perverse little power trips people liked to lay on you: habitual tardiness, last-minute changes of plan and schedule, calculated indecision.

For most of July, then, I kept to myself. I went to a lot of movies in real movie theaters, not screening rooms in which slippered Filipinos passed popcorn in silver salvers. I stayed out of the known haunts of the kiwi-fruit crowd. And there was a lot going on at AbCom.

Predictably, X's announced policy changes had been news and had stirred up the expected reactions. The American Association of Advertising Agencies had denounced the proposed curtailments on political and credit commercials as a rank violation of the First Amendment. Telegrams had been sent to members of Congress, the Federal Communications Commission, GBG's affiliated stations, and so on. BLEEP took out after X from its weekly Op-Ed pulpit.

"Blah, blah, blah," said X when he read the AAAA and BLEEP pieces. "Just so much mush." He was disappointed. He'd hoped to elicit a comment from Erwitt, but the President had made no comment, even though *Newsweek* had pointed out that GBG's decision, if it spread to the other networks, could drastically affect Erwitt's reelection strategy, which was essentially based on saturation advertising.

Toward the end of July, X announced the sale of One AbCom Plaza, just months away from occupancy, to a tax-shelter syndicate organized by First Stuyvesant. The cash to AbCom wasn't that much, about $25 million, the building having been financed with six or seven layers of debt, a "pousse-café of leverage," as Duncan put it. But X seemed to regard its continued presence on his horizon as a symbol.

Shortly afterward, he spent a small part of his growing war chest buying in GBG's "commitments." These were "pay or play" deals the network had made to keep happy or tie up the talents—producers, writers, actors—associated with past and existing winners, everyone from Bernie, Isaac, Fred, and Leo to the Polynesian dwarf who starred in "Resort."

"This way we choke off a great deal of prospective garbage we'd otherwise be obliged to show," he informed an analyst from Donaldson, Lufkin. "We spent twenty-nine million dollars buying in our outstanding commitments, which in most instances were nothing else than substantive payoffs and which can prove disastrous, as they did for my old friends the Sarnoffs." His grin was tigerish. "That sum represents the discounted present value of our estimate of future liability." He was proud of his growing grasp of the new language of the Street. "This network," he announced proudly, "is no longer a sewer into which certain people have a contractual right to dump their garbage!"

He was all over AbCom now, commissioning pilots, restudying accounting procedures, moving and replacing people, looking at acquisitions. He bought a quarter interest in a cable financial service and added two special-interest computer magazines to the publishing stable.

"Not that I really believe in all this computer blather," he told me. "I don't think it's all it's cracked up to be. Take the weather. Twenty years ago we'd just call Philadelphia when we were predicting for New York. Now I've got computers and satellites and I'm paying that idiotic woman nearly a million dollars a year to read the forecasts, and we're still wrong five days out of six."

He began to spend one day a week at GBG Labs, his favorite brainchild. Under Abner, the Labs had been relatively quiet; Abner preferred to purchase proven technology rather than risk money creating it. Once or twice I accompanied X to the Labs' rusticated compound in central Connecticut.

"I'm just a tinkerer at heart, Sam," he announced as we were driven through the stone gates. He slipped easily and with great charm into his fantasy roles. "Just a Yankee tinkerer in a garage, that's me, and this is my garage.

"We're really doing a lot of interesting stuff up here," he said enthusiastically, plunging down a corridor flanked by workrooms and laboratories filled with electronic equipment. "New laser-based recording techniques, digital sublimination, high-speed long-range transmission, over-the-air pay television that works. I tell you, Sam, this is the most exciting part of Granite!"

We spent the better part of the day there. To me, the technical palaver was as tiresome as always; I had no mind for this sort of thing, and not much interest either, and differences of degree, so exciting to X's scientists, had little significance for me. I made admiring noises, and some of the stuff was pretty remarkable; the holographs produced as good an illusion as any magician could ask for, and some of the subliminals were downright hypnotic. It was all a good show but, as far as I could see, small potatoes compared to the real excitement at AbCom, which was the programming that would be going on the air next fall.

At the beginning of August, X screened the first five episodes of "First National" for a group of around fifty critics gathered from around the country. They loved it. The scripts were strong and the characterizations deft. The show was entertaining and involving, and it rang true, it smelt real. X had taken pains to see that it was simultaneously authentic, credible, and understandable. "The most important thing," he said, "is to get the business part so the man on the street can grasp what it's all about; if we're going to make him productively angry with the system, we've first got to show him how it works."

A second screening a few days later for the network's salespeople and a few advertising types was less generally applauded. "First National" was hardly an anthem to the nation's banks and bankers. "Citicorp is gonna shit when they catch this show," Duncan told me that night. The next day, my tapes confirmed his observation. There had been a private audience for AbCom's sales and advertising people.

The first voice I recognized was the GBG vice-president for marketing. "Well, sir, it's a good strong show, no doubt of that, but I think it's going to be a tough sell. The banks aren't going to like it. Not one bit!"

"Really?" I heard X say. "Why? It's very true to life." I could tell he was having fun.

"I think what Jack's getting at"—another voice, one I didn't recognize, presumably one of the agency heads—"is that there are a lot of potential buyers for this show, consumer goods companies, maybe the bottlers, who are gonna get leaned on by the banks."

"Leaned on?" X sounded scornful. "And how, pray tell? Will their loans be called in? Will their checks be bounced?"

"Look, Mr. Monstrance." The unknown voice spoke again. "Let's not kid each other. The banks are gonna crap in their pants if you put this on. That episode you showed us, that was every goddamn banker I ever knew, and I've been on the Chase account for ten years! The banks see that, they're gonna lay on the heat: redline you, me, any sponsor; shit, they'll try to get the names of the Nielsen households and lean on them!"

"Well," said X, "I guess we'll just have to see what happens. I'm putting the show on the air September fifteenth, sponsors or no sponsors. Nine o'clock. We'll lead in with 'Shield Two Sixty-two.' I'll make you a little bet, Arthur. Say a thousand dollars or lunch for two at Le Cirque, whichever is more. I'll wager you that by the November ratings period, 'First National' will have a forty share. Until then, if no one buys the show, we'll carry it; we can afford to. Come November, when the Nielsens are in, I'll guarantee you sponsors will be fighting to get on it."

"I'll fade you the grand, Mr. Monstrance. But even if you win, I still say it's gonna be a bitch!"

"So is life, Arthur," I heard X say calmly, "so is life."

His next announcement, that GBG was going to expand the evening news to forty-five minutes, followed by a nightly fifteen-minute in-depth special report on consumer and economic affairs, raised unshirted hell within the GBG family. The new half hour would replace "That's Unreal!," a popular and profitable nightly trash heap devoted to spectacularly deformed people, singing dogs, and the like. The affiliates raised hell; he heard from over a hundred and ninety out of two hundred. X was skilled at retreat, and he traded off a compromise: the reformatted news would run three nights a week, until they could see how it did, with "That's Unreal!" remaining in its accustomed slot Tuesday and Thursday.

"Did you ever hear such shortsighted bushwah?" he said. "Bunch of darn fools. Don't they realize that all that anyone thinks about these days is the economy? For forty years, we've underreported business and money and the economy, let people like this chap Rukeyser steal our thunder. We give 'em a montage of the stock exchange trading floor and a Dow Jones graph and a sentence about some economic index or other, and that's that. And, of course, we throw in a film clip giving them the party line from Washington. Well, we're going to change that, I can tell you, affiliates or no affiliates!"

The new shape of the GBG schedule gradually emerged on the programming board which ran the length of one wall of his office. Whole stretches of the inherited programming lineup were left untouched. The daytime hours, for example, remained a wasteland of game shows, soap opera, point-and-tell confessionals, and talk shows of the sort that had spawned the President. "God help us that this chap in San Francisco doesn't turn out to be another Erwitt," X said one day of a phenomenally popular new GBG talk-show host who specialized in exhibiting other people's misery and aberration.

He tinkered with the network's early morning wake-up show, which had never done well against ABC and NBC and was back and forth for last place with CBS. He wanted to pitch the show at the millions of men and women washing and dressing on their way to work; advertisers wanted demographics that emphasized housewives in curlers. As the fall season approached, he hadn't found the key.

He continued to spend really big money building up the preemptive position GBG had in sports, the key to the high-ticket fatcat market. While the other moguls basked in the Hamptons with their thumbs up their asses, X moved quickly and preemptively to strike a series of major deals. Abner had given him a head start: GBG already shared rotating rights to the World Series and the Super Bowl, as well as the U.S. Open and Wimbledon, and had an exclusive lock on the NCAA Final Four, National Conference of the National Football League, Wednesday night baseball, the New York City Marathon, and Notre Dame football. Now, for another $600 million payable over three years, he bought a revision of GBG's deal with the NFL, essentially acquiring the right to pick and choose its weekend pro football lineup without regard for local markets or live attendance. It represented an inevitable final step for the league's owners; they had now sold out their hometown fans completely. In the next few weeks, he concluded negotiations that gave him exclusive television rights to televise a national collegiate football championship playoff; a two-year elimination tournament to determine, once and for all, the world's boxing champions; the World Cup in soccer. In the process, he rinsed GBG's schedule of bowling, roller and demolition derbies, celebrity triathlons, and other junk sports. The market loved it. Big-time sports had the puncture-proof demographics which would ring the bell on the bottom line. AbCom stock nudged close to $100 in a lifeless market.

In all X had done, his timing was impeccable, and he had Branch Rickey's luck. Eldonomics was turning out to be the big lie that people had suspected, and the markets had been in for a rough spell as investors took a reef in their sails. Volume dried up; the share prices of the big brokerage houses plummeted as their overleveraged, overbuilt operating bases led to plunging earnings. The price at which X had spun off Financial Assets Management now looked like a master stroke, but original investors still owned the stock at a decent profit. The consolidation of BizNet with Eric Shaughnessy's CNI had been no less fruitful. AbCom's remaining stake in BizNet was worth close to what the whole had been.

Never one to let the propitious moment slip by, Duncan persuaded X to hold a two-day powwow for big investors early in August at Dunecrag. The instant it was announced, it became the hottest ticket on the Street. I heard from "friends" I never knew I had. Buck called to beg an invitation.

In the end, a blue-ribbon collection of roughly sixty analysts, investment advisers, trust officers, and money managers was bidden to Dunecrag for two days of hearing about AbCom. Many had summer homes nearby; the others, along with a score of AbCom types, were billeted at an East Hampton inn. The dozen bedrooms at Dunecrag were parceled out among the host crowd, including me, Duncan, and Eugenie, and a number of showbiz guests, including Bernie, Isaac, et al., and the stars of "River Oaks" and "Resort," there to add glitz to the occasion. Cass would be on hand too. I really hadn't expected to see her, nor had I laid eyes on her yet this summer, most of which I knew she'd spent in Europe. I doubted she would be coming to my room after curfew.

"Having her was the Chief's idea," Duncan told me two nights before the conference. We were in his apartment, which had been completely redone to resemble X's office. The sparse geometries of the decorative scheme I'd first seen had given way to a contrived clutter of wooden furniture, moth-eaten fur throws, and old glass. There was quite a bit of brass, and yards of paisley hung in great swags around the windows.

"Actually, I make it for kind of an ego trip, between you and me," said Duncan. "Makes him look like a stud, but with taste. A great-looking but obviously classy woman, not a different starlet after every meal. There's places where the Zanuck bit—the hookers and the rest—works, but not with this crowd."

"She was my girlfriend, you know."

"So I heard. You crying on the inside, laughing on the outside?"

"No. That was in another country—"

"And, besides, the wench is dead," said Duncan. "Actually, what Marlowe wrote was: 'It was a long time ago, in another country. . . .' *The Jew of Malta*. Marlowe shoulda been with me yesterday. I went to this place, Dean and DeLuca, in East Hampton. Scouting the territory. How about ten bucks for peanut butter, huh? Marlowe woulda written 'The Jew of East Hampton.' This is gonna be some f—— show!"

I enjoyed the two days at Dunecrag. Unlike Duncan, I had no responsibilities, other than to watch and report. I dutifully attended the presentations, screenings, slide shows, buffets, previews, and briefings and kept the right glasses filled, principally my own. None of my money was on the table. I assumed I was part of the AbCom team, part of the entertainment world, and thus entitled to all rights and privileges therefrom accruing, so I contrived to make it out to the dunes with the cute brunette who played the third female lead on "River Oaks," the one married to the Nicaraguan who thinks he's an heir to the fortune. I conducted some basic research: her breasts were just as extraordinary and gravity-defying as they'd seemed in *Playboy*, good enough to make me overlook the fact that it was surely possible to look in one of the young lady's ears and straight out the other without encountering anything but air. Just as things were proceeding agreeably, the wind changed, bringing a wet mist in off the ocean, and so discommoding her bleached Santa Monica sensibility that she rushed from the scene with a tiny cry, leaving me in a state of extreme dishevelment and excitation. When I looked for her later, I saw that her heart had been stolen by a certain former football player of my acquaintance.

For most of the two days, X remained apart, an aloof, enticing presence. Between the plenary sessions, he mingled, let them rub up against him, feel the alluring heat of his aura. He wooed them by indirection, with his wealth, his taste, the fruits his genius had brought him. He orchestrated an exercise in the sheer eroticism of riches and power, making them seem mellifluous and treasurable as honey. He led them among the silver frames from which Presidents and megastars smiled back at them; he shared with them the pleasure of admiring his Lichtensteins and Dines and Calders, and the Pollock which had been painted not twenty minutes' drive from Dunecrag, which he'd bought right off the artist's floor. In the pool house they gazed enviously at the Stronzos and Sporcas he'd bought through Cass, and at the huge new Scheisstueck triptych, "Vicksburg II," an interpretation of the battle that appeared to have been confected of shredded Tupperware but which had been reproduced in *Vogue* and was thus significant. These were massive productions of the artists of the moment, whose work people like these trooped dutifully to SoHo on Saturdays to puzzle out. Having such paintings stamped X as totally contemporary, as young in spirit as any of his guests.

He made his formal appearance just before dinner the second night.

"He's got 'em lickin' the crumbs from his hand," Buck declared. "He's shown 'em somethin' they want so bad they can taste it! Most o' these folks're just clerks makin' half a million a year. They're shittin' with happiness just to be where he can see 'em!"

That afternoon, they'd seen the first public previews of "First National." The segments this audience had been shown were selectively less "controversial" than what the critics and agencies had seen. Duncan had also dropped hints about the political series.

X was asked about production arrangements for the new series. GBG was filming them itself, he answered. Wasn't that illegal? Networks weren't supposed to control syndication rights. Quite right, he said; but the syndication rights in the shows had been donated to Yale and New York Hospital; the two institutions had entered into private arrangements with Lorimar to market the shows for syndication. This would give GBG creative control and, down the road, a nice tax deduction.

Another questioner raised the rumor that advertisers were upset with the political content of certain of the "First National" episodes, none of which had been shown here, that were said to be violently anti-bank and anti-business. X slipped the question with smooth assurances that there wasn't anything planned for the series that this audience wouldn't find realistic.

Someone asked about hearsay that the administration was unsympathetic to X's proposed limitation on political advertising and might take action in the courts. Wasn't it true, she added, that GBG was limiting Mr. Erwitt's exposure on its news broadcasts? Surely, a hostile administration couldn't be good for the company and its stockholders?

X threw his questioner his slickest, most ingenuously reassuring grin.

"You know," he said, "I've heard those rumors myself. I don't believe them. For one thing, the President and I have known each other a long time, and I'm certain he has the same feelings about the political process as I do, as must concerned Americans everywhere. As for the second part of your question, I will admit that we here at Granite *are* trying to report real news. I bow to no one in my admiration for the effectiveness and dedication of Mr. Erwitt's press office, but there has been a tendency, undoubtedly thanks to the overzealousness of some of his aides, to reduce the news content of the Presidency to a series of press releases and photo opportunities. Now, I think you'll all agree that you'd find that unacceptable in your business of making investment decisions about companies; you need hard facts, and the less peripheral matter the better. Well, it's just the same in ours, so I hope you'll understand. As for singling Granite out, I would doubt it, especially now that our competitors seem to be following our lead. And now, I know that Jacques has made a special effort, so I think we'd best go in to dinner."

Everyone agreed that it had been a sensational two days. The next morning, ABI opened at $101.

CHAPTER 19

I stayed over after the conference ended, while X and his AbCom consort, and the guests, were flown off in enough helicopters to have evacuated Saigon.

Cass remained too; an AbCom chopper would be returning later in the morning to ferry her to Newport. We had coffee on the porch. It was weird to be chatting as uninvolvedly as if we had just met and were trying to sell each other life insurance. I heard about her new business: advising on corporate art purchases; besides AbCom, she now had, mainly thanks to X, a handful of other big clients, names so loaded for artistic bear that she could cut her own deals along Fifty-seventh Street and West Broadway.

"How's the book going?" I asked, trying to sound genuinely interested.

"Not to worry, darling. You won't recognize yourself. I must say, you seem better. H.H. says you had a fling with that Clerc woman. I can tell you he was not at all pleased. Anyway, did it do the trick? Get you over me, I mean?"

"Barely." I made a series of loud, obvious, panting sounds. "God, it was hard! How's your love life, if it comes to that? Age and beauty still do the trick?"

"Don't be nasty. I'm much too busy. I've never been happier."

When she left, I gave Clio a call, thinking that I might cruise over to Southampton and pay my respects. She sounded pleased to hear from me. She was driving Abner up-island to talk to a specialist at North

Shore Community Hospital, but they'd be back for dinner. Would I stay over? I would.

"A specialist?" I asked. "Anything wrong?"

"I don't really think so. He has these little lapses now and then, really just more of the same, but I don't think much has changed."

"Why drive all the way up there? Why not get a helicopter from AbCom? I'm sure X'd send one."

"I don't want any favors, not from him. Anyway, that sort of thing's completely unnecessary now. We have nothing but time on our hands. Abner'll be thrilled you're coming for dinner. Where are you staying, with that stockbroker friend of yours? Do you want to bring him? Abner told me how much he liked him the time you played golf."

"Actually, I'm at Dunecrag. X just got through a dog-and-pony show for the institutions."

At the other end I heard a sigh that spoke her thought: must he be everywhere in our lives, these lives that he's ruined?

In the course of the evening, it was clear to me that Abner was losing ground. More than once he drifted away from us, losing the thread of what was being said and how we had gotten to where we were. Momentary lapses, to be sure, but obviously more than daydreaming, and certainly more pronounced than any I'd seen before.

"He does seem a little tired," I said after dinner, wanting to be tactful. Abner had gone off into the study to watch a baseball game on television.

"You noticed, didn't you, Sam? I try to make myself not see it, but he is getting worse, isn't he?" She lit a cigarette and blew the smoke out with exasperation. "Well, how was it at Dunecrag? How is H.H.?"

"Strictly late Picasso. Lusty, protean, full of ideas, scared of time, creative as all hell, oversexed. What's new? He's extraordinary, no matter what else you may think of him. Haven't you seen him recently? He's only twenty minutes down the road."

"Not since Abner came back from Los Angeles. I think his father believes him to be damaged goods. He doesn't like that, you know. Just ask Eugenie!"

"Do you see her?"

"Quite a bit. She came by last weekend. She's taken a terrible great barn of a place on Meadow Lane. I can't imagine what she does with herself here. She hates big overdressed parties, and that's all Southampton is now. I'm putting this house on the market in the fall. That ghastly little Cornara man came by the other day; not to see Abner, but to make me an offer. I told him to double it, and he accepted on the spot! I just want to be away from the Monstrances and their endless, endless quarrels! Aren't you tired of them too?"

"I suppose so. I'm not really in the line of fire. Abner's the way he is, and Eugenie's been keeping a low profile since she had that blow-up with X. I don't think she comes into the office much."

There was evidence in the sports pages for that supposition. The Boroughs had led their division through the middle of May; then a couple of shifts in personnel had been made, and the team had lost two thirds of its games since.

"You'll wear out too," Clio said. "Just wait. Sooner or later."

Just then Abner wandered back into the room, his face wreathed in a smile of unstained, boyish pleasure.

"Sam, you really ought to come watch. You wouldn't mind, would you, Clee? This is terrific! It's two–two, bottom of the ninth. Come on, Sam, whyn't you watch with me? Just till the end, please."

In mid-August, X fired a direct salvo at President Erwitt. He and Cass—she called to tell me—were leaving for Salzburg, where they would attend the festival as the guests of Bud and Marie, who had rented a whole bunch of schlosses for their many new friends. According to my gossip sheets, Salzburg was the place to be in August, now that the Hamptons were invaded by newer, or this year's, money. Anyone could rent a yacht, but it took real dollars to rent Mozart. I had a mental picture of Salzburg: the women batting their jewelry at each other in the courtyard of the opera house or the lobby of the Goldener Hirsch Hotel; in the evenings, their husbands would snooze through *The Magic Flute* or Mahler's Fourth, heads afloat on pillowing dreams of telexes bringing news of fresh deals and percentage rentals. I said bon voyage without envy.

Erwitt had set one of his rare press conferences, now limited to three or four a year, for a Tuesday at his Iowa farm, where he was vacationing. In accordance with his politics of simplism, the President took frequent vacations; the nation seemed to find reassurance in this: if its chief executive made the exercise of his office seem less complicated and demanding than running a corner garage, why worry?

The four networks alternated the job of running the pooled camera feed for the presidential press conferences. It was not a demanding job. The sessions were carefully rehearsed and orchestrated. The interrogatory battle order was as established as an Edinburgh reel: first the two ladies from AP and UP, then the veterans of the press corps, finally the TV and radio people. Because forty years before the camera had atrophied Erwitt's ability to improvise, the President worked from a seating chart and a TelePrompTer that cued him on the questions his aides had given various favorites in the press corps to ask.

This particular press conference was apparently important. The President had preempted an hour of prime time, from 7:30 to 8:30 EDT, but as far as anyone knew at GBG, which would be operating the pool transmission, there was no special news. There was nothing surprising about that. One of Erwitt's pet tricks was to put the drama into the announcement and then say nothing, comforting the nation by deflating its illusory anxieties.

I knew something was up, however, because Duncan and I had been summoned to X's apartment to watch it. We stopped for a couple of shooters at the Pierre and presented ourselves as commanded, spiffy in mental dress whites, precisely at seven o'clock. It was just the three of us. We ate on trays in the study: baby potatoes crowned with red caviar and cold veal birds, with a snappy California Riesling. X talked of Salzburg, about going there in 1937 to hear Toscanini conduct *The Magic Flute*; about returning again at the end of the war after seeing Auschwitz. He was starting to tell me how wonderful Vienna was, unaware of my little private fixation, when the presidential seal materialized on the four-screen console. X muted the ABC, NBC, and CBS pictures; the sound came up on WGBG.

Erwitt looked tanned and confident. He began in his customary folksy way. "My dear friends, I don't know why we . . ." and launched into a jovial attack on the economists who were currently assaulting his selectively free-market economic policies. His tone and terminology were genially overblown, the language of the high school debating society, Middle American oratory, a bit strained, but in its way the mild awkwardness was comforting. It was "just folks" raised to a fine art; words and delivery chosen to let his audience know that this was what a President had to do, even if he'd just as soon be on the store porch arguing batting averages and waiting for the evening's TV. He conveyed the image of a man who was no better or worse than the rest of us, no smarter, no abler, but just a mite luckier, although maybe it wasn't all that lucky, being made to do all this work and worrying about the Bolshies and such. This evening's chat was in anticipation of Labor Day, and all this talk about how American management was overpaying itself, when the hardest laborers were the unsung managers who kept the wheels turning.

The script had been written by someone at BLEEP, or possibly one of

Duncan's opposite numbers at United Technologies or Mobil, the current ranking corporate apologists for Eldonomics. Erwitt spoke about American grit and creativity, about entrepreneurialism, about the business spirit. As usual, he resonated history without once referring to a fact of that history. The past has no reality for this man, I thought, but then, as X pointed out, neither did the present, and as for the future, forget it!

When he concluded, he called for questions. The AP and UP ladies beamed under outlandish hats and asked outlandishly simple questions. Next in the interrogatory minuet was the capital's chief sycophant, the *Time* columnist, whose wet lips had been pressed to the fundament of every President since Roosevelt. He bootlicked his way through a dialogue about El Salvador. Other questions followed. A hand went up in the second row. X leaned forward expectantly.

"Yes, Roger?" said the President.

The man who rose, however, was not Roger Stirling, GBG's White House correspondent. This was a younger man, diffident, by appearance Jewish, with a high, trickly voice.

"Martin Melstein, Mr. President, filling in for Roger Stirling. Would you comment, please, on the decline in last month's productivity index?"

"Decline?" Erwitt looked around, in momentary confusion, as if something had gone wrong with the TelePrompTer. "The index didn't decline."

"I'm sorry, sir," said Melstein, "but according to our source at the Department of Commerce, the figures to be released tomorrow show a three point four percent seasonally adjusted annual rate of decline in gross industrial productivity."

"Well, Mr. Melberg," said Erwitt, voice rising, obviously angry, working hard to maintain his mask of geniality, "how can I comment on something I haven't seen? Do you know how many pieces of paper emerge from this government every day? Four hundred million! And still America's on the move again. I can't help it if you've gotten some bum dope from some sour grapes negativist leaker somewhere. Why just last week I had a letter from a fellow in Spokane . . ."

Accomplished performer that he was, Erwitt wiped all traces of irritation from his face and voice and launched into an anecdote involving a Washington fruit grower and a crossbred heifer, defining Administration policy in the vernacular of a Lamb's Club "roast." Vintage Erwitt: defusing a loaded situation by retreating into amiable boobery. His punch line drew a pleased little rivulet of applause from the press corps.

Melstein, however, was still on his feet.

"Mr. President . . ."

Erwitt paused. He beamed glorifically down on his persistent interrogator.

"I thought I'd answered your question, Mr. Melstone."

"It's Melstein, Mr. President. S-T-E-I-N, sir. Anyway, about the decline in the productivity index—"

Erwitt seemed to flush, difficult as it was to tell under the layerings of makeup. He looked at the camera, but with the deflected focus that told me he was asking his TelePrompTer for help.

"Mr. Melstein, it's obvious you're using figures which I am unfamiliar with. You know we country people have a saying."

He reached deep into his resources of jocularity and dragged the folksy aphorism to the surface like a huge inert fish pulled from the depths of a lake.

"Anyway," he concluded with a patient smile, "we'll have a statement for you tomorrow morning. We've been pretty darn busy around here getting ready to greet our returning heroes from Manila!" The corners of his mouth turned down and he spoke with pious sorrow about the heroism of the Special Forces detachment that had been dispatched to Manila to pull out the Marcos family and their courtiers. Then he grinned, as if he'd remembered something really neat. "Mr. Melberg, you can rest easy about one thing. The economic recovery is still under way. As a matter of fact, the market-basket cost of the average American family declined last month by almost five percent! And you can tell that to your quisling friends!"

The President turned away and started to point at another questioner. But Melstein didn't sit down. He addressed the President over impatient hisses from the rest of the press corps.

"As a matter of fact, Mr. President, our figures from the CBO indicate that the market-basket price increased last month at an annual rate of eleven percent. Your figure of five percent is incorrect. Would you care to comment on that?"

The President glared. Then he smiled and moved into the old Erwitt routine, the tried-and-true evasion.

"Five percent?" A big grin crossed his face. "Did I say that?" The rest of his answer was lost in a chortle from the reporters, as if Erwitt had set a mechanical toy off. The *Time* correspondent reached up and tugged at Melstein's sleeve. Someone from NBC jumped up and hurriedly asked about the President's vacation plans. Erwitt kept smiling; he started to wax rhapsodic about the beauties of the Tetons. In a few minutes, the press conference was over.

"Now comes the good part," said X enthusiastically. "Let's see if I know Eldon as well as I think I do. He's a terrible bigot, you know."

On the console, the other three networks shifted back to the studios for the usual punditry. The GBG screen stayed with the scene of the press conference, tracking the President as he strode into a hall leading, I assumed, to the farmhouse kitchen. It stayed on the President as he stopped to address an aide, angrily. The President's voice came from the screen as clearly as if he were sitting next to me in X's living room.

"How'd that sheenie homo get in there?" asked the President of the United States in the full hearing of however many millions of people were still tuned in to GBG. "Find out who let that happen and kick his keister out of Washington! And tell Roger Stirling I want to see him first thing tomorrow. Nine thirty sharp!"

He strode fuming down the hall. GBG cut to its own pundits. X clicked the remote control, and the four screens went dark.

"How about that?" X said gleefully. He got up. "A little champagne, boys? Good old Eldon. He's an ignoramus, he's a liar, and he's a bigot, as I well knew, and he delivered on all three!" He lifted his glass. "Three cheers for the boys at the Labs! That new microphone of theirs'll pick up a whisper in Times Square!"

Duncan sipped his wine reflectively. "I hate to say this, Chief, but this could cause a lot of deep shit."

"Not at all," X replied in his most hyperconfident fashion. "Our apologies will be profuse. You can draft the letter tonight, Fergus. You know what to say: mixup in the broadcast van; unauthorized use of experimental equipment; appropriate disciplinary remedies and future safeguards already taken, et cetera, et cetera, et cetera. Appeal to Eldon's infinite ego."

He raised his glass again.

"A toast, gentlemen! This'll bring the wrath of the Israeli faction down on his head, but nobody else will care. Only Eldon will feel the sting."

I knew what he meant. We were going through one of those periods when no issue, from dairy subsidies to the humidity, could seemingly be discussed without the matter of Israel being dragged in. Zionism had temporarily overplayed its hand and overstayed its rhetorical welcome. This would be strictly a three-day wonder.

"I hope so," said Duncan. "You know, this is the goddamn President of the United States!"

"Fergus, don't concern yourself. Eldon's just another man, like thee and me. The office is no larger than he is. And that's what we're going to prove. I can count on you two to stand with me, I'm sure."

He got up and went to the piano. Duncan muttered to me, "Erwitt's shit may be the same color as mine, but he's the f—— President, so there's a whole lot more of it."

X started to play the duet from *Forza del Destino*. *"Solenne in quest' ora,"* he sang in his gruff baritone. He thumped away with great passion. It was a strangely moving moment. *"Giurarmi dovete. . . ."* Duncan went over and stood by X, humming along, faking it but obviously touched.

X hammered the last chords.

"Well, boys," he said. "Think I'm ready for Salzburg?"

As usual, he had accurately gauged the consequences of Erwitt's televised gaffe. "Sheeniegate" ran its course in less than a week. The *Daily News* headlined the episode PRES BOMBS JEWS. In the *Times* Safire got on his hobbyhorse and called for Erwitt's impeachment. That was the extent of the negative clamor, apart from a spate of full-page newspaper ads signed by hundreds of rabbis and proctologists. The President himself simply claimed that he had been misheard, that he had said something else, that he had many good Jewish friends. Despite the contrary evidence of several million pairs of ears, such was Erwitt's semantic magic that his explanation went down. In other circles, there was satisfied opinion, confirmed on the quietus by aides instructed to spread the word, that the slip of the presidential tongue hadn't been that accidental, considering that the nation's Israeli connection was screwing up the oil industry with the Arabs. GBG's letter of apology was accepted with mistrustful, grudging resignation. The President ambled serenely off to the Tetons; the uproarious waters calmed; and life, like Melville's great ocean, swept on unruffled.

I got back to New York late on Labor Day night after spending the long weekend on Cape Cod to find that all hell had broken loose on my answering service.

They were in a panic. It hadn't occurred to me to leave a number. Mother was in Oregon; X was in Salzburg. All was quiet at the magazine. I had no friends and relations in harm's way that I knew of.

The calls had started coming in late Saturday and had continued right up until an hour before I checked in. It only took a few moments to put two and two together. Most of the calls were from the 503 area code; the minute I recognized it as Oregon, I knew the worst. Some of the names were friends of Mother's; others I didn't know: two doctors. One call had been at 12:07, just when I was starting in on the first of many Pimm's Cups on a lawn in Wellfleet. Terror, panic, and a horrible certainty started to mount in me. There had been three calls from Austria. Buck had called twice, and Margarita from London, and Cass, and a Mrs. Monstrance from Southampton. The whole world had been looking for me.

Except Mother—and I knew why, as I picked up the phone and dialed the doctor's number. Life was calling in another loan.

The doctor was kind. He had bad news, he said. Very bad news. I fought back the sobs and the terror. She had gone sailing with friends in a small open boat. A squall had come up and they'd had to put in at a small offshore islet, nothing more than a rock. The rain had been fierce, the temperature had dropped precipitously, and when they got Mother to shore, pneumonia had set in.

"But pneumonia!" I protested dumbly. "That's a nineteenth-century disease! Surely—"

"It wasn't any use, Mr. Monstrance," the doctor said. "We put her on the respirator, but her lungs were gone, as it turned out. She was emphysematic, and the X-rays showed pretty severe lesions. She had lung cancer, sir. It was hopeless."

"Lung cancer?" The idea was incredible. "Did she know it?"

"We can't say. Because of the respirator, she couldn't talk. She was barely conscious when she got here. It happened very quickly. Cancer can sometimes be kind. What we need to know is—"

"Oh, Jesus," I moaned, "don't just throw her out. Can you . . . can you keep her? I'd just like to see her once more. Please. I'll get there as soon as I can."

"Of course," he said soothingly. "And if there's anything else I can do—"

I put down the phone and cried, quietly. Mother wouldn't have wanted keening. This is what she would have wanted: no agony for me, no vigil, no crowds. To die in the care of strangers.

The phone rang. It was one of X's secretaries. He was on his way back from Austria. One of the GBG Gulfstreams was standing by at LaGuardia to take me to Oregon and bring me and Mother back. Then Cass called, and Buck, and Margarita. And then Clio. And then finally X himself, patched into me from his plane through one of the transponders circling the earth on Telsat. They all called, but it didn't help.

At three in the morning PDT, I saw her in the hospital, cold and gray and silent. I felt horribly guilty; I had deprived her, and me, of the one ultimate privilege of life: the right to speak and hear the last words; to know and to be told what is seen in that last fatal, flickering, approaching light. I kissed her cold cheek and said foolish things to her, pretending that this body could hear me and somehow absolve me. I thought about Jacob Polhemus's description of hell. I asked God, to whom I was a stranger, to take care of her.

Her friends were solicitous and kindly, but they were old people and not anxious to have the word of death's sojourn amongst them. From Mother's cottage I took the few things I wanted: a picture of my father, a few photographs, a couple of books, things invested with memories too proprietary to let fall even into the hands of friends. I invited her friends in the colony to come into the cottage and choose something of hers in remembrance of the good times they'd shared with her. The rest I gave to her housekeeper. I met with a real estate agent and arranged to put the cottage on the market, priced for ready sale.

I wanted to close it all down, so when I got back to New York, I drove immediately to Bridgehampton. It never occurred to me that I should take over the house. It had been her house; now it must belong to strangers, but not to me. So it goes. I took her ashes with me: they were in a sort of tarted-up coffee can. I carried them out into the field that ran down to the bay and stood there for a moment, feeling the sun, the air still sticky with summer, trying to be a proxy for sensations she had loved, and then I closed my eyes and tipped the can and let her ashes join the earth. As I did, a large cock pheasant burst squawking from a nearby remnant of tall hedges, another denizen soon to be displaced from the only place he'd ever known to love.

As I had in Oregon, I went through the house. There were too many memories to confront, too much memorabilia, too weighty a past. I dropped a tear or two. Here were records, *Manhattan Tower, South Pacific, Kiss Me Kate*, my Kostelanetz albums; their jackets hauled me back through time, to memories that were not only of her but of years that looked golden from here; in the attic I found cartons of my books, *Freddy the Detective, The Kid from Tomkinsville, Goldfinger*. She had stored my childhood under her eaves. In a carton at the back, I found the salmon reel: TO S.A.M. VI FROM H.H.M. ('X'). Rosebud.

I got another carton from the kitchen and began to fill it: the reel, my old fielder's glove, still faintly perfumed with neat's-foot oil, some books and records. Then I said the hell with it.

I let it all go. I was too old for Oz books, and New York, New York wasn't such a wonderful town any more. Let Lipshitz figure out what to do with my souvenirs; I could get by on the memories. I took only a little watercolor of the Shinnecock dunes by William Merritt Chase, some scrapbooks and family papers, and the four pictures of gentians I'd given her for Christmas. I arranged for the books to go to the local library and the few good paintings to go to the Parrish Museum. I called Nilsson in Southampton and asked him to make me an offer on the rest. I arranged to have the house cleaned up and put on the market. The agent told me it would bring $800,000 easy. So what, I thought.

A week later, a memorial service was held in the chapel at St. James's. Mother's will had been very specific about the sort of service she wanted. She wanted a hymn "that old voices could sing." She would consider it a favor if one of her old actor clients could read a brief eulogy. She wanted the service to be brief.

From the vestry, I watched the chapel fill up. The ranks were shrinking; night now came on with a rush for these old people. I wondered about the purpose of this, thinking how entirely at our own convenience we came to God, imploring him to preside at funerals and weddings and the christenings of our friends' children and to remain in the closet for the rest of time. To my pleased surprise, I saw Cass and Clio come in together. When the time came, I went alone into the front pew. Above the first strains of the organ processional, while I tried to remember prayers learned thirty-five years earlier in the basement classrooms of this very church, I heard the congregation behind me murmur, a sound I'd first heard thirty, nearly forty years earlier, at a Parents' Day, and then the sound of footsteps in the aisle.

X slid into the pew, next to me, and knelt for a moment, praying. I felt as if a mountain had suddenly loomed beside me. He smiled and placed a comforting, steadying hand on my forearm. I suppose I should have been irritated; this was a private, personal moment, and he had seized the stage. But I was moved and grateful he had come. So enormous was his presence that it was as if a giant umbrella had been spread over us all, as if he were an all-consoling Misericordia, taking us into the sheltering folds of his charity. I felt then, rightly or wrongly, for better or worse, that I loved him.

CHAPTER 20

The fall season began the apogee of the Age of X. Nothing went wrong for him or for AbCom; each day brought a new brisk and brassy triumph.

But not for me. Perhaps it was the cumulation of so much in my life: Mother's death; Margarita's leaving; the sad ongoing threnody of Clio and Abner; a delayed reaction to Cass and how she'd turned out. It happened virtually overnight, in time with the changing of the leaves and the freshening of the air. One night, it seemed, I went to bed intoxicated with the thrill of it all, infatuated with the great, pulsating machine of which I was a part, the throbbing heart of influence and manipulation, convinced it was the true religion and the right, and when I woke up I was sick of it. The sky was bright over the park, the colors of the city sparkled crystalline, and I patted myself and asked the day whether I'd been in a trance for the last six months.

The all-disguising excitement was certainly gone. I didn't belong here, I knew. This wasn't my sort of world. It was too big for me, too tangible, too reified, a world that talked of millions with the same indifference with which I spoke of postage stamps. I was used to, and happy with, the stakes of art and the spirit, of truth and style, of a kind of integrity that couldn't be suborned except in the hyped-up netherworld of Cass's gallery or of publishers like Cutter and Glemp. X might think he was professing the same thing, but he wasn't. Business was not art; politics was not art, though there was an art to each. Somehow I had gotten on the wrong carousel, and now, suddenly, the music had faded away, the centrifugal pull had dwindled, and I had to get off.

I went to X and the editor and told them I needed a change. I wanted to go back to writing about soup and nuts, to dig my mind out of the channel. It was agreed that I could reduce my commitment to GBG to two or three mornings a week. There wasn't anything for me to do anyway. I could help X with his speeches, and assist in the researching and writing of a batch of public service commercials designed to discomfit Erwitt, and fiddle with the language of various sorts of AbCom propaganda, stuff I'd been working on all along but which now seemed to fill up no more than a tiny corner of my time. The first, overwhelming rapture was gone, and that was what had taken over my days, seeming to expand my waking, working minutes into hours with the excitement of observing and participating. The AbCom landscape was no longer mysterious and fragrant; it tended toward rankness.

The editor understood. Besides, he could use me. There was a lot going on that needed to be punctured.

X didn't care. The tape recorder in my desk would keep rolling, and as long as I remembered to change the cartridge every couple of days, I could keep on top of things. He could spare me now; supportiveness was currently in oversupply both at AbCom and out there in television land.

"First National" was an immediate hit; by the mid-November sweeps it had built to a forty-five share, which won X lunch at Le Cirque, and ranked eleventh nationally and fourth in New York. *TV Guide* described it as "the 'Hill Street Blues' of money." It featured rapidly crosscut plotlines to create an alarming corporate world in which everything was subjugated to a drive for short-term results, dosed with managerial egotism. It was an expensive show, shot on a tight schedule so as to interweave and connect with the banking news of the day, from the Brazilian loans to credit card usury and many forms of computer sleight-of-hand. It had good guys and bad guys, inside and outside the eponymous bank, entrepreneurs, financial reporters, community-spirited loan officers. Above all, it had a point of view; and, in its way, it was educational on any number of levels. It was showing millions of ordinary people just exactly what "bottom line" thinking meant to their lives.

As X had predicted, the show was hardly a success in the banking community. A couple of weeks before the sweeps, I had a call from Florrie Grosvenor, who was just passing through town on her way to Stockholm. She had left the IMF and was now working for the Comptroller of the Currency. She was off to spend about ten thousand of the taxpayers' dollars observing Swedish banking at work and play.

The big banks were going wild, she said.

"This show is doing to Citibank what Nader couldn't!"

"Isn't that a good thing?" I asked. The most recent episode had centered on First National's forcing a marginal cement plant to close down, at a cost of a few hundred jobs, by calling its loans, in order to finance its takeover and conversion into mini-warehouses by a wealthy Arab customer. The parallel was clear; all the papers had been screaming about a New York banking group closing down a Queens chemical company and forcing its sale for ten cents on the dollar to a group of Kuwaitis.

"Probably," Florrie said, "but that was playing with a stacked deck."

"Cut it out. You're the one who told me to keep an eye on the banks."

"I know, I know. But do you know how many calls we've gotten, asking us to get this show off the air? The Comptroller even had a personal visit from the boy wonder at Citi; you know, Mr. Deregulation himself. This is the guy that's been trying to get the Comptroller's office abolished, and he came trooping in here with about fifty acolytes lugging attaché cases and demanded that we do something!"

"What can you do? Lean on the FTC or the FCC? The show's a hit. The public's eating it up. Besides, how can you? Erwitt's told the agencies to lay off."

"So far. But let's not be naive, sweetie. This Administration is committed to making the world safe for the Fortune Five Hundred and their bankers! I heard there was a high-level meeting over at Sixteen Hundred Pennsylvania Avenue with the man himself yesterday. All the big hitters: B of A, Citi, the Chase, First of Chicago, Mellon, Texas Commerce. McNeery, naturally. These guys are deeply unhappy!"

"Truth always stings."

"That may be," she said, "but you ought to see our mail. Mostly from the great unwashed, from small savers and depositors. Stephen King couldn't dream up horror stories like we're hearing. They want us to do something. No wonder the banks are nervous! This isn't some professor having himself off in *The Nation*; there are forty million people watching that show, and it feels like about half of them are writing us. And to the Congress. If they suddenly discover that they've got some character and courage, and some constituents to protect, watch out!"

"X'll be pleased to hear that. The show's his baby."

"I can't knock the show, honey. Personally, I love it, but that's strictly under the table. I think you can look forward to some noise from BLEEP.

Strictly a show of support by the business community for its friends in the banks. I hear they got some hotshot from BBDO to write some ads."

She was right. A few days later, full-page ads appeared over the BLEEP seal, a Prudential-type rock with angel's wings, and the same old tired signatures of McNeery and a half-dozen former Cabinet Secretaries. The ad attacked "First National" as "a crudely drawn, deceptive, inaccurate attack on a banking system which is a monument to the enterprise of the free citizens of a free country." There were a lot of graphics emphasizing amber waves of grain and spacious skies. Viewers were asked to write anyone they could think of: their Congressmen, X, the sponsors of the show. It stated that conscientious, patriotic businessmen would not buy time on the show. I noted BLEEP was careful not to hint at any sort of collusive boycott.

Business went on as usual, however. Time buyers looked at "First National"'s ratings and demographics and left the ideology to others. Automobiles still needed to be sold and rented, and flights to Jamaica, and cream sherries, and personal computers, and cans of beer. Prospective sponsors were lined up around the block. X ordered two more seasons of the show: twenty-six episodes.

There was a certain amount of editorial flak in the papers. The Administration's mouthpiece, *The Wall Street Journal*, lambasted the show as "a vicious caricature." *The National Review* accused GBG of "a crypto-socialistic smear" and made it clear that it esteemed the banks as the noblest, most selfless creations of the mind of man.

X was unruffled.

"More mush," he said. He grinned. "If they hate 'First National,' wait till they see 'Statehouse'!"

No show in the history of television ever caused so great a commotion as the first episode of "Statehouse" did. X had commissioned Nielsen to track the show in five-minute segments. Led in strongly by "River Oaks," it inherited that show's thirty-three rating and a forty share, but opened at around a nineteen share, as viewers deserted GBG for CBS and "Dallas." Then the ratings began to rise, inexorably, as those viewers, alerted by others, switched back.

As the title credits scrolled soundlessly, an airborne camera bore the viewer at a high rate of speed across a broad, varied landscape. The one-minute journey began with a sweep down forested mountains, across meadows and plains bisected by a broad river. The camera followed the river's course; gradually houses appeared, then hamlets, exurbs, suburbs, until on the horizon loomed the high-rising core of a decent-sized city. By now the landscape was densely populated: apartment buildings, factories, shopping centers, schools, and hospitals. The camera sped along a broad, fairly heavily trafficked avenue toward a grand, gold-domed, redstone nineteenth-century building. The pace slowed: the camera entered the door, moved uneasily past uniformed state troopers and down halls past offices marked SHERIFF, FINANCE COMMISSIONER, COMMISSIONER OF PUBLIC SAFETY, STATE ATTORNEY GENERAL, and the like. The halls were busy with people. The camera entered a richly paneled elevator and rose; it exited and moved along a carpeted hallway, past administrative offices and file rooms. It passed between rows of desks of functionaries, past three desks manned by secretaries, and into a large round office, at the end of which, in front of an array of flags, a man sat at a desk, head bent, writing.

"Governor Miller?" asked an offscreen voice.

"Yes?" said the man at the desk. He looked up. The camera closed on him.

It was Eldon Erwitt.

"Ho-ly shi-it!" Duncan whistled. We were watching at my place.

Of course it wasn't Erwitt, but it was very like him, very, very like him. There was a strong physical and vocal resemblance, but not a mimicry. This wasn't an actor "doing" the President of the United States, like Rich Little or Frank Gorshin "doing" Cary Grant or Cagney, not an impression or impersonation. The combined genius of the people who had put the show together had somehow captured the essence of Eldon Erwitt without falling into the trap of trying to counterfeit the man. The result was that the show seemed real; it played on and fused the hundreds of thousands of Erwitt images and impressions filed away in the audience's collective memory, the sum total of forty years of being watched and listened to; it activated those images, coalesced them with the character on the screen, and out of that fusion created its own truth. The barriers raised by artifice and impersonation seemed to melt away. Even I, skeptical as I was, sophisticated as I fancied myself, couldn't avoid the feeling that what was being shown to me was absolute real life, was the way things were.

It was true of the other principals in the cast. "Governor Morton Miller"'s wife "Eileen" was Darlene Erwitt, desiccated and faded, not especially intelligent, and full of airs. "Commissioner of Public Safety Herman Pflug" was Secretary of Defense Oscar Felsenstadt, and so it went, with "Sheriff Al McGregor," "State Assembly Leader 'Red' Reilly," "Special Counselor Bob Lewis," feisty industrialist "Vito Camora," and so on. Even former President McNeery was represented, as retired Assemblyman, now lobbyist, "Julius 'Jiggs' LeMaster."

"Ho-ly shi-it," said Duncan several more times in the course of the hour. He made himself four hefty bourbons during that time.

The show declared itself ideologically from its first scene, although in no wise so bald a fashion as to slide over into satire or demagoguery. This was real, serious stuff; the implicit declaration was: Look closely, viewer, because these are who and what they are, and this is the way it works. It depicted a political nexus in thrall to wealthy interests and outdated ideas, wedded—like the Erwitt Administration—to the paradoxical notion that good government is no government. The "Statehouse" writers had gotten the tone just right: the President's partiality for crackerbarrel anachronisms, his intellectual simplism, his infectious, confident geniality, his offscreen meanness. "Governor Morton Miller" took his orders, read the scripts he was handed, fronted for the dealmakers; with the familiar special mixture of glibness and charm, we watched him paper over scandal, racism, economic bigotry, spiritual decrepitude, hypocrisy; his only intent moments were depicted as being taken up with reruns of "Magnum, P.I." and the tea-cosy fripperies of his little wife. By the time the show ended, with the Governor saying to the Commissioner of Public Safety, "Don't worry, Oscar, what the darkies don't know won't hurt us," I was pretty sure that a lot of preconceptions had been shaken up in a lot of living rooms.

The phone rang almost at the instant I flicked my set off.

"Well," shouted X, as exuberant as I'd ever heard him, "what do you think?"

"I think it's great," I said, "but I don't count. I wonder if they were watching at the White House."

"Who cares?" he rumbled. "The country was! The switchboard at Granite's lit up like a Christmas tree! Over four hundred calls by the first commercial break! I just had a call here at home from the marketing vice-president of Chrysler. They want to preempt five minutes an episode!"

"How are the calls running?" I asked. "Yea or nay?"

"About fifty-fifty. There're a lot of dummies in this country to begin with, and a lot of dopes who think it's never all right to take after the President, and more particularly the President's wife, not even if the White House is occupied by Mr. and Mrs. Hitler!" He laughed; I could tell he was very pleased with himself.

"What do you think the reaction in Washington will be?" I asked.

"Zero. They've got to stonewall it. To do otherwise would be to admit the show's on the mark. Eldon'll try to pretend it doesn't exist. Just watch!"

He was right. At a briefing on the deteriorating situation in the inner cities, Presidential Press Secretary Ted Chitter responded to questions about President Erwitt's reaction to "Statehouse" by saying that the President hadn't seen it, and that it wasn't policy in any case to comment on particular aspects of an industry of which the President had been a proud and luminous part, and which he still held dear to his heart.

It would have been impossible for "Statehouse" to sustain the impossibly high, Super Bowl–level ratings of its first few episodes. But it held a fifty share and vaulted right over "60 Minutes" and "Dynasty" into the number-one slot in the regular weekly ratings. It seemed to carry GBG along with it. When the November sweeps came in, GBG had seven of the top ten regularly programmed shows, and four of the top five. "Statehouse" was practically out of sight, with an average 41.2 rating and a 54.1 share. Its first three episodes finished one-two-three among all shows, knocking off the other networks' stew of specials, a papal visit, and a two-hour "Dynasty" retrospective.

X had enjoyed any number of triumphant moments in his life, but there could have been no time, save possibly when Selena had said yes, like those three weeks at the end of November and the beginning of December. *Newsweek* rushed a cover story into print, with a specially commissioned silk-screen portrait by Sporca; it was rumored that X looked like a sure bet for *Time*'s "Man of the Year." There were stories under way for *People* and the Sunday *New York Times Magazine*.

He was feeling his oats, but none of us close to him suspected how strongly; none of us guessed how far he might go. GBG was building the national power base he'd forecast. The Senate Banking Committee reported out a bill to protect small depositors which was almost verbatim a proposal outlined in an early episode of "First National" and—in an instance of X's increasing use of symbiotic cross-reference in his two big shows—vetoed out of hand by the governor on "Statehouse." He had lured the tart-minded editor of a leading financial journal into doing a ten-minute weekly business critique called "Steal of the Week" at the tail of Thursday's "GBG Evening News with Loomis Hartley," and the first segment had caused such a stockholder uproar that a particularly juicy, fee- and perk-laden leveraged buyout of a large publicly owned food packager was derailed. His decision that GBG election coverage would no longer feature predictions, exit polls, and other forms of tampering with the normal workings and intentions of the political process became policy at the other three networks, after an all-day huddle at Dunecrag, while BLEEP gnashed its teeth in the background.

Each of these would have been satisfaction rich enough for a normal man, but the South Bronx referendum in early December was the zinger.

At issue was voter approval of a billion-dollar bond offering to finance the creation of a South Bronx Development Bank, a kind of local RFC that would underwrite the working-class rehabilitation of an area that made Hiroshima look like the Augusta National. Low-rent housing would be built with low-cost loans, as would small businesses, using minimally skilled local labor. Large, now-desolate tracts of land would be taken by eminent domain and reclaimed from blight. It was, on paper, a daring economic and social experiment.

It was the New York governor's baby and had even won the grudging endorsement of the city's unpredictable mayor, as well as a host of local councils and improvement groups. Opposed, however, was the real estate gang, thugs in Dunhill suits with pocketsful of million-dollar lawyers, who owned the Republican State Assembly. It read like an episode of "Statehouse." The real estate boys weren't content with having parlayed a dozen years' worth of Manhattan tax handouts into ten-digit property fortunes. There were murmurs at the breakfast tables in the Regency about a deal with Albany to demarcate the area as a "free casino zone," to plow under whatever still stood to make way for a Babylon of glitz, something that would make Atlantic City look as if it had been designed by Baron Haussmann. Trump was said to be in the deal, Sinatra, big Arab money, the Reichmanns. Reading about it reminded me of the Scottish "clearances" of the nineteenth century, when the peasantry was driven from their homes to make room for the Duke of Sutherland's sheep.

The matter had dragged on for a year, like Westway, and finally the governor had agreed with the Assembly Leader to put the issue to the voters. The Republicans and real estate guys liked that. It was cosmetically OK, and the early betting put the odds at 4 to 1 against. Upstate voters would see it as another giveaway to the blacks and Hispanics, who didn't vote anyway. BLEEP arranged for President Erwitt to tour the area; his face radiant with disdain for the way these people lived and took care of valuable property, he spoke on television; this was a real opportunity for the private sector, he told the cameras, his grin crinkly in the brisk wind; for people who cared enough to put their money where their mouth was, who could make something of economically viable land which its indolent occupants no longer deserved to live on.

Throughout the summer, there had been court delay after court delay, as every interested party and ax grinder weighed in, but at last the referendum was set for the second Tuesday in December. The way the pundits were calling it, the only way the SBDB had a snowball's chance was if the minority vote turned out in historically unprecedented numbers. That was out of the question. For one thing, who could expect these people to turn out when all they could think of was the game at Shea Stadium, the Sunday following the referendum, between the New Jersey Jets and Eugenie Monstrance's Vandals?

The Vandals had moved into Shea when the Jets decamped for the Meadowlands, their owner—whose fortune was estimated at several hundred million dollars by *Forbes*—miffed at receiving too small a cut on hot dog sales. It was a performance that prompted Buck, who still valued the game that had made him, to remark, even over the chance to turn a few quick millions, that "we sure got the scummiest buncha billionaires in the whole recorded history of money."

Something had ignited the Vandals. Even though Eugenie's involvement with AbCom was no longer consuming, the team was transformed from the sad lot I'd watched at training camp the year before. They had real "quality people" at the "skill positions" now, including a Bronx-born Puerto Rican scatback receiver out of Power Memorial via UCLA, who'd busted four games already. And three of the team's down linemen on defense were black inner-city kids, two originally from Erasmus High via Kansas and SMU, the other from Tilton via Florida State; together with a quarter ton of jet sinew from Michigan State, they were known collectively as "the Ebony Hammers."

The Vandals were looking at their first playoff season ever. They were 6–6 on the season, and it was going to take at least 9–7 to get in as a wild card. They had four games left: Tampa Bay, which was a 4–8 nothing; the Jets, who were 7–6 themselves and needed this one desperately; the Lions, a sure pushover at 3–10; and the Rams, a powerhouse at 11–2, whom the Vandals were unlikely to beat. The Jets were the key; the Jets were their best shot, and given the ethnic accent of the team, the ghetto was having the first good, hopeful time it had had in a decade.

Sheer good luck placed me in the right place at the right moment. Eugenie had invited me to sit in her box at Shea. The game was a rout, the Vandals winning 27–6, and although I missed seeing live what I learned had been watched by 74 percent of the watching homes in the metropolitan area—namely, X coming on television himself to make a personal statement—I was present for the blowout.

I saw the tape later. At the first time out, instead of cutting away to the Lite Beer repertory company and the tire ads, Steve Albert, who was doing the play-by-play, had simply introduced X by name. He looked very gritty and distinguished onscreen, dressed in a quiet tweed jacket and a dark tie, a man to take seriously. He described himself as Chairman and President of GBG, and then, very calmly, but with real and convincing sincerity, he advised the viewers that it was the duty of the GBG Network and WGBG-TV, as responsible corporate citizens, to do what they could to ensure that a free democracy worked as it should, to improve the possibility of making a better life for its less fortunate citizens. Next Tuesday's referendum, he said, was a watershed. Every New Yorker owed it to himself and to his fellows to vote. Accordingly, he said, unless 75 percent of the registered voters cast a vote one way or another, WGBG-TV would not televise the following Sunday's crucial game between the Jets and the Vandals in the New York market. No bread, he was saying, no circuses!

The announcement was repeated three times in the first half and three in the second. We heard about it almost immediately, however, from one of Eugenie's overseas guests who was watching the game on television in the warm sanctuary of the bar behind the owner's box. "Is this not your father?" he called out. Eugenie watched, incredulous, and then rushed to the phone and dialed the announcing booth. She slammed the phone down.

"He's insane! He's up there, but he won't talk to me!"

She snatched the phone up and made a hurried series of calls. From what I could overhear, she was trying to track down the NFL commissioner, who was out in Cleveland watching the Browns.

When she hung up at last, she said to me, "He's certifiable, Sam. What in heaven's name can he imagine he's doing?" The phone rang and she grabbed it, listened, then thrust it at me. "It's for you!"

It was Duncan. "Some fun, eh?" he said.

"Where the hell are you?"

"Up here in the booth with the Chief." I looked up and saw him waving. "What the hell is all this about, Fergie?" I asked.

"Patriotism, Sam," said X's voice. "See if you can make Eugenie calm down, it's very unseemly. I can hear her caterwauling from here."

I hung up, very pleased. I didn't have much in the way of strong, personal politics, but as a Southern senator once put it, better than I could, I did believe that the jam belonged on the lowest shelf, where everyone had a chance to reach it. If X fomented any kind of a turnout north of 96th Street and in Bed-Stuy and Crown Heights, the governor might just get his redevelopment bank. I could imagine what was going on at NFL headquarters, but I was sure X had an impregnable contractual position. He was simply exercising discretion he'd paid for, and Plastic Man and the league owners had damn near worn the tassels off their Italian loafers hustling to the bank to cash GBG's check. Washington would scream too, but after all, X hadn't told anyone how to vote, just to do it.

As expected, all hell broke loose on Monday. X received a state visit from Plastic Man, the NFL commissioner, who went on at length about the network's obligation to the New York fans. X remained obdurate. Throughout the city, posters blossomed, exhorting voters in three languages to vote. NO VOTE, NO GAME! was the simple message. The real estate boys found themselves in a corner. They could find no way to put the fix in. Their customary strategy of bleeding their enemies to death on the spike of litigation wouldn't work; the NFL-GBG contract had been blessed by a million dollars' worth of legal time. President Erwitt flew to New York Monday night and made a last-minute appearance at a Catholic Youth Organization dinner; he fulminated folksily against "those who manipulate the minds of a free people" and received a plaque from the Cardinal.

Tuesday broke bright and chilly, a fine day for voting, or so the 83 percent of the registered electorate who showed up to vote appeared to feel. The SBDB won a thin victory, a matter of four percentage points, so the property magnates lost their casinos, the South Bronx got the money for its greening, and the people got their game.

X had spotted a chink in the NFL contract and driven a political truck through it. Now, all over town and in Washington, sharp ears could pick up the squish of legal putty being forced into such other cracks and crevices. Florrie called; the mood in Washington, patient at first with the vagaries of an old man, was turning ugly. She had heard that the Federal Communications Commission had been asked to go over GBG's broadcasting licenses with a microscope; the Administration's congressional hitmen were trying to drum up support in camera for a bill establishing a new Broadcasting Code, and the FCC had been instructed to stop its efforts to water down the Fairness Doctrine.

"It's all pretty nebulous, so far," she told me. "The last thing the Administration wants is open war. But it seems that certain people who write pretty big checks and see that others just as big get written had their eyes on that property. It didn't turn out the way the script said it was going to. Erwitt knows he's around only so long as he reads the scripts convincingly enough to sell the product. These people can't have old man Monstrance running around squeezing the Charmin. Any screams from sponsors? BLEEP's got to start leaning pretty soon."

There'd been no problem, I told her.

"What's really burning them," she said, "is that the stock's going up." It was true. ABI had closed the day after the referendum at almost $110. As Buck said, "Any ol' boy that put that kinda bulldo across is sorely deservin' of a better PE."

For the next three days, the heartbeat of the city was the heartbeat of its beloved Vandals. Then, on Friday, after a hundred column inches a day on the team, fate struck another of its curious blows.

No one knew how it had happened. Gutierrez, the wide receiver who had become the guts of the team, sure hands atop a sprinter's speed, and the heart of a Secretariat, had simply gone to Third Avenue with a few teammates for a couple of beers. Somehow they got separated in a Third Avenue bar. The next thing any of us knew, some girl was screaming rape, there'd been police, the kid bleary and unable to remember what had happened, how he'd gotten into this predicament, and the *Post* had somehow been right there to take photographs, which it ran under the glaring headline: EXTRA! INTERCEPTED PASS!

Eugenie suspended the receiver pending a full investigation. Across America, the bookies took the Jets-Vandals game off the board. The city wept.

The whole business stank. It smelled of frame-up. There was a lot of talk about how the bookies were swamped and had put the fix in. There was even talk that the real estate boys at the Regency had set it up, a little act of retribution against the Vandals fans who'd voted away their cookie. Even the league office issued a statement saying the known facts were inadequate to warrant a suspension. But Eugenie stuck to her guns, arousing a chorus of wimpish praise from the knee-jerkers for the indomitable courage of her convictions.

My heart was with the Vandals, though, and if I wasn't keen to watch a rout, I was not about to quit on them either. So when Eugenie invited me to join her for the second Sunday in a row, I accepted.

The atmosphere in her box was about as genial as a funeral service. Her guests deferred to Eugenie like mourners in the widow's parlor. I put my field glasses on the visiting owner's box across the way. Well, surprise:

McNeery was there, along with a few pillars of the Regency crowd, Arnold Plume the takeover lawyer, some familiar Wall Street faces, and a clutch of fur-draped women. There to gloat, as the Jets ate up the Vandals.

Then came the other surprise: the Vandals beat the Jets 17–14!

They did it the way the inspirational textbooks say it's supposed to be done: with pride and desire. They dug in, and gutted it out, and gang-tackled. It was obvious within five minutes they were playing for something bigger than money. It was something I'd seen maybe a half dozen times in the pros: Willis Reed going out on a bum leg and stuffing Wilt Chamberlain and the Lakers; sitting with X and Abner in the Yale Bowl in 1956 watching Yale beat Army; both Sugar Rays; Fisk taking Pat Darcy downtown to win the sixth game of the '75 World Series for the Red Sox. Around me, almost tangible, I sensed thousands of other such memories, rising in the air like a bright, inspiring emanation.

When it was all over, I turned to puff my laryngitic congratulations to Eugenie. She was sitting staring at the field, her head turtled down in a swath of sable. Her face was set in a fierce mask, holding back chagrin and vexation. Her eyes were squeezed shut against tears; tears, I knew, of anger and blinding disappointment. It shook me. Moira's diagnosis had been right: Eugenie had wanted this team to lose. It was terrible knowledge to have.

On Monday the girl in the Gutierrez incident came forward and said it had all been a mistake.

On the following Sunday, Gutierrez caught six passes for 153 yards and two touchdowns against the Lions, and the Vandals were safely in the playoffs. I watched the game on the tube. Eugenie had invited me to go with her to Detroit, but I declined. I'd seen enough.

The year's final quarterly meeting of the AbCom board was held in New York ten days before Christmas. Jacob Polhemus came down from Boston to attend and invited me to take lunch with him.

I had spent the morning over at the magazine, putting a piece on the South Bronx master plan into the Wang. I was feeling good; the Vandals were set for the playoffs, the words were coming easily, and the enemies of truth and beauty seemed to be in disarray. I met Polhemus at a new, fancy restaurant on the East Side. I was interested in seeing the place. Duncan, always in the vanguard of discovery when it came to chic eating, had described it as "a monument of Franco-Islamic cuisine de luxe: a good French restaurant filled with a lot of very rich Arabs."

Polhemus looked sprightly and fit. He apologized to me for not having called about Mother, but he'd been in Europe when it happened, and then he'd let it slip his mind, and so on. I absolved him; I knew how he felt: too often we let things go until the iron seems humiliatingly cold. He looked about the restaurant. X had apparently recommended it—and made the reservation, I guessed, since we'd been put at what was obviously the best table, to judge from the sniffy curiosity with which we were being examined by the people installed to either side.

After we'd ordered, Jake said, "Well, things seem to be really popping. I must say, though, I think Xen gets carried away sometimes. I can safely say that 'Steal of the Week' is much watched by my friends on Congress Street, if not loved by them. I never thought the day would come when we'd see intelligent financial reporting on the network news."

"Not loved" was an understatement. First Stuyvesant Company, once AbCom's investment bankers, together with American Patent, one of its clients, a fledgling company specializing in patent acquisition and exploitation, had filed a $225 million lawsuit seeking triple damages against GBG, most of its affiliates, the journalist who did the show, and X and the AbCom directors, for queering a $75 million initial public offering. AbCom's attorneys were confident that we would win; all that "Steal of the Week" had done was to analyze the American Patent prospectus in detail, taking the viewers through the numbers and pointing out that the company's financial statements appeared to have been prepared by the same team that wrote Mother Goose. In the wake of this particular show, about forty affiliates had dropped "Steal" and substituted "Celebrity Weather."

The first course came. I'd followed the captain's recommendation and ordered some kind of a warm salad involving strips of veal and pheasant, walnuts, and field salad, "this year's 'in' roughage," in a light Roquefort dressing. The mixture was improbable, as was most fancy new cooking these days, but it was very tasty. The wine waiter poured from a bottle of Bernkastler Pfalzgraben that was on the menu at fifty bucks. Jake picked at a tricky sashimi française. Around us rose the idle babble of rich Manhattan gathering itself for the final mad rush to Christmas.

"I must say I rather like the way Xen's stirring things up," Polhemus said. "I've become positively addicted to that program about the bank. It's very good, really. I can't get over how banking's changed. Not necessarily for the better, may I say. All those computers. You know, my old eyes and ears may be deceiving me, but there are times when it seems to me that a great many of these very crisp young men and women are actually trying to think and sound like computers. One would have hoped it would be the other way round."

The next course arrived. Small paillards of veal and chicken, accompanied by a many-hued palette of vegetable purees and a bottle of Mouton-Rothschild that wasn't much younger than I.

"Of course," he said, "so little of this brave new financial world makes much sense to me. The object seems to be to protect the bankers' profits and prestige no matter what the consequences to the rest of us. I think that's a mistake. A country that dispenses welfare to its privileged, and not to its helpless and undefended, is headed for trouble. Mind you, not that my people haven't seen to it that we've taken advantage of Mr. Erwitt's myriad tax blessings. But he doesn't make it much fun to be rich. I feel guilty most of the time, as if I've cheated at cards."

"Well, the deck is rigged, isn't it?"

"Indeed it seems to be. But no one complains, and that I don't understand. Is Xen the only man of principle in the press?"

"It sometimes seems that way. He's trying to make things hot for Erwitt."

We finished lunch over small talk and swapped reminiscence. Polhemus signed the check and accepted the restaurant owner's salaams, and we walked out onto the sidewalk. What had been a blustering gray morning had settled into a calmer afternoon, the dreary drifting clouds here and there breaking open to reveal scraps of pale sky.

"I thought I'd take a turn through the Frick Collection," Polhemus said. "Why don't you join me?" He adjusted his hat. The soft dark fedora, slightly oversized, combined with his fur-collared overcoat to create a strikingly old-fashioned appearance. He looked like an old-time Manhattan dandy.

We walked up Madison Avenue. Jake returned to X's vendetta against Erwitt.

"I do hope Xen protects his flanks," he said. "This fellow McNeery may look like a Neanderthal, but my friends in Washington tell me he's not as stupid as he appears. He has a sort of native slyness you often find in men of small intellect. Nowadays, it doesn't seem necessary to know anything to know everything, if you see what I mean. Are you enjoying your stint at AbCom, by the way?"

"I did. But I'm not really at home there. I've gone back to writing, which is where I belong. It was pretty exhilarating, though, for a time!"

We reached the Frick and went in. As always, it seemed a perfect oasis of peace and order. Mother had started bringing me here when I was about nine or ten, in the old days, before kids were shut out. I'd loved the place and had made a dozen resolutions to visit it regularly and, like most New Yorkers overwhelmed by options, had failed in my resolution. New York was too much. How to cope with the surfeit of choice: the Metropolitan Museum, the Museum of Modern Art, the Whitney, the Guggenheim. A hundred plays on and off Broadway; God knows how many art galleries; dance and ballet companies by the score; twenty concerts and recitals a night; medicine for the soul in a city compulsively addicted to action.

We walked swiftly through the galleries, pausing only when something snared Jake's attention. "It doesn't change, does it?" he remarked, pointing to the wickedly observant Gainsborough of ladies walking out in St. James's Park. "They still look each other up and down. People in society seldom look at each other; they merely appraise each other's parure. It reminds me of the restaurant we just left."

We strolled into the long room where Frick's own portrait hung, the tycoon posed thoughtfully against a desolate landscape, the blackening of which had made him wealthy and brought all these beautiful things to Seventieth Street. Was the trade-off worth it? I wondered. Probably. If not Frick, then surely someone else, someone worse, someone who might have eluded the grasp of Duveen and Wildenstein and Knoedler, who would not have left these treasures by way of recompense.

Our next stop was in front of a tiny Duccio.

"I should have bought one of these myself," Jake said, "when the Rockefellers decided to sell. I always wanted a first-rate thirteenth-century picture. I was quite an aesthete as a young man, you know."

"I didn't."

"Oh, my goodness, yes. Camping it up at I Tatti with the Berensons. Staring soulfully at the Arno of many an evening. Writing windy sonnets about Botticelli. Then I came back and got involved in lesser matters, but I never lost the love of art. The Rockefeller Duccios got away from me. One went to Fort Worth, and Heinie Thyssen bought the other."

Along the way, we stopped to admire a painting I particularly liked, or rather the subject of the painting, Valerie, Lady Meux; Whistler had devoted considerable attention to her dark looks and mythic bosom.

"Like that, do you?" asked my companion.

"I always wonder what she'd look like with her clothes off," I said.

"So I expect did her husband," Jake murmured. "She was a very naughty girl. Ah, now here's the way I fancied myself as a young man."

He looked up at the other big Whistler in the room, a portrait of Robert de Montesquiou, an elegant stiletto of a man, known to be one of the models for Proust's Baron Charlus.

We walked out into the sculpture court.

"Let's sit for a minute," Jake said.

I looked around. "This place would have suited X," I said. "It's his kind of palace."

"Indeed. I sometimes think Xen took this as an exemplar. I brought him here just before it opened to the public. My father was a friend of the Fricks. He was very taken with it."

"I suppose he likes to think of himself as a robber baron, a condottiere of commerce. He runs AbCom as if he were leading troops into battle."

"Xen does like a good fight; often, I've thought, as much for its own sake as for the prize to be gained. He's never been one for the contemplative life, his recent protestations to the contrary. I was terribly surprised when he went to ground in London. Xen's not happy without a lot of commotion going on around him."

"And you?"

"I like cypress alleys and noon in Florence. I think that's why we've stayed friends. We don't compete. I enjoy great events as much as the next man, but I don't want to be running the show. Xen has to run things. He'd like to run the world, and Lord knows he's got the energy and intelligence, but he's shrewd enough to see that there's no chance of that, so he settled for something less cosmic, but only moderately so."

"How do you think it will all come out?"

"I won't be surprised if he gets his way with history. A hundred years from now, assuming that mankind lasts that long, Xen is going to be seen as one of the pivotal figures of this century, for better or, as I fear, for worse, seeing how we've turned out as a nation."

"Wouldn't you want that kind of fame for yourself?"

"Oh, I'm famous enough in my own estimation. I think I've led a useful life, not totally selfish. I hope I've done more good than ill." He got up. "Come on, let's go see the Holbeins."

I was filled with admiration. Polhemus had outlasted wealth and flattery and the graspings of ambition. He'd had the character to keep his life and himself in balance, and yet he'd made a difference. Other men in his position might have welcomed the chance of being swept into still, lazy backwaters. I had friends like that, who ran trusts for people who still trusted; who did old-timey business on the Stock Exchange; who saw about the placid work of small foundations.

We examined the pair of Holbein portraits. Adversaries in posterity as they had been in life, Sir Thomas More and Thomas Cromwell faced each other across a short space of pale velvet, with Saint Jerome mediating between them: Cromwell shrewd, mistrustful, cruel; Thomas More the very model of the probity on which history insisted.

Looking at Cromwell, I was struck by a resemblance to X, especially in the smart, small eyes. I remarked on this to Polhemus.

"I don't think Xen would much like that," he chuckled. "He rather fancies himself in the More mold, especially these days. But they both lost their heads on Tower Green."

"Is that a prophecy?"

"Not really. Anyway, we don't use axes any longer, do we? Just lines of credit and proxy statements. So much more surgical."

Outside, early twilight had fallen, bringing with it a sharp wind that whistled angrily out of Central Park. Jake and I shook hands; I thanked him for lunch and for suggesting the Frick.

"I must caution you," Jake said as we parted at Madison Avenue. "I wish I could share Xen's confidence that this will all go just as he pleases. I have the feeling that he may see what's going on in Washington strictly in terms of politics. I happen to think that Erwitt's the first truly ideological President we've had since Wilson. Not that he thinks for himself, of course, but there are enough men anxious to do that for him. There's also a very great deal of money at issue, and I don't think Xen has really ever properly estimated the true power of money. It's one of the problems of being too well brought up."

Or an artist, I thought. I was struck by how closely Polhemus's thinking paralleled Margarita's farewell speech to me.

The morning of Christmas Eve, I called Margarita in London to say happy, happy and see what was up. I caught her on the verge of going down to the country. She had sort of a present for me, she said, too late in the giving, but I must appreciate the sweetness of the thought. I told her how awful the season had been in New York.

"Why don't you come here, if it's so awful there? I need company. Pierre and I have decided to pack it in, and I find it upsets me."

I liked the idea. This had been the most vilely crowded and clamorous

334 | MICHAEL M. THOMAS

holiday season I could remember, and the night before I'd awakened, sweating, realizing that I had no family.

"Do you really mean that?" I asked. "Shall I hop the Concorde and be in your arms as Christmas dawn glints purple on the sweet-flowing Thames? You know my situation."

There was an instant's silence. "I guess not. Not just yet. Better that I go to my aged aunt in Bourton-on-the-Water. But I have a better idea. Why don't you come to Venice in April?"

"Venice?"

"It'll be lovely then. I'm going out to visit Mother. She's got a very pretty house on the Dorsoduro."

"Promise me no German tourists in huge orange shoes?"

"Promise."

She asked about X. He was well, I reported; the latest Gallup Poll still placed him second to Erwitt as the most influential American, but he seemed to be gaining. She sounded happy to hear it. I gathered she hadn't talked to him, but I didn't ask. X had a way of scrubbing people.

Again, I wished her love and Merry Christmas and Happy New Year. Hanging up, I thought how consoling it would be to be again enfolded in her strong, damp, raucous embrace. I recalled every aching detail of our exhalations and explorations. Still, why fool ourselves? Better to take things as they happened and not press against the natural flow, looking for feelings that weren't there, confusing sensation with emotion or, as she had put it, preoccupation with love.

Instead of running for the Concorde, therefore, I went to X's for Christmas Eve.

I suppose in the course of the evening at least four hundred people passed through his Fifth Avenue apartment. It was a rout, a riot, a revel, a perfect, exquisite production, a consummate manifestation of X's unquenchable thirst for admiration.

"Beauty and the Best" was how Duncan described it. He came wheeling out of the crowd, a big grin on his face. He was pretty drunk.

"Look around, look around, look around," he chanted. "Beauty and the Best! Pretty good, huh? Hey, you know something? You and I are the only help here. 'Cept of course some newsroom pussy the old man's rung in to add the requisite holiday jiggle."

"Where is X?"

"Over in the next room, doing the Death of Sardanapalus bit, surrounded by his court, 'cept he's still alive, of course."

I thought of Delacroix's painting of the pasha, done to death by luxury and voluptuousness and not enough calm, surrounded by his treasure and his concubines. Not bad, Fergie, I said; as in death, life. Feeling pretty profound, I took another glass of champagne from a tray proffered by a Glorious Food altarboy and asked Duncan what else was new.

"Well, I talked him out of doing a number on Mrs. Erwitt. You know they had the tree-lighting ceremony last night at the White House? Fags on parade? Oom-pah-pah and wiggle your buns! Everybody gives each other cute little presents? This year she sent out orchids. From one to a treeful, depending on how rich you are."

"So what happened with X?"

"You may not know this, but the White House press office has laid down some strict rules about camera angles for shooting the First Lady. I don't know if you ever checked her out from the knees down, but it's strictly Redwood City. She's got a set of pins like Babe Ruth's favorite bat. Which is why the White House TV people have made it clear: no shots of Darlene Erwitt from within fifty feet except above the waist, always shoot down at her. Well, you can guess what the Chief had in mind."

"Shoot up at her?"

"You got it. All that fashion shit she goes in for, and this'd make her look like Sequoia National Forest. I talked him out of it. Told him it wasn't in the Christmas spirit."

"Sam! Sam, darling!"

Cass rushed up, waved a sprig of mistletoe over my head, and kissed both my cheeks.

"You look great," I said. She did. "How's everything?"

"Fantastic. And you, my sweet?"

"No complaints other than the usual miseries of this time of year. What's new?"

"Busy busy busy. My book's almost done. Foster's very excited."

"And the art?"

"Busy busy busy. Have you been into the living room? No? Well, take a look when you do. I found H.H. the most fantastic Scheisstueck diptych."

"I thought he had one already, in the pool house. Isn't one enough?"

"Darling, when he saw this one, he just had to buy it. Dieter's so hot it's a scandal. I mean, there's this Italian that has an open bid on everything Dieter does. H.H. is lucky to have gotten this one. I had to beg Dieter for it."

"You and old Dieter sound pretty chummy."

"Don't be absurd." She pressed a girlish hand to her bosom and gave a pretty shrug.

"Well, I can't wait to meet him," I said. "I heard Abner and Clio were here?"

"I think so. I haven't seen them, though. H.H. said he was going to invite them. They're coming to Little Gourd at some point. We're off tomorrow! Christmas in the tropics, don't you love it? H.H. has put together the most wonderful party."

She lost interest in me; with a wave of her mistletoe and a shriek, she rushed off.

I found X at last, in the center of a crowd. He was grinning broadly, his thick frame enclosed in a belted velvet jacket with a quilted collar. He needed only a Turkish cap to complete the effect. Around him rose a positive steam of sycophancy.

"Hello, X," I said. "Happy Christmas."

"Sam!" He embraced me and introduced me.

By ten the crowd had thinned, and I still hadn't found Abner and Clio. They must have zigged while I was zagging. People started to leave. Even these people had families, I suspected, children to be wakened and kissed, elders to be fussed over. I had no one; I sat by myself on a sofa as the party bravely went on, thinking New Year's Eve thoughts on Christmas Eve: thoughts of Mother, and of other losses, of changes in life and the world, none of them much for the better, many of them clearly for the worse. I was joined by a reasonably pretty woman who did something with some law firm. She chatted away engagingly. For a moment, I was tempted to take pot luck. She was probably alone too, but there was something sacrilegious, it seemed to me, about trying to get laid on Christmas Eve, so I nodded and smiled until she went away.

Around eleven, X was persuaded to go to the piano. He played carols; the courtiers joined in; I listened. He played "Adeste Fideles" and "Silent Night" and "God Rest You Merry, Gentlemen." He saw me sitting there, grinned, and launched into the Starbuck hymn. I went over and joined in: ". . . for the good or evil side . . ."

And then, suddenly, it was midnight and Christmas.

And then, just as suddenly, it was Christmas morning, ten o'clock, me in my apartment with little memory of getting home, and my phone was ringing. It was Clio.

"Oh, Sam, I hope I'm not bothering you." She sounded very measured. "I'm looking for someone to go to church with me. Abner doesn't feel up to it. I tried to find you last night."

"You have your man."

Forty minutes later I met her outside St. Thomas's. It was a clear day but bitter cold. Huddled in a dark fur coat, with a big fur hat, Clio looked fine. Again I was struck by the differences from her sister.

We read the lesson and sang the hymns and listened to the famous men's choir sing Tallis and Handel. I waited while she took communion. Afterward I walked back to her apartment building with her. I wasn't sure what to say. She didn't seem to want to talk about Abner. She spoke without enthusiasm about their plans, about going to Little Gourd Key after New Year's and then to Palm Beach again. I could see the lamps in her life were going out one by one. I felt I desperately wanted to do something for her, to hold her, to tell her some good things. Was there something growing between us?

I wasn't sure, Cupid always turns out to be such a liar. But she looked very beautiful.

She asked me to come up, but for some reason I couldn't. I made an excuse which I hoped didn't sound as patently false to her as it did to me. Then I made my way across town to my apartment, and listened to "A Night in Venice" with Gedda and Schwarzkopf, and uncorked the last bottle of Margarita's Bowmore and got drunk. Merry Christmas.

CHAPTER 21

In its first issue of the New Year, even with the election impending, *Time* named X as its Man of the Year. The cover story was so pious that I accused Duncan of having written it.

"Not merely content with having achieved one legend in his lifetime," began the cover story, "H. H. Monstrance has now guaranteed himself a double dip of immortality." The piece went on to praise him for "reforesting the vast wasteland of television, in presiding over a media revolution that is remaking the spiritual map of America."

Hyperbole aside, there was no question that X was making things run his way. "Statehouse" and "First National" had become central rituals in American life, impregnably anchored in the first and third slots in the weekly Nielsens. Best of all, Erwitt seemed to be slipping; a *Washington Post*/ABC Poll indicated that while the President still enjoyed a positive perception relative to what he had done for the economy, he was beginning to give ground on the intangibles: trustworthiness, capacity for the job, integrity, compassion, fair-mindedness. "Statehouse" had dramatically personified Erwitt's habit of bailing out on domestic issues by beating the foreign policy drum. Sixty-two percent of the poll's respondents were on record as believing the President should devote more time and study to the nation's deep-rooted domestic problems and leave Central America to the State Department. A startling 80 percent believed he should restudy American history.

"First National"'s impact was more direct. Five state legislatures had introduced bills to prevent banks from milking their customers on the float. The letters columns of leading papers were full of ire: people wanted to know why bank profits were at record levels while interest rates seemed stuck at an altitude that priced the average guy out of the American Dream. There were rumors that the Congress was mulling a mandated ceiling on interest rates and a temporary prohibition on take-over loans. Talk in this vein became so loud and frequent that BLEEP took full-page ads to argue the free market case, which somehow seemed self-contradictory when the stock market jumped twenty points on a rumor that a House subcommittee was in fact about to report out a bill limiting interest rates.

X spent the first three weeks of the new year on Little Gourd, and with nothing going on at the magazine or AbCom, I accepted Buck's invitation to be his guest at the Bob Hope Desert Classic. I thought it might make an interesting counterpoint to the piece I'd written the year before on the Masters. Palm Springs was one of those places I hated on principle without ever having been there, Vienna in reverse, an air-conditioned Hades, but for its citizens, leathery political troglodytes and their sun-embalmed wives, the Promised Land of Eldonomics.

On the way out, I stopped in Los Angeles to see a Harvard classmate who was now working as a producer at GBG Studios. I met him for dinner at a place on Melrose that specialized in Chinese pizza. He was full of beans and excitement. He'd just wrapped a three-hour "State-house" special.

"Three hours? That sounds odd," I said.

"The man himself ordered it. Completely hush-hush. Closed set: 'need to know' only. The works. Just like the Manhattan Project."

After dinner, while the parking attendant fished out my friend's pearl-gray Bentley, he asked me conversationally whether I wanted to get laid. How nice, I thought, that at least LA hasn't changed, it's still an island of prurient looniness in a shifting world; but I said no, thanking him anyway. It was just age, I told him, not ingratitude. He wished me happiness at the Hope and pressed on me a couple of numbers "in the Valley" to call in case I needed to get my ashes hauled.

I stayed with Buck at a cottage he'd rented at the El Dorado Club, the only place I'd ever been where the pro shop sold white mink jackets and television sets. The golf course wound its way among the swimming pools and patios of glass-coated, low-slung houses. Above the crisp line of the encroaching mountains, the smog of Los Angeles, a hundred miles distant, hung like a faraway explosion. We took our meals in the club-house dining room, which was about as charming and stylish as Love

Field. The rest of our party consisted of a bunch of insurance company executives with whom Buck was putting together what he called "a greenmail fund."

Dinner took an interesting turn one evening, however, when our table was joined by none other than former President McNeery, the shining light among the tournament's "celebrities": a sorry lot of Vegas lounge performers, vaguely remembered TV actors, and over-the-hill astronauts. It was that kind of a tournament anyway, strictly Kelvinator dealers and guys who sold commodity options. The upmarket pro-am crowd preferred the Crosby, which would be played three weeks later in the Del Monte Forest.

McNeery knew one of Buck's guests. When we were introduced, I mentioned that I had been a fellow guest at Clio and Abner's party two years before.

"Oh, yes, Mountcastle," said McNeery. "Aren't you writing a book about AbCom? It's a real tragedy what that old man's done to one of the great American corporations."

He spoke with heavy regret, as if X had taken a paint sprayer to the facade of Chartres.

"Abner Monstrance was a great American," McNeery continued. "A great leader, a patriot, a man of infinite promise."

"It's sad how things worked out," I said.

"A great tragedy, sir," said McNeery, giving it the full Senator Claghorn treatment. "I spoke with Abner's lovely wife just the other day. The situation is not improving. Sad, sir, sad."

The others at the table nodded sympathetically. Whether it was Abner's plight or X's squandering of corporate assets that tore at McNeery's and their hearts wasn't clear. The former President got up and left to rejoin his party.

"The President's right," said one of the men at our table. "Have you seen that 'First National' show? Straight Communist propaganda. Just like in *The Spike*. They ought to lock that old man up! Or shoot the son of a bitch!"

I said nothing. There was no point in starting an argument. I'd been around the man who'd spoken long enough to make him for a rabid Eldonite, a fellow who probably had a framed copy of Andrew Carnegie's Gospel of Wealth over his desk and who, by speaking seriously of the "philosophy" of William E. Simon, had caused me to miss a three-foot putt. Anyway, I was Buck's guest and he was playing for big money.

In a properly ordered world, January, especially in a beehive like New York, would be a time of respite, a month for huddling indoors out of the cold and taking stock, or at least catching breath. But too much of the two weeks following my return from Palm Springs was taken up with high life. Florrie Grosvenor arrived for a five-day weekend, having designated me as her escort of choice for a ballet gala, three dinner parties, and the Winter Antiques Show; I threw in X's Super Bowl Party as my contribution. She had changed jobs again. Now she was working for Merrill Lynch in mortgage-backed securities. I was happy she was coming; after the alien culture of Palm Springs, here was someone I could be calm with, who understood me, who was my sort of people.

The day before she arrived, I hunted down Duncan and asked him if he knew anything about X's three-hour "Statehouse" special.

"Uh-uh. The Chief came banging in here the day before he left for the island, woke up everybody on the Coast, and ordered three hours of the show. Who knows what he's up to? Shit, this place is a circus!"

"What else is going on?"

"You know that spade who plays quarterback for the Techs?"

"Henry Morrow?"

"That's him. The Chief sent one of the Gulfstreams to Houston for him; snatched him after Super Bowl practice and brought him up here for dinner. They ate in the Chief's office, just the two of them. Then we flew him back to Texas."

That was odd, I thought. Henry Morrow, of all things a black quarterback from, of all places, Princeton, had led the Silicon Valley Techs into the Super Bowl against the Browns. The Techs were an expansion team that had come into the NFL the same year as Eugenie's Vandals. Morrow was the perfect leader for a team that *Sports Illustrated* praised for its "calculated, entrepreneurial football." He was six-three, one hundred ninety pounds, and could forward-pass a football from five to fifty yards in more trajectories and velocities than NASA. Henry Morrow was also a *cum laude* graduate in political science, a second-year law student at Yale, and a civil-rights activist who had served a term as a staff assistant to Ted Kennedy. Buck thought he was the greatest player to come out of the Ivy League since Calvin Hill and, naturally, himself.

"What the hell was Morrow doing here?" I asked Duncan.

"Beats me. Maybe the Chief thinks he's gonna be the next Bryant Gumbel."

Florrie arrived on Thursday evening. She called me after she checked into the Carlyle.

"Pick me up at seven fifteen," she instructed. "I've planned a quiet night for us." She had tickets for a play at the Public which I'd been meaning to see; we could eat afterward.

She looked great. I guessed that at least ten pounds were gone; her hair was cut shorter; I felt that I was seeing her for the first time not as an extension of the debutante I'd groped and grappled twenty-odd years ago but as the different person those twenty-odd years had made her.

So it was probably logical, after the play and dinner, and a brandy and just enough Bobby Short in the Carlyle bar, that when she asked me to her room for a nightcap, I accepted.

I can't say that the earth moved, but I can't say, either, that it didn't. I do know that as she took me into her I had only Florrie on my mind, that no fantasies of others known or craved crept into my awareness or were summoned by it. On the other hand, I felt that neither of us truly felt that this was the big one that lifetimes are built toward and upon.

Somewhere in the middle of the night, when we were languidly perched on the edge of the precipice of sleep, we talked.

"What brought you up here, Flor? Business—or me?"

"A little of each. I just got the feeling the time might be right for you and me. I was lonely. I heard you were."

"From whom?"

"It doesn't matter. You know how people talk. Maybe I didn't hear it. Maybe I just knew it; what does it matter? Should I have married you, Sam? You were the boy next door."

"Why do you say that?"

"Oh, I don't know. We just got to know each other so well. It suddenly seemed a pity to have wasted all that, chasing after strangers."

I turned on my side and let my hand rest on her hip.

"I'm not sure I know you as well as I thought, my little one," I said. "Where'd you learn all this X-rated stuff?"

"When I was in India. I got to know a Kathakali dancer pretty well. He was very inventive. Didn't you enjoy it?"

"Well, it's been a few years since my legs fell off."

"Oh, good. Why don't you just plan on overnighting while I'm here?"

"Why don't you stay with me? It's less commercial."

"That may be, but here, at least, I don't know who's been in this particular bed doing what. Two, you don't have room service. You probably have one of those bachelor refrigerators with nothing in it but flat champagne and one withered rose."

I let this slander pass. We drifted off into our own cocoons of unconsciousness, waking again an hour or so later to find each other, to try new ways.

Afterward, she said, sleepily, "Will it be fun to go to Mr. Monstrance's? I hate football, but I'm dying to see his paintings."

"The fact is you're dying to see X," I said. "And I daresay when he sees the all-new slender you, he'll be only too happy to show you not only his paintings but his extensive collection of etchings, especially if I was to tell him of your intimate knowledge of the trickier parts of the Kama Sutra."

"Don't be ridiculous. He's a hundred years old."

A few days later, toward morning, back at the Carlyle, Florrie remarked, "You're still holding out, aren't you? How come?"

"Holding out?"

"For the one and only, the perfect big true love?"

"I don't know. Isn't everyone?"

"I hope not."

Over breakfast, she said, "You know, people in Washington are saying Mr. Monstrance has got some kind of grudge against the President. Something about the old days in television."

I explained it as far as I dared.

"It's ceasing to be amusing down there, you know. Did you see last month's consumer credit figures? Down at an annual rate of almost fifteen percent. That's bad. If the public goes cold turkey on borrowing, who pays for Wall Street's caviar?"

"I suppose you have a point, although I thought the idea was we should save more. I expect McNeery's been seen quite a lot in the nation's capital?"

"BLEEPing away for all he's worth. He's the messenger boy between the Gorse Club and the Oval Office. Come over here; I just remembered something that might amuse you."

She snuggled next to me and became very distracting; all political discussion ceased.

On Sunday afternoon, the Super Bowl was not scheduled to start until five o'clock, and we passed up X's invitation to lunch, preferring a hamburger at Melon's and a stroll among the Impressionists at the Met, just like a real couple. At four thirty, we rendezvoused with Buck outside X's apartment building and went up. There were about a hundred people there.

"I thought we were here for a football game," Florrie whispered. "It's all the same people from the antiques show."

"It's just 'le tout New York,' my love," I said. "These people would bust their butts to watch dogs screw if the invitation came from X."

Our host saw us and bustled across the room. As usual, the fawning of his guests seemed to have renewed his tan. His smile brightened when I introduced him to Florrie. He turned on the charm, spinning it about us like a web. I saw Florrie give a little shiver of pleasure.

"Hello, darling." Cass presented cheeks first to me, then to Buck. "Why, hello, Buck; fancy seeing you here."

Buck made a parody tug at an imagined forelock. "I just got me a new party suit and reckoned I'd show it off."

"And can that really be you, Florrie?" said Cass. Cheeks were pressed and acknowledgments exchanged.

"Cassandra, could you see if everyone's got what they need," said X. He looked at his watch. "Ten minutes to game time. Why don't you come over here by me, Florence, and you too, Buck." He draped his arm over Buck's shoulder. "I'd be most interested to have your views of the game. It should be a dilly."

He turned to me.

"Sam, would you do me a simply enormous favor? Eugenie's back in my study, sulking. I don't know why she bothered to come at all." He reached up and gave my arm a confiding, man-to-man squeeze. "See if you can cheer her up. She likes you, and this way she's no damn good to me."

I said I'd be happy to try. He led Florrie and Buck off to a couch set in front of one of the three oversize screens that had been installed in the drawing room.

Eugenie got up when I came in. We embraced. I was startled by her appearance. The way X had talked, I'd expected her to be even more gross and swollen. Instead, she looked trimmer, much lighter. There were two empty Tab cans on the table.

"How've you been?" I asked.

"Oh, fair," she said.

"Somebody told me you took a place in the Caribbean?" I asked, looking for a subject.

"I bought a house in Antigua, but I hate it there, it's so boring. I think I'll sell it. I thought about Jamaica, but Jamaica's so pushy. I'm looking at Mustique. There are a lot of English there. The English are nicer."

"It was too bad the Vandals had to draw the Cowboys in the opening round. They had a hell of a run this year."

"Yes, didn't they," she said. She went over to the refrigerator. "Would you like a drink?"

"I don't think so. I've drunk every drop of alcohol in the free world in the last few days. An old friend's been in town, and she's run me ragged."

She smiled. When she opened the refrigerator door, I could see it was filled with diet sodas.

"Who do you like in the game?" she asked. "I suppose Father sent you in here to keep me company? He thinks I'm in some kind of a funk. He didn't even notice that I've lost more than twenty pounds."

"A new doctor?"

"Purely firm resolve." She was warming up. I wasn't surprised that X hadn't noticed. He had his "idea" of Eugenie, her form and function, and that was that. What a sorry state of affairs, I thought.

We ended up betting five bucks, with me taking the underdog Techs plus seven, two less than the Vegas line. As we shook on it, I supposed that giving up my edge so easily was just one more indication of my unsuitability for business.

For once, the Super Bowl was a hell of a game, by turns clawing, dumb, heroic, brilliant, slick, agonizing. The momentum ebbed and surged. It was 21–17 Browns at the half; 31–31 going into the fourth quarter; 34–31 Browns with ten minutes left, then with five minutes left, and then with a minute fifty-two seconds, when the Techs recovered a fumble on their own 37. Three plays nudged the ball to the Browns' 42, where it was fourth and one with twenty-eight seconds. The Techs made it by an inch. Morrow threw three incompletions. Fourth and long, out of range of the Techs place kicker, ninety million people in America knew it had to be a pass. The Browns sent in everybody but Mickey Mantle. The Techs came to the line. Summerall's voice was frayed to a whisper; Madden was silent. All the world to play for, now.

Morrow dropped back, slipped the nose tackle busting in, and looked downfield. The Techs had three burners deep left on parallel fly patterns with a pair of cornerbacks on each; Morrow looked them halfway to the goal line and pump faked; on the other side of the field, the strong safety and the nickel back sneaked a peek and bumped each other, which was when the tight end broke out of his crossing pattern and headed for the corner, a step in the clear. Morrow, with seven hundred pounds of Browns linemen pushing at him, started to go down, reached into himself to wherever it is that champions come from, and threw the ball at the ceiling—and when it came down in the tight end's hands, it was Techs

37, Browns 34, with zero seconds left on the clock. They never bothered to kick the extra point.

"Whoof!" I said, and moved as rapidly as the tight end to make myself a stiff Scotch. The television showed the two teams filing into their dressing rooms, the Techs a triumphant rabble of exultant white and black faces, fists and index fingers raised, with great, gap-toothed grins and shouts of "Hey, Mom!"; the Browns downcast, heads lowered, feet dragging, here and there a tear.

The door to the study opened, and X joined us. On the screen Irv Cross was talking to Art Modell, the Browns' classy owner. The scene shifted to the winners' locker room, a bedlam of shouting and squirting. A platform had been set up. On it stood the Techs' managing partner, the NFL commissioner, Henry Morrow, the Techs' coach, and Brent Musburger of CBS.

After a few words, the commissioner presented the Super Bowl trophy to the Techs' owner, a young guy who'd made about a billion in microchips. I felt X lean forward on the back of my chair.

"This ought to be pretty good," he said.

Onscreen, Brent Musburger was handed a wireless telephone. Then the screen divided, and there was Eldon Erwitt in a cardigan and open-necked shirt, the great Dad of us all, sitting by an open fire with a hound at his feet. He looked expectant, waiting for his cue.

"There's someone here who wants to say something to you, Henry," said Musburger, handing the quarterback the telephone. Erwitt smiled.

"Well, Henry," said the President, giving the camera his full genial wattage, "when I told the Russians about our guided missiles, I should have mentioned you." His voice was patronizing: nice job, boy, good pass; an extra slice of watermelon for you tonight. He continued, "Why, I—"

Morrow looked at the camera. I felt he was looking into the conscience of every one of us. Then, in front of seventy million people, he hung up on the President of the United States.

"I don't have to listen to this garbage," Henry Morrow said. He handed the telephone back to Musburger, stepped off the platform, and vanished among his teammates. On the left, Erwitt's avuncular smile collapsed into a venomous look that would have done a Grand Kleagle proud; he began to comb his hair furiously. The commissioner looked poleaxed; the Techs' owner suppressed a smile; his coach tugged puzzledly at his cap. Musburger gesticulated, and the screen shimmered, scrolled, and then came alive with Warner Wolf flirting with Michelle Marsh.

"Sam, Eugenie," X said, lifting his glass, "I give you the health of that splendid young man!"

"Are you mad, Father?" Eugenie propelled herself from her chair; she was flushed with rage. "Are you absolutely certifiably insane? That was the President of the United States! Father, what are you doing?"

X ignored her. He gripped my arm.

"How about that Morrow, Sam? That's the kind of young man I want at Granite; thank heaven we've signed him to a lifetime contract."

"Father!" Eugenie lunged forward, knocking over her Tab, and grabbed X's arm. "Father! What are you doing? Do you want to destroy our company?"

X looked down at the puddle of spilled cola. "I think you'd better ring for Hideki," he said.

She began to sob. I hated the cruelty of the moment and, more than that, loathed them both for making me witness it. "You can't ruin it, Father," she wailed, "you can't! It's not yours! It's mine too! Oh, God, you awful old fool, I . . . I hate you!" She heaved great gulping breaths.

X looked at her disgustedly, then turned to me. "You know," he said, "I thought about giving Morrow a little more material to work with, but I decided against it." Eugenie continued to retch dryly, shoulders jerking spasmodically. He opened the door for me and took a key from his blazer.

"I'll have Hideki let her out when she's got control of herself."

I hated this moment. Did there have to be this much blood on the floor between father and daughter? She was all he had left. Except Granite, of course; except Granite. He was pushing her, I could see; provoking her, enraging her, driving her right to the edge. I found myself hoping he didn't succeed. I don't know why; I just did.

There was one question that needed asking.

"X," I inquired as we walked back to the drawing room, "what if the Browns had won?"

He gave me an infuriatingly enigmatic smile. "Oh, goodness, Sam, you don't think an old shark like me doesn't have his bets hedged? Anyhow, I think that Someone up there wants us to win this one." His face gleamed with the ardor of the righteous.

I woke up the next morning at home, alone. Florrie hadn't wanted me to come up. Tired, she said, and due downtown bright and early. I read the papers. As I expected, the sports pages were more about Henry Morrow's postgame performance than about the game itself. At a press conference in Houston, the commissioner, "speaking on behalf of the entire league," made a formal apology to President Erwitt. Morrow was suspended indefinitely "for conduct detrimental to the league." No surprises there. Twenty-five of the thirty-two owners were signatories to BLEEP.

I went to the magazine and then to AbCom. The place was a-twitter. Eugenie Monstrance had resigned as an officer and director. X had pushed her over the edge.

I met Florrie for a valedictory lunch and played my hunch as soon as we were seated.

"How was it last night at Fifth Avenue? Doth age improve the shining hour?"

She laughed. "I thought you'd guess, but I had to give it a try. If I tell you, is it deep graveyard?" She winked.

"Absolutely!"

"Well, it was really very quick. And very sweet, and in a way quite touching. I felt honored to be asked to serve; that was the strangest thing. He was celebrating and I was part of it. He just needed a new body for reassurance, that's all. He was dear and tender and he wanted me—it— so badly." She gave herself an instant with the memory, then said strongly, "But that's all there was, believe me. If you think I'm going to say he was better or worse than you—"

"No need. Any other news transmitted upon the steaming pillow?"

"Don't be ridiculous. People like him don't get to be people like him by tattling in bed. On the sofa, actually. He was very impatient."

"How colorful, how romantic. Was he pleased with his little Super Bowl skit?"

"He didn't say. But it might interest you to know that I talked with a chum in the White House. I rang him, just for your sake. The things I do for you. He wants something I have, and he thinks he'll get it by telling me exciting gossip. Besides, he's like a lot of people in the White House. He can't stand Erwitt, but the power of the place is simply too seductive. Anyway, apparently our Chief Executive was heard to use the word N-I-G-G-E-R several times, which is very unbecoming for the President of all the people. Apparently there's a council of war this evening. Erwitt, the Veep, the counselors, that clown from the USIA, and McNeery, of course, since this is a 'private sector' matter. The bottom line is that GBG's going to be taken very seriously from now on."

When we parted, she asked, "The next time can I stay with you?"

"Of course you can. Whenever you want."

I meant it. Florrie was real value. She wouldn't come to me again until her powers of darkness told her the time was right for both of us. We said goodbye without regrets, and with deep fondness.

"If she hadn't quit then, she sure as hell would have quit now," declared Duncan. He'd hustled over to my place that evening to brief me on the morrow's newsbreak. X wasn't giving the White House much time to take him seriously. The release was just going out that the GBG network would not be carrying President Erwitt's State of the Union speech the following evening but would broadcast instead a three-hour special of "Statehouse." The newspaper accounts were accompanied by full-page GBG ads and a hailstorm of thirty-second spots across the network's Tuesday afternoon and evening schedule.

Duncan swore he hadn't known about it until around seven o'clock that night. By eight, there was insurrection within the AbCom family.

"Naturally, we telexed the affiliates first. We started hearing from them about an hour later. A hundred of 'em say they're not gonna carry the 'Statehouse' special and that what the Chief's doing is unpatriotic."

"What's X say?"

"Bullshit, or words to that effect. He says just watch the ratings and leave it up to the people to decide. It's their airwaves, he says. The guy at the *Times* called just before I came over; the Chief told him what's the difference? It's just one TV fantasy against another. The Chief says the affiliates'll get out their calculators and by air time we won't have lost more'n a dozen."

"What about advertising?"

"We got some, which is a plus, since otherwise it was dead time. The best part is, the Chief's gonna run a bunch of those 'Army/Navy/Air Force/Marine' spots for nothing. They buy a lot of expensive time on the NFL and so on, so why not scratch their back a little? He doesn't want a lot of commercials, anyway. Maybe ten minutes' total over the three hours; he says it would be injurious to the country's mental health to have people zapping us to go over to Erwitt."

"The Chief" was right as usual. He knew his market. X's head-to-head confrontation with the President pulled a fifty-two rating and a sixty-five share for the "Statehouse" special. The President's State of the Union address got a twelve rating and a twenty share on the other three networks combined.

I expected to find X jubilant the next morning, but he seemed pensive.

"I've won the easy shots," he said, "but now Eldon'll start to fight back. I expect the going will be considerably harder from here on out. I trust your loins are well girded."

"How do you think they'll play it?"

"I think we'll start to see pressure put on our advertisers, lenders, and suppliers; certain of our stockholders. Nothing too blatant, though. Eldon has to be aware that the press is crawling out of its slime of complaisance and lining up behind us. But some of our affiliates have sensitive commercial and personal concerns, and efforts will be made to trade on those. Any number of them are ideologically in Erwitt's camp or leaning that way. They'll see this as a test of the profit motive. We'll hear a lot from BLEEP, I dare say."

"You don't sound hysterical with fear."

"Oh, my goodness, no! After all, the sponsors still have things to sell, and they want to make money, and Granite's still the best at doing that for them. Our shares are holding at a hundred sixteen, even after those nervous nellies sold out. We have six hundred million dollars in cash, so we can take a bit of a pounding, if it comes; what price would you put on the consistency and dedication of our audience? And I hardly think Eldon's going to nationalize the industry. It's bad enough that he's probably going to have to nationalize the banks."

"Do you want to talk about Eugenie?" I asked.

"What is there to say? She's like Ab, ruled by her emotions. This business is too tough for her. But I let her keep some of her ties; she's still the trustee for the pension funds and a director of the Foundation. Those are good for her self-esteem."

X had once said that he expected to be compared to everyone from Christ to Caligula. In the week after the Super Bowl/State of the Union fuss, the accent was definitely on the latter.

First, BLEEP ran full-page ads headed AMERICA, WE APOLOGIZE! in leading papers across the country. The thrust of the advertisement, signed by McNeery above the usual list of Wall Street and corporate leaders, was that of solicitous parents apologizing for a rogue child. The Murdoch papers produced a thundering attack on AbCom as a font of anticapitalism and called on X, now personally identified for the first time as the perpetrator of villainous heresies against the Great White Father, to journey to Canossa, kiss Erwitt's ring, and beg his forgiveness. *Forbes* said more of the same, comparing X to a great Clos Vougeot that had corked. Mobil and United Technologies, the Bobbsey Twins of corporate philosophizing, produced jaunty homiletic "advertorials" on the interrelationship of free enterprise and political responsibility. The ripples spread, and spread, and then, just as predictably as they had appeared, vanished into the muck of public apathy, leaving its surface clean and unruffled.

"All that's just bullshit," Buck said on the telephone when I called to ask how he read the entrails. "They got to do something like that. What'll count is when they get together in the back room and figure out what they can really do."

X got off Erwitt's case for a while. AbCom was flourishing, and he wanted to reconsolidate his stockholders' goodwill before once again making them nervous. Things quieted down, and confidence returned overnight. Although the stock market was going through a phase that was charitably described as "uneasy" in *Business Week*, AbCom held its own. The Dow Jones was off about 12 percent from its late summer high, but AbCom seemed rock firm at around $115.

By the time X left again for Little Gourd, even life within the company moved at a deceptively calm pace. I found myself more involved at the magazine. Winter ground on. I was now all set to go to Venice to visit Margarita in early April, but that was still long weeks off. I stayed close to home, got drunk a couple of times with Duncan, fooled around and screwed around some, and let myself drift.

The day after X's departure, I was working in my apartment when the bell rang. It was the elevator man with an AbCom envelope addressed to me; I figured it must be something from Duncan.

I opened it to find a microcassette and a note in X's strange, tiny hand. I had been brought up to believe that great men, from dictators to tycoons, must write in a grandiose, illegible scrawl, like Beethoven or Louis XIV. X wrote in a minuscule, absolutely clear script.

The note said:

Sam. For your Granite archives. I had a meeting Saturday. I had to go by taxi to some dreadful rooms in the Waldorf Towers, which is where people of this sort seem to feel most powerful. I took the precaution of having myself "wired up" by the Labs people. I must say it's rather fun, at my age, playing secret agent.

I put the tape on.

There was the sound of a knock, which had to be X announcing him-self, then other sounds, and a voice (which I didn't recognize) said: "Mr. Monstrance? President McNeery's expecting you."

Then more sounds, then: "H.H!" McNeery, ebullient. "How good to see you! I'm glad you could take the time to come."

X (very matter of fact): "Mr. President."

Sounds of chairs shuffling; McNeery asking if X wants anything to drink; X declining. Sound of a door closing, signaling, I guessed, the departure of whoever it was that admitted X.

X: "Well, Mr. McNeery, here I am."

McN.: "H.H., I really am very glad you could come. It's been a long time, hasn't it?"

X: "Well, there was that time at my son Abner's—"

McN.: "Yes, of course, a most tragic thing, that. And before that?"

X: "Washington, I think. Almost ten years ago."

McN.: "Indeed, indeed. Those days seem lost forever now, don't they. So much has changed. You know, H.H., I never thought that a political animal like myself would find life as a private citizen so—well, re-warding."

X (dryly): "I daresay. What is it you wished to see me about?"

McN: "I . . . we—the Bilateral Liaison, that is—feel that there have been some misunderstandings that really could be cleared up by a little good-faith, face-to-face, heart-to-heart conversation of the kind we're having. I might add, incidentally, that President Erwitt is quite upset personally. That some misunderstanding should have occurred between such old friends as the two of you."

X: "That's typically presumptuous of Eldon. He was always a much better friend of mine than I was of his."

McN (placatory): "Well, obviously I can't discuss that, H.H. What we do need to discuss is that this is a pretty critical time for the President's program for economic revival."

X: "It is? I wasn't aware that Eldon was doing much in the way of reviving anything except the bank accounts of the sort of people I used to see at the Bohemian Grove." (chuckle)

McN: "And then there's the threat of the worldwide Communist con-spiracy."

X: "Mr. McNeery, is Eldon seeking my advice about Russia? If he is, there must be some confusion. I am not an expert on Russia, nor do I hold any strong opinions on the matter of Russian policy except that our present shoot-first approach seems pretty darn silly."

McN (again placatory): "Of course not, H.H., of course not. Heh, heh. The Russian problem is just one of many that this President faces. It's important that he be given every chance to present a strong face to the public, a face of dignity, of trustworthiness, of—"

X: "Mr. McNeery?"

McN: "Yes?"

X: "You and I are busy men. It's Saturday, and I'm sure we both have errands to do. Can we cut across this? Do I gather from your drift that you are trying to say something about the programming policies of my network?"

McN: "Well—umm, that was . . . H.H., the fact is, these shows and policies of yours have not been helpful. It's disturbing. It seems to be affecting public confidence in the President's program, in his ability, and in his—well, good faith. AbCom is a great and important member of the American community of corporations. Your own son, bless him, was a founder of the Bilateral Liaison. You yourself are one of us—"

X: "I beg your pardon."

McN: "What?"

X: "I believe, Mr. President, that you said I was one of you."

McN: "Well, yes. You're the head of a major company, a wealthy man—"

X: "Mr. President, I may be a rich man. I am the chief executive of Granite, but I am assuredly not one of you. I am not one of you by birth, by education, by point of view, or by preference. I have known Eldon Erwitt longer than most men he knows, certainly much longer than any of the people whom he is said to regard as friends and from whom he derives advice and financial support. I know him for what he is. He is an image, no more substantive than smoke."

McNeery's voice took on an edge. "H.H., the rules have changed; the game, in fact, has changed. You'd better understand that. The old club doesn't exist. Most of the members are dead and the clubhouse is boarded over. You people controlled things and you let the bleeding-hearts take over, and they got this great country of ours into a mess, and now we in Washington and the private sector are going to get out of that mess whether you are with us or against us!"

X's reply was equally testy. "Mr. McNeery, you people speak of something called Eldonomics, which consists of auctioning off the nation to the rich and making sure they get all the credit they need to pay for it. You speak of something called foreign policy, which consists of making war, generally upon small backward nations. You speak of free markets, which you subsidize and wall off from competition and the risk of loss. I think this is wrong. The whole weight of the past suggests this is wrong."

When McNeery spoke again, it was soothing. "H.H., there's no point in you and me arguing politics. We're practical men, businessmen. I think we should put these small differences aside and see how we can work fruitfully together. The main reason I asked you here today was to indicate that a number of our members at the Bilateral Liaison have expressed interest in some of your activities, and in seeing AbCom grow back to its old prominence, and they'd be prepared to work closely with you—"

"Meaning what?" asked X.

"Well, in very general terms, and of course this is highly confidential and conceptual, of course, since I can't speak for them, but there has been talk of a guaranteed advertising base, several billion a year over, say, five years, and of course you have other divisions—"

"Mr. McNeery," said X cheerily, "I'm honored. Honored and flattered."

"Really," said McNeery, sounding somewhat surprised.

"Yes," said X. "Unless I'm grossly mistaken, you have just offered me the largest bribe in the history of the Western world."

"Well, now—"

"Now, now, that's perfectly all right. It's understandable, and, as I say, I'm flattered. Sadly, though I recognize that ninety-nine out of a hundred men would have jumped at your offer, certainly ninety-nine out of a hundred of the sort of people for whom you speak, I must decline. I'm an old man. Money can't mean that much to me any more, even if I weren't already wealthy. The wealth I have is really my memories and my dreams. The one drives the other, you see, and they both push me along, irresistibly."

There was a shuffling sound, presumably X getting up.

McNeery said, "You should reconsider, H.H. You should think it over. You don't know what you might be costing yourself. Or your people. Or your stockholders. Our people estimate that the sort of working relationships we were considering would virtually assure that your shares sell at two hundred dollars."

"That's quite a sum, Mr. McNeery. I have considered what you urge, however. Please don't think I haven't. There are greater risks in life than the price of shares, sir, even if people these days don't think so. What more can it cost me, anyway? It has, in a way, as you know, cost me my only son."

There was a pause, then X went on.

"Mr. McNeery, may I ask you one thing? These days one does hear tales about some of Eldon's people. Has this conversation been taped without my knowing it?"

"You must have a low opinion indeed of us," said McNeery harshly. "Of course not! I must say, the President will be very disappointed, H.H.; he often speaks of you with great warmth."

"I'll bet he does," said X. The two men said goodbye and the tape began hissing.

Well, I thought, now all the shoes have dropped. Now it begins.

CHAPTER 22

"It reminds me of the first time Cassie and I went to Paris," Clio said. "We did what all tourists do, especially American girls with their heads full of romance: we climbed up to Sacre Coeur at midnight and watched the city go to sleep. It never wholly did, of course, but we watched the lights twinkle out, one at a time. Cassie said each one was like a little death—she was in her poetic phase then."

She was talking about Abner, who had taken a turn for the worse. Whatever physiological or chemical deterioration was taking place within his brain had accelerated. She was jumpy and worried.

We were in a restaurant in North Palm Beach; Abner had been left at home with his watchers and his television set. I wasn't sure what I was doing in Florida. It was too easy to blame the slush of March. For the first time since Cass and I had called it quits, I was lonely, very much aware of the absence of dependable, recurrent female companionship. At sixes and sevens, I considered radical solutions: a week at a Club Med or the Gardner tennis ranch; a blind date through Buck. When I dropped in at AbCom at the end of the day, which was how I'd finally compromised with X, Duncan beseeched me to join him on a pub crawl, but the prospect of waking up with someone I'd have to explain to myself appalled me.

X was on Little Gourd for most of March. The editor went off to Zermatt to ski; the thought of him making his dignified way down the glaciers brought some amusement, but not enough. Even *alt Wien* failed to do the trick; I'd put on Schwarzkopf or an operetta and snap it off again.

The winter had come up short in terms of scandals, scoundrels, and poseurs, and I couldn't find the energy in myself to scout up subjects where there probably weren't any. I decided to try to draft a couple of chapters of the X/AbCom story. The meeting with McNeery would be a watershed, I thought, in whatever happened. So I made a great show of resolution and organization, putting my papers and notes in order, neatly relabeling my growing collection of cassettes, and decided to hie myself off to the sun somewhere, to labor in solitude for two weeks. I borrowed a condominium about thirty miles north of Palm Beach, in a development where Buck was an investor, which wasn't far from a couple of golf courses where I was pretty sure I could cadge a game, bought myself a snappy new Hermès portable typewriter, and set off.

After forty-eight hours, more "surf 'n' turf" and exotic frozen cocktails than I'd eaten or drunk in a lifetime, and a mercifully unconsummated flirtation with a skinny divorcée at the bar of a plastic-palmed joint in Vero Beach, I had written exactly three not-very-good paragraphs and then picked up the phone and called Clio. In so doing, I was admitting that she was the force that had pointed my compass needle in this particular direction and that the person whom my writerly paraphernalia had been intended to fool was myself. She invited me down for a drink. Abner greeted me affably enough, but he soon lapsed into himself, as if he were watching a movie inside his head. Clio was jumpy; she said she'd like to get out of there, but she hated all the usual places in Palm Beach, so we drove over to the mainland and up Route 1 until we found a place that looked OK. It was all very Elmore Leonard.

"Is it going to get worse?" I asked.

She shrugged. "That's what they guess. Nobody seems to know. They do agree that he's unlikely to get any better." She looked fine and sad in the dim light of the restaurant.

"I thought maybe I'd see if he'd like to play a little golf. I'm staying not far from Seminole." I was scattering small sympathetic noises like bread crumbs, trying to attract her, unsure of the right way into her feelings.

"I don't think so, Sam, but you're sweet to ask. I took him over to Everglades the other day, to give him a chance to play. He was very excited. It was early and there wasn't anyone on the course. He played four holes. Then, poor darling, he just dropped his club and wandered off and sat under a palm and asked the air where his daddy was. His father has totally vanished from our lives, of course. He doesn't like flawed things."

I didn't say anything. For a minute or two, we ate in silence, trying to figure ways of escape from the impasse the very thought of X created.

"I sometimes wonder," she said, shaking her head as if she found life entirely disbelievable, "how it might have worked out if Cassie had been the one who got Abner. That was what she had in mind, you know."

She didn't mean it to be wounding, and I was past being shocked.

"Abner and Cass?" I made a diffident grunt.

"Yes, really. I think she would have made things work out differently with his father. She's so ambitious."

"Don't tell me!"

"Besides, if Cassie had gotten Abner, he wouldn't have been in Virginia with me that morning and one thing wouldn't have led to another."

I reached over and patted her hand, trying to seem avuncular. The mourner with his hand under the widow's skirt.

"Yes, he would," I said. "He would have gone after that farm no matter whom he married."

"I suppose you're right."

On the way home, she asked me if I could scare up a black tie and be her escort the next evening at a party in Palm Beach. Abner wasn't up to it; the woman who was giving the party was one of the few who still made an effort.

I said I would, and did, and showed up the next evening in a rented dinner jacket that cost me the small residue of whatever notions of elegance I'd ever had about myself. Abner was glad to see me.

"Sam, when'd you get here?"

"Last night." He'd forgotten I'd been there the night before.

"Any chance of getting in some golf?"

"Not this time, I'm afraid." I saw Clio looking at me. "I have to leave first thing. Something's come up." Which was true. A month earlier I'd signed a contract on Mother's house; that morning I'd received a call from my lawyer: the purchaser wanted to accelerate the closing and was prepared to pick up half the broker's commission if I agreed to do so. That came to more than $20,000. I nodded to Clio to signal that I wasn't fibbing and flattered myself that I saw a look of disappointment pass across her face.

"Gosh," said Abner. "That's too bad." He sounded like a small boy refused a game of catch. Then his expression seemed to lose focus. "Where is he?" he asked; I heard a small note of anxiousness.

Clio went over and touched his face. "Who, love?"

"Dad," said Abner. "Where is he? Where's Dad?"

"He'll be coming soon."

Abner smiled. He settled back. He began to hum, a private child's song, the words and meaning secret. Watching him, I wondered whether there had come, while he lay comatose in the Virginia hospital, an onrush of monstrous dreams, dreams peopled with demons wearing his father's face, demons which had torn his mind loose from the stalk of reality. It must have been something like that.

The party Clio took me to was predictable. The Palm Beach season was down to butt ends; people who had little enough to say to begin with now had nothing left. "Why did you and Abner ever come here?" I asked Clio on the way back to her house. "Everyone here was born seventy years old and retired."

"Abner liked it. He felt safe and superior here."

"I wouldn't think that would be difficult."

"Most people come here reflexively. They don't really know why."

It's called "being rich together," I thought; similarity breeds affection, or at least reassurance.

I pulled the car into their driveway and stopped.

"Well," I said, "I have an early plane. I'll stay in touch." Then, without thinking, I leaned across and kissed her. I'll say for the record I meant just to kiss her on the cheek, a wordless brotherly *Wiedersehen*. She was the one who altered the angle of her face so that our lips met.

"Ummm," we both said.

The kiss had been more than sisterly, more than friends, but she kept her mouth closed. "I can't stay out too long," she said.

I think all we intended was a little light necking, teenage stuff, or teenage the way I thought of it. A temporary palliative for her isolation and my loneliness. We weren't kids any longer, however, so our kisses intensified, inspired investigation; at this age we both knew where the treasures were to be found, and our hands acquired lives of their own. I shifted, to undo the waistband of my trousers and felt her tense uneasily. "No, please," she said. "No farther than that. Here." She took my hand; it seized the hint and seemed to find its own way under the fabric; by itself it closed over her; she felt like silk, like syrup.

"That's right," she said. "Oh, please, just keep that up. Please; oh, just like that; just exactly like that. Oh, my God!"

I wanted to be inside her so badly I felt as if I would shatter like crystal if I couldn't. But I couldn't break the rhythm of what we were doing, either: our hands on each other; the two of us breathing in time, long heavy breaths, moans that seemingly rose directly from where we touched each other. I wanted so awfully to be above her, to be in her, to get for myself that soft, slick, long release I knew she would give me, but she didn't want it, and I didn't want to stop what we were doing, and sure enough, soon enough, I felt her slide away into a rippling series of jerks, felt her push her pelvis against my hand, and felt through her lips her breath coming first bulletlike and then dying into sighs. I felt all of that in her and through her, felt it for about a millionth of a microsecond that lasted about as long as the history of all time, and then it was my turn to gather behind myself stiff as a stick and blow apart like a balloon.

Afterward, we lay back against the seat, blowing for air. I riffled through my brain for something to say that would let us segue back into polite society and mere friendship. Something to put a light face on our lack of control, our faithlessness.

"If this were a John O'Hara novel," I said, "I would excuse myself to adjust my clothes."

"And I would pull my top up, and my skirt down, and dash from the car, with a light but throaty sob, and run into the big house." She gave a resigned little laugh that indeed sounded close to a sob. The moonlight splashing through the windshield caught her profile. "And tomorrow, if we met, I'd cut you dead."

"You look terrific, Clee. You are terrific."

"Am I?" She reached down and touched me again; it was like being brushed by an electric feather. It made me shudder.

"You better not do that," I said. "Murder by ecstasy is punishable by something. Even in Palm Beach."

She took her hand back and looked at it curiously. "Goodness," she said. "Half the population of China in this pale little hand."

She laughed quickly, an ironic little chuckle weighted with faint regret. She reached up and turned my face to hers.

"You do understand, don't you, Sam? Why I can't; much as I may want to now? Why I probably never will."

"I think so. Never say 'never.'"

"Not while he's alive, Sam; not while he's mine to care for, while he's close. Not here; not in his house or in his garden."

"They're yours too."

"You know what I mean. Kiss me just once more, will you? Just touch me. Here. Aah, that's nice."

Afterward, I walked her to the house. Through an otherwise darkened window, I saw the flicker of a television screen and heard crowd noises; he must be watching an exhibition game. I kissed Clio quickly; her kiss said we were back to being friends again, or at least friends more than anything else.

The door closed behind her. If and when, I thought. The story of all of our lives: if and when we can sense and seize the opportunity; if and when we can undo what we have done. By mistake or mismatch, out of desperation and anxiety and loneliness, we forge chains that constrain us through our lifetimes. We would have made a great pair, Clio and I, but I'd heard that from me before, and by now I knew enough to be skeptical. I headed back toward North Palm Beach. It was still early. Fragments of music hung like moonbeams in the sultry night; along Worth Avenue, people patrolled the shop windows, gearing up for tomorrow's spending. A truly contemporarily romantic scene, I thought, and I a truly modern-day romantic hero: forty-four years old, trousers sticky with recent passion, driving alone at one in the morning to a borrowed condo in North Palm Beach.

The agent was proud of the price he'd gotten me for Mother's house. It was all right; it was money, and the market was such that the sort of people to whom I would have liked to see it pass couldn't have afforded it. The guy who bought it was a junior-grade Bud, very much on his way, a young financial futures trader at Bear, Stearns who spent the hour and a half it took to close telling me how he'd made $500,000 before lunch that day.

It made me sad to see the house go, but not sad enough. It was an old house, and it and its ghosts would survive a hundred years of futures traders if it came to that, just as it had outlasted who knows how much godawfulness before Mother, and there would always be happy moments under its roof to penetrate the gray spells. I shook hands across the bank's conference table, silently bid goodbye to a large part of my past, and walked across Broad Street to Buck's downtown office with the check. I prided myself how thoroughly up to date I'd become. Ten years ago, I'd have stuffed the check in my pocket until the next time I had to go to the bank. But one day's interest came to $201.03, as I'd figured on my lawyer's calculator during the closing, and that was lunch money.

I took a cab uptown from Wall Street to the AbCom Tower. I'd been busy for most of the week helping X and Duncan put the finishing touches on X's letter to the stockholders for the annual report. I was really enjoying this, because, to quote Duncan, "This ain't no annual report, it's a goddamn manifesto!" It was also a useful distraction; Margarita had gotten involved in some sort of special project, and our trip to Venice had been pushed into April. Actually, until Margarita called, the day after I got back from Florida, I had forgotten all about it.

X accepted a number of my suggestions, mostly on matters of phrasing and emphasis but also with respect to a couple of ideas. I thus felt a surge of pride of authorship when the report came out, toward the end of April, and caused the stir it did.

The summary figures were glowing. After setting aside profits from the sale of AbCom's financial services and real estate divisions, and the 51 percent interest in BizNet, and after reflecting the reductions in revenues and income resulting from those divestments, AbCom had still pulled in consolidated revenues of just over $7 billion, for a net profit on continuing consolidated operations of $512 million, or $7.90 a share.

The first hint that this was to be an unconventional report came in the presentation of AbCom's 49 percent equity in BizNet's net income; the $62 million attributable to AbCom's interest was broken out as "unavailable investment income." Most companies I knew would have merrily included this sum in profit, through "equity accounting," even though the money was being held and used elsewhere and wasn't theirs to control or demand.

The letter to stockholders followed. We knew it was addressed to a euphoric audience, since AbCom, even at $110 in a weak, listless market, was still almost double from when X had taken over. X therefore figured on a certain "emotional elasticity," his term for the indulgence he expected his shareholders would grant to his somewhat radical ideas.

He began by talking about GBG News:

> GBG operates by grace of public consent in the sense that it transports its product through the public domain, the airwaves. We pay no right-of-way for the use of what is by any standards public territory, which is a de facto subsidy as against other communications companies, which are obliged to lay cable, string wire, or construct microwave facilities in order to deliver revenue-producing products and services. Accordingly, it is your management's belief that some quid pro quo is called for. At AbCom, through our GBG News Division, we seek to provide this in the form of an enlarged, enhanced news effort aimed solely at increasing our audience's awareness and informedness. We believe that efforts to sell news as a form of entertainment or propaganda or as an outlet for personality exposure are insulting, wrongheaded, and, in the last analy-

sis, dangerous. In the most recent fiscal year, losses sustained in your company's broadcast news operations approximated $67 million, largely as the result of upgrading facilities and increasing personnel without a commensurate increase in advertising rates. Your management regards that cost as small recompense indeed for the economic advantage of unlimited access to the public airwaves.

We'd gone on from there, taking our chances. The letter concluded:

As stewards of a public stockholder-owned company, your management is obligated to utilize all available legal and fiscal opportunities to increase your company's profits. In recent years, federal economic and tax policies have made available to corporations specific concessions and adjustments which, while they have no meaningful effect on the efficiency, modernity, or productivity of your company's operations, nevertheless permit your company to significantly reduce its obligation to pay federal taxes on income. Accordingly, for the most recent fiscal year, your company had a taxable income, the excess of revenues over all operating costs and other cash and invoiced expenses, of $967 million. Thanks to Administration-mandated tax credits, offsets, and intangible deductions, your company paid on this profit a total of $12.8 million in cash to the Internal Revenue Service, for an effective income tax rate of 1.3%. In addition, your company paid cash dividends on its common stock of $2.80 per share. Of these dividends, which aggregated approximately $181 million, $118 million was paid on shares owned by foundations, pension funds, and other holders specifically exempt from federal income taxes, leaving $63 million distributed to individual stockholders in varying tax brackets. Accordingly, on a profit of close to $1 billion, notionally taxable at either the corporate or stockholder level, the Federal Government received an estimated total of approximately $43 million, or 4%.

The financial reports that followed were unlike any the investment community had ever seen. The company's income statement was set out in the normal fashion, encrusted with the accountants' customary impenetrable gobbledygook, but right next to it was a line-by-line recapitulation of AbCom's true cash results for the year, understandable to anyone who ever tried to match his salary to his cost of living. It showed that AbCom had actually collected receivables on the order of $6 billion, and that the company had paid out, in everything from X's salary to taxes to the production costs of episodes of "Statehouse" that wouldn't be shown until later this fall, around $5.2 billion, which meant that its cash earnings per share, instead of being the $7.90 that conventional accounting showed as reportable profit, were in fact more on the order of $12.35.

The rest of the financial data were displayed in the same fashion. It set out an estimate of AbCom's film library and other assets, how much it owed and when exactly it was due, all liabilities that "normal" accounting wouldn't have required to be reported beyond a nodding, obfuscated mention buried in an undiscoverable footnote.

The final table was a real stunner. Headed APPRAISED AND MARKET VALUE and prepared by independent experts in various areas of valuation, it showed, in considerable detail, what the company's assets were worth at current prices. It worked out to around $125 per share.

In assembling the report, X knew he was mounting a challenge to the assumed proprietary right of managements around the country to exclusive possession of the numbers that really mattered: actual cash flow and the true going value of assets. He knew he was picking a fight with the entire business world. This radical annual report was going to be sent not only to every AbCom stockholder but to every government official above the level of GS-12, to every member of Congress, to every federal commissioner, judge, and attorney. Copies would go to every registered representative of every large brokerage firm, to the media, to each of the 15,000 investment institutions and money managers listed in *Reich's Directory*, and to the heads of every registered trade union and government lobby. And a copy would go to every one of the nine million names in the computers of AbCom's Direct Mail division.

"Direct Mail's gonna really hit the spot," said Duncan. "It's going out with an insert that this billion-dollar company which paid a whole four percent in taxes last year gets to send out this glossy report letter for less than it costs some dinge in Newark to send money home to Georgia."

"You sound suspiciously like a reform-minded liberal, Fergie. Have I won you over?" I asked.

"The Chief and you have given me back the old fire in the belly. I was head of the Young Marxists in high school. I heard you were in Florida. How's the kid?"

"Not so hot. How'd you know I was there?"

"The Chief knew. He talked to the kid's wife. Say, you know who was on the island? Old girlfriend of yours; I rode back on the plane with her."

"Cass Hargrove?"

"Nah, I know her. This's another one. Got about five names. The Chief tried some fast moves, but he never got a glove on her."

"Florrie Grosvenor."

"That's the one." Duncan left me pondering the implications of that.

Since his meeting with McNeery, X had remained quiet on the Erwitt front. To some extent, he was distracted by the uproar caused by our annual report. He commented gleefully that he had been cut dead by other moguls at the Gorse and the Praetorium; two large advertisers canceled. *The Wall Street Journal* reported that ninety-three large corporations had been besought by newly organized stockholder groups to emulate AbCom in the public presentation of their figures. Five Senators had sensed a potentially hot issue and were sponsoring "stockholder need-to-know" legislation. This wasn't the whole story, though. I got the feeling from him that he'd decided, almost on impulse, to pull back for a while, to let McNeery and the rest of Erwitt's hoplites conclude that X's grave brave talk at the meeting with McNeery had been just so much bluster and that the former President had in fact made him reconsider.

Not that the administration wasn't continuing to feel the sting of earlier GBG sorties. Against what we understood to be the advice of the Attorney General and the personal urging of the President and McNeery, a former Undersecretary of Defense had filed suit against GBG for libel and defamation, seeking damages of $600 billion. The suit had been provoked by a "Statehouse" episode which depicted an Assistant State Highway Commissioner tipping off his mistress's brother about forthcoming projects that were to be let for bids. The script implied that money had changed hands.

The television episode closely paralleled the circumstances surrounding the recent resignation of an Assistant Secretary of Commerce, a well-known North Carolina textile executive, who was named by a Congressional committee as having leaked confidential trade figures to a lady with whom he was alleged to enjoy "a confidential, close relationship." The lady was said to have made a $380,000 profit shorting the dollar.

X was gleeful. "Now the entire seamy side of Eldon's administration will have to come out in court! We're not going to settle; you can count on that! Boys, it's just like the Marquis of Queensberry tricking Oscar Wilde into suing him! And the dummy fell for it!"

Unfortunately, however, cooler heads and the interests of discretion prevailed, and the suit was withdrawn.

The other litigation did not involve GBG directly. A trillion-dollar class action suit had been brought by a small Arkansas bank against the

Comptroller of the Currency, the Federal Deposit Insurance Company, and the Federal Reserve Board. The three federal agencies had collaborated in guaranteeing the deposits of a major money center bank whose mismanagement and pellmell lending practices had caused a run by large depositors. The bailout so clearly favored the large over the small that one financial daily described it as "not merely violating the spirit of the legislation which established the FDIC, but raping it!" In an interview in *The American Banker*, counsel for the Arkansas bank had admitted that his client had been inspired by a segment of "First National" which had dealt with cozy understandings given the big banks that Uncle Sam would be behind them no matter what.

Moreover, the press reaction to the annual report had been exactly what X had intended.

The *Times* had given it a front-page play. ABCOM ANNUAL REPORT ASTONISHES INVESTORS, STUNS BUSINESS COMMUNITY, ran the heading. The piece began:

> In a total departure from common practice and norms of corporate behavior, AbCom Inc.'s annual report, released yesterday to stockholders, the media and, in an unusual step, to the more than 9 million names on file with the broadcasting/communications giant's Direct Mail Division, contained detailed and clear presentations of the company's financial condition, including cash flow and asset appraisals, which corporate managers have been historically loath to reveal.

The article continued into the business section and went on to describe X's reform of AbCom's executive compensation formulas, which were now directly tied to real stockholder benefits, principally dividends and absolute and relative market performance. In a sidebar, the paper reported the reactions of a spectrum of corporate executives, small stockholders, Naderites, accountants, union leaders, and money managers. Opinion was all over the place, but it confirmed the hostility X had reported in his clubs. McNeery was quoted as saying that broad dissemination of the type of information set forth in the AbCom annual report, "at a time of watershed in America's business recovery, risks letting vital corporate secrets fall into threatening hands and could be just about on a par with the Rosenberg traitors giving atomic secrets to the Soviet Union."

Duncan had caught hell too, from his colleagues in CCEA, the Corporate Communications Executives Association. Although he was the brightest star and best-known of the group, he'd been invited in for a light brushing-over with truncheons and rubber hoses. His peers had not regarded the annual report as a high point of contemporary disclosure standards and practices, but Duncan remained unruffled. He was with the Chief all the way.

Then in late April, hard on the heels of the release of the annual report and virtually on the eve of the annual meeting, X opened fire again.

I was tipped by Duncan. X was away in California.

"You know that congressional runoff in Iowa? Well, tune in to next week's 'Statehouse.' The Chief's decided to take a hand at the table."

The entire nation knew about the Iowa runoff, which was being contested within the party for the right to run for the seat representing the President's own home district. It pitted the President's influence against a set of existential facts: the district had been hit hard by farm closings and unemployment. Even the big Deere plant that Erwitt had porkbarreled had laid off four hundred people.

The Erwitt candidate, for whom the President had already stumped personally, was a millionaire realtor who preached big bang defense, limited, standoffish government, and the beauty of massive economic units. His opponent, a professor of agronomics from the state university at Ames, liked small business and small farming, entrepreneurialism, and asserted that lasers in the sky and battleships off Cancún, the cornerstones of Erwitt's foreign policy, were of less moment than county unemployment rates.

The professor won.

There had probably never been such intense coverage and so many and extended postmortems of an off-year local election in history. Despite what the analysts claimed, it could not be conclusively established that the "Statehouse" episode which had aired nationally a few nights before the runoff, and which had mysteriously found its way onto the local cable system for two election-eve reruns, was the primary cause of the Erwitt candidate's narrow defeat.

Nevertheless, it must have been a catalyst. It was a strong show, revolving around the governor's buying new police cars with federal money allocated for crop relief, arguing amiably that the crops might fail anyway, and since crop failure meant unemployment and unemployment meant crime, better to buy the police cars now. It was an effective allegory, and it must have touched real nerves, plucked real strings.

It was small potatoes, though, compared to X's next step.

CHAPTER 23

I had breakfast with X at his apartment the day of the annual meeting. He was understandably upset; he'd been awakened early with a terrible piece of news. Jacob Polhemus had suffered a stroke in the night and was in Massachusetts General Hospital; he was unconscious and it was uncertain whether he would live. That morning, for the first time since we had come back into each other's lives, I could see X's big, usually confident features furrowed with intimations of mortality.

"First Ab, now Jacob," he said. "Now there's just you and Duncan."

There was certainly no point in even mentioning Eugenie. She had virtually disappeared from AbCom, as far as I knew. I intended to disappear too. I'd enjoyed the work on the annual report, and playing the limited role I had in sticking it to the fatcats, but I wanted to get back to my other life. I was due to leave for Venice the next night, and I thought that would usefully make the break. After that trip, I intended to limit my visits to the company to perhaps an hour or two a week, just to keep abreast, and to make exceptions only for major occasions, such as the affiliates' meeting, this year in Dallas, at the end of the month.

I hadn't spoken with Clio for a while, so I asked X how his son was doing.

"Not well, I'm afraid. We've had to send him away for a while. We found a nice place near Millbrook." As he described it, it sounded a cross between Silver Hill and Bedlam.

"Ab's just like a two-year-old, Sam," he said. "It's worse than Alzheimer's. He's not even continent." He spoke as if speaking of a dead man, but without bereavement. He found Abner's condition too ugly to merit mourning, just as Eugenie's plainness had been too uninteresting to merit affection.

"And how's Clio?" I asked. X's use of "we" had set a small bell tinkling. Had he finally gotten through to her? Worn her down by solicitousness, already worn down as she was? It occurred to me that I might also ask him about Florrie. Cass, Margarita, Florrie, now Clio. Was there a pattern in this?

"She's taking it extremely well," he said. "I've persuaded her to stay at Dunecrag this summer. It wouldn't do for her to be alone. Her sister will be there."

How cozy, I thought. There was something faintly repellent about all this.

"I think there'll be trouble today," he said.

I thought I knew what he meant. AbCom stock had been behaving badly; the night before, it had closed at $105 and a fraction. There were reports of restiveness among certain large holders, in particular a story in *The Wall Street Journal* that quoted "a major fund manager" as expressing apprehension that X might be jeopardizing AbCom's future growth by alienating advertisers and regulatory authorities. The paper's own position seemed to be that life was difficult enough for the big banks without washing their linen in public the way GBG was doing with "First National." In the *News*, Dorfman had quoted a West Coast newsletter which had put ABI at the top of its list of issues ripe to be shorted.

Instinctively I tried to put a good face on things. I don't know why. At that moment, I wasn't especially well-disposed toward X personally, even though, ideologically, he was still my main man. I let my ideology speak for me.

"It looks as though Erwitt's really starting to feel the heat," I said.

The latest *Washington Post*/ABC poll had been full of good news. The President's trustworthiness rating had sunk somewhat, but his skill rating, the measure of the respondents' confidence in Erwitt to deliver, had plummeted. Sixty percent of those polled agreed with the proposition that the President "is unfair in his mind." Less than 40 percent indicated confidence that the President was intellectually up to his job.

X took my encouragement in stride. "Speaking of that," he said, "there's something I want you to see. I know you're trying to keep a balanced approach here, Sam, and I can understand that, but this is important." He told me to be at the GBG screening room that evening at seven.

I said I looked forward to a stellar performance at the annual meeting.

"Don't worry," he said, the old confidence magically returning. "I was in Germany just after I got out of Yale. I'm not about to be pushed around by amateurs. I saw the real thing in Nuremberg, and I'm not going to be bullied by a bunch of brownshirts in pinstripes."

He was true to his word. He got through the formal part of the annual meeting quickly enough. I could tell the mood was completely different from the year before, when the stockholders had echoed the affiliates' contentment. The euphoria was gone; in its place, like damp seeping through a wall, was an uncertain suspicion. Once, X's audience had assumed that the legendary old man who addressed them was solely concerned with making money for them. That assumption was now confounded by the evidence of recent months. They weren't sure what to make of him now.

The stock had opened that morning at $102, off more than a point, which didn't help things. I called Buck from a pay phone outside the Pierre ballroom, X's lucky venue, and he reported that more institutions were known to be lightening up.

"A lot of these folks've had a real fat ol' time. A lot of brokerage accounts are goin' long-term, too." He confessed to "takin' a li'l short position myse'f; just a trade, old buddy. Don't mean a thing, loyalty-wise!"

So the magic was definitely compromised; a hairline crack, a trace of mildew, had appeared on the golden egg.

The trouble didn't start until the question-and-answer period, when truculent questions came from all parts of the room, from different sorts of people, none of them the persistent professional agitators, the tired, familiar veterans of thirty years of putting up one failed resolution after another. The group which began to work X over was new. I had been to a lot of annual meetings in my career, and this struck me as a put-up job. The questioners were too diverse; the questions too studied. X's interrogators could have come out of Bishman's casting pool.

To begin with, the questions touched on a great many issues, none in themselves surprising except for the fact of being asked at all. Why had Eugenie Monstrance resigned as a director? What was the purpose of the accounting changes? Was it true there had been advertising losses on both the affiliate and network levels? Allegations and rumors were paraded before X for comment, confirmation, denial, and explanation. Once or twice he was sharply interrupted. A young man on the right side of the

Pierre ballroom and a young woman on the left, sexually indistinguishable in similar three-piece outfits and neckties, started to monopolize the interrogation, trying to shout X down, to halt him in mid-answer, pulling up fractionally short of being downright insulting. It was obvious their intent was to goad X into behaving like a fuddled, angry old man and turn his audience against him.

They had stepped up too far in class, however, in taking on someone as experienced and clever as X. He was, quite simply, out of their league. He held his ground and controlled the meeting. Patiently, tactfully, he refused to be provoked. He defended the business logic of his policies and actions and riposted as uncandidly as they thrust, disavowing any taint of ideology, of Erwitt-baiting. He turned aside his questioners with lordly, measured good humor. When the meeting broke up, the mood of the audience seemed lighter-hearted, more at ease.

And yet I wondered. Had he come across as too much the proprietor, not enough the steward? Had he been too patrician, too condescending? These people were AbCom's owners too. Had he behaved too feudally with them? They were no longer toiling in the shadow of the castle. The order of life had changed.

When I showed up, as bidden, at the screening room, I complimented him on his performance.

"That was very cool, X."

"Why, thank you, Sam. I'm glad to have it out of the way. I think you know everyone?"

There were only three to know: besides X, Duncan was there, and Eric Shaughnessy.

X made a brief, introductory speech.

"What you're about to see is the fruition of something Eric and I have discussed for some months now. One of our great concerns is that the American voter seems to be suffering from a peculiar form of amnesia, or that he's just plain forgetful. Either way is just as bad, since it means that politicians are no longer held accountable for their promises, their statements, and their records. What you're about to see is what Eric and I believe to be a pretty good way of force-feeding the public memory."

He signaled and the lights went down. A screen descended from the ceiling.

The first image was the logo of CNI, Shaughnessy's company, surmounting the corporate slogan, AWARENESS IS OUR BUSINESS. A voice-over informed us that the following announcement was being presented as a public service, and repeated the CNI motto.

The next picture was of Eldon Erwitt, grinning. The camera closed in. The President's face assumed an expression of mild, amused incredulity. "Did I say that?" he asked the camera.

It was the President's most famous, notorious evasion, his way of shrugging off his looseness with fact and declaration. Erwitt played many changes on it, numerous variations of intonation and gesture. The effect was always the same: challenged to explain some gross inconsistency, the President could somehow convince the camera that his earlier statements or declarations, now confounded or canceled by fact or expediency, had somehow been placed in his mouth by the malefic sorcery of his opponents, a bunch of disgruntled, misguided, elitist plotters against America.

The main body of the spot consisted of a highly charged presentation showing a politician contradicting himself, breaking a promise, turning upside down. Altogether, we were shown a dozen. Only three were of Erwitt; the others showed everyone from a well-known governor to the mayor of a major city. Dates and places were shown in strong graphics. At the end, the image returned to Erwitt, an image different from that with which the spot opened, but once again centered on the President saying, "Did I say that?" The spots closed with the AbCom logo and motto, and a repetition of the "public service" voiceover.

As the lights went up, Duncan nudged me. "Strong, huh? He's got fifty of 'em. Only about a dozen on the President, but he's at the top and bottom of every one, so the point ain't about to be lost!"

It certainly wouldn't, I thought. The spots achieved their purpose, which was to establish Erwitt typologically, as the epitome and avatar of political duplicity and self-interest. The implication was unmistakable. The main body of each spot might show the Speaker of the House, or the leader of the state assembly, or the governor, but these were merely manifestations and changelings, disguises adopted by Erwitt, the Merlin, the single spirit, the Supreme Liar.

There was a brief discussion afterward. The first spots would go on over the weekend. I was glad I'd be in Venice. Duncan promised to keep me posted.

I heard from him in the middle of my stay. Margarita and I had spent the day in a long ramble under warm, hazy skies. Our stroll had taken us all the way over to the Madonna dell'Orto, where we admired the big Cima and the startling Tintorettos.

It was good to be under a spring sun. When I had left New York, the days still wore themselves out in gusts and long, chilly, soaking rains; from the window of the train which carried me from Milan to Venice, I could see that Italy was in flower, the fields sprouting and the sun bright. The water taxi took me from the station mainly along back canals; the Grand Canal was closed for the repair of the Accademia Bridge. From every window flowerboxes hung, adding a measure of cheerfulness to the expectant joy I felt just at having come here, a joy that redoubled when I caught sight of Margarita, together with a wiry, uniformed servant, waiting for me on the Campo di San Vio.

When I climbed up from the motorboat, there was an instant when neither of us was quite certain what to do. Not all lovers come together the way they seem to in deodorant commercials, loping in slow motion through sunny fields of millet. We pecked at each other, and I squeezed her and told her how wonderful she looked, which was true, and she said something of the same to me, and then we squeezed each other and took each other's hand and followed the manservant back to her mother's house, which was just off the Calle delle Mende, not far from the Anglican Church of St. George. It was a pale yellow house of four narrow stories, slightly peeling; within and without, it gave off that distinctly Venetian mixture of decadence and artful dilapidation, qualities I cherished in Venice as much as risotto or the profile of the Salute at twilight.

Margarita's mother was a spry, elegant wisp in her late seventies. She treated me with warm formality. "Samuel," she said, "I am deeply glad that you have come to us." On the short walk from the landing, Margarita had warned me that her mother could not conceive of "Sam" as anything but a contraction of "Samuel," and so Samuel I remained for my fortnight in Venice.

That first night Margarita came to my room. Out of courtesy for her mother's sensibilities, she muffled her moans and sobs, but she tore into me with a vengeance. I didn't flatter myself that our lovemaking was much more than a monument to months of separation and lust. There was no metaphysical dimension lurking behind our heavings and strokings, and, in a way, that was nice. I knew afterward, lying beside her in the dark, my hand on her stomach, fingertips just tracing the first tendrils of the thatch at her crotch, that we were to each other just as we ought to be, just as we had to be. We were of good use to each other, but neither of us was destined to be the other's answer to the great puzzles.

Oddly, it wasn't until our walk to the Madonna dell'Orto that we even mentioned X, who had brought us together. We had talked about every-

thing else under the sun: about the possibility of my doing a series of
pieces on cultural politics in New York, and what I was doing at AbCom;
about her excitement at the whispers that she was being considered as a
Fellow of All Souls; about whether Vivaldi's greatness would survive
"The Four Seasons," now played by string ensembles in hotel lobbies;
about Erwitt and his crazy new ideas about NATO; about the ten most
overrated people, books, restaurants, and so on in New York and London
and anywhere else. We were just too busy with ourselves and Venice to
think about X, and then we became self-conscious about having stayed
away from the subject, so it became a kind of deliberately childish game
not to bring him up.

When we got back from the Madonna dell'Orto, having soaked up the
afternoon's last full rays over coffee and a Punt é Mes at a café near the
Accademia, we found Margarita's mother waiting for us in the *salone*. She
held out a fat envelope, an express letter from Duncan.

He wrote that the CNI "Did I Say That?" spots had really stirred
things up. X had gotten his wish; Erwitt had come out of his lair. Duncan
enclosed a clipping, which I scanned. At a press conference, the President had been asked about a possible vendetta with X and had replied,
"It's really nothing to worry about. Mr. Monstrance was a great figure in
the broadcasting industry. It's sad to see him turn out to be just another
sorry old man yearning for the age of Teddy Roosevelt—or was it
Franklin?"

There were other enclosures, which I passed over to Margarita. A
Times editorial praising GBG and CNI for "opening people's eyes to the
cavalier disregard for accuracy and factual reality which has characterized
American politics in the Age of Television, shown in so direct, visually
uncomplicated, and irresistible a manner that not even the most uncon-
cerned voter can ignore it!" There was a front-page center-column story
from *The Wall Street Journal*. Under a sketched portrait of X, the article
was headed REBEL WITHOUT A CAUSE? ABCOM'S FOUNDER INTEN-
SIFIES ATTACKS ON PRESIDENT AND ADMINISTRATION. IS LEGEND-
ARY BROADCASTER H. H. MONSTRANCE BACKING A CAUSE OR A
VENDETTA? STOCKHOLDERS GETTING EDGY.

There was a photocopy of a "Flash Report" under the Institutional
Equities Associates logo, signed by the redoubtable Ms. Pfannglanz. She
reviewed AbCom's numbers, analyzed GBG's apparently inexorable increase in market share, reviewed the company's other business, and concluded that everything looked rosy. She saved her caveat for last:

While prospects for AbCom's having another banner year, with earnings per share advancing perhaps to the $9.00–$9.50 level, remain excellent, much depends on the degree to which management avoids having its energies unconstructively diverted. We continue to regard ABI with extreme favor, maintaining it as a PRIORITY HOLD/BUY, but we will be monitoring developments closely.

Duncan wrote that the reason he was sending me this stuff was because it was wet and cold in New York, and because the Chief was raising hell on about ten fronts, and because he knew that I was probably going to Harry's Bar and drinking Bellini cocktails and eating cuttlefish risotto and doing Ernest Hemingway imitations and a lot of other wholesome, fun things, including "molto screwing," and he therefore had a lot of envy to work off, which he could do by ruining my idyll with a "harsh jolt of reality." The calligraphy of the note suggested it had been affected by copious infusions of Old Granddad. He added that Jacob Polhemus was not gaining and that Abner was "back from the funny farm."

After dinner, Margarita and I saw her mother to bed and went out. We took a vaporetto across the Bacino to the Molo and walked through the Piazzetta into St. Mark's Square. The weather had definitely changed: it was distinctly cold; a front had obviously swept down from the Alps. Steam seemed to rise from the ground.

We found an open café and went in for coffee and a *grappa*. I could see she was preoccupied.

"He's really in deep now, isn't he?" she asked.

"I think so."

"He won't win, you know." There was deep sadness in her voice. She cared. We both did. There was nothing to say. We finished our coffee and walked back through the Campo Moise. Cats scuttled at our approach. The canals exuded tendrils of mist.

"You don't see Venice like this often, darling," she said. "Someday you must come when the city's flooded, to see the *acqua alta.*"

"Someday I will." My life seemed to consist of nothing but somedays. That night I asked her, "Why did you go to bed with X?"

We were lying, cupped like spoons, I still inside her but all energy expended, just lying there, coupled, wanting to keep the closeness.

"At first I thought it was all that power and genius. Those are very compelling to any woman. I think, though, that it was probably that he wanted me so badly. It almost made me sad for him. I wanted to do something, and that was it."

About the same answer Florrie'd given me. Still, there were plenty of things, plenty of women, I'd wanted, and no one had felt compelled to see that I got them.

The next morning, it was as if, during the night, a giant hand had scoured the sky of all pleasant things; clouds and sunbeams and blue patches had all been dashed away, like china swept off a tabletop. We spent the day indoors, away from the dull rain and the cold, reading. That night, Good Friday evening, we went to hear sacred music in the Frari church. Behind and above the players and choristers, Titian's "Assumption" hovered in the candle smoke, adding exaltation to a moment already wholly enchanted.

Afterward, Margarita said, "You know, that was kind of Duncan to send you those clippings. He knows you're involved and would want to know. It's written all over you, love."

"Is it becoming?"

"Quite, really. Kenneth Clark once remarked, 'Men of action are sometimes useful in the world of scholarship.' You're rather the other way round, don't you think? I wish Duncan could be here. He's a nice, funny, devoted little man. What is it he calls Horace? 'The Chief'?"

"He worships X."

"And does Horace treat him well?"

"He likes him. Duncan's become his all-purpose factotum. His court jester."

I stayed two more days. Easter Sunday dawned gloomy and drizzling. Foul, vaporous mists still hung in the air. We went with Margarita's mother to church at St. George's, heard the lesson read by a thin-lipped curate with a thick Midlands accent. Not the sort, I found myself thinking, who would have preached to the *milordi* in olden days. That night I left by the evening train for Milan, from where I would fly back to New York early the next morning. "Samuel, you must come back as often as you like," said Margarita's mother. I kissed her hand—it seemed absolutely the right thing to do, and she showed no surprise—and thanked her. Margarita and I had said one set of specialized, thankful farewells the night before in her bed. Now she rode with me to the railway station.

"I had a wonderful time," she said.

"Me too."

"It was just what I needed."

"Me too."

Her dark eyes clouded. She reached up and brushed a hair away from her forehead. I looked at her closely and saw for an instant how old we both were, and how fortunate to have preserved what few threads of youthfulness we still had.

"Be careful, Sam," she said after a moment. She reminded me of Mother. She stared at the palazzi lining the canal, their brilliant, cake-fancy facades dulled by the gloomy day. "Be careful. You know, the longer I was in New York, the more I watched Horace and all of this begin to unfold, the more I felt like a child who hears a noise in the distance, over the hills perhaps, and creeps closer to investigate, and sud- . denly knows that the sound is gunfire, and then before knowing it, really, the battle sweeps over the child, trampling it under, unless it is very, very lucky. Another random casualty; another accident of war."

"Don't worry, I'm keeping my distance." I told her about my new schedule.

She shook her head. "I hope so," she said. She didn't sound convinced.

We kissed each other in the boat. I told her not to wait. The train's departure wouldn't be for another half hour. Just as when I'd arrived there had been no slow motion, now there would be no pat phrases of farewell, no premeditated slow dissolves for our parting. We had no re-grets, either of us. We had shared this time together, and something like it might be repeated by us somewhere, someday, but the bonds we had weren't even near to being a lifetime's bonds, no matter how compatible our minds or how fantastic the sex was. That was the trouble with pas-sion—and Venice. It was always necessary to go back through the door into real life. Or what passed for it.

CHAPTER 24

"**D**on't look so gloomy, boys. There's a point in every love affair when the kissing stops for a while." X didn't sound the least bit disheartened or discouraged. Duncan and I were; the annual affiliates' meeting had been a disaster, by comparison with the evangelical fervor of the year before.

It was plain bad luck to have inherited Abner's choice of Houston as this year's venue. This was Erwitt country, especially now that the billion-dollar helping hand the Administration had extended the banks was said to be about to reach out to the oil industry. Houston was bidding hard for the convention four years out, over which Erwitt, if reelected, would preside as the outgoing lion of his party, a convention which would also be a celebration of his leavetaking. This was a city which calculated its few crusades by the penny saved and the criminal jailed, which ranked life-style well ahead of virtue on its roster of civic aspirations. The only really favorable coverage X received in the local papers centered on the grand and superb scale of his way of life and entertaining. "Superb" seemed to be a word they used a lot in Houston.

Although no one came out and said as much, it was obvious from the first function, a reception for GBG's Texas affiliates, sponsors, and important connections, that people had uneasily accepted the idea that X, for his own reasons, had declared war on the President. It wasn't until the next day that we found out that members of the executive committee of BLEEP, most often McNeery, had been quietly contacting GBG affiliates around the country. So far, the results of that effort were nominal:

stations in Midland and Norfolk–Virginia Beach had dropped the nightly news completely and bought a Metromedia–CNN package, and a small station in up-country Alabama had gone so far as to disaffiliate. The sorest issue was the "Did I Say That?" spots X had positioned on his highest-rated programs; the affiliates were stuck with them, but they were loudly pressing for their cancellation.

Our biggest problem were the rumors, which were all over the lot. Someone had heard from a guy who knew someone at BBDO that Pepsi was thinking of dropping "First National." Another had it on reliable information that Chrysler was getting edgy about "Statehouse." Three big independents, which between them held nine important GBG-affiliated stations, were going to walk, which would panic Madison Avenue. Someone else had a friend in Washington who knew a guy in New York who had whispered that big legal trouble was coming, that the American Banking Association, the Investment Banking Association, the Securities Industry Association, and the Insurance Company Institute were joining in a multibillion-dollar lawsuit against AbCom, GBG, and every GBG affiliate individually, for restraint of trade in restricting financial advertising, and that the departments of Justice, Treasury, and Commerce were going to join in the suit as amici curiae. Buzz buzz buzz, it went, rumor feeding on rumor, no matter how farfetched or improbable, and it worked, sending the hand to the hip to make sure the wallet was there, to the throat to check the pearls. This was an uneasy crowd, unnerved to the edge of hostility. Buck had always told me that Homo sapiens Americanus worried about only two vital organs, his heart and his wallet, and that in a crisis there wasn't any question which got protected first. Looking at these people, I knew Buck was right.

Through it all, X stayed upbeat. He was consistently at his best: by turns jovial, lordly, reassuring, confidential, personal, philosophical, or mantled in rectitude, projecting the conviction that there was not the smallest fraction of any aspect of any action he took or programming decision he made that wasn't the best for the GBG family and, more importantly, which wouldn't line the family's pockets with richer seamings of gold.

In head-to-head sessions he confronted the affiliates' questions and tried to allay their suspicions. Would the current limitation on paid political advertising apply to the presidential election this fall? No decision had been made, X answered; the dollars involved, several hundred million, were so considerable that the matter was being rethought. Did GBG have any other highly controversial programs in the works for next season?

Not at the moment. Wasn't he worried that his "depersonality-ization of the evening news," as *Ad Week* called it, would lower the ratings? Not really: the extra fifteen minutes of in-depth financial news that had been tacked on to "The GBG Evening Report" was unarguably the most popular such segment in the history of television newscasting; it had no dominant personality, no Rukeyser, and the ratings were bringing in the advertisers. He handled these questions with a grin or a look of grave concern, with ebullience or intensity, as the occasion demanded; as he saw one visitor after another out of his suite at the Remington, I was sure there was no doubt in his mind that he had put this particular set of demons to flight.

With one enormous exception, and that was the problem he couldn't deal with because he refused to accept it as such. These people for the most had torn loyalties. Many of them were new to the game; to them X's place in their heart was only as strong as last week's Nielsens. They were as much a part of the ascendant new rich as Bud and Marie, even if they hadn't had their accents buffed and their social personas patinated by the New York life-stylers. The man who owned their hearts was Eldon Erwitt. X might make money for them, but Erwitt let them keep most of it; Eldonomics urged them to enjoy it, flaunt it, walk it in public in a rhinestone collar. Erwitt was their kind of folks. X recognized that, hated it, refused to accept it. When they urged him to tone down "Statehouse," he bridled.

But X was a realist, and his notion of loyalty was unequivocal, at least to the point of paying lip service to the preferences of these middle-class people who had put him back in the driver's seat at AbCom. He listened to Duncan, who urged moderation on him. When he addressed them on the last night, it was not of familial pride and a sense of mission that he spoke, but mainly of dollars and cents. To be sure, he left certain moral inferences in the air, faintly perfuming the smoky ballroom with evanescent hints of a higher calling and nobler values. But the priorities he stressed were GBG's financial impregnability and the earnings of the network and its affiliates; he delineated a future illuminated by a hard golden gleam, a horizon dominated by a Stonehenge of giant dollar signs, even though I knew he thought that to do so was like affixing a lead weight to a nightingale. Toward the end of his remarks, therefore, he returned to his own sense of things.

"We here in television, all members of this great Granite family," he said, his voice sounding husky in the smoke, "as well as our brethren at the other three networks, must continually remind ourselves that we enjoy a public trust, at a very attractive cost of entry."

Around the room chairs shuffled; there were murmurs and mumblings. Oh, shit, the room was grumbling under its collective breath, not this crap again.

X continued unperturbed.

"I think none of us can turn away from the fact that there appears to be ever-increasing evidence and thoughtful opinion that, unwittingly or not, our industry has had a considerable influence on the political process. Most opinion appears to believe that this effect has been less than constructive; that it has been distortive, perverse, and, to those holding the extreme liberal end of the spectrum of opinion, even pernicious."

More murmurs. We don't want to hear this, the room was saying. This was news twenty years ago. The world's changed; get with it, old man. I heard murmurings of unadulterated greed, no different in its emotional purity from the cries of infants mewling for the nipple.

X didn't seem to hear.

"I think we are all entitled to our own opinions on this crucial matter," he continued. "Each of us must be the keeper of his conscience. Nevertheless, the evidence is overwhelming that the reliance on television advertising, with its associated costs, has to some extent poisoned the well of the American political process."

The murmurs verged on groans now.

"This network has always been a leader," X said, eyes rotating around his audience, his gaze moving from one table to the next like a searchlight. "We must continue to lead. In the last three days, a number of you have inquired whether it is Granite's intention to apply our present limitations on paid political advertising, on a national basis, to the presidential election to be contested this fall. I have told you that the matter was under advisement. I think you are entitled to something more definite than that. The answer is: Subject to drastic rethinking, those restrictions will apply."

There were angry stirrings. "Aw, come off it," said a voice somewhere, bringing on its owner a barrage of reproachful "Shh's." Let's not forget, the shushings seemed to say, that it's H. H. Monstrance, *the* H. H. Monstrance, up there talking to us.

X smiled, as if he had trapped his audience in a little personal joke. "Provided," he said, his grin lighting up the farthest reaches of the room, "provided this can be done with no adverse financial impact on you."

Everyone seemed to relax suddenly. Now the murmuring said, Didn't I tell you? He never really lets us down. One scornful look from Casey, I thought, and the multitude was awed.

"Based on the most recent presidential election year, our research department has estimated that total television expenditures by the presidential candidates will be on the order of three hundred and fifty-five million dollars, an increase of some thirty percent, or approximately seventy-five million over the last election, principally as the result of the implementation of the FCC's third-stage deregulation, which will permit the number of permitted commercial minutes to increase to twenty-eight per broadcast hour."

Duncan had showed me the figures. Of the $275 million spent on TV advertising in the last election, my memory reminded me, nearly 70 percent, or almost $200 million, had been spent by the Republicans to elect Eldon Erwitt.

"Assuming our dominant position in the ratings should continue, we would expect that around thirty-five percent of the total amount, or nearly one hundred million dollars, would be used to purchase national and local advertising on the Granite network. This is a substantial sum. No right-minded businessman could consider forgoing revenues of this magnitude, most particularly those of you who, like ourselves here at Granite's parent company, have public stockholders to whom we are accountable. It is not a sacrifice we could ever ask you to make."

The room was still. He'd bought their attention.

"Accordingly, to the extent we are unable to replace forgone political sales with other sponsors, GBG will make you whole by purchasing time, on a predetermined affiliate-by-affiliate basis, to compensate you."

Little splashes of applause broke out around the room. Then gradually these linked up, and soon the whole room was on its feet clapping. But it was reflexive; it lacked the heartbeat I'd heard in Los Angeles. X was losing these people.

He knew it too. When we repaired back to the hotel for a nightcap and a postmortem, no one was fooled. The first rhapsodic rush, the unopposed march through open fields, was over; from now on it was going to be a hard slog up-country. The sharpshooters were moving into position behind the hedgerows.

Back in New York, things started to happen.

First, Buck told me something that I found disquieting. It seemed that

in the course of lunch with a guy he knew, a member in the highest
standing of the Bishman fraternity of financial public relations firms,
there had been some boastful talk of a hush-hush golf outing down at
Pine Valley which had been attended by none other than President
McNeery. Buck's lunch companion had produced a list of the thirty-odd
guests, which Buck had kept. He now passed it across the table to me.

"Funny," he said, "I ain't heard of most of these guys, but that ain't
exactly a diddley-squat bunch of companies you're talking about."

It wasn't. Represented on the list were the names of ranking corporations in various industrial oligopolies: two out of this "Big Three"; six out
of that "Big Eight."

"McNeery don't show up to go eighteen with the ribbon clerks," Buck
observed. "It makes me a mite curious. I b'lieve I'll just have to scratch
the itch. Quickest way to get poor is not to take that extra l'il sniff. Poor
or dead."

Duncan scratched my own itch when I showed him the list.

"Hey, man, you know who these guys are? These are the big deals in
CCEA. My opposite numbers."

He restudied the list.

"I think we better talk to the Chief. Look at this list. I'd say there's
maybe three billion of advertising here."

X didn't share Duncan's and my apprehensions.

"You young men are downright paranoid," he said, when Duncan and
I voiced our suspicion that McNeery's little golf outing had been a summit meeting of some kind.

The next shock, however, was more deeply personal, and it came just
when X was on a high. For the first time, I saw in X's face a shadow of
the realization that his enemies were capable of doing some wounding of
their own. He had never considered Erwitt and his allies as real, in the
way that a puppet is seldom more than wood and string to its maker, and
the overconfidence this instilled made the shock all the more sudden.

It happened in early June, just after X had received honorary degrees
from both Harvard and Yale. It was the second time he'd been so honored
by his alma mater, so now he had a Yale LL.D. Hon. to go with the
honorary Doctorate of Humane Letters he'd been granted years before.
The Harvard degree was especially satisfying. X's position on the use-
lessness of MBAs had become policy at AbCom; the company wasn't
hiring them. Apparently, objections to his honorary doctorate had been
raised by the Business School, but the lobbying had been a failure.

The degree citations in New Haven and Cambridge emphasized X's

role in revitalizing the nation's politics and rejuvenating its most important medium of communication. I'd ridden up to Yale with him. In the
academic parade, X, rigged out in his robes and floppy velvet cap, looked
more than ever like Holbein's Cromwell. Watching him, I shared his
pleasure and pride: his designs on a certain kind of immortality were well
advanced.

Watching him, I also pondered my own position. I had vowed to keep
my distance, but my journalistic instincts had me like a snaffle, and I
couldn't stay away. Something was brewing, and I found myself spending hours just following X around. There was another thing, too. I had a
rooting interest. I wanted to be there if he needed me, to fight the good
fight or bear witness or whatever, because the cause was just and the
stakes were great.

He returned to New York euphoric. On the following Monday, however, the spell was broken. Eric Shaughnessy came in to inform him,
shamefacedly, that CNI was withdrawing its sponsorship of the "Did I
Say That?" spots.

"I thought the Chief was gonna lay the old 'sharper than a serpent's
tooth' number on Shaughnessy," said Duncan, "but he just let him go.
Shaughnessy felt awful. But what could he do? He told the Chief he's
catching unbridled shit from his stockholders and lenders. Plus he got
booted off the next ComSat launch."

"So what does it mean for the network?" I asked.

"In terms of money, it means shit! As a symbol, that's something else.
You saw what the Street did."

The stock had been off nearly three points on the Shaughnessy news,
sinking to $95.

"What's X going to do?" I asked Duncan. "Pull the spots?"

"Shit, no," said Duncan. "That's what he ought to do. No one's going
to touch those spots. He couldn't give 'em away. Not and do any business
in D.C., or so we hear."

"Shaughnessy said that?"

"He as much as said it. One of our FCC law firms down there does
some work for CNI. Apparently Shaughnessy got the word on a big
contract that he's been working on to hook up Commerce and HEW
around the country. They told Shaughnessy: blow or go. He blew. I can't
blame the poor bastard. Shit, he's got a public company too. Anyway,
the Chief's gonna ride with the spots, he says. Carry 'em ourselves. I told
him he's making a mistake; he can sell that time to someone else. No, he
says, this is bigger than time sales, Fergie. And he's going fifty-percent

Erwitt with 'em. That'll really raise a shitstorm. The only good thing is, I told him, at least Eugenie's not around to get on his case."

"Where is she anyway?"

"Who cares? Out west, I hear. Some spa. Her nine hundred and ninety-ninth weight-loss program."

The weather went from drizzly late winter to viscously steamy summer overnight. Spring, at least as I remembered it, was no longer a season on New York calendars. May had been more or less like February; now June was like August. Suddenly, too, the Monstrances disappeared from my life.

X went to California for most of the month: to clean up operations at GBG Studios, according to Duncan, and to personally oversee the production of a couple of "made-for-TV"s. When I observed that was pretty unusual, Duncan surmised that the Chief was really determined to ring the bell with some big specials, and anyway it would be good for him to take his mind off Shaughnessy's capitulation, the first direct hit suffered at Erwitt's hands. Things seemed deathly quiet suddenly. Clio and Abner were said to be in Arizona, talking to yet another team of specialists. I heard from Cass fitfully at the beginning of the month; then she fled into summer with the glitter people. Even Duncan took a week off. I declined the opportunity of accompanying him to the Club Med on Guadeloupe, tempting as I found his prayerful assurances that the scoring would be unreal.

The next weeks went by in a delirium of tedium. Duncan returned—scoreless, I inferred—and kept me up to date on X. The returns were mixed. The Chief had won a bunch of citations from parents' groups for the improvements he had wrought in GBG's children's schedule. His invitation to attend the Bohemian Grove was withdrawn. Nothing much seemed to be happening, and I filled my days making work for myself at the magazine writing fillers and snippets.

X returned from the Coast on the third of July and summoned me to lunch at the Praetorium, the first time in a year we had lunched outside his office. He spoke mostly of his plans for reforming GBG's election coverage, but I knew his mind was really on something else. After lunch, he got a briefcase from the cloakroom and led me to a secluded corner of the club library. He looked around conspiratorially. A few members scratched away desultorily at writing tables; others read or dozed in the heavy chairs. I found myself thinking how surprising it was to see X with a briefcase. Men like him had people to carry their papers, not briefcases.

"This is deepest graveyard, Sam," he said. "I want you to look at a tape of a show I'm thinking of doing, possibly as a miniseries, four or five hours. There's some other stuff in here, too, that I want you to read."

He handed me a video cassette and a manila folder. Why was he asking me? I thought; he's the expert, the great showman, the man with his finger on the pulse.

"I think this is pretty hot stuff," he said, and I saw he wasn't after my opinion at all; he simply wanted to show off for me, to demonstrate that he hadn't lost his fast ball.

I opened the folder. The sheet on top was erratically typewritten, probably by X himself. It was headed THE LEAGUE OF DYING MEN.

"Very catchy, X," I said. "Very cheerful, too. Just the thing for a cold winter evening." I promised to read them, to watch the tape of the pilot, to think about them, and to report back.

Which I did about a week later, under less than ideal conditions. The mano-a-mano evening implied in his invitation turned out instead to be a play and supper afterward, in the unlikely company of Clio and Cass. I was uneasy most of the evening; there were too many complex and prickly dimensions to deal with, too much going on, as if X had invented an immensely, indeed, impossibly difficult board game in which we were players and pieces both. Mainly I wasn't sure how to behave with Clio; I looked for signals from her and received none. Again and again, I asked myself what she was doing here with X, once the archfiend. Each time, I satisfied myself by extrapolating from a feeling that had grown on me through the relative stillness of June that something might be imminent, that we might be like gulls gathering on the high ground before the storm, pulled together by the magnetism of impending crisis. The problem with that feeling, however, was that it found no hard evidence in fact. Nothing much was going on.

I had plenty of time to reflect in the theater. The play was typical and awful, from the moment the curtain had gone up and the audience had vigorously applauded the scenery. It was a musical, actually, with a book and score that wouldn't have cut it at the Starbuck Academy Athletic Awards Banquet and Annual Frolic. Liza Minnelli sang about three bad songs; at the end of each, a lot of chaps in the standing-room section whooped and shrieked and hopped up and down.

We had supper at Elio's. X busied himself playing little head and body games with Clio and Cass, dispensing precisely measured scintillas of charm and attentiveness first to one and then the other, punctuated with overly casual touches and strokings. To my gross dissatisfaction, Clio didn't push him off, at least not overtly. Cass chatted on, and I turned my mind from the confusions of affection and passion to the material X had given me to look over.

The two-hour tape, "The League of Dying Men," was either the pilot for a series or the extended first installment of a serial. The idea was ingenious and the production values astonishing, especially the concluding special effects. As I passed through the several stages of my reaction to it, from gut feeling to reasoned analysis, I concluded that I had been dazzled and then frightened, and that, in the end, I violently disapproved. The tape seemed to contradict so much of what X had claimed he had set out to do.

The show began with a meeting of minds between two doctors. One was a specialist in a large urban cancer center; the second was a psychologist specializing in the mental aspects of dying, a thanatologist. Together they conceived a scheme whereby they would inspire, encourage, and guide certain of their terminal patients, doomed men and women still able to think and act, to rid the world of people the doctors identified as societal vermin.

Basically, it was still a good guys–bad guys show, but marked up to a more elevated level: "The A Team" with George Kennan as Mr. T, "The Untouchables" with Albert Einstein as Elliot Ness. The instruments of fierce justice, the dying men, were depicted as noble kamikazes willing to yield the remnants of their lives in grand, apocalyptic, apotheosizing gestures. No Arthur Bremers here, or Hinckleys, or Oswalds. No diseases of the mind. The enemies weren't the usual, either: no dope pushers, comic Central American dictators. Mafiosi, evil geniuses with atom bombs on call. No Fidels or Dr. Nos. The bad guys were specifically the people for whom X held contempt up to the point of hatred—as did I, as did everyone of a certain background, upbringing, education, morality.

The taped pilot laid the conceptual groundwork, got the ball rolling, and then quickly sketched in its target: the vulgar, expedient, advantage-seeking new rich, homegrown and émigré—Bud and Marie and the Cornaras. The indictment was vague and, to be honest about it, flimsy. That was what bothered me, because the show escalated what was basically a resentment into a jihad. It dressed it up with notions of urban malaise; shuttered limousines splashing gutter puddles on ragged, homeless, hungry black children, the usual repertory of life's unfairnesses translated into something much grander. The show peddled the notion that if somehow all these new rich people were gotten rid of, and their greed and vulgarity and self-involvement expunged from the life of our times, things would be a whole lot better and the peaceable kingdom would be restored on earth.

But oh, how well it peddled it! What was essentially a conventional story line unfolded visually and dramatically into an aphrodisiac of violence. It culminated with the explosion of a truck bomb, a terrorist weapon familiar from the papers, not at a military compound or chancery of state but against a large charity party in a building that was unmistakably the Trump Tower on Fifth Avenue. In the final scene, the camera focused first on the bejeweled gathering in the garish atrium, the orchestra on a balcony, champagne fountains, heavily made-up old faces, the same overfed, overpleased herd I'd seen at a hundred such affairs; signs and posters and bunting in the background made it clear that this was a function with political overtones; the face smiling from the posters, glimpsed only fleetingly, suggested Eldon Erwitt. Now it shifted to a truck moving slowly through the Central Park transverse, driven by the obviously decent young middle-class man whom we'd watched be enlisted, exhorted, and excited through most of the show. Watching, my own emotions were stirred, my own loathing animated. It was a feeling that needed some violent catharsis to settle. I'd felt that urge before; more than once, walking on Fifth Avenue, I'd looked up at the Trump Tower and wished I could blow it away, for no more particular reason than a vague, generalized loathing of its presumption and vulgarity, its total contemptuous affront to a difficult world seething with suffering and a need for compassion.

So I felt that it was me driving that truck, as it emerged from the park, went down Fifth Avenue past the Tower, turned west on Fifty-fifth Street, north again on Sixth Avenue, and east again on Fifty-sixth Street, coming to idle about halfway down the block. The late-night streets were virtually empty. It seemed to be winter. There were dirty patches and ruts of snow on the paving.

The camera cut back to the atrium and panned around the throng. Then back to the truck. The engine noise increased. A car crossed Fifty-sixth Street, then the intersection was clear; the lights on Fifth Avenue changed, and the truck leaped forward. A cut to the atrium; a last cut to the driver, blond, serene, at peace, knowing how meet and right it was that he—that I—do this thing. Then the truck, jumping the curb and smashing through the heavy glass doors, screams, the grinding of metal; and then the explosion. The camera cut back, watching as the building collapsed inward on itself amid a hail of splintered glass and bursting shrapnel. It was as good a special effect as I had ever seen.

I'm not sure that I didn't lick my lips in relish as it happened. My mind closed the gap between the screen and reality; I savored the atomization, the bloody fragmentation of Bud and Marie and all their detestable ilk.

Then, just as suddenly, I realized how utterly I'd succumbed to the manipulations of the film. In real life, I didn't hate those people, not that much! Cass would have been in there, in real life, and others I knew. These people deserved chastisement for their arrogance and vulgarity, but the proper punishment was to be held up to the light for close inspection, to be mocked and tickled and embarrassed—not murdered, not for the sin of grossness. The awful building should be smeared with paint and excrement, not blown up. Blowing it up would prove nothing. Violence in such cases was an inadequate substitute for derision; it made martyrs out of sleazebags, and, since it is through martyrs that religion is perpetuated, it could only be self-defeating.

That was the chicken view, however. Violence was no answer, never could be, much as I'd have liked, myself, to have kicked Bud right in the nuts and then again right in the center of his fat, greedy face. These were powerfully bloody instructions X was teaching. I read the papers in the folder X had given me. It was more of the same, one substantially complete teleplay and four brief treatments. Each of them drew on resentments and violent urges and channeled them toward targets at the top of the heap, focusing known if unlocated rage and disgruntlement with the intensity of sunlight through a magnifying glass. One depicted a black Air Force veteran, riddled with an Agent Orange carcinoma, renting a small plane and napalming a private compound unmistakably copied from the Bohemian Grove. Another dealt with the torture and elimination of a comedian; the central figure was obviously modeled on a celebrated singer notorious for his arrogant manners and rumored gangster connections, who was at the Erwitt White House more frequently than the Secretary of State. A third culminated in the explosion of a bomb at a stag fatcat political dinner; the treatment was loaded with approving parallels to the Stauffenberg attempt to kill Hitler. The fourth incinerated a famous television evangelist known for his right-wing politicizing skill, along with his famous glass house of God and his mailing-list computers. The last was amusing, if horrific to a certain audience. It postulated a high IRS official who, out of a mixture of patriotism and disgruntlement, released the tax returns of the *Forbes* "400 Richest" to *The Washington Post*. Again, the parallels to real persons and institutions were unmistakable. From the raggedy typing and the emendations marked in X's precise little hand I gathered he'd pecked them out himself, probably on the portable in his office that he claimed to have been given by Faulkner.

In each, from what I could gather, could be found the same unspecific allusions to Erwitt as had been intimated by the political banners and posters in the tape I'd seen: vague visual hints, nothing to pin down exactly, fogged images loosely suggesting the President, physiognomic shadows and highlights only. The purpose was unmistakable. X knew the susceptibilities and suggestibilities of his audience; he knew that somewhere out there among the two hundred million would be a mind diseased or sick at heart, a life sunk in despair or animus, that would take him up on his notion and cause the television show and reality to coalesce, fatefully. In effect, X was putting out a contract at large on the President and his circle of interest.

He had to be talked out of it.

When supper was over and I had gotten my line of reasoning as organized as was likely, I indicated to him that I awaited his pleasure. He obviously wanted to talk too. We dropped the ladies off and went back to Fifth Avenue.

"Well," he said expectantly. "Good stuff, eh?"

"Very strong," I said, "but I don't think you should put them on, X. This isn't the time. They're too damn good. There're a lot of crazy people out there with a lot of grudges. Christ, that Bohemian Grove number I read! Some nut case out there, or some guy with a beef, he's gonna figure, Hey, I can take out the President and his buddies! All it takes is a rented Cessna and a little napalm on the VISA card. You're telling them to put a torch to the big house on the hill just because it's big and because it isn't theirs!"

"Nonsense," he said. "This is just a good strong show. Pure pap for the ratings; something to put a little backbone in the people who doubt some of the things we've been doing around here." He grinned engagingly at me. "Not that I don't think they're ideologically sound, of course."

I had to laugh. "No shit, X!" I modulated my voice. I didn't want to seem to accept being brushed off; that was an old and many times proven trick of his: getting people to strip their own words of gravity. "Seriously," I said, "nobody agrees with you about Erwitt more than I do, but this is pushing it. You're too damn good. Jesus, watching that Trump Tower bit, I felt like getting up myself, and loading up my Uzi, and strolling over to Le Cirque to do my bit to make society better by wasting a few of those assholes. I won't, because I was brought up to control myself, but a lot of people aren't."

He simply chose to disregard me. I could see he was on a roll. I tried another tack.

"You know, X, this is going to make you look like the all-time hypocrite! Talk about violence on the tube! You talked about feeling the clammy touch of the future; like Marley's ghost, you said. Wait'll the ghost of Dr. Wertham gets ahold of this!"

"Sam," he said with infuriating patience, "calm down. There are a few other things you ought to know about. We're onto something at GBG News. Deep graveyard?"

"Deep graveyard."

"We've got a lead from someone in the budget office. Strictly on the QT. There's reason to believe that someone's been tinkering with the GNP figures to make Eldon look good when the campaign starts. I'm going to do a special in October!"

His voice resounded with chuckly, malicious satisfaction. I examined him carefully. Something had altered, almost imperceptibly. He was carried away, I could see, with the momentum of his imagination. I decided instinctively that I didn't believe him about the GNP numbers.

"That's pretty hot stuff, X," I said, probing. "If you're right, it's merely the biggest news story since Hiroshima. Ninety percent of Erwitt's popularity is based on the economic outlook, and you're saying that they're making up the statistics?"

"I said only that we had some reason to believe so." His tone was altogether too sly. "I told you, Sam, that Eldon's a master of disinformation."

"The phrase you used was 'emotional' disinformation. It was a question of mood. This is something else; this is outright lying. This makes Washington about on a par with Moscow, if you accept the notion." I sounded truculent. I looked at him squarely. "Of course, if all the gloves come off, anyone in a position to spread the word can do his own disinforming, can't he?" He smiled back; his expression said maybe yes, maybe no.

I said nothing further, but I felt somehow that I had put my dart somewhere close to the center of the truth. He kept smiling, in a way that I could see was designed to disarm, to put the restless mind at ease. At that moment, strangely, he reminded me of Erwitt, grinning away trouble, mistrust, doubt, and suspicion. Paradoxical, I thought; but then, not so, perhaps. Locked in combat, we must become tinged with the qualities of our foe, with his sweat and spit and smell, not just his blood.

"We're going to beat Eldon," he said, and his jubilation was real. "Elections are won in October, and that's when we'll lick him. I happen to know that the plan is to keep Eldon hidden away in the White House. But our new season'll change that!"

He told me some more. There would be a new, sympathetic character added to "Statehouse," a living simile for Erwitt's opponent. X was certain this would do the trick.

I supposed there was some reason for his confidence. The public, a large and growing part of it, at least, seemed to regard "Statehouse" as a truthful and accurate metaphor of the White House. X was a genius at creating surrogates and personifications of people's aspirations and resentments. There was no reason he shouldn't succeed with this.

I felt tired and in need of a kind of reassurance I wasn't going to get here; I was worn out with conjecture, tired of listening to means-justifying. I said good night, but once outside, in the wider night air, I found I still felt like talking. There was a pay phone on the corner, and I went to it. Duncan would still be up, I was sure, and he was.

CHAPTER 25

It was, on the whole, a miserable summer. It rained every weekend, or seemed to, from the St. Lawrence to Rehoboth, and with each gloomy day my own mood darkened. I wasn't restless; that was the strange part. I felt no compulsion to hop up and down the Eastern seaboard. For one thing, I doubted that distraction would take care of what was bothering me. Apart from a golf weekend with Buck in early August, and Labor Day in Amagansett with friends too long-standing and kind to be put off any longer, I made no social plans. There would be some business travel; otherwise I intended to remain in New York, hunkered down in my mire of depression, discontent, and world-weariness, a twentieth-century victim of that miserable amalgam of boredom and depression the Middle Ages called "accidie," a paralyzing world-weariness.

All at once, I was fed up with what I did for a living. Until I became bored with the effort, I tried to figure out why. It seemed to me that magazine writing of my kind was about as lasting, in memory and influence, as a tickle. I had been given a taste of large causes, thanks to X, compared to which, win or lose, agree or disagree, writing sharp little pieces about the matters and men of the moment seemed totally trivial. No matter how artful I was, or clever, or insightful, I was still fenced in, a prisoner of the corral of topicality. It ws true of all of us who did magazine work; we were spared the discipline and continuity of the journalistic beat, and we never got far enough into anything—with the rare exception of some of our brethren on *The New Yorker*, who were really publishing books in installments—to earn any kind of permanence. We were voguish and transitory, something to put out each Monday with the trash as new sensations knocked at the front door.

Normally, I would have expected this sort of mood to produce a fever of work on X's story, but it didn't. I would need to get away to do that, I felt, and how could I?—what with my magazine assignments and, on top of that, the fact that X's story had barely begun to play itself out on the scale he'd envisioned those many months before in London.

My high-principled disagreement with X over his programming plans had faded, done in by the practical consideration that there was nothing I could do about it anyway. I was still rooting for him, at least in terms of the big picture, and he wasn't doing so well currently. The honeymoon with the investment community was definitely over, and the market was jumpy.

Things came to a head the second Monday in August. I'd spent the preceding weekend with Buck; our golf games at the National and Maidstone had been washed out, confining us to quarters, to fiddle with books and papers and watch exciting events like the Memphis Buck and the Rockford All-Star Bowling Tournament on the tube. By Sunday, Damon and Pythias would have started to get on each other's nerves. Buck was definitely the tetchier; Friday night he'd gotten "drunk as a hooty owl" at Bobby Van's, where I, not much soberer, had insisted on driving through rain and fog for old times' sake. Saturday, at a dinner party, he'd been merely "Indian drunk."

Around eleven the phone calls started coming in: from Buck's "monitors" and other market players. I heard him talking about ABI and watched his mood improve with each call. I knew he was still nursing a considerable short in ABI, but the stock had recently come back to $99 after having sold as low as $93, where Buck had shorted a bunch more. If it was good news for him, it had to be bad news for X. I heard him call an associate and instruct him to see if he could get off another hundred thousand ABI short on the Hong Kong and Zurich exchanges, while New York was still asleep.

"Well, golly gee, old buddy!" he said, voice and eyes suddenly bell clear. Money did that to people like Buck. "Guess what? They lost a sponsor on 'Statehouse'! The first one. That Jap outfit makes computers. My Washington spies say ol' whatever-his-name-is at Trade Relations leaned the ass off 'em!"

"So what?" I commented, sounding, after the fact, altogether too defensive. "'Statehouse' is pulling close to a fifty share. I'd guess there'd be no problem finding sponsors to pick up that slot."

"Good buddy, 'so what' is that the Street's been wantin' trouble; them boys is tired of ABI, but they need an excuse to hit the silk. Now they got it! Plus, IEA's taking ABI off its BUY list. Ms. Pfannglanz's had a mood change, or maybe she's having her period. We're livin' in an age of moods and perceptions and analysts on the rag, old buddy. I know it don't mean diddledoo that some Jap's dropped the show. I know it, and Pfannglanz knows it and so does the Morgan, and the Chemical, and Fayez Sarofim and Joel Leff and Barton Biggs, and ever' last one of 'em knows ABI's second quarter was up a smooth thirty percent, or about three times the rate of IBM, and ever'one knows the old sumbitch has got hisself fourteen of the top twenty shows, but I promise you, old buddy, when they ring the bell tomorrow morning they gonna shovel ABI out like shit on a goose farm!"

He was right. In the specialists' words, uttered pretty much from the sidelines, "the stock found its level" at $94, off four and a big fraction on over 800,000 shares.

I checked in with Duncan at the end of the day and found him somewhat shell-shocked, preparing, he declared, to go out and get magisterially drunk; he muttered harsh words about betrayal. The IEA thing had hit them hard; apparently Ms. Pfannglanz had weekended at Dunecrag not long before, and relations had been extremely cordial. Anyway, Duncan said, the Chief was taking direct action. For one thing, he was dropping "Did I Say That?" It had served its purpose, and it made people too nervous to be worth it.

"Actually," Duncan said, "the Chief's not really dropping 'Did I Say That?' He got a bid from the Dems, so he sold them the spots. We got over two hundred in the can now. Would you believe one guy could lie that much? Starting October you won't be able to watch fifteen minutes on CBS, ABC, or the peacock without seeing Erwitt lying about something."

"Be generous, Fergie. Only about half of what Erwitt says is lying anyway," I commented. "The rest of the time he forgets, or didn't know in the first place, or just makes it up. So X 'got a bid,' did he? Out of the blue, eh? For two hundred spots showing the President smiling and saying day is night? I'll bet the Democrats really had to twist his arm."

Duncan didn't hear me. It was only a matter of time, he averred, before the Street regained faith. The next three quarters were in the bank, and the numbers would be strictly Cooperstown Hall of Fame material. He invited me to join him in getting hopelessly loaded; I declined, but not before thinking it over seriously. I reminded Duncan that alcohol had much to answer for, and to stay out of trouble.

A week later, Duncan had more news.

"Guess who paid the Chief a state visit? His holiness the NFL commissioner."

"Plastic Man? What'd he want?"

"Wanted to talk about advertising for next year's Supe. Apparently the FCC's gonna drop all restrictions on commercial time next year. We can run forty minutes of commercials if we want."

"They'll have to start the Super Bowl at nine in the morning to get it over in time for the eleven o'clock nightly news."

"That's the commish's idea. He also wanted to talk 'policy.' Make sure there was nothing 'controversial.' No more Henry Morrows. He tried the buddy-buddy approach with the Chief."

"That generally doesn't play. How'd X react?"

"The Chief gave him an evasive answer. Told him to stick 'controversial' up his ass. Quoted the contract to him."

"Hey, guess what, I saw Eugenie the other night. At least, I think I did. At McMullen's. I was pretty tanked up. Say, she didn't look too bad. Thinner. I sat with 'em for a while. Man, I don't think stingers're too good an idea for a man my age. She has a mean hand with a cocktail."

"How do you know?"

Duncan leered. "She invited me back to her place. Shit, we got talking about the company and the Chief and all, and suddenly McMullen's making closing noises, so she asked me back. She was really interested." He leered some more, opening a path of inquiry which I declined to follow. I felt a clammy tingling at the back of my neck.

"You didn't discuss any of that stuff I told you about, did you?"

"You crazy?" Duncan sounded legitimately aggrieved. He leered again. "Shit, man, we didn't have time!"

Late in August I went to Texas for a few days to gather material for an article I was writing on art collecting in the Sunbelt. I caught up with some old friends and made some new ones and, generally, behaved myself. I saw some extraordinary houses, was shown new frontiers in home electronics and plumbing, and found very few works of art worth remembering or writing about. I saw a lot of Monets and Renoirs and a lot of very expensive, safe New York School stuff, de Kooning, Lichtenstein and Johns, one decent Pollock.

On the way back to New York, I ran into a guy I knew in the boarding area. We'd been at *Newsweek* together, crossing paths on the sports desk. He was a real football nut, and he'd followed his mania into real life, working first in public relations for the Giants and then moving into management. Now he was assistant general manager of Eugenie Monstrance's Vandals. He'd been in Dallas trying to pry a second-string pulling guard out of Landry. It had been at least three or four years since I'd seen him. We arranged to sit together on the plane.

"How's it going?" I asked when we were aloft and had drinks before us. "You damn near took it all the way last year."

"We would've, too, if we hadn't cut a couple of kids that most of us wanted to keep: that boy who went over to play free safety for Denver, and a kid who's on the taxi squad at San Francisco. He could've filled in when our center went down; the boss wouldn't pay what the Saints were asking for their backup. He was too old, she said, except the guy she ended up getting for us could have been his father. She cut the two kids because she said she didn't like their attitude; she just knew, she said, they wouldn't cut it psychologically. Shit, man, you don't block Too Tall Jones or Randy White with your psychology. Anyway, what's a boy to do? It's her football."

"And her baseball and her basketball and her hockey puck. You ain't alone, cousin."

"I know. I've been talking to the guys on the Boroughs and the Buckets. You know, she's got us all together in this building she owns on Twenty-third Street. Piece of shit from the outside, but the offices are really nice. Anyway, we get together for a pop after work and everybody's got the same story. Mind you, Sam, we love her. Her heart's in the right place, and she's one smart lady, and God knows I think she wants to win worse than any of us, but she just keeps screwing up! Winning is about eight percent the talent you can put on the field and the rest is chemistry and don't ask me what, because I can give you a hundred different answers. The problem is it's got to be a hundred percent to take it all the way. Anything less might as well be zero. Anyway, I think we're going to have a shot at the blue ribbon this year."

"You had a hell of a draft."

"That's only part of it. You remember how well the baseball club did when she was dicking around at her old man's company. Well, now it's our turn."

This was news. "She's out of the company," I said.

"I know; now she's all of a sudden involved in some big charity deal.

Or maybe it's politics. Started a few weeks ago. She didn't even come to training camp this year. She turned that big house of hers over to the coaching staff. She's running this thing out of the office in the city. She and that guy McNeery."

"Who?" My question was entirely for effect. I was getting that old clammy feeling.

"McNeery. The guy that was President for about ten minutes. Before we elected the Late Late Show."

This is very peculiar, I thought. "What kind of charity?" I asked.

"I'm not actually sure. It's some big deal, though. They're putting the arm on a lot of corporations, I gather. Apparently McNeery's a big cheese on some kind of business supergroup. They seem to be buddies, him and the boss, and he probably needed a place to work in the city, so she gave him some offices. He's got about six people there. They put in their own phones. I must say, being a former President's a pretty good deal. A bunch of guys come up one day—you know, Secret Service, guys with the little doohickeys in their buttonholes—and install the equipment. Same-day service. Try getting that these days from Ma Bell. Christ, the phone service has gotten so bad it cost me the chance to get a real stud tackle from the Bucs—"

"Is McNeery there often?" I interrupted. I was very curious. I didn't identify Eugenie with McNeery. Of course, they had been on Abner's AbCom board together. There was probably an explanation.

"He comes in maybe twice a week and stays over a day or two. Makes a bunch of calls; takes a few. Holds meetings. I saw that lawyer up there, the one that's general counsel for the Jets. He's our counsel now. Arnold Plume. What a stuffed shirt he is. He sure likes his freebies. I had to move half the season ticketholders around to get him a box. The boss kisses his ass, though. Anyway, so far it's no big deal with McNeery. And it keeps the boss out of the way, thank God."

At LaGuardia I wished him luck for the season. Riding back into the city, I wondered if I was in possession of a useful piece of information. When I got home I called Duncan at his apartment and told him about my conversation on the plane.

"Didn't I tell you about that?" he said. He sounded as if he'd had a few: quite a few. "Shit, that's old news. BLEEP's got some kind of corporate United Way going on. Eugenie volunteered. She even called the Chief about it."

"And?" I started to ask Duncan if he was absolutely certain that he hadn't talked to Eugenie. I was worried about my own responsibility, of course. I'd phoned Duncan to voice my apprehensions about "League," about the GNP scam, about "Statehouse" fielding a real-live opponent to Erwitt.

"And what?" Duncan remarked. "He patted her on the ass and told her to go to it. He signed us up for a hundred grand. Something about orphans or something. Who gives a shit?"

When I hung up, I did. Life didn't seem as simple to me as the power people made it out to be. Sure, there was nothing to go on, and it was faint, this uneasy tickle of suspicion, but it kept me awake for most of the night.

When X invited me to beg off my Amagansett plans and instead stay at Dunecrag over Labor Day, I declined, but I couldn't refuse his insistence that I come to a party he was giving that Sunday night.

"It's gonna be a big deal," Duncan told me. "Four hundred people: Peter Duchin on the ivories, ninety fags from Glorious Food to pass the chow; ten thousand bucks' worth of flowers from some broad on Eighty-fourth Street your ex turned up. I wouldn't be surprised if Kissinger sang the national anthem!"

I could tell from his tone of voice he hadn't been invited. The path to the summit was very carefully ordered. Maybe next year.

X's invitation made it a weekend for dues-paying, and I figured I'd sweep the table, so, after calling first, I drove down via Southampton and paid a call on Clio and Abner. I'd been pretty pissed off at what I took to be her capitulation to X, and I hadn't seen or spoken to her since our evening at the theater.

I was shown through the house onto the porch overlooking the pool. Clio was there alone, reading. When I came in, she put down her magazine and got up.

"Hello, Sam." We rubbed cheeks. She looked tired, noticeably so, even though it had only been a matter of weeks since we had dined together after the theater; it was plain that she had lost the capacity to draw energy from Abner's condition. The challenge was no longer to be wife, nanny, nurse. The challenge was to survive the awful gray boredom. She was trapped in Abner's illness as much as he was.

"How is he?" Certain occasions yank dumb questions out of us like teeth.

"Bad," she said. "He doesn't like to come out of his room at all, now. He's happier in there with his nurses. My three ladies in white. All paid for by AbCom. He likes them better than me, anyway. You know, he can't sleep with the lights out?"

"What are you going to do?"

She shook her head. "You really must stop asking me that every time I see you."

Stop trying so hard to be concerned, I scolded myself. I tried another angle.

"You look wonderful," I said, careful not to add "considering." She did look well, considering. Tired, yes: but not gray, not wrinkled, not shriveled with vexation and frustration.

She smiled. "Why, thank you, sir." She came over and kissed me lightly on the mouth.

"Duncan said you were thinking of putting Abner in some kind of another home—at least for a while."

"I don't know what I'm going to do. I'm thinking of moving west. I sold this house, you know."

"To Cornara?"

"To the Shrecks, actually. Marie says her Agawam neighborhood is going to the dogs."

"How just, I guess. Where out west?"

"There's a place in Santa Barbara. It costs three thousand dollars a day, but that doesn't seem to matter. The doctors tell me I'll probably be a widow in a year or so, the way things are going. A rich widow, I suppose."

She looked up.

"Will you marry me?" She was being bantering, insincere.

"Of course." So was I.

"If he doesn't get me first," she said disgustedly.

"Who?" I knew. "X? Don't be silly."

"Don't you be silly, Sam."

"Has he asked?"

"Not in so many words. But he will. He wants everything Abner ever had. I'm part of that!"

She laughed nervously and lowered her eyes.

"Well," she said, "I suppose it might be better than ending up with some polo player with flashing eyes and the sexual and mental equipment of a stallion."

She saw me watching her.

"I'm as frail as an eggshell, aren't I, Sam?" She spoke slowly, as if the pace of her words could slow the pulse of her feelings.

"You've been through a tough time," I said.

I saw her smile to herself suddenly, a thin smile awakened by an uncertain inner joke; her smile widened and her eyes warmed—responding, I thought, in phase to an irony growing more assured, more confident.

"You know," she said. "Maybe I should give everything to Cassie. She's always wanted to be rich."

"Rich and famous," I added.

"Rich and famous and everything else. She and Abner's father were made for each other; they're just alike."

"Maybe that's why they don't get along."

"Don't they? No, I suppose they don't, really."

We were fencing. And fenced in. That was the trouble with real life. In a romantic novel, the tension between us would have collapsed like a plaster wall, and we would have been in each other's arms, with the promise of eternity pealing like Bow bells, and I would have taken her right there, as two years before I had wanted to take Margarita Clerc, right there on the blazing beach not ten miles from here.

But this was the real world, and we were who we were, where we were, and how we were, and so we played pitty-pat with words while inside Abner sat with his nurses and chortled at cartoons and "Sesame Street." It made me ache.

I declined to stay for lunch, wondering if I too was deserting her, but I saw that she was relieved. I could sense that she wasn't happy about her feelings for me, whatever they were. I supposed she might even have loved me, in a way, as I loved her, in a way. Surely she liked me; probably she even needed me. But there was too much sorting out to be done. I knew it would never work. It wouldn't, would it?

She walked with me to the door.

"I'm glad you're a gentleman, Sam, even though we did have that little slip from grace in Florida."

"A gentleman? In what way?"

"You're considerate. I know you have a lot of things you think you want to say to me. Maybe there are feelings I have. Maybe they should be said; maybe some time they will be. But it won't be now. It means a lot, believe me, this way you're willing to put yourself at the back of the line."

I suppose I should have taken it from there. People like us couldn't keep up with all these pushers and shovers, these dynamos and dominators. We were strictly back-of-the-bus types who should find solace with each other, be each other's consolation and comfort. We were likely to be all there was for each other.

The Montauk Highway was already choked with traffic, so I cut off onto Mecox Road. I thought for a second about driving by Mother's house to see what changes had been wrought; the lilac beds and hedges had probably been uprooted in favor of a covered pool and a sunken tennis court. No, I figured, let's leave it in memory, as far as it goes.

X's party wasn't a total loss, because Florrie showed up. I'd hoped she would; I needed her sort of company. I separated her from a chubby commodities tycoon who was licking her naked with his eyes, and took her off to a distant table in the garden.

"How goes the struggle?" she asked when I'd gotten us each a glass of champagne.

"As the man says, it naught availeth. And you? Are you staying here? Tell me you're not."

"Alas, I am, naturally. You?"

"I was staying with friends in Amagansett, but it's Sunday and we've jollied each other into a state of absolute hostility. I'm going to blow this pop stand after dinner and drive back into town."

"You can't! S. A. Mountcastle Vee Eye, you absolutely cannot! I've got things to discuss with you. So does H.H."

"X? He's been in a bit of a snit with me. I was surprised he asked me for the weekend. Or was I to be for you?"

"No, he said he needed to talk to you. He's a big fan of yours." She reached over and patted my cheek. "Besides," she said, "I want to see you." She looked terrific. She'd lost some more weight, and for me it had been a long time.

"Do I sense the renewed stirrings of ancient longings?" I asked. "What about the master of the house?"

"He got his last night," she said without a blush, beaming mischievously. "Cass's on duty tonight. Besides, here at Dunecrag, *mi casa es su casa.*"

I heard my name called, and X came striding briskly through the garden tables. He looked at me earnestly.

"Where have you been, Sam? I've absolutely got to talk to you about something. I need your help."

"X, I've got to get back to town. I'm on deadline. Do you want to talk about it now? I'm sure Florrie will excuse us."

"I can't just now, Sam. The Shrecks have brought some captious jackass from Lehman Brothers and insist that I pay attention to him. Right now I need Wall Street, so I agreed. Can you come for breakfast?"

"I've checked out of my hosts' life, X. I'm bedless." I looked crestfallen. "I suppose I could sleep in the car."

"Nonsense. There's plenty of room. Florence, tell Hideki to make up a room. There must be one. I'd be most grateful."

X was grateful to lesser men about once a decade, so I thought I'd be well advised to relent. I also guessed there'd be a dividend, a sweet dividend. So I said I'd stay.

It was not long before dawn that I dragged myself up to the third-floor room which had been made up for me. As I had guessed, Florence Mary Ashley Grosvenor Nuywaerts da Sola Basto arrived not long afterward.

"Hmmm," she said, reaching for me as she slipped under the covers, "it appears you've been expecting me. How very flattering."

I thought of all sorts of smart answers, but she stopped them in my throat.

We drowsed off afterward, for perhaps an hour, and then awoke to make love more quickly and conventionally. For some reason, perhaps old acquaintance, the sex business worked wonderfully.

"That was a terrible party," I said.

"How could it not be? I've never seen people like this. The Virginia hunt country may be stuffy, and Georgetown's pretty awful too, but it isn't this. You'd think with her money that Getsmore woman could afford a few diction lessons."

"I didn't see any Monstrances."

"There weren't any, silly." She stretched. "Clio won't come; not while Abner's still home, and Eugenie's back to not speaking to H.H." She rolled over to look at me. "Do you still fancy yourself in love with Clio, Sam?"

"Am I as transparent as that? What did I tell you the last time? I don't know. Yes—no—maybe."

She rolled back and pushed her face into her pillow. Then she lifted it, screwing her mouth into a tight, reflective grimace, like a little girl deciding whether or not to be naughty.

"Sam," she said after a pause, "do you know anything about some screenplays?"

"Screenplays?"

"Something like that: screenplays, scripts, TV pilots. A tape of some new show of H.H.'s?"

The tickle of apprehension came alive again.

"No, I don't think so," I said, trying to sound calm. "Why?"

"You know I've been seeing a man who works in the White House?"

"I seem to remember your saying something about that."

"Well, I'm getting bored with him, but he likes me, and I know a lot of people in Middleburg and Georgetown, which impresses him. He's trying to keep me on the string by feeding me tips from the top, real inside White House dope. People in Washington do that a lot; they think it's seductive. All it is, really, is indiscreet."

"Just give the news, please. What's this about scripts and pilots? What does it have to do with X?"

"I'm not sure. Apparently there's one about the GNP figures being faked. Everyone's in a flap, especially now that the campaign's for real."

"Which means what?"

"I don't know. No one does, for sure. There's just a lot of loose talk about 'fixing' H.H."

"Did you say anything to X?"

"Not yet. It could be just another White House uproar. Every time they turn around over there, they think they see a man in a bear suit brandishing a club. I didn't want to ruin his weekend."

My worst suspicions were confirmed to my satisfaction. Lying there, I wondered where the hell I'd find Duncan.

"Come here." Florrie's mind had moved to other subjects. It was hard to think straight.

"You know I'm not getting any younger," I gasped. "I'm not sure—"

"Of course you can, darling. Why, it seems like only yesterday that we were children at Maidstone, and then there was the Carlyle, and . . . goodness, it's grown bigger and stronger since then, but then it's had so much practice, you bad thing. Ah, yes. Ah, yes!"

A table had been set for X and me under the awning on the porch. Bright and cloudless and warm, the weather seemed to be making amends to the South Fork for the last six miserable weekends. X settled into his chair and stared thoughtfully out at the beach and the white foamy crusts of the waves.

"I appreciate your staying over, Sam. I really do need to talk to you." He drank his grapefruit juice.

"You've gotten to be pretty close to our friend Fergus, haven't you?" he asked.

"I suppose so. I like him."

"Coffee?" X poured from the silver pot.

I looked down at the place setting. Perfection of silver and china and linen. Revere and Meissen and Queen Anne. Very comforting.

"He's a good man and a loyal soldier, Fergus is. I'm fond of him too. Very fond. Which is why I'm concerned."

Do you know that Erwitt knows, I thought? Have your hundred, your thousand wires plugged in everywhere brought you a warning? Have you been tipped about the White House? Only three of us knew about "The League," I thought, X and me and, thanks to me, Duncan. I hadn't talked, and I was sure X hadn't, and that left only Duncan. He had told Eugenie—hadn't he?—and she had seen it as the chance for which she'd waited and hated all these years, and she'd told McNeery, and now something was cooking. X was talking about Duncan. Did he presume to appoint me to carry to Duncan the news of his banishment? What about me?

"What's the problem?" I asked.

"Sam, I'm afraid the pressure's gotten to Fergus. It's this business about the share price. One has to be philosophical. As the elder Mr. Morgan said, 'the price of shares will fluctuate.' But it seems to have gotten him down. The fact is, he's drinking too much. It worries me. It's doing him no good, I can assure you."

"And I infer from your tone that you'd like me to have a little chat with him?"

"Precisely. Coming from me it might have the wrong sort of ring. More like a command. and that's not what I want. You can assure him, in any way you choose, that he continues to enjoy my every confidence. You'll do it, won't you, Sam? I'd be most grateful."

Of course I would. He beamed, as much as anything reassured of his prodigious powers of persuasion. The talk I had in mind for Duncan would be different indeed from what X envisaged.

He began to discuss the market. He had decided to take his show on the road, to calm the institutions before the campaign heated up. This panicky selling was ridiculous: ridiculous and irresponsible, especially by institutions that bore the public's trust. It wasn't that way when he'd started Granite. Eric Shaughnessy was right. This currying favor with institutional investors was a two-edged sword. He remembered when it had gotten started, back in the mid-sixties. Then everyone told you that you couldn't have institutions owning enough of your stock. They were rock solid, everyone said. Buoys in the fog, groins against a sea of unease.

Fiddlesticks! Jake had warned him. Don't fall for it, Jake had said. Without traditions, the sort of long shadows from the past that played about a place like Starbuck, an institution was just so much stone and mortar, just a building. It was the people, Jake had said; they were changing. Tradition? Just something to be painted over like last year's wallpaper.

He went downstairs with me. I asked him how Jake was doing.

"No good. It's virtually all over. Just days, weeks, they tell me."

He shook my hand and looked into my face.

"Don't get old, Sam. It's awful. My oldest friend's dying. My son's a vegetable. My daughter hates me. I crave company, and the best I can get is what you saw here last night. All I have left is what I've started. When this thing with Eldon's finished, I'll probably die too, like a bee without its sting."

He sounded properly tragic; then, before I could say anything, he brightened. Martyred Caesar's bloody garment, rent and stained, vanished, replaced by the imagined raiment of a perfect gentle Christian knight.

"Of course," he said, his words bobbing like corks on a suddenly unleashed torrent of self-confidence, "we're going to win, and that'll show them! The greater good, Sam; the greater good!" He squeezed my arm at the bicep, as if the gesture somehow bonded us forever.

As I drove down the long driveway, I looked back in the mirror at Dunecrag, at its great shingled hump crowning the line of the dunes. I saw X raise his hand, however, in a faint, sad old gesture that brought back the farewell my mother had made two years earlier, at a time when there weren't so many ghosts howling on the wind as now.

Ghostly, too, was the chill I felt as I drove toward New York, although it was a pleasant day and I had left the windows open. What exactly did you tell Eugenie, Fergie, I asked? How much? How much did I tell you? I turned the questions this way and that, exhausting hypotheses and speculations, until, at blessed last, the profile of the city pushed through the haze and I was able to find other troubles to think about.

CHAPTER 26

When we told X what we'd done, he was surprisingly magnanimous. "Boys will be boys," he said, "and this isn't the first indiscretion ever committed over a glass of whisky." There had been no point in embroidering the recital of our betrayal by going into whatever other adventures Duncan might have had that evening.

"The important thing is," he continued, "what do Eugenie and Mc-Neery think they're up to? Making trouble with our advertisers, stockholders, and affiliates? Probably. Now that the campaign's under way. Some sort of boycott? Very likely. If so, it'll show up pretty damn quickly in the affiliates' clearances."

"Maybe they're trying to put together a deal to take over the company," I ventured.

"With whom?" asked X. He proceeded to answer his own question. "I can't think of any likely candidate, and if I could, I would hold up the license transfers till kingdom come. The FCC may be bent on pulling out its own teeth, but the law's still the law." He grimaced—thinking—and then smiled. "Of course, I'm sure Eldon would like the government to take us over. Once you nationalize the banks, people like us are the next logical step, especially if it can be done in the name of private greed."

"I'm checking around," said Duncan. "I've got a few due bills out—and there's one or two things I know about a couple of guys. One thing:

according to Sam here, McNeery's been on the phone since last month and the stock's done nothing. If there was a deal in the wind with someone, I would've heard about it. Someone woulda talked. These guys can't keep their mouths shut; they like to have their edge and toot their horns about it."

Duncan was right about the stock. ABI was doing nothing, meandering along in the low $90s, on normal volume, a few hundred thousand shares a day. I asked whether it might not make sense to put out some feelers to the other side.

"Sue for peace?" asked X. "Possibly, although I think not just yet. To all outward appearances we must continue to give the impression that this great bark sails serenely on."

"I think we better get Bouverie, Marcus in," said Duncan. "There's gonna be an investment banking angle to this, and they'll have their own ways of scouting the Street. Bishman too. And I hate to say it, but we probably ought to talk to the legal eagles."

X told him to set up a meeting for the next afternoon, and Duncan left the office. "Poor old Fergus," X said. "He feels terrible about this."

"So do I. I shouldn't have told him. None of this would have happened. You can count on me for whatever I can offer."

He smiled in a way that closed the circle. "All I ask, Sam, is that you stick by me here for a while. I may need a shoulder to lean on, and with Jake out of the picture, you're my last strong reed." We were both silent for an instant; then he stood up, his voice now brisk. "I'm afraid there's no time for recrimination."

"Speaking of which, you don't think you can talk Eugenie off? Make a deal with her?"

"I'm afraid too much has taken place between us. Besides, having her around here all the time would very likely offset whatever pleasure I get out of this place."

Duncan returned to say that the meeting was all set.

X got up. He looked tired, but he produced a last comforting smile.

"Don't look so down, gentlemen. The damage is regrettable but, it is to be hoped, not terminal. We'll have to wait to see what, if anything, the other side has in mind. It may be nothing."

His voice was brave, but it was with the courage of his hopes.

"Another thing," he said, "class tells, as they used to say around the prize ring. I suppose neither of you remembers when Granite still had the Kentucky Derby? I brought Jack Drees over from ABC to call the race for us, best racing announcer there ever was, you know, and Jack had this wonderful phrase he'd always use if it was close as they turned into the home stretch. 'And here's where they run on their pedigree,' he'd declaim. I never failed to get a thrill when I heard him say that. Well, gentlemen, it seems that's where we find ourselves: heading for home and running on our pedigree. And I don't for a minute suspect that it will fail us, not against the likes of Eldon and McNeery and the rest of their sorry crowd."

The meeting next afternoon was relatively brief. The lawyers went over the legal options in the event another company or outside group made a bid for AbCom. As X had surmised, the only real peg was to hold up the transfer of licenses at the FCC and in court.

"I must say," X commented when the attorneys had finished, "that I'm dubious about the amount of help we can expect. I'm inclined to view all this talk of lawsuits and regulatory proceedings as just so much piffle. I'm of the opinion that if we're going to have to fight on the grounds of public interest, we're going to have to do it with the public."

Small consolation came from Hillhouse of Bouverie, Marcus. The investment banker obviously liked the prospect of a fight, as much out of sheer competitiveness as for the promise of a multiplicity of fat fees. The disturbing thing about Hillhouse's takeover rhetoric was that it seemed to make no distinction between, say, a tractor company and AbCom, which was potentially a conduit into the spirits of a hundred million people. To Hillhouse, a deal was a deal.

"Well, sir," he said to X, looking and sounding positively Churchillian, an effect heightened by a fat panatela which he alternately rolled in his fingers and slurped at reflectively, "we can go poison pill, we can go scorched earth, or, if that's too much for you, crown jewels; or we can talk to your banks and be ready to go Pac-Man when, as, and if; or we can hunt up a White Knight."

X smiled at him patiently and requested clarification. Hillhouse was pleased to explain. "Poison pill" meant that AbCom would issue a dilutive new stock, either with special or multiple voting rights or with a triggered takeout price that would double or triple the cost of AbCom to an unfriendly acquirer. "Scorched earth" would involve selling off the company's central assets, beginning with its "crown jewels," the five owned-and-operated television stations in major markets, or its 49 percent of BizNet, now the largest factor in electronic mail, or its software division. "Pac-Man" would involve borrowing billions for a counter-purchase; AbCom would gobble up him who intended to gobble up AbCom.

"We'd recommend a credit facility of a minimum four billion, sir," said Hillhouse in a measured voice. A sum this large demanded a respectful mien.

"I suppose we could do that," X said. He turned to his chief financial officer. "You'll talk to our banks, won't you, Harvey." He looked back to Hillhouse. "It may be that we'll encounter some resistance. Some of the things we've been doing around here haven't exactly made us the fair-haired boys of the banking community."

"Not to worry," said Hillhouse. "Banks are whores. They'd lend money to a guy who wanted to take them over. Don't waste time worrying about the banks."

"I see. Have you other thoughts?"

Hillhouse reached down beside him and extracted a computer printout from his briefcase.

"Yessir, we've done a little background work on prospective White Knights. Our group has developed a program we call 'King Arthur.'"

X chuckled. "To show that chivalry isn't dead, eh?"

Hillhouse returned the grin and nodded.

"Yessir." He read off a list of company names, principally oil and insurance companies. "These are the ones big enough to go the whole shooting match. Then we've got another list who could swing a deal on the crown jewels, or maybe go for a blank check preferred. You know, make sure that when the Lone Ranger comes riding over the horizon, his six-shooter's loaded with silver bullets."

Hillhouse's jargon seemed to me to trivialize this whole business, to turn it into an episode from a comic book. Behind all these stylish, crisp, pat phrases, I wondered, did Hillhouse feel any qualms? Did he realize that he was dismissing, in his drugstore snappiness, whole lifetimes, other people's lifetimes, of planning, dreaming, creating, bringing into being? I doubted it.

X looked at the list briefly. He remarked that at first blush he didn't see much in the way of business or attitudinal compatibility. Then he turned back to Hillhouse.

"There's one thing that seems most incongruous about this, Mr. Hillhouse, although I'm perfectly willing to accept that the rules have changed."

"And what's that, Mr. Monstrance?"

"It strikes me that there's little difference between this company being taken over, on the one hand, and, on the other, proceeding with the measures you recommend. One way or the other, the Granite my son and I built ceases to exist. Either someone else comes in or else Granite, as we know it and want it to be, is gutted or has borrowed so much money its financial integrity is impaired, not to say destroyed. I find it paradoxical; in other circumstances, I might even find it amusing that you recommend self-destruction as a form of salvation."

Hillhouse looked at X as if explaining a basic algebra problem to a dull student.

"Mr. Monstrance, what we're trying to do is come up with something to run the guys in the black hats off the spread. Failing that, the big thing is to make sure they don't win, period."

"Even if Granite is destroyed in the process?"

"Sometimes you got to break a few eggs to make an omelet."

"I see," said X coldly.

"Anyway," said Hillhouse, placatingly, "between us and your lawyers, I think we can Stalingrad 'em to death."

"Stalingrad?"

"You know: snow 'em under with paper. Russian winter with subpoenas instead of snowflakes. Like Napoleon and Hitler. FCC, FTC, SEC, Sherman Act. Every state in which you operate. All that stuff."

X said all this would be taken under advisement. He instructed the professionals around the table to do what they could about erecting the recommended barriers quietly. He did not wish to appear suspicious. This ruled out going to the stockholders for "poison pill" authorization, although the documentation could be drafted by a top-secret working party. The bank line would be set up; the banks could be told AbCom was looking at an acquisition of its own. Obviously, no approaches could be made to White Knights, although the list could be refined in preparation against the day trouble might come.

While Hillhouse and the lawyers busied themselves digging trenches and piling up sandbags, X did his best to ensure that his forthcoming foray among AbCom's big institutional stockholders would be nothing less than a triumphal progress. He barraged them with good news. He put $150 million on the table and secured first domestic exhibition rights to the next Star Wars film, which, within thirty-six hours, he resold to sponsors for close to $300 million. He announced a study to determine the virtue of spinning out the software businesses to ABI stockholders. Duncan made sure that the market knew all about the progress of future earnings.

And yet ABI stock did nothing. It was obvious the market was sullen, suspicious. If it bothered X, he didn't show it. He was confident it would all come right when he got a chance to work his face-to-face, heart-to-heart magic on the boys and girls in the trust departments and pension funds.

Then, the afternoon before I was to leave with X on the long-planned institutional foray, as part of my compact to stand with him, I was shuffling papers and closing out my open assignments. I had been candid with the editor. He understood; this was family business.

I was just about to leave when Buck called. "Anything special going on at AbCom?" he asked, too innocent-sounding to be merely curious.

"Why?"

"You see the stock today?" I hadn't. "Well, the sumbitch been bumpin' along doin' nothin', and then in the last hour it kinda broke out. Volume's already nine hundred thousand and change, and they've marked her up two points. And she's headed north."

He called me again about an hour after the close. ABI had finished trading at 96⅛, up over three points on the day, on over a million shares. The rumor was that the company had asked the Exchange to look into the trading in AbCom. What Buck heard, which was the funny part, was that the boys upstairs were kind of dragging their feet on this one. Usually they jumped when this sort of thing happened, with noise and press releases and a considerable display of public virtue.

"Jes' talked to the Coast, old buddy. Jefferies and Company's tryin' to put together a block of two million shares for a buyer. Somethin's goin' on. It smells like 'deal'! You remember that time we went fishin' for blues off the Shinnecock inlet, and you said a school of bluefish smells like melons? Well, old buddy, this sumbitch smells like money!"

He told me he expected me to tell him everything and anything I heard. I demurred. I told him that people who peddled inside information either went to jail or got appointed to Erwitt's cabinet, neither of which was a destiny I had in mind.

"Besides," I said, "I thought you called yourself a 'risk' arbitrageur."

"That's just so the public doesn't find out how easy it is. Shit, ol' buddy, ninety percent of makin' money is keepin' the public in the dark; otherwise they might get the idea to use their money on themselves. You keep me posted, hear?"

"If I hear anything, which I doubt, I'll think about it. And you?"

"I'll call you, old buddy. Promise. Just as soon as I call my broker, you'll be the first to hear. I tell you, Sam, somethin's comin'. My old country nose don't lie. That sumbitch is out there, somewhere, just like an ol' bear, just snuffling in the brush and stinkin' all the way to Valdosta, comin' close, comin' close."

But nothing happened. After the first flurry, which left the stock at 98 after two days of furious trading amid a hurricane of gossip, things quieted down again. ABI backed off a point or so, although volume on the Big Board remained relatively high.

X kicked off his institutional campaign in Boston. It went all right, although one hard-eyed young man at Fidelity kept insisting that ABI management "had no right to play your politics with our money." We flew on to Philadelphia and to Pittsburgh (where the Mellon fell all over X); then we cut back south, to Richmond and Atlanta, and back up to Nashville. Next it was Cincinnati, Detroit, and Chicago, then a haul due south to Houston and back up through Dallas to Kansas City. We didn't spend more than a single day in any city. The schedule began with breakfast and continued through dinner, the hours in between being broken up into sometimes as many as six separate appointments. X insisted on going one-to-one, and his strategy seemed to be paying off. He was a celebrity in his own right, and the doors he wanted opened to his knock. He saw bank trust officers, mutual fund managers, men and women who ran large pools of pension money, family offices responsible for hundreds of millions of inherited money. He made a point of paying a courtesy visit to the GBG station in every city we visited.

By the time we reached Kansas City, we'd been on the road, in Ab-Com's new Gulfstream IV, for twelve days. The rest of us were beat, exhausted by repetition, by hearing the same old song over and over again, but X seemed tireless.

As far as I could judge, the trip was turning out to be a success, if not quite the Caesarian triumph he'd envisioned. He was invariably received warmly. Although what he had to say was convincing, it was the simple fact of his presence that most often carried the day. That he brought good news about AbCom and its prospects obviously counted for something, but what hooked his listeners was that H. H. Monstrance himself had stooped to come to them.

The stock was reacting favorably, moving up on modest volume, giving and gaining. The morning we reached Kansas City, it was back to over 100.

Nevertheless, X's limitless energy failed to conceal an uncharacteristic lack of exuberance. People were Benzedrine to him and yet he was off his usual near-manic feed. Something was bothering him. It was in Kansas City, while we were finishing a nightcap, he let his feelings slip to Duncan and me.

"I feel like Custer," he said. "It's a fine night up here on the mesa. Stars, moon, the works. But I hear 'em moving down there in the river bottoms, boys. Schooling up. Getting ready to jump us."

CHAPTER 27

And jump us they did, just a day later, when we were at forty-seven thousand feet between Kansas City and Seattle.

Later, when I thought more about it, it was apparent that someone had been tracking N261GB through our flight plan filings, helpfully furnished by the FAA. When they hit, we were just coming up over the Idaho border. It was 11:28 Mountain Daylight Time when the call came, a minute to be marked indelibly on my memory, the way people remember Pearl Harbor or the day Kennedy was shot.

X had been stretched out on a banquette, feet up, reading a script. Duncan was drinking coffee in the back with the steward—just like Mr. Roberts, I later thought, when the kamikaze got him. I was checking some galleys. One of X's secretaries had rotated into our trip at Kansas City; she was seated at a computer terminal which was patched by satellite into the central word processor at AbCom.

Hillhouse's voice was elated. Combat at last! He summarized the contents of a letter which had been delivered a half hour earlier to AbCom. The message had simultaneously appeared on the Dow Jones and Reuters wires about ten minutes ago.

EmpCom Holdings, a newly organized Delaware corporation, was offering $140 per share, net, for any and all of the 64,786,476 outstanding shares of AbCom, for a total of $9,070,106,640. The nine-billion-dollar offer was unconditional and would expire in fourteen days. Stockholders who tendered would be paid within twenty-four hours of depositing shares in good order at various specified depositories. The tender offer was being managed by the investment banking firm of First Stuyvesant and Company. Hillhouse added, gratuitously, that Street gossip had it that First Stuyvesant was being paid close to $50,000,000 for handling the deal for EmpCom.

"Who in tarnation is EmpCom!" X blasted at the loudspeaker.

"It's some kind of consortium company. A bunch of names. We're trying to find out about it right now. When can you get back here, Mr. Monstrance?"

X checked with the pilot. We'd have to refuel; the plane didn't have enough fuel on board to turn around and make it back to LaGuardia nonstop. Unaccountably, we'd come out of Kansas City a little light; the fixed base operator somehow hadn't followed instructions to fill us up, but since we had plenty of fuel to get to Seattle, and X had been in a hurry to get wheels up, the pilot had gone ahead with his flight plan. The best thing would be to fly on to Twin Falls, which was another twenty minutes but wasn't as busy as the more easterly airports were likely to be, refuel and refile there, and head for New York. With luck and no traffic or weather delays, we could be at LaGuardia by eight o'clock their time.

X advised Hillhouse of this, patched into his office, and started giving instructions. A meeting would be set up at AbCom; have everyone standing by starting at eight o'clock. The financial officer was instructed to start buying ABI shares for the company's account and to activate the $5 billion standby credit which had been negotiated with a global banking group. As soon as the lawyers could get their ducks in a row, they were to kick off the paper blizzard that would bury the invaders. There was nothing else to do. X signed off and turned away, staring out the window at the mountains.

I didn't like any of it. The coincidences were too perfect; an oversight in refueling; the offer being announced exactly to catch us in the air with our pants figuratively down. A consortium company? Exactly what I had feared had happened: they were trying to take X's company, his life, away from him, and it was thanks to my big mouth.

It was finally close to midnight when we touched down at White Plains, LaGuardia having been closed to incoming traffic. Our problem hadn't been adverse traffic or weather on our way back to New York. Everything had simply gone very precisely, organizedly wrong. The delay at Twin Falls had been a put-up job, I was sure of that. As soon as the pilot had radioed in the course change, the gremlins went to work. We were held over the field on various pretexts for close to an hour. The pump on the fuel truck broke down. The radar in the tower went out. A tire blew out on landing and had to be replaced. All in all, we were stuck there for four hours. And every pay phone in the small airport wore an "out of order" sign.

I rented a car—I guessed that whoever it was who was calling the signals to keep us behind schedule and incommunicado wasn't worried enough to put the fix in at Avis—and drove until I found a gas station with a bank of pay phones. Now it was my turn to call Buck.

"What the hell's going on?"

"Where you been, ol' buddy? I've been trying to call you."

"Twin Falls, Idaho."

"That don't strike me as the best place for Mr. Monstrance to be hangin' out when they're trying to buy his company."

"Cut it out. Who's 'they'? Who in Christ's name is EmpCom Holdings?"

"Now, old buddy, just you guess. What a question for a smart boy like you. And a wordsmith, no less. Lessee now; what word begins with 'emp'?"

"Emp . . . empire . . . emperor . . . empress. . . . Empress! Holy shit! Eugenie!"

"That's what I hear. The skinny says everyone's in this one. I mean ever'body! I'm talkin' 'bout the *Fortune* 'ten thousand'! People been buying the stock all goddamn night. Singapore, Hong Kong, then switched to Zurich. A guy I know over at Boesky says the gloves are off. They ain't no ceilin' on this one. It's a lock. Hey, you know sumpin'? Just bein' your friend cost me money, old buddy. Apparently McNeery let a few folks in on the big secret, just to get a few million shares in safe hands, long as they did it nice and quiet. McNeery's the hoss on this one. He put it together piece by piece, him and Eugenie."

"And it's a consortium? Who's in it?"

"Ol' buddy, you bet your sweet bippy it's a consortium. Five hundred big companies each put up ten million apiece for some nonvoting preferred stock. That was the first five billion. Eugenie put up seven hundred million for the common stock. A bunch of banks and insurance companies loaned the other four-odd billion."

"Where'd Eugenie get seven hundred million, borrow it?"

"Hell, no, old buddy, that's the beauty part. She tendered her AbCom at one-forty a share first thing this morning, for a cool seven hundred big ones, immediate payment; then she just turned right around and reinvested it. She's now the hundred-percent owner of EmpCom, which aims to be the hundred-percent owner of AbCom. Sweet deal, huh?"

"A hundred percent. How about the banks and the companies that put up the main money? Where's their pound of flesh?"

"You can't answer that, 'cause you just been with him. The ol' boy got too sassy, old buddy. It's been a good game for these folks, and they're right nervous he may spoil it. This way, he goes and it don't cost them nothin'. Shit, they *spill* ten million dollars! And I don't have to talk about the way the banks feel. I mean, that show's been right funny and all—"

"It's going to be bloody," I said, interrupting, feeling angry at the world, at all the bloodsuckers, at Buck.

"No, it ain't. They ain't gonna be no problems. Eugenie's already a control stockholder. My Washington guy told me the FCC just hung up the gone fishin' sign."

"What about insider trading?" I was inventing my own straws to grasp at.

"Now, grow up, ol' buddy. These days, how bad you done is jes' a function of how big you is. This's a big 'un. I only got me 'bout three hundred thousand shares, thanks to hanging around with you, but it's a lock. They ain't goin' to be no trouble, nowhere, nohow. This ain't Dr. Pepper, old buddy. Ever'body's rootin' for this deal!"

For most of the endless flight to LaGuardia, further discouraging bulletins kept coming in. X was silent for most of the trip; he just sat staring out the window, mind working, but I could see from the expression on his face that he was frustrated: his intelligence wasn't giving him the solutions he needed, and the situation wouldn't allow the small appeasement of losing his temper. That he had been outflanked and very probably outgunned by Eugenie and the likes of McNeery and Erwitt—that Eugenie, a Monstrance for all her faults and deficiencies, should even have made cause with the likes of Erwitt and McNeery, should have turned on AbCom, on Granite—gouged at him worse, I was sure, than that daughter had turned against father.

Just east of Indianapolis, we lost our airborne voice. According to the pilots, something had glitched with the AbCom ground station; we were connected to the world only by our emergency frequency. In a way, it was a relief to have the flow of bad news stanched, but no consolation for the knowledge that our bad luck was now being managed for us—but that, for a long time previous, it had been managed by us.

It was a rumpled, tired crew who awaited us in the AbCom offices, too tired even to try to keep the true awfulness of X's situation out of their faces. Even the Bishmans' practiced toughness looked frayed. At least, we didn't have to face the press. All that greeted us outside the AbCom building area was a weary reporter from the *Post*.

We gathered in the conference room; X's secretaries had ordered in a light supper from "21," which we picked at. I watched as Duncan poured himself a vodka that would have poleaxed a Russian poet. I supposed he would soon be getting around to blaming himself for all that had happened. I promised myself to keep an eye on him, to do my duty as a friend when the time came to see him through the "If only I hadn't" crisis that would have to come.

"Well, gentlemen, what's the state of play?" X looked around the table. "We might as well get right to it." It was plain that everyone was past dissembling the extent of the crisis with small talk. "Mr. Hillhouse?"

"I'm afraid they've got us in kind of a box, sir."

"No bear hugs, are there, Mr. Hillhouse? No Pac-Men to come gobbling to our rescue? No White Knights?"

"All the possible White Knights seem to be in EmpCom, sir."

"What about Shaughnessy? CNI?"

"They're in too, sir." Hillhouse looked at the table. X said nothing, but his shoulders seemed to shrink.

"So there's nothing for us to hug or gobble, Mr. Hillhouse?"

"It'd be a hell of a bite, Mr. Monstrance." Hillhouse fished in his pocket and produced a sheet of paper. "EmpCom's corporate stockholders, the public ones, had a total market value of three quarters of a trillion dollars as of today's close. You couldn't make much of a dent in that."

"It's academic anyway, H.H." AbCom's chief financial officer spoke for the first time. "The banks have pulled the plug on us. The credit facility's closed down."

"Didn't you have a signed agreement?" X asked angrily.

"Of course we did." The financial officer looked offended. "We signed it up just as you instructed. But the banks are pleading *force majeure*. You see, their biggest customers and some pretty tough competitors are all on the other side. Plus we hear Washington's dangling a bailout on Brazil and Argentina if they flush us. Plume worked it out with the Fed through McNeery."

X smiled ruefully and shook his head. "It would appear that everyone's against us."

"Not quite everyone," said the financial officer. "I did hear from Shaughnessy. He couldn't get through to you. He wanted to explain. His business is on the line; he said he thought you'd understand. He's offered us a hundred million if there was any way we could use it. On the QT, of course. He insisted on that. I think he feels terrible."

"I see." X looked down the table at his lawyer. "Well, Francis, I always thought that litigation was the last resort of a scoundrel, but it seems I've come to that unlovely pass. Is there anything to be done? We appear to have the better part of industrial America lined up against us. Is there anything in that, perhaps something with an antitrust flavor? Or are you about to tell me that Stalingrad, too, has fallen?"

The lawyer looked rueful. "I'm doubtful, H.H. The Administration's policy on antitrust is pretty clear. There's no such thing."

"Any possibility of some form of injunctive relief?"

"As a matter of fact, they beat us to the punch on that one. Eugenie secured an injunction against your using your veto power on the Foundation's stock to block its being tendered. We'll knock that one out, however, on appeal. And we've sued in Wilmington for disclosure. There may have been some insider fun and games. I'm afraid, though, H.H., we haven't got a great deal to stand on legally. It's the wrong era for you and me."

X's eyes ran around the table, looking for a life ring, and settled on Audrey Bishman.

"What about you, Ms. Bishman? Is there any mind-bending we can do with our loyal stockholders?"

"Well, I was just whispering with Duncan here," she replied in her hard, street voice. "Our only hope is to politicize this. Work the media. Public opinion. It's our best shot; it's our only shot. And try to get some of our big stockholders to sit still. There's no time to do a personalized number on the little guys like we did last time. We gotta go at them through the media: TV, editorial pages, interviews, get the juices riled up. Talk to some of the big players; get 'em to sit on their fannies for a while, buy us some time."

Hillhouse seconded her.

"If we can hold 'em for a week, I think we might make it. These consortiums tend to hang together by very thin threads. After the first excitement, everyone goes back to thinking about himself."

"If we blitz 'em in the media," added Audrey Bishman, "identify 'em, dig up the dirt, keep it hot and steamy, make 'em sweat, there's a shot."

For the first time I felt some sense of optimism flicker around the table.

"I think we ought to bid them up, too," said Hillhouse. "At least as far as we can. Take some of the arbitrage gravy out of the deal by running the price up toward the tender price; cut the spread back to where the Arabs have to take a second look at their cost of money. How much can you raise?"

He looked first at X, then at his financial officer. Quick calculations were made. Between AbCom's war chest, X's personal fortune, Shaughnessy's secret pledge, the Foundation's non-AbCom holdings, and what could probably be raised in Zurich and Hong Kong, where Eldonomics was viewed with feelings between trepidation and hatred, the figure came to around a billion and a half.

"Good," said Hillhouse. "Assuming we wanted to push the stock to one forty-five, that'd give us the firepower to buy about ten million shares. With the Polhemus stock, and yours and the Foundation's, we'd have over twenty million shares."

"Mr. Polhemus is still in intensive care, Chief," said Duncan. His eyes were downcast; he doodled fitfully on his yellow pad.

"That's all right," X said. He had brightened enormously. I could see what he was thinking: I can win this one on showmanship. And so you might, I thought, if that was what it came down to. If that was all it came down to.

"I know the people who run Jake's family office. They know how it is with Jake and me."

We broke up in a pugnacious if not jubilant mood.

My enthusiasm evaporated when I talked to Buck after the word got out that AbCom was buying its own stock in the market.

"Bullshit," he said. "The old boy's just pissin' in his hat. This deal ain't about what the stock's worth. This ain't some oil play where ever' time the takeover price gets bumped you got to refigure the price per acquired barrel of reserves and refining capacity to see if you're getting close to go– no go. These boys want that old sumbitch out of there. At first he was kind of a joke, the way I hear it, even sort of useful, to show there was some opposition out there. So what if he gets the spics all riled up about the South Bronx? That's democracy at work, and all that's lost is the opportunity cost on maybe a hundred million dollars. Sam, these boys don't even take it out of their pants for a hundred million."

"What do they take it out of their pants for?"

"What's on the table. Owning the country on their terms. They don't give a shit about deficits, and they ain't buyin' no fifty-thousand-dollar home, so interest rates don't make a shit's worth of difference to them, not with what they stand to make on what they got in mind. Let me see if I can put it in perspective. What's next year's defense budget?"

"About two hundred and fifty billion."

"OK: that's 'billions' with a capital B. And nobody gives a shit how much of that is profit or makework either, not with this Administration! That's the way Erwitt works, see. He gets a big report about government waste and blames it on some guy who was President ten years ago, and everybody says how awful and goes about selling ten-cent screws to Uncle Sam for five thousand bucks a copy! And how about deregulation? How about instead of owning just five TV stations, a boy could own, say, ten or fifteen?"

"That'd be a lot of money."

"And suppose they turned Social Security over to the insurance companies and such to run it on a fee? And started leasing their F-Fifteens from GE Credit? And how about the banks and so on? Do you get my drift?"

"I got it." It was just what X had said, but coming from Buck it wasn't made to seem so awful.

"Well, that's the point, and folks like me are making it all come true for them by buying AbCom at a hundred thirty-two, which is where it closed today, and tendering it at one-forty, plus commission."

"What makes America great, huh? Don't you feel like a shit? What about the larger issues?"

"What larger issues? That's for you people who write books. That's what you chose, ol' buddy. Me, I chose money, 'cause at least I know what money can do!"

"Everything, it seems."

"Not always. But right now: yes. I ain't crazy about the idea that right now, the way things is, I can borrow twenty million to play this AbCom offer when there's folks out there can't eat or keep their business; I ain't crazy about the fact that I ain't paid taxes since Nixon was President; I ain't crazy about Nixon, comes to that, but here he is, bigger'n life and ever'body kissin' his ass. But that's the way it is. So I jes' go with the flow, I make money the old-fashioned way—"

"Yeah," I said, unafraid to show my disgruntlement. "You earn it— with inside information and a fat line at the bank."

"Old buddy," Buck said mildly, almost plaintively, "I didn't make the rules. That's what you jes' don't seem to see. These boys been workin' on this set of rules for about twenty years now; all it lacked was a guy who could put it over with the folks that do the votin', and they found him. They ain't gonna let nobody spoil this party."

But it looked for a while as if Buck was going to be proved wrong. X's initial media charge was, frankly, breathtaking. He was all over the place: powerfully favorable interviews in the *Times*, *USA Today*, *The Los Angeles Times*, *The Washington Post*, painting himself as the Establishment's Thomas à Becket. Even the attacks on him were quality, coming from the sort of enemies it suited a decent man to make: *The New York Post* ran a story comparing him to Alger Hiss and Eugenie to Whittaker Chambers; *The National Review* montaged his face onto a photograph of William Randolph Hearst. He appeared on "Good Morning, America" and the "Today Show," flew to the Coast to trade jabs and jibes with Carson, and demonstrated a flair for coming across as venerable and august on "Face the Nation" and "Meet the Press."

Not that he didn't have the press on his side to begin with. It was obvious the EmpCom takeover bid was a present danger to the First Amendment, but there was nothing actionable about it. EmpComp's preferred stockholders would have no vote. Rumors were around that EmpCom's bank lines were in effect collateralized by advertising guarantees of the type McNeery had once offered X, and although Duncan got a story to this effect into *The Boston Globe*, where it appeared loaded up with allegations of collusion, nothing could be proved. All the heavyweight columnists, from Joseph Kraft to Murray Kempton and even George Will, weighed in for X. As Buck said, however, it was just words against bullets, or, in this case, bucks. Not even when Jack Anderson broke the story that the other three networks had split $20,000,000 of EmpCom preferred among them, presumably with the more purely economic objective of taking a token participation in the surgical elimination of a dangerous competitor, did any meaningful outrage spread beyond the editorial pages.

Nevertheless, we ran uphill with full hearts for almost a week, bolstered by the support from the press, from the dozen university endowments which announced their loyalty and refused to tender their stock, from the small stockholders who wrote X cheery, applauding letters: notes scrawled on lined paper; elegant spidery billets-doux on engraved paper; resolutions signed by school classes and labor unions and investment clubs. We were fooling ourselves, of course; people like X and me tended to overrate the quality of our supporters, but it was quantity that counted in something like this. Overall, there wasn't much stock involved, four or five million shares at most, but the psychological boost it gave to our beleaguered team was tremendous.

I thought of myself as part of "us" now, of "we" against "them," something I'd sworn never to do when all this started. Over the last two years, I'd seen much about X that made me question the sincerity of his commitment to the virtues and values he'd enumerated in London back on that buzzing late May day when he'd summoned me from Scotland. Now, however, I felt involved in something worthwhile, something that made transcendent my own dissatisfaction with my world. It was as if the battle for GBG was somehow the last redoubt, the final test for the new religion of which Eldon Erwitt was the prophet, which proclaimed that everything had its price and by rights belonged to him who could pay it. The editor had once described our magazine as Fort Zinderneuf in a Sahara of cant. Well, here I was on another besieged rampart.

For a while, there were enough tendrils of euphoria and possibility to make us believe we might yet clutch them and swing across the abyss to safety. But on the Sunday before the EmpCom offer was set to expire, Eldon Erwitt sent our Sisyphean boulder tumbling down the hill for the last time. He broke in on "The NFL Today" to announce, with a proud tear in his eye and "Hail to the Chief" blaring in the background, that at the request of the French Government he had dispatched a task force to the French overseas territory of St. Pierre and Miquelon to subdue a threatened uprising by Quebec nationalists. In making these two small islands, which I vaguely remembered as curiosities in a stamp collection I'd once begun, secure for a valued NATO ally, the President said, America could stand straight and look itself in the eye. The operation had been swift and surgical, Erwitt said, a testimonial to American military technology, deft and daring: the only casualties had been a Miquelon lobsterman who had perished when a Navy Tomcat mistakenly nailed his dory with an air-to-surface tactical missile, and a Marine lance corporal who had been run down by a bull and sustained a broken leg.

In his peroration, Erwitt said, "This shows our country is on the move again, and that we are ready and prepared to answer forcefully any threat to our allies and ourselves. No less must we be ever vigilant, with God's help, against those within who would seek to curb this great American resurgence, who would impugn the honor and intention of our dedicated public servants with ill-conceived mockery, who would array themselves against the very forces that have permitted this nation to hold its head up and walk straight and tall and tell the world, 'Watch out, America is back.' If you listen to their doubting, negative talk, which says we don't need a militarily strong America, an America in which a man can still become wealthy without being criticized out of envy and in spite of big government, just ask our good friends the oppressed peoples of St. Pierre and Miquelon what America means to them. Fortunately, when such a threat arises, we have shown ourselves in our private sector to be ready to defend our sacred honor."

The "Star-Spangled Banner" had broken out. Darlene Erwitt materialized to clutch her husband's hand, and a misty-eyed Erwitt asked the nation for a moment of silence for the brave fighting men far from home on the distant, cold Newfoundland fishing banks, having to forgo a Sunday of professional football.

Afterward there'd been a briefing and question-and-answer session with the Secretary of Defense, during which, in response to an obviously planted question, he'd made it clear that the President was in fact referring to AbCom, and that he did sympathize with the EmpCom tender, because the prevention of abuse by the media was just as important to every American as the First Amendment, and that, by golly, he, the Secretary, although he couldn't speak for the President, thought that every darn one of the fine American corporations which had subscribed to EmpCom deserved a Medal of Freedom.

That did it. X might come and X might go, but the President was going to be around, and a fat and pleased nation had been assured of its deserving permanence. War always took precedence; nothing captivated like military adventure. AbCom/EmpCom was relegated to the financial pages.

On Monday, Hillhouse came to X to inform him that Bouverie, Marcus was obliged to withdraw as AbCom's financial advisers. It was the pressure from the banks, Hillhouse said.

"What you're really saying," X replied tonelessly, "is that Wall Street is no longer a place where relationships predominate."

"Mr. Monstrance, I won't quarrel with you," said Hillhouse. "It's the way things are. We now make most of our money on trading positions, big ones. My firm is run by people who in your time would never have made it out of the order room; maybe that's a good thing, maybe not. We didn't want it this way. When they pushed through the business about shelf registrations, which we thought wouldn't be very good for the public, we went with Goldman and Morgan Stanley in fighting Rule Four-fifteen, but Salomon and Merrill and Lehman carried the day. How can we relate to our clients if they won't relate to us? How do we justify the time and effort to cultivate a relationship when that relationship's treasurer will throw fifty years out the window because Salomon offers him an extra five-hundred-thousandth on a bond deal? Nowadays, we have to bid 'em, buy 'em, take 'em into inventory with borrowed money, and pray to God we can parcel 'em out at a profit. So our bank lines are like arteries, and half a dozen of my partners and I got the word from our biggest banks that they don't like us doing business with you. You've been pretty rough on them, not that they don't deserve it. The trouble is, they're the guys with the dough. And I'm just one of seventy partners."

"Is it that many now?" X asked. He sounded old, tired, and elsewhere. "Goodness me. I remember when Granite made its first public offering. Henry Bouverie was alive then. He came on our board. Well, times change. I wonder how Henry would have reacted?"

"Who can say, Mr. Monstrance? Times change; people change. Maybe he would have backed off too. Maybe he would have gone down with the ship. I can't tell you."

"I can," said X.

The psychological coup-de-grâce came two days later, on the eve of the EmpCom offer's expiration, when we flew to Boston to talk to the Polhemus people.

CHAPTER 28

After five minutes in the conference room, it was clear to me that, to the young woman portfolio manager with whom we were meeting, the opportunity to piss all over a living legend, and a man, yet, was too rare to be passed up and should be savored in full, tortuous measure.

"That may be, Mr. Monstrance," she said, after X had opened by going over the length and depth of his friendship with Jacob Polhemus, still comatose in Mass General, alive in name only, "but absent specific instructions from Mr. Polhemus, this office is constrained to act in what we believe to be the Polhemus group's best interest. After all, we are talking of roughly eight hundred million dollars."

Deirdre Goswell—"Ms. Goswell" to us—was very blond and put together; she spoke with a much-practiced, bloodless, uppity precision. The instant I saw her I made her for one of the hundreds annually cloned and cookie-cuttered out on Storrow Drive at the Harvard Business School. It was obvious she would be trouble.

According to Buck, the ball game was over. His mole at Certified Guaranty National Bank, which was acting as depository, had told him in dark confidence that over thirty-five million AbCom shares had been tendered, which gave Eugenie and McNeery an outright majority. Nevertheless, if it was the time for last hurrahs, X said, it was necessary to go to Boston, if only for the comfort of knowing that Polhemus would be with us until the last wave washed over the fo'c'sle.

Looking around him as we were led to a conference room, X remarked that he didn't recognize a single face. Nor will you recognize a single mentality here, I felt like adding, remembering something he'd said to me once about no longer recognizing Abner's mind. In his heart, I knew he was still clinging to the notion that if only he could find one staunch ally, one cow with whom to bell the institutional flock, he could pull it out. I subscribed to his delusion. I, too, wanted to postpone the inevitable final disillusionment, the moment which would bring me up against the fact of my part in all of this.

I sat across the table from Ms. Goswell as she put X by turns through his paces and the wringer. She was all right there on the surface, all consumption and calculation and received opinion. There would be a husband just like her, probably working at the John Hancock or the Boston Consulting Group or Arthur D. Little, and a restored barn out near someplace like Framingham, matched Volvos in the garage to go with the matching Rolexes, a weekend cabin in New Hampshire and tickets to the Pops and the Symphony, but only when they played Mozart and Dvorak, and a bookcase full of Robert Ludlum, and a kitchen with nine different vinegars, with a genteel scrimmage each morning to be first with the bran and the business section, and, on Sunday nights, "Masterpiece Theatre" on the high-tech TV monitor.

Not exactly X's cup of tea. I wondered how he would try to manage her. She came not merely from another generation but from virtually another civilization.

As I guessed, he soon abandoned logic and tried to come on to her, to gaff her with the Monstrance charm that had once left gasps and sodden panties from Malibu to Montevideo. He didn't understand the new, sexless, Yuppie feminism, and Ms. Goswell wasn't buying his charm. Offhandedly, I found myself wondering how Ms. Goswell looked with her clothes off; how Goswell made out when he dragged himself home from Ropes and Gray or wherever, and the lights were down low. Not so good, I imagined. Bed would be strictly a weekend thing, between trips to the Museum of Fine Arts to look at Korean pottery and hours over the stove with a tricky new pasta sauce. I'd have bet my last dollar that Ms. Goswell was on at least half of AbCom Direct Mail's lists.

What X was talking about held no reality for her, I could see. "Real life" was five-day stretches of computers and quote machines and wires to New York and Singapore and Geneva. She was anti-men in a sort of frozen, neutered way, not like the sixties Women's Lib survivors I'd known who'd handled their femininity like a slave rebellion.

She heard X out, fending off his logic and his seduction. Then she said, sorry, but the Polhemus group would tender its 5.7 million shares of AbCom. She would have tendered to Genghis Khan or Hitler if she'd liked the price. There was no point even in suggesting she think it over. The $140 being offered fully discounted the "best-case" earnings prospects for AbCom. She used words like "scenario," terms like "DCF" and "ROI," manipulating them like foils to fence away X's arguments. She had no more time, let alone further truck for ideas. She had been taught that the sole function of the American corporation, whether it sold widgets or truth, was to earn the highest return for its stockholders.

Finally, in desperation, X produced a letter from Jake Polhemus. Old and yellowing, written years before, just after the war, X had once shown it to me as evidence of what real friendship was. In it, among a great many other sentiments, Polhemus had remarked that he would stick by X through "fire and brimstone."

Ms. Goswell read it through calmly. When she'd finished, she shoved it back across the table to X.

"Mr. Monstrance, we have been confronted with any number of so-called 'handshake' arrangements in this office since Mr. Polhemus fell ill, and we have disavowed them all, absent suitable documentation in proper legal form. It was a technical weakness of Mr. Polhemus's otherwise successful business practices, which we are attempting to bring up to date. If, however, you would like to speak with counsel, your friendship with Mr. Polhemus certainly requires the courtesy of our—"

"No," X said, sounding reedy, hollow. "No . . . it was just . . . just a letter."

"I'm sorry," said Ms. Goswell.

The only pity she felt for this broken titan sitting across from her was for his failure to perceive the consequences of the sweep of time and progress. She couldn't spare wielding the lash one last time.

"Mr. Monstrance," she said, "Mr. Polhemus used to say that each new generation on Wall Street makes its fortune recapitalizing America. He used to say that was the point of Wall Street. That's all this is, Mr. Monstrance. Progress."

We were shown out. Waiting for the elevator, X said bemusedly, "You know, Ab told me the same thing, just after he came back from business school."

"What did you answer?" I asked.

X shook his head sadly. "You know, I can't remember." He forced a smile. "Don't be bitter, boys," he said. "You know, perhaps we should be somewhat grateful to be part of so important a process as progress, even just as victims. And after all, it's just a company." He rallied; his grin returned, and he draped his arms across our shoulders. Duncan, I saw, was having a tough time holding himself together.

When they fished Fergie Duncan out of the Charles River and did the autopsy, it turned out he was dead even as he hit the water. The autopsy disclosed cyanide; his "holocaust" pill, I guessed.

He would have wished to sink forever from our lives, I knew, but it had just been his bad luck that a couple of students had strolled by the Harvard Bridge at dusk, just as he'd fallen into the water. He must have been sitting at the base of the bridge for a while, thinking things over, waiting for it to get dark. Steeling himself, too; the police turned up a half-empty fifth of Stolichnaya by the bridge abutment. When he felt the time had come, he'd simply stood up, bitten into the pill, and toppled into the river.

All he had in his pockets was about five hundred dollars in cash, a gold initialed pen that had been a recent present from X, and a slip of paper with my name and address on it, so the Boston police called me just after eight o'clock on the night we returned from Boston. I managed to make the nine o'clock shuttle back up, and by midnight I had identified the body, fought through the paperwork, and made arrangements to have him cremated first thing the next morning. Afterward, I took the small box which now contained all that there was in the world of my late friend and flew back to New York.

As I came into my apartment, the phone was ringing. I knew somehow it was X.

"Sam, where in thunder have you been? And where's Duncan? I thought he said he was coming back this morning."

"He probably did," I said. "Who knows? Maybe he lost his beeper." Duncan had taken great pride in the electronic umbilical which connected him to the Chief, the one he worshiped most. I said, "Where are you? I've got to see you."

"At the office, naturally. I've got an all-hands meeting set for eleven thirty. I've got to find Duncan; I need him!"

"I'll come on over now," I said. "Maybe I can help."

". . . And so," I told X, "I guess he wanted to do it away from New York, in a way that looked like he'd never be found. He didn't want to cause you any more trouble than he had already."

"Terrible," X said. "Terrible." He rubbed his face despondently.

I said nothing.

Finally he said, "Sam, this must have been awful for you."

"It was just something that happened. I was the name they found in his pockets. I was afraid Fergie might do something."

"He was a loyal soldier. And very bright too, Fergus."

Yes, I thought, he was lots of things, just like every one of us: some good things, some not so hot. None of us knowing the troubles the other has seen. It was natural, I thought, and fitting, that he'd found his way out by Harvard at the end. That world he'd never made, for all his trying.

"Sam." His tone said that X was straining to hold himself within a fragile membrane of self-control. "I have a meeting scheduled in forty-five minutes. I'd like to be alone until then, if you don't mind. Just to gather my thoughts."

I started to leave.

"And Sam," X said, "don't say anything about Duncan, will you? I think it's my job to tell them."

As you wish, I thought. A curiously normal human reaction, this compulsion of ours to want to be the first to tell the news of a death?

I went downstairs to the cafeteria and had a cup of coffee. Then I went to my AbCom office and called Margarita in London. She would want to know.

"Poor man," she said when I told her.

"You were right to leave here," I said after I'd gone through the whole thing. "You were right about the way it would come out. This has been a brute."

"It must have been. How is Horace? I'm sure he still expects a miracle."

"We're out of miracles. Anyway, the age of miracles is over; the sooner we realize it the better. You were right about X. I see that now. He was never going to win. There was too much money on the table."

"And you, Sam? How are you?"

"Fair. This business with Duncan has hurt. And you?"

"I'm really very well. Very busy."

"I thought I might come over when all this gets wrapped up. Would that be a good idea?"

"I'd love to see you, Sam. I really would. I am"—from across the ocean I heard her breathe deeply—"seeing someone, however."

Well, I said in farewell, find me someone to make a fourth.

The old gang was ranged around the boardroom table: the Bishmans, the lawyers, the financial man, even Hillhouse had turned up out of respect, although strictly ex officio. All of us save one.

X came in. He looked ravaged: old and defeated. I wondered if he'd shed a tear in the solitude of his office.

He attempted a weak smile. "I feel more like Lear than ever," he said wistfully. "My daughter's sold me out, and now my poor fool is dead." He told them about Duncan.

My poor fool: Duncan would have liked that, I thought.

X sat down and rested his hands on the table. "Do you know," he said, "his real name was Grodnick. Herman Grodnick. There's a sister living in Jackson Heights. If any of you care to write, my secretary has her address. I've arranged a brief service tomorrow in New Haven, in the Yale Chapel. It's the least I can do. I hope you'll all attend. He wasn't the greatest man I've ever known, but he fought the good fight."

The Yale Chapel, I thought. The Ivy League at last. Good for you, Fergie. Good for you, X. Class tells.

X's voice strengthened, became more practical. "I've asked you to come here, very possibly for the last time on this matter, to see if anyone has any ideas. No wild surmises, please. It's been a very tiring day."

He looked around the table in an unhopeful way. His listeners looked at their hands or scribbled nervously on their scratch pads. Finally Hillhouse raised a tentative hand.

"Well, sir, sometimes in these things, there's a certain satisfaction in seeing that the other side doesn't win even if you don't either. Especially given the circumstances of the opposition."

"Are you suggesting we scorch the earth, Mr. Hillhouse? Break up Granite?"

"It's just a thought, sir." Hillhouse's voice was tentative. "We could find buyers for the pieces very quickly."

"May I assume your firm has tested the water with potential buyers? Strictly off the record and *en principe*, of course?"

"I won't deny it."

"Well, we have a week to decide. They've extended the offer a week.

They want my stock. Mine and the Foundation's. They've made it clear they want unconditional surrender, so let me think it over."

"It's a lot of money either way," said Hillhouse.

X smiled at him. "That it is. But then again, if it's no more than money, if that's all it is, perhaps it's nothing at all, no matter how consequential the sum. Nothing at all."

He looked down at himself briefly, like a woman appraising her body. Then he looked back up to us.

"Well, Mrs. Bishman, gentlemen, it's been quite a run. You'll be called if you're needed." He got up. One by one they filed by, shaking his hand; it reminded me of the postlude to the Stanley Cup. A last ceremonious pretense that the world was a gentler place than it seemed. That it was all just a game, and that life would just go on, and we could all go back to being friends and to doing whatever it was we thought we did under a sun that would keep coming up, no matter what.

He gestured me to stay.

"Well, Sam, it was quite a dream, wasn't it?"

"It was dynamite!"

"Quite a dream," he repeated. "I wonder, does anyone still read Yeats? Do you know the line: 'I am worn out with dreams'? That's how I feel. I hope I can count on you for the weekend?"

And so I spent a last, dismal weekend at Dunecrag. On Saturday morning, a GBG helicopter took us to New Haven, where we mourned and prayed over Duncan's ashes, and then on to Dunecrag. As we landed, X levered open his window and shook Duncan's ashes loose in the prop wash.

"He always liked it here," he said. Now, I thought, there are two I know here, part of the land.

I was surprised to find Clio waiting for us. X hugged her warmly and told her how touched he was that she'd come. When he went upstairs, she turned to me.

"How are you, Sam? How is he? He begged me to come. I'm praying he won't be impossible."

"He's tired. I think he's a little confused. It's a lot for an old man. How's Abner?"

"In the city. I'm taking him to Santa Barbara next week. I don't know why I'm here. It's just that for some reason I owed it to him, I thought. Don't ask me why."

"I am surprised."

"So am I, but there it is. I dread this weekend. You won't believe this, but he's accepted to go to a dinner party tomorrow night in South-ampton. He wants to fly the flag. It's at the Shrecks'."

"Bud and Marie? Jesus! Where is Cass, anyway? Why isn't she here?"

"Who knows? I don't think she was asked. Anyway, she's got a new beau. A rich Swiss with a large cantankerous wife he keeps in Lucerne. They'll probably be here tomorrow."

The three of us dined alone that night. It was a feast: fat gray caviar; a special bottling of Bollinger; quail; what X said was the last of the '49 Cheval Blanc. Afterward cigars born under Batista and a cognac dating from the Crimean War.

He only alluded to the EmpCom business once during dinner. "I couldn't ever be a party to dismembering Granite," he said quietly. "I know you both understand. It wouldn't be fair to either of us, not to me, not to Ab. It's all we really had together." Then he looked at us. "Well, we're all orphans now," and he raised his glass with forced joviality. "We might as well face the morrow with confidence." But he wasn't up to the act.

But after dinner, over coffee, some of the old, unquenchable high spirit returned. "Was old Curwen still around Starbuck when you and Ab were there?" he asked.

"Only as a sort of living monument," I replied, memory bringing back the image of a tall, crop-headed figure looming over the football sidelines and frowning in the back of the debating room. "He was retired by then."

"A great man, Curwen," X said. "He used to say that losing in the right was vastly better than winning in the wrong." X shook his head, in-wardly contemplating the needless destruction of something harmless. "We boys didn't believe him, of course. All that Henry Newbolt stuff. 'Play up, and play the game!' He was pretty good at it, though. The sort of thing boys believe because it sounds the way things should be, until life makes a lie of it." He shook his head again, and then grinned. "Well, it looks as if I'll have plenty of time to savor the truth of Curwen's observa-tion, but I can tell you, right now it tastes downright awful!" He chuckled.

The next night, after a perfectly awful evening at Bud and Marie's, we drove home through a thick ground fog. It had been a sour few hours, and none of us said much. Bud and his chums had discovered shooting, and most of the conversation revolved about how much Purdey shotguns cost and what a decent Highland moor rented for these days and who was going to have which duke or viscount in whose shooting party. Cass was there, with her new beau, a stolid man pronounced Al-*fred*. She was full of herself and her book. Al-*fred* was a bore, interested only in the likelihood of Erwitt's reelection, which—he said several times—would be most beneficial for the Swiss franc. X was treated as a somewhat dotty and decrepit elder: to be indulged as a matter of courtesy but no longer of much use or interest. What he now had left to give, as far as these people understood him, they already possessed. They had aped his china and plate, and bought the same great wines that lined his cellars, and built their own big houses, and made lists of his friends and purveyors. At one point, I overhead Bud snigger behind his fat hand that he'd made a bundle on the tender.

In the middle of the night, in the midst of a nightmare in which I dreamed I plummeted from a great height, noises intruded on my uneasy sleep. Waking, I heard plaintive sounds, then gruff ones, as if the wide world had burst into rut.

I slipped on my bathrobe and padded down the hall. The sounds were coming from Clio's room. The door was barely ajar. I couldn't see in, although there was a slice of dim yellow light under the door. I listened.

I heard Clio say, "No, please; no!" Then X, gruffly whimpering, "Please. Please." A noise which might have been fabric. Then Clio again; then a gruffer, stertorous, growling, throaty puffing and grunting, and nothing from Clio, and finally a hoarse, deep groan, which I recognized for what it signified. I knew what it had to be. There had been a time when it would have enraged me; now I felt only sick, only sad.

I lingered in the darkness of the hall. After a while, I heard X go back up the corridor to his room. His steps were those of a very old man, a wheezy shuffle brushing across the boards. When I heard his door close, I went down to Clio's room.

She was sitting on the edge of the bed, her bathrobe gathered around her, hugging herself as against a chill and rocking slightly.

"I heard something," I said. "Are you all right?"

She looked at me dully.

"Oh, it's you, Sam."

I said nothing. I saw her awareness of me sharpen. Her voice rose.

"And what did you hear? Did you watch, too? Did it excite you?"

I shook my head. "Clio, please." Very tentatively, I reached out.

"No, no." She shivered and drew her robe around her. "I didn't want this, don't you see? But it never would have ended. He begged. I felt so sorry for him. He needed something. I don't know; I don't know. . . . "

"Did he attack you?"

She laughed bitterly. "Attack? Good God, no! He's an old man. He needed me, someone, anyone—just to prove that he was still real!"

I took a step toward her. All I wanted to do was console her. What had happened with X was nothing. How she felt was everything.

"You saw, Sam," she said. She sounded like a small, bruised child. "He licked me, Sam. Licked me like a puppy. His slobber's all over me. Then he just sort of pushed at me until . . . Oh, God, I feel so filthy!"

She saw me reach toward her and held up a hand. Her eyes sparkled wet and mistrustful.

"Of course," she said, suddenly calm. "You want me too, don't you, Sam? We've got unfinished business, don't we?"

I shook my head.

"Yes, we do." She turned away. "Just wait, I won't be a second." She walked quickly into the bathroom. I heard water running; the toilet flush. She came out a minute later.

"There," she said. "I've washed him away. All gone. I've washed away all traces of him, whatever they were. Now it's your turn, Sam. Now you can do it to me properly. Just like we promised each other: in a proper bed. Here."

She pulled the front of her gown apart. I suppose I just stood there staring. I'd touched her before in Florida, but I'd never had the full sense of her body. I'd never seen it. It was a true "lady's" body: the breasts firm, their tips pink; the flesh was unpuckered; between her legs the fleece was pale, the color of honey, neither truly dark nor truly blond.

"Do you like that?" she said. She rucked the gown over her waist and pivoted. "And this?"

Her bottom was firm and clear-skinned. Clio had the body every Starbuck boy had lain awake nights dreaming of, the body which all those Farmington and Garrison Forest and Foxcroft girls had hidden away under those austere school uniforms and the Christmas tulle and the tennis clothes.

"I've held up nicely, haven't I?" Clio said, turning back to stare at me. Her hands let the gown drop. I stared at her.

"Poor Sam, you are excited, aren't you? You can have me. Now."

"No," I said. "No. I just wanted to hug you. That was all."

Her face fell apart and she sat down, hard, on the bed. Then she looked at me.

"Would you go now, Sam? Please." She began to cry softly. I went over and kissed her hair, and guided her under the covers. She wept quietly. I sat on the edge of the bed, not touching her, until at last she fell asleep.

On the way back to my room, I heard a sound coming from downstairs. I paused on the landing to listen. The air inside the great house seemed compressed, vile. Someone started to play the piano. The playing was clumsy and tentative: a Chopin nocturne. I went stealthily down the front hall, by the drawing room. As I drew abreast of the door, hidden in the shadows, the music changed. "Once to ev-ry man and nation/Comes the moment to decide. . . ." X's voice sounded frail and reedy, graveled with age and dejection. The words slipped away into a vague humming. I went back to my room. Minutes later, I heard him come back upstairs.

I wrote a note to him, and to Clio, and packed my bag. I made my way downstairs. Through the window I could see the sun make its way above the horizon. I went out on the veranda overlooking the dunes. The air was fresh, the sea gentle. As the sun rose, the sky took on infernal colors, fiery pink, blazing orange, striations like the earth's deepest flaming layers.

It took me an hour to walk to East Hampton. The sky was forcing itself to a paler gray when I got to the railroad station to wait for the milk run.

I never saw any of them again.

Except Eugenie.

On Monday morning, a week into GBG's new fall season, with the most potent new episodes of "Statehouse" still unshown, X handed over his sword and tendered the Foundation's shares and his own. It was announced that EmpCom would move swiftly to elect a new board of directors and to install Eugenie and McNeery as Chairman and President/Chief Executive Officer, respectively. X resigned.

He didn't call me at home or at the magazine. My note to him had not been angry or remonstrative. But I felt that I had done all that could be asked of me and that our lives had once again parted.

There was only one errand I had left, I felt, one still loose, strictly journalistic thread, and that was to see Eugenie. I telephoned for an appointment and was told that she'd be happy to see me, although, for the time being, at least, whatever was said would be off the record. I agreed.

She had taken up residence in X's old office. I thought, looking around, that this was the third metamorphosis I'd seen in so many years. First, Abner's spartan technocratic setting. Then X's men's club jumble. Now Eugenie. She had completely redone the place in the fashion of the moment, what Florrie called "English Indistinguishable": a dozen chintzes;

ten paintings, mostly crude, of Jack Russell terriers; a single check's sim-ulation of a lifetime's picky gathering of objects: Vaseline glass, Battersea boxes, treen.

Eugenie looked out of place in this fatuous clutter. For one thing, she was thin, perhaps another thirty pounds lighter than the last time I'd seen her. She was drinking iced coffee.

She looked no happier, however, than she had all along, and the hand she gave me, though less fleshed, was still lifeless. After the initial pleas-antries, when I was seated, she began to talk of the glorious plans she and McNeery had for AbCom and GBG. I listened agreeably. She wasn't fooling either me or herself. She wanted a body to gloat over, a mourner to gloat to, and here I was. My hope was that if I stuck it out, listened attentively, I might be treated to a confidence or two as compensation.

When she had finished, I said, "It's too bad X never knew how much you hated him, Eugenie. Did you always?"

"Always? Good Lord, no! I loved him for so long. I spent most of my life trying to please him, trying to be something special. But I couldn't be special in the only way he understood a woman could be special, which was to be beautiful, alluring, and sexy or to have perfect taste. I wanted to make him happy, Sam, but over time I realized I couldn't, and shouldn't, not if the price to me for making him happy was me! Nobody can be made to pay that price."

"That's the price most fathers want, it seems to me."

"I can't say. He wanted us to worship him. We went to Sunday school, Abner and I, and were taught to worship God the Father, and then came home and worshiped Father the God. Still, I managed until a few years ago, when I just couldn't stand it. I decided if I was to be a sacrifice to his ego, well, I'd do it my way: I'd become a living reproach, an embarrass-ment. I got fat. I bought the teams."

"The teams?"

"You never caught on, did you? Any of you? Men! Oh, he and Abner hated it, that my teams lost. It wasn't easy, you know, all that losing."

"Tell me about it."

"It took talent, too, don't you see? It took brains and persistence."

"To do what?" I knew where she was going.

"To lose, don't you see? I had to decide what trades to make, what players to cut, how to break their spirit when they started to win. How to do all those things and yet make it seem as if it was done for the best motives and the most careful reasoning. Can you imagine the kind of imagination it took to do that, Sam?"

I took a deep breath and asked, "What about the players? What about them?"

"Sam, I used to worry about that. Believe me, I did, until I realized that all they really cared about was the money. That's all. They had agents who only cared about contracts, who didn't care about the game, and the players learned from them. In time, they became just bodies to be bought and sold. Maybe there were a dozen who really cared. No more!"

She must have noticed the expression on my face.

"Oh, don't look so shocked, Sam. Everything's different now. Look at you and Abner and Father. So smug in your memories. You thought you had everything. Now I have!"

She slapped a large hand on the desk, rattling a small company of Chelsea figurines.

"Father threw everything back in my face. Now it's my turn. I won't stop. I'll pursue him beyond the grave. You don't know how I hate him, Sam! How I loved him!"

Inexplicably, for a woman who had everything, she began to cry, wailing to herself. There was nothing to be said. I watched for a moment and then left, leaving her to herself and her misery, eyes bubbling and nose streaming in this, her great hour of triumph.

CHAPTER 29

For a long while after X's capitulation, well into November, after Erwitt's landslide reelection, I mopped up and moped around. I put in listless days at the office and pretty much stuck to myself in the evenings, having lost, overnight, my taste and need for connections. My mood was gloomy and confused; I tried the old remedies in extenso, but they didn't work. I listened to my Viennese music until I was choking on czardas and *Gemütlichkeit*; I devoured P. G. Wodehouse and Ogden Nash and Perelman and saw an entire run of Preston Sturges comedies at the Regency.

The whole business had left me mentally exhausted and concussed, exactly as Margarita had predicted: a shell-shocked survivor—like a character in Stephen Crane or Stendhal—of a battle into which I'd been conscripted by curiosity and old loyalties.

Naturally, I couldn't settle down to work. My editor tried to coax me along, cooing about the Pulitzer Prize, but after a couple of weeks he gave up. Nobody had to tell me that I was sitting on a hell of a book: potentially even bigger than *Indecent Exposure* because at least in this tale one or two of the players had a touch of class and character. I had my notes and my tapes and my recollections; all the raw material was at hand, but after two or three fitful starts, a few preservable paragraphs at best, I put them aside.

New York had turned into a hostile phantasm, unreal and unknown.

Once-familiar itineraries were now traversals of alien, unrecognizable territory. The hobnailed ambitions of the Shrecks and Trumps had ground my city to dust; not that it had ever been mine, of course; New York gave herself over and over again to new and richer suitors.

I needed, also, to get away from writing. For over twenty years, I'd been listening to people and watching them, dowsing for the truth of their motivations, probing for what exactly was going on, and then—as the poet said—trying to get the words right. It was as if all that effort at discovery and self-discovery had finally culminated in exhaustion. Life was too complicated, too inconstant. I began to brood on vanished friendships, devoured by lust or distraction or ambition. I found the metaphor I wanted, oddly, at the dentist's. The technician showed me an admonitory slide of the bacteria ravaging my gums. There we are, I thought, just like all those millions of bacilli on a laboratory slide, wiggling and flexing desperately, our constant motion the only verification of our existence, forming and reforming, joining and separating. I promised the dentist to use my Water-Pik diligently and went off troubled, but not by my teeth and gums.

My gloom wasn't improved by a message that came, as it were, from the other side of the grave. A few days after X surrendered, I got a postcard. It reproduced one of my favorite paintings: Degas's "The Artist's Father Listening to Pagans Playing the Guitar," from the Boston Museum of Fine Arts. The picture was about young men and old and about the inner music old men hear behind the sounds the rest of us make. My name and address were scrawled in Duncan's handwriting. The card was postmarked the day he drowned. In the message space was written, simply, *Henry VIII, 3/2. 429.*

I thought I knew what it meant. I took down my beaten-up India-paper Oxford Shakespeare, the same edition I'd seen on Duncan's bookshelves. On the flyleaf my grandfather had written: *To S.A.M.VI from his loving grandfather (S.A.M.IV).* I turned to the citation, to find what I expected—Wolsey's sad, final speech: "Cromwell, I did not think to shed a tear/In all my miseries. . . ." I read it slowly, right through to the end. "Had I but serv'd my God with half the zeal/I serv'd my king, he would not in mine age/Have left me naked to mine enemies."

It rang old bells: walking with Jake through the Frick, looking at Holbein's "Cromwell" and thinking how much it resembled X; scene after scene of Duncan speaking of "the Chief." So much. Then I laid the postcard aside; Duncan was dead; Jake had died three days after him; it was all dead, after all: as dead and drowned and finished as Duncan was. I wanted an end to valedictories.

I tried to make something of what I had. I rustled up Moira at *Newsday* and took her to lunch and told her about Eugenie's confession.

"So, didn't I tell you?" she said. She looked around Mortimer's, at the raucous, tinny people of the moment, shook her head, and dug back into her chicken hash.

"Who's going to believe it if you print it?" she asked when she surfaced. "Especially now that the Vandals are leading the division. Anyway, honey, you think our lawyers would let me run a story like this, especially with the Empress as tight as she is at the White House? Shit, everybody knows what happened to old man Monstrance. Freedom of the press has a price, sweetheart."

She was seriously thinking about getting married, she informed me at the end. To a young man who drew editorial cartoons for a syndicate. They might live in Bucks County. He hated New York, hated all cities. She was going to freelance; *Newsday* had promised to take some of her stuff: travel pieces, things like that. She wanted to try a novel.

"You ought to get away," she said. "This place has become a bummer. Even just since I was a kid in Park Slope. I hate to think how it must have changed for an old guy like you."

She grinned and poked at me with her fork.

"I'm not kidding," she said. "I got to see Mantle play, at least, and Conerly. Now what have I got? Donald Trump talking about the Generals and a guy like Steinbrenner owns the Yankees, and a total whacko in Gracie Mansion, and horns blowing every two seconds, and shit in the streets, and a hundred bucks a copy for dinner, and a mugger on every block."

"Don't you appreciate how 'vital' all that is?" I asked sarcastically. "Don't you read *Town and Country?*"

"Vital, schmital. About ten thousand people are making out in this town, and about a tenth of those are making ninety percent of the noise and a hundred percent of the money. Go away for a while, Sam. Stop trying to get laid and fall in love and be Mr. First Nighter. Do it the old-fashioned way. Fall in love and then get laid. And you can give away the Father Knickerbocker suit; it's a nice shtick, and you're a cute guy, but it hasn't played since about 1968, and even if it did, nobody gives a shit. It's all nostalgia, Sam, and there's no money in that, so do what the song says, my dear, Get out of town before it's too late!"

That was just about how Cass, that quintessentially up-to-date young woman, had disparaged my sense of my city: Stuart Little stuff, too much memory. I wished Moira love and luck, and we promised to keep in touch, knowing that our string had been cut too.

I heard from Cass a couple of times and learned that X had gone back to London. The Fifth Avenue apartment had lasted on the market for one day and had been bought by Marty and Shermie Getsmore for seven million dollars. Bud and Marie had rented X's house on Little Gourd Key for three years to use for guests; Cass was going to spend Thanksgiving with them. She and Al-*fred*.

It didn't surprise me that X had left without calling me. He probably felt shamed, and shame is one form of misery that doesn't want company. I understood—and admired him for it. X was out of the old school: disgrace meant something to him; it would be intense, haunting, lasting, not just a moment's flicker of regret to be effaced as the broken pieces were swept aside in bustling on to the next deal.

Clio had taken Abner to Santa Barbara. In my heart, I wished her well, and him too, poor kid. Two more broken or wounded to be added to the body count. I wanted no more casualties in my life, no more hungers, no more rages, no more unfinished businesses, at least none that weren't strictly and entirely of my own making.

From time to time, over those weeks, EmpCom/AbCom/GBG broke into the news. I watched the gradual emasculation of "Statehouse" and "First National." It was cleverly and quickly done: Bernie and Isaac and Fred were pros, and since the ratings were holding up on these "brand name" shows, they would have been compliant. So the bite and edge were removed from them ever so gradually; they were ethically sterilized a vein at a time. By Thanksgiving, they were notionally the splendidly successful shows X had created—the November sweeps were sensational—but they had been downgraded to extended soap operas, of a piece with "Dynasty" and "Dallas." But if the audience noticed the change, they made no complaint, and that was the saddest part.

In mid-November, after the election, an investigative reporter for *The St. Louis Post-Dispatch* got hold of a complete list of EmpCom preferred stockholders. It suggested that either X had offended everyone or there were just too many who stood to profit from an electorate soothed into helplessness by their easy spokesman. All the expected corporate names made the list: the defense contractors, oil companies, every big name imaginable. Labor was represented in spades. The UAW and the good old reliable Central States, Southeast and Southwest Area Pension Fund of the Teamsters, and the Players Association of the NFL and the USFL, and a bunch of big real estate associations, and seven out of the Big Eight public accounting firms. Arnold Plume's law firm, the one X had fired, was there, and an entire cast of merger-and-acquisition comprimarios: proxy solicitors, law firms, arbitrage houses. Anyone who had an interest in getting a regulation selectively relaxed or tightened or a contract fixed. Wall Street was along for the ride, too; the list of banks and investment banking names looked like the top bracket in an IBM tombstone. And the big advertising chains and the chemical companies and all the other poisoners of mind and atmosphere and earth, and so on and so on. Worthy foes.

Poor X, I thought. He'd imagined his crusade against Erwitt to be about politics. But politics and money were fused and indistinguishable; just as Buck had seen from the first, the one was the other.

By Thanksgiving, I had decided to leave, at least for a while. There was no way I could handle a New York Christmas, not with the tumult of resentments that had risen within me. I had no connections and no dependencies: no parents, children, nieces, or nephews, no cousins I knew, and few friends. Florrie did call to suggest that I join her on a trip to Cartagena: two weeks in the sun and bake it all out. It wasn't my scene.

I settled on Scotland. I liked the prospect of long winter nights. I had the place in my mind: somewhere along the Moray Firth, near Inverness. Somewhere I could hide away and yet get away from if I needed. A friend in Edinburgh suggested an inn near Forres, about thirty miles from Inverness. The rooms were spacious and the food good. That suited me; I wasn't about to take care of myself. I knew the region. It was good country for anything: in the spring there would be great golf. If I wanted, I could ski in the Cairngorms or Aviemore. It wouldn't be like sequestering myself in Patagonia. Inverness was a legitimate city; if I got desperate for larger human commotion, there was Edinburgh and, in extremis, London. I asked my friend to book a small suite of rooms for me through June. June, I thought, would be time enough to get through to whatever the next step would be.

My "account" at the magazine was in good shape. I didn't owe any pieces and I had plenty of money. A stroke of good luck sent an Oxford friend of Margarita's to me; he was spending a year teaching at the Institute of Fine Arts across the park, and I rented him my apartment for a few hundred dollars a month and the satisfaction of knowing that my few treasures were in good hands.

I arrived in Scotland ten days after Thanksgiving. It was blowing cold, with a hint of snow, and I took my time driving across from Prestwick. In the back of the rented station wagon were my clothes and my golf clubs and a duffel filled with the shards and leavings of X's adventure: tapes, and notes, and halfway startings of pages and paragraphs, and bits of this and that. Another bag held my little Vienna, my tapes of Tauber and Strauss and Grete Keller; a few books. Against the off chance that the muse might reappear, I'd brought a typewriter.

My inn proved a delight. I had a comfortable sitting room and an agreeable bedroom, furnished in a simple, good manner: heavy, hefty stuff, with thick, rough covers on the bed. I had a decent bathroom and an alcove with a hot plate to keep the tea warm. Each evening a fire was laid in the sitting room grate.

The food at the inn was good, straightforward fare: lamb and beef and salmon. There was malt whisky beyond praise and adequate wine. For company, there were the innkeeper and his wife, the giggling girls who set the table and made the beds, and a friend who would be newly made, an Englishman, like myself a fugitive from harassment and buzz. After a month we took to dining together, and to sharing whiskies before and after, and splitting a bottle of claret, sometimes two. Sometimes three.

I wanted to be away but not cut off. I arranged with a newsagent in Forres for a daily transfusion of the London papers and the *Paris Herald*. A care package from the editor arrived each week: the *Spec*, *Time*, *Sports Illustrated*, *New York*, *The New Yorker*, *The New Republic*, *Golf World*, and *Golf Digest*. The newsagent in Forres kept me in Penguins, and there were decent bookstores in Inverness and in Elgin to the east. When I read about something I had to have right away, I called Heywood Hill in London. Gradually, as always, stacks of books, many bought on impulse and destined to go unread, built up in my sitting room.

Thus I passed the winter. I walked away the days, which were short, and read in the evening, and ate, and sometimes watched television in the downstairs parlor. I made excursions around the region: dutifully visiting the Speyside distilleries; tramping Culloden Moor, the stones and cairns by which my ancestors had fallen. I soaked up the rich, wonderful wholeness of this beautiful, mysterious, windy country. Mostly, though, I read. The forward stretch of unused days was at first easing; I really got into Proust for the first time, and over the winter, I finished. Often I thought about New York, but it seemed distant, as remote as another galaxy. The notion that I might never again live there seemed possible; it wasn't that you can't go home again, but that you might not want to.

By February, however, the skein of dark, damp days looked as if it would unreel forever, and I fled: to Edinburgh twice and once to London.

It was a treat; I was a city boy and I knew how to hide in cities, how to have my way of them. In London I lunched with Margarita, abloom with love. X was around, she said, but she knew no one who'd seen him. He was probably recuperating. Behind her voice I heard the message: he wasn't her problem any longer. She was too happy; there would be no more volunteering for service in other people's wars; there wasn't enough time left.

One evening, with the darkness settling, I came out of the Tate Gallery and for some reason turned right. I walked east along the Thames in the dusk, until finally I fetched up across from X's house. It was fully lit, yet I had the feeling that there wasn't any life behind the warm, welcoming glow of the windows. I thought for an instant about ringing the bell, but only for an instant; then I signaled a taxi coming off the bridge and returned to the lighted heart of London. The next day I flew back to Scotland.

February turned out to be full of excitement. Eugenie had said she would pursue X his whole life through, and she was making good on that threat. On Valentine's day, the London papers reported that President Erwitt had nominated her to be Ambassador to the Court of St. James's. That was the one thing X had failed to win for Selena; now Eugenie had it. I wondered what the Queen would make of this tall, awkward, unsexed woman, spayed by hatred.

On what would have been the Washington's Birthday holiday, I received an express parcel from my editor. "You'll probably want this," read his covering note, "although it seems pretty thin, niminy-piminy stuff to me." It was the bound galleys of Zero at the Bone, a novel by Cassandra Hargrove. I retreated to my room, filled more with irritation than with dread, and opened it. It was dedicated "To some who dare . . ." which meant as little, I was sure, to the book's author as to its readers, but which sounded appropriately febrile.

It was about what I expected, written in a rat-a-tat, aphoristic style, with quiddly little paragraphs dancing across the page like florists at a wedding. The first chapter began: "Will he know, I wonder, that this might. Might. This. That this might have been. Don't you see. But then there was her and the moules marinière and thus might became wasn't." It went on from there for a hundred and ninety pages, at $14.95 bad value even for a Foster Greenglass production. The people in the book were thinly veiled; the women all had male given names, and the male characters' first names all seemed to be last names. I made out X, Clio, and several that represented weak or nauseating aspects of myself. There were quite a few brand names and addresses. At least we were spared recipes.

Well, good luck to you, my love, I said when I put it down. May it bring you what you want.

And it did. In March I had a letter from Florrie enclosing a bunch of clippings. The litcrit androgynes had flipped over Cass's book. *New York* had sent its resident arselicker off to explore the raging talent which had produced this work; he anthemed Cass's "twitchy, quirtlike intellect," her "fibrous, feral, emotional perspicacity." Most of the other stuff, principally from seminal literary journals like *Vogue*, ran along the same lines. According to Florrie, Cass was on all the talk shows and at all the right parties. The people, places, and scenes on which the book was based had been leaked in considerable specificity to the columns, and Cass was having the time of her life embroidering them on the airwaves.

Ah, well, I thought, it is the way of the world that we are all rungs on someone else's ladder. At least she has her own celebrity now, not another's reflected glow.

The winter wore on: I read my Proust and my Powell, tried to write, and didn't get very far, while the days and evenings ran into each other: waking and walking and sleeping; the daily papers, a fire in the grate and, at bedtime, a gill of Glenmorangie, with the real world out there somewhere beyond vision, like a vague, threatening front.

X died in the spring, in April, the Friday after Easter.

In Scotland it had been a fair day. I'd played that morning at Lossiemouth, over the links of the Moray Golf Club. The air had been soft, with a bright sun barely dulled by a high wash of clouds, and only the merest dying hint of chilliness on the breeze that blew in off the Moray Firth. It had rained that day in London, the paper reported; in New York it would be hazy and unseasonably warm.

He had died in his sleep, the papers said, in his house on Chelsea Embankment. The paper briefly recited his accomplishments and named his survivors, most prominent among them the Honorable Eugenie Grace Monstrance, Ambassador of the United States of America to Her Majesty's Court at St. James's. That alone would assure royalty in the front pew at St. James's, Piccadilly, where a service of thanksgiving for the life of the Hon. Horace Hubert Monstrance, B.A., L.L.D. (Hon.), D.H.L. (Hon.), L. juris. D. (Hon.) was planned for early May. Other services would be held in New York and Los Angeles. And at Starbuck, I thought; that would be the most important to X, from wherever he might be watching.

I had no intention of going to the service in London. I wasn't about to participate in what I was certain would be an effort by Eugenie to convert the occasion to a further moment of triumph and vindication. Anyway, I thought, my business with the Monstrances was now forever finished, over, done with; and then knowing, in the instant the thought came to me, that of course it wasn't.

That night I drank too much whisky and read *East Coker* over and over until the print blurred. I thought of Mother derisively describing X as "Mr. Valiant for Truth." Well, he had been, I thought sadly, and I hoped that the trumpets had indeed sounded for him on the other side. X always liked trumpets. When I finally stumbled to bed, I couldn't sleep; my twilit imagination projected a Dickensian procession on the screen of my mind, each coming forward to take a last bow: X and Mother and Duncan and Abner, now locked forever in the cryogenic clench of death and trauma; poor, sad Eugenie; Cass and Clio holding hands, curtsying prettily in unison; then the Bishmans, and the merger experts from First Stuyvesant, that odd couple, and Hillhouse; and Ms. Pfannglanz and Goswell, oddly Sapphic, smiling secrets to each other; and the obvious villains, fat, swart Arnold Plume and beady-eyed McNeery, bobbing in the flickering footlights, and, last, Eldon Erwitt, grinning and nodding, waving a white card like a child's flag, while about him rose a roar like the sea that finally sent me to sleep.

In the morning, I woke convinced that some sacrifice, some gesture was due from me. It was all very well to sit here swaddled in my fine feelings, my calibrated aggrievements and disillusions, bathing my exquisite wounds and feeding my sulks with choice little morsels of *Weltschmerz*, in my way every bit as phony, presumptuous, and self-indulgent as a cowlike Marie Shreck queening it over her dinner table, picking her way through a plate of fancy vittles. More was required—a pound of flesh or soul or faith. I had been X's friend and his ally, I had borne witness, I had been his confidant and had broken his confidence, and I owed him something for all that, not to mention the gamble he had taken and lost for all of us. My account with him was not yet closed.

I thought about it through the day and again that night. I knew finally what would be appropriate, a suitably grand and sacrificial gesture. In the morning I called Inverness and booked a ticket to Vienna.

I never got there, of course. I did get as far as Heathrow, past the customs, as far as the moving sidewalk unscrolling its way to the gate where the Vienna flight waited. I suppose, as in many things, it was necessary that I get my nose jammed right up against the rough wall of reality, like a burglar being frisked, before I could begin to see the picture and to understand how insubstantial my sadness was, more pique than grieving, and what in fact I should do.

Suddenly I realized that the last thing X would have asked of me was what I proposed to offer up: my last remaining secret place of the heart. X understood about dreams and memories, and he valued them, and he was a builder. He wouldn't want something thrown away or torn up, something abandoned for the momentary relief gotten from a theatrical gesture; he would want something created, grown, planted. What he would want of me was exactly what he had asked from the beginning: that I write down his story. Perhaps I couldn't give him exactly the posterity he'd craved, immortality made to measure, a monument carved to exact specifications, but at least I could render him a kind of permanence. *Hic jacet Xenophon Horace Hubert Monstrance, "X." De mortuis nihil nisi verum.* Just the truth.

Now, as in a revelation, after months of stumbling petulantly around in my private grievances, acting as if I'd been the one most deeply wounded, the "idea" of the book came to me. It would have to go beyond a recital of proxy fights and corporate stratagems, of money and tactics and bids and prices and ratings and politics, and reach for the darker side of these obvious instrumentalities of the way things were now. It would have to face up to the dark consequences of letting present and future be swept along on a wave of greed and carelessness, ours, theirs, everyone's, until when at last we got around to sticking to our guns, it was too late in the day, always too late. It would have to treat of the paradox of the favored and fortunate in a world in which, no matter how sterling our characters, the only mintage that paid the piper was hard cash, so that our talents and principles ceased to be strengths and became shackles; so that we found ourselves not exalted but enfeebled by our best and noblest qualities, left by the roadside to scavenge among our memories while the rest of life rushed by, noisy and heedless and hoggish.

It would be about how people like the Monstrances can be as much trouble to themselves as to the rest of us, but that that didn't make it any better. How they arrive in our lives, generally unbidden, with their money and power and infinite means of seduction; how they appropriate the pieces of us they want—our space, our calm; they casually sever our old friendships by proffering new temptations and advantages; as it suits them, they alter the things we've known, the old familiars, the takings for granted on which we've built ourselves, the houses external and internal in which we dwell, our most personal territories. More often than not, the trouble they make for us is a careless by-product of the trouble they mean to make for each other. They are big enough, or important enough, to cause ripples; the rest of us are merely innocent civilians, victims of the bombing and the cross fire. It was just as Clio had said, they have a power, because of who they are, because of what they have, to extract tribute from the rest of us, to make us bend. And yet, at the going down of the sun, what have they got, except more money?

The only safe haven was in that dim corner of our hearts in which we stored our memories. How had Eugenie put it? That X and Abner and I were smug in our memories. She'd said it in a voice like a curse, and of course I suppose that's what memory was for her. Smug in our memories, I thought. Nicely put, Eugenie. Smug and, at the last, snug and secure, beyond the reach of others, in our one ultimate impregnable, un-purchasable redoubt.

In a world in which money alone had value, an Erwitt world, a Mc-Neery world, an Abner world, the worth of memory slipped by unre-garded. Having no present barter value, it had no relevance, except to those of us who fancied ourselves keepers of a flame that flared, near extinguishment, only in the anger and longing of those of us who knew the way it used to be and hated the way it had become.

In the end, a decent book about X would have to memorialize his anger and longing, which were my anger and longing. It would personalize those feelings, give them an effigy, poignant and grand like carved tombs in old and vast cathedrals, perpetuities that the Erwitts and the Buds and the McNeerys, crashing about with their hired guides and drivers and loud voices, might suddenly come upon and know to be awed.

Scotland, with its old stones, would be a good place to make a start on such a book. Along the road I could feel my way back into life through my friends. Maybe Buck would like to come over for a week or so: we could golf at Moray and Buckie and Nairn and go north, across the Black Isle to Tain and the regal links at Dornoch, and to Golspie and Brora, where X had hunted me down when all this had begun. And I had a feeling that when the weather got warmer, Florence Mary Ashley Grosvenor Nuywaerts da Sola Basto would turn up. Perhaps she'd stay a while, to read in the garden while I wrote. What were old friends for? She'd like Scotland, and we could try London for a few days, and then it would be time for both of us to go back to New York. Vienna would keep.

I walked back toward Immigration, thinking about the book. Ideas and phrases and perspectives suddenly crowded upon me. I let them mingle noisily in my head, each clamoring for attention; it didn't matter, I would get them all down, and try to sort them out, and then the editor would do what he was there for: to help me get the book I wanted to write from the book I had written.

I closed my mind to these noises, needed to refocus on what I would say to the Immigration people, how I'd explain my turnabout, how I'd get my bag back. For an instant it all seemed a terrible bother. But then I thought: these people see all sorts, and they'll have seen plenty like me before: orphans of the storm, driftwood washed ashore by the complex tides of life, looking—like everyone—for love and explanation.